THE CHILDREN OF THE GODS SERIES BOOKS 35-37

DARK SPY TRILOGY

I. T. LUCAS

Copyright © 2021 by I. T. Lucas

All rights reserved.
No part of this book may be reproduced in any form or by any electronic or mechanical means, including information storage and retrieval systems, without written permission from the author, except for the use of brief quotations in a book review.

NOTE FROM THE AUTHOR:
Dark Spy Trilogy is a work of fiction!
Names, characters, places and incidents are products of the author's imagination or are used fictitiously and are not to be construed as real. Any similarity to actual persons, organizations and/or events is purely coincidental.

CONTENTS

DARK SPY CONSCRIPTED

1. Kalugal	3
2. Jin	6
3. Jin	10
4. Jin	12
5. Jin	17
6. Jin	20
7. Jin	24
8. Jin	28
9. Jin	31
10. Jin	35
11. Jin	39
12. Kian	42
13. Arwel	45
14. Jin	48
15. Mey	51
16. Arwel	54
17. Jin	57
18. Arwel	60
19. Jin	63
20. Mey	65
21. Kian	67
22. Jin	69
23. Arwel	72
24. Jin	74
25. Kian	76
26. Arwel	79
27. Kian	82
28. Jin	84
29. Arwel	87
30. Kian	89
31. Arwel	92
32. Jin	95

33. Mey	98
34. Jin	101
35. Kian	104
36. Jin	106
37. Arwel	109
38. Jin	113
39. Mey	115
40. Jin	117
41. Arwel	120
42. Kian	123
43. Kian	126
44. Arwel	129
45. Jin	132
46. Kian	134
47. Jin	137
48. Arwel	140
49. Jin	143
50. Arwel	147
51. Jin	150
52. Kian	153
53. Jin	156
54. Arwel	158
55. Jin	161
56. Kian	164
57. Arwel	166
58. Jin	168
59. Kian	171
60. Jin	174
61. Arwel	177
62. Jin	179
63. Arwel	182
64. Jin	184
65. Arwel	187
66. Jin	190
67. Arwel	192
68. Kian	195
69. Jin	198
70. Kian	201
71. Jin	203
72. Arwel	205

DARK SPY'S MISSION

1. Kian — 211
2. Kalugal — 215
3. Jin — 218
4. Arwel — 221
5. Jin — 224
6. Arwel — 226
7. Kalugal — 229
8. Syssi — 233
9. Kian — 236
10. Jin — 239
11. Arwel — 242
12. Jin — 245
13. Arwel — 248
14. Jin — 250
15. Arwel — 253
16. Kian — 256
17. Jin — 260
18. Arwel — 263
19. Jin — 266
20. Arwel — 269
21. Jin — 272
22. Arwel — 275
23. Jin — 278
24. Arwel — 281
25. Jin — 285
26. Arwel — 288
27. Kian — 291
28. Jin — 294
29. Kalugal — 297
30. Arwel — 300
31. Jin — 302
32. Mey — 305
33. Vlad — 308
34. Wendy — 311
35. Vlad — 314
36. Wendy — 317
37. Arwel — 320
38. Kalugal — 323
39. Jin — 325

40. Kalugal	328
41. Jin	331
42. Arwel	334
43. Kalugal	337
44. Kian	340
45. Jin	343
46. Arwel	346
47. Jin	349
48. Arwel	352
49. Jin	355
50. Yamanu	358
51. Jin	361
52. Vlad	364
53. Jin	367
54. Arwel	369
55. Wendy	372
56. Jin	374
57. Vlad	377
58. Wendy	380
59. Kian	384
60. Jin	387
61. Kalugal	390
62. Arwel	393
63. Jin	396
64. Arwel	399
65. Jin	402
66. Arwel	406
67. Kalugal	408
68. Jin	412
69. Arwel	415
70. William	417
71. Jin	419
72. Kalugal	421
73. William	424
74. Jin	426
75. Kian	429

DARK SPY'S RESOLUTION

1. Kalugal	433
2. Kian	436

3. Jin	439
4. Arwel	442
5. Turner	445
6. Kalugal	448
7. Jin	451
8. Turner	454
9. Arwel	456
10. Kian	458
11. Kalugal	460
12. Kian	463
13. Kalugal	466
14. Yamanu	469
15. Mey	472
16. Lokan	475
17. Magnus	478
18. Kian	481
19. Kalugal	484
20. Wendy	487
21. Vlad	490
22. Kian	493
23. Arwel	496
24. Jin	499
25. Kalugal	502
26. Kian	505
27. Kalugal	507
28. Jin	510
29. Annani	513
30. Arwel	516
31. Kian	520
32. Jin	522
33. Kian	526
34. Kalugal	529
35. Wendy	532
36. Vlad	535
37. Wendy	537
38. Vlad	540
39. Kian	544
40. Kalugal	547
41. Jin	551
42. Arwel	554
43. Wendy	557

44. Vlad	560
45. Wendy	562
46. Mey	564
47. Wendy	567
48. Vlad	569
49. Kian	571
50. Arwel	574
51. Jin	577
52. Kian	580
53. Jin	583
54. Kalugal	586
55. Kian	589
56. Jin	592
57. Arwel	594
58. Kalugal	596
59. Jin	599
60. Arwel	602
61. Jin	605
62. Kalugal	608
63. Arwel	611
64. Kalugal	613
65. Jin	616
66. Kalugal	619
67. Arwel	621
68. Kalugal	623
69. Jin	626
70. Kalugal	629
71. Jin	632
72. Kalugal	636
73. Jin	639
74. Arwel	643
75. Jin	645
Dark Overlord Excerpt	649
The Children of the Gods Series	657
The Perfect Match Series	667
Also by I. T. Lucas	669
FOR EXCLUSIVE PEEKS	673

DARK SPY CONSCRIPTED

1

KALUGAL

Three years ago.

Kalugal stood in the backyard of his new mansion and watched the excavator dig into the ground. The bunker he planned on building was massive, much bigger than what he needed, but he had long-term plans that might or might not come to fruition before he was forced to move again.

Hopefully, it wasn't going to be anytime soon.

He liked the area, and his ambitious plans required proximity to the startup center of the world.

"Are you going to stand here all day?" Rufsur sidled up to him. "I vote for taking another trip to Berkeley."

Kalugal cast him an amused glance. "What's wrong with the locals? Couldn't find any hotties?"

Rufsur grimaced. "If I were into MILFs, there are plenty to choose from. But I like college girls." He licked his lips. "Berkeley is like a buffet. Plenty of delicacies, and they come in all flavors."

The analogy was apt, and Kalugal shared Rufsur's preferences, but as with all things, he wasn't satisfied with anything but the best. "I prefer Stanford girls."

"That's because you are a cheap bastard. You want to screw them and pick their brains at the same time."

The guy was loyal to a fault, and Kalugal counted himself lucky for having him as his second-in-command, but he was also crass, and Kalugal liked more refined company. He had it in his other right-hand man, but Phinas was a dry stick and not much fun to be around.

With a shrug, Kalugal turned around and started walking. "I like intelligent women."

Offended on behalf of his chosen female student body, Rufsur frowned. "It's not easy to get into Berkeley. Those accepted are far from stupid."

"Yeah, but Stanford girls are smart and driven. That's more my type."

"I wonder about you." Rufsur clapped him on the back. "What do you do with the chicks you pick up, talk all night?"

Sometimes.

Kalugal appreciated the company of his men, and he considered the warriors who had stayed loyal to him over the decades as close friends. But he enjoyed female company more and not just for the sex.

"What I do or don't do is none of your business." He glanced at his watch. "I have an appointment in the city. Are you coming with me, or are you staying to supervise the work?" He walked out through the open gate.

His Lamborghini was parked on the street at a safe distance from the dust surrounding the excavation site. In a fancy neighborhood like that, there was little chance anyone would try to steal it, even if the keys were left inside. His other luxury cars were stored in a warehouse he'd rented in an industrial park outside the city, and once the construction of the bunker was completed and the car lift installed, he was going to move them into their new home.

"I'll come with you. I don't like it when you go out alone."

"You're just paranoid. No one knows who I am, and I'm perfectly safe."

Rufsur shrugged. "On the off chance that someone can see through your shrouds, I'd rather have your back. Who are you pretending to be this time?"

"A Chinese investor."

"That's new."

As Kalugal got behind the wheel and turned the engine on, the powerful purr brought a smile to his lips.

"The oligarch disguise was getting old. Besides, technology attracts more Chinese investors than Russian."

As a matter of policy, Kalugal never met with anyone without shrouding himself in one disguise or another. On the rare occasions that he'd encountered humans who were immune to his tricks, he hadn't stayed for longer than had been absolutely necessary. Pretending to be an assistant with a message from the boss, he'd left as soon as possible.

Even the best of deals was not worth exposing his identity.

Even after the long decades that he had spent in New York, working the stock market and accumulating his wealth, none of those he'd harvested for insider information could pick him out of a lineup.

Besides his activities being illegal, Kalugal also had his father to worry about. There was no doubt in his mind that Navuh was still searching for him.

He didn't hate his father, but he was smart enough to fear him.

At the time of his escape, Kalugal's powers were not nearly as formidable as Navuh's, and even though they had grown over the years, he doubted that they had reached his father's level. The guy had an entire island under his compulsion, while Kalugal couldn't even control all of his men at the same time.

Not that he'd tried it for any purpose other than testing his ability.

Whoever wanted to leave was free to do so, and some had chosen to do just that and had gone on to seek their own fortunes. Most had left at the beginning, when Kalugal had still been struggling to find his way in the new world. Some had left later, with his permission and his blessing.

Rather than having a large force that was a mixed bag, he preferred having a small group of men who were loyal to him out of their own free will.

Unlike his father, Kalugal didn't want to rule with an iron fist, and he didn't want to watch his back for fear of betrayal or assassination.

But just like Navuh, Kalugal had aspirations of one day ruling the world.

Except, his way of achieving that was not going to be by force, and his rise to power was not going to involve climbing over piles of bodies and sailing over rivers of blood.

The days of brute force were over, and the technological revolution had ushered in a new dawn, heralding the arrival of a different type of conqueror.

2

JIN

Two months ago

"Jin! Get your freaking phone!" Gabi yelled. "I hate that spooky seventies ringtone you assigned to your sister." She slung the strap of her purse over her shoulder and left their dorm room in a huff.

Drama queen.

It was the theme song from *Doctor Who*, and for some reason, it freaked her roommate out. Not that Jin was going to change it just because Gabi didn't like it. It had been her and Mey's favorite television show when they were girls.

Heck, it still was. Whenever they had the chance, they would cuddle on the couch under a blanket and watch it while sipping cocoa, and on a hot day, they would just blast the air conditioner until it was cold enough to do that.

Except, ever since Mey had moved in with Oliver, they hadn't done it. Jin didn't like the guy, and she didn't like going over to their place.

Pulling her earphones off, she leaned and snatched the phone off the charger. "I was wondering when you were going to call. Do you want to grab a cup of coffee? I've missed you."

It had been a whole week since Mey had flown out for a photo shoot. She'd called almost every day, but now that she was back, Jin wanted to do more than just chat over the phone. Perhaps they could catch a movie.

"I've broken up with Oliver." Mey sniffled. "The bastard cheated on me while I was gone."

Jin sat up straight. "Where are you now?"

"I'm crashing at Tatiana's. Actually, it's more permanent than that. Two of her roommates are moving out later this month, and I'm going to share the apartment with her and Josephine. I left my place with just the things I had with me on the trip, but I'm going to get the rest of my stuff tomorrow when the jerk is at work."

"How did you find out?"

"The moment I entered the bedroom, I smelled another woman all over the bedding. He tried to deny it, calling me a paranoid bitch, but I know what I smelled. You know how good I am at sniffing things out."

Obviously, Tatiana was in the room, so Mey couldn't talk about how she'd really found out about the bastard banging another woman in her bed, but Jin had no problem filling in the blanks.

Mey had heard the echoes of what had gone on in that bedroom while she'd been away.

Her sister's ability to hear echoes left over in the walls was a secret only Jin was privy to, and the same was true of Jin's special talent. No one other than Mey knew what Jin could do, which was even weirder than having the walls tell stories of past conversations.

They were the freak sisters.

Not only were they both six-foot-tall Asian females, which was enough to turn heads wherever they went, but they could also do those bizarre things that no one else could.

Poor Mey. Coming home and discovering what her boyfriend had done must have felt like a punch to the gut.

"What a colossal jerk." Jin plopped back on the bed and draped an arm over her eyes. "Good riddance, that's what I say."

Once the initial shock had worn off, rage started building up in Jin's gut, and it needed an outlet. She felt like hopping on the subway, going over to Mey's old place, and beating the crap out of Oliver.

How could he have done that to her sweet, beautiful sister?

Mey was not only gorgeous, but she was also a wonderful person. She hadn't demanded anything from the asshole other than fidelity, and he couldn't give her even that.

Paying half of the rent on their apartment had been the extent of his contribution to their shared household. Mey had been doing all the cleaning and laundering, as if the maggot was some fucking prince.

Hopefully, Mitch wasn't like that.

He and Jin had just started dating, and he seemed like a great guy, but she was going to keep a close eye on his behavior. If he showed even a tiny hint of Oliver's entitled attitude, she was going to get rid of him so fast that he wouldn't know what hit him.

"I know." Mey sighed. "I keep telling myself that it's for the best, and that it's better I discovered it now, and not while I was married to the jerk. But it still hurts. I'm lying on the couch in Tatiana's living room, feeling like I have a huge boulder sitting on my chest. I can't breathe."

"You don't want him back, though, right?"

"Never. The hurt is not so much over the loss of the relationship. It's the insult and the unfairness that gets me. How could he have done it to me? I was good to him."

"Too good, that's for sure."

"I wonder if that woman he was banging is going to move in with him. I don't want to ever touch any of my beautiful bedding again, but I'm not going to let them enjoy it either. When I go back for my things, I'm going to put on a pair of gloves, put all of it in a trash bag, and throw it out."

"Don't throw everything away. You can take the clean stuff from the closet."

Mey wasn't a big spender, but she had a thing for luxurious bedding. She must've spent a small fortune on it.

"God knows how many women he's screwed when I was away on photo shoots. I bet this wasn't the first time."

"I don't want to say anything in his defense, but it probably was. Otherwise, you would've known, right?"

Mey would have heard the echoes of any other times as well.

"Yeah. You're probably right. Nevertheless, I don't want to take anything other than my personal things. I'm going to donate everything else to charity, and that includes the furniture that I paid for."

"I'll come help you. But first, I'll go there while Oliver is home and touch the bastard, so I can spy on him later. I'll probably do that by punching him in the gut and slapping him silly. Then when we go to collect your things, I'll tune in to him, so we can check where he is and what he's doing. We don't want him to catch us clearing out the place. Things might get ugly."

"I don't want you to do that."

"Why not? What's the point of having a freaking paranormal talent if I don't get to benefit from it?"

"I don't want you to get contaminated." Mey lowered her voice to a whisper. "The special connection you create is personal. So far, you've only used it on a couple of your friends and me. I'm afraid of what will happen if you leach into a scumbag like Oliver."

Jin shivered. "Why did you have to use that word? You made me feel like a bug."

"I'm sorry. I didn't mean it. I blame the margaritas. It's the third one that Tatiana's made for me."

Jin chuckled. "I thought that you and your model friends counted every calorie."

"These are skinny margaritas. Tatiana says they have less than a hundred calories each. But back to my poor choice of words. We've never figured out what to call what you can do."

"I've given it some thought lately. I don't know why, since I haven't used it on anyone in ages. Well, that's not exactly true. I know why I was thinking about it. I've started to date a new guy, and I'm still debating whether I want to tether him or not."

"Is it serious?"

Jin chuckled. "You know how I am with guys. I get bored after a couple of dates. But Mitch is fun to be with, and he is tall, so I might keep him for a little longer."

Mey groaned. "Forgive me for not gushing all over the place. Right now, I think of all men as scumbags."

"You have good reason. Anyway, tethering is how I think of it. When I touch someone with the intention of keeping tabs on them, it's like I'm inserting a hook into their psyche and tying a string of my consciousness to it, creating a tether."

"I like it. Hook, line, and sinker, but with a twist."

Feeling somewhat offended again, Jin huffed out a breath. "You make it sound like a bad thing. I'm not deceiving anyone, just spying on them. Although if they don't know that I'm doing it, you are right about it not being kosher."

3

JIN

Six weeks ago.

As Jin left the classroom, she pulled her phone out and checked her messages. There was one from Mitch, asking what she wanted to do to celebrate the end of her senior year, one from Mey, asking how the last test of the semester had gone, and a voice message from a number she didn't recognize.

Most likely, it was one of those scams that were going on lately. Everyone she knew was getting fake phone calls about their social security number being compromised. The scammers kept switching numbers, so blocking them did not solve the problem.

Still, on the remote chance that it was something important, she put her earphones in and pressed play.

"Hello, Jin. My name is Maria Savino, and I'm a headhunter. Given your stellar academic record and impeccable work ethic, you are just the kind of candidate my client is looking for. I would like for us to meet and discuss the details. I can't say much over the phone, but I can assure you that this is the most exciting and generous offer you, or any of your classmates, are going to get. I'm in town only for a couple of days, so please call me as soon as you get this message."

Staring at the phone in disbelief, Jin replayed the voicemail.

None of her friends had gotten calls from headhunters, and some of them had grades as good as hers and were just as hardworking.

This was weird.

Still, there was no harm in calling the woman back and hearing more details about the supposedly fantastic offer. Perhaps it was legit?

As Jin returned the call, it was answered immediately. "Hello, Jin. I'm so glad you called me back. When can we meet so I can tell you all about this amazing job offer?"

Apparently, Maria was a get-straight-to-the-point kind of gal. Jin liked her already.

"Whenever you want. I've just walked out from taking my last test, and I'm free as a bird."

Maria chuckled. "I still remember the feeling. But now, years later, I realize that this was the best time of my life." She sighed, a bit too dramatically. "Where are you now? Are you still on campus?"

"I just got out."

"Wonderful. I'm staying at the Dominic. Do you know where it is?"

"Yeah, I do."

It was a fancy hotel, which Jin viewed as a good sign. If the headhunter could afford to stay there, she was being paid well.

"You can either walk over here or take a taxi. I will reimburse you, of course."

"I can walk. Are we going to meet in the lobby?"

"You can come up to my suite. I'll let the front desk know that I'm expecting you, and you can come right up. I'll order dinner for us. Any preferences?"

Jin was taken aback. Meeting in a hotel room was not her idea of proper interview etiquette, and if Maria were a guy, she would've said no thank you.

But what if Maria was only pretending to be a woman? Or worse, what if she was luring Jin for someone else to rape?

A girl could never be too careful.

"How do I know that you are who you claim to be?"

The woman chuckled. "I like you, Jin. You are smart and careful. I'll meet you down in the lobby, and we can go to the hotel bar. You can check my credentials before we go up to my room to discuss the job offer. The reason I have to do it this way is that the information I'm going to share with you is highly confidential. I cannot discuss the details in a public place, and I don't have an office in New York that I can use. I travel all over the country, recruiting talent."

That sounded logical, and meeting Maria in the lobby seemed safe.

"Okay. I'm walking toward the Dominic. How will I recognize you?"

"I know what you look like. I'll come to you."

"I see that you've done your research."

"Of course. My client is very discriminating, and he only wants the best."

Flattered, Jin walked a little straighter. "Can't you at least give me a hint about the job or the company that wants to hire me? I'm dying of curiosity."

"Patience, my dear. You'll find out shortly." Maria ended the call.

Just to be safe, Jin sent a text to Mey. *I got a call from a headhunter, and I'm meeting her in ten minutes at the Dominic hotel. Her name is Maria Savino. In case she is a serial killer, I want you to know where I'm going.*

Mey's text arrived a moment later. *Good luck. Let me know how it goes.*

I will.

Jin copied the text she'd sent to Mey and sent it to Mitch, but with an added comment about postponing their plans for later.

He texted her right back. *Good luck. Call me when you are done. We still need to celebrate tonight.*

4

JIN

As Jin entered the lobby of the Dominic, a thirty-something average-looking brunette walked toward her. "Hello, Jin." The woman affected an overly friendly smile. "I'm Maria. Thank you for agreeing to see me so soon."

Curiously, the headhunter didn't offer Jin her hand. Maybe she was waiting to see what Jin would do? It could be part of the interview process, checking for social skills and confidence level.

Jin had no problem with either.

Flashing a smile of her own, she extended her hand. "Thank you for inviting me."

Maria ignored the offer. "The hotel's bar is over there." She pointed and started walking.

Shrugging it off, Jin followed the woman. Not everyone shook hands. Some people were germaphobes, and for others, it was a cultural thing.

The bar was pretty full, but they managed to find a table for two in the back.

"This is perfect." Maria waved the waitress over. "We'll have some privacy."

"What would you ladies like to drink?" the waitress asked.

Perhaps this was another test to see if she ordered alcohol. "I'll have a coke, please."

"Black Russian for me."

"Would you like an appetizer?"

"No, thank you. That will be all." Maria didn't even look at the waitress, her eyes never leaving Jin's.

The dismissal was somewhat rude, as was not asking Jin whether she wanted something to snack on.

Maria must be in a hurry.

As soon as the waitress had left, she put her palms on the table and leaned toward Jin. "First order of business. Everything that transpires between us must be kept confidential, which means you can't tell anyone about me, my employer, or what this job offer is about."

Jin swallowed. "I told my sister and my boyfriend that I'm meeting you here. I always do that when I go somewhere alone at night." She smiled, hoping that she hadn't just ruined her first interview. "Better safe than sorry, right?"

The woman nodded. "Absolutely. Since you are a smart young woman, I expected you would do that, which is why I didn't give you my real name."

Alarm bells went off in Jin's head. She'd never had a headhunter contact her before, but she was pretty sure they didn't use fake names.

"That's highly unusual. Do you do that with all of your recruits?"

Maria smiled indulgently. "You can trust me, Jin. When I show you my credentials, you will understand the need for secrecy."

Suddenly feeling ridiculous for imagining the worst about the woman, Jin let out a breath. What possible nefarious plans could Maria have for her other than offering her a job?

"Okay. I promise not to tell anyone about you, your employer, or what this job offer is about. All the secrecy makes me even more curious to hear it."

The waitress's arrival with their drinks meant another delay. "Will there be anything else, ladies?"

Maria shook her head. "Just the check, please."

"Are you guests at the hotel?" The waitress pulled out a folder from her apron pocket and handed it to Maria, or whatever her name was.

"Yes." She signed the bill, included the room number, and handed it back.

When the waitress left, Maria pulled her wallet out and handed it to Jin. "Open it."

Arching a brow, Jin flipped it open and read the laminated identification card. "National Security, Agent Marisol Ortega." It had the headhunter's picture on it.

The woman nodded. "That's me. Flip it to the other side."

Jin did as Marisol asked and found a West Virginia driver's license with the same name and picture.

She handed the wallet back. "Two identification cards prove nothing. They could be fake, not that I think they are, I trust you, but what on earth can a business major do for national security?"

Marisol laughed. "Every organization needs an accounting department to keep an eye on the costs. It also needs cleaning crews and cafeteria servers and countless others who are not agents."

That made sense.

"Why me, though? I don't have work experience."

"You don't need any. We prefer to hire young people who haven't been molded by the corporate world yet, and we provide them with training. You have a proven record of academic excellence and a strong work ethic, which is what we are looking for."

She'd said that before, but it was nice to hear it again.

"So, what's the job? Am I going to join the accounting department?"

"Before I give you any more details, you have to sign a nondisclosure agreement." Marisol smiled. "I need more than a verbal promise." She pushed to her feet. "Let's continue this in my room, where we will have more privacy."

As they headed toward the elevators, Jin asked, "Can you at least tell me how much they are offering? I'm sure that information is not a national security item."

Marisol waited until they were alone inside the cab before leaning to whisper in Jin's ear. "Two hundred and fifty thousand dollars a year, and provided that your performance is exemplary, a million-dollar bonus at the end of the five-year contract."

That couldn't be real. Jin had anticipated fifty or sixty thousand a year, which was the best a business major could hope for. The exception was investment banking, which paid much better, but she hadn't specialized in that.

"You're joking, right?"

Marisol shook her head. "No joke, trust me."

Exiting the elevator, they headed down the corridor to the very end, where Marisol opened the door to the corner suite.

Talk about impressive.

Jin had been prepared to see a nicely appointed room, but this was on an entirely different level. She'd never been inside a luxury hotel suite before, and she was trying hard not to gawk like some country bumpkin.

"The view of the river is beautiful." She walked over to the windows overlooking the water.

"Make yourself comfortable." Marisol pointed to an armchair. "I'll get the paperwork."

It occurred to Jin that she should have an attorney go over the contract, but she didn't know any. Not only that, the need for secrecy probably precluded it.

"Here is the nondisclosure agreement." Marisol put a stapled bundle of pages on the coffee table. "Read through it and then sign at the bottom. I'll notarize it once you are done."

That was convenient. The recruiter being a notary saved time, but it seemed somewhat shady. Then again, given the secrecy, it was probably necessary to do it like that.

"Do you need my driver's license?"

Marisol chuckled. "I have a copy. Working for the government has many advantages."

It would seem so.

As Jin read through the thing, she had no idea whether the list of draconian repercussions was standard for agreements like that. Bottom line, she couldn't tell anyone anything if she didn't want to end up in jail and stay there for a very long time.

Nevertheless, she signed it.

This was just about keeping her mouth shut, and she could do that. She wasn't agreeing to anything yet. Besides, what choice did she have?

Without the nondisclosure, she would never learn what this was all about.

Then there was the money.

The dollar signs in her eyes were blinding her to anything else. With that much money, at the end of her five-year contract, she and Mey could open the fashion business they had been fantasizing about for years.

Up until now, that plan had seemed like an impossible dream.

Except, Jin's gut was churning with unease despite Marisol's reassurances.

The effect the woman had on her was strange because Jin wasn't the trusting type. On the contrary, she was always suspicious of people's motives, but something about the woman inspired trust.

The agent flipped through the stack of papers, making sure that Jin had initialed everywhere it was required. She then pulled out a notary's journal from her briefcase, took Jin's fingerprints, and then had her sign the journal.

"Beautiful." Marisol closed it and put it in her briefcase together with the nondisclosure agreement. "Now, to the offer itself." She pulled out another stack of papers and handed it to Jin. "Take your time reading through it."

The prudent thing to do would have been to read every line, but Jin was out of patience. She flipped to the section about compensation, verifying that the amounts Marisol had quoted were real.

The woman chuckled. "Every recruit does the same thing. But I suggest that you go back and read all the details."

Jin smiled sheepishly. "I had to make sure that I heard you right. Those sums sounded so fantastical."

"They are. But once you read the job requirements, you will understand why our government is so generous."

Jin ended up reading through the contract twice.

Basically, the government was going to own her for the next five years, and she would have to live and work in a secret facility. During the training period, which was six months long, communication with family members and friends would be limited to pre-screened text messages. She would be allowed short visits with them only after completing the training.

The one thing that was missing was an actual job description.

She lifted her eyes to the recruiter. "It doesn't specify what I'm actually going to be doing."

Marisol smirked. "You'll do whatever you are told to do. But don't worry, you won't have to kill anyone or sleep with anyone that you don't want to."

Jin looked down at the stack of papers. "I wish it said so explicitly. I would feel better about signing the contract."

"Don't you trust me?"

"I do. But not everything is up to you."

With a sigh, Marisol lifted the contract and took another pen out of her briefcase. "I'll add a note explicitly stating that killing and sex are not going to be part of your job."

Oh, damn. That would look so stupid. Jin lifted a hand. "Don't."

"Are you sure? Because I have no problem adding the provision. You belong in this program, and your fears are unfounded."

"Whoever looks over the contract will just think that I've watched too many spy movies."

"Have you?"

Jin nodded. "It's my favorite genre."

Given Marisol's broad grin, that seemed to please her for some reason.

"Mine too." She handed the packet back to Jin. "Are you ready to sign?"

"I am." Jin grabbed the pen and scribbled her signature quickly before she had a chance to chicken out.

"Wonderful." Marisol took the contract, looked it over, and put it in her briefcase. "Now that all the legalities are out of the way, I can tell you why you've been chosen."

"I'm all ears."

"Given your penchant for spy stories and your special talent, you are going to love it. I told you that you belong in the program. Never doubt me."

The words 'special talent' sent shivers down Jin's spine. "What special talent?"

Marisol smirked. "I believe that you call it tethering."

5

JIN

Butterflies in her stomach, Jin looked out the jet's window at the narrow runway it was aiming for and prayed the pilot wasn't going to miss it.

Given that she was flying in a military transport, the fear was illogical. The pilot probably had thousands of flight hours under his or her belt. Except, she'd never flown on a small plane, and it was much scarier than flying commercial.

Next to her, Marisol closed her laptop and buckled her seatbelt. Smiling, she glanced at Jin. "We are almost there. Are you excited?"

Jin nodded.

Marisol hadn't talked much during the flight, working the entire time on her laptop or pretending to do so. Jin had a feeling that the woman had a problem connecting with people, and that she liked her solitude. Still, it was nice of her to offer Jin a free ride to her new place of employment.

Then again, it was likely that the agent had done it to ensure that Jin actually got to where she was supposed to and didn't pick up and run the other way. Marisol had even come to collect Jin from the dorms, driving her to the military airport and then joining her on the flight.

It made Jin feel important, but it hadn't been necessary.

She'd had no intention of running.

Now that she knew the real reason behind the government's willingness to pay her the obscene amount of over two million dollars over five years, she actually felt better about taking the job offer.

She might not like spying on people, but at least she was going to earn her pay. No one else could do what she could, which made her extremely valuable to her employer.

Hopefully.

She hadn't tested her ability on anyone in years, and never on complete strangers. It might not work.

"What if I can't do it? I mean tether to strangers. I've never done it before."

Marisol cast her an amused glance. "Don't worry. With our help, you will learn to hone your special talent and use it at will. Most of the people we get have a very loose grasp on their abilities and little control over them. That's what the training is for."

"I'm looking forward to meeting the other people in the program."

That was the most exciting part of her new job. After a lifetime of believing that she and Mey were freaks of nature, Jin was going to be among others like herself. Other than the money, helping her country was a significant bonus as well. Marisol hadn't had to work hard to evoke Jin's patriotic feelings. She loved both of her adoptive countries.

Both had been kind to her.

Except, thinking about the type of work that would be required of her, Jin felt conflicted. Because of her looks, she would most likely have to spy on Chinese officials, and she was not looking forward to that. After all, China was her birthplace, and perhaps her and Mey's biological parents still lived there.

As the jet touched down, Jin released a shaky breath. "Thank God. I was afraid the pilot was going to miss the runway. It's so narrow and short."

Marisol unbuckled and got up. "Military pilots are the best. There was no reason for worry."

Outside, a car was waiting for them, and the driver helped load their suitcases into the trunk.

"Thank you." Jin smiled at the young soldier.

The guy was cute and looked to be around the same age as her. Since she'd broken up with Mitch before leaving, Jin was a free agent, so why not?

"You're welcome." He smiled back, but that was it.

Marisol's stern scowl probably scared him off.

Less than half an hour later, they reached their destination, and Jin's jaw dropped. "Are we going inside the mountain?"

Marisol nodded. "It's incredible. There is a whole city built inside. For the next six months, you will be living underground. By the way, if you want to send your sister a text that you've arrived safely, this is the time to do it. You'll have to leave the phone with the guards."

It had been one of the provisions in the contract, but Jin had forgotten about it. Now that it was time to part with her phone, she felt like she was leaving part of herself at the gate.

She wrote the text, which Marisol checked before she could send it, and then handed it to the soldier who checked the driver's and Marisol's credentials.

"There is no reception inside anyway," Marisol said. "You can use only landlines, but you won't get the code for an outside line until your training is done."

"Yeah, I know. I actually read the contract."

Other than not getting to spend time with Mey, this was the hardest part. Worse, she hadn't told Mey about it either. The prohibition on revealing any details included the communications restriction.

As the enormous gate started lifting with hardly any sound, Jin swallowed. She wasn't claustrophobic, but the thought of not seeing sunshine for six months was disturbing.

Once the gate was open, they entered a well-lit tunnel that was four lanes wide. If necessary, tanks and even small planes could make it through.

"How many people live here?"

"Several thousand. Your program is just one of many. As I said, it's a city, with buildings and shops and cafeterias, except you don't have to pay for anything." She chuckled. "It's an all-inclusive resort."

"What about sunlight? Doesn't it get depressing to be underground?"

"The simulated light is incredible. After a day or two, you'll forget that it's not real."

6

JIN

"*I* get my own place?" Jin turned in a circle. The studio apartment was simply furnished, but it was about ten steps above her dorm room. First of all, there was only one queen-sized bed, so it looked like she wasn't sharing it with anyone. There was a sitting area with flat-screen television and even a kitchenette with all the necessities.

Many New Yorkers paid a fortune to live in a place like this. There was even a window. It was looking out into the underground street and the building across from hers, but still, it was an actual window, and the simulated light outside did a damn good job of making it look like early evening.

It was simply amazing.

Marisol smiled. "You're an adult with an important job. Of course, you don't have to share an apartment. You can invite people over, and if you meet someone you like, he can spend the night. What you do in your free time is nobody's business."

Jin felt like hugging her recruiter, but Marisol had made it clear that she didn't want to be touched. At first, Jin had thought that it was a personal preference, but after learning that her recruiter knew about her secret, the reason for the no touching had become apparent.

Marisol feared Jin's tether.

"You still didn't tell me how you knew about my ability."

"I'll leave it to the director to explain. Come on. He's waiting for you."

Jin looked down at her jeans and T-shirt. "Shouldn't I change first?"

"No time, and no need. Let's go."

As Jin followed Marisol out, the door closed behind them with a click, the mechanism locking it a couple of seconds later. She'd gotten the code to open it, but since her phone had been taken away, she had to memorize it. Living without that device was certainly an adjustment. Jin was used to storing all important information in the various applications that organized it neatly. Her own brain's memory functioning was out of practice.

As they walked outside, Jin looked around, but the street was deserted, which meant that most of the underground city's inhabitants were still working. Occasionally, an electric golf cart would pass by, and Jin noticed that some of the people riding them wore uniforms while others had civilian clothes on.

"Am I going to wear a uniform?" She climbed into Marisol's vehicle.

"Your department works with the military, but it is not part of it. So, no."

That made sense. If the paranormal department's job was to train special spies, uniforms were counterproductive to that. "By the way, am I allowed to talk about it with the people living and working here?"

Marisol shook her head. "As I said before, you can talk with everyone in the paranormal program about what you are doing but not to outsiders, and that includes any of the people working here that are not part of the program. And just to close any possible loopholes, you are not allowed to use any form of paranormal communication to connect with anyone in the outside world or anyone not in the program. So, if in addition to your hooking and tethering you also happen to have telepathic ability, you can only use it with others in the program. All of your communication with people outside this underground must get screened first." She pinned Jin with a hard stare. "Repeat what I've said."

Jin rolled her eyes. "I'm not allowed to communicate with anyone outside of this underground in any way without it getting screened first. And with those living here, I can't talk about the program unless they are part of it."

Marisol nodded. "You got it."

"So, what do I tell people when they ask me what I'm doing here?"

"Since everyone here is working on one secret project or another, no one is going to ask you that. But if someone does, you can say that it's confidential, and that will be the end of it."

Jin tilted her head. "Do you know what the others are working on?"

"No clue. I'm only affiliated with the paranormal department, and I don't ask questions that I know I'll get no answers to."

"Am I going to get my own golf cart?"

Marisol laughed. "No, my dear. You are going to walk. The distances are not that great, and it's not like the weather can get inclement here. It's always a pleasant seventy degrees."

"I figured as much."

Once they cleared the residential area, the structures became squat, and the numbering changed to lettering.

As they reached the building marked with the letter H, Marisol parked the cart next to several others.

Inside, a receptionist greeted them with a smile. "The director is expecting you. Go right ahead."

Jin lifted the identification card Marisol had given her. "With all the secrecy, I assumed that I'd have to put my card through scanners before being allowed to get in."

"It was scanned."

"How?"

Marisol shrugged. "I'm not a tech person, but the card in your pocket got scanned as soon as we approached the door. It wouldn't have opened otherwise."

Impressive. This was even more advanced than the imagined futuristic technology in *Star Trek*. Had it been developed right there in this underground city by one of the teams who were working on space-age security measures?

As they walked down the corridor, Jin noticed that there were no names on the doors, and they were distinguished from one another only by numbers.

Marisol knocked on the one marked with the number five.

The lock clicked, and the door opened on its own.

Inside, they were greeted by a distinguished-looking gentleman in his late sixties or early seventies. With his full head of gray hair, a neatly trimmed beard, and frameless glasses, the guy reminded Jin of her economics professor. They were about the same age and had the same intelligent and cunning eyes.

"Hello, Jin. Welcome to the program." He got up from behind his desk and walked around it to offer her his hand.

She looked down at it. "Aren't you afraid to touch me?"

His laugh was good-natured. "I am not. My special talent is immunity to all the supernatural tricks paranormals can pull. Many have tried, but none have succeeded." He took her hand and covered it with his other. "But you are welcome to try it as well."

As kind and as grandfatherly as the director appeared, Jin knew in her gut that it would be a huge mistake to try and succeed.

"I haven't tethered anyone in ages. My first try should be on someone easier."

He nodded. "You'll get your chance soon." He motioned to a chair. "Please, take a seat."

"Do you need me to stay, sir?" Marisol asked.

"You can leave. And thank you for delivering Jin to me."

"You are welcome, sir."

As Marisol left without sparing her a second glance, Jin's chest squeezed with apprehension. Up until now, the woman was her liaison, her instructor, the only person she knew in this strange new world, and now she was gone.

"Don't worry." The director smiled. "She'll be back tomorrow. By then, you will have met all of your teammates and made plenty of new friends."

"I hope so. I'm eager to meet other people like me." She hesitated for about ten seconds before asking. "How did you find out about my talent? No one other than my sister knows about my talent."

"Does your sister share it? Talents usually run in families."

If he didn't know about it, Jin wasn't going to tell him. Until she found out what all this was about, she was going to keep Mey's talent secret.

"No, she doesn't." And that wasn't a lie. Mey couldn't do what Jin could.

"That's a shame. Two are always better than one, right?" He smiled his kindly smile, but Jin wasn't sure she was buying it.

"You still didn't tell me how I got discovered. I've been very careful not to mention it to anyone. Even my parents don't know about it."

Leaning forward, he looked at her with an indulgent expression on his face. "An intelligent girl like you should have been even more careful. Everything you say over a cellular or internet connection, every text, every email, they all leave a trail. With computing power growing exponentially, it's become easy to search this endless stream of information for trigger words. Mostly, it is used to find out about terrorist activity and all kinds of plots against our country, but it is also useful in identifying special talents."

Jin felt the blood drain from her face.

Marisol had contacted her shortly after the phone call in which she'd offered Mey to attach a tether to that cheating scumbag Oliver.

Luckily, Mey hadn't mentioned anything about her own talent. But surely there had been other phone conversations and texts in which they had talked about it.

Her only hope was that the search for paranormal talent had started only recently, and that the bots were not going to screen past communications.

Crap, how was she going to warn her sister if she couldn't communicate with her?

More importantly, why did she feel the need to shield Mey?

So far, everything looked great, and Jin was excited to meet the other talents. Except, she couldn't shake the nagging feeling that things were not as they seemed.

7

JIN

"Team, say hello to your newest member, Jin Levine." The director put his hand on the small of her back, urging her forward.

It was a small classroom, but there were no desks, and the twelve people she'd counted were sitting in a semi-circle as if they were a support group for recovering substance abusers or trauma victims.

In a way, they were.

After all, life hadn't been easy for any of them. Feeling like freaks was not conducive to well-being, and hiding their paranormal talents made getting close to people nearly impossible.

What surprised Jin, though perhaps it shouldn't have, was the wide age spread. There was a guy who looked to be in his late fifties, and a boy who couldn't be older than twelve.

Now that was totally wrong.

Taking a kid out of his home and putting him inside a bunker with a bunch of adults bordered on child abuse.

Several people said hello, others waved, and one guy gave her an appreciative look-over. He was mildly attractive and looked to be in his mid-thirties, which she was okay with if he passed the height test. Given her statuesque appearance, Jin couldn't date short men. Well, couldn't wasn't the right word. It just made her uncomfortable.

"Hello. I'm so glad to meet others with paranormal abilities."

"Welcome to the freak show," the older guy said.

"Now, James" The director scowled at him. "You know that I don't like that word. You are all gifted individuals, the next step in human evolution, not freaks."

"Yay, us," someone murmured.

"That's the spirit." The director grinned as if the comment was genuine. "Let's introduce ourselves, shall we? James, you start."

The guy nodded. "Hi, I'm James, I'm fifty-five years old, and I am a remote viewer."

Next was the kid. "Hi, I'm Andy, I'm fourteen, and I am a telepath."

So, he was a little older than he looked, but he was still too young to be there.

The girl sitting next to him raised her hand. "I'm Jacklin, but everyone calls me Jacki, and I am twenty-two years old. I'm clairvoyant, which means I can sometimes see the future."

The thirty-something guy was next. "I'm Richard, and I am thirty-four years old. I'm a sensory telepath. Which means that I need to touch you to create a mental link."

"Cool. That's similar to what I can do."

Behind her, the director chuckled. "Richard can sense what the person is feeling only while touching them. Your talent is on a whole different level."

Richard didn't seem happy to hear that, while the others looked curious.

"Jin has the most unique talent." The director turned to her. "Why don't you tell the group about it? I'm sure you can explain it better than I can. We can continue the introductions after that."

Feeling extremely uneasy about telling the group what she could do, Jin reluctantly nodded. "I also need to touch a person to create a link. But once I put my mental hook into their psyche, I can tie a string of my consciousness to them, and from that moment on, I can see and hear what they see hear and see. But not all of the time. I need to focus and follow the tether to the person, and then I can only see and hear what is going on at that moment. I have no access to their past experiences." She chuckled nervously. "Which can be really embarrassing. I can follow the tether while they are sitting on the toilet, or taking a bath, or being intimate with someone. That's why I haven't done it in years. I'm not even sure if I can do it to people I don't know. I've never tried."

As she'd expected, the room fell silent, and everyone was kind of gaping at her.

The director put his hand on her shoulder. "Thank you, Jin." He pulled out a chair for her and put it in front of the semi-circle. "You can sit down." Turning back to the class, he waved his hand. "Let's continue with the introductions. Jeremy, you are next."

She looked at the guy the director had pointed at. He was sitting with his elbows propped on his knees, and his head cradled in his hand, and as he lifted his eyes to hers, Jin's breath caught in her throat.

It wasn't that he was handsome. Jeremy's face was too thin, and his nose was too long, but he had the most amazing eyes she'd ever seen. The irises were turquoise, rimmed with dark blue, and his lashes were so long that they looked fake. In fact, if she'd seen him on the street, Jin would have thought that he was wearing contact lenses and glued-on lashes.

Perhaps he was?

"Hi, I am Jeremy, I'm twenty-four, and I am a remote viewer like James but with a slight twist. While James can remote view in the present, I can remote view in the future. Regrettably, my ability is much less useful than James's because there are many possible futures. What I see may or may not happen."

The director waved a dismissive hand. "Don't sell yourself short, Jeremy. Your talent has been proved to work."

Jin rubbed her chin. "Forgive my ignorance, but what is the difference between a clairvoyant and a future remote viewer? Isn't it the same thing?"

Jeremy shook his head. "Jacki sees what's going to happen. She might not know when and where, but there is a high probability of her visions being true, and it's mostly about major events. I see snapshots. Sometimes they are of future technology that doesn't exist yet, or cities of the future, bridges, dams, futuristic buildings." He chuckled. "I think of myself as a modern Jules Verne but without the writing talent or Leonardo without the artistic ability. I rarely see people or events in my future viewing. It's more about things."

Fascinating. So far, it was the only talent Jin wished she had. To foresee what would be invented and where humanity was going technology-wise could be very useful. "It's a shame that you can't write about it or draw it. I would have loved to see what you see."

Jeremy seemed pleased. "Can you draw or write?"

"Unfortunately, no."

"That's a real shame. I could have described to you what I saw, and you could've translated it into words or pictures."

Was that a pick-up line?

Jin wasn't sure, but provided that Jeremy passed the height test, she hoped that it was. He seemed like a nice guy, was her age, and his eyes were gorgeous.

The director walked up to him and put a hand on his shoulder. "The way technology is advancing, you'll soon be able to describe your visions to a computer, and it will create a story or a drawing from it." He turned to the girl sitting next to Jeremy. "Wendy, it's your turn."

"Hi, I'm Wendy, and I'm nineteen. I'm an empath."

And so it went.

"I'm Abigail, I'm thirty-two, and I'm an energy healer."

"Naomi, I'm twenty-one. I have psychometry. I can get information from objects." She smiled shyly. "Sometimes."

That sounded similar to what Mey could do, and Jin made a mental note to ask Naomi later what exactly she could learn from objects. Was it visual, auditory, or both?

"Spencer at your service, ma'am. I'm seventeen, and I can read auras. Yours is very strong. You are driven, resourceful, and you don't take crap from anyone."

Jin laughed. "Thank you, Spencer. That's a great conversation starter. I bet you have no trouble with pick-up lines."

He grimaced. "Most auras are not as flattering. So, unless I lie, I can't use my talent for that."

The director pointed to the girl sitting next to Spencer. "Sofia, your turn."

"I'm eighteen, and I have a tiny bit of telekinetic power. If someone flips a coin, I can make it fall in a particular way, and the same is true for dice. But I can't move them unless they are already in motion."

"Thank you, Sofia." The director pointed to the woman sitting next to her. "Mollie."

She nodded. "I'm forty-six, and I'm post-cognizant. I see past events."

"I'm Dylan," said the last member of the group. "I'm thirty, and I have claircognizance, which basically means that I get good hunches. Personally, I count myself lucky for having this ability, but it's not very useful for others."

He was right. Although fascinating, half of the talents were useless for spying, and Jin wondered why they had been recruited. Perhaps the program wasn't exclusively about that?

Still, everyone seemed to be okay with being there, and it didn't seem as though anything nefarious was going on.

Smiling, she looked at her new teammates. "Thank you for sharing your talents with me. I have to admit that I've never heard of some of them. I'll do my best to remember all of your names and who does what, but if I don't, please don't get offended. I have a sucky memory for names."

"I have a question," Jeremy said. "Do the people you touch feel when you create the connection?"

Mey had, but Jin wasn't going to mention that. In fact, she was going to say as little as possible about her sister. Maybe she could even lie and say that they weren't close.

"I don't think so. But the last time I tethered to someone, I was fourteen, and I haven't followed that thread in years."

That wasn't a lie, just not the entire truth.

None of the team members had said anything about detecting lies, so she might get away with that. Except, perhaps the two empaths could feel when a person lied, especially if said person felt guilty about it.

Why should she feel guilty, though? She was protecting a loved one, and that was a good thing.

But why did she feel such a fierce need to protect Mey?

Everyone seemed nice, including the director, and she'd accepted the offer out of her own free will.

Still, somewhere in the back of her mind, suspicion lurked, prompting Jin to keep her guard up.

8

JIN

Marisol sat on the couch, crossed her legs, and lifted the cup of coffee Jin put on the side table for her. "So, tell me, how are you acclimating?"

Jin hadn't expected house calls from her recruiter, but it seemed like Marisol wanted to stay in touch.

"I'm good." Jin sat next to the recruiter, but not too close. Marisol still wouldn't shake her hand or touch her in any other way. "I was bummed about missing the weekly outing, but Director Simmons said that I needed to catch up to the group and has had me studying my ass off since day one." She sighed. "I thought I was done with school, at least for several years, but here I am, doing homework again."

She'd also discovered that each group member was assigned different study material, and they had instructors come in and work with them individually. In her case, she was studying Mandarin, which made the director's future plans for her quite obvious.

Jin was going to spy either on Chinese officials or business people. Not a big surprise there. She was perfect for the job.

Theoretically.

Mandarin was damn hard to learn, and Jin doubted she would ever get fluent in it or master the proper accent. Except, maybe it wasn't necessary. It was enough that she understood what the people she was spying on were saying.

Marisol leaned forward. "Is there anyone in the group who has caught your eye?"

That was unexpected. Suddenly they were BFFs?

Jin shrugged. "Jeremy is cute, and he has the most amazing eyes, but he is too short for me. Besides, he and Naomi seem to have a thing going on."

"How about Richard?" Marisol asked. "He is handsome, and he is tall."

Jin waved a hand. "Too old for me."

Marisol chuckled. "A ten-year difference might seem like a lot to you now, but it really isn't. And your talents overlap. It's much easier to have a relationship with someone similar to you."

"I guess. He is okay, but I'm not attracted to him."

"That's because you've got it in your head that he is too old. Give the guy a chance. He might surprise you."

For some reason, Marisol's suggestion suddenly seemed like a good idea. It wasn't as if there were a lot of guys to choose from.

Only Richard and Spencer passed the height test, but Spencer was still a kid. James was in his fifties, Andy was fourteen, and Dylan and Jeremy were too short, and both had eyes for someone else.

"He doesn't seem interested in me."

Marisol snorted. "You are so naive. Every guy in that group, including the fourteen-year-old boy, is stealing glances at you. They are just afraid to approach you because you are such a badass."

"Why would they think that? I'm polite to everyone, doing my work and helping others whenever I can, and I don't argue with anyone."

Uncrossing her legs, Marisol smoothed a hand over her slacks. "It might be because of what Spencer said about your aura. Or, they are just intimidated by you. You're very tall, beautiful, and you are smart. Most guys would hesitate to approach a girl like you. I'm sure Richard just needs a little encouragement." She waved a hand in a circle. "Flirt with him a little. You don't strike me like the shy type."

"I'm not."

Jin was still stuck on the aura reading. Marisol hadn't been in the room when Spencer had read it.

"How did you know about the aura reading?"

"The director told me."

Jin narrowed her eyes at the recruiter. "What else did he tell you about me? And why? Isn't your job with me done?"

Marisol smiled, but as always, the smile didn't reach her eyes. "My job is never done. For now, I'm like the homeroom teacher, making sure that everyone is getting along with everyone else. Once the group gets significantly larger, Director Simmons may hire someone else to take over this part of my job."

Jin leaned back and crossed her arms over her chest. "I hope that you'll get many more people into the program so we can be divided into teams according to talents. It makes no sense for an energy healer to learn the same things as I do. In fact, I shouldn't be here at all. They should have assigned me to a spy unit. That's all my talent is good for."

"That's the long-term plan. Except, it's not easy to find talent. Most of what the bots flag is nonsense. They have a team of twenty-five people working in that department, sifting through all the garbage that the bots are throwing at them."

"That must be a very frustrating job."

"It is. But at the rate artificial intelligence is advancing, I expect that the entire department will be replaced by a supercomputer soon."

"You really think so? I think it will take several decades before computers can understand human conversations and analyze them in depth."

Marisol's eyes sparkled with excitement, which was quite jarring since they looked kind of deadened most of the time. "You're wrong. It's going to happen much sooner than that. And when it does, it's going to be done at amazing speed. I'll be hopping from city to city, collecting the talents."

Jin laughed. "You will need a team of assistants."

"No way. I'm not splitting my commission. Do you have any idea how much I get per head?"

Jin had heard somewhere that headhunters were paid ten percent of the recruit's first-year salary, which meant that Marisol had pocketed twenty-five thousand for bringing Jin in. It was a lot of money, but it wasn't a fortune. Still, given that the thirteen people in the program had all arrived in the last three months, that added up to quite a lot. At that rate, Marisol would be making more than a million a year.

Not bad at all.

"If everyone's pay is similar to mine, I assume that you are getting twenty-five thousand per head."

"Good guess." Smirking, Marisol leaned forward. "But I get double that, and all my expenses are paid. I'm going to retire a wealthy woman."

Jin whistled. "Can I have your job? I mean once you retire?"

The recruiter chuckled. "You don't have the necessary qualifications." She pushed to her feet. "Promise me that you will give Richard some serious thought. Flirt with him, show him that you are interested."

Jin didn't want to promise anything, but for some reason, it was impossible to refuse Marisol.

"I promise."

"Good girl." The recruiter smiled. "Oh, I almost forgot the main reason for my visit." She pulled Jin's phone out of her purse. "Since you missed the outing, you didn't get a chance to send a message to your loved ones, and I promised you that you could." She handed her the phone. "Type it, and as soon as I'm in an area that has reception, I'll send it out for you."

That was nice of her. Or maybe not.

Jin typed the most generic message to Mey, saying that she missed her, was very busy with work, and would send another message next week.

"Thank you for doing this for me." She handed Marisol the phone. "I'm sure my sister and my parents are worried because they haven't heard from me."

"We can't have that." Marisol dropped the phone into her purse and smiled. "My job is to keep everyone happy."

It seemed like the woman had many responsibilities, but with what she was getting paid, it was only fair that her bosses expected a lot in return.

9

JIN

"That will be all for today," the fitness instructor announced. "Good work, everyone."

"Thank God." Jin huffed out a breath. "I don't think I could have lasted another minute. Who do they think we are, special ops commandos?"

"Yep, I guess they do." Jacki wiped the sweat off the back of her neck with a towel. "It makes sense for you because you are training to become a spy, but why do I have to suffer?"

"Or I," Mollie groaned. "I'm way too old for this."

Over the past two weeks, the three of them had become good friends, spending their free time together, or rather what was left of it after classes, homework, and dates.

Homework took at least an hour a day, Mollie was dating James, and Jin was dating Richard. Only Jacki was adamant about remaining single despite Dylan's desperate flirting attempts, and he wasn't the only one. Jacki was getting covetous looks from all the other male team members, the instructors, and even from Director Simmons, who wore a wedding ring.

The girl was hot, and it wasn't only because of the waist-long cornsilk-blond hair, or the enviable cleavage and long legs. She seemed mysterious and unapproachable, and that was enough to drive any guy nuts. It was good that Jin had no self-esteem issues and believed herself to be just as hot, or she might have developed an inferiority complex.

Jacki didn't act like a queen bee, though, and she treated her looks more as a hindrance than an asset. She wore no makeup, her clothes were baggy, and her gorgeous hair was usually hanging in a messy braid down her back.

"I still didn't show you the turbines," Jacki said.

Jacki found the inner workings of the enormous mountain cavity they were living in fascinating. For days, she'd been nagging Jin to come see the heavy machinery that made life underground possible.

The problem was that Jin was only mildly interested, and between dating Richard and studying her ass off, she had no time for sightseeing. Still, she couldn't keep coming up with excuses and disappointing Jacki. It was best to get it over with instead of getting reproachful looks from her new BFF.

"Do you want to do it now?"

Jacki's eyes widened. "I can't believe that you actually said yes. Sure, ready when you are."

"Then let's go." Jin wrapped the towel around her neck. "I don't need to shower and change first, right? We are just going to see some dusty, noisy turbines."

"They are noisy, but they are not dusty. Maintaining them in perfect working condition is crucial. Without them, we would have no fresh air coming in."

Jin glanced at Mollie. "Do you want to come?"

"Some other time. Right now, all I want to do is go home, shower, put my PJs on, and collapse in front of the dumb box. I'm exhausted."

For some reason, Jacki seemed relieved that Mollie had declined the invitation. Perhaps the walk to see the turbines was an excuse to have a heart-to-heart conversation.

Except, there had been plenty of opportunities for them to have girl talk when Jacki had come over to Jin's place or vice versa.

"How are things going with Richard?" Jacki asked a few minutes into the walk, confirming Jin's suspicion.

"Okay, I guess. We both keep running hot and cold." She shrugged. "I've never dated a guy for longer than a couple of weeks, so it might be my fault. One day I think that he is the sexiest guy on the planet, and the next, I wonder what I see in him."

Jacki nodded solemnly as if it made perfect sense to her.

"Did you ever experience that before with a guy?"

"I didn't date much, not even before I got here."

"Why not? You are seriously gorgeous and a swell human being."

Jacki smiled. "Thank you. I don't like having to keep secrets, that's one reason. The other is that when I get close to people, I start seeing glimpses from their future." She shook her head. "Imagine having to keep that a secret."

They were getting closer to the turbines, and Jin had to raise her voice to be heard. "Yeah, I can see how that could be a relationship killer. On the other hand, it can save you heartache. Take my sister, for example. She came home from a photoshoot, and right away smelled another woman all over the bedding. If she could have foreseen that her boyfriend was a cheating scumbag, she wouldn't have started dating him in the first place."

Jacki nodded and took Jin's hand, leading her into a narrow pathway. On one side of it was a wall with a two-foot-tall concrete ledge, on the other side a long line of massive ventilation turbines. A metal railing separated the path from the heavy machinery, allowing visitors a clear view.

Jacki kept walking, crossing at least a hundred feet until she stopped and sat on the ledge, pulling Jin to sit beside her.

"Impressive!" Jin yelled to be heard.

Jacki leaned closer, covering her mouth with her hand while speaking into

Jin's ear. "The turbines are not the reason I brought you here. It's the noise. This is the only place where I'm absolutely sure we can't be overheard."

Jin lifted a brow but said nothing.

"If you want to say something, cover your mouth so the cameras can't see your lips moving. And don't look for them. Just nod if you agree or shake your head if you want to talk."

Jin nodded.

"I have another talent no one knows about," Jacki said. "I'm immune, like the director. Compulsion doesn't work on me. It does work on everyone else in the program, though. And that's how Marisol has a hundred percent success rate. She compels the recruits to sign the contracts."

Jin frowned.

Was it possible that she'd been compelled?

She shook her head, and they switched places. Jin leaned into Jacki's ear and covered her mouth with her hand. "I was compelled by the money. I don't think Marisol needed to do anything else."

Jacki shook her head. "Did she tell you to trust her?"

Jin nodded.

"And you did, even though you had no reason to?"

Jin nodded again.

"That was compulsion. Did she tell you to flirt with Richard?"

Unease starting to churn in her belly, Jin nodded.

"She did the same to him. That's why you are both running hot and cold. It's hot right after she has a talk with you, and then it runs cold when she is away. Am I right?"

Thinking back, Jin realized that Jacki was right. The cooling off usually started a day after Marisol left. Suddenly, a lot of little things that hadn't added up before started to make sense.

Jin nodded.

"She tries to do the same with Dylan and me, but I pretend to be pitching for the other team. She thinks she can override even that, but at least she is not suspicious."

Jin shook her head, and they switched places again. "If she didn't compel you, why did you join? And before we switch again, is there a way for me to override the compulsion?"

"I came because of the money. I was a foster kid with no prospects, so this was a lifeline for me. She didn't need to work hard to convince me. And as for overriding the compulsion, I don't think anyone can do it on their own. But when you think about it, the compulsion is only about keeping the program secret and about trusting Marisol. We can still run."

Jin shook her head, and they switched again. "Why run? I don't like the compulsion part, but I really like the money. After five years, I'll have more than two million dollars. My sister and I will have enough to open our dream business."

They switched. "Think about the big picture. Why is Marisol trying so hard to pair us up? Why are we all in the same program even though it's obvious our talents have very different uses?"

Jin shrugged, indicating that she didn't know.

"They want us to make babies with each other and produce even stronger talents. Do you think they will let you go and take that child or children with you? And what about having kids with a man you don't really love but are compelled to be with? Is that worth the money?"

A cold shiver running down her spine, Jin shook her head. "I didn't have sex with Richard yet, and now that I know what Marisol is doing, I'm not going to. She might be able to force me to date him, but not to sleep with him."

Jacki shook her head. "Don't be so sure. Marisol is subtle, but she is powerful. Besides, your sister is coming for you."

Jin jerked away, but Jacki pulled her down again. "In the vision I had, she approaches you in the mall that they drop us at in Harrisonburg. She has a couple of guys helping her, and she asks you if you are here voluntarily. That's all I saw, but it's enough. On one of our future outings, your sister will come, and you can escape with her."

Jin shook her head. "What about you?"

"If she's willing to take me, I'll come along. I have a good feeling about this. I don't think we will have another chance to get out of the program."

It was Wednesday, and the next outing was on Saturday. Jin had until then to decide whether she wanted to stay or not.

First, though, she had to verify if what Jacki had said about the compulsion was true, and Jin knew precisely how to test it.

Over the past two weeks, there had been many instances when she'd been tempted to follow the tether she had to Mey. Getting a small glimpse at her sister's life and making sure that she was okay was not violating the program. But every time the thought had crossed her mind, Jin had been reminded of her promise not to communicate with the outside world in any form and had stopped.

Later tonight, she was going to follow the tether to Mey no matter what, but if she couldn't, then Jacki was right.

10

JIN

"Can you sever the tether once it is created?" Dr. Roberts asked. The guy was an actual medical doctor, but in addition to making brain scans while they were using their talents, he also worked with them on gaining better control of their abilities.

Jin hesitated. She could easily claim that she could, and no one could prove otherwise.

The truth was that she'd never tried.

Before joining the program, she had only tethered to people she cared about, and she avoided following the string of consciousness unless she was worried about them.

Now, she had a tether to each of the teammates, including Jacki, which proved that it worked on everyone. Which made her regret that she hadn't hooked the director when she'd had the chance.

Still, it was not too late. Since he didn't know about Jacki's immunity, he also didn't realize that his own probably was not going to protect him from Jin. He might offer her his hand again.

"I'm not sure."

The instructor nodded. "Then let's give it a try." He turned to look at Jeremy. "Attempt to release him. First without touching him, and if that doesn't work, with touching."

None of her teammates had been happy about her hooking them, but she'd promised never to spy on them unless it was during the many exercises Doctor Roberts insisted on. She'd even asked the two empaths to verify that she'd meant it.

Nevertheless, since that day, they had all started treating her differently, and she couldn't really blame them for that.

"Ready when you are," Jeremy said.

She waved a hand. "Give me a moment. I need to concentrate."

"Take all the time you need." The instructor walked over to Jeremy. "I want you to focus inwardly and see if you can feel the tether releasing."

Closing her eyes, Jin did the reverse of what she did when inserting a hook. She imagined unraveling the string of consciousness she'd previously tied to Jeremy and then pulling out what she imagined as a shiny little hook made from light.

"I feel it," Jeremy said. "It's so strange. I didn't feel it when Jin hooked me, but now that she's released the hook, I feel a little lonely, abandoned." He made a pouty face.

Naomi elbowed him in his side. "Watch it. You're making me jealous."

Doctor Roberts lifted his hand to stop the banter. "It could be a placebo effect. Jeremy, I want you to walk out of the classroom and do something unusual." He turned to Jin. "When he is out, check if you can still follow the tether to him."

As Jin waited for Jeremy to walk out, she debated what to do in case the tether was still there. Lie and say that she couldn't see what he was doing? Or admit that she still could?

Luckily, Marisol hadn't compelled her to tell the truth, just to trust her and to lust after Richard.

Jin's inability to follow the tether to Mey had proved beyond doubt that she was under Marisol's compulsion. All that her many attempts had managed to achieve had been severe headaches.

The compulsion was impossible to shake, and even though she knew now that the feelings were not her own, she had a hard time overriding them. It was doubly difficult with Richard. He was convinced that he wanted her as well and was very upset about her refusal to get intimate with him.

Jin had lied, saying that she had a rule against going to bed with someone she'd just met. The truth was that it didn't really matter. Since she was on the pill, he couldn't make her pregnant, and as far as she was concerned there was nothing wrong about two adults scratching an itch.

But it was the principle of it.

She wasn't going to have sex with a guy because someone was compelling her to lust after him. Except, if she continued to stall, Marisol was eventually going to force the issue. Jin figured that the only reason she hadn't done it so far was that she didn't know that Jin and Richard hadn't had sex yet.

"Well, what's the verdict?" Doctor Roberts asked.

"Oh, I haven't tried yet. Give me a couple of moments."

Concentrating, Jin tried to find the thread and follow it to Jeremy, but it was really gone.

Letting out a relieved breath, she shook her head. "It's not there. I can't see what he's doing."

As the others started murmuring about getting released as well, Doctor Roberts lifted his hand to shush them. "One at a time, people."

As Jin unhooked each of her teammates, some reported the same sensation of abandonment as Jeremy had, while others reported feeling nothing.

Jin felt lighter. Letting go of so many tethers at once was like freeing her mind of background noise. She hadn't been aware of it, but, apparently, tethering twelve additional people had an adverse effect on her.

Being able to sever the tethers was good news.

She'd often wondered what would happen when she was sent out on missions and had to hook into people that she had no desire to be tethered to. Knowing it would be only temporary was a huge relief.

When the class was over, the looks she got from her teammates were much friendlier than the polite ones she'd been getting since the experiment had started.

Jacki walked over and wrapped an arm around Jin's shoulders. "I haven't shown you the water pumps yet. Are you up for a walk?"

That was code for going somewhere noisy to talk.

"Sure. You've infected me with your fascination for heavy machinery."

They didn't talk much on the way, and when they reached the fenced-off area, they sat down on the concrete floor and looked at the pumps through the crisscrossing wires.

Jacki leaned closer. "I think your sister is coming for you this weekend."

It hadn't happened the previous Saturday, but the upshot had been that Richard had stayed behind to catch up on homework, and she and Jacki had sat in a coffee shop right by the entrance, talking without fear of being overheard.

Naturally, they had checked their clothes and shoes for bugs, going as far as leaving their purses on the bus and just taking some money and their driver's licenses in their pockets.

Jin had thought that Jacki was being paranoid, but she'd followed her example anyway. They'd spent the entire time talking in hushed voices and glancing through the window in hopes of seeing Mey.

She hadn't shown up, which was good since Jin still wasn't a hundred percent sure that she wanted to leave. Giving up two million dollars was not an easy decision, and she still wasn't sure that Jacki was right about the program being designed to breed the next generation of super-humans.

Marisol and the director could have had other motives for pushing teammates into each other's arms. Doctor Simmons was big on team bonding, and pairing them up might have been part of that.

But there were other bothersome aspects to the program.

Like the kids.

Last week Marisol had arrived with another fifteen-year-old girl, which brought the number of underage participants to three out of fourteen.

That was wrong no matter how much the director and Marisol had tried to cloak it in good intentions.

She leaned toward Jacki. "I wonder whether I should offer the teenagers a chance to come with us. Except, I'm still not sure that I should escape. Giving up all that money and then spending the rest of my life in hiding doesn't seem like a smart move to me. I'd rather stay the five years, collect my bonus, and then leave."

Jacki snorted. "First of all, you are not going to walk away with the whole amount. Did you forget taxes? You're only going to get half of that. Secondly, do you really think they will let you walk away? You are the most valuable asset they've snagged so far—the ultimate spy. And besides, you are still compelled to feel that you belong here, and that's why you can't see what's wrong with this place."

"And yet you came out of your own free will. No one compelled you."

Jacki shrugged. "I was blinded by the money, and I was curious to meet others like me. I also wondered if my ability could be enhanced. Naively, I didn't expect them to push drugs on us. When they started that, it cemented my decision."

"They said that hallucinogens are harmless and that they have no side effects and don't cause long-term damage. They helped you with your visions."

It had been a freaky experience, but Jin had no problem experimenting when she knew it was safe. They had a medical doctor supervise it, and other than Mollie, no one had freaked out. Well, James had had a scare because of his heart condition, but the doctor had reassured them that it hadn't been because of the drugs. But what if it had?

Nah, doctors were sworn to do no harm. He wouldn't have let James participate in the experiment if he'd thought that it was dangerous for him. Besides, even if the doctor didn't give a shit, James's talent made him a valuable asset to the program.

A remote viewer was good for spying.

Shaking her head, Jacki leaned into Jin. "And that makes it okay to give them to impressionable teenagers? Come on, Jin. If not for Marisol's compulsion, you would have felt just as awful about it as I did. Try to shake it off and think. God knows what else they are going to have us do. Five years is a long time."

It was difficult to feel alarmed by Jacki's words when all Jin heard in her head were Marisol's reassurances. She'd said that the drugs were perfectly safe and that they had the potential of unlocking more hidden talents she might not be aware of.

So far, no new talents had surfaced, but they had only done the drug experiments twice.

"I wish I could remove the compulsion from you," Jacki said in her ear. "If you decide not to go with your sister, do you think she will still help me escape? Because I want out. I'm sick of living underground, and I'm sick of feeling like a bug under a magnifying glass, with cameras and listening devices recording everything I do and say."

Jin shook her head. "How are we going to make it out there? We will need new identities, or we will have to move somewhere far away from here." She smiled as an idea blossomed in her mind. "You can come with me to Israel. We can hide there."

"First, let's make it out of here. Then we will worry about where we are going."

"We need to plan for it now. My sister served in intelligence, and she might know someone who can help us. Maybe she and her friends can help the entire team escape. I'm sure Israeli intelligence would love to offer each of us a job, and they can provide everyone with fake identities."

"And what would we achieve by that? Change one secret organization for another? No, thank you. I want my freedom. As sucky as my life was before I signed the deal with the devil, I'd rather have it back than stay here."

Yeah, Jacki was right. Jin would have liked to believe that Israeli intelligence held itself to higher moral standards, but she had nothing to base it on. The higher-ups over there might be just as unscrupulous as those over here.

11

JIN

The artificial glow outside Jin's window mimicked dawn at precisely six o'clock, the same as it had done every morning since she'd arrived at the belly of the mountain.

Except, today was Saturday. The day Jacki had predicted Mey showing up at the mall and offering Jin help to escape the program.

Jin was excited, scared, and conflicted.

She'd signed a contract, and as she'd told Mey in her text, she wasn't a quitter. Turning her back on obligations that she'd committed to felt wrong. Also, there were many other things she was going to regret if she ran. Like not having had the chance to shake the director's hand and tether to him. If she did that, she could find out whether Jacki was right about him and the breeding plan and all the other things she'd accused him of. Like planning to keep the recruits in the program forever.

Perhaps once she got out, she could tell someone about his plans and at least get the kids out. Except, she wasn't going to see Director Simmons before getting on the bus with the rest of her team.

Damn, she was going to miss her new freaky friends, and she was going to miss Richard as well.

Talk about guilt.

Her feelings for him weren't real, but knowing that logically didn't help the way she felt about leaving him behind without a word of warning.

There was no way she could risk saying goodbye to him or even hinting that she was leaving. The poor guy would feel so betrayed. Just like her, he was under Marisol's compulsion, but unlike her, he didn't have Jacki to whisper the truth in his ear.

And then there were the little things, like not having gone to see the underground lake yet. She should have done it while she still had a chance, but things had been hectic. Between the long hours in the classrooms, the grueling physical training, the homework, and spending time with Richard, there hadn't been much time left over for hiking trips to see the natural treasures of the mountain.

Perhaps she should leave Richard a note? Something he would find after she was gone?

And say what?

It was better not to say anything, especially since she didn't know whether Mey was going to show up for sure.

Last week, Jin had stuffed her backpack with all the things she'd thought she couldn't live without, but Jacki had told her to leave it because it could be bugged. Jin had spent most of the ride to Harrisonburg thinking about the contents of that backpack and whether she could live without them. The answer was that there had been nothing really important in there, just a couple of favorite shirts and a few knickknacks that she'd brought with her. Those had sentimental value, like the small jewelry box her mother had given her for her sixteenth birthday, but they were replaceable. The contents of that box were so few that she could wear all of them at once, and it wouldn't look weird.

This time, she was not going to take anything with her. Not even her purse. Her wallet could go into her pocket.

With a sigh, she looked around the lovely studio that had been her home for the past month. She was going to miss having her own place too.

Where was she going to live?

She couldn't stay with Mey because that would be the first place they would come to look for her. Her best bet was to go back to Israel. Could they get to her there as well?

Probably.

The more Jin thought about escaping, the more impossible it seemed. There was nowhere to run, and the benefits of running were not as clear to her as they were to Jacki.

Perhaps she should wait and see what Mey had planned. Her sister was a smart woman, and she wouldn't have organized an escape for Jin unless she had all the details figured out.

But that was assuming that Mey was indeed coming to whisk her away and not just to check whether she was okay.

Except, if Mey had managed to figure out where to find her, she must have had help. Probably old buddies from her army days. Though that didn't make much sense either. How would they have access to such information?

The most likely explanation was that Jacki's vision had been wrong, and Mey wasn't coming.

Jin let out a relieved breath.

Yeah, she'd been working herself up for nothing. If she really wanted to run, she could just walk out of the mall and keep on going. The one supervisor who had accompanied them last week had spent the entire time just walking around the mall and going in and out of stores. He hadn't been paying much attention to them until it was time to head back.

Which reinforced Jacki's claim that they were all under compulsion. No one had expected them to run, or even to try to contact their families. It could have been as easy as walking into the bathroom and asking a random person to borrow her phone for a moment. And yet, it hadn't even occurred to Jin until now.

With a groan, she draped an arm over her eyes.

Why hadn't she called Mey last Saturday? And why hadn't Jacki thought of that either?

Jin was under compulsion and not thinking straight, but Jacki wasn't, and she wasn't stupid either.

As the dim light outside got brighter, Jin glanced at her watch and gasped. It was five minutes to seven, and by seven-thirty, she was supposed to be ready and waiting outside together with the rest of the team for the minibus to pick them up.

12

KIAN

Present day

As everyone assembled around the dining table, Kian caught Mey looking at him expectantly, either waiting for his reassurance that things were going to turn out okay or perhaps just wondering if there were any last-minute updates.

"Let's have breakfast first and then go over the plan one last time." He reached for his coffee and smiled at her. "Everyone will pay better attention after they are caffeinated and their bellies are full."

Mey nodded. "Thank you again for doing this for me. Without your help, I couldn't have found Jin, let alone gotten her out of that program. I'm forever grateful to you all."

Yamanu took her hand, clasping it between his two. "You don't need to thank us. We are your family."

As Mey tried to discreetly wipe the tears misting her eyes, Kian pretended not to notice. The poor girl had been through a lot recently, and she was handling it like a trooper.

Less than a month had passed since she'd met Yamanu in New York, and her life had changed in so many ways that it was a wonder she was holding up as well as she was. Her transition hadn't been difficult, but growing fangs had, not so much physically as emotionally. A female Dormant growing fangs was an anomaly, and it had been upsetting to Mey. Developing a physical trait that was typically male had bothered her greatly, but the ladies had done a superb job of cheering her up, all claiming to be envious of her fangs.

He wasn't sure whether they were sincere about it, but he appreciated what they had done for Mey, helping her make peace with it.

Pouring himself another cup of coffee, Kian leaned back in his chair and waited for everyone to be done with breakfast.

Once Arwel returned from feeding Eleanor, Kian addressed the group. "Let's go over the plan one last time. Julian and Brundar. You are going to stay with Eleanor. Once we have Jin, you are going to take Eleanor back to the resort, put her in the hotel room, and plant evidence of drug use. Brundar, you are going to shroud the three of you from the moment you arrive at the hotel's parking lot. Once you are done with Eleanor, go into the security office and erase any footage of that and of passing through the lobby, etc."

As the two nodded, Kian continued. "You are going to take the new van that Turner has arranged for us, and once you leave the area, change the license plates. If everything goes according to plan, we will meet you at the airfield."

Callie lifted her hand. "What I don't understand is why are we driving all the way to Washington DC if we are going to board a private cargo plane in a tower-less airfield outside the city? That's adding two unnecessary hours to the escape route. Couldn't we fly out from a nearby airfield?"

"That's a good question, and I asked Turner the same thing. He made a compelling argument for his choice. Once Jin is reported missing, they will start an investigation, and after checking all the commercial flights going out from around the area, they are going to move to the private ones. But since there are thousands of rural tower-less airfields throughout the country, they are not likely to check all of them. The further away we go, the better chance we have of avoiding detection. And we are not flying straight home either. We are going to Nebraska to another rural airfield first, boarding a different private plane to Alabama, and from there, flying on our own jet home."

Syssi sighed. "That's going to be a long day."

"At first glance, it seems like overkill, but we can't be too careful." Kian rubbed a hand over his jaw. "As it is, we are taking a huge risk by poking the bear."

Mey groaned. "What if Jin refuses to come with us? I can just imagine how much this is costing the clan. It would be such a colossal waste."

"Don't worry about it," Kian said. "Even if Jin stays, we still need to be extra cautious because we abducted Eleanor, and she might remember what happened to her despite the drugs. And as to the cost, I consider it money well spent. We've learned a lot from Eleanor. We know now that she is a recruiter of suspected paranormal talents. Following her, we will be able to identify those paranormals and go after them once they are done with training and sent out on missions. That could be a great source of Dormants that we wouldn't have had access to any other way. The government is actually going to help us in our search."

"Did you implant Eleanor with a tracker?" Ella asked.

"We've considered it, but even though it could have been beneficial to us, we've decided against it. If the tracker is discovered, it could lead back to us, and that's a risk we cannot take. Given the level of secrecy and security around the program, we should assume that the personnel working there are routinely screened."

Ella nodded. "So, how are you going to follow her?"

"Hopefully, she will keep her current fake identity, and if she changes it,

William and Roni can find her new one. Whenever she books a flight, we will know."

"What if she uses military transport?" Mey asked. "In the same way that we managed to stay under the radar, she could be moving around the country completely incognito."

"It's possible but not likely, for the simple reason that she doesn't need to be that secretive. On the face of things, everything she does is legal."

13

ARWEL

As good as Kian's plan was, Arwel still felt uneasy about it.

Eleanor, aka Marisol, was way too confident about their inability to convince Jin to come with them. She hadn't even asked what they were going to do if Jin refused to leave.

Obviously, she wasn't telling them everything. The group of paranormal talents might have more security personnel with them than the one escort Eleanor had mentioned, or they might be implanted with trackers, which the handheld device Turner had sent them wasn't going to detect. It was only good at detecting devices hidden in clothes and perhaps implants that were just under the skin. But if an implant was buried deep inside the body, medical-grade equipment was needed to detect it.

Another possibility was that the government was using a different kind of tracker which the device wasn't engineered to detect. But as long as it wasn't implanted inside Jin's body, they had a simple solution for that. The plan was for Jin to dump what she was wearing and change into an outfit that Mey was going to give her. But if the thing was inside her body, they were screwed.

Bridget was going to meet them at the keep and run Jin through her medical equipment the way she'd done with the Doomers, so the village would be safe no matter what. Still, they were running the risk of exposing the keep, and it would be a shame to lose the place. Having another secure location for their people was an essential precaution in case the village was compromised.

Kian continued. "Once the bus arrives, we are going to wait until everyone disembarks and goes into the mall. Hopefully, people are not going to wander off to other places because it would force us to split up, and we don't have enough Guardians."

Amanda huffed. "You wouldn't have that problem if you let us come along. Dalhu and I can thrall, and so can Wonder."

"I don't want to leave Syssi, Callie and Ella without protection. Besides, you,

Dalhu and Wonder will attract too much attention. None of you can blend in easily."

Crossing her arms over her chest, Amanda stuck her chin out. "We can shroud ourselves."

Kian arched a brow. "For how long? Five minutes, ten? That's not long enough, and Dalhu can't shroud at all."

The guy grimaced. "I've been practicing, but I'm not good at it."

When Amanda sighed, conceding defeat, Kian continued. "Anandur and I are going to stay outside and take care of the bus driver and those of the group who might decide to venture outside the mall. Mey, Yamanu, and Arwel will follow Jin inside under the cover of Yamanu's shroud. We don't want Jin to see Mey before we can isolate her from the group. Her initial reaction to seeing her sister might alert their escort and ruin the entire plan." He turned to Arwel. "This will be your job. You will need to thrall Jin to go into the ladies' bathroom or a clothing store's changing room."

Arwel nodded. "In case Mey and I get separated, a photo of Jin would be useful."

"I can send you several," Mey said. "But I doubt you will need to look at photos to spot Jin. She is probably going to be the only six-foot-tall Asian girl in the whole place."

"You never know," Amanda said. "Expect the unexpected. There are many tall Chinese people, and a female basketball team from China might be visiting that mall right at the same time. Sūn Mingming is the tallest professional basketball player in the world at seven feet and nine inches. Or was. I think he is retired."

"Right." Mey chuckled. "As if that is likely to happen. I'm going to send them to all of you." She pulled out her phone and selected several photos. "I'm group messaging Jin's pictures to everyone on the team."

As Arwel's phone pinged with an incoming message, he flicked the application on and touched on the first picture to enlarge it without really taking a good look.

Stifling a gasp, he stared at the face on his screen, trying to figure out why he'd responded so strongly to it.

He'd never been into Asian beauties, or into brunettes in general, and certainly not into six-foot-tall females. His ideal type looked a lot like Carol and shared her personality. He liked petite, curvy blondes, with flirtatious attitudes, sunny dispositions, and strong personalities.

There was nothing sunny or flirtatious about Jin. She radiated power, a smart badass with a no-nonsense attitude. Her gaze was so intense that Arwel felt as if she was looking out of the picture straight into his soul and issuing a challenge.

He could almost hear her whispering, *do you think you are man enough for me?*

And the funny thing was that he responded with a resolute, *heck yeah.*

He was probably overreacting, and it was nothing more than his hormones going into overdrive. He hadn't been with a woman since before the trip to New York, and this was the first pretty face he'd seen that wasn't mated to one of his friends.

Shaking his head, Arwel switched to the next photo, hoping to see a different aspect of Jin's personality. A smile would be nice, something to soften the effect.

Big mistake.

The first one was only of her face. The second one was a full-body shot, and Jin's was spectacular. Despite her height and slimness, she was all female, with delicate curves in all the right places.

As if having a mind of its own, his finger brushed lovingly over the screen.

Perfection.

"Arwel?" Kian asked.

He lifted his head. "Did you say something?"

Several chuckles answered his question, and Julian clapped him on the back. "That's how it all started for me. One look at Ella's picture, and I was a goner."

Arwel shook his head. "Jin is very pretty, but it's not like that. I'm just memorizing her features."

Liar.

Julian clapped him on the back again. "Right. Don't say I didn't warn you."

14

JIN

"You feel tense," Richard said. "What's going on?"

Jin shrugged. "It's the Mandarin. I'm struggling with the most basic stuff. I'm going through a list of phrases I'm trying to memorize, but I keep forgetting words. It's just so difficult, and the pronunciation changes the meaning. The same word can mean ten different things depending on the tone and the emphasis."

That was all true, so Richard wasn't going to detect a lie, but it was a mild stressor compared to the big one of possibly escaping the program.

They were on the bus, on the way to their once-a-week leave, and having Richard's arm draped around her shoulders meant that he was privy to the storm going on inside her.

"I can help with that." He started kneading the tense muscles. "Do you want to practice Mandarin on me?"

"Not really. If I keep at it, I'm going to get a headache."

Richard was a decent guy, and Jin felt bad about her initial unfavorable impression of him. He'd seemed so full of himself, and she had no patience for arrogant pricks. Except, there was more to him than his inflated ego, and it came out in moments like this, when he was doing nice things for her.

Crap, it would have been easier if he hadn't done that.

Leaving him behind without a word was a bitchy move, and she hated having to do it. Some of her friends thought nothing about ghosting a guy they didn't want to see again, not answering phone calls or texts, but that was wrong on the most basic level of common courtesy. It was a coward's way out, and Jin was no coward.

Except, that was true for all things romantic, not daring escapes from secret government programs. She was scared shitless.

Jacki turned around and smiled. "You can practice on me tomorrow. I promise to listen to every word." She winked.

The girl had nerves of steel. She was sitting next to Wendy, who was an empath, and the girl hadn't said a word about Jacki being stressed. Perhaps her immunity to mental tricks made her emotions undetectable too?

Lucky girl.

Jin wished she was an impenetrable vault like that. If Marisol's compulsion hadn't worked on her, she wouldn't be sitting on this bus with a bunch of other freaks that she was going to miss terribly.

Only a month had passed since she'd joined the program, but everyone in it felt like family to her. They were her tribe, her kind of people.

As the bus stopped near the entrance to the mall, Doctor Roberts stood up in the middle aisle and lifted a plastic bag full of walkie talkies. "Don't forget to take your device before leaving the bus, and make sure that your name is on it, so you don't take someone else's. If you need me for whatever reason, don't hesitate to contact me. No one is to wander away from the mall without checking with me first and without a buddy to accompany them. No exceptions."

It was the same speech as last week, only delivered by a different instructor. They'd had Shannon, the fitness teacher, accompany them the other time.

Richard took her hand. "Where would you like to go?"

"Jacki and I want to check out the clothing discount store."

"I'll come with you."

Crap. That wasn't good.

She smiled and kissed his cheek. "That's so sweet of you to offer, but we are going to the intimates sections to stock up on panties and bras. You'll get nasty looks from the ladies shopping there." She leaned to whisper in his ear. "They'll think you are a pervert checking out female lingerie."

He pulled her closer to him. "I've shopped for lingerie before, and no one gave me nasty looks."

Jacki turned around and pinned him with a hard stare. "You are really thick, Richard. Jin is trying to be nice about it, but the truth is that I don't want you hanging around when I'm trying bras on." She followed Wendy down the steps.

Richard frowned. "You should have said so in the first place."

"I'm saying it now. Isn't there a hardware store you want to visit? I'm sure you'll find it more interesting than lingerie."

Richard pretended offense. "That's such a sexist thing to say. I'm going to report you to the PC police."

The four of them were the last ones on the sidewalk, and Jin glanced around, checking for her sister even though she doubted Jacki's vision was going to come true today.

"Can I come with you?" Wendy asked.

"Do you need to shop for tools?" Richard winked at her.

She rolled her eyes. "No, I want to go with Jin and Jacki to try on bras."

He put a hand over his chest. "No one wants to be with me. I'm deeply hurt."

Letting out a breath, Wendy threaded her arm through his. "Fine, I'll come with you. But on one condition."

"Name it."

"You buy me ice cream later."

"You've got yourself a deal." He started walking, then looked over his shoulder at Jin and Jacki. "And you two aren't getting any because you are a couple of meanies."

Laughing, Jin sent him an air kiss.

"Oof." Jacki let out a breath. "That was a close call. We don't want either of them hanging out with us."

As a pang of sorrow speared through Jin's heart, she ran after the two and pulled them both into a quick hug. "Now, am I getting ice cream?" She tried to cover up for her emotional outburst.

Richard let go of Wendy and pulled Jin against his chest. "A kiss, and it's yours."

15

MEY

Mey tapped her foot on the floor and looked out the café's window. It was across the street from the main entrance to the mall, which was where the bus was supposedly going to drop the trainees off.

Hopefully.

The driver might deviate from his routine and drop them off at the parking lot in the back or next to one of the other entrances. And that wasn't the only problem. Lokan was late. He'd been supposed to be there over half an hour earlier.

Mey and her team had arrived early, right when the café had opened, and no other customers were there yet. As soon as they'd entered, Yamanu had shrouded the place, making it look as if it was closed so no one else would come in. Kian had taken care of the two guys behind the counter, thralling them to ignore their group and the lack of incoming customers.

They were in an invisible bubble, watching the street, and waiting for her sister to arrive.

"Where is Lokan? He should have been here already." She looked at Kian. "Can you call him?"

"He'll be here at any moment. Carol texted me that they were stuck in traffic, leaving Washington. A three-car collision was blocking two lanes of the freeway."

Arwel lifted a brow. "Is Carol coming with him?"

Kian chuckled. "You know Carol, she wouldn't want to miss out on all the excitement."

Mey appreciated having another woman on the team. Carol had been very helpful with Eleanor's interrogation, and they had been lucky that she'd shown up with Lokan. She might be helpful again, and Mey was glad Carol hadn't asked anyone's permission to join.

As wonderful as her mate, Arwel, and Kian were, they were a bunch of chauvinists who preferred to leave the women behind, where they knew they were safe.

The only reason Mey was included, grudgingly, was because she'd convinced Kian that Jin wouldn't come willingly without her there. They could have used compulsion or thralling to make Jin cooperate, but that was riskier. No one knew for sure whether Jin was susceptible to thralling, and it was better not to take a chance.

Mey's presence guaranteed that Jin would at least listen to what they had to say.

As the door opened and Carol walked in with Lokan, Mey puffed out a relieved breath.

"Sorry we're late," Carol said. "I guess we arrived on time, though." She glanced out the window. "Since we cleared the traffic jam, Lokan has been driving like a maniac. I don't know how we weren't pulled over by the police."

Lokan pulled out a chair for her. "I told you that you had nothing to worry about. I'm an excellent driver."

"Of course, you are, my love." She sent him an air kiss.

Now six people were looking out the window, but only two were anxious. She and Arwel.

Mey didn't need a paranormal empathic ability to sense the Guardian's inner turmoil. Even her pre-transition human senses would have picked it up.

For some reason, Arwel had been off since that morning. His usual long-suffering expression had been replaced with a determined one that Mey hadn't seen on him before. Usually, he was such a mellow guy, but now he was buzzing with barely suppressed energy as if he was preparing for battle.

Was he sensing something the others were not?

Being a powerful empath, his senses were probably reaching far and wide, and he was collecting information that was not accessible to the others.

"What's the matter, Arwel?" Mey asked. "You seem on edge."

He cast her a scowling look. "I'm getting ready for surprises. I don't trust our source as far as I can throw her."

Everyone agreed with him. Marisol was a rotten person through and through, but that was nothing new. Something else was going on, and Mey wondered whether Julian had hit the nail on the head with his remark about Arwel being infatuated with Jin.

Mey stifled a smile. She couldn't have chosen a better mate for her sister if she'd tried. The question was whether Jin would feel the same about Arwel.

The girl was extremely picky when it came to guys she dated. Her list of requirements was ten pages long, and no living man could match them all. Arwel was very handsome, and he was a couple of inches taller than Jin, but was he tall enough? Was he too mellow? Not mellow enough?

Mey sighed. If Jin stuck to her list, she was going to remain single forever, but not if Mey had a say in it. The moment Jin was safe with them, she was going to put her matchmaker hat on and go to work.

"A minibus is pulling up," Yamanu said. "Did Eleanor say a bus or minibus?"

Mey's heartbeat accelerated. Could this be it? Was she going to see Jin?

From where they were sitting, they had a perfect viewing angle of the vehicle, but they couldn't see the people getting off until they took several steps toward the entrance.

The first two were a couple holding hands; following them were a boy who looked to be no more than twelve and a girl who was a little older. Those couldn't be the people from the program. They were probably a family, a mom, a dad, and their two kids.

Mey sank back in her chair and crossed her arms over her chest. "It's not them."

"I think it is," Arwel growled as if he was ready to tear someone's throat out.

Lifting her head, Mey looked at the sidewalk again, and her breath caught in her throat. Was the girl who was passionately kissing a guy her sister?

She was tall, and her long dark hair was gathered in a ponytail, but with her face glued to the guy's, it was hard to tell for sure. Except, Mey recognized the blouse Jin was wearing. It was one of the many she'd borrowed from her and had never returned.

Pushing to her feet, she was about to run out when Yamanu pulled her back down. "Not yet. We have to wait for them to go in."

"They have children in that fucking program," Kian spat. "Did you see that boy? He looks to be Parker's age or younger."

"And the girl looks no more than fifteen or sixteen," Carol commented. "Eleanor said nothing about kids."

"Of course not," Arwel hissed. "She didn't want us to think any worse of her than we already do."

"Can we get them out?" Carol asked.

"I wish we could." Kian looked out the window, watching the group enter the mall. "But we can't, and not only for security reasons." He turned to look at Carol. "The kids didn't sign the contracts, their parents did, either under compulsion or not. Their families probably depend on the contract money. Once the training is over, they will get to see their children again. The best we can do is to keep tabs on them and approach them when they are adults."

"By then, it'll be too late," Carol said. "They will be fully indoctrinated. But you are right. There is nothing we can do."

16

ARWEL

As Arwel tried and failed to stifle the growl that had started deep in his throat, Anandur got up.

"I'm going for the bus."

Strolling casually in a wide circle, he walked up to the rear of the vehicle and attached the tracker.

"It's a shame that we will have to remove it once the driver's memory is taken care of," Kian said.

Following the signal back to the base would have given them valuable information, but they couldn't chance it being discovered. It was supposed to look as if Jin had just decided to run on her own and hadn't been aided by anyone.

Although, given the fervor with which she was kissing that dude, Arwel was afraid that Jin might refuse to leave even after Lokan freed her from Marisol's compulsion. She wouldn't want to part with her new boyfriend.

Except, if the guy were dead, she wouldn't have a reason to stay, which Arwel could arrange.

Damn. Where had this rage come from?

So what if Jin was kissing some dude? She didn't know Arwel, nor was it her fault that he had developed an idiotic, totally unwarranted obsession with her. She didn't owe him a thing.

What the hell was wrong with him?

He was so agitated that even Mey's anxiousness didn't register until she put a shaky hand on his arm.

"Can we go now? Yamanu will shroud us, so there is no point in waiting until they enter the mall."

"Two more minutes." Arwel glanced at Kian, who nodded his approval. "It's better to wait for everyone in the group to get inside first and disperse. Some of them might be immune, and I prefer to have the cover of other people when we follow them."

He also needed a moment or two to regain control. If he got out now, he was bound to attack the boyfriend.

Her lips drawn in a tight line, Mey nodded.

Closing his eyes, Arwel took a deep breath and then another, forcing himself to relax. After the mission was over, he was going to schedule a session with Vanessa because it seemed like he was finally losing his fucking mind. Centuries of suffering the onslaught of human emotions hadn't broken him. Still, one look at a picture of a pretty face apparently had.

But maybe it was just the last straw.

Going on two missions back to back meant that Arwel hadn't been drinking to drown the emotions of others, and dealing with that while sober had taken its toll. On top of that, he also hadn't had sex for far too long.

Was it a wonder that he was at breaking point?

A vacation was in order, a real one. Yeah, a few sessions with Vanessa and some time off would do the trick.

In the meantime, though, he had to get his head in the game.

As the last of the bus's passengers got out, and it drove away, Yamanu got up. "Let's move."

Fortunately for everyone involved, Jin had parted with her boyfriend at the entrance, and while the guy and the brown-haired girl continued in one direction, Jin and the blonde went in another.

Arwel and Yamanu walked behind the two, while Mey, Lokan, and Carol headed toward the restrooms where Arwel was going to later send Jin with a thrall.

It should have been easy for him to sense Jin's feelings and figure out how deeply she felt about the boyfriend, but he couldn't get a grip on them. First of all, she wasn't projecting much, and secondly, he was too worked up to make sense of what she was feeling.

Mostly, she was anxious.

Or maybe Arwel was projecting his own emotions onto her?

His empathic ability had always been too strong, but today it was malfunctioning. He couldn't read the blonde at all, and what little he was getting from Jin didn't match her expression or her behavior.

Joking and laughing with her friend as if she had no worries in the world, Jin didn't seem anxious at all.

He felt a nearly unstoppable urge to reach into her mind and dig around for information about the boyfriend, and also to check whether she was anxious or not.

But that was wrong, and it wasn't sanctioned. All he was supposed to do was thrall her, planting the need to visit the bathroom.

Except, as the two entered a department store and headed for the lingerie department, the blonde turned around and looked at him and Yamanu. Her eyes widening in appreciation, a flirtatious smirk lifted one corner of her mouth.

She shouldn't have been able to see them through Yamanu's shroud, but she obviously did.

Jin's friend was an immune, and that complicated everything.

"Drop the shroud," he whispered as the blonde nudged Jin and motioned at them with her head.

If Jin couldn't see what her friend was seeing, it would alarm both of them. Since they were aware of paranormal abilities, they were not going to dismiss it.

Instead, Yamanu grabbed his elbow, turned them around, and ducked behind a clothing rack before Jin had a chance to turn her head.

"Do it now," Yamanu whispered. "Send her to the bathroom."

Arwel couldn't figure out why Yamanu hadn't just dropped the shroud, but he did as his friend suggested, planting in Jin's mind an urgent need to pee.

"Oh, crap." She crossed her legs and started rocking in place. "I need to find a bathroom right now, or I'm going to wet the floor."

"There is one a two-minute walk away," the blonde said and threaded her arm through Jin's, leading her back the way they'd come.

Jin hissed. "I hope I make it."

As the two rushed out, Yamanu called Mey. "Jin is on her way to the bathroom, but she has her friend with her. The bad news is that the friend is an immune."

17

JIN

*J*in felt like any moment now, she was going to embarrass herself.
That would be just great. She would have to purchase new clothes and dump what she was wearing in the trash because there was no way she was lugging around a shopping bag with pee-soaked pants and panties.

Gross.

"I don't know why I need to pee so badly. I only had one small bottle of water on the bus."

"Let me distract you." Jacki lengthened her strides. "Did you catch a glimpse of the two hunks that were walking behind us?"

"What hunks?"

"You must have missed them by a second. I think they are the ones I've seen in my vision together with your sister. The tall one for sure. That's one hell of a mouthwatering specimen of manhood."

Right now, the last thing Jin cared about was some hunky dudes that Jacki had dreamt up. All she was interested in was the bathroom sign, which was glowing about fifteen feet away.

"Salvation is near." She pulled her arm out of Jacki's and ran the rest of the way, barreling into the first stall and pulling her pants down before even closing the door.

"Thank God," she breathed as the pressure eased.

She'd been expecting to pee gallons, but surprisingly there wasn't that much.

Damn, could she be coming down with a urinary tract infection?

The uncontrollable need to pee was one of the symptoms. Still, absent was the stabbing pain and the burning sensation that usually accompanied it.

Hopefully it wasn't that because it couldn't have happened at a worse time. Nothing other than antibiotics would help with that damn infection, and spending the rest of the day in excruciating pain would be a nightmare.

Except, Doctor Roberts could probably write her a prescription. It was such a stroke of good luck that he'd accompanied them on the outing.

Outside, she heard Jacki ask someone what she was looking for.

"I lost a contact lens, and it's impossible to find it on these blue tiles." The woman sounded distraught.

"When did you notice that it was missing?" Jacki asked.

"It was right outside the bathroom when I rubbed my eyes, and I felt it pop out. Usually, it just gets caught on my clothes, so I came in here to look for it in a better light. I swear that I heard it fall and hit the tile, but I can't find it."

"Show me where you were when you rubbed your eye."

"Right outside the bathroom. Thank you so much for helping me. I'm blind without it, and it's really hard to find something when you can't see."

"No problem, I'm glad to help." Jin heard two sets of footsteps walk away from her.

As one of the stall doors opened, and someone walked out without flushing the toilet, Jin shook her head. Some people were just gross. A moment later that same someone walked over to her door and knocked. "Jin, it's me, Mey. Open up."

Even though Jacki had warned her, Jin gaped at the door, too stunned to respond.

"I know that you are in there. Open up."

Leaning forward, Jin unlocked the door.

Mey walked in and flattened herself against the side panel to close the door. "Are you still not done peeing? We don't have time. My friend is keeping yours busy outside, and we need to sneak by her somehow."

Shaking her head, Jin found her voice. "If I'm going, Jacki is coming with me. She is a clairvoyant, and she foresaw you coming for me."

Mey sagged against the stall's door. "That complicates things. I don't know if we can take her."

Wiping quickly, Jin pulled up her pants and flushed the toilet. "I want to hug you so badly, but I need to wash my hands first."

"Don't be an idiot." Mey pulled her into her arms, crushing Jin to her chest. "I was so worried about you. Do you know that you were compelled to sign that contract?"

"Um, can you let go? I can't breathe."

"Sorry, I'm still getting used to my new strength. But never mind that. We need to hustle."

What new strength? Had May started weight training? She would have to ask her later.

"Jacki is not a problem. She is the one who actually wants to leave. She convinced me that I should accept your help and run, but I'm still not sure that this is the best decision for me."

With a sigh, Mey nodded. "I had a feeling you might say that." She pushed the door open. "Come on, let me introduce you to my friends."

Jin didn't know what to expect, but it certainly wasn't a gorgeous guy who looked like he had stepped off the cover of a romance novel. One of those about hot billionaires.

"This is Lokan, and he is here to free you from the compulsion."

The guy smiled and offered her his hand, but Jin didn't take it.

"Give me a moment to wash my hands."

He dipped his head. "Of course."

Such a gentleman. Was that Mey's new boyfriend? Lucky girl.

As Jacki and a petite blond entered the bathroom, Lokan offered his hand to Jacki.

"So, you are both a clairvoyant and an immune. Fascinating."

She eyed him suspiciously. "How do you know?"

"I overheard Mey and Jin talking about you. I'm Lokan."

"Jacklin." She shook his hand. "You know that this is the ladies' room, right? Someone might come in and see you here."

"We have friends outside, making sure that we are not disturbed until this is done."

"What is done?"

After drying her hands with a paper towel, Jin offered him her hand as well. "Hi, thanks for coming to help us."

The petite blond smiled and put her arm around Lokan's middle in a show of ownership. "I'm Carol. Nice to meet you all."

Putting her hand on her hip, Jacki struck a pose. "What are we still doing here?"

"Talking, dear," Carol said. "We need to make sure that Jin wants to come with us, but to do so, we need to free her of the compulsion first. And that's what my guy is about to do."

Jacki frowned. "Is this your talent? Compulsion removal?"

He shook his head. "I'm a compeller like the lady who recruited you. In theory, one compeller can remove the compulsion placed by another, or rather override it."

"In theory," Jacki repeated. "You've never tried it?"

"This is my first time."

Leaning against a sink, she crossed her arms over her chest. "Good luck then. As far as I know, Marisol compelled Jin to trust her, which was probably why Jin signed the contract in the first place, and she also compelled her to think that she is attracted to Richard because the director wants to create super-babies. There might have been smaller compulsions, but if you remove those two, I believe that Jin will be free to make her own decisions."

18

ARWEL

Outside the bathroom, Yamanu created an illusion that both the men's and the ladies' restrooms were closed for cleaning, complete with a sign that pointed toward the bathrooms at the other side of the mall.

"I hope this girl is the only one who is immune," Arwel said.

"Why don't you go in and ask? I'm sure she knows whether there are others like her in the program."

"In case there are, I need to stay here and guard the entrance. If thralling and shrouding don't work, old-fashioned lying about a mess in the bathrooms will."

It was just an excuse. Arwel didn't want to go in and face Jin. If she was in love with another guy, hearing that she wanted to stay because of that was sure to send him over the edge.

As it was, he was struggling to keep his head from going places it shouldn't.

Leaning against the wall, he folded his arms over his chest and listened.

"Good luck," he heard Jacki say. "As far as I know, Marisol compelled Jin to trust her, which was probably why Jin signed the contract in the first place. And she also compelled her to think that she is attracted to Richard because the director wants to create super-babies. There might have been smaller compulsions, but if you remove those two, I believe that Jin will be free to make her own decisions."

Arwel felt as if he had suddenly grown wings and was about to soar up to the sky while singing hymns to the merciful Fates. Jin wasn't in love. She'd been compelled to like that guy, and once the compulsion was removed, she would be free to fall for Arwel.

As if things were ever that easy.

Arwel raked his fingers through his shaggy hair, regretting not getting a decent haircut. He was also sporting stubble, and his clothes were not exactly GQ style. Still, he had been told that his eyes were his best feature, and, hopefully, Jin would notice them and ignore the rest.

"I'm going in," he told Yamanu. "Are you going to be okay here shrouding on your own?"

"Piece of cake. I can do this and fight off hordes of bathroom seekers all by my lonesome."

Smoothing his hand over his untamed mane, Arwel squared his shoulders and walked into the bathroom.

"Who are you?" Jacki asked.

It was good that she was the one asking because he doubted he could have answered Jin.

In person, she was even more impressive than in her pictures and so beautiful that he couldn't take his eyes off her.

On her part, she didn't seem bothered by his stare. In fact, she stared back, and her lips parted.

Was he imagining it, or was she gaping a little?

With his own emotions in overdrive, his empathic ability was rendered worthless. All he could feel was his own turmoil, which was louder than the entire mall full of human feelings.

"I'm Arwel." He finally managed to put two words together.

"Are you also a compeller?" Jacki asked.

Still looking at Jin, he answered, "I'm an empath."

"Cool. So, who are you people? A private organization of paranormal talent?"

That was actually an excellent cover. They couldn't tell Jacki who they were because she was an immune. She might be a Dormant, but until it was ascertained that she was, she couldn't be told anything.

Damn, he should have called Kian and given him an update about the unexpected additional escapee. His brain was really not functioning right.

"Yes," Carol said. "That's precisely who we are. We are trying to keep others like us safe from our government's clutches. And not only ours. Other governments, as well as various shady organizations, would just love to get their hands on what we can do. We keep each other safe."

"What's your talent?" Jin asked.

Carol struck a sexy pose. "Isn't it obvious? I'm a seductress."

Lokan chuckled. "Can we keep all the explanations for later? Now is not the time for this." He reached for Jin's hand. "First order of business is freeing you from the compulsion."

As another growl threatened to escape Arwel's throat, he turned his back on Lokan and Jin and their conjoined hands.

Leaning against one of the sinks, he pulled his phone out and texted Kian. *We have a complication. Jin's friend is an immune and she wants to come with us. What do you want us to do?*

He could only imagine the litany of curses leaving Kian's mouth. Jacki was a pain in the ass. They couldn't bring her to the village, and they couldn't release her into the wild either. Not only that, with her around they would have to pretend to be human, which was going to complicate explaining the situation to Jin.

Kian's return text arrived a whole minute later, probably because he needed a moment to calm down. *We have no choice but to take her. Make up a story about who we are. We are going to put her in the keep until I figure out what to do with her.*

Arwel texted back. *She might be a Dormant.*

I'm well aware of that. What I'm trying to figure out is how to introduce her to potential mates.

Arwel chuckled softly. *That's not going to be a problem. Jacki is a bombshell.*

Kian responded. *Are you interested?*

Not really.

Figures. Keep me updated.

Damn. Julian's stupid comment at breakfast had outed Arwel before he could even process what was going on with him. Now everyone was assuming he had a thing for Jin.

Which he had, so they weren't wrong. Except, he would have liked to have kept his feelings private.

"How do you feel?" Lokan asked Jin. "Can you tell that the compulsion is gone?"

19

JIN

How did she feel?
    Jin wasn't sure.
Pulling her hand out of Lokan's, she tried to delve inward to examine her feelings, but all she could think about was Arwel's amazing eyes.

She'd thought that Jeremy's were beautiful, but they were dull compared to Arwel's, which were a deeper shade of turquoise and seemed to be glowing with an inner light.

But it was not just that. For some reason, Arwel evoked a longing in her that she'd never felt before. And that was even before Lokan had removed the compulsion.

Jin had felt attraction before, but not like this. It wasn't even sexual, or rather not entirely. The longing felt as if her soul was craving his. It was a need to connect that she'd never felt before toward any of the guys she'd dated or hooked up with. Even with Mitch, it had been mostly about having fun.

Why the hell was she suddenly thinking about long talks into the night with a guy who wasn't even her type?

She liked guys who were mindful of their appearance, while Arwel was the definition of a schlump. His hair was messy but not in a stylish way, and his clothes were loose and baggy, and the colors didn't match. He had a five o'clock shadow at eleven in the morning, and it wasn't the styled scruffy that some guys cultivated with care.

On the positive side, he was a couple of inches taller than her, and he had the most amazing eyes. He might also have a good body under the ill-fitting clothes, but it was hard to tell. He could be a little overweight or maybe a bit too skinny, but none of that mattered. Jin wanted him and hoped that he wasn't taken.

On the other hand, Lokan, who was precisely her type, had stirred no physical attraction or longing in her, even before Carol had made it clear that he belonged to her. Jin had acknowledged his good looks, but that had been the extent of her interest.

"Well?" Lokan asked again. "Anything?"

"I'm not sure." She pushed a strand of hair that had escaped her ponytail behind her ear. "I liked the money, and I liked the idea of meeting others like me, so I think I would have signed the contract even without being compelled to do it. I still feel uneasy about going back on something I committed to."

"What about Richard?" Jacki asked. "Do you still want him?"

That was an easy answer, but Jin had a feeling it had nothing to do with compulsion or lack of it. After looking into Arwel's incredible eyes, Richard was the furthest thing from her thoughts. She still liked him as a friend, but the attraction she'd felt for him was gone.

"No, I don't want Richard. But I still feel bad about leaving him without a word of explanation. That's mean."

Out of the corner of her eye, she caught Arwel's shoulders sagging in relief. Apparently, she wasn't the only one who felt the connection.

Jacki shook her head. "Don't forget that Richard's feelings for you are not real either. Maybe Lokan could free him as well, and then he won't be upset about you disappearing on him."

Lokan shrugged. "If you point him out to me, I can give it a try. But right now, I'm not sure if I managed to override Marisol's compulsion. Jin seems unsure."

Pushing away from the sink, Jacki put her hand on Jin's shoulder. "How far do you trust Marisol?"

"Just as far as I can throw her. She is an evil witch."

Jacki smirked. "There's your answer. Before Lokan did his thing, you would have answered that you trust her completely."

"No, I wouldn't. I knew that she'd compelled me to trust her."

Throwing her hands in the air, Jacki looked at Mey. "I give up. It's your turn."

Mey nodded. "Would you all mind giving us some privacy?"

"No problem." Lokan draped his arm over Carol's shoulder, and the two walked out. "Just be mindful of the time. The longer we stay here, the riskier it gets."

Arwel cast Jin a quick glance before taking Jacki's elbow. "Let me apologize in advance for taking you into the men's bathroom, but we can't have others from your group see you with us."

She grimaced. "How gross is it in there?"

"Gross. I suggest that you cover your nose. By the way, are any of the others in your group immune?"

"I'm the only one."

"Good. We might get away with just standing at the entrance to the bathroom."

She frowned. "Why?"

"It's a long story."

20

MEY

Mey waited until Jacki walked out with Arwel, trusting that he would keep her from hearing what she was about to tell Jin.

Jacki being an immune was a problem.

Kian would never allow her in the village, and Mey had no idea how they were going to figure out whether Jacki was a Dormant or not. As far as she knew, all the other female Dormants had entered a romantic relationship with a clan member first and were induced later by their partners. How was it going to work in reverse?

Taking Jin's hand, she walked her to the furthest corner away from the entrance. "I couldn't tell you anything while your friend was here, and I can't give you the entire long explanation either because we don't have time. My friends are not a group of talented paranormals, they are a clan of immortals. You and I are carriers of their immortal genes. I was activated, and now it's your turn. I think immortality trumps anything the government is offering you. No contract is worth giving that up."

Gaping at Mey as if she had lost her mind, Jin lifted her hand and put it on her chest. "I can accept people with special abilities, but what you are saying sounds crazy. A clan of immortals? Like in *Highlander?*"

Mey chuckled. "Most of them were born in Scotland, so you are not far off. I know it's hard to believe, but I can show you proof." She grinned, letting Jin see her new fangs.

Her sister's eyes widened. "What the hell, Mey? Have you lost your mind and had your teeth filed into points?"

Ugh, it was so frustrating. Maybe she should call Arwel in and have him show Jin his fangs. The guy was obviously attracted to Jin, so having his fangs elongate in her presence shouldn't be a problem.

"When I entered transition, my canines fell off, and these little fangs grew instead. It's not common for a female to grow fangs, but we are the freak sisters, so naturally, we have to be different. When you go through your transition, you will probably grow a set as well."

Jin leaned in closer to take a better look. "Can I touch them?"

"Sure." Mey opened wide.

Reaching with a finger, Jin touched one pointy fang. "Oh, wow. They are really sharp." She put the finger in her own mouth to lick the scrape. "So, you want to tell me that you are immortal now?"

"Yep. And it comes with a lot of other advantages. I'm stronger, my vision, hearing and sense of smell are more powerful, and I can eat whatever I want."

Jin smiled. "Immortals don't gain weight? That alone is worth the price of admission." She frowned. "What is the price? I'm sure that there is one."

Smart girl. But it was too early to go into all that, and definitely not in a public restroom in a mall.

"Immortals can gain weight, but I guess it would take real binging to do so. I can eat whatever I want because I'm not going back to modeling, so I don't have to worry about my weight anymore."

"Why not? You are not going to age. You can go on modeling for as long as you want."

Mey shook her head. "First of all, immortals have to live in hiding, which means no modeling or acting or even politicking. We need to stay away from the limelight. Secondly, I've been followed around, and my apartment was bugged. The same people who hired you were probably trying to figure out if I had an interesting talent as well. Needless to say, I had to go into hiding, and if you come with me, you will have to do so as well."

"I didn't tell anyone about your ability."

"I know. That's why they were following me around. If they knew for sure that I had a talent, they would have sent Marisol after me as well."

"How do you know about her?"

"It's a long story, but we found her first and had her tell us where to find you."

"Did you have to torture the information out of her?"

Stifling a chuckle, Mey nodded. "My friends tied her to a chair and didn't let her go to the bathroom."

"Ouch. After my experience from half an hour ago, I can sympathize. I needed to pee so badly that I would have told anyone anything they wanted to hear in exchange for toilet privileges."

21

KIAN

Kian put his phone away and leaned against the side of the bus. "We are actually lucky that the driver has given us the slip."

They had followed the tracker to the parking lot behind the mall, but the driver had left already, and they were waiting for him to come back.

Anandur arched one red bushy brow. "How so?"

"One of the other talents is an immune and a clairvoyant. She predicted that Mey was coming for her sister, and she wants to come with us. Since she is immune, we have no choice because she can rat Jin out if we leave her behind."

Frowning, Anandur scratched his head. "If she is an immune, what does she need us for? She could have walked out during one of the other mall excursions. She is not compelled to stay."

"True. She could be an informant. But even if she is not, her vision of us coming for Jin is troubling news. She doesn't know who we are, but there might be others in the program who can use their powers to find out who we are and where we are hiding. Normally, that wouldn't be a problem because no one would have taken them seriously. But given who they work for, that is a security risk for us." He chuckled. "And for the Doomers, but that's their problem. I wouldn't mind if they are found out. That could take care of Navuh for us."

Anandur's frown deepened, his entire forehead creasing with worry lines. "That changes things. This is no longer about getting Jin out because of what she can do and because we know that she is a Dormant. If these people are a security risk for us, shouldn't we take them all?"

"That wouldn't solve our problem. On the contrary. Whoever is running the program will get more talents and have them focus on finding the missing paranormals. And if they are any good, they might lead the government straight to us."

Anandur shook his head. "So, what are we going to do?"

"Continue with the plan but modify it for Jin's friend. Instead of making it look as if just Jin ran away, we are going to make it look as if Jin and Jacki left together. But because Jacki is an immune, we need to pretend to be human and bring her to the keep instead of the village."

"We can also drop her off somewhere. But on her own, there is a high chance of her getting caught. She will talk."

"Precisely. Besides, she is a possible Dormant. It would be a shame to let her go."

"Yeah, but how are you going to test her? We can't bring her to the village. How is she going to meet her mate?"

Kian crossed his arms over his chest. "That's what I'm trying to figure out. We can bring her to the keep and tell her that it's a temporary hiding place until the storm blows over. In the meantime, we can have a different Guardian watch over her every day and see who she clicks with. Arwel says she is a knockout, so that shouldn't take long."

"Jacki must be the blonde with the long hair." Anandur smirked. "The one who was standing next to Jin when Jin was kissing that guy. She is a looker, and I'm sure there will be no shortage of volunteers to induce her, but that's not the same as finding her fated mate. She is an outsider with no ties of loyalty to us, and a potential spy. Unless she forms a bond with one of ours, we can't trust her with the knowledge of who we are."

"I can't argue with any of that. If she doesn't bond with one of the men, we will have to let her go. I can't risk bringing her to the village even if she turns. In fact, I don't want anyone to have casual sex with her without protection. She should only be induced by her fated mate. If she finds him."

Anandur rubbed his jaw. "I've been thinking about something. What if we find a lesbian Dormant? How are we going to induce her transition if she can't have sex with a male?"

"That's a problem. Unless she is bisexual, I can't see how that could happen. But just like with any other Dormant, she would have to find her truelove mate first, except, in her case, it would be another female."

Males had it easy. Typically, a Dormant male needed to fight an immortal opponent, spurring enough aggression in him to produce venom and bite him. Nothing else was required.

A female, on the other hand, had to be bitten during sex. Perhaps females who were not interested in sex with males could be induced in the same way males were?

But could the bond form without the help of their mates' venom?

The other problem would be finding partners. The clan was small, and the selection wasn't big to start with. There would probably be only a handful of males and females to choose from.

Then again, Kian was learning to trust the Fates and their matchmaking acumen. For those who'd earned the boon, they would find the right partner.

22

JIN

As Mey's phone buzzed with an incoming text, she glanced at it and then smiled apologetically. "Give me a couple of minutes. I'm getting instructions."

"No problem."

It gave Jin time to examine what was stored in her head without the compulsion muddling things up.

What had been her own decision, and what had she been compelled by Marisol to do?

As much as she resented the woman, Jin was glad that the extent of her torture had been not letting the recruiter use the bathroom.

Mostly, Jin was angry about Marisol pushing her into Richard's arms and him into hers. She could have forgiven the extra push to sign the contract, and she would have been fine staying in the program if the people running it didn't have nefarious intention of never letting the trainees have a life and breeding them to produce super-babies.

Had that part been sanctioned by the higher-ups? Or was it something the director had cooked up in his sick brain?

Couldn't they have waited for nature to take its course?

A small group of people spending days on end with each other would have eventually produced couples without any outside intervention. But then they wouldn't have the right combination of talents to create the type of offspring the director was hoping for.

How far were he and his supervisors willing to go to get that?

If they were willing to compel people into having sex with each other, she wouldn't put it past them to go one step further and harvest eggs from the females and sperm from the males. If they did that, they could cook up super-babies in a lab and experiment with different combinations.

Jin shivered.

Yeah, that was definitely wrong, and she couldn't stay and allow that to happen. Her children would arrive the natural way, born out of love, and raised in a loving home. They were not going to be part of an experiment, their future decided for them by power greedy government officials.

As Mey put her phone away, Jin put her hand on her sister's arm. "I'm coming with you."

Mey smiled. "I knew that you would not turn your back on immortality."

"I wasn't even thinking about that. I don't want my children to grow up in a lab and get raised to serve their puppet masters."

Mey tilted her head. "What are you talking about?"

"Never mind. We will have plenty of time to talk once we are out of here. What about Jacki, though? You didn't want her to hear you telling me about the immortality part, so I assume she is not a candidate for that?"

"She might be. But until we know for sure, we can't bring her into the clan's secret hideout. We will have to put her in another secure location."

"I understand. Which probably means that I can't tell her about the clan and the immortality."

"Correct. It's going to be difficult for everyone involved, but my friends are going to pretend that we are a group of talents in hiding. Carol already did a great job with that. All we have to do is stick to what she said."

"How are they going to determine whether Jacki is a candidate or not? And how do they know that I am?"

"Because I already transitioned successfully, there is no doubt that both of us are carriers of the godly genes. You are a Dormant for sure. Jacki might be just a paranormally gifted human. I'll explain later about how it is done."

Jin shook her head. "Hold on. You lost me at the godly genes. Godly?"

Mey smiled. "You heard me right. We are the descendants of gods."

"Cool. I can't wait to hear that story. But back to Jacki. I'll go with her to that other place. She is my friend, and I don't want her to be all alone and freaking out in some safe house or wherever they plan on taking her."

"I was afraid you were going to say that. But just so you know, the clan's hideout is a beautiful village steeped in greenery, while the other place is an underground facility."

Jin grimaced. "I really don't like living underground. But it's only temporary, right? Until they find out whether Jacki is also a descendant of the gods." She shook her head. "I wish I could tell her that. She would lose her shit, and just so you know, Jacki never loses her cool. This would be so worth seeing."

Mey laughed. "When the time comes, I'll do my best to ensure that you are the one delivering the news to her."

Jin leaned against one of the sinks and crossed her arms over her chest. Now that she'd made her decision, apprehension gripped her as she thought about the actual escape.

What if someone noticed her and Jacki walking out? They were supposed to inform Doctor Roberts when they wandered outside the mall. Would anyone check with him?

"So, what's the plan? How are we getting out of here?"

Mey smiled. "We had an ingenious plan that hit a snag when Jacki joined, but

Arwel came up with a solution." She patted her phone, indicating that this was what the texting exchange had been about.

An image of deep turquoise eyes flashed in Jin's mind, momentarily distracting her. "Are you going to tell me about it? Or is it a secret?"

"It's not a secret, and we need you and Jacki to point out to us each of the other trainees and the group's escort. Arwel is going to thrall them to remember that you and Jacki came down with the flu and stayed at the base. My other friends are going to do the same with the bus driver. That will buy us many hours of a head start. By the time they get back to base, and the guard checks the roster, we will be on the other side of the country."

Jin lifted a hand to stop her sister. "First of all, what the hell is thralling? And secondly, the trainees are scattered all around the mall. If you make someone forget that Jacki and I came along, but then he or she sees us approaching someone else, it's going to ruin it. We will be going in circles."

"Thralling is like hypnosis, it's a mental suggestion, but an immortal doesn't have to actually say anything to the subject. They can enter their minds and plant the suggestion. And as for being seen, that's not a problem either. Yamanu, who is my mate, is going to shroud us, and no one is going to see you or Jacki. It's good that she is the only immune, or it wouldn't have worked."

"Wow, my head is spinning with what these people can do. How are we going to explain to Jacki what's going on?"

"Easy. We stick to what she assumes. We are a group of people with various paranormal talents. The other option is to pretend as if I'm the one performing all those fabulous tricks."

"Can you?"

"Not yet. I'm a baby immortal. The other former Dormants who I've spoken with can't do any of those things either. It takes time and practice, and most of them don't bother because they have no use for thralling or shrouding. There is a bunch of rules for when it's okay to thrall and when it's not, and I don't have them down yet, but from what I've seen, it's only reserved for emergencies and to hide the clan's existence."

"I'm glad that they follow rules of conduct. The ability to manipulate minds can lead to corruption."

Mey nodded. "The Clan Mother is very wise. She keeps her clan members in check."

When Jin opened her mouth to ask who that was, Mey lifted a hand to stop her. "Later. We need to go."

23

ARWEL

With Yamanu shrouding the entire bathroom area, Arwel didn't need to hide Jacki in the men's room, for which he was grateful. He wasn't a clean freak like Anandur, but even leaning against the wall felt gross.

It didn't seem to bother Jacki, though. Despite being a knockout, she wasn't acting like the typical pretty girl. She had a no-nonsense attitude and a ruthless vibe that reminded him of Eva. And she was also highly suspicious, which might be the reason she was immune to mind manipulation.

In fact, she emitted very little emotion. She was right next to him, leaning on the same wall beside him, but he wasn't suffering the onslaught of emotions such proximity to a human would have typically brought.

It reminded him of Eleanor. Except, Jacki wasn't a borderline sociopath like Ella's aunt, who had mental walls up that were a foot thick. Was it because she was protecting her mind from invasion by other paranormals? Or was it something deeper than that?

Perhaps a hard life experience had caused her to erect protective shields that strong.

"How did you know where to find Jin?" Jacki asked.

"We got lucky. Someone who knew Marisol mentioned something about her moving to West Virginia, and we found a travel guide in Jin's room with the Quiet Zone earmarked. Two paranormal talents traveling to the same place could have been a coincidence, but we decided to follow the thread. We found Marisol, and we got her to tell us where to find Jin."

Jacki's eyes blazed. "Did you torture the bitch?"

He chuckled. "If you count preventing her from peeing as torture, then yes, we did."

"That's all? I was hoping for much worse."

It was a harsh thing to say, but it wasn't accompanied by extreme emotions, which he found strange. Then again, Jacki might be feeling angry but not broadcasting it.

"Do you hate her that much?"

Jacki shrugged. "I've met worse. I hate her type, and unfortunately, there are many more like her out there. I wish I was an empath so I could tell the bad from the good. But all I get are visions of future events that usually have nothing to do with me. A worthless talent, if you ask me."

"Count yourself lucky. I'm an empath, and most days, I have to get stupid drunk to drown out the emotions of others."

"How did you people find each other? I know that the government is using sophisticated equipment to flag people talking about paranormal stuff, but I'm sure no private organization has access to something like that."

"Psychic conventions." He blurted out the first thing that popped into his head.

Luckily, Jacki wasn't an empath, so she couldn't tell that he was lying.

"Really?" She arched a brow. "It would have never occurred to me to look for paranormals in those freak shows. Most of the participants must be fakers and crazies."

That was what Julian had reported. And yet he'd found Vivian in one of those, which had led him to Ella, his fated mate.

"You are right about that, but a few are the real thing. You have to sift through the grit to find the gold."

The answer seemed to satisfy her. "So, what do you do? You approach someone who you suspect of being golden and offer them membership in your club?"

"Something like that. We follow them around for a while before we approach them, though. With the government collecting talents, it's risky to just walk up to someone and tell them about us. We need to be careful."

"Who foots the bill?" She glanced at Lokan. "He looks rich. Is it him?"

Arwel really didn't enjoy lying, but it was necessary, and since he'd started weaving a certain story, he decided to go with it. If Jacki turned out to be a Dormant, he would apologize to her later.

"We have several members who are very wealthy. The telepaths usually are." He thought of Kalugal. "Imagine walking into the stock exchange with insider information that you've gathered from the minds of CEOs. You could make a killing. Or being a compeller like Marisol and pocketing huge amounts of money for every recruit she brings in. She has a hundred percent closing rate."

"How much did she get for each of us?"

"Headhunters get between ten to twenty percent from a recruit's first-year salary. If she got twenty percent, that's fifty thousand per head. But since each of you signed a five-year contract with a large bonus at the end of it, she might have gotten more."

Jacki whistled. "Not bad. There were fourteen of us in the group. That's seven hundred thousand excluding the bonus in three months, and she didn't even work full time. She spent one day convincing us to sign the contract, and another day to deliver us in person. That's just twenty-eight days."

He nodded. "That much money is one hell of a motivator. She didn't feel even a smidgen of remorse for making you sign your lives away."

24

JIN

As her sister called the others to come back, Mey's boyfriend had to stay outside and keep shrouding them, and that was a damn shame. Since the shroud affected Jin like everyone else in the mall, she hadn't seen him yet, and she was dying of curiosity.

For some reason, Mey called him her mate, and Jin had made a mental note to ask her about it later. It was one more in the ten thousand questions she had.

This was so exciting. She'd thought that meeting other paranormal talents would be fascinating, and it had been, but that couldn't compare to meeting an entire clan of immortals and learning about their godly origins.

Was she dreaming all of this?

Was it just one of the hallucinogenic trips, and now was she back at the base, reclining in an armchair after being forced to experiment with drugs?

Those trips felt incredibly realistic while they were going on, and only later would she realize how impossible it was for any of it to be real.

Was Arwel a product of her imagination as well?

Those turquoise eyes that were staring at her so intently could belong to Jeremy, but maybe she was seeing someone else because of the damn drugs.

"Are you okay?" Mey asked. "Your hands are trembling."

"She is having a panic attack," Arwel said.

"No, I am not. I'm just hallucinating. All of you are part of a drug-induced trip."

"I'll take care of it," Jacki said as she walked up to Jin. "This is real. You are not hallucinating." She pinched Jin's arm hard. "Does that feel like anything that belongs in a trip?" She pinched her again. "Or this?"

"Stop it." Jin caught Jacki's hand before she managed another one. "You've proved your point." She massaged the offended spots. "You are so mean."

"Yeah, but effective. We don't have time for dramatics."

Jin showed her the finger. "I'll get you back for this."

"Yeah, yeah. You'll thank me later." She turned to Mey. "Are we going to hang around here for much longer? Because I could use something cold to drink. I hope you have provisions in your escape vehicle."

Carol chuckled. "I like you. A practical girl who doesn't beat around the bush."

"Let me bring you up to speed," Mey said.

After she was done, Jacki shook her head. "I don't know how good your shrouder is, but we might have a problem with the empaths. They are going to feel you messing with their heads."

"That occurred to me," Arwel said. "We will deal with each case individually. Lokan is going to accompany us, and he can compel those who we can't thrall for some reason."

Carol rubbed her hands. "Let's do it."

"One second," Jin said as they started turning toward the exit. "I have a small favor to ask from Lokan."

The thing that had been bugging her the most about running was leaving Richard without a word. Especially since he was still compelled to have feelings for her.

Lokan arched a brow. "What is it?"

"Can you remove the compulsion from Richard? Marisol has done to him the same thing that she did to me. I don't want him to suffer, thinking that the woman he loves left him without a word of explanation. If you remove the compulsion, he won't be heartbroken because he will realize that he never loved me. And maybe I can tell him what's going on before Arwel thralls him, and then he can thrall him to forget that too." She shook her head. "I'm making no sense. If Richard is going to forget what I've told him, then there is no point in telling him anything."

"I've already agreed to free him from the compulsion," Lokan said. "Just point him out to me."

Carol sighed. "You are such a nice girl, Jin. But you know what they say. Nice girls finish last. To compel Richard, Lokan would have to approach him and talk to him. That's adding an unnecessary risk factor."

Unbidden, Jin's eyes turned to Arwel. "It's important to me. I want to leave with no regrets."

After staring at her for a long moment, he nodded. "It shall be done."

She let out a breath. "Thank you."

25

KIAN

As Kian read Arwel's message, he exhaled in relief. "Jin is ready to bail."

"I thought she'd already decided that she was coming with us." Anandur pushed away from the bus's side, which the two of them had been leaning against for the past hour, waiting for the driver to come back.

"Apparently, she needed a little more convincing. They are going after the other talents now."

"Do we tell the rest of the team to start moving out, or do we wait until Jin and Jacki are in the car with us?"

"They should get going. By the time they are done loading Eleanor and everything else into the vans, Arwel will be done. I estimate that it will take him no more than an hour to thrall the other team members. Making them forget about Jin and Jacki coming to the mall this morning won't be a problem for him."

"Should I let Wonder know?" Anandur asked.

"Sure. I'll text Brundar and Syssi."

Kian texted Brundar first, giving him the green light to take Eleanor back to the resort. He then texted Syssi, letting her know that everything was moving according to plan. More or less. Jacki was an unexpected complication, but then every mission had one. 'Expect the unexpected' was the standard operating protocol.

"We have to find the damn bus driver. I should have stuck the tracker to his ass."

Anandur had already removed the tracker from the bus's rear fender, but he would probably need to stick it back on if they were to leave the spot and go searching for the driver.

"Did you get a good look at him?"

Anandur nodded. "I will recognize him. The problem is where to start looking. It's too early for him to hit a bar. Maybe Arwel should ask Jin to keep an eye out for him. He might have gone into the mall. It's not like there are many places around here that he could have gone to."

"For all we know, he could have family in town, and he went to visit them."

"Not likely. He would have taken the minibus with him. What are the chances of them living within walking distance from the mall?"

"True." Kian pulled out his phone again. "Stick the tracker back on the bus. We are going to check the local bars, and I'm texting Arwel to look for him in the mall. If we have to wait for him to come back, we are going to lose most of our head start. We have to find the bastard."

As Anandur reattached the tracker, Kian searched the map app for bars and taverns in the vicinity of the mall. There was one about ten minutes' walk away and another a little further out.

He was betting on the closer one.

Falling into step with Kian, Anandur scratched his beard. "If we can't find the driver, and if he doesn't come back until we are ready to move, we should view it as a sign from the Fates that we need to take everyone with us."

Kian cast him a sidelong glance. "And how do you suggest we do that?"

"Easy. We wait until the driver comes back to collect the recruits and thrall him to head out of town and then stop at the side of the road because there is something wrong with the bus. But instead of calling the base or the nearest mechanic, we will implant our phone number in his head. We get on that bus, thrall everyone to get out and follow us into our vehicles. Then we thrall the driver to fall asleep until the next morning."

"It's doable, but not advisable. As much as I would like to get everyone out of there, we can't risk a manhunt. If only Jin and Jacki go missing, they will assume that one of them had a hidden talent and made everyone forget that they were on that bus. That's a plausible scenario. But they probably know that neither of them is a compeller, so there is no way they could have convinced everyone to come with them."

It was a fucked-up situation, and Kian's conscience had a hard time leaving the kids behind. But taking them was out of the question, and not only because of the risk factor. Those kids had families, and as bad as the program was, they were still allowed to see them. If the clan took them, that would not be possible, and it would also be wrong. They had no right.

"I know," Anandur said. "What I'm saying is that if we can't find the driver, we should seriously consider doing that. If we have to wait for him to come back, it will leave us with only two hours of a head start because the moment he gets back to the base, they will realize that two of their recruits are missing. That's not long enough. But if he doesn't come back, they will first try to contact him, then they will send people to investigate, probably the local police, and all of that is going to give us at least another hour if not more. Three hours are enough for us to get to the airfield near Washington and take off. By the time they find the bus, we will be in the air."

"All of that is true, and we might be forced to do it your way. But let's hope that we find the driver, and it won't be necessary."

Anandur nodded. "It's up to the Fates, and I trust their judgment on this. But just in case, I suggest that you call Syssi and tell her to wait. If we have to take everyone, we will need them to come over with the other two vans, and Lokan will have to take a couple of the recruits in his car. Which means that he also has to wait for us to find the driver."

26

ARWEL

"Two down, ten to go," Jacki said after Arwel was done with a kid named Spencer.

Surprisingly, he had encountered a lot of resistance from the kid as well as the guy before him. Arwel had a feeling that they had been compelled into distrusting strangers.

After he was done, Yamanu brought him back under the shroud.

"I really hate this," Jin said. "I know that you are all right here with me, but I can't see you. It was easier when I could at least see Arwel." She turned to where she thought they were. "Can't Yamanu exclude me from the damn shroud?"

Arwel was glad that Yamanu was covering their voices as well as their bodies because Jin wasn't keeping hers down. Poor girl didn't know how far from her they were. She was the only one in their group who was affected by the shroud like everyone else in the mall and felt completely isolated.

Jacki was immune, so the shroud didn't work on her, and the rest of them were immortal, so it didn't affect them either.

Naturally, Yamanu couldn't release Jin from the shroud's cover because it was crucial that none of the recruits saw her or Jacki. Besides, it wouldn't help her to see the others, and she would be just as isolated.

But he could exclude Arwel. If Jin could see him, she wouldn't feel alone, and he could tell her what the others were saying.

He nudged Yamanu. "Take the shroud off me. This will save you the trouble of taking me out when I approach a recruit, and it will be easier for Jin if she can at least see me."

"No problem. It's done."

Jin puffed out a breath. "Thank you. That's much better."

He nodded and then whispered, "I'm not covered by the shroud now, so I can't look at you or talk to you without people noticing that I'm talking to thin air. But you are covered, so you can talk to me."

"That's so weird. But at least I don't feel like I'm floating in limbo."

"The first two were hard nuts. Do you remember Marisol compelling you to distrust strangers?"

She shook her head. "But that doesn't mean anything. She had a way of compelling without it being obvious. Like she told me to trust her, and that covered a lot of things. I trusted her to be truthful, and I didn't doubt anything she said. She might have said something about trusting only her or something like that. I don't remember. But anyway, I trust you. So, it would seem that she didn't do it to me."

That was nice to hear. But then he had her sister vouching for him, so maybe he didn't fall under the definition of a stranger.

As the others hung back, giving him and Jin some space, Arwel wondered whether they were doing it consciously because everyone was hoping that he and Jin would become a thing.

He hoped so, but he was so off his game that Jin was probably not impressed.

"There is Wendy." She pointed. "Richard was supposed to be with her, but I guess he went looking for Jacki and me."

"What's Wendy's talent?"

"She is an empath."

Arwel stopped and turned around, lifting his hand to indicate that the rest of the group should hang back. When they gathered around an indoor tree, he turned to Jin. "They are all standing next to the tree. Go join them. I'll approach her by myself."

Jin nodded and did as he asked.

Still, when he walked up to the girl, she was radiating stress by the gallon. She was looking in the direction of the tree as if she could sense that there were people there, and it was making her nervous that she couldn't see them.

Wendy must be a powerful empath to feel their emotions and be able to pinpoint their location by that.

"Excuse me." He smiled his most charming smile. "Do you know where the restrooms are?"

She glanced at him for a second and then shifted her eyes back to the group. "I don't know. I'm not from here."

He reached into her mind, but there was a thick blanket of mistrust mixed with angst that was hovering over everything in there like smog on a bad day in Los Angeles. Now he was convinced that Marisol had used some form of compulsion on the recruits or a subconscious suggestion not to engage with anyone outside the program.

Perhaps Lokan should override it before Arwel attempted a thrall, but that meant that Yamanu had to remove the shroud from Lokan, and Wendy was looking right at them.

Pulling out his phone, he texted Yamanu with instructions to hide on the other side of the tree and release Lokan.

The group changed locations, and several moments later, Lokan emerged from behind the tree and sauntered toward Wendy. "Hello, pretty lady. My name is Logan, and I'm the most trustworthy guy you'll ever meet. In fact, I'm the only one you can trust, and I'm also the best-looking one."

That should have taken care of Eleanor's compulsion for Wendy to trust her.

Except, the girl looked Lokan up and down. "Does that line work for you? Because it's pretty lame."

He made a pouty face. "And here I thought that I was being so suave." He offered her his hand. "Let's start over and introduce ourselves. My name is Logan, and I would love to invite you for a cup of coffee. We can talk, get to know each other, and then I will no longer be the pesky stranger to be wary of. I'll be your friend."

That was good. It should override Eleanor's compulsion to mistrust strangers.

"I'm Wendy," she said shyly, her tone lacking its prior hostility.

Lokan grinned. "A pleasure to make your acquaintance, Wendy."

It was progress. Still, when the girl smiled and took Lokan's offered hand, Arwel was taken by surprise. But the moment their hands touched, Wendy's smile disappeared, and her expression turned serious. "Take me with you."

Lokan swallowed. "To the coffee shop?"

Holding on to his hand, she shook her head. "I know that something is going on. I know that you and your friend with the beautiful eyes want to make me forget something. You both have paranormal talents, but you are not connected to the program. Are you here to take someone? Because I can sense that you have good intentions but that you are also feeling sorry for me. I didn't feel it before. You did something. You broke through some barrier that was blocking me."

Arwel and Lokan exchanged glances.

Well, this was a pickle.

"Please?" She held on to Lokan's hand. "Don't leave me behind."

In a last desperate attempt, Arwel reached into her mind, but it was no use. Wendy knew he and Lokan had paranormal abilities, and she knew that they were about to free someone. She wanted to run so desperately that no other thought could penetrate that whirlwind of need and want.

Even if he could somehow thrall her, Arwel had no heart to leave the girl behind.

"Let's take her to the others."

Lokan nodded. "Kian is going to throw a major tantrum."

"Who is Kian?" Wendy looked at him with frightened eyes.

Lokan patted her hand. "You'll find out soon. But don't worry. His bark is much worse than his bite."

27

KIAN

"Are they fucking kidding me?" Kian wanted to hurl the phone at the pub's wall. "They are bringing in another girl."

Instead, he slammed it on the table, causing several people to look at him with a mix of worry and annoyance in their eyes.

Damn, he should be able to control his temper and avoid attracting attention. And as always, the failure to do that only angered him more.

"What happened?" Anandur put his hand over the phone while casting the barflies a reassuring smile.

Kian leaned toward him and lowered his voice to a near whisper. "She didn't respond to Arwel's tricks and somehow guessed what he and Lokan were up to. She has the same ability as Arwel, but that doesn't explain how she could have possibly known what he was planning when he approached her."

Anandur grinned. "She must be very powerful."

"It would seem so. She begged them to take her with them."

"I think that the Fates had something to do with it. Maybe they decided that we need her."

Kian shook his head.

He should have never said anything about believing that the Fates were real. Ever since he had, everyone around him was invoking them left, right and center, and that was a recipe for disaster.

Decisions shouldn't be made based on faith, only on facts. Once every last detail was taken into consideration, and a solid plan was made, then it was okay to hope and pray and do all the other silly things that people did in the face of uncertainty.

"We should keep looking for our guy." Kian pushed to his feet and dropped a couple of twenties on the table.

They hadn't found the bus driver in the pub, but Anandur had been thirsty, so they had stopped for a drink and had grabbed a bite to eat while they were at it.

Outside, Kian checked the location of the other bar on his phone before heading in that direction.

With Wendy bringing the number of passengers to eight, one of them would have to sit in the trunk area of the Suburban. The other option was for Lokan and Carol to take Wendy in their car and deliver her to the meetup point where the two other vans would be waiting for them.

"We don't have enough space in the dungeon," Anandur said. "There are only two nicely furnished cells. Even if Jin and Jacki share the bigger one, the other one would be taken by a Guardian." He smirked. "Probably Arwel. He will want to stay close to Jin. And if you want to bring more Guardians to try their luck with Jacki, they will need a furnished cell or two as well. But even if they stay in the apartments upstairs, we still need one more for the new girl."

Kian nodded. "That's not all. We will have to feed them too. Three meals a day."

"And they will need to have the freedom to move around the underground. They are not prisoners." Anandur scratched his head. "Well, technically they can't leave, but we don't want them to feel as if they are."

Kian chuckled. "So, what are you suggesting? That we tell Ingrid to get in there and decorate the dungeon level to look like a high-end hotel?"

"That's not a bad idea. But at the very least, the girls should be able to use the gym, the pool, and the theater. Those are all on different levels. You will have to grant them limited access to the elevators. Do you think that William can do that?"

"I'm sure he can. He will have to program their thumbprints into the system but allow them access only to those levels."

Kian pulled out his phone and checked how far they still had to walk to the other bar. According to the map application, they would reach it in seven minutes.

"I'm going to text Onegus. He needs to get ahold of Ingrid and have her start working on the other cells."

Anandur nodded. "The girls will also need clothes and toiletries, and whatever else females require to feel comfortable. Normally, Amanda would take care of that, but she is here with us, so Ingrid will have to do that as well."

"Right." Kian shook his head. "You know that saying about no good deed going unpunished?"

"What about it?"

"It never fails."

As Anandur opened his mouth to answer, Kian lifted a hand. "Please, don't say that the Fates are going to reward us for it. I'm sick of hearing that."

Anandur snorted. "I don't have to. They already have."

Kian glanced at him. "What's that supposed to mean?"

"Look." Anandur motioned with his head at the middle-aged guy walking toward them. "That's the driver."

28

JIN

When they found Richard in a sports store, Jin tugged on Arwel's hand. "The guy sitting over there and trying on shoes is Richard. Can Lokan remove the compulsion from him?"

Arwel turned around and pointed. "He needs to find a spot where he can materialize without anyone seeing him."

"Can Yamanu remove the shroud from me as well? I want to talk to Richard."

Arwel frowned. "Why? That's not a good idea. He can't remember seeing you here, so what's the point? I will have to remove the memory of whatever you say to him anyway."

"I know. But I have to find out if my feelings for him were really the result of compulsion." She threaded her arm through Arwel's and whispered in his ear. "I like Jacki, but I don't trust her completely. She wanted out, and she might have used me to do it."

Turning toward her, Arwel regarded her with those intense turquoise eyes of his. "Are you still not convinced that you were compelled?"

She nodded. "I'm coming with you, so it's not about that. But I didn't feel a major change after Lokan removed the compulsion. Well, except for disliking Marisol, but I didn't like her before either. She is far from charming, and her sleazy personality bubbles to the surface no matter how much she tries to cover it up."

"Is there anyone else from your group inside the store?"

Jin shook her head.

"Fine." Arwel turned to where she guessed the others were and pointed at an alcove on the other side of the indoor street. "Come with me." He took her hand and led her toward it.

Jin didn't feel any different, but when Lokan suddenly appeared next to her, she figured that the shroud was off of both of them.

"Walk between Lokan and me so we can block you from view."

"Okay."

They were both taller than her, but not by much. Luckily, both men were blessed with broad backs and impressive shoulders, so they had enough bulk to offer her solid cover.

Walking behind Arwel, she held on to his belt and slouched to make herself smaller. Lokan was right at her back.

When they entered the store, she went ahead, while Lokan and Arwel stood shoulder to shoulder with their backs to her and Richard, blocking their view from outside the store.

"Hi, Richard." She sat next to him on the stool. "Getting new shoes?"

He smiled and wrapped his arm around her. "What do you think?" He lifted his foot. "You approve?"

"They are very nice."

Examining her feelings, she realized that what she felt toward Richard was friendship. His arm around her didn't bother her, but it didn't excite her either. She liked him, but she wasn't attracted to him.

Turning toward her, he frowned. "What's the matter? You are still tense as hell."

She shrugged. "I'm probably getting my period. I turn into Godzilla a day or two before." The lie tumbled effortlessly from her mouth.

Her periods were not remarkable, but her former roommate's were epic, and Jin had channeled that.

As she'd expected, Richard affected a compassionate expression and nodded. "Poor baby. Is there anything I can do to help?" He leaned and kissed her lips.

Jin recoiled, the intimacy suddenly feeling all wrong to her.

Apparently, the compulsion had been real. That had been a very different response to Richard's kisses. Before, she used to like them.

Frowning, Richard leaned away. "You feel odd. Is that also because of the period? I sense something more is going on."

Since Arwel was going to thrall Richard anyway, there was no harm in telling him about the compulsion.

"I need to tell you something. What you are feeling for me is not real. I found out that Marisol is a compeller, and she's been playing matchmaker. Did you notice that all the couples were arranged according to talent? They want us to pair up and produce babies with enhanced abilities."

He looked at her as if she had lost her mind. "That's insane. It makes perfect sense for people with similar talents to be attracted to each other. The opposites attract theory is a myth."

"Let me ask you something. Before I joined the program, who did you fancy?"

"That's easy. Jacki. But she's an ice queen. She never responded to me."

"Did you feel attracted to me from the first moment or only after Marisol had a talk with you?"

"You are gorgeous, so of course I was attracted to you from the start. But I thought you weren't interested. Marisol convinced me that you were just shy and that I should try again."

Jin snorted. "Shy? You know me better than that. But that's beside the point.

I met someone who can remove the compulsion from you. Let him do his thing, and then you'll know what I'm talking about."

"Sure. Bring him over." Richard's tone was mocking.

Lokan turned around and leaned down to offer his hand to Richard. "I'm Logan. Everything Jin said was true. Don't trust anything Marisol has told you, and you should be fine. You are free to feel whatever you want toward anyone you want."

Pulling his hand away, Richard shook his head. "Oh, wow. That was intense. I feel as if a fog has lifted from my brain, and I can think clearly again. Thank you."

That was a surprise. Why had the compulsion removal made such a profound change for Richard and a barely noticeable one for her?

Had Richard needed more convincing than she had?

That was an unflattering thought.

She patted his knee. "Good luck on finding a real girlfriend next time."

He caught her hand. "Are you leaving?"

"Now that you are free to think for yourself, I'm sure that you don't want us to keep dating."

"That's not what I meant, and you know it. You were saying goodbye to me. Are you running away?"

She nodded. "I couldn't leave you without freeing you first. I felt so bad about how hurt you would feel if I left without a word. You are not going to remember any of this because my other friend is going to make you forget this conversation. But your mind will remain free, and you won't feel bad about my disappearance."

While she'd been talking, Arwel had turned around and was now glaring at her.

"Take me with you. You can drop me off somewhere. I just want to get away."

Arwel groaned. "We can't. I'm sorry."

"Please? I can pay you. I have money saved up."

"It's not about the money."

29

ARWEL

As soon as Jin had opened her big mouth and told Richard about the compulsion, Arwel had known that things were going to get messy. But then she had spilled the rest of the beans, telling the guy basically everything.

Thralling him to forget would be impossible, but Arwel had to try. And if that didn't work, Lokan would have to compel him into silence.

Except, if Lokan could remove Eleanor's compulsion, Eleanor could probably remove his, and then the entire operation was screwed. She could force Richard to talk even if under normal circumstances he would have kept his mouth shut to protect his friends.

Bottom line, it was up to Arwel, and if he failed, Kian was going to have his and Jin's heads.

Fuck.

As mad as Arwel was at the girl for letting her mouth flap, the thought of Kian berating her enraged him. Never before had he imagined punching his boss's condescending face until Kian apologized to Jin.

That wasn't good.

He hadn't exchanged more than a few sentences with her, didn't know if she was even interested in him, and yet he was behaving like a mated man.

Probably worse. Arwel was willing to bet that Yamanu had never had even one disrespectful thought about Kian.

Taking a deep breath, he was about to reach into Richard's head, when Jin put a hand on his forearm. "Please, Arwel. Can Richard come with us? I'm sure he can be valuable to your organization. It's not fair to bring only girls." She winked at him.

Damn, she had a point.

The clan females would appreciate having a Dormant man who was free for the taking. So far, the Fates had favored the clan males, and more Dormant females had been found.

The question was what Kian would have to say about it.

"I have to check with the boss."

Richard lifted a pair of pleading eyes to him. "Tell me what I need to do in order for your boss to approve me, and I'll do it."

Arwel regarded the guy with suspicion.

How come they had to convince Jin to leave, and that was with her sister vouching for them, while the others were begging to be allowed to join?

Wendy's reaction had been similar to Richard's.

"Why do you want to leave so badly? We had to persuade Jin to come with us."

"I didn't want to join the program. I was engaged to be married, but thanks to fucking Marisol, I broke off with my girlfriend and signed the damn contract. I don't want to do anything for those fuckers, and if I go back, that bitch is going to become my puppet master again."

The vehemence in Richard's tone hadn't been faked. His resentment towards Eleanor and the others in charge of the program was so intense that Arwel felt like he was getting hit with wave after wave of dark energy.

He cringed. "Okay. Calm down. I'm going to explain the situation to my boss."

"Yeah, Richard. Tone it down a bit. Arwel is an empath, and your tirade is hurting him."

Arwel was surprised that Jin had realized that, and he was touched that she cared.

Pulling his phone out, he typed a lengthy explanation to Kian, detailing Richard's reasons for wanting to join them. Hopefully, that would lessen the boss's wrath.

30

KIAN

"You are turning red." Anandur peered over Kian's shoulder at the phone's screen.

"I'm ready to blow."

At this rate, they were going to take everyone despite having found the driver and thralling him to forget that Jin, Jacki, and Wendy had been on the bus that morning.

"Relax. At least we got the driver."

After Kian had stopped him to ask for directions and thralled him, they followed the guy back to the bus to remove the tracker. He had gone inside and, taking advantage of the long bench at the rear, had gone to sleep.

That was most fortunate because now they had to thrall him again to forget Richard.

"Not only do I have to thrall that man again, but the team also has to go back and thrall the other recruits again. And when they go back, there will be another one who will resist and want to join us and then another, and we will end up with everyone coming with us."

Anandur shrugged. "That wouldn't be so bad. More Dormants to go around, and more special talents to take advantage of. If they are willing, of course. I don't want them to think that we are anything like Eleanor and her bosses."

"You are such a fucking optimist, Anandur. Frankly, I'm sick of you trying to push me into taking all of them. As it is, four out of fourteen is going to trigger a massive manhunt, which was precisely what I wanted to avoid."

"There isn't much difference between three and four. Besides, what can you do? If you off the guy, it will still be one more recruit missing."

Anandur was joking, but Kian wasn't amused, especially since he was still not sure that he was doing the right thing by leaving ten of the talents behind.

The kids bugged him the most, and he'd been wracking his brain how he could take them and return them to their families. He would have to compensate them for the earning potential lost, and he would also need to relocate them and give them new identities. And after all that, the government was most likely going to find them again because they wouldn't be careful enough, and because it was really difficult to hide an entire family from Uncle Sam.

The first option was still the best.

He was going to wait for those kids to reach adulthood and then approach them. They would probably get new fake identities, but if he had pictures of them, William could find them with his facial recognition software.

With input from four people, Tim could draw amazingly accurate portraits of the ten remaining recruits.

Better yet, the team could snap photos of them.

He typed a text to Arwel, telling him to do just that and to go back and thrall the others to forget Richard. Hopefully, that was the last complication for the day.

Still peering over his shoulder, Anandur approved. "Good thinking. I wonder why none of us has thought of it before."

"I'm sure Turner did but thought that it went without saying."

"Perhaps you should call him and ask him for advice."

"It has crossed my mind, but what is he going to tell me? It's not like we have a choice."

"Right. But since we are already taking four, maybe he will suggest taking everyone?"

Kian pinned him with a glare that had absolutely no effect on the big oaf. "You are still pushing and you're getting on my nerves."

"I like to examine all options. That's all."

Just to get Anandur to finally shut up about taking all fourteen recruits, Kian typed a long message to Turner, explaining the situation and what he thought was the best way of handling it.

The answer surprised him. *I'm crossing my fingers that no more will join. Stick to the original plan and take only those you must. You cannot and should not take everyone.*

"Ha." Kian shoved the phone in Anandur's face. "Is that going to finally shut you up?"

The Guardian shrugged. "Turner has his opinion, and I have mine."

Seeing the jolly red giant crestfallen, Kian heaved a sigh and clapped Anandur on the back. "This is not the end. Eventually, we are going to get them all, or rather those who turn out to be Dormants. We will approach the older ones as soon as they finish the program and start going out on missions, and the younger ones as soon as they turn eighteen."

That seemed to cheer Anandur up. "I wonder if the facial recognition program would work on the kids. Their faces are going to change."

"I'll have to ask William. But in any case, I'm sure that Tim can draw a portrait adjusted for age." He chuckled. "I'm the champion of new technologies, and yet when I thought about taking their pictures, the first option I came up with was having Tim draw their portraits. Only a moment later, I realized that we can tell the team to snap photos while Arwel is thralling them."

Anandur draped his arm around Kian's shoulders. "We are a couple of old-timers, my friend."

"Tell me about it. This year I'm celebrating my bi-millennial birthday. Not that it's such a great reason for celebration. It just reminds me of how old I am."

Anandur grinned. "You are so full of shit, Kian. This will be the best year of your life. You are going to become a father."

31

ARWEL

With Richard also covered by Yamanu's shroud, neither he nor Jin could see each other or the rest of the group. Only Arwel remained visible so he could communicate with both of them.

The problem was that Richard and Jin solved the invisibility problem by walking with their arms around each other.

Yamanu hadn't added the sense of touch to his shroud, and Arwel was contemplating asking him to do that. Even though Jin and Richard's feelings for one another were limited to friendship, watching them walk together like a couple of lovers was driving Arwel nuts.

Perhaps he should just try to avoid looking at them.

He had to calm down.

Going back and thralling those that he had thralled before and adding Richard to the roster of people who had stayed behind because of the flu, meant a third thrall for two of the recruits. It was risky, and he had to be diligent, performing a very precise thrall without disturbing much else. Usually, not a problem for a gifted thraller like him, but not when his own cranium was home to a storm.

Sidling up to him, Mey put her hand on his arm. "What's troubling you? Usually, you are the calm and mellow one, and today you look like you are about to murder someone."

For a moment, he was tempted to admit his feelings. Perhaps confiding in Mey and telling her that he wanted her sister like he had never wanted anyone before would ease the pressure in his chest. But what if it freaked her out?

She'd just found Jin, and the last thing she wanted was to deal with an overzealous admirer.

Besides, he needed to sort out his feelings and get himself under control first. Everyone was already suspecting that he had a thing for Jin, and it was difficult to pretend that she was just Mey's little sister and not a woman he desperately craved.

"Kian asked that we snap photos of the talents we are not taking with us. I'm worried that the extra focus is going to alert them, and more will want to come with us."

It wasn't a lie. It was a real concern, just not his only one.

She nodded. "So, let's not do it at the same time. First of all, the rest of us should keep our distance when you approach a talent. Then once you are done thralling them, I'll wait a couple of minutes and then get closer to take their picture."

"Sounds like a plan. I'm going to tell Jin and Richard."

Mey glanced their way. "It's odd to think that they can't see or hear each other, only feel their arms around one another."

"Yeah. Odd."

She cast him an amused glance. "At this point, he is just a friend."

"I know." He patted her arm before quickening his steps to catch up with the pair. "Slow down," he whispered.

"What's up?" Jin asked.

"From now on, when I approach a talent, I want you to stay back, and by back, I mean at least fifty feet away. I don't want them to get a whiff of your emotions. It's especially important when dealing with empaths and the aura reader."

"His name is Spencer," Richard said. "He is seventeen, and he has reddish-blond hair."

"I know. I took care of his memory once before already."

The guy was trying to be helpful, but it only irritated Arwel more.

"I didn't know that."

"We are not sure whether Yamanu's shroud can hide our auras, so when I approach Spencer, you should duck into a store. I'll tell the others to do the same."

"I feel so bad about leaving him behind," Jin said. "I wish we could take him as well. His talent is so rare."

"We can't take anyone else." Arwel walked away to avoid further discussion and joined the rest of the team. "Did you hear what I said about Spencer?"

Carol nodded. "When we see him, we should get into a store and mingle our auras with those of other people."

"Right."

Jin tapped him on the shoulder. "The balding guy holding hands with the woman wearing a pink T-shirt. Can you handle them together?"

"Remind me what their talents are?"

"James is a mediocre telepath, and Mollie has post-cognition."

Great, one could sense Arwel's intentions, and the other could see what he had done before. Dealing with paranormally talented humans was not as easy as dealing with regular ones.

"Got it. Turn around and start walking in the other direction. I want you far away from them."

"Yes, boss." Jin saluted, and she and Richard turned around like one unit and walked away.

The rest of the team followed them.

Taking several deep breaths, Arwel calmed himself down as much as he could without the help of booze and walked over to the couple.

32

JIN

Given the boss's negative reaction to Richard's addition, Jin tensed up every time Arwel approached one of the trainees.

Watching him do his thing from behind the store's window display, she saw James and Mollie glance around nervously. Her stomach churned with worry that they might resist the thrall and demand to join the escape as well.

When Arwel nodded and waved, she let out a relieved breath.

Richard squeezed her shoulder, which was the only way they could communicate while under Yamanu's shroud. This was certainly going down as the most bizarre experience of her life.

So far.

God knew what else was in store for her.

The one good thing about it was that she couldn't talk with Richard or Mey or anyone else other than Arwel and had time to process what was happening to her.

It occurred to her that no one had thought to ask her to tether her friends, and Jin was grateful for that. She would have refused, but that would have caused tension between her and the boss for sure. The question was whether it was a careless omission or a deliberate decision in accordance with the high moral standards that the clan was supposedly holding itself to.

She hoped it was the latter and not the former. If the clan was about to become her extended family, it was reassuring to think that she was joining good people who valued the concepts of personal freedom and consent.

That being said, thralling people to forget that four of their friends had been on the bus with them that morning was not exactly kosher, but it was unavoidable.

On the other hand, asking her to tether her friends so they could be more easily located in the future was not necessary since they could be found by other means.

Still, if that were the only thing her tether could do, it would have been fine, but obviously it wasn't. It had much more nefarious potential uses. Like finding out what her friends were working on and who they were spying on.

That it hadn't even crossed the boss's mind spoke volumes about his moral makeup. She couldn't wait to meet him and thank him for coming to Mey's aid.

By the time Arwel was done with the last of the recruits, he looked like he'd been run over by a bulldozer, which made Jin feel guilty for the immense relief she felt that no one else had asked to join the escape.

"You look awful." She put her hand on Arwel's arm. "Thank you for doing this. I know it took a lot out of you."

A smile tugging on his lips, he nodded. "Thralling paranormal talents is difficult, especially when they've been compelled to avoid contact with people outside the program."

As a soft hand landed on Jin's shoulder, she knew immediately who it belonged to and rested her cheek on it. "Hi, Mey. Did you get everyone's pictures?"

The answer came in the form of a gentle squeeze.

"Can we get out of here so Yamanu can drop the shroud, and I can finally see and hear everyone?"

Arwel took her hand, beating Richard to it. "The Suburban is parked behind the café, but we can't fit everyone in it. Lokan will have to take two in his car. I hope no one is there because we can't just have people materialize out of thin air in front of spectators." He led her toward the mall's exit.

"Are the others behind us?"

"Yes. Jacki is holding Wendy's hand because she is freaking out the same way that you did. And Richard is on your other side."

Arwel's tone had changed when he said Richard's name, making her realize that he was jealous.

She'd never had a boyfriend who was jealous over her. Not that Arwel was her boyfriend, not yet. Hopefully, that was going to change.

He hadn't said anything to indicate that he was interested, but there had been neither the time nor the opportunity for it. Still, if he was the shy type, she would have to do something about that.

As gorgeous as he was, Arwel seemed oblivious to his appeal, and he dressed as if he couldn't care less whether the ladies found him attractive or not. And unlike other guys, it wasn't because he was full of himself. He just was too preoccupied with all the emotions coming at him to bother with his looks.

She was going to take care of that as well. When he was hers, she would make sure that he never left the house looking so schlumpy.

Except, that fell under the category of trying to fix a guy, which everyone claimed to be a girls biggest relationship mistake. The advice she'd read in magazines was to either accept a guy the way he was or move on to the next one. Apparently, men didn't like it when women tried to fix them.

They liked to feel like the big honchos, the protectors, the providers. Or at least the good ones did.

Damn, she was so clueless.

Up until she'd met Arwel, dating was a casual thing for Jin, and her longest relationship had been with Mitch, which had lasted about a month. She'd felt no need to fix him, though, and it wasn't because Mitch was so perfect. She simply hadn't thought of him as a keeper, so it hadn't mattered if he fulfilled all of her expectations or not.

Perhaps she should talk with Mey. Except, her sister had crashed and burned so badly with damn Oliver, so evidently she wasn't an expert on relationships either.

Jin hadn't met Mey's new boyfriend yet. All she knew was that he was a powerful shrouder, and that Mey's eyes sparkled whenever she talked about him.

Her sister was in love, that was obvious, and hopefully she wasn't going to get disappointed this time. If Yamanu pulled a stunt like Oliver had, Jin was going to teach him a lesson he was never going to forget.

Arwel's hand tightened on hers. "What has gotten you upset all of a sudden?"

She shrugged. "I was thinking about Mey's ex-boyfriend. What's her new guy like? I hope he's a mensch."

As Arwel laughed, his turquoise eyes shone from the inside. "He is the best guy on the planet. I'm just glad that I've recently gotten a crash course in New Yorker slang. Otherwise, I would have thought that you were insulting my best friend."

"Yamanu is your best friend?"

"We were roommates before Mey moved in with him. Naturally, I moved out to give the newly mated couple their privacy."

There was that word again. "What does it mean to be mated? Is this Scottish slang for being in a relationship?"

"Sort of. We will have plenty of time to talk about this on the plane."

33

MEY

The closer their group got to the parking lot behind the coffee house, the tenser Mey became.

She wasn't looking forward to seeing Kian angry. The guy was intimidating as hell when he was trying to be nice. Right now, he was probably sprouting horns and spitting fire from his throat because of the three extra people he had been forced to take with him.

He was going to blame her for that, and rightfully so.

Mey hoped that he'd had enough time to cool down, and that he thought of the additional escapees as potential Dormants and future members of his clan, and not three more mouths that he had to feed.

Heck, feeding them was just the tip of the iceberg. If they were not Dormants, he would have to arrange new identities for them and cover the cost of their relocation.

And then there was the security factor, which was the gravest concern. Four people missing instead of one would make a big difference in the scope of search the program's supervisors were going to launch. It was almost as bad as absconding with the entire busload of trainees.

Next to her, Yamanu was walking with that faraway expression on his face, concentrating on the shroud, and she didn't want to disturb him by engaging him in conversation.

When they reached the Suburban, Kian stepped out, and poor Wendy swayed on her feet. Still remembering her first reaction to Annani's son, Mey could sympathize. He really looked like a god, and thankfully, he didn't look majorly pissed.

Just mildly so.

But it was enough to make poor Wendy shake in her boots.

Surveying the group, Kian zeroed in on Lokan and motioned for him to step forward.

"I need you to take the three additional trainees to the meeting point. We don't have enough space in the Suburban."

They could have taken one of them in addition to Jin, but Mey was glad that Kian was sending the other three to the other car. That would allow her and Jin to talk freely.

"No problem," Lokan said. "We are heading in the same direction. Who do you want us to take?"

As if it wasn't obvious.

"Jin will want to be with her sister, so you take the others."

"My car is over there." He pointed at a black Mercedes sedan.

Without knowing much about cars, Mey was sure that it was the firm's flagship model. It wasn't that Lokan was a show-off, it was more that he really thought of himself as a prince, and frankly, he fit the role.

Then again, Kian was driving a Suburban, so there was that. Except, he probably had a fancy vehicle at home, and the modest one he was using now was part of their cover.

Checking that there was no one else in the parking lot with them, Kian motioned for Yamanu to drop the shroud.

"Oh, my God." Wendy plastered herself against Mey's side. "I must be dreaming."

Mey patted her arm. "It's okay. Pretend that you are Alice and that you went down the rabbit hole. That's how I deal with it."

Wendy and the other two didn't know that the rest of the group could see and hear each other while shrouded, and it was important to maintain that illusion.

Richard stepped forward and offered his hand to Kian. "Thank you for agreeing to take me. I just want you to know that I'm at your service in whatever capacity you may find me useful."

Kian looked down at the offered hand and shook his head. "I accept your gratitude, but I'm not going to shake the hand of a sensory telepath until I'm sure that I can trust you, and I'm not the trusting sort."

Richard's face reddened, and he dropped his arm. "Reading you wasn't my intention, but I understand your hesitation. No hard feelings."

Kian nodded, then looked at Jacki and Wendy. "I'm going to save the introductions for later. Please join Richard in Lokan's car."

As the three left with Carol and Lokan, the rest of them got into the Suburban. Arwel and Yamanu went in the back, Jin and Mey in the middle, and Kian sat next to Anandur, who was the designated driver.

Once Anandur pulled out from the parking lot, Kian turned back and offered his hand to Jin. "I'm Kian, and I want to officially welcome you to the clan, Jin. I couldn't say that in front of the others."

She smiled and shook what was offered. "Thank you. And a big thank you for taking my friends too. Mey explained why that's such a hassle. I understand that you are taking them to some secret facility?"

He nodded. "It's crucial for our safety to fiercely guard the clan's location. Only members of the clan and their mates are allowed in. But since your sister is mated to Yamanu, and you are devoted to her, I'm making an exception in your case. Besides, I'm sure you will find a mate in no time."

"Everyone keeps saying mate and mated. What does it mean? Is it like a husband?" She narrowed her eyes at Mey. "Because if you got married without me, I'd be really disappointed."

"Never." Mey took Jin's hand and squeezed it. "I would have never gotten married without you. Mate means a life partner, and for immortals, that's like saying forever. The bond between mates is much stronger than marriage, and no ceremony is required for two people to be acknowledged as mates. But if a couple wants to have a big party to celebrate their bond, that's more than okay. In fact, the Clan Mother loves to preside over weddings, and she's just waiting for Yamanu and me to decide on a date."

34

JIN

In the brief moments between Yamanu dropping the shroud and everyone getting into the cars, Jin had caught a glimpse of Mey's new guy, and she was duly impressed.

He was the most stunning man she'd ever seen, and that included Kian, who looked like a god. But where Kian was intense and intimidating, Yamanu was like calm waters. His strange pale blue eyes were kind, and the bright, welcoming smile he'd cast her had been genuine. Without exchanging a single word with the guy, Jin already liked him a lot.

But as gorgeous as those two were, neither had Arwel's amazing turquoise eyes and kissable lips. Now wasn't the time to be thinking about kisses, though.

Turning around as much as the seatbelt allowed, she offered Yamanu her hand. "We didn't have the chance to get introduced properly."

Yamanu enveloped her hand in his huge paw, but his touch was just as gentle as she'd expected. "I've heard a lot about you, and I'm glad to finally meet you in person. With you joining the clan, Mey's happiness will be complete." He glanced lovingly at her sister.

Jin stole a sidelong glance at Arwel, who so far hadn't said a word. He still looked exhausted, and she wondered how immortals recuperated. Did he need to eat a big meal? Or maybe sleep it off?

With the way her list of questions was continually growing, it would soon be as long as the Scroll of Esther.

Mey chuckled. "Almost. I will also need a bunch of kids running around for my happiness to be complete. And maybe also have their grandparents nearby, but I know that's asking for too much."

Her sister had always wanted to have a big family with lots of kids, but that was supposed to happen sometime in the future, after they had their business up and running. Except, it seemed like that dream was not going to happen. Mey had jumped over it straight to the marriage and kids stage.

That was a shame, but Jin couldn't begrudge her sister the happiness she'd found with Yamanu. Besides, she loved the idea of having a bunch of nieces and nephews. She was going to be the cool aunt that they told all their secrets to.

That was in the future, though. In the meantime, her practical mind was trying to organize this new world into manageable bits.

"Marriage first," Jin said. "What about Mom and Dad, though? They will also never forgive you if you don't invite them to your wedding. How are you going to explain what's going on to them?"

"We will probably need to use Lokan's services again. He can compel them into silence about our immortality."

Kian turned around.

"I want you to tell me everything you know about your three friends. Is there a chance that any of them are plants? Jacki knew that Mey was coming for you, and she could have been cooperating with the bosses by organizing a spy team to infiltrate our organization."

Jin was taken aback. Her first instinct was to dismiss Kian's suspicions, but that would be naive of her. If not for Jacki, she would have never suspected that Marisol was a compeller, and that she was pushing people into relationships that would produce super talents for the government.

"Frankly, I don't know. I think Arwel can do a better job of assessing their motives than I did. Maybe once he has rested a little." She glanced back and smiled at him. "Thralling ten talented paranormals, some of them three times, took a lot out of him."

Kian nodded. "I understand that you are not a telepath or an empath and that you know only what you see. But you've spent time with these people. Are you at all suspicious of their motives?"

"Wendy is just a kid, so I would be very surprised if she is hiding something. Jacki is my best friend from the program, but she is also crusty and suspicious, and I don't know whether it's the result of growing up in the foster system, or because she is deceitful and therefore thinks everyone else is as well."

"Did she ever lie to you?"

Jin shook her head. "Not that I know of."

"What about Richard?"

"He was my boyfriend, but that was because of Marisol's compulsion. I would have never gone for him otherwise. First of all, he is full of himself, and I don't like arrogant men, and secondly, he is ten years older than me. I've never dated a guy that old."

It suddenly occurred to her that Arwel might be ancient and that she'd just blabbered about not being interested in older men. "Not that age is a big deal, I've just never done it before. Other than that, Richard is a decent guy. Or at least I think he is, and I really think that he had no ulterior motives when he offered you his hand." She chuckled. "I've never seen him turn that particular shade of red before."

Kian arched a brow. "What other instances cause him to blush?"

"Richard hates losing or being second best at anything. Whenever someone did better than him, he would turn red."

"A sore loser," Mey commented.

"Not necessarily. He was never mean about it or claimed that it was a fluke or that he wasn't at his best or some other nonsense like that. He would just turn red and then try harder the next time."

Kian still looked skeptical. "Did you believe Jacki that Mey was coming for you?"

"I did, and I didn't. I wasn't sure."

"As a touch telepath, Richard must have felt your anxiety."

She waved a hand. "I told him that studying Mandarin was stressing me, and he believed it."

Mey squeezed her hand. "Not knowing whether I was going to show up or not must have been stressful for you."

"It was. Jacki knew that you were going to approach me in the mall, so last Saturday, I was a nervous stress ball. But after you didn't show up, my enthusiasm diminished, and I wasn't as excited this time." She cast Mey an apologetic look. "I wasn't sure I wanted to leave. And I didn't really believe Jacki's claim about Marisol compelling me to sign the contract and then to date Richard."

"But now you believe her, right?" Mey asked.

"I do. But I also know that I would have signed that contract even without compulsion. The money was a good enough motivator. The reason I agreed to run is their breeding program and the realization that they were not going to let me leave."

"What breeding program?" Kian asked.

"They wanted to pair complementing talents in the hopes of producing super-babies. Like I can touch people and then see what they see and hear what they hear, Richard can touch people and know how they feel. Imagine someone with our combined powers."

35

KIAN

Kian tried to wrap his head around what Jin had said. He could see the government using coercion and even compulsion to get the people it wanted. But a breeding program?

That was something a lowlife like Navuh could come up with, not a branch of a democratically elected government.

Except, it was a huge organization. Kian had no doubt that some of the more prominent cogs in the system took matters into their own hands and played God with the lives of the people they were in charge of.

It was abhorrent, but it wouldn't be the first or the last time it had happened, and there was nothing he could do about it. What he could do, however, was to make sure that he was not leading those unscrupulous individuals to the clan's hideout.

The meetup point was at a rest stop about twenty minutes' drive out of the city, and Kian had spent half of that time questioning Jin about her friends.

He'd hoped to get a better assessment of them before deciding on what instructions he should give the rest of his team members, but Jin hadn't been much help in that regard.

First of all, he needed to reiterate the importance of keeping up the pretense of being a group of humans with paranormal abilities. Secondly, he was going to use the same precautions with the four trainees as he had used with the captured Doomers.

Regrettably, he didn't have the equipment needed to check them for implanted trackers, and it would have to wait until they were in the keep. He should let Bridget know so she could get ready and assemble the equipment she needed in her old clinic in the underground.

That could wait, though.

Getting rid of their clothing was the first priority, since it was more likely that if they were tracked, the devices were hidden either in the garments they were wearing or in their footwear.

A quick text to Amanda solved that issue.

When they reached the rest stop, Anandur eased into one of the two spaces between the two vans, and Lokan into the other. They were parked near the picnic area, which was thankfully deserted.

Amanda opened the side door of one of the vans and waved. "Girls change in here. Boy, on the other side."

Jin looked at Mey. "What's going on?"

"You are about to change into my clothes." Mey smirked. "Nothing new there."

Kian waited until the other three had gotten out of Lokan's car before explaining. "Everything you have on goes into a trash bag except for the cash. You might have hidden trackers on you. We have a handheld device that can detect some of them, but not all, and we don't want to waste time patting every seam and hem. My teammates have organized a collection of clothes and shoes for you to wear until we get to our destination. You'll get a new wardrobe when we get there."

"What about credit cards and a driver's license?" Richard asked.

"You can't use either, so there is no point in taking them. We will get you new fake IDs."

The guy rubbed the back of his neck. "I appreciate the help and everything, but what are we going to do for money?"

It was a little late in the game to suddenly be concerned with practicalities. Richard should have thought about that before forcing them to take him.

"You are going into hiding, so you will not need money. Later on, we will figure out something."

Jacki clapped Richard on the back. "When you decided to run, you should have realized that you'd be starting from scratch. Get used to the idea of a career as a janitor named Pablo Cusinovich." She smiled at Amanda and offered her hand. "I'm Jacki."

"Nice to meet you. I'm Amanda." She pulled on the girl's hand, helping her get into the van. "Choose whatever you like. Unfortunately, you will be going commando for the duration of the trip. None of us had new underwear, and I know I wouldn't want to wear someone else's undies even after they were washed."

"No problem." Jacki ducked into the back.

"Are we going one at a time?" Jin asked.

"Hop in." Amanda waved her on. "We made room." She looked at Wendy. "You too."

"Yes, ma'am."

After she'd pulled the girl inside, Amanda closed the sliding door.

Richard was still standing next to Lokan's car, looking lost.

Yamanu put a hand on his shoulder. "You need to get moving, buddy. Everything is going to work out fine. You'll see."

Richard lifted his head and looked at Yamanu's smiling face. "You really believe that, don't you?"

"Of course. I trust the Fates."

36

JIN

"Welcome to Amanda's fashions," the beautiful brunette said as she pulled Jin into her arms. "And welcome to the clan," she whispered in her ear.

They were standing bent over in the middle row of the van, while Jacki was in the back with Wendy, already undressing.

"Thank you. Mey said that she left some clothes for me."

Amanda shook her head. "Kian put me in charge of collecting clothes for the four escapees, and it was easiest for me to just grab some of mine for you and Jacki. Ella donated hers to Wendy because mine would have been too long on her. But you and Jacki are going to look fabulous in what I've selected for you."

"I'm Ella." The girl sitting at the shotgun seat waved. "Nice to meet you, Jin."

"And I'm Callie," the one behind the wheel introduced herself. "Wonder and Syssi will be back in a minute. They are using the facilities."

Amanda glanced at Jin's cleavage. "You are a little bustier than Mey and me, but I don't think that will be a problem. The shirt I got for you is stretchy."

"Oh, my goodness," Jacki gasped from the back. "Is this a Prada T-shirt? I can't put this on." She had already pulled on a pair of leggings and was sitting bare-chested and holding the shirt out.

"Nonsense, darling. The fabric is very soft."

Jacki lifted a pair of wide eyes to Amanda. "I'll be afraid to breathe in it. What if I accidentally stain it?"

Amanda shrugged. "Then you'll have a stained Prada shirt. It's yours to keep. I'm not taking it back."

Jacki lowered her head. "Then I really can't take it. Can I have some of Ella's clothes as well? I don't mind if they are too short. It's just for the road."

It took Amanda a moment to realize how what she'd said had sounded to Jacki. "Oh, darling, it's not because you will be wearing it. I never wear an outfit more than two or three times, and I've already worn that damn shirt more than that. If you don't want it, I'm going to donate it to charity, like I do with all my used clothes."

Jacki clutched the shirt to her chest. "I'll take it, and I'll also take anything else that you want to donate. Consider me your private charity project."

Amanda laughed. "Done."

"I hate being short," Ella murmured from the front of the van. "Amanda could dress the entire village with what she throws away, but who has a body like hers?"

Amanda cast her a hard stare, and Ella covered her mouth. "I meant an entire village of women."

There was no harm in saying the word village. Jacki and Wendy didn't know that it was a specific place. Nevertheless, Jin decided to divert the conversation to more practical matters.

To afford top designer brands like Prada and toss them after two or three uses, Amanda must be a rich woman. And she was obviously interested in fashion. She could be the money partner Jin and Mey needed to launch their future clothing line.

"So, you are the group's fashionista?"

Amanda nodded proudly. "Indeed, I am."

"My sister and I want to create fashion for tall women. You could become our consultant."

This was a soft approach, just testing the waters. If Amanda took the bait, a serious pitch could come later.

"I would love to."

"What do you do now?"

"I'm a neuroscientist. I research paranormal phenomena."

Jin's jaw dropped. The woman was unbelievable. Gorgeous, smart, and rich?

Amanda chuckled. "Naturally, I couldn't indulge my fashion obsession with what the university pays me. I come from a very old and wealthy family."

Yeah, she came from a clan of immortals who lived forever, but that didn't explain her wealth. Ella was dressed modestly, and so was Callie. Neither had that aura of royalty about them either.

Jin would have loved to know Amanda's real story, but it would have to wait for later, without Jacki and Wendy listening in.

Once they were done, they exited the van, and Jin went to the backseat to change. The two items left were another pair of super soft leggings and a long-sleeved shirt that at first glance looked like a simple Henley. Except that it wasn't.

"How are we going to do this?" Jin asked as she pulled her pants and underwear down. "Who is riding with whom?"

Unlike Mey, who was used to undressing in front of people, Jin felt shy, and talking while she was at it helped.

"I'm sure you want to be with your sister and talk freely. So, you should ride in the Suburban with Kian and Syssi, Yamanu, Mey, and Arwel. Jacki and Wendy can ride with me, Dalhu, Callie, and Ella. Richard can ride with Anandur and Wonder. Am I forgetting anyone?"

"Brundar and Julian," Callie said. "But they are going to meet us at the airfield."

"Where are we going?" Jin asked. "Mey didn't tell me."

"Los Angeles, but we are not flying directly there." Amanda took the trash bag with the old clothes and opened the back door. "I'm going to give it to Arwel to check for trackers and then get rid of it."

"Why bother checking if Arwel is going to dump the bag in the trash anyway?"

"Curiosity. Kian wants to know if you had any on you."

37

ARWEL

As Yamanu cast a small shroud, Arwel ignited the contents of the trash can.

Before dumping the bag with the trainees' clothes, they had swiped the tracker detection device over it, but the thing kept flashing green, which was worrisome.

Arwel found it hard to believe that the recruits hadn't had any on them. Were they tracking them through the walkie talkies that they had left behind in the mall? Probably, but not only. The government must have developed trackers that the device couldn't pick up.

Regardless of the technology and materials used though, the fire would take care of that, melting the delicate circuitry in the miniature devices.

As he and Yamanu waited for the smoke to disperse, the rest of the team went to load up on snacks from the rest stop's vending machines. It was miserable fare compared to Jackson's pastries and sandwiches, but that's what was available, and it would have to suffice until they found a decent takeout joint.

Finally, when the smoke was gone, they walked over to where the rest of the group was waiting.

"I'm going to miss you all so much." Carol hugged Arwel and then Yamanu.

She'd already shed quite a few tears saying goodbye to Ella and her other friends.

It seemed to bother Lokan.

Standing with his hands in his pockets, he looked on with a grim expression on his face, and it wasn't because he was jealous that his mate was hugging and kissing her male cousins.

The feelings that Arwel was picking up on were helplessness and irritation, the second probably resulting from the first. Lokan didn't like seeing Carol sad, and he liked even less not being able to do anything about it.

"I'll see you when I see you." Carol wiped a tear with the back of her hand. "You should come to visit me. It's much easier than the other way around."

"I'll do my best." Arwel cast a glance at Jin, who was talking with Syssi.

It wasn't going to happen anytime soon because he was going to be busy wooing a girl.

How? He had no clue. Not yet.

Lucky for him, Arwel had no shortage of advisers. Amanda would gladly put her matchmaker hat on and assist, and he might even enlist Mey's help. She should know what her sister liked or disliked about guys.

After another round of hugs and kisses with the girls, Carol took Lokan's hand, and they got into their car.

"Why is she so sad?" Jin asked.

Syssi put her hand on her shoulder. "Carol and Lokan live in Washington DC, and she misses her family."

"I get it," Jin said. "I missed Mey during the month that I didn't see her, and I miss my parents terribly." She sighed. "I don't know when I'll be able to see them again. This really is like diving into a rabbit hole."

Syssi laughed softly. "I felt the same way. But I find the world on the other side of that wormhole beautiful." She glanced at her mate. "I have more than I could've ever dreamt of."

Jin looked like she wanted to ask Syssi questions, but Jacki was standing right next to her.

"Okay, people." Kian lifted his hand to get their attention. "Time to move out. Richard, you are going with Wonder and Anandur."

Anandur clapped Richard on his back. "You won the lottery, buddy. You get the entire back seat to yourself. You can take a nap."

As the three of them entered the van on the left, Kian motioned to the one on the right. "Jacki and Wendy, you are with Amanda, Dalhu, Callie, and Ella. The rest are with me."

"Who is going to drive?" Yamanu asked.

"I am." Kian got behind the wheel, and Syssi joined him in the front.

"I guess we are in the back again." Arwel motioned for Yamanu to go in first. "Or do you want to sit with Mey?"

"I do, but I'm a considerate guy." He ducked to the backseat and waited for Arwel to join him. "Mey and Jin want to talk."

"I love you." Mey sent him an air kiss.

They were so cute together that it was sickening. Arwel was glad that he'd moved out because watching and sensing their mutual adoration would have been too much for him to handle.

Hell, was he jealous?

As Kian eased into traffic, Yamanu leaned into Arwel. "What's eating you?" he whispered.

The sisters were deep in conversation, and as far as Arwel was aware, Mey's hearing hadn't improved significantly yet. Still, it was probably much better than Jin's.

Nevertheless, at some point he was going to ask Mey's advice anyway, so it didn't really matter if she heard his conversation with Yamanu.

"Jin. I'm so obsessed with her that I can't think straight."

"I knew it!" Yamanu's whisper was so loud that both sisters turned around.

"What did you know?" Mey asked.

Arwel braced for the most embarrassing moment of his life, but Yamanu proved that he was great at improvising. "That the Lakers were going to win against the Hawks."

"Oh." Mey and Jin both lost interest and went back to talking in hushed voices.

"Good save," Arwel whispered.

"That's great news. You found your mate. Why are you upset?"

"I'm not upset. I'm nervous. She is so strong-willed and so outgoing, and I have no idea how to approach her. I don't know how to woo and how to date. I only know how to seduce, and I'm not that good at it either. Usually, I just let the eyes do the work."

Yamanu arched a brow. "The eyes?"

Arwel pointed at his peepers. "The ladies love them. When I go hunting, it's enough that I look at a woman, and she does the rest."

"Hmm." Yamanu rubbed his chin. "Perhaps you should go with that. If it's worked for you so far, it might work with her as well." He motioned with his head at Jin.

"I don't know if she's interested in me."

Both of Yamanu's brows shot up. "You are an empath. How can you not know?"

Arwel pushed his overgrown bangs back. "Since I saw her picture, I've been a nervous wreck, and my empathic ability has gotten all jumbled up. She is not broadcasting much, and I have a hard time quieting my inner turmoil enough to distinguish between my own feelings and hers. It's even impacting my work, which stresses me even more."

Nodding, Yamanu put his arm around Arwel's shoulders and sighed. "Love has a way of messing with our heads. But the moment you give in and admit your feelings to your lady, the storm becomes a gentle breeze." He chuckled. "With the occasional thunder and lightning."

"It's not love. I don't know her well enough to love her. It's a crazy attraction, that's all."

Yamanu grinned. "Yeah, keep telling yourself that."

"I'm not in love."

"Maybe not, but you will be. This is more than attraction, though. This is the Fates at work."

Arwel rolled his eyes. "You and your Fates. I don't want to belittle your faith, but I don't share it."

"Bullshit. Deep down, you believe in them too. You are just not secure enough in your masculinity to admit it." The idiot leaned back and crossed his arms over his chest.

"You are so full of it, Yamanu. Faith or the lack of it has nothing to do with my dick."

Both May and Jin turned their heads and looked at him.

What a great way to impress Jin. Now she could add crass and unsophisticated to schlump.

"My apologies, ladies. I didn't realize that I raised my voice."

Jin chuckled. "No apology is needed. I agree with you. One has nothing to do with the other."

38

JIN

Arwel must be really old-fashioned to apologize for saying dick, or really old, not just old-fashioned.

Jin had used that word in conversation and had never felt the need to apologize for it. It was mild compared to the language her friends used, but no one got offended by any of it. So far. The PC police were adding to the list of prohibited words by the day, but for some reason, the worst of them hadn't made it there yet.

Glancing out the window at the farmland they were passing by, Jin wondered why Arwel's age wasn't creeping her out. It boiled down to perception. He looked like he was in his late twenties or early thirties, and that's how she thought of him. Did it really matter how old he was?

And how old was Yamanu? Did it bother Mey?

There were still so many questions she wanted to ask her sister. They would have to drive all the way to Los Angeles for her to have time to ask them all.

"How long is the drive to the airfield?"

"About an hour and a half," Mey said. "Do you want to take a nap? All this excitement must have exhausted you."

"I don't think I'm going to sleep anytime soon. My head is buzzing with ten thousand questions. But first, I want to hear all about your new pointy teeth and about turning immortal and all the other goodies you dangled in front of me but never got to explain."

As Mey glanced back at Yamanu and Arwel, Jin followed her eyes. The two were busy whispering in each other's ears like a couple of yentas, and in the front, Kian and Syssi were holding hands over the center console.

Was Mey checking if they were listening? And what if they were? Everyone knew about her fangs, so it wasn't as if she was going to divulge some clan secrets.

"I'm waiting." Jin nudged her. "You spaced out on me."

"Sorry. I was just trying to figure out the best way to explain it." Mey pushed her hair behind her ears. "Immortals have fangs, but they are not the same for males and females. Females have tiny ones that look like pointy canines, similar to what I got. Males have really big ones that elongate and retract more or less on demand. They also have extra glands that produce venom in response to two different triggers. One is aggression, and the other is arousal. The venom produced differs according to the trigger, but both kinds can induce transition in a Dormant. Naturally, to induce a male, the immortal needs to get aggressive, and to induce a female, he needs to get aroused."

"I saw Amanda's, and hers are barely noticeable. Yours are longer. How come?"

Mey groaned. "Because we are the freak sisters. I told you before that this is uncommon, but the truth is that this is the first time it's happened. The clan females have those tiny fangs that look like sharp canines, but since they are induced when they are little girls, they grow them together with their adult teeth. Aside from me, none of the other adult Dormant females lost their canines while transitioning, and they didn't grow fangs."

Frowning, Jin leaned back and crossed her arms over her chest. "Any explanation for that?"

"The clan's doctor thinks that our ancestor might have been a goddess who had fangs. Aside from the recent influx of Dormants, everyone in the clan descends from one goddess, and she is a petite, gorgeous redhead with glowing skin." She chuckled. "The formidable Clan Mother looks like an otherworldly eighteen-year-old. Only when you look into her eyes, you realize that she is ancient."

Jin gaped. "No freaking way. The Clan Mother is a real goddess? And she is still around, and you saw her?"

Mey laughed. "I was so nervous, but she is so nice and friendly and not scary at all. Yamanu told me to think of her as a queen and act accordingly, and that's what I did. But after half an hour, I was calling her by her first name and chatting with her as if we were best friends. She is awesome."

Syssi turned around. "I love Annani. She is the best mother-in-law."

"Figures." Jin tapped her temple. "That's why Kian looks like a god. He is Annani's son."

"I'm right here," Kian muttered.

"I'm sorry. You are right. When I saw you, I thought that you looked like a god. A stormy god of thunder."

Rolling her eyes, Mey elbowed her.

Me and my big mouth. Jin never knew when to put a sock in it. "I mean, you are gorgeous, and you look formidable," she quickly added.

He chuckled. "Thank you, but there is no need for flattery. I'm well aware that I'm an intimidating asshole, and that is on a good day."

"No, you are not." Syssi cast him a reproachful look. "You have a lot on your mind, and you are always stressed, which makes you frown a lot and look intimidating, but you are a kind and loving man."

He lifted her hand and kissed the back of it. "I love you."

39

MEY

Mey and Jin exchanged knowing smiles.

Love could blind a woman and make her see only the good side of her partner. It was true that Kian was kind, and he was entirely devoted to his clan and deeply in love with his wife. That being said, he was also gruff, demanding, and not very friendly. Still, his positives outweighed his negatives by a wide margin. He was a good man and an excellent leader.

"I will probably get fangs too." Jin dipped her head to take a better look at Mey's teeth. "They are not too bad. Are they still growing?"

"God, I hope not. As they are, I can still pass for a human, but if they get any longer, I will have to have them filed down on a regular basis. One of the perks of immortality is that everything grows back. Forget about tattoos and piercings. We can't have them."

Jin cast her an amused glance and leaned to whisper in her ear. "I can live without those, but big freaking fangs could be problematic, and not only aesthetically. How do the immortal males kiss? If their fangs elongate when they are aroused, which happens when people smooch, they could cause some real damage." Jin frowned. "And if their glands produce venom when that happens, I guess it has to go somewhere. Do they bite only to induce transition or every time they get randy?"

Crap. That wasn't a talk Mey wanted to have with her sister in front of others, but knowing Jin, she would just keep pestering her until she did. She had two options. She could either state things matter of fact like a mother explaining the birds and the bees to her daughter, or she could talk in vague terms and not go into intimate details.

Except, explaining the fangs and the venom bite without mentioning that sex was part of the deal would be misleading.

Damn, what to do?

Jin and Arwel were obviously interested in each other, but the moment Mey explained about sex being a necessary part of transitioning, Jin would feel pressured to choose an immortal male to induce her, and that would kill the romance.

"They know to be careful when they kiss. And even if they nick their partner by accident, their saliva contains healing properties, so no harm is done."

"Yeah, but it must hurt, and then the mood is gone."

Mey leaned and whispered, even though she knew it was futile. "It hurts only for a split second, and when you are all excited, it hardly registers. Besides, sometimes, a little hurt can enhance the pleasure."

That was vague enough. Hopefully, the explanation would satisfy Jin for now.

40

JIN

Mey was being evasive, but given that they weren't alone, it was understandable.

There was no point in pestering her for more details because she was obviously not going to supply them until they had a chance to talk privately. And that wasn't going to happen for many more hours.

Still, Jin could deduce things from what little Mey had told her.

Since the males' fangs elongated when their venom glands got activated, it meant that whenever a guy got aroused, his fangs would grow large in tandem with the other part of his male anatomy that responded to sexual stimuli in the same way.

It didn't make sense for that to happen only when an immortal male was about to induce a Dormant.

When the venom got produced in response to an aggressive trigger, it was designed to aid the male in a fight. And when it was produced in response to a sexual one, it was designed to be used during sex.

Why?

That part was unclear. Perhaps they marked their partners? Was the venom a catalyst to the strong bond mated couples shared? Mey had said that immortals stayed mated for life, so that was probably what made it possible.

Except, if the females didn't have venom, how was the bond created in both partners?

That would be question number ten thousand and one.

Bottom line, biting was part of sex. Which meant that in order to transition, Jin would have to get bitten, and that would probably involve having sex with an immortal male.

She didn't mind the sex part, especially if it was with Arwel, but she did mind getting bitten.

Ouch.

Then again, judging by the passionate looks she and Yamanu had been exchanging, Mey didn't seem traumatized or reluctant to engage in bed sports. On the contrary, the two looked as if they couldn't wait to jump on each other, and the same was true for Syssi and Kian.

Jin leaned and whispered in Mey's ear, "I know you can't talk, but just tell me one thing. Does the bite make the sex hotter?"

Mey blushed, which didn't happen often, and then nodded.

As Syssi chuckled softly and Kian shook his head, Jin realized that they had heard her question, which meant that Arwel and Yamanu had heard it too.

Turning to look at Arwel over her shoulder, Jin expected to find him smirking, but he appeared to be absorbed in whatever he was reading on his phone, or perhaps he was just pretending for her sake.

It was nice of him to try to save her the embarrassment, but she wasn't shy, and her question had been one hundred percent legit.

Despite Mey's explanation, she still couldn't figure out how kissing would be possible once the fangs elongated, and she wasn't sure how she felt about getting bitten either. In theory, it might have been hot. In reality, it probably hurt like hell. Besides, it was weird. Jin had never fantasized about having sex with a vampire and found the whole sucking of blood thing disgusting.

She wasn't a Twilight fan.

Except, the immortals didn't need blood for nourishment, hopefully, and they bit for different reasons, which were still not a hundred percent clear to her.

Mey couldn't or wouldn't tell her more with the others present, and that was a major bummer. They were not going to be alone for the duration of the trip, and once they reached their destination, they would probably part ways. Mey would go back to the lovely village, and Jin would accompany her friends to the underground facility.

Ugh, she hated living like a freaking mole.

Now, that was funny. A mole that didn't wish to live as one.

Except, she was no longer training to be a spy, and hopefully the clan wouldn't ask her to serve in that capacity. She'd been willing to sacrifice five years of her life to save up for her and Mey's dream, but she wasn't willing to spend her immortal life spying.

Perhaps others found it exhilarating, but not Jin.

Her excitement was all about building a business and running it honestly and successfully with no spying involved.

There were so many things she wanted to talk with Mey about. "I wish I could come with you to the village, but I really can't leave my friends. They regard me as their representative."

"They'll be fine," Kian said. "You should go home with Mey and Yamanu."

Right. Jin had no wish to become the third wheel and ruin their honeymoon. "I can't." She turned to Mey. "I hope that you'll come to visit me often. We have so much to talk about."

"I have an idea." Mey's eyes widened with excitement. "If you can't come to live with us in the village, perhaps Yamanu and I can come live with you in the underground facility." She leaned forward between the two front seats. "I assume that you will want to post Guardians to keep an eye on the trainees. Yamanu and Arwel can do their guard duty there."

"Do we have enough furnished cells?" Syssi asked.

Cells? Jin and her friends were about to be locked up in a freaking basement, and Mey was okay with that?

"Are you putting us in a dungeon?"

Syssi turned around. "Relax. It's not what you think."

Kian cleared his throat. "It's exactly what she thinks, but we are not going to lock anyone up. We have a nice one-bedroom apartment that is beautifully furnished. In fact, my sister and her mate spent quite some time in there. We also have several studio style rooms, but only one is furnished. I called our interior designer and asked her to prepare three more for our guests. But if Mey and Yamanu are going to join you, I need to tell her to prepare another one."

Syssi smiled. "It's really not as bad as it sounds. Each of the rooms has its own bathroom, and the underground has a gym, a swimming pool, a movie theater, a commercial kitchen, offices, classrooms, and even a banquet hall and an assembly hall. It's like an underground city."

"I just came from one," Jin said. "And although what you are describing is impressive, it's nowhere near on the scale of that facility. The place is so big that there are streets with electric vehicles traveling back and forth. They have simulated lighting that mimics the real thing, and there are windows in the buildings overlooking the streets. Still, it's located in the belly of a mountain, and living there is not the same as living topside."

Kian glanced at her through the rearview mirror. "How many people live in there?"

"I don't know the exact number, but I estimate thousands. The place was designed as a fallout shelter, but it is currently used for countless secret projects. Don't ask me what they are because I don't know. We were instructed to keep what we did secret, and so were the others. But there is cooperation. Like I was taking classes in Mandarin with normal future operatives, and our group practiced in the same shooting range as everyone else."

Kian nodded. "I wonder if Turner knows about it."

"The place itself is not top secret," Jin said. "Many people probably know that it exists, but they think it's only a doomsday shelter facility. They don't know how large it is or what it is used for."

Kian's hands tightened on the steering wheel. "I don't get envious often, but I would like to have a place like that at my disposal in case of a catastrophe. Knowing that I had a safe shelter that I could move all of my people into would make me sleep better at night."

41

ARWEL

The jet Turner had arranged to pick them up was so old that Arwel felt wary about boarding it.

"Trust the Fates." Yamanu chuckled and clapped him on the back. "It only looks old. I'm sure Turner wouldn't put us in danger."

Kian went past them with a suitcase in each hand. "It belongs to an ex-Air Force pilot. You have nothing to worry about." He climbed up the stairs with Syssi right behind him.

So far, their luck had held.

They had encountered no roadblocks, and the one police car blaring its siren had shot past them in pursuit of a speeding car.

"Nebraska, here we come." Arwel slung the strap of his duffle bag over his shoulder and picked up one of Amanda's suitcases.

"Welcome aboard the Thomas express," the pilot said with a heavy southern accent. "We might be low on luxury, but we are high on hospitality. You will find refreshments in the cooler." He winked. "You are in for a surprise."

"Let's have a look." Anandur popped the lid and grinned. "Hallelujah, bless Turner." He pulled out a Snake Venom beer bottle. "Who wants one? There is plenty for everyone."

Arwel lifted his hand. "Toss it."

He caught the bottle and hugged it to his chest. "Thank the merciful Fates."

Yamanu chuckled. "Now you thank them."

"Is it good?" Richard asked. "I've never heard of this brand."

"The best." Smiling evilly, Anandur tossed him a bottle. "Catch!"

Arwel expected Richard to read the label and realize the alcohol content, but the dude just popped the cap and took a swig. His eyes bugged out, but he swallowed it and only then looked at the label. "What is this shit, and how can you drink it?"

Yamanu clapped him on the back. "It's from Scotland, our homeland," he said, letting his Scottish accent out.

Standing up, Amanda lifted her hand to get everyone's attention. "We didn't have time for proper introductions at the rest stop, and not all of our team members were present." She pointed at Julian. "This is our doctor, so if you have any medical emergency, Julian is the guy to turn to."

As the introductions continued, Arwel walked over to where Jin and Mey were sitting, took the seat behind them, and popped the cap on his beer. Lifting it to his mouth, he took the first swig and then another, enjoying the pleasant burn as it went down his throat.

Regrettably, he couldn't allow himself to get drunk with Jin present. He wanted her to think of him as the clan's amazing empath, not the clan's drunk.

Besides, he didn't even have a good excuse to indulge.

Immortals didn't broadcast their emotions as loudly as humans, and surprisingly the paranormals didn't either, so it wasn't about drowning out other people's feelings. This time it was about drowning out his own.

On the way, he'd listened to Mey telling Jin an abbreviated history of the clan, and Syssi and Kian had answered some of her questions.

It irked him that he hadn't been the one to reveal the immortals' secret to Jin.

In Arwel's mind, the telling of the clan's story and how it had all begun was part of the bonding process between a Dormant and her or his immortal truelove. And even though he hadn't dared hope for a mate, he'd secretly been rehearsing the reveal and imagining her awed responses.

He should have been the one to tell the story to Jin.

But that was water under the bridge and not really relevant at this point. When they reached the keep, he would step up his game and try to spend time alone with her, but since Mey and Yamanu were moving into the one-bedroom apartment, that wouldn't be easy either. The sisters would want to spend every waking hour together, and he would have to steal moments here and there.

Surprising him, Jin got up as Yamanu walked over with a beer in his hand. "I've monopolized enough of Mey's time. You two should sit together." She moved to the seat next to Arwel.

Yamanu remained standing. "I don't mind. You have a lot of catching up to do."

"That's okay. I think Mey wants to take a nap, and I'm sure she'd rather snuggle with you."

He smiled. "You've said the magic word. I can't say no to snuggling." He sat next to Mey and draped his arm over her shoulders. "Did you miss me, love?"

Leaning, she kissed his cheek. "I missed this."

As the smooching began, Arwel tried not to look, but it was impossible since they were sitting in front of him. He could either look out the window, which would be rude to Jin, or look at Jin and hope that his fangs behaved.

Jin grinned. "I love seeing her like that."

"Same here. Yamanu has been lonely for a very long time."

She arched a brow. "Really? A handsome guy like him? He probably had to walk around with a fly swatter to keep the girls away."

Yamanu chuckled and turned his head to her. "You know that I can hear you, right?"

"So what? I'm not revealing any big secrets. You are one hell of a hunk."

It was good that Yamanu was happily mated. Otherwise, Arwel would have had a big problem with his buddy.

"But you have the most gorgeous eyes of them all," Jin whispered in his ear.

Had he been so obvious?

"Thank you. But that's okay. I'm used to turning invisible when Yamanu is around, and not because he is shrouding me."

"You are not invisible." She leaned her head against his shoulder and sighed. "You are very handsome too." Sighing, she closed her eyes.

The girl wasn't shy, that was for sure. Or maybe she didn't think of him as a potential boyfriend and therefore was treating him just as a friend. Concentrating, he tried to read her emotions, but she'd fallen asleep already.

That wasn't a good sign.

He could have never dozed off next to a woman he was craving, which meant that Jin had put him in the damn friend zone.

For now, he would go along with that, but in time he was going to change her attitude. When they reached the keep, he would ask Amanda to stay and give him a haircut.

Someone had to order clothes for the four escapees, and knowing Amanda, she would want to be in charge of that. He could ask her to order some nice stuff for him because if he did it, he was going to end up with the same loose cargo pants and button-downs he always got.

Then again, he shouldn't look as if he was trying too hard or making too many changes to impress the girl.

Stifling a groan, he took another swig from his beer.

Why did things have to be so complicated?

Couldn't he just point to his chest and say, 'Me Tarzan,' then point to her and say, 'You Jane,' throw her over his shoulder and carry her off to his jungle lair? Or in this case, one of the keep's upper floor apartments?

42

KIAN

"Thank you so much." Syssi smiled at the pilot who'd graciously helped them unload their luggage despite their protests.

Kian offered the guy his hand. "Thank you." Looking into the pilot's eyes, he thralled him to forget their faces, implanting other ones in his mind.

Not that Turner's buddy was going to talk, but Kian preferred to play it safe. Just like the previous pilot who had taken them to Nebraska, this one would remember a middle-aged, nothing-special group of people.

A few minutes after the plane took off, their own jet landed. It was like a well-synchronized dance.

"Hello, everyone." Charlie stood at the top of the stairs. "Welcome aboard."

Kian walked up. "Thank you for picking us up." He shook Charlie's hand and leaned to whisper in his ear. "Don't mention our destination in front of our guests. I don't want them to know where we are taking them."

Charlie lifted a brow. "Any idiot can recognize L.A. from the air."

"I'm going to have Yamanu and Julian put them to sleep."

"Roger that." Charlie saluted.

Kian came back down, and as the rest of the group started boarding the aircraft, he put his hand on Yamanu's shoulder. "I need a word with you before we board." He waved Julian over as well.

Nodding, Yamanu followed Kian a few feet away from the plane, with Julian joining them a moment later.

"I told Charlie to keep quiet about our destination. As soon as we are in the air, I want you to put our guests to sleep, and I don't want them to wake up until we put them in their beds in the keep."

"No problem. I can thrall Richard and Wendy, and they will sleep until I tell them to wake up, but you'll need our esteemed doctor to take care of Jacki."

"I can do that," Julian said. "I can either give her a shot or put something in her drink." He chuckled. "I have plenty left over from dear Aunt Eleanor."

"I was meaning to ask you about that. You mentioned complications?"

"Nothing major. There was a guy who seemed to be able to see through Brundar's shroud. He was staring in our direction as we carried Eleanor into the lobby. But it turned out to be a false alarm." Julian raked his fingers through his hair. "Well, not exactly false but close. He was looking at a woman, and then we walked right in front of her, and she got accidentally shrouded as well, so she disappeared from his view for a moment. I noticed that and told Brundar to keep going with Eleanor to the room, while I went back and thralled the guy's memory of the incident away."

Yamanu shook his head. "That's the problem when I'm not around. When I shroud, I don't only hide things from view, I also substitute so there are no gaps."

Unfortunately, Yamanu could not be in two places at once, and his skill had been more needed at the mall. "I hope no one else noticed anything."

Julian shrugged. "There weren't many people in the lobby, and Brundar took the emergency stairs. So, I think we are good. Eleanor is not going to wake up until tomorrow morning, and when she does, it will be in a room full of drug paraphernalia."

"Good job."

"I heard that Arwel had trouble thralling the talents," Julian said. "Perhaps I should put the other two to sleep with a shot or pills instead of Yamanu trying to thrall them."

"It's not going to be a problem for me," Yamanu said. "They are calm now, so they don't have their defensive walls up, and if they need additional calming, I can sing them a lullaby."

Kian chuckled. "That would put everyone on the plane to sleep, including the pilot. Your lullabies are dangerous."

That was an exaggeration, but not a big one. Yamanu's voice had a hypnotic quality to it even when he was just talking. When he sang, the effect was almost overpowering.

"I'll sing quietly, so only our four new friends will hear me."

"You don't have to put Jin to sleep," Julian said. "She knows where we are heading."

"I'll do it for Arwel. Poor guy seems like he wants to crawl out of his own skin."

"Why is that?" Kian asked. "I get that he is attracted to Jin, and that's great, but why does it make him miserable instead of happy?"

Yamanu shrugged. "Maybe he is insecure. Guys get weird when they really want to make a good impression on a girl and don't know how. It's easy to be confident with casual hookups because they don't mean a thing. But when you know that your future rests in the hands of that one lady, it can get stressful. Especially when a guy isn't sure that she reciprocates."

Frowning, Kian pushed his hands into his back pockets. "It is obvious to everyone that she likes him. That's a good start. Besides, can't he feel her emotions? As an empath, he doesn't need to guess."

Yamanu rubbed a hand over his jaw. "I don't know whether Jin is subconsciously muting the broadcasting of her feelings, or she just doesn't feel much in general. She also might not be as intensely attracted to Arwel as he is to her.

Which makes me think that we shouldn't take it for granted that she is his fated mate. When it's meant to be, the powerful attraction is mutual. It doesn't seem to be the case here."

Julian shook his head. "Maybe Lokan didn't remove the compulsion entirely. When Ella seemed less passionate about me than I was about her, I thought that it was because of the trauma she'd been through, and so did she. But it turned out that Lokan had compelled her to feel attraction only toward him and no one else. Once that was removed… well, things changed."

That was an interesting thought.

She was no longer attracted to Richard, so that part of the compulsion had been overridden, but maybe Marisol had done more than compel Jin to want Richard?

"You might be on to something. Lokan freed Jin from the compulsion to crave Richard, but there might be another component to it that he didn't address. Perhaps Marisol compelled her to ignore all other guys."

Yamanu shook his head. "She isn't ignoring Arwel. Jin likes him, just not with an all-consuming passion, and that's what is bugging him. He knows that something is off, but he doesn't know what it is."

"That's exactly how Ella was," Julian said. "She liked me and wanted to be with me, but the passion was lacking until Lokan removed the compulsion."

Kian didn't comment, leaving things at that. He hoped that Julian was right, but he couldn't dismiss the possibility that Jin wasn't Arwel's fated mate.

Not everyone got so lucky.

43

KIAN

*Y*amanu's observation about Jin kept bothering Kian throughout the flight from Alabama to the clan's airstrip.

If Jin wasn't Arwel's fated one, the guy would be devastated, and there was nothing Kian could do about it.

The thing was, Yamanu was right.

By now, there had been enough fated matings in the clan for the pattern to be clear. Aside from Ella, who had had several factors working against her, all of the mates had felt a powerful attraction to their partners.

There could be four possibilities why Jin didn't seem as passionate about Arwel as he was about her.

The first and the most obvious was that so much was going on in her life that it was a wonder the girl still appeared relatively calm and collected. Jin was either one hell of a tough cookie, or she was great at putting up a façade.

Still, it was possible that Jin was interested in Arwel, but she wasn't his fated mate.

The other explanation could be what Julian had suggested. Perhaps Marisol had put an additional compulsion on Jin, which was acting as a suppressor on her arousal toward any guy who wasn't Richard.

The fourth option was that Jin's feelings weren't as transparent as a regular human's.

Kian wasn't an empath, so it was difficult for him to gauge the level at which Jin broadcast her feelings. And Arwel was too emotionally involved to make an objective assessment.

Perhaps Wendy could help with that?

He could ask her to assign projection scores to different people as a test of her skills and include Jin in it. That way, Arwel wouldn't realize what he was attempting to do.

Damn, this wasn't something that he should stick his nose into, and it made him feel like a yenta. This was more up Amanda's alley. But Kian cared about Arwel.

The guy was just as deserving of a boon from the Fates as Yamanu.

Instead of choosing an occupation that didn't expose him to constant contact with humans or working from his home as many of the clan members did, Arwel had chosen to serve the clan in the best way he could. And by doing so, he put himself through constant suffering.

That sacrifice deserved a big-ass reward.

Then again, if Jin could dim the broadcasting of her emotions as a human, as an immortal she would be an impenetrable wall and the perfect mate for Arwel. If that was the case, the Fates were even better matchmakers than Kian had given them credit for.

As the jet came to a stop, Anandur opened the door and lowered the steps. "I can't wait to get home." He glanced back at their sleeping guests. "But first, we need to unload the cargo at the keep."

As people started getting up, Kian lifted his hand. "My apologies for dragging everyone to the keep, but it makes more sense for Okidu to pick us all up with the bus rather than have several people come with their cars."

"No problem," Callie said. "I want to see what Ingrid has managed to do with the dungeon to make it look more hospitable."

"Yeah, I'm curious too." Amanda stretched and yawned. "I napped, so I'm good to go."

Once the luggage and the sleeping guests were loaded on the bus, the rest of them got in. Charlie stayed behind to service the plane, but he had his own vehicle parked next to the hangar.

As Okidu put the bus in drive, Kian pulled out his phone and called Onegus.

"Welcome home," the chief answered. "How was your trip?"

"Long. We are on the bus on the way to the keep. Is everything ready?"

"Ingrid got the five additional cells furnished and decorated. The bars are stocked with snacks and drinks, the bathrooms have towels and toiletries, and the closets are filled with new stuff from Anandur's favorite store."

"Walmart rocks." Anandur high fived Wonder. "You can get everything you need in one place and without breaking the bank."

Amanda snorted. "Yeah, if you have no standards."

Looking smug, Anandur sent her an air kiss. "I love you like a sister, but you are a snob."

She sent him a kiss back. "No argument there. I like quality." She wrapped her arm around Dalhu. "In everything."

"What about food?" Kian asked. "All we have eaten since yesterday morning is junk."

It was after two in the morning, and he was famished.

"Okidu and Onidu prepared a meal in the keep's kitchen, which has also gotten revamped by Ingrid. The woman is a miracle worker."

"How did she manage to get everything done so fast?"

"She mobilized half of the Guardian force and several unfortunate civilians. The furniture, decorations, bedding, and many other items came from the unoccupied homes in the new phase, and the rest from Walmart. We used the bus to transport the stuff."

"Smart."

"Indeed. Ingrid is waiting for you in the keep, so don't forget to compliment her."

"Don't worry," Syssi said. "We are all going to ooh and aah."

44

ARWEL

As Okidu drove the bus into the clan's parking lot in the keep, Arwel wondered whether it was smart to break from protocol when secrecy and security were at an all-time high for this mission.

Since the clan had moved into the village, the directions had been to park in one of the high rises across the street and use the underground tunnel. They even had a golf cart they could use, so transporting the sleeping guests wouldn't have been a problem.

Still, if they had trackers implanted in their bodies, that security measure would have been useless anyway.

"You are so strong," Jin said as Arwel picked Jacki up.

He liked the compliment but not Jin's lack of jealousy. He was holding a sexy young woman in his arms, and it didn't bother her one bit. "Immortals are stronger than humans."

"Still, you did it without even huffing out a breath, and Jacki is not a small woman." Jin chuckled. "Just don't ever tell her that I said so. She will be offended."

"No worries, I won't."

She looked over her shoulder at Anandur, who was carrying Richard. "I'm glad he is asleep for this. Being carried like that would have been hard on his male ego."

Kian held the elevator door open for them. "I suggest that we take turns instead of trying to squeeze everyone in at once. Guests and their carriers go first." He motioned for Arwel and Anandur to get in, then waved for Syssi, Jin, and Wonder to join them.

Yamanu, who was carrying Wendy, got in the other elevator with Mey and several of the others.

"I'm excited to see what Ingrid has done with the place," Syssi said.

She didn't have to wait long.

As soon as the elevator door opened, the first thing they saw was a large framed picture hanging over the wall across from it. And it wasn't the only one. The entire corridor was lined with framed art reproductions, transforming the place from stark and dreary to almost warm. The lights were still fluorescent, and the floor was concrete, but given the limited time Ingrid had had to perform the transformation, it was impressive.

"Nice," Syssi said. "All we need now is a new carpet and light fixtures, and this will look like a hallway in a hotel."

Kian grimaced but said nothing.

Jin glanced at the art as they walked by it, but she didn't seem overly impressed.

Arwel was starting to get a feeling that she really wasn't projecting much, and that was why he wasn't sensing her feelings, not because she didn't have them. The question was whether it was her natural state, or she was somehow suppressing them.

She wasn't a blank like Turner, but her emotions were muted.

Still, she could be just an unemotional person.

As they reached the first redecorated cell, Syssi stopped and peeked inside while the rest of them kept going. "Come back, you have to see this."

Kian rolled his eyes but did as his wife asked. Naturally, everyone followed.

It was one of the smaller cells, but Ingrid had managed to transform it into a comfortable studio apartment. There was even a couch, a narrow coffee table in front of it, and a television mounted on the wall across from it.

"You can put Richard in here," Kian said. "We will put Jacki in the next one."

"Gladly." Anandur walked into the room, while the rest of them remained out in the corridor.

Looking like she hadn't slept in days, Ingrid walked out of one of the cells and came over. "So, what do you think?"

"You did an awesome job." Syssi pulled her in for a quick hug. "I don't know how you managed to do it in one day, basically."

"With a lot of help from my friends." Ingrid peeked into the room. "And who is that?"

"His name is Richard," Jin said and offered Ingrid her hand. "I'm Jin, Mey's sister. Thank you for making this place look less like a prison. I really appreciate it."

"You're welcome. It was a challenge, and I'm not done yet." Ingrid glanced at Kian. "With the boss's approval, I would like to do more." When he shook his head, Ingrid lifted her hand to stop his retort. "I'm mindful of the budget. Nothing fancy, I promise."

He nodded.

"Thank you." She looked at Jacki. "Let's put this one in the next room."

After Yamanu had deposited his cargo in the third room, they continued to the one-bedroom where he and Mey were going to stay, but instead of going in and checking it out, Mey wanted to see Jin's room first.

"It's the one right next to it," Ingrid said.

It was the one Arwel had stayed in when he'd been keeping an eye on Lokan, and for some reason, it pleased him that Jin was staying there.

"I love it." She walked in and sat on the couch. "This is comfy." She looked up at Ingrid. "Where is Arwel going to stay?"

"The next one over." The designer waved her hand. "Come, I'll show you."

It was one of the newly redecorated cells, but Arwel wouldn't have cared if it had only a cot and a blanket. As long as he was right next to Jin, he was good.

But just like the other cells in which they had deposited their guests, this was beautifully done, with a carpet on the floor, and artwork on the walls, and furniture that was very similar to what Arwel had in his home.

Not that he counted it as such.

It had taken him a long time to call the place he'd shared with Yamanu that, and now that he had moved in with Ben, it was going to take even longer. Ben was a nice guy, but they weren't buddies. Not yet.

Besides, if things turned out the way Arwel hoped they would, he wasn't going back to that house.

He and Jin would be moving into their own.

45

JIN

The studio wasn't as big as the one Jin had had in the government facility, but everything in it was of higher quality. The couch was so soft that it felt as if it was stuffed with feathers and down, and it probably was. The television screen hanging on the wall in front of her was at least sixty-inch, which was overkill for the small space, but since the designer had taken it from the homes in the village, the size made sense.

But despite Ingrid's efforts, she couldn't hide the real purpose of the place.

Jin had noticed the thickness of the doors and the small windows on the bottom that were there so food could be shoved through them without opening the doors. And there were no handles, which made her wonder how she was supposed to open and close her door.

But the worst part was the lack of windows. Inside the mountain, she at least had the illusion of normalcy.

"What's the long face about?" Mey asked. "You don't like it?"

"No, I do. It's just that I don't like living underground, and this is even worse than where I lived for the past month."

Mey sat on the bed next to her and wrapped her arm around her shoulders. "It's still not too late to change your mind and come to the village. You don't have to stay here."

Jin glanced at Ingrid. The woman had gone to so much trouble preparing all those units that changing her mind about staying would have been a really flaky thing to do. Besides, she didn't really have a choice.

"I need to stay until the situation with my friends is resolved." She smiled. "That's okay. I'm sure we are going to have lots of fun here. We can go swimming in the pool, watch a movie in the theater, and cook things in the kitchen." She cast Mey an apologetic glance. "I just feel bad about dragging you here with me. You don't have to stay."

"Nonsense. I don't mind the underground, and I want to be with you." Mey looked up at Callie, who was standing outside in the corridor and looking in. "My new friends can come to visit us. Callie can give us cooking lessons. That would be fun."

"I'll be happy to," Callie said. "And perhaps Dalhu can give you drawing lessons."

"I can't teach." The big guy came to stand next to Callie and Brundar. "But I can draw your portraits if you want."

"Of course, you can teach, darling." Amanda walked in and sat on Jin's other side. "You can show them how to use charcoals and how to blend. That's good enough. It won't make them artists, but it will give them the tools to start practicing. Right, Jin?"

"Sure. I can learn how to sketch my design ideas."

Amanda leaned closer as if she wanted to tell Jin a secret. "Do you know that Dalhu and I stayed in here?" She smirked. "Kian wasn't overly thrilled with my choice of mate. You see, Dalhu used to be a Doomer."

"A what?"

Amanda looked at Mey and then at Yamanu. "You didn't tell Jin anything yet?"

"We did," Mey scrunched her nose. "But we kind of skipped around a lot, and some things got left out."

Amanda sighed. "Never mind that then. What's important is that Dalhu and I stayed in the larger apartment, and then other couples stayed in there too for different reasons. So even though this is a dungeon, there is a lot of love in these walls."

Mey let out a relieved breath. "Good. I was afraid of hearing echoes of torture."

"No one has ever been tortured in any of these rooms," Arwel said. "And it's not just a dungeon, it's also an emergency shelter. You and your friends are not prisoners here. You can move around the underground facility freely."

Jin looked at the door. "There are no handles, how are we supposed to get out? Just leave them open?"

"The doors are very heavy, and even if they had handles, they would be difficult to move. They are controlled with an application. I'm sure that our tech guy brought phones for you and your friends with the application already installed on them. In fact, we should find William."

"We also need to eat," Amanda said. "I heard there is food in the kitchen."

"Shouldn't we wait for the others to wake up?" Jin asked. "They are probably hungry too."

"Right." Yamanu pushed away from the wall he'd been leaning against. "I should wake them up."

46

KIAN

"I'm hungry," Syssi said. "Should we wait for the others or head to the kitchen?"

It had been a long day, and all Kian wanted to do was take Syssi home, draw her a bath, and hope that she was up for some lazy lovemaking.

Regrettably, that wasn't on the menu for tonight. By the time they got home, she would be asleep, and he would probably have to carry her to bed, undress her, and tuck her in.

"I need to wait for William, but you go ahead. I don't want you to wait. When you're hungry, you should eat."

"Wasn't Bridget supposed to be here as well?" Syssi asked.

"She is in her old clinic, getting ready to check our guests for bugs."

Syssi grimaced. "How about we leave all that for after we eat? I know that you are hungry too."

"Not a bad idea. But we should wake the three sleeping beauties first."

"Just not with kisses." Syssi affected a stern expression. "Especially not Jacki."

He laughed, then leaned to plant a soft kiss on her lush lips. "I have eyes only for you, my love."

"Yeah, but you still have eyes, and you are a guy. All men look when they see an attractive female. Even you."

"Damn eyes." He covered them with his hands for a moment. "But seriously. It's an instinct, and it means nothing. No one other than you stirs anything in me."

She cupped his cheek. "I know. I was just teasing. Let's wake them up and go to eat."

"Who do you want me to wake first?" Yamanu asked.

"Let's start with Richard." Kian headed toward the guy's room. "For some reason, that guy worries me the most."

"Why?" Yamanu followed him inside.

"I don't know. Something about him feels insincere."

"You should bring Edna to probe him."

"Already arranged for tomorrow afternoon."

"Are you going to use Andrew as well?"

Kian shrugged. "I haven't decided yet. It depends on what Edna has to say."

The sound of something being wheeled had Kian turn his head and look out into the corridor.

"Don't wake him up yet." Bridget walked in, pulling some kind of medical contraption behind her. "I want to check him for trackers first."

"What is this thing?" Kian waved a hand at the equipment.

"It's a mobile ultrasound."

"How long is it going to take?"

"Long. I have to get him undressed, and then go over him inch by inch."

"Can I watch?" Ingrid entered the room.

It was starting to get crowded in there, and Kian had no intention of waiting for Bridget to test all three sleepers. "Wouldn't it be simpler to just stick them into the MRI?"

"Of course. But I thought it would be better to search them while they were asleep."

"There is no need for that. They know that they are going to get checked, and that includes Jin. They might have been implanted without their knowledge."

Bridget shrugged. 'It's up to you. Anyway, I'd rather go say hello to Jin than stay here and check this man."

"Mind if I do it?" Ingrid asked.

As everyone turned frowning faces at her, she laughed. "Just kidding, you people. Where is your sense of humor?"

Kian pushed the ultrasound cart aside. "I don't have any when my stomach is empty."

"Should I wake him now?" Yamanu asked.

Kian nodded.

The Guardian put his hand on Richard's shoulder. "Wake up, buddy. There is chow in the kitchen," Yamanu sing-songed in his hypnotic voice.

As his eyes flew open, Richard sat bolt upright in bed. "How did I get here?"

"Anandur carried you." Yamanu patted his shoulder. "Now, let's get up nice and easy so you don't get dizzy and head to the kitchen."

Shaking his head, Richard put his legs down and then took Yamanu's offered hand. "Why did you have to carry me? Did you guys put narcotics in my drink?"

"Nah." Yamanu put his arm around Richard's middle, helping him get steady on his feet. "I sang you a lullaby, and you fell asleep like a baby."

Richard wasn't a fool. Narrowing his eyes at Yamanu, he asked, "Did you hypnotize me?"

"I did."

"Damn." He looked around. "This is not bad. Who's the decorator?"

He'd meant it as a joke, but Ingrid answered, "That would be me." She flashed him a bright smile and offered him her hand. "The name is Ingrid, interior designer extraordinaire."

He took her hand and brought it to his lips for a kiss. "A pleasure to meet you, Ingrid. I'm Richard." He glanced at Yamanu. "I've noticed that no one is using their last names. Is there a reason for it?"

"We like our anonymity." Yamanu led the guy out of the room.

"Are your first names even real?"

"Some are, and some are not," Kian said. "Are you okay to walk on your own? Because Yamanu needs to wake Wendy up."

Julian was taking care of Jacki, who he'd said was supposed to wake up any moment now. He'd slipped her a sleeping pill on the plane, which fortunately she wasn't immune to.

It was good to know that even immunes could be handled with medication. Not that there were many immunes, but it seemed like there was a higher percentage of them among the paranormal population.

47

JIN

"Would you mind if I do it?" Jin stopped Julian as he was about to enter Jacki's room. "She is going to be less mad if I wake her up."

He seemed relieved. "Sure, go ahead. She should be waking up on her own any moment now."

"Thanks," Said Jin and went inside.

"Wake up, Jacki." She shook her friend's shoulder.

Jacki groaned, opened her eyes, and then quickly closed them, draping her arm over her face to hide from the glaring light. "It's too damn bright in here. And where are we?"

"In the underground hideout."

"How did I get here?"

"Arwel carried you."

She shook her head. "I feel groggy. Did you drug me?"

"Not me personally." Jin sat on the bed next to her. "I didn't know that they were going to do that, but can you blame them? When they took you and Wendy and Richard, they exposed themselves to a huge risk. This was just a small safety measure to mitigate that."

"Yeah, I get it. No hard feelings." Jacki sighed. "I'm starving. Is there anything to eat?"

"We were just waiting for you and Wendy to wake up. Richard is already awake. So, get your ass in gear and let's go. I'm hungry too."

"You said the magic words. Give me a hand?"

Jin pushed to her feet and then pulled Jacki up. "Your flip-flops are to your right."

With a hand on Jin's shoulder, Jacki pushed her feet into the flip-flops and took a look around. "Nice room. Where is everybody?"

"Outside in the corridor, waiting for us."

"Were you and the others drugged as well?"

"I fell asleep on my own, and Yamanu hypnotized Richard and Wendy to sleep and then to wake up on his command."

"That guy is handy."

"And he is also very nice. My sister is lucky to have found such a wonderful man."

Naturally, he'd heard her, and as she and Jacki walked out of the room, he was grinning from ear to ear.

"We are the last ones," Mey said. "Everyone else is already there."

Jin quickened her steps. "Then let's hurry before there is nothing left for us."

"I wouldn't worry about that. Knowing Okidu, he cooked enough for an army."

Jin frowned. "Wasn't that the name of the bus driver?"

"Same guy. He is Kian's butler," Mey said.

The kitchen was on a different level of the underground, and they had to take the elevator to get there. Jin hadn't noticed before, but to activate it, Yamanu had pressed his thumb to the scanner.

"Are there stairs that we can use to get around?"

"There are, but you don't have to use them unless you want the exercise." Yamanu held the door open for them. "William is going to program your thumbprints into the system, and you'll be able to use the elevators to get to the floors approved for your use."

"So, we are prisoners here," Jacki said.

"You are guests," Yamanu corrected. "But we have to be cautious."

"Yeah, I get it. But we are still prisoners, just with benefits."

As they walked along, the voices got louder, and when they entered the large commercial kitchen, Arwel waved them over. "I saved seats for you."

Everyone was seated on swivel barstools around the super long center counter, while the butler was rushing around and loading people's plates.

"Energetic fellow," Jin said.

Mey pulled out a stool. "Okidu is a rare find."

"I bet." Jin sat next to Arwel. "Thank you for saving seats for us."

"I was afraid that all the good appetizers would be gone by the time you got here, so I put some on your plate."

"You are awesome." She leaned and kissed his cheek, causing him to gape. "Thank you."

For an immortal who was possibly ancient, Arwel seemed awfully inexperienced, but that only made him sweeter to her. He was genuine, and his care for her was real, not something he was doing to ensure a later hookup. She was so sick of guys putting on an act only to get what they wanted.

Sometimes she wondered whether they even liked her, or women in general. It seemed as if they were only after the sex and had no interest in learning anything about her.

The dearth of basic communication skills was the plague of her generation, followed closely by selfishness and lack of common courtesy.

It would be nice to be with someone who had grown up in a different era. Then again, he might be a chauvinist, which was an affliction the older generations of men suffered from.

If she was lucky, though, Arwel was the rare lover of women who appreciated everything a woman could offer, emotionally and intellectually, and not just sexually.

Those were few and far between.

48

ARWEL

"Hello, everyone." William walked into the kitchen as everyone was ready to fall off their stools, sated and tired and ready to sleep.

But there were still a few things that needed to be done before those staying in the keep could retire for the night. The others could have left, but since they were all going back to the village on the same bus they had arrived on, they had to wait for Kian, and he wasn't going to leave until everything was taken care of.

William wasn't carrying anything, but given that all the pockets of his cargo pants were bulging, he hadn't come empty-handed.

"That's our tech guy," Arwel whispered to Jin.

She chuckled. "He looks it. He also looks like he hasn't slept in days."

Kian pushed away from the table and walked up to William. "Let me introduce you to our guests."

"I'm sorry for coming so late. My thumbprint reader malfunctioned, and since I didn't have the right replacement parts, it took me hours to fix it."

Kian lifted a brow. "Couldn't you have used an old-fashioned stamp pad?"

"I didn't think of that." William chuckled. "It would have saved me a lot of grief."

Kian clapped him on the back. "That's the problem with being so smart. You overcomplicate things." He led him to Jin. "This is Mey's sister, Jin."

William shook her offered hand and then reached into one of his many pockets. "I have a present for you."

When he pulled the phone out and handed it to her, Arwel saw that there was a label attached to it with her name on it. Apparently, each of the newcomers was getting a different phone.

Reaching into another pocket, William pulled his scanner out and turned it on. "Would you mind putting your thumb on the screen? You can put both or just one, it's up to you. Just remember which one you gave me when you want to activate the elevator."

"This one." She lifted her right one. "I'm right-handed, so if I'm holding my phone with my left hand, my right will be free to press the button."

Arwel loved how open she was and unapologetic. Jin seemed to be very comfortable in her own skin, which was rare for a young woman her age. She was plagued by none of the insecurities that seemed to bother her sister, like the fact that she was a six-foot-tall Asian girl with an unusual paranormal talent.

Then again, maybe she was a bit of a show-off and was good at hiding the things she wasn't confident about.

Not being able to get a clear reading on her emotions bugged him and intrigued him at the same time. On the one hand, he wondered why she was hard to read, and on the other hand, he was glad of it. This gave him a chance to explore the mystery of her, which was curiously exhilarating.

Jin pressed her thumb to the screen, and a moment later, it beeped.

"It's the same technology as the phones have. Keep pressing your thumb until all the lines are filled."

She looked at him and smiled. "You should get with the times, William, and switch your elevators to facial recognition. This is old technology."

For a long moment, William just stared at her, and then he laughed. "You are absolutely right. Why didn't I think of that? Facial recognition is what I do all day long."

"Because you were busy," Kian said, his gruff tone reminding William that he couldn't talk freely in front of the new guests.

"Yeah, I was very busy." He lifted the scanner and typed Jin's name under the thumbprint. "Who's next?"

Jacki lifted her hand and waved. "I am."

The gulping sound William made as he looked in her direction was so audible that Arwel was sure the humans had heard it as clearly as he had.

"That's Jacklin, Jin's friend. She is an immune," Kian said.

"Yeah, I know." William was still gaping.

Jacki was a knockout, so the guy's reaction was understandable. Except, William wasn't the easily excitable sort. Then again, she was a possible Dormant, and that made her even more attractive.

Arwel had no doubt that once the news of possible Dormants spread throughout the village, Guardians, as well as civilians, would come storming the place, hoping to snatch one for themselves. Which meant that he had to stake his claim on Jin before any of the men got ideas about her.

The problem was that he had no chance of accomplishing that in time.

If no one stopped them, they would start arriving tomorrow, and some other male might catch Jin's eye.

He couldn't prevent her from checking out other males, but he could convince Kian to wait for a couple of days before he allowed anyone in. The new arrivals needed to rest, further tests had to be conducted, and so on.

Once William was done with Jacki, he walked over to Richard.

"I don't want to give you my thumbprint." The guy crossed his arms over his chest. "What are you going to do with it?"

"Program the elevators to recognize it and allow you access to several of the underground's levels."

"What else?"

William shrugged. "Nothing. You heard the lady. This is an obsolete technology. It's all about facial recognition now." He pushed his glasses back on his nose. "Unfortunately, it's very easy to obtain a good photograph of you and program it into the system. Even a driver's license mugshot would do. So, the only reason to worry about giving your thumbprint is if you plan on perpetrating a crime and are afraid of leaving incriminating evidence. But if you do, just wear gloves, and you'll be fine."

Rolling his eyes, Richard pressed his thumb to the screen.

Once William was done distributing the phones, Bridget got up and waved her hand.

"I'm Doctor Bridget, and I will be checking you for implanted trackers. Please follow me to the clinic."

"Can't it wait for tomorrow?" Wendy asked. "I'm tired."

"I'm afraid not."

49

JIN

"Let me show you how to work the app to open your door," William offered. "I want to make sure that all of the newcomers know how to operate it before I leave."

Was it a hint that Jin should leave Mey's apartment and call it a night?

If it had come from anyone other than William, it would have been likely. But he didn't seem like the type to throw hints around.

Jin pushed to her feet. "Yes, please. I don't want to be stuck in the room without being able to get out or call someone. These doors are so thick." She leaned and kissed Mey's cheek. "Good night. We'll talk more tomorrow, and tell Yamanu good night from me."

He'd gone to take a shower and was either taking a very long one or had fallen asleep.

"You betcha."

After the doctor had tested all four of them, thankfully finding no implanted trackers, everyone who wasn't staying the night had left.

Except for William and Ingrid.

William's pretext was that he wanted to make sure that everyone knew how to operate everything, and Ingrid's excuse was that she wanted to double-check that everyone had what they needed, and nothing was missing.

Jin suspected that the two had more selfish motives. William was lusting after Jacki, who surprisingly hadn't rebuffed him yet like she had every guy who'd tried to flirt with her in the program. And Ingrid was after Richard who, naturally, loved the attention.

It made Jin happy that he had moved on so quickly and freed her from any lingering feelings of guilt.

William walked into her room and picked up the receiver of the landline phone. "You are not going to get stuck even if you forget your code or how to use the app. Dial zero and someone in security will answer you. They can open the door remotely."

"That's good to know." And a little disconcerting.

It meant that her door could be opened by someone other than her. Not that it was a big concern in the clan's highly secure hideout, but what if someone working in the security office was a pervert?

It could happen. Every community had them, no matter how highly moral the majority of its members were. Immortals could be perverts too.

"I did a lot of prep work before your arrival to make this level of the underground function more like guests' quarters than a dungeon."

"Much appreciated. But nothing can mask the function of this place with those thick doors and the small delivery windows at their bottom." She looked at the door to her room. "Mine doesn't have one, though."

"This is one of the real guest rooms. The others were designed as cells, but we haven't had much use for them. If you hand me your new phone, I'll show you how the app works."

"Thank you."

"It's really simple. If you want to close the door, press on the button that says close and enter your code when the app asks for it. Like so."

William must have memorized all the codes because he hadn't asked for hers, and she knew that each code was different.

"To open, you press the button that says open and put in the code. Easy, right?"

"Very. Thank you." She took the phone from him. "Can I make calls on it?"

He smiled apologetically. "You can't call anyone who isn't programmed into your phone. I put in the numbers for everyone staying here with you, my number, Bridget's, and the security office's. I also programmed Kian's number, but don't call him unless the place is on fire, and no one else answers."

"Trust me, I won't." She leaned closer and whispered in his ear. "You should add Ingrid's number to Richard's phone and give her his."

He leaned away and pushed his glasses up his nose. "Do you think that something is going on between them? I usually don't notice things like that."

Jin shrugged. "I might be wrong, but she seemed very interested, and Richard seemed to eat up the attention."

William nodded. "Thanks for the tip. I'll ask her."

As he lingered a moment longer, Jin wondered if he wanted to ask her about Jacki and was either too embarrassed to do so or maybe searching for the right words. For her part, Jin wasn't going to say anything until she talked with Jacki and checked whether her friend was interested in the tech guy. He seemed like a very nice man, or rather immortal, and he was obviously very smart, but that didn't mean that Jacki was necessarily attracted to him.

In fact, Jin wasn't sure Jacki was interested in men at all.

After William had left, Jin checked out the contents of the closet. Everything was brand new and still in its original packaging. She pulled out a pink pajama set, a pair of undies, and walked into the bathroom.

Several jars of facial creams and lotions were lined up on one side of the sink, two hairbrushes in different sizes, and a hairdryer on the other, and there was even a pouch with makeup essentials.

Curious, Jin unzipped it and checked the contents. Two eyeliner pencils, one black, and the other blue, mascara, and two lipsticks. Ingrid had even thought about including nail clippers, a nail file, and tweezers.

Jin was going to thank Ingrid again tomorrow. Even though she must have been under a lot of pressure to achieve all that in one day, she had still put a lot of thought into making them comfortable in the dungeon and providing all the necessities.

As she took her borrowed clothes off and stepped into the shower, Jin felt her stress melt away under the hot spray. It had been a long and exciting day, and Jin couldn't wait to get into bed.

Except, once she was actually under the covers, she couldn't sleep. Staring at the ceiling, she kept thinking about what would have happened once their absence had been discovered.

Were people searching for them? Putting out wanted posters?

In her imagination, she saw their mug shots on a bulletin post, claiming that they were bank robbers, armed and dangerous.

Jin chuckled. If they had robbed a bank, they would at least have some cash. It didn't feel good to have nothing and to depend on the charity of others for everything, starting with underwear. In her case, it wasn't as bad as it must be for her friends. Depending on family for help was not as bad as depending on strangers. But still, it was an uncomfortable feeling, especially since Jin had no idea how long she would have to live in this limbo.

Almost an hour later, Jin was still awake despite being exhausted.

Perhaps she couldn't sleep because there were no freaking windows, and she felt claustrophobic in the room. Were the others experiencing the same thing? Maybe she could go to Jacki's room and climb in bed with her. It wouldn't feel as bad if she wasn't alone.

Throwing the comforter off, she swung her legs over the side of the bed, put her flip-flops on, and pulled out a hoodie from the closet.

It wasn't until she went to the door and remembered that she needed to use the app to open it that it dawned on her that Jacki's door would probably be closed.

Still, on the remote chance that it wasn't, Jin stepped out of her room and headed in the direction of Jacki's.

Except, all of her friends' doors were closed, and so was Mey's. Heading back, Jin didn't stop at her room and continued to Arwel's.

His door was open.

Knocking lightly on the metal, Jin peeked inside, but seeing that it was pitch black in there, she retreated.

"Come in," Arwel said. "I'm not sleeping." He turned on the bedside lamp.

She took a step in and then stopped. He was still in bed, and she wasn't sure what to do. They weren't close enough for her to go over and sit beside him, and sitting on the couch while he was in bed would be weird.

Standing in the doorway, she whispered, "I couldn't fall asleep, and yours was the only door that was open."

"Forgive me for not getting up, but I'm naked under here. Can you toss me those pants?" He pointed at a pair of sweatpants that were draped over the back of the only chair.

It was good the room was dark because imagining Arwel in the nude had her cheeks flame hot.

"I should go."

"Don't, please." He waved his hand in the direction of the pants again.

Reluctantly, she walked all the way in and did as he asked.

Pulling the sweatpants under the blanket, he shimmied into them and then tossed the comforter aside and got up.

Holy guacamole, talk about abs.

And not only abs. Shoulders, pecs, biceps, the guy was built to perfection. Athletic, but not overly buff. Why the hell was he hiding all that under baggy, unflattering clothes?

Actually, she was glad of it, and also for the shaggy hair. If not for that, Arwel would have been either snagged a long time ago or developed an ego the size of Jupiter with all the attention he would have been getting.

50

ARWEL

*J*in walking into his room was proof that sometimes wishes come true.

Arwel had been lying awake and thinking about her, wondering if she was okay and whether she was sleeping peacefully or tossing and turning as he was.

She looked adorable in the pink pajamas and Hello Kitty hoodie over them. But even in that getup, she was all woman, curvy in all the right places, and her breasts were pushing the fleece out just right.

He was glad that she had come, but he hadn't expected it. If he had, he would have left his pants on and would have gotten rid of his worn-out fuzzy slippers.

Thankful for the dim light and for her human vision, he kicked them under the bed. Anandur was right. It was time to toss them in the trash and buy some sexy ones instead. Was there such a thing for men, though? Or were manly men supposed to walk barefoot or wear boots at all times?

Rubbing a hand over his stubbled jaw, Arwel stifled a chuckle. "Would you like some coffee? Or will it keep you up all night? What's left of it, that is."

"Usually, I can sleep no matter how many cups of coffee I have." She sat on the couch, tucking her hands between her knees as if she was cold. "I think that I might be a little claustrophobic, and that room without windows makes me feel trapped. Or maybe it's just the adrenaline still coursing through my body. This has been one hell of nearly twenty-four hours."

"Whatever it is, I'm glad that you came. I couldn't sleep either." He took a bottle of water and poured it into the little machine. It worked on capsules, and there was an entire box of assorted flavors in the cabinet.

"Any preference as to strength? We have mild, medium, and strong."

"Medium, please." She pulled her knees up, tucking them under the sweatshirt.

He took two mugs and put them under the twin nozzles.

The small cell didn't have a built-in minibar like the one Jin was staying in, but Ingrid had put together a makeshift one similar to the ones found in hotel rooms. A cabinet housed a mini-fridge on the bottom and a coffee maker on top. The fridge was stocked with snacks, water, several bottles of his favorite beer, and one bottle of good whiskey.

Since he was on duty, so to speak, he hadn't touched the alcohol, saving it for when reinforcements arrived in the morning. Surprisingly, though, he wasn't craving the booze.

What he was craving was the young woman sitting on the couch and hugging her knees to her chest. She was bracing the balls of her feet on the sofa and wiggling her dainty little toes, and he had the absurd urge to kneel on the floor and kiss them one at a time.

One day he would, but not yet.

This wasn't about a meaningless hookup, and he couldn't rush things.

On the other hand, he didn't have much time. Kian was probably sending more Guardians in the morning, and the race was going to begin, whether he was ready or not.

Turning his back to her to hide his glowing eyes and elongating fangs, he concentrated on the coffee and tried to think about anything that might subdue his libido.

"I wonder how seriously they are searching for us," Jin said. "Do you think they would go as far as putting an APB out on us? Or wanted posters?"

"I'm sure there is an APB. I can check if you want." He pulled two creamers and four sugars from the cabinet. "And I'm pretty sure they are not putting up posters." He chuckled. "One look at Wendy's innocent face, and people will wonder what the hell a kid like her could have done."

"Hey, what about me? Don't I look sweet and innocent?"

Chuckling, he lifted the mugs from the coffeemaker and brought them over to the table. The thing was only a little over a foot wide and about two feet long, but that was enough for two cups of coffee and for the bag of cookies that he'd found in the fridge.

"How about mysterious, alluring, intriguing." He sat next to her. "Should I go on?"

"Definitely." Smiling, she put her feet down and reached for the packets of sugar.

"Beautiful, confident, assertive, comfortable in your own skin." He could go on, but then words like sexy and hot would come out, and that was going too far too soon.

She stirred the creamer and sugar in and then brought her feet back up. "Usually, I don't believe guys when they start gushing like that, especially when they've just met me and don't know jack about me. But since you are an empath, I believe that you meant them. Thank you. Those were all very nice things to say."

Arwel rubbed his hand over his jaw. "I have to confess. For some reason, I can't feel your emotions as easily as I can those of other humans. In fact, yours are more muted than those of most immortals."

She frowned. "Interesting. Maybe that's because I'm a Dormant?"

"I've experienced that with only one other Dormant, and that was Ella. She is a strong telepath and can actually talk with her mother telepathically. But only with her mother. Since she was born with the ability, she built strong protective walls to keep her mother out of her head when she wanted privacy in there."

"What about Mey? Could you read her easily before she transitioned?"

"During the entire time that I've known her, she has been so stressed out that this one emotion masked all of the others." He smirked. "I felt her attraction to Yamanu, though. But then she wasn't trying to hide it. The one who was doing his damnedest to ignore it was Yamanu."

"Why?"

Arwel shook his head. "That's their story to tell. I can only talk about my own observations."

"I respect that." Jin smiled and then yawned. "I'm wondering if Mey and I are just different." She yawned again. "The freak sisters."

He didn't want her to go, but it was evident that she couldn't keep her eyes open.

"I think you should go to bed."

"Can I sleep here on your couch? I really hate being alone in that room. That thick door makes me feel as if I'm being locked up in a safe."

Taken by surprise, Arwel was nevertheless delighted that she felt safe with him. "Of course. But you can sleep in my bed. I'm going to sleep on the couch."

"No way. I'm not taking your bed." She glanced at it. "But if you don't mind, we can share it. It's big enough for two."

Jin closed her eyes and leaned her head against his bicep.

This was going to be torture, but he couldn't tell her no. She would either get offended or think that he was an old-fashioned prude. A moment later, there was no one to talk to anyway because she was already asleep.

When he picked her up and carried her to his bed, Jin mumbled something, and when he tucked her in, she smiled and snuggled into the blanket.

Standing next to her, Arwel debated what to do. Now that Jin was already sleeping, he could go lie down on the couch. All he needed were three to four hours of sleep, which meant that he could wake up before her and then join her in bed. She wouldn't know that he hadn't spent the entire time there.

Except, that wasn't what he wanted.

Arwel wanted to lie next to Jin and look at her beautiful face, smell her alluring scent, and feel her warm body snuggled against his.

That was well worth the torture of a raging hard-on and pulsating fangs.

51

JIN

Jin hugged the pillow, sniffed it, and smiled. The delicious male scent was the best reminder of where she'd spent the night.

This was Arwel's bed.

Except, he wasn't there, and as she opened her eyes, she saw that the door was partially open. Had she chased him out of his own bed?

She would die of embarrassment if he'd run away because of her snoring. It didn't happen often, and usually only when she was really tired, which she had been last night.

Where had he gone? Maybe he had slept in her bed? As a Guardian, he probably had the codes to all the doors on the dungeon level.

And were the others awake as well? Anyone passing by Arwel's room could peek inside and see her sleeping in his bed.

It wasn't that she was embarrassed about spending the night in his room, but she didn't want to advertise it either. People would jump to conclusions and talk. She'd just broken things off with Richard, and even though their relationship had been the result of compulsion, it wouldn't look good for her to jump into bed with someone else the following night.

With a groan, she pulled the blanket over her head and then put the pillow on top for good measure. If she couldn't hear or see anyone, she could pretend that they couldn't see her either.

It was an ostrich move, but whatever. She was still tired and wanted to sleep a little longer. Or at least that's what she was going to tell anyone who asked why she was hiding under the blanket.

"Good morning, or rather good afternoon." The bed sank as Arwel sat on it. "I brought breakfast."

"You shouldn't have left the door open," she said from under the blanket.

"Right. I wasn't thinking. Sorry about that."

She put the pillow aside and lifted the blanket off her head. "I'm not embarrassed or anything. But you know people. They make assumptions, and they gossip."

He chuckled. "No worries. The only ones awake aside from me are Yamanu and Mey. Your friends are still sleeping."

Jin pushed up on the pillows. "Did Mey see me?"

"No, she is still in bed. Yamanu and I decided to pamper you two with breakfast in bed."

That was so nice. Oliver had never done that for Mey, and Mitch hadn't gotten the chance to do it for Jin. She'd never slept over at his place and had always gone back to the dorms for the night.

"What did you make?"

"Coffee." He handed her a mug. "And a turkey sandwich."

"Yummy." She took a sip from the coffee and sighed in delight. "You made it just the way I like it. Thank you. You are the best."

Looking embarrassed by her compliment, Arwel shrugged. "It's not a big deal. I saw you fixing your cup last night."

"Yeah, but you paid attention and remembered. Most guys don't bother. Not even married ones who should."

"Really?" He arched a brow. "I would think that people who cared about one another would pay attention to their partners' likes and dislikes."

Jin cupped the mug in her hands. "Don't underestimate people's selfishness. They only think about what they want and what they think they deserve."

"I wouldn't want to be with a person like that."

"Me neither. But that was how Mey's ex was. I have no idea why she tolerated him for so long. But I shouldn't talk about it. After all, it's her business, right? It's just that I was so mad." She made an angry face and fisted one hand. "I wanted to punch him so badly."

Arwel chuckled. "You look adorable when you try to look dangerous."

"I *am* dangerous." She mock pouted but then sighed. "For real. Maybe I can't do much damage with my fists and beat scumbags up, but I can spy on them."

Arwel tilted his head. "You don't like doing it, though."

"I definitely do not. When I first discovered my ability, I thought it would be great to keep an eye on the people I loved and know that they were okay. The full potential of what I could do didn't even occur to me, and when it did, I felt really lousy. It's like discovering that you are good at killing people, like being a sniper with a perfect aim. I don't want that."

"What do you want?"

Jin smiled. "Mey and I dream of having our own business. I have a good head for money, and Mey has great design ideas." She leaned closer to him. "Do you think I can persuade Amanda to invest in it? She is obviously rich, and she has excellent taste. Not only that, we want to make a fashion line for tall women, and Amanda is tall."

Lifting the sandwich, he handed it to her. "I think that it's a great idea. But you should eat first."

That hadn't been the response she'd been hoping for. Arwel seemed as enthusiastic about her idea as if she'd been talking about plans for doing laundry.

"You're making fun of me." She took a bite. "But since you make great sandwiches, I'll forgive you."

"I'm not making fun of you. I think it's admirable that you have a dream and that you are tenacious about following it. But you should hurry up and eat your sandwich, and then get dressed. Kian is going to be here in less than an hour, and he is bringing the heavy artillery with him."

Jin paused with the sandwich an inch from her mouth. "Heavy artillery? What do you mean by that?"

"One is Edna, who has the ability to dig deep into a person's hidden layers and figure out their motives and their core makeup. The other one is Andrew, who is a lie detector. Jacki's immunity is not going to protect her from either of them. Their abilities seem to work on different wavelengths than ours."

"Mine works on Jacki. Perhaps Mey and I are more like these two." She took another bite of the sandwich.

"That's an interesting observation. I didn't know that Jacki is not immune to what you can do."

"Do you suspect her?"

"I suspect everyone who wanted to come with us. That was an unexpected turn of events. Given what you have told me, it wasn't that bad in the program, and it didn't make sense for these people to be so desperate to want to leave it and go into hiding. Not only are they saying goodbye to a lot of money, but they are also leaving behind their families and everyone they know. After the six-month training was over, they would have been allowed to see them again. I don't know when and if it will be possible now. That's why it seems suspicious to me. But we had no choice. We had to take them or risk them spilling the beans."

Even though the same thing had occurred to her, Jin still felt as if it was her duty to defend her friends. Besides, the same suspicions applied to her.

"What about me? Do you suspect me as well?"

"Of course not."

"Why? You said that I'm mysterious and that I don't look innocent. What if I have a hidden agenda?"

She wanted him to deny it, to say that he trusted her implicitly and that he could feel how good she was on the inside. Instead, he smiled and patted her leg. "Finish your sandwich. If Edna is going to probe you as well, you will need your strength. I hear that the experience is draining."

Great. It seemed like she was a suspect too.

52

KIAN

As Anandur parked the Lexus in the lowest level of the high rise across the street from the keep, Kian waited for the gate to roll back in place before getting out.

This space was reserved for the clan's use, but officially it was called storage. Empty crates and cardboard boxes were stacked against the far wall to reinforce the illusion.

"Would you like to take the golf cart?" Brundar asked as he opened the back passenger door for Edna.

"If you don't mind, I'd rather walk." She glanced at Andrew.

"Same here."

"Then let's walk." Kian punched the numbers into the fake storage room's keypad, and the five of them went in, only to step out into the tunnel on the other side.

"It's cold in here," Edna said.

If he were wearing a jacket, he would have offered it to her, but it was the weekend, and Kian had forgone it.

"Here." Brundar shrugged off his leather coat and handed it to her.

"Thank you." She smiled at him. "But aren't you going to be cold?"

He shook his head. "I only wear it to conceal my weapons."

"So that's why it's so heavy."

It was late afternoon on Sunday, and Kian felt bad about taking Andrew away from his family, but he didn't want to wait. The sooner it was done, the better.

Other than Jin, he didn't trust any of the newcomers, not even the innocent-looking nineteen-year-old. In fact, after he'd given it some thought, he trusted her the least.

Jacki knew about Mey coming for Jin, so if she was cooperating with the government, she would have told the higher-ups about it, and security would have been tighter during the mall outings.

Richard was a suspect too, but he might have jumped on the wagon to be with Jin. He could have had feelings for her that hadn't been the result of the compulsion, so its removal wouldn't have changed things for him.

Wendy was the only one who hadn't had a strong enough motive to join them. Still, it was possible that she was the impulsive type and that she hadn't thought through her decision to run.

"Where do you want to conduct the tests?" Edna asked.

"In my old office. William arranged it so they could move freely around several of the underground levels."

"Is it clean?" Anandur asked.

"Okidu was there yesterday, and he even restocked the bar."

"I might not be able to conduct all three tests in one day," Edna said. "If any of them is as complicated as Lokan, the session is going to exhaust me."

"Who are you going to test first?" Andrew asked.

"Wendy."

Anandur's brows lifted. "Why her?"

"A hunch."

Kian pulled out his phone and called Arwel. "Bring Wendy to my office."

"Jin is asking if she can come with her."

Kian glanced at Edna.

"If Jin's presence would help the girl calm down, I'm all for it."

"She can come."

"I heard. Also, are you sending more guardians in?"

"Not yet. I want the testing done before I expose our guests to more of our people."

"Good thinking. I'll get Wendy, and we will head to your office."

Smirking, Kian closed the phone. Arwel had sounded relieved to hear that no new Guardians were coming in. Obviously, he wanted some time with Jin before competition showed up.

"Anyone want something to drink? Anandur pulled out a couple of bottles of water from the fridge.

"I'd like one," Edna said.

Kian waved a hand. "Just bring all the bottles over to the conference table, and if there are any more in the cabinet, put them in the fridge to chill."

"Yes, boss. Do you want me to bring the beer too?"

Kian would have loved one, but this was an interrogation, not a social visit. "Save it for later."

Edna unscrewed the cap and took a sip. "Just so I know what to focus on, what exactly do you want me to search for?"

"Subterfuge and ulterior motives. Both will produce feelings of guilt, and that should be easy for you to find."

"Wendy could feel guilty about losing the income." Anandur pulled out a chair next to Kian. "It probably goes to her family."

Kian wiped the condensation from the bottle. "Did you get a chance to talk with her?"

"Sorry, I didn't. I had my mate with me. Wonder is not the jealous type, but

Wendy would have been suspicious if I sat next to her instead of sitting with my girl. I saw Ella talking with her, though. You can give her a call and ask her what she learned."

"There is no time for that. Besides, I'm going to ask Wendy about her family anyway because I want Andrew to verify her answers."

"How do you want me to do it? Overtly or covertly?" Andrew asked.

"Covertly. If she is lying, scratch your stubble."

"Got it. So, you don't want me to say anything when she is telling the truth?"

"Right."

"What about the others?"

"Same thing, unless I decide otherwise. You'd better sit across from me, so it won't be too obvious that I'm looking at you for verification."

53

JIN

Arwel closed his phone. "We need to get Wendy."

"She is going to freak out." Jin put down her third coffee cup of the day. "I should go first."

"It's not up to me, and I don't know if Kian has plans for you to go through it at all."

"Then I'll volunteer. I have nothing to hide."

Across the kitchen island, Richard shook his head. "I'm surprised he doesn't want me to go first. If I were Kian, I would have suspected me the most of having ulterior motives."

Jacki stretched her arms over her head and yawned. "Since no one can get into my head, I have nothing to worry about. Not that I have anything to hide either." She chuckled. "Except for the shoplifting I did as a teenager. But I don't think that's what Kian is looking for."

Perhaps Kian was right about wanting to interrogate Wendy first. If Richard and Jacki weren't worried about being questioned, that left only Wendy.

She hadn't joined them in the kitchen, preferring to stay in her room to watch anime on one of the streaming services. Not that it was suspicious. The girl was technically still a teenager.

What was suspicious was Mey claiming to still be exhausted and going back to bed, with Yamanu joining her. After spending more than a week with a bunch of people who had exceptional hearing, those two were probably having fun behind the thick dungeon walls.

Pushing away from the counter, Arwel lifted his phone. "I don't know how long it's going to take with Wendy, so keep your phones nearby. I'll call to let you know who's next."

When they got to Wendy's room, they found her door closed.

"Maybe she went back to sleep? We can have either Richard or Jacki take her place."

Arwel shook his head. "I'm calling her."

A moment later, Wendy answered, and he told her that he was activating the door.

The thing was so heavy that Jin doubted she could push it closed without the help from the pneumatic mechanism.

"What's up?" Wendy asked once the door opened.

Arwel motioned for her to step out. "It's time. Edna and Andrew are here."

"Oh." The color drained from the girl's face. "Let me brush my hair and put my flip-flops on." She looked down at her feet. "I wish I had proper footwear."

Jin grinned. "Amanda promised to come back with supplies. I can't wait to see what she gets us."

"Yeah, but she's not here now, and I have to meet important people in flip-flops."

"No one cares about that," Arwel said. "But they do care about having to wait. So, hurry up."

"Yes, sir." She padded to the bathroom.

"You are right," Jin whispered to Arwel. "She looks so innocent. But for some reason, that makes me more suspicious of her, not less."

Smiling, he lifted his hand as if meaning to touch her, but then let it drop by his side. "You have a suspicious mind. Perhaps you are better suited to being a spy than you think."

"Nah." Jin waved a hand and leaned to whisper again. "It's just that in all the books and movies, the least obvious character ends up being the one who's done it. So that's what my mind is programmed to think. You are the empath. What is your impression?"

"She is scared. That's all I'm getting. But that doesn't mean anything. If I had to go through Edna's probe, I would be scared too."

"Why? Is it terrible?"

"I hear that it's very intrusive. I only get what people project; she can actually reach in and pull it out."

"Sounds ominous, but I'm not scared. There is really nothing going on inside my head that I want to hide. What you see is what you get." She snorted. "Except for the tethering. That's my biggest and only secret."

Arwel glanced at the closed bathroom door. "What's taking her so long? She said she was only going to brush her hair, not wash it."

"She is probably putting some makeup on. Either that or she is talking to herself in the mirror, rehearsing what she's going to say."

As Wendy stepped out of the bathroom, a line of a blue pencil around her eyes and black mascara on her lashes, Jin lifted her finger. "And the correct answer is number one."

54

ARWEL

On the way to Kian's office, Arwel kept stealing glances at Jin, wondering how to move their relationship from friendly to romantic.

They'd been spending nearly all of their time together, but there had never been a moment where he felt that it was the right time to put on his seducer's hat and lean in and kiss her.

Had Jin caught him staring at her lips?

If she had, she was pretending that she hadn't.

He wouldn't have minded spending weeks getting to know her before making his move, but with the arrival of new Guardians, Jin would have a lot of suitors to choose from, and he would lose his advantage.

Except, what if he made his move prematurely and spooked her? She might not give him another chance.

As they arrived at the glass doors to Kian's office, Wendy sucked in a breath. "I'm scared. I can feel the powerful empath."

"Edna is not an empath. She is something else."

Jin reached for Wendy's hand. "If it will make you feel any better, I'll go first."

Looking at Jin over Wendy's head, Arwel cast her a stern look. She shouldn't have said that. What if Kian refused her offer to volunteer?

Kian waved his hand. "Come in."

"Hi," Jin said. "Thank you for letting me join you."

Kian nodded. "You're welcome. I hope you are all sufficiently rested?"

"Oh, yeah, I slept like a baby." Jin smiled at Arwel. "I didn't wake up until two in the afternoon."

"Good. Pull out chairs, and let's get the introductions over with." Kian waited for them to be seated. "On my right is Edna. She has the special ability to detect intentions and assess the general make-up of a person."

Edna smiled. "Hello."

"The guy sitting across from me is my brother-in-law, Andrew."

"Hi. Welcome aboard."

"Thank you," Jin said.

Wendy looked terrified.

Per Kian's instructions, Arwel hadn't told anyone other than Jin about Andrew's ability to detect lies. He hoped Jin had remembered not to say anything.

"Nice to meet you. I'm Jin, Mey's sister, but you already know that. And this is my friend, Wendy."

"Hi." Wendy's whisper was barely audible.

Jin cleared her throat. "Is it okay if I go first? Wendy is a little scared. Seeing me going through the probe might help her relax."

Edna groaned. "Arwel, you really shouldn't have told them that it was a probe. No wonder Wendy is scared." She turned to the girl. "You are an empath, right?"

Wendy nodded.

"What I can do is very similar to your ability. The difference is that I'm able to peel away the outer layers and look at the core inside. Usually, what I find there is purer than what's on the outside."

Releasing a panting breath, Wendy nodded. "I don't know why I'm freaking out. In the program, we used each other to test our abilities, and I had other empaths examine my emotions. It's just that I don't know anyone here."

"I promise to be gentle." Edna pointed to the chair to the left of hers. "Come sit next to me."

"So, I'm not going first?" Jin asked. "Because I'm really curious to check out what you can do. My ability is uncommon too…" She smacked her forehead. "That's why you don't want to test me. You are afraid that I'll attach a tether to you. But I don't do that without asking permission first."

Arwel stifled a chuckle. The girl was tenacious and had no filter. He loved it. Jin really was the 'what you see is what you get' type.

Edna smiled indulgently. "I'm not afraid of attaching your tether to me. In fact, I would love for you to do that later on because I'm curious as well. I want to find out whether I can feel it, and even more than that, I'm curious to find out whether I can disconnect it on my end."

"I see." Jin nodded. "That should be interesting. I've never considered the possibility that someone could sever the tether from their side."

When Jin opened her mouth again, no doubt to keep arguing, Arwel put a hand on her arm. "Give it a rest."

Deflating, she slumped in her chair and cast Wendy an apologetic glance.

"It's okay," Wendy whispered. "I hope."

"Give me your hands, and look into my eyes," Edna instructed.

"Okay."

"Don't fight me. Let me in, and it's going to be over in no time. If I have to force my way inside your head, it's going to be difficult for both of us."

Wendy nodded.

The room fell silent, with no one daring to breathe too loudly while Edna did her thing. It was like witnessing a delicate operation and not wishing to distract the surgeon.

The others had no clue as to what was going on within the connection that

Edna had created, but as an empath, Arwel was in a unique position to feel the emotions of both the tester and the tested.

The longer Edna spent in Wendy's head, the sadder she became. Wendy, on the other hand, seemed to loosen up. It was almost as if Edna had cut into a festering wound and relieved the pressure.

When she was done, the judge let go of Wendy's hands and leaned back. "Don't worry, I'm not going to share with anyone what I have learned, but I would like you to talk to a friend of mine. She can help you."

Wendy shook her head. "I don't need to talk to anyone. I'm fine."

Andrew scratched his jaw, which Arwel assumed was the agreed-upon sign for when he detected a lie. Except, no one in the room needed a lie detector to realize that.

Wendy was obviously not fine.

Edna leaned forward and took the girl's hands. "Would you like to talk to me? I'm a great listener. I can make cupcakes and come to visit you. We can have a girl talk. How about that?"

Arwel almost spat out the sip of water that he'd taken. Edna making cupcakes? Having a girl talk? Was the world coming to an end?

To everyone's surprise, Wendy nodded. "I would like that."

"Then it's settled." Edna turned around and faced Kian. "Wendy has no ulterior motives, and the things she hides are personal in nature. She poses no danger to our group."

Arwel didn't need a degree in psychology to figure out what Edna had found in Wendy's head. Years of empathic exposure to humans had taught him all he needed to know. That didn't mean that he could help Wendy or anyone else, though. There was a big difference between being able to uncover a problem and knowing how to fix it.

Kian nodded. "That's good to know. I have a few questions I need to ask, if that's okay, Wendy. Are you up to it? Some people feel very tired after a session with Edna."

"I'm fine. She was very gentle." The girl turned to the judge. "Thank you. That wasn't bad at all."

"I'm glad." Edna patted her knee.

55

JIN

*J*in had no intention of letting Wendy keep her terrible secret, whatever it was. As soon as she could have a moment alone with the girl, she was going to gently probe her.

In fact, she felt offended that Wendy was willing to talk to Edna, a complete stranger, and she hadn't thought to confide in Jin or even Jacki. If she'd been having a problem, in the program or outside of it, they would have helped her in any way they could.

But maybe they couldn't help, and that was why Wendy hadn't said a thing. Still, just talking with someone would have eased her in some way. On the other hand, if her problem had been connected to the program, talking about it would not have been smart with all the surveillance equipment monitoring the trainees and everyone else inside the mountain.

Insisting that the only safe place to talk was next to noisy machinery, Jacki might have seemed paranoid, but she was probably exaggerating only slightly.

Damn, as Jin tried to imagine what could have happened to Wendy, the scenarios she was coming up with were one worse than the other. Hopefully, none of them were what had really happened.

"Tell me about your family," Kian said.

He was going for gentle, but that wasn't much improvement over his usual tone. The guy probably sounded gruff even when whispering sweet nothings in his wife's ear.

"My father raised me alone after getting full custody of me because my mom was a drug addict. Over the years, many girlfriends came and went, but I guess none wanted to stick around and raise me. He finally got married after I graduated high school. When Marisol approached me, I jumped at the opportunity to get out of the house."

"What about college?" Kian asked.

She shrugged. "I went to community college. But I quit when I got the offer.

Marisol said that the skills I would learn in the program would be much more useful than anything I could learn in college."

"Why did you decide to run?"

She dipped her head. "I don't want to talk about it."

Edna put her hand on Kian's arm. "That's okay. I know why, and it's private. It's up to Wendy to decide who she wants to talk to about it and when."

"I understand." He looked at Wendy. "I have no further questions for you. Thank you for cooperating."

"Who's next?" Edna asked.

"Jacklin." Kian turned to Arwel. "Please escort Wendy back and bring Jacki here."

"I'll come with you." Jin pushed to her feet.

Edna leaned back in her chair. "If you stay, we could test whether I can detect your tether and sever it."

That was a tempting proposition, but Wendy needed her. "Maybe after you test Jacki. I want to make sure that Wendy is okay."

"I'm fine," Wendy said. "I'm just going back to watching my favorite anime. I have four more episodes before I catch up."

Sometimes zoning out was the best strategy, and it was apparent that Wendy wasn't in the mood to talk.

"Are you sure?"

"Yes. Stay."

"Do you want me to bring Jacki up right away or wait?" Arwel asked.

"Bring her up," Edna said. "By the time you get here, our little experiment will be done."

After Arwel and Wendy had left, Edna motioned for Jin to take the seat that Wendy had vacated. "Do your thing. Attach a tether to me."

Jin hesitated. "Just so you know, I can't see anything that happened in the past or what will happen in the future. My tether is like a surveillance camera. I only see and hear what's going on at that moment."

"That's fine. If I can't cut the line on my side, I assume that you can cut it on yours?"

"Yes. We tested it in the program. I tethered to each person in the group and then cut the connection. I even did it to Jacki, who is immune to all the other tricks."

Edna pursed her lips. "I wonder if she is immune to mine as well." She offered Jin her hand. "Let's shake on it?"

Taking a deep breath, Jin clasped her hand and imagined a string of consciousness extending from her to the woman, entering her mind, and hooking up to her cranium. It was no more and no less difficult than with the other people she'd done it to.

"Can you feel it?" she asked.

Edna nodded. "I think I do, but if I hadn't known it was coming, I would have never noticed it. Do you hear and see everything double now?"

Jin laughed. "No. But if you want to test it, I can go out into the corridor. When I'm out, say something I could have never guessed."

"Okay. Let's do it."

Jin walked out of the office, closed the door behind her, and kept on going, making sure to go far enough not to hear anything.

Leaning against the wall, she closed her eyes and concentrated on her connection with Edna.

"Jin looks a lot like her sister," Edna said. "But their personalities are different. Mey is more gentle and accommodating, while Jin is assertive and uncompromising."

Jin frowned. She was assertive, but it wasn't true that she was uncompromising. Well, maybe a little. But she wasn't a stubborn ox. When necessary, she was willing to bend a little.

"You can come back now," Kian said.

The downside of her talent was that she couldn't say anything back. If that was possible, she would have told Edna to try to cut the connection. It would have saved her another trip to the corridor.

"So, what did I say when you were gone?" Edna asked as Jin walked into the office.

"That I look like Mey but that I'm a different person. Mey is gentle and accommodating while I'm assertive and uncompromising, which is a nice way to say that I'm stubborn as an ox."

Edna laughed. "You don't mince words, do you? That's exactly what I said. Now for the second half of our test. Go stand over there." She pointed at the sideboard. "After I cut the tether, I'll write something down, and let's see if you can read it through my eyes."

"Sounds good. At least I don't have to go out into the hallway again."

It was wide and well-lit, but it still felt like a freaking dungeon even though this level seemed to be occupied by offices and classrooms and not cells.

"Did you feel it?" Edna asked.

"What? You mean the severing of the tether?"

"Yes."

"I didn't feel a thing."

"Tell me what I'm writing."

Jin closed her eyes and concentrated, following the wispy thread of consciousness to Edna. It was still there, but it felt as if the hook was no longer attached. Jin tried harder, imagining reinserting the hook, but without touching the woman, she couldn't do it.

"I can't. You actually managed to sever it."

56

KIAN

Kian watched Jacki walk into the office with the swagger and confidence of someone secure in the knowledge that her brain was inaccessible.

Hopefully, she was in for a surprise.

"Hi, everyone." She looked at Kian and smiled, then waved at Jin and the others.

Gutsy girl, challenging the alpha first. Or a very good faker. As an immune, she was not susceptible to thralling and compulsion, but she wasn't a blank slate like Turner. Kian could still sense the slight whiff of apprehension that was coming from her. But it was much more subtle than what he would have expected from the average human or even an immortal.

"Hello, Jacklin," Edna greeted her. "I'm Edna. Please come sit next to me."

Jacki sat on the chair Edna had indicated and crossed her legs. "What do you call your ability? Are you an empath?"

"I guess it belongs in the same cluster, but it's different. I can sense intentions and core predispositions." Edna leaned forward. "Please give me your hands."

"Does that enhance your reading?" Jacki took Edna's hands.

"I don't really need it for the reading itself, but sometimes my subjects have the urge to pull back. Holding hands keeps that from happening. I suggest that you try to relax and don't resist me. It will go easier for both of us if I don't have to break through walls of resistance."

Jacki smirked. "I'm immune to paranormal manipulation, so it doesn't matter if I resist or not. You won't be able to access my mind anyway."

"Let's give it a try. As I said, my ability is different than empathy. You may say that it operates on another wavelength of consciousness."

"Hmm." Jacki tapped her chin. "I never thought about it that way. Do you think that consciousness produces a wave? Like a radio wave?"

"It hasn't been proven scientifically, but I believe so. How else can you explain paranormal abilities? Gifted individuals probably have special receptors that can detect those waves and even manipulate them, like in the case of thralling, shrouding, and compulsion."

"That is certainly food for thought." Jacki leaned forward, her eyes issuing a challenge. "Go for it."

For the first ten minutes or so, everyone was quiet, watching the two locked in what looked like a battle. But as the clock kept ticking on, people started shifting impatiently in their chairs, reaching for their bottles of water, sipping on them, putting them back, and then picking them up again for another sip.

Kian wanted to snap at them for disturbing Edna's concentration, but by doing so, he would disturb her even more. Instead, he gritted his teeth and watched.

Almost an hour had passed when Edna finally let go of Jacki's hands and leaned away with a sigh. "You are a complicated lady, Jacklin."

Jacki lifted a brow. "Really? How so?"

"Let's start with how hard to read you are. I think your immunity stems from the thick walls that you have erected around your mind and your heart. You don't allow yourself to trust anyone or feel anything for anyone. At first, I thought that you might be a sociopath, but when I dug deeper, I realized that your soft spots are covered with thick layers of scabs. You've been hurt."

For a brief moment, Jacki's bravado wavered, and her eyes misted with unshed tears. But she was a tough cookie and refused to show weakness.

Folding her arms over her chest, she shrugged. "What can't kill me makes me stronger. That's the motto I live by."

"Indeed." Edna nodded. "But you are among friends now, and you can let your guard down at least a little."

Jacki lifted a brow "I reserve judgment on that. I'm grateful for you taking me in, but you are keeping me locked up and putting me through a psychic interrogation. That's not very friendly."

"We have to protect ourselves," Kian said. "You and your friends are unknowns. I'm trying to mitigate the risk you represent."

Letting out a breath, Jacki unfolded her arms. "I understand, and I would have done the same thing if I were in your shoes. Heck, I would have probably refused to take three stowaways."

"I'm glad we understand each other." Kian turned to Edna. "So, what's your assessment?"

"As I said, Jacki is complicated, and I can't give you a black and white answer. I didn't sense any nefarious intentions, but since so much is buried and inaccessible to me, I can't say for sure there aren't any. Jacki doesn't have any regrets that I could detect or feelings of guilt, but that doesn't mean she has no malicious plans. She might believe that what she is doing is right. I'm not saying she does, though, only that it's a possibility."

Kian hated ambiguity, and this was as ambiguous as it got.

Edna smiled apologetically at the girl. "I'm sorry that I can't vouch for you. You'll have to prove your good intentions on your own."

Jacki shrugged. "What else is new?"

57

ARWEL

"Are you okay?" Arwel held the elevator door open for Jacki.

She let out a breath. "It was weird. I could actually feel her going in and digging inside of me. I've never experienced a psychic invasion before."

He pressed the number for the dungeon level. "I meant about not getting the all-clear."

She arched a brow. "Did Wendy get it?"

"Yes. Edna hinted that there was a good reason for her wanting to run away from the program."

"Oh, yeah? What was it?"

He had a good idea, but he wasn't going to speculate, and he wasn't going to betray Wendy's confidence either.

"I can't imagine what it could be."

She cocked a brow. "You are an empath. Didn't you feel something?"

"Her anxiety was so strong that it masked everything else." That was more of an exaggeration than a lie.

Jacki tilted her head. "Do you want me to talk to Wendy?"

"Only if she brings it up. Don't tell her that I said anything because I probably shouldn't have."

"I'll try to be circumspect about it." She shook her head. "I wonder if Marisol's compulsion could prevent someone from feeling certain things. What if she told Wendy to feel alright about something that she shouldn't have?"

"I know it's possible to compel someone not to feel attraction for a particular person or anyone other than who the compeller chooses. Is that what you are referring to?"

She shook her head. "No, forget that I said anything."

"Come on. You had an idea. Let it out."

"It was a stupid question since I know the answer already. If Marisol told Wendy to feel attraction toward a guy, which we know that she has done with several people, and Wendy had sex with him, she wouldn't have felt that there was anything wrong with it until the compulsion was removed. But once it was, she might have felt violated. The thing is, Wendy didn't date anyone in the program, so maybe it was about something else."

As they passed Mey and Yamanu's room, Mey waved them over. "Where is Jin?"

"She stayed in Kian's office, why?"

"Amanda just called and said she is on her way with a bunch of clothes for the girls. I thought it would be fun to try them on together. Yamanu is going to hit the gym, so we will have the place to ourselves."

Jacki's mood improved in an instant. "I'll get Wendy, and Arwel can send Jin down when he delivers Richard." She turned to him. "Does Kian want Jin to be there when Edna probes Richard?"

"I don't think her presence is required."

"Great. Send her down." Rubbing her hands, Jacki joined Mey on the couch. "I can't wait to see what Amanda has gotten for us. I'm willing to become her cleaning lady just so she gives me her clothes."

Arwel chuckled. "Amanda has a butler."

"That's a shame." Jacki slouched against the pillows.

"Have fun." Arwel waved and continued to Richard's room.

He found the guy watching a boxing match on one of the streaming services.

"Your turn, buddy. You can pause it and continue watching later."

Richard pushed to his feet. "I'm ready. I was just killing time." He followed Arwel out into the corridor. "I don't mind a day or two of vacation, but no more than that. I need something to do. Is there any job your group needs done? I don't care what it is as long as it keeps me busy."

Arwel leaned against the elevator's wall. "What did you do before joining the program?"

"I was a real estate agent. But I can do many other things. I'm a quick learner."

"Maybe after the interview you can ask Kian, but I doubt there is anything you can do from here, and for the time being, you are not going anywhere."

"For how long?" Richard followed him out of the elevator.

"I'm not sure. There are people looking for you. You need to hide."

"I'm an average-looking guy. I can change my hair color, wear sunglasses, and use a fake identity. I know how to stay under the radar."

Arwel arched a brow. "Have you been in trouble before?"

"Not really. But I've watched a lot of spy movies and read many spy books. Some of them were written by real operatives, so don't scoff at them as a source of information."

"Did you get any spy training in the program?"

"I did, and it only reinforced my opinion that those writers really knew what they were talking about."

So far, nothing in Richard's behavior or feelings had aroused Arwel's suspicions. He was the high-energy, restless type, and he was anxious, but given the situation, that was understandable.

58

JIN

"Callie!" As Jin saw her new friend from the doorway, she rushed into Mey's living room and hugged her. "I'm so glad you came." Next, it was Wonder, and then Syssi, and lastly Amanda. "Where is Ella?"

"She couldn't come," Wonder said. "She's buried under a ton of homework, but she sends her love."

"I'm glad that's behind me." Jin let out a breath. "I thought that I was done with homework when I finished college, but then I joined the program and had to work even harder than before. I was good at business and economics, so it wasn't hard for me. But don't start me on Mandarin. That must be the most difficult language on the planet. Anyway, I'm happy to be done with that and never have to do homework again."

Amanda leaned against the media cabinet. "Never say never. You might decide to go back one day. Either to get your master's or even a PhD."

"Not me." Jin pulled out a chair next to Wendy. "I'm done. I want to go straight into building my business. Except, I need to work to save up money for it first. Now that a million-dollar bonus is no longer in my future, I need to find a new way to make money fast."

That wasn't the pitch she'd had in mind for Amanda, but as always, she was running her mouth before thinking.

Wendy groaned. "I was counting on that too. I thought that after five years in the program, I would be set for life. Except, they had no intention of paying it out."

Jin frowned. "What do you mean?"

"You should have read the small print. It said that you will get the bonus if you perform your job to their full satisfaction."

"I planned on doing that."

"Yeah, we all did. But they never planned on paying out no matter how well you did. They were going to come up with excuses, and you were never going to get it."

"What about the annual salary? That wasn't shabby either."

"That part, they had no choice but to honor. But what got us all into the program was that freaking bonus."

"How do you know that they never intended to pay it? Did you overhear something, or is this just speculation?"

"I overheard. They were going to do a six-month assessment, and whoever's talent proved useless was going to be kicked out. That was another small-print provision that hardly anyone paid attention to. But those who got terminated were the lucky ones. Those who proved useful would never be released. They would keep extending their contracts and dangling that bonus in front of their noses. And if that didn't work, they would come up with other methods of persuasion."

Jin nodded. "Especially in my case because I could make such an amazing spy. I don't remember reading a small-print provision for that in the contract, but I came to the same conclusion."

"You're smart. I had no idea until I overheard the director talking with Marisol."

Jin dipped her head and looked into Wendy's eyes. "Is that why you decided to get out?"

She nodded, but Jin had a feeling that it was not the only reason. In time, she was going to get it out of the girl. It wasn't healthy to keep things bottled up inside, and it helped to talk with someone who cared.

Jin had the opposite problem. She talked too much and kept too little to herself. That wasn't the best strategy for success, either.

"Shall we begin the fashion show?" Amanda pushed away from the cabinet and opened the door to Mey and Yamanu's bedroom. "There are outfits galore spread over the bed. On the right is my stuff that is going to fit Jin and Jacki, and on the left is stuff for Wendy, donated by several good-hearted shorties, mostly by Ella and her mother. I also bought shoes for all of you." She looked at the plain flip-flops the three of them were wearing and grimaced. "Those belong in the trash."

Jacki, who up until now had been uncharacteristically quiet, jumped up. "Can I go first?"

Jin waved a hand. "Be my guest. Even though I plan on launching a fashion business, I'm not a fashionista. My idea is to make everyday, comfortable clothing that would be appropriate for work and for leisure."

That was more like it. At least she'd managed to tell Amanda a bit more about her and Mey's plans.

Except, Amanda didn't respond to that last bit. "All three of you can go in together if Jacki promises to behave and not beat up Jin over clothes."

"I promise." Jacki saluted Amanda, then offered Jin a hand up. "Come on. I've never even been into a store that sold that kind of stuff, let alone worn it."

Smiling, Jin let her friend pull her to her feet. She was fine with the clothes that Ingrid had bought for her in Walmart, and when she wanted something nice, she could always borrow stuff from Mey. But watching Jacki go crazy over Amanda's designer hand-me-downs was going to be fun.

"Wendy, you too." Amanda pushed the girl's chair. "Please come out in every outfit you try on. We want a fashion show."

"We need to make room for a runway." Mey got up and started pushing furniture around.

"I'm going to make everyone drinks," Callie announced. "Except for Syssi because she is pregnant and Wendy because she is not twenty-one yet."

Amanda waved a dismissive hand. "Who is going to card her? Give the kid a margarita, just make it weak. We will pretend that this is England, where the legal drinking age is eighteen."

In the bedroom, Jin leaned against the dresser and watched as Jacki attacked the pile of clothes.

"Look at this!" Jacki lifted a bikini swimsuit set. "And there is another one in blue. I was just thinking that we needed bathing suits to use the pool. I'm not shy, but skinny-dipping is not my style." She lifted the other one and dangled both in front of Jin. "Which one do you want, the blue or the red?"

"You pick one, and I'll take the other."

Jacki walked over to the mirror and held both next to her face. "I'll take the electric blue. It goes better with my coloring. The red is going to look amazing on you." She handed her the two-piece.

Wendy lifted a one-piece bathing suit. "Ella is so sweet. She must have thought of the pool too. And it's black, so it's going to hide my tummy."

"What tummy?"

Wendy rolled her eyes. "This one." She pushed it out.

"Don't be silly," Jacki said. "You have feminine curves. That's sexy."

"I could do with a little less femininity."

"I guess we are going to the pool later?" Jin asked to change the subject.

She didn't like the self-deprecating attitude that Wendy had going on.

"Naturally," Jacki opened the bathroom door. "We promised the girls a fashion show first, though."

"Right." Jin grabbed the hem of her T-shirt and pulled it over her head. "Let's see if it fits. Amanda said that I'm bustier than her, and so are you."

"It will fit. As long as it covers the nipples, it's not indecent, and I really want to check out the pool."

"So do I." Jin put the bikini top on and tied it in the back. "It fits."

In fact, it made her look sexy as sin, so naturally, it made her think of Arwel. Hopefully, he would join them, so she could admire that spectacular body that he was hiding under his schlumpy clothes.

59

KIAN

"There is a lot of anger in you." Edna let go of Richard's hands. "And it's all right there underneath the surface. It's still fresh."

Kian straightened in his chair. Was Richard the mole after all?

Not that he had reason to believe that any of them were anything other than what they claimed to be, but Kian wasn't the trusting sort. In his eyes, they were guilty until proven innocent. It wasn't fair to them, but when it came to the safety of his people, Kian didn't give a fuck about fairness. His number one job was ensuring his clan's survival.

Except, finding mates for his people was part of that as well, and the newcomers were all potential Dormants.

Still, Dormants or not, he wasn't going to cut them any slack.

Richard nodded. "I broke up with my fiancée because of damn Marisol and her compulsion. I'd been so sure that it was my decision and that I'd made the right one. Then your guy removed the compulsion, and I realized that I'd been coerced into leaving my life behind to join the program. Are you surprised that I'm mad? Wouldn't you be?"

"Furious," Edna said. "But you didn't love your fiancée."

Richard, who'd proven to be quite the talkative fellow, fell silent. For a long moment, he just stared at Edna and then shook his head. "What makes you say that? Did you look into my subconscious or something? Because I was sure that I loved Clara until Marisol convinced me that I didn't."

"I didn't see your subconscious. I just didn't detect any feelings of deep love. Not in the present nor the past. You've never been in love, Richard."

Slumping in the chair, Richard looked lost. "That's not true. I've had many girlfriends, and I had feelings for them." He sounded unsure as if trying to convince himself more than them.

Edna shook her head. "Perhaps you thought you loved them, but it was probably just lust and like. You've never gone deeper than that."

Deflated, Richard let out a breath. "What are you trying to say? That I'm incapable of love?"

"I didn't say that. You just haven't met the right woman yet. When you do, you'll know the difference."

Tapping his fingers on the conference table, Kian was waiting for the talk about irrelevant stuff to end so he could ask the pertinent questions.

When there was a momentary lull in their discussion about love, he interjected, "What about motives?"

Edna turned around to face him. "Richard is curious. He wants to find out who we are, who do we work for, and who finances us. But I don't get a sense that he wants the information for someone else. He wants to know for himself. He's also thinking about how to best take advantage of the situation and become a member of our group. He wonders if there are any private-sector jobs for people like him that don't involve solving cases for the police or spying for the government. He thinks that there could be much more money in the private sector."

Surprised, Kian leaned back. "You learned all of that by looking into his soul?"

Edna had never been so detailed with her observations, and he'd always thought that she could only get impressions of motives and underlying currents. This sounded as if she had read Richard's mind.

Perhaps the guy was that obvious and unguarded?

Edna smiled apologetically at Richard. "Some of the things I'm going to say may seem offensive to you, but I think it's better that I say them in front of you rather than behind your back."

"Go ahead." He shrugged. "If I'm getting a free shrink session, I should at least hear what you have to say."

"Thank you." She turned to Kian. "Richard is not very deep, that's why it's so much easier to read him than the two women. Men in general are less complicated creatures, but I have encountered enough hard nuts not to allow myself to prejudge. Richard is also vain and very competitive. Success means a lot more to him than relationships, and he is willing to work hard to achieve it."

Kian cast a glance at Richard. "I don't see anything wrong with that."

"My thoughts exactly," Richard said. "Why did you think that I'd find the assessment unflattering? Because you said that I'm not deep? I know I'm no philosopher. I'm a get-it-done kind of guy and damn proud of it."

When Kian nodded in agreement, Edna cast both of them indulgent smiles.

"I love seeing male bonding in action. But you are right, nothing so far was truly objectionable. My worry is that you are too self-serving, and because relationships are not important to you, you might be incapable of loyalty."

Kian was glad that Jin had left before Richard's interrogation had started. Even though her feelings for him hadn't been real, it would have been embarrassing to hear that her ex-boyfriend was a self-serving bastard who didn't have it in him to develop deep feelings.

If Richard were younger, Kian would have attributed his attitude to immaturity, but at thirty-four, the guy had a fully developed personality, and it was doubtful that he could change.

What Edna had said was troubling. Even if Richard were a Dormant, without the ability to form a bond with an immortal mate, the guy couldn't be trusted to join the clan.

Richard nodded, not trying to deny it. "There is something to it. I am self-serving, but I'm also smart, and I will never betray a group that I'm part of. Especially if my freedom depends on it. If you allow me to join you, and if there is a way for me to earn a decent living in any capacity that you may deem me useful in, you will have my loyalty. Not because of nobleness, which I seem to lack, but because it's beneficial to me."

60

JIN

Out of the huge pile of clothes that Amanda had brought, Jin had come away with the modest loot of four T-shirts, one short skirt, two pairs of gorgeous jeans that had been thankfully too small for Jacki, and the red bikini, which was the best find. She looked terrific in it, if she said so herself.

Arwel was going to salivate and hopefully make a move.

Usually, Jin didn't have a problem with flirting, and she was quite forward when the occasion demanded, but for some reason, she was holding back with Arwel.

The guy was probably centuries old and had old-fashioned ideas about courtship. If she came on to him, he might not like it and lose interest.

Besides, it would be nice to be treated like a lady for a change, to get wooed and courted, wined and dined, and to not have to act all macho because the guys of her generation were wusses who waited for the girls to do all the work.

Jin glanced at Jacki, who'd put the bikini back on and was admiring herself in the mirror. "Do you think I can just wrap a towel around my middle and go to the pool like this?"

"I don't see why not."

Jacki scrunched her nose. "Mey and Yamanu might have a problem with us taking their towels. Is there a laundry machine we can use somewhere in this place? Because if I take a towel to the pool, that will leave me with only one for showering."

"I'm sure we can have things laundered. It's not like we are staying here for a day or two. I'm just going to put a T-shirt on so I don't parade around with my boobs on display."

Wendy was already ahead of them, pulling her sweatshirt on. "It's cold in here. I wonder where we are. Did they take us up north somewhere? Or is it cold because we are underground?"

Both girls looked at Jin, waiting for her to supply the answer.

Pretending not to get it, she wrapped the towel around her hips. "You are right. It is damn cold in here. We should turn the thermostat up."

Casting her a narrow-eyed glance, Jacki opened the bedroom door. "Richard is back."

"Just in time to join us." Jin followed her out. "How did it go?"

"Edna declared me a self-serving prick, vain, and highly competitive."

"Ouch. Are you okay?" It was right on the money, but Richard had plenty of redeeming qualities as well. "I'm sure she had some good things to say about you too."

He shrugged. "I don't think of what she said as bad. I'm a go-getter and proud of it. Not everyone can be the sensitive poet type."

Arwel clapped him on the back. "I agree."

Jin wondered if Arwel was one. As an empath, he was super sensitive to other people's feelings, but after centuries of that, he might have become desensitized.

"We are all going to the pool," Jacki said. "Do you want to come?"

"I need to check if Ingrid bought swimming trunks for me."

Yamanu got up from the couch. "If she didn't, I can lend you a pair of exercise shorts."

Richard looked up at the tall guy. "I don't think yours will fit me."

"How about you, Arwel?" Jin asked. "Are you coming with us to the pool?"

For the first time since they'd met, he looked her up and down. "I wouldn't miss it for anything."

There was a sultry quality in his voice that she hadn't heard before.

Yamanu chuckled softly and ducked into the bedroom, proving that she hadn't imagined it, and Mey was grinning like she'd won the lottery.

Her sister was less than two years older than her, but sometimes she behaved like her mother. It was annoying and sweet at the same time.

Jin cleared her throat. "Go get changed. I'm already wearing the beautiful bikini that Amanda donated to the cause."

"Me too," Jacki said and looked at Amanda. "Can I be your maid?"

"Why would you want to?"

Jacki rolled her eyes. "Because the maid always gets the hand-me-downs. I can be fabulously dressed and also make money by selling some of them. These hardly worn designer labels will sell like crazy on eBay."

"You don't need to be my maid. I've already told you that they are yours and Jin's."

"Yay!" Jacki pumped her fist. "I can live like a queen."

Amusement dancing in his incredible eyes, Arwel put his hand on Jin's shoulder. "I'm going to my room to get changed. I'll meet you at the pool."

"Okay."

"Have fun." Amanda lifted her purse and looked at Callie and Wonder. "Do you want to ride home with me? Or are you going back with Kian and your guys?"

"We are going back with Kian," Wonder said.

Callie sighed. "I wish I had my swimsuit with me." She pushed to her feet. "Next time."

"Can you come tomorrow?" Wendy glanced up at Amanda. "We can have fun together." She looked genuinely sad to see them go.

"Come here, kiddo." Amanda pulled the girl into a quick hug. "I'll come, and I'll try to get Dalhu to join me and give you, Jin, and Jacki a drawing lesson. I don't think Richard will want to participate."

"Why not?" Richard asked. "Maybe I like drawing?"

Amanda lifted one perfectly shaped black brow. "Do you?"

"Not really, but what else is there to do here? I might as well learn a new skill."

61

ARWEL

As Arwel changed into his swim shorts, he was reminded of the time he'd watched over Lokan. After Carol had left for her mission on the Doomers' island, he and Lokan had spent long hours at the pool each night. Lokan had been trying to exhaust himself by exercising and swimming so he could fall asleep in the morning and meet Carol in dreamland. With the time difference between the island and Los Angeles being twelve hours, his day had been Carol's night. Arwel, who wasn't a great fan of swimming, had spent most of that time sitting on a towel or lying down and reading.

Remarkably, he remembered his time with Lokan and Carol fondly.

Lokan was a pleasant enough fellow, and observing his and Carol's bond forming and solidifying had been fascinating. It had provided Arwel with a rare opportunity to be so close to fated mates that he could share in their experience.

There had been a Peeping Tom aspect to it, but since Arwel had been put in charge of guarding Lokan, there hadn't been much he could have done about it.

Had he learned anything from it, though?

The most astounding aspect was the speed at which it had happened. The problem was that Lokan and Carol's lightning-fast bonding had created certain expectations for how it would be when Arwel found his own truelove mate. He'd expected the attraction to be just as overpowering and the bond snapping into place just as fast.

Except, it appeared that he'd been wrong, and things moved at different speeds for different people.

Then again, he'd only met Jin yesterday morning. It just seemed as if he'd known her for much longer.

Patience.

Usually, he was a laid-back kind of guy, and waiting patiently for things to unfold had never been a problem for him. As an immortal, time was of little consequence. So why the hell was he stressing over how slow things were moving with Jin?

Pulling a fresh T-shirt out of the duffle bag, he combed his hair with his fingers. There hadn't been time to ask Amanda for a haircut and style advice, but he should really get on with it before the keep got swamped with eager Guardians who were all much better groomed than he was.

As Arwel slid the phone into a pocket in his swimming trunks, he was tempted to pull it out again and text Amanda, but the truth was that he was embarrassed to make the request. Perhaps Magnus could help him out?

He was a suave dresser, but his style was too formal and polished for Arwel. Magnus was also always perfectly groomed, but Arwel doubted that the Guardian cut his own hair or even did the trimming on that stylish goatee of his. The best Magnus could do was refer Arwel to his barber.

It had to be Amanda.

With a groan, he pulled out the phone and typed a text. *I'm sorry to bother you, but I was wondering if you could do me a favor. I know that you helped Anandur when he was courting Wonder, and he actually looked great for a couple of weeks until he let his hair get unruly again. I'm in desperate need of a haircut, but I can't leave the keep at the moment. I could also use some style advice on how to dress casually but more elegantly without looking as if I'm trying too hard.*

Fates, he sounded like a teenage boy asking his big sister for dating advice.

Not expecting a response anytime soon, Arwel put the phone back in his pocket and headed for the pool.

Except, the thing rang a moment later.

Damn, he'd hoped Amanda would save him the embarrassment and text her response instead of calling him.

"Darling, of course I'll help you. It's a shame you didn't ask me yesterday. If you had, you would have been a new man today. I'm going to come around tomorrow straight from the university and give you a whole new look."

"Thank you. I don't want anything too drastic."

She chuckled. "You've let yourself go, Arwel. Even a simple haircut will be a drastic change."

"I will leave it up to you. Can we do it discreetly, though?"

"I have a splendid idea. I'll get Eva to come with me, and we will give the girls makeovers. While we are at it, I'll offer you, Richard, and Yamanu a makeover as well. That way, no one will know that you asked for it, and I can go all out on you. I can turn you into a supermodel."

The woman was a genius. "You are the best, Amanda. I mean it."

"I love you too, Arwel. I'll see you tomorrow."

62

JIN

"The water is cold," Jacki complained.

"Isn't the pool heated?" Jin sat down next to Jacki and dipped a toe in. It was cold.

"If it is, it's not enough."

Sitting on the edge and dangling her feet in the water, Jacki seemed more interested in watching Yamanu and Mey splash around than getting in herself.

The two looked perfectly happy to fool around and didn't seem bothered by the water's temperature. Apparently, being impervious to cold was one more of the many advantages that immortals enjoyed.

Richard and Wendy were in the pool too, though, and they were still human. Perhaps she and Jacki were just being wussy.

It still made Jin's head spin every time she thought about Mey being immortal. Sometimes, she would forget that her sister was no longer human, but all that was needed to remind her was Mey smiling and flashing her new fangs.

Those were hard to ignore.

"Come on." Richard splashed her and Jacki. "Get in. It's only cold for the first second or two." He turned around to point at Wendy, who was on her sixth lap. "She doesn't mind the water being a little cold."

Wendy lifted a hand and waved. "He is right. Get in."

Jin glanced at the double doors. Arwel should be walking in at any moment, and she wanted him to see her in the bikini before she got her hair wet.

On second thought, she might look sexier when wet. But for him to see her in her hot bikini, she would have to get out of the water, and since it was cold, she would have to cover herself up with a towel, and that would defeat the purpose of wearing it.

"I'm waiting for Arwel."

Her friend eyed her from under lowered lashes and leaned to whisper in her ear. "What's going on between you two?"

"Nothing." Jin smirked. "Not yet, anyway. I'm waiting to see if he makes a move. If he doesn't, I'll have to be the one to initiate it."

Jacki arched a brow. "And that's a problem because?"

"I have a feeling that Arwel is old-fashioned."

He was probably centuries old. What was the etiquette about asking an immortal his age? Was it considered impolite? Was it okay?

There were so many things to learn about their society, and it was so difficult to do while pretending they were just paranormally talented humans. Perhaps she should have listened to Mey and gone to the village instead of insisting on staying with her friends.

Doing the right thing was sometimes inconvenient, but Jin preferred that to choosing the easy way out.

Besides, if she'd gone with Mey to the village, she wouldn't be with Arwel in the keep. Would he have even stayed on if not for her?

His job was to keep an eye on her friends, but Jin had a feeling that Arwel would have asked for someone else to be tasked with that job if she wasn't there.

He liked her.

She should be more patient and give the guy some time. After all, they had only met yesterday, so it wasn't as if he was dragging his feet about it.

What if he had someone else? It hadn't occurred to her before, but he might have a human lover stashed somewhere.

If he had an immortal mate, Mey would have known and warned her. Still, Yamanu and Arwel seemed to be close friends, so even if Arwel was seeing a plain old human, Yamanu would have known and would have told Mey.

All that was true, but Jin couldn't help the suspicion that she was missing an important piece of the puzzle. She'd spent a night in Arwel's bed, giving him the perfect opportunity to start something, and he hadn't done a thing.

Maybe he thought her too young? Too tall? Too skinny? Too forward?

Damn, she was driving herself crazy. Jin had never obsessed before about whether or not a guy liked her, and she didn't like the feeling of not knowing where she stood.

As the doors to the pool room swung open, Jin looked up and sucked in a breath. Arwel wasn't bare-chested as she had hoped for, but the simple white T-shirt he had on didn't do much to hide his body. Unlike all of his other clothes, it wasn't loose. Stretching across his chest, it showcased the defined muscles beautifully. And as a bonus, she finally got to see his legs, which were just as powerfully built.

Some guys worked out in the gym, focusing only on their upper body and neglecting their legs, which resulted in what she called the Chicken-Big body—broad shoulders, massive arms, and stick legs. But not Arwel. The guy was perfectly proportioned as if he had been sculpted by a loving hand.

As he walked up to her, his eyes never left hers. "Are you waiting for me?"

Was he trying hard not to stare at her boobs?

She was okay with a quick look. After all, she was sitting there in a bikini, freezing her nipples, not because she wanted him to admire her eyes.

"The water is too cold."

"It is?" He pulled his T-shirt over his head and dropped it on the concrete next to her. "I'm going to check it out."

Leaping into the air like some freaking dolphin, he gained an altitude that was impossibly high and then dove into the pool on the other end, cutting into the water so swiftly that barely any of the spray reached her and Jacki.

"Show-off," Jacki murmured. "But I'm impressed. Who knew that he was hiding all that under those baggy clothes." She fanned herself. "I think that I'm hot enough to give the water a try."

Jin leaned closer to her friend's ear. "Don't get any ideas. He's mine."

Jacki smirked. "I know. I was just teasing." She motioned with her head toward the water. "Go in. He's waiting for you."

"He's not. He is still showing off."

Swimming butterfly style, his powerful arms propelling his body forward, Arwel was a sight to behold. Even Richard had stopped swimming and was watching the action with a gaping mouth, while Wendy clung to the side, swimming slowly and ignoring the spectacle going on in the center of the pool.

Mey whispered something in Yamanu's ear, and a moment later, he joined Arwel, the two of them giving dolphins a run for their money.

"Yamanu is not bad either," Jacki said. "Want to place bets?"

"Arwel is going to win."

"Oh, yeah? I'm betting on Yamanu. He is taller, and his arm span is longer."

Jin winked. "Yeah, but he's already gotten the girl."

63

ARWEL

Why the hell was he showing off?

This wasn't something Arwel had done even as a teenager. He'd never felt the need to impress a girl or his friends, especially when it meant winning against someone else.

He wasn't competitive. The opposite was true.

His entire life, he'd been doing his best to make others feel good, and if that meant giving up a win to someone else, he had done it gladly. The influx of positive emotions was much more valuable to him than his own satisfaction.

Jin had changed all of that.

As he felt Yamanu's joy at the prospect of friendly competition, Arwel's first instinct was to slow down and let him win. Imagining the taste of Yamanu's satisfaction was like imagining a sumptuous dessert, and it usually would have been sweeter than any victory.

But this time, there was another variable, one that was overshadowing everything else.

Arwel had to win because Jin was watching, and a more primal instinct had taken over. It wasn't logical, and it wasn't civilized, but the urge to prove his worth to her was so strong that all other considerations had been pushed aside.

As a moment later, his friend shot past him, his long arms eating up the distance much faster than Arwel's, a surge of adrenaline propelled him forward. His muscles straining, he gave it all, overtaking Yamanu and getting to the finish line first.

Except, Yamanu wasn't done. Flipping inside the water, he pushed himself against the pool's wall and started for the other end. Arwel followed, overtaking Yamanu and hitting the end a split second before him.

Somewhere in the back of his head, he was aware that they shouldn't be putting their immortal speed and strength on display in front of the humans. But that was his logical brain thinking, and at the moment, it was occupying a tiny part of his cranium, while the primitive beast was thinking only about the win and the female who was going to reward him with her favors.

Luckily, Yamanu was still thinking, and at the end of the next lap, he stopped and conceded defeat. "You win." He huffed, exaggerating just a little. "I can't do another one."

From up on the ledge, clapping started.

As he looked up, expecting to see Jin and Jacki, Arwel was surprised to see everyone else had gotten out and joined the two to watch the competition.

"What the hell was that?" Richard asked. "Are you guys on steroids? I've never seen anything like it."

"Energy drinks," Yamanu said. "I need to check what they put in that stuff."

Richard shook his head. "Whatever it is, it must be dangerous."

"Nah, Arwel and I are strong swimmers. We've been competing for years."

Yamanu was a good liar, or rather an excellent twister of the truth. He hadn't actually said that he and Arwel had drunk energy drinks, just that he needed to check what was in them. And the part about the competition had only implied that they had competed against each other while stating that they'd been competing in general.

The guy should give lessons on fooling empaths and lie-detectors. Not even Andrew could have called out any of it as a lie.

"I think I'm done with the pool for today." Arwel put his hands on the ledge next to Jin and pushed himself up.

Reaching for his towel, she wrapped it around his shoulders. "That was impressive. You and Yamanu gave us quite a show." Jin leaned toward him and smiled. "Since I don't have a gold medal to give you, I'll reward you with a kiss."

It was only a quick peck on the cheek, but it meant more to Arwel than any medal because it was accompanied by a faint scent of Jin's arousal.

If they weren't surrounded by people, he would have put his arms around her and kissed her properly.

Instead, he pulled the towel down and put it over his groin, hiding his own arousal, which had become very obvious and was still growing by the second.

"You should put your shirt on," Jin said. "It's so chilly in here that you might catch a cold."

Had she forgotten that immortals didn't get sick? Or was she giving him a way out?

Glancing at her smiling eyes, he realized it was the latter, and decided to follow her lead.

"It really is cold. I should take a hot shower and then crawl under the blankets."

"That's an excellent idea. I'll come with you and make you hot tea." She lifted her legs out of the water and swung them over the ledge. "Here is your shirt." She handed it to him and then bent to lift hers. "Wrap the towel around your wet swim shorts."

"Yes, ma'am."

64

JIN

It had been a bold and impulsive move, but Jin had seen an opportunity and had taken it.

No guts, no glory, right?

Besides, Arwel's eyes were glowing, and Jacki was looking at him and frowning. If her hunch was right and his arousal had caused the glow, his fangs were probably going to elongate as well, and that would be very hard to explain.

He had to get out of there pronto.

Wrapping the towel around his hips while he was still seated was telling, but it diverted Jacki's attention away from his eyes.

Her friend smirked knowingly and winked. "Make sure to tuck him in."

"I will." Jin pulled her T-shirt over her head, wrapped a towel around her waist, and together with Arwel, headed out.

To break the awkward silence, she asked, "Is there a laundry facility down here? We are going to run out of towels and clean clothes soon."

"There isn't, but it's a good idea to add one. I'll take care of it."

As the pool room's doors closed behind them, Arwel let out a breath. "Thanks for the save."

Jin threaded her arm through his. "You're welcome. Is that a common thing for an immortal's eyes to start glowing when he is excited?"

Once again, her mouth had run faster than her brain. Embarrassed, she hurried to press the button for the elevator.

Arwel chuckled. "Yes, and it affects females as well." His words came out a bit slurred.

Blushing, she cast him a sidelong glance. "Did your fangs elongate as well?"

He nodded.

"Can I see?"

When he opened his mouth, she gasped. "They are huge!"

"Not so loud." He put a finger on her lips to shush her and then leaned closer, bringing those monstrosities to an inch away from her ear. "They are not even at their full length yet. Do they scare you?"

The implied threat stole her breath away.

As it was, the trickle of fear that his fangs and his hot breath on her ear were evoking had already caused a delicious tingle in her core. His suggestive tone amplified the effect tenfold.

The elevator arrived, and as the door opened, Jin dared a closer look. "How do you kiss with those things?"

"I can show you." Arwel wrapped his arms around her, lifted her, and walked with her inside the cabin.

When the doors closed behind them, fear gripped Jin.

Rationally, she knew that there was no reason for worry. Arwel was a gentleman, and whatever he did to her with his fangs was going to bring her pleasure, not pain.

Still, she was trapped in a small place with a predator, and her body responded with the instinctive fight-or-flight.

Pushing her against the cabin's wall, he brought his mouth to a fraction of an inch from hers.

Jin closed her eyes, waiting for him to close the rest of the distance, but he didn't.

Instead, his arms loosened their grip on her, letting her feet touch the floor. "Say no, and I'll stop."

Was he kidding her? She'd been dreaming of this moment since the first time she'd seen him. He must have sensed her fear, and that was why he'd stopped and asked.

Letting out a breath, she opened her eyes and smiled even though she was still scared. "Kiss me."

His arms tightened around her once more, and as he pressed his body against hers, she could feel his long erection through both towels.

She moaned even before his lips brushed over hers. The soft touch was enough to send an electric current through her, and Jin shivered involuntarily.

He pulled back, his eyes glowing like flashlights. "Don't worry, I'll be careful. I'm not going to nick you."

At some point, the elevator doors had opened, but neither of them had noticed.

"I'm not worried," she whispered. "I've been dreaming of your lips on mine since I first saw you. I'm just hyper-sensitive right now."

His eyes softened, and he cracked a smile. "You were dreaming of kissing me?"

As the doors started closing, Arwel reached with his hand to stop them, and then pressed his body against hers once more.

Loving how it felt, Jin closed her eyes and imagined how much better it would be with no barriers between them.

Without warning, he lifted her into his arms and carried her out. "I hope you don't mind."

She wrapped her arms around his neck. "I've never had a guy carry me before. I like it." Especially since he was doing it so effortlessly.

The cave girl in her got a thrill out of having a powerful man carry her off. The question was where to, and to what end?

Were they going to kiss and neck or go straight for the sex?

They were both adults, and neither was a virgin, so there was no reason to hold back. And since dating was not really applicable to their current situation, it made even less sense to wait.

Except Jin didn't regard Arwel as a casual hookup, and she was interested in building a relationship with him even more than she was in the sex, which at the moment she was extremely interested in.

65

ARWEL

Arwel strode down the corridor with Jin in his arms and stopped in front of his door. "My room or yours?"

"Your choice."

Jin was making it too easy for him, and he didn't know whether to be glad about it or not. The hunter in him appreciated the chase, but he was also out of time. The sooner he claimed her, the better, and she'd just offered him the perfect opportunity.

"Your sister might come looking for you in yours, so we'd better hide out in mine."

Fortunately, he'd left his door open, so no acrobatics were needed to reach for his phone while holding Jin up.

Giggling, she buried her face in his shirt. "It's embarrassing that everyone will know what we've been up to."

He walked into his room, set her down on the bed, and then pulled out his phone to close the door. "Does it bother you?"

As much as he wanted Jin, he wasn't going to push her into anything she wasn't a hundred percent sure of.

In response, she reached behind her neck and pulled on the string that was holding her bikini top up. "Not enough to stop. I want you." She released the other string, letting the top fall into her lap.

For a moment, Arwel stood gaping. Her breasts were beautiful, plump, and topped with hardened nipples that were begging for his attention.

His swimming suit was still wet, so he couldn't sit on the bed, but it was too soon to take it off. Except, what choice did he have? Get underwear from his duffle bag and put them on?

That was ridiculous, and in the background, the imaginary clock was ticking the seconds away. If he delayed for too long, Jin would start wondering what he was waiting for.

"My swimming suit is wet," he admitted.

She smiled. "Take it off."

When he hesitated for another moment, she lifted up and slid the bikini bottoms down her long, long legs.

What happened next was unclear.

One moment, Arwel was standing next to the bed with a towel wrapped around his wet swimming trunks, and the next, he was pressing his nude and cold body against Jin's warm one.

"You're cold." She wrapped her arms around his neck and pulled him on top of her. "I'll warm you up." She lifted her head up and kissed him.

There was nothing shy or hesitant about her kissing, and as she licked into his mouth, her tongue brushing against his fangs, the passion he'd been tamping down for the past thirty-six hours erupted with an uncontrollable force.

Taking over the kiss, Arwel banded his arms around Jin and penetrated her mouth with his tongue.

Arching up and pressing her beautiful breasts to his chest, she moaned into his mouth.

Nothing had ever felt so right. She tasted sweet and innocent, but the way she moved under him was all woman.

When he realized that she needed to come up for air, he lifted his head and stared at her gorgeous face with wonder. "You are so beautiful."

She smiled with the confidence of a woman who knew this to be true and cupped his cheeks. "I could stare into your eyes forever."

He kissed her again, going a little slower this time. Skimming her sides, his hands were gentle, caressing. He wanted to savor their first time coming together, to go slow, but his hunger for her was too powerful, and soon the kissing turned rough.

In the back of his mind, Arwel tried to remind himself that he needed to be mindful of Jin's human fragility, but forcing his body to comply with his brain was a struggle.

Especially since Jin wasn't protesting any of it. The rougher he got, the more aroused she became, her short nails digging into the muscles of his back as if she was afraid that he might stop kissing her.

He had no intention of doing that. But when she undulated under him, her hard nipples scraping against his chest and her core rubbing against his shaft, he had to let go of her mouth and take care of that ache for her.

Sliding down her body, he cupped both plump mounds. Pushing them up, he licked one nipple and then the other, going back and forth between the two.

Jin's hips moved under him in sync to his licking, and as he took one peak between his lips and sucked it into his mouth, she arched up hard, lifting both their bodies off the bed.

The girl was stronger than she looked and just as impatient to consummate their lovemaking as he was.

Except, Arwel was not going to give in to their primal urges.

This was the first of hopefully an eternity of passionate lovemaking, and he was adamant about making it as memorable as he could. If he let go, he would be inside her in a split second, and a moment or two later, his fangs would send her soaring into the clouds. When she came back down, all Jin would remember were those scant moments that had led to the bite.

That wasn't how he wanted her to remember this.

66

JIN

*J*in was burning up.

She had no patience for the slow foreplay that she usually favored. With Arwel, she felt an unstoppable urgency, a deep need to make him hers as quickly as possible.

But he had other ideas, and as much as she wanted him to make them one, she also wanted to learn everything there was about his body, his mouth, his hands, his taste. She wanted to touch him all over and learn every muscle, every bone, every sinew, kissing and licking every inch of his skin.

The hunger and thirst were so overwhelming that she felt lost, unable to decide what she wanted to touch or taste the most, and what to do next. In the end, she'd chosen the easy way, letting Arwel dictate the pace and everything else.

It wasn't like her. Usually, Jin was as assertive in sex as she was in any other situation, but with Arwel, she felt different. It was okay to let go because she trusted him like she'd never trusted any other man.

Why?

Was it because Mey had vouched for him?

Because he was an immortal male and she needed him to transition?

None of that rang true.

The feeling was inexplicable, and although her rational mind was rebelling against the realization, she had no choice but to concede that their coming together felt fated.

It seemed as if everything that had happened to her since she'd first met Marisol had led to this moment. So maybe the woman wasn't evil incarnate but the messenger of fate?

Right now, though, Jin didn't want to think about freaking Marisol. She wanted to concentrate on the moment and commit every detail to memory.

"You have gorgeous breasts that I could spend days worshiping." Arwel kissed each one in turn as if saying goodbye to them. He then slid further down, wedging his broad shoulders between her spread thighs. "But I need a taste of this too." He pressed a soft kiss to her folds.

"Oh, God." Jin arched into his mouth.

He chuckled. "Thank you. But Arwel will suffice."

She reached for his hair with both hands and grabbed fistfuls of it. "Don't tease me."

"I wouldn't dare." He treated her to a long lick. "You taste amazing."

He kept sliding his tongue around her folds, dipping it inside her, and then going back to licking her as if her feminine parts were made from ice cream.

Was he going to take a bite?

That was a scary thought, but then he slipped a finger inside her, and Jin stopped thinking. As her sheath clenched around the penetrating digit, she bit her lip to keep from screaming his name.

Brushing soft kisses against her swollen clit, Arwel was too gentle, teasing her despite his previous claim.

She pulled on his hair. "I need more."

He added another finger, kissing her lightly as he pumped slowly in and out of her.

She pulled harder. "I need to come."

He could either bring her to completion or lose fistfuls of hair. She wasn't giving him another choice.

Reaching up with his hands, he pinched both nipples, and at the same time closed his lips over that most sensitive bundle of nerves that he'd been kissing so softly and sucked.

First, Jin mewed, and as the orgasm washed over her in a tidal wave of excruciating pleasure, her thighs closed around Arwel's head, locking him in place, and the sound she made as she came was one she'd never heard herself emit before. It was primal, it was loud, and it made her feel free and wild and more authentic than she'd thought possible.

Somehow, Arwel had awakened the tigress that she hadn't known had been dormant inside her.

"You are magnificent," he whispered as he slid up her body.

Taking her mouth in a crushing kiss, he surged into her with one swift thrust.

Jin came again, her sheath squeezing around the length that was filling her up so perfectly that it felt as if it had been made for her.

Before she had a chance to come down from her second orgasm, Arwel started moving. Riding her fast and hard, he was going to bring her to the edge once again.

67

ARWEL

The feeling was incredible. They fit together as if they were made for each other. With each thrust, Arwel became more consumed with the need to possess Jin, to mark her as his, the wildness overtaking him so intense that it was scaring him.

What if he was too hard on her?

She was still human, and he was supposed to be mindful of her fragility, but she seemed just as wild as he was, meeting him thrust for thrust, as if she couldn't get enough either.

There was no stopping this, and as he pistoned in and out of her, he felt the bond dancing on the edge of his consciousness. Any moment now, it would snap into place, and they would be mated for life.

Except, the bond refused to obey, shimmering like a mirage and blinking out of existence no matter how frenzied Arwel's shafting was or how loudly his heart thundered in his ears.

Perhaps to seal the deal, he needed to bite his mate.

Yes, that was it.

Going even harder and faster, he began to orgasm.

Instinctively, Jin turned her head, exposing her neck. And as he bit down, she moaned and climaxed instead of crying out in pain.

He kept pumping into her as he filled her with his venom, and she kept orgasming until he withdrew his fangs and licked the puncture wounds closed.

When it was done, Jin's body went utterly lax, her head falling back with a euphoric expression spreading over her beautiful face.

Picking the towel up from the floor, Arwel tucked it under Jin's bottom before pulling out. They hadn't used a condom, but he was quite sure that Jin was on birth control, so pregnancy wasn't an issue even if a miracle could have happened. He wouldn't have minded in the slightest, but Jin would. Coming from the human world, she wasn't ready to accept him as her mate yet, not after knowing him for such a short time, and she certainly wasn't ready for a child.

The thing he wasn't sure about, though, was whether she could enter transition while on the pill. He wanted her to turn immortal as soon as possible, but he hadn't asked for her consent first.

It was safe to assume that she wanted it, but he still needed to ask.

As he lay next to her, his heart swelled with gratitude. How had he gotten so lucky?

Jin was so perfect in every way.

And yet, for some reason, the bond hadn't snapped into place, and now that the frenzied lovemaking was over, he couldn't even feel it dancing in the periphery of his consciousness as he had before.

Maybe it wasn't common for the bond to solidify during the first lovemaking like it had for Carol and Lokan. Perhaps other couples had to build it up slowly.

Hell, if he hadn't been in the next cell when Carol and Lokan had bonded, he wouldn't have even known that anything was amiss.

"Hey." Jin lifted her hand and cupped his cheek. "Why are you frowning?"

That was some fast recovery. Usually, after the venom bite, human females were out for hours. It seemed that his girl was unusual in every possible way.

"I was too rough." That hadn't been the reason for his frown, but it wasn't a lie either.

"Let me be the judge of that." She leaned up and kissed his jaw. "I loved every moment of it. But that bite was something else. Wow." She closed her eyes and smiled. "The psychedelics they gave us in the program didn't come anywhere close to that."

Fighting the sudden flare of anger that her comment had evoked, he wrapped his arms around her and pressed his body to hers. "I feel like ripping their throats out for forcing you to do that."

She sighed. "Don't. This moment is too precious to spoil with bad thoughts."

"I agree a hundred percent. How are you feeling?"

"Euphoric. Dreamy. A little loopy."

"Does anything hurt?"

She brought her hand to where he had bitten her and touched it with her fingertips. "There is no sign of your bite. It's like it never happened."

"Both my venom and my saliva have healing properties."

"That's a shame. I would have loved having a reminder." She smiled. "A mark would have served as an instant turn on."

"I love how strange you are."

She lifted a pair of smiling eyes to him. "Why am I strange? How is it different for the others?"

He chuckled. "I have no idea. It's not like the couples share details with the bachelors. But I've never heard any of the females lament about not having a mark left on them. Also, the euphoric effect usually lasts for a lot longer than it did for you. You woke up only a few moments later."

"How long does it last for others?"

"Hours. Sometimes all night."

"The freak sisters must be different in every way," she murmured. "I'll have to ask Mey how long it lasts for her."

68

KIAN

As Kian opened the door to his office on Monday morning, he wasn't enthused about going back to work.

The vacation, even though it had been a working one, had been fun. He'd enjoyed spending long days with Syssi. He'd even enjoyed hanging out with the rest of the bunch. Cohabiting in the chalet had been more pleasant than he'd expected.

The break from his routine had been refreshing, and they had been more successful in what they had set out to do than they could have hoped for. Not only did they have Jin, but they also had three more possible Dormants.

Or spies.

Despite Edna and Andrew's tests, he still wasn't sure about those three. The blessing they supposedly represented in the form of possible mates could be a Trojan horse situation.

That's why he'd summoned both Turner and Onegus to discuss safety protocol. Turner was just paranoid enough to foresee possible threats from the three that even Kian couldn't imagine, and Onegus was sufficiently practical and level-headed to offer solutions.

Kian was quite proud of himself for calling this meeting instead of deciding everything on his own. Even at almost two thousand years old, he was still learning, which was good.

Damn, his bimillennial birthday was fast approaching, and knowing Amanda, she was planning a big-ass surprise party for him. He didn't mind the party, but he didn't like surprises. Should he tell her that?

"Knock, knock." Onegus strode into the office with a tall paper cup of steaming coffee. "Turner is on his way up."

"Good morning." Kian leaned back in his chair. "How were things here in my absence?"

Onegus shrugged. "Nothing interesting to report from the village, but we have good news from the team in the Bay Area. Magnus told me that he updated you on the latest."

"He did. Are he and Vivian coming back later today?"

"Most of the team is. I decided to leave Kri and Michael there just to make sure that our guy doesn't run without us knowing about it."

Turner walked into the office with his briefcase tucked under his arm and a paper cup with coffee in his hand. "Good morning."

"What happened to your thermos?"

"It broke. I've ordered another one, but it hasn't arrived yet."

Kian waited for Turner to get comfortable before getting down to business. "I need to discuss with you what to do about the three paranormal talents we picked up along with Jin. I had Edna test them, and Andrew was there while I questioned them, but I'm still not sure they are not Trojan horses." He looked at Turner. "What do you think?"

"They could be. But since you have the best spy in the universe, you can keep an eye on them, so to speak, at all times. Have Jin hook into them and let them know that they are under constant surveillance. They wouldn't dare do anything."

"She is not going to like that. They are her friends."

Turner shrugged. "Does it matter if she likes it or not? If she considers them her friends, she probably wants to help them. Lifting the constant cloud of suspicion hovering over their heads would be helpful."

Kian raked his fingers through his hair. "I need her to spy on Kalugal, and I haven't asked her yet. The girl is a straight shooter, and spying is not something she is comfortable with. Having the ability is different from wanting to use it. I'd rather force her hand with Kalugal than waste it on our three uninvited guests."

Turner nodded. "I would like to meet Jin. Do you want me to talk to her?"

"Why? Do you think you can do a better job of convincing her to do it?"

"If she is such a straight shooter, she will appreciate being told things as they are. As the leader of the clan, you are better suited to present the situation to her, but if you are uncomfortable doing so, I have no problem doing it for you."

"I'll do it. Jin knows me, and she is not intimidated by me, which says a lot about her character."

"Do you want to wait until after your talk with Jin to send Guardians in?" Onegus asked. "I've given instructions to those on rotation in the keep to stay away from the underground for the time being."

That was what Kian had instructed the chief to do. He needed to decide on a strategy before the new arrivals met anyone else.

"I haven't decided yet if I want to leave it up to chance or send those who might be best suited for the two females. We also have the male to think of. How are we going to introduce him to the clan females? Don't forget that they will need to keep their immortality a secret and pretend to be part of a society of people with paranormal abilities. The problem is that most of them don't have any."

"They can make them up," Turner said. "It can be obscure things like talking to ghosts, like Nathalie's talent. No one can prove that they can't actually do that. Or they could claim an uncanny business acumen like yours or a strategic planning one like mine."

Folding his arms over his chest, Onegus leaned back. "You could ask Amanda to organize a party and invite a select group. She's a pro at those."

Turner cast him an amused glance. "How come you are not rushing to the keep to check out the selection?"

Onegus shrugged. "I don't think my fated one awaits me in the keep. I'm not even curious to check the two out. One is a nineteen-year-old girl, which is way too young for me, and the other is an immune. I'd rather wait patiently for the right one."

69

JIN

"Hey, sleepyhead, it's time to wake up."

Jin smiled and cuddled closer into Arwel's muscular chest, happy that he hadn't put a shirt on. "What time is it?"

"Ten in the morning." He kissed the top of her head. "Yamanu called asking if you were with me. I told him yes. I hope that's okay."

She opened her eyes. "Of course, it is. Otherwise, they would have searched the entire underground for me. Did he ask you anything else?"

"No, and I wouldn't have told him anything if he did."

She cupped his cheek and planted a soft kiss on his very kissable lips. "So, what do we tell the others? Are you my boyfriend now?"

"I hope that I'm more than that."

She thought he was teasing, but he looked dead serious. "Meaning?"

"I hope that I'm your mate."

"What's the difference?" she asked, before remembering what Mey had told her.

Damn, he couldn't be serious.

"A boyfriend is a temporary status. A mate is forever."

Apparently he was.

Jin stroked Arwel's cheek with her fingertips, scratching at the stubble. "We've known each other for forty-eight hours. I think it's too early to be talking about forever. Let's stick to boyfriend for now."

Arwel seemed disappointed, and she hated that, but as much as she liked him, and as perfect as the sex had been, they weren't even in love yet. They didn't know each other well enough for that.

"You are right. As far as the others are concerned, we are dating." He took her hand and put it over his heart. "But in here, I know that you are my mate."

She could live with that. "Okay."

"You need to get up. Kian texted me that he's coming to talk to you, and he asked that you be ready by eleven."

"That's plenty of time." She stretched her arms and yawned. "I just need to get some clothes from my room and eat something. I'm starving."

They had made love twice last night, but Arwel hadn't bitten her the second time. Apparently, immortal males needed almost no recovery time to have sex again, but there was a limit on venom production. The downside of that was that she was a little sore this morning.

It was well worth it, though. Arwel had changed her perspective on sex forever. She'd enjoyed it before, but not like that. It was like comparing drinking tea to sipping on the best wine ever made. The first was pleasant. The second was habit-forming.

And that bite. Oh, God, that bite. That was seriously addictive, and she couldn't wait to experience it again.

"I'll get the clothes for you. I don't want you parading down the corridor in my T-shirt and no underwear."

"Fine with me. Choose something nice. I want to look decent for my meeting with Kian. Do you know what he wants to talk about?"

Arwel nodded and then shook his head. "I'm not sure, and I don't want to speculate."

It was probably about her friends. Kian seemed worried about the security risk they posed, and she couldn't fault him for that. Not only did they all possess paranormal abilities, but they were also connected to a government agency that was aware of the existence of paranormal talents. That could pose a real threat to the clan.

Keeping their immortality secret was a matter of survival for Kian's people.

"Can you also get my toothbrush while you get my clothes?"

He pretended to frown. "Are you moving in with me?"

"I'm not. My room is bigger, so you are moving in with me. But you don't want me walking out of here with no underwear on, right?"

"Absolutely." He got out of bed in one fluid motion. "I'll be back in a minute."

"Take your time." She pulled the blanket up to her chin.

"Don't fall asleep."

"I'm not. I'm just closing my eyes for a moment."

Arwel chuckled. "Right."

Hearing the door open and then close, Jin turned on her side and tucked her hands under the pillow.

A forever mate. What a concept.

This was another thing she needed to talk with Mey about. Except, perhaps she should speak with Arwel instead and ask him to explain. Mey was still learning, and she didn't know all the details.

Was there a manual the clan provided Dormants with?

If there wasn't, someone should put one together. Perhaps she'd do it after she'd learned all that there was to know about it.

When the door opened again, she turned around and smiled at Arwel. "That was quick."

"Not really." He grimaced. "I barely managed to dodge Jacki. Prepare for an interrogation."

Jin laughed. "I should prepare an official announcement." She pretended to hold up a scroll. "Hear ye, hear ye! Last night Arwel and I had mind-blowing sex, and we are moving in together so we can have more."

70

KIAN

"I thought that we were going to your old office." Anandur arched a brow as Kian pressed the button for the dungeon level.

"I'm following Syssi's advice to have the talk in a more informal environment. We are meeting at Mey and Yamanu's place."

Syssi had brought up a valid point. Since Mey knew of his interest in Jin's talent and what he needed her to do, she might have mentioned something to Jin already, and if she didn't, she could help present the case to her sister.

"Good choice," Brundar said. "Jin is not going to like it. You might need Mey to convince her."

Whether Jin liked it or not, she was going to do it. He needed her help, and after he'd rescued her and her friends from the program, she owed him a favor. He would have done it regardless, but the bottom line was that he couldn't infiltrate Kalugal's lair in any other way.

The door to Mey and Yamanu's apartment was open when they arrived, and Kian was glad to see that none of Jin's friends were there.

"Good morning," he said as he walked in.

"Good morning," Jin smiled at him. "Would you guys like some coffee? We have a fresh pot."

"Sure," Anandur said. "Where are your friends?"

Yamanu got up and pulled three coffee mugs from the bar cabinet. "William brought over the video game that he developed to search for paranormal talents, and he is showing them how to play it."

"Interesting." Kian crossed his legs at the ankles. "He didn't tell me that he was planning on doing that."

"Really?" Yamanu handed him a full mug. "I thought that you'd sent him to keep them busy while you talked to Jin."

"I didn't think of that, but I'm glad of his initiative. Would you mind closing the door?"

He waited until the door clicked into place before turning to Jin. "Has Mey told you about Kalugal?"

"Who?"

"Apparently not." Kian sighed. There was a lot of background to the story, but he didn't want to waste too much time on it. "I'll try to be brief. What I'm about to tell you is top-secret, so please don't repeat it to anyone."

Jin nodded. "Of course."

"Kalugal is Lokan's brother. They are both the sons of our arch-nemesis, Navuh. However, their mother is our Clan Mother's sister, who we've just recently discovered is still alive and living in seclusion in Navuh's harem."

"Wait." Jin lifted a hand. "Did you say harem?"

"Yes, but from what we've learned, Navuh keeps the harem just for appearances. Areana is his truelove mate, and he's been devoted to her through all those years. But that's a whole different story. Back to Kalugal. His mother told us that his abilities rival those of his father, who is believed to be the most powerful immortal ever born. Fearing that his father might regard him as a threat, Kalugal faked his own death during WW2 and escaped with a large number of immortal warriors. We think we've found him living in the Bay Area, but we don't know what he is up to and if we should approach him or not. That's what we need your help to find out."

"You want me to tether him?"

Kian nodded. "We can find out when he visits a certain café or restaurant in the area, and all you will need to do is bump into him and then report to us what he is doing."

"Is he dangerous?"

"We don't know. From the information we have on him, he seems to be focused on making money. Which in his case is easy, since he is not bound by the same moral rules we uphold. With easily obtained insider information, he could have made a fortune on Wall Street."

"Do you know for a fact that he did?"

"We believe so."

"What are his powers?"

"He can thrall and compel immortals as easily as we can thrall and compel humans."

"Oh, wow. I thought that immortals were immune to those mind tricks."

"The Clan Mother can thrall other immortals if she so wishes because she is a goddess and a very powerful one, but immortals usually can't do that to each other. The only exceptions we know of are Navuh and Kalugal."

"Is that why Edna had me try it on her? To make sure that my talent worked on other immortals?"

He nodded. "If it worked on Edna, who is powerful, we can safely assume that it would work on any immortal, including Kalugal."

71

JIN

*J*in cast a sidelong glance at Mey.

Her sister didn't seem surprised by Kian's request, which meant that she'd known it was coming.

The traitor.

She should have said something.

Not that Jin could say no. Not after what the clan had done for her and her friends. But at least she would have had time to mentally prepare. They were going to have a talk later on, and she would give Mey a piece of her mind.

And Arwel.

He had obviously known about the spying gig as well. Was that why he had seduced her? Had all the talk about forever mates been a bunch of baloney? A scheme to make her cooperate?

Both felt like betrayals. But if her sister and her lover had worked in sync to trap her into doing this, Jin was never going to forgive either of them.

Nevertheless, she had no choice but to agree.

"I'll do it, of course. I owe that to you. But is that going to be my job in the clan? Am I going to become the clan's in-house spy?"

That wasn't the kind of life she wanted for herself.

"I will never force you into doing work that you detest. But in this one instance, I have no choice. No one else but you can get inside information about Kalugal and what he's up to. Naturally, if you decide to make a career out of it, I would be very happy to offer you a Guardian position after your transition. As Arwel and Yamanu can attest, we pay our Guardians very well, and they are held in very high regard."

"Are Guardians soldiers?"

"They are a cross between warriors and police officers. Right now, most of the work they do is focused on rescue missions. The clan dedicates a lot of our resources to saving girls and boys from traffickers and then rehabilitating them so they can have a chance at a normal life."

That was so incredibly admirable that suddenly all of Jin's prior misgivings felt childish and petty. She felt honored to be part of such an organization.

"God, you are putting me in such a difficult position. I want to help as much as I can with that, but I also have other dreams and aspirations. I studied business because Mey and I wanted to one day open a business of our own. But compared to what you are doing, that seems like such a frivolous thing. Who cares about fashion for tall women when lives are at stake?"

Leaning forward, Kian took her hand. "You do, and so does Mey. One does not exclude the other. You can have your business, and on the rare occasions that we need your special talent or Mey's, we will ask for your help. Does that sound doable to you?"

"Definitely. And anyway, the business idea is something for the future. We don't have the money to start it yet."

Kian grinned. "As a business major, I'm sure you can put together a detailed business plan and a profit forecast, right?"

"Of course."

"Then make one and present it to me. If you can convince me that investing in your fashion line is going to turn a profit for me, I'll invest the clan money in your business. After all, that's my special talent. I know which businesses are going to succeed."

Jin's heart skipped a beat and then started racing. She glanced at Mey, who was grinning as happily as Jin felt. Their dream might come true sooner than they ever thought possible.

"You've got yourself a deal." She squeezed Kian's hand. "My talent is at your disposal whenever you need it and for whatever reason, and so is Mey's." She glanced at her sister. "Right, Mey?"

"Definitely."

He smiled. "It's good that you phrased it like that. I also need you to tether your friends and let them know that you did it."

That hadn't been part of the deal, but she'd painted herself into a corner by promising Kian the use of her talent whenever and for whatever.

"Why?"

"It's for their own benefit. I can't shake the feeling that one of them might be a Trojan horse. If they know that you have access to them twenty-four-seven, they won't dare betray us even if they previously planned on doing so. It would give me peace of mind, and if they prove to be Dormants, it would mean faster integration into the clan for them."

She nodded. "I really don't like this, but I understand the logic. They are going to hate me for doing that."

"Can you think of a better way to ensure the clan's safety?"

She shook her head. "Unfortunately, I can't. But I'll think about it. Perhaps I'll come up with a better solution. How soon do you want me to do that?"

"I would like you to tether your friends by tomorrow morning. As for Kalugal, it can wait until you feel rested enough to embark on a new adventure."

72

ARWEL

"Jin needs at least a week to rest and get acclimated," Arwel said. "This is all new to her, and she still has a lot to learn about the clan. To face an immortal like Kalugal, she needs to be in peak condition."

It was all true, but he had a selfish reason for wanting to postpone her mission. They needed time to nurture their nascent relationship, and he wanted their bond to be firmly in place before she faced the charismatic and charming Kalugal. The guy had seduced the young Eva, and she was the toughest lady Arwel knew. As assertive and as confident as Jin was, she would be putty in the hands of someone like that. He could seduce her even without thralling or compelling her, which he could do as well.

After all, Kalugal was an ex-Doomer, and those guys had no qualms about taking a woman against her will, if not by physical force, then by thralling her.

It was still rape.

Hopefully Kalugal was a decent guy, but they couldn't count on it. Jin would have to go in with a strong Guardian backup, and Arwel was going to make sure to be as close as possible to her without alerting the guy.

"I second that opinion," Mey said. "We have a lot of catching up to do, and a week of nothing but recreational activities would be good for Jin."

Jin lifted her hand. "I appreciate everyone's concern for my well-being, but you are all forgetting one important detail. I am a wanted woman, and I'm supposed to be in hiding. Isn't it dangerous for me to be seen in public?"

"You can wear a disguise," Kian suggested. "There are special glasses that can fool facial recognition cameras, and you can put on a lot of makeup and a wig."

"I am not easy to disguise. There is no way to hide my height or my Asian features. Both are going to give me away."

"Not necessarily," Mey said. "Wait until you see what Eva can do. She can make you look like an old lady or even a man. It's not like you need to flirt with Kalugal, you only need to bump into him and touch him."

"That could work. Disguised as an old woman, I can ask him to help me to my table, or trip next to him and let him catch me, or something like that."

Kian shook his head. "That won't work with Kalugal. You forgot about immortals' sense of smell. An old lady or a man smell differently than a young woman. Kalugal would know right away that something was wrong. Not only that, the latex that the prosthetics are made from has a distinctive smell as well. You will have to work with more mundane methods like makeup, contact lenses, hair color, and the like. Changing your age or your gender is not a viable option."

Frowning, Jin crossed her arms over her chest. "I think that this job requires more than one person. Jacki should come with me. First of all, she is an immune, so he can't thrall her like he can do to me. And secondly, she has chutzpah in spades."

"How are we going to explain it to her?" Mey asked. "She is not supposed to know about immortals."

"There is no need to tell Jacki that Kalugal is an immortal," Jin said. "We can tell her that he is just a guy with impressive paranormal abilities who is suspected of doing all kinds of illegal stuff. Your organization wants to know what exactly he is doing because you want to recruit him, but not if he is a criminal."

"I'll give it some thought," Kian said. "But before we involve Jacki in our plans, I want you to tether her. I need to make sure that she is not going to betray us."

"Yes, sir." Jin saluted.

Kian put the mug on the coffee table and rose to his feet. "I'm glad that we've reached an understanding." He offered Jin his hand. "Thank you for agreeing to help."

She shook it. "It's the least I can do after all that you and the clan have done for my sister and me."

He nodded. "Nevertheless, I know that this is not something you enjoy doing. I appreciate the sacrifice."

Once Kian and the brothers had left, and Yamanu closed the door behind them, Jin turned around and pinned Arwel with a hard stare. "You should have told me about Kian's plans." She looked at her sister next. "And you knew about it too and didn't say a word. I'm mad at both of you."

"I didn't know he would do it so soon," Mey said. "We've barely had time to talk about anything. There are so many things I still need to tell you."

Jin's expression softened. "Okay, you are forgiven." She turned and pointed a finger at Arwel. "But you are not."

He cringed. "Can I make it up to you?"

"How?"

"Just name it, and I'll do it."

A wicked smile lifting her lips, Jin walked up to him and wrapped her arms around his neck. "I can think of a thing or two. But let's start with the proclamation. Except, you are going to recite it, not me."

He shook his head. "Please, not that. Can you think of something less embarrassing?"

"Na ah."

"I forgot how it went."

"Nice try. Hear ye, hear ye!" She waved her hand in a circular motion. "Go on, you can do it. Man up."

"Hear ye, hear ye!" Arwel rolled his eyes. "Last night, Jin and I made mind-blowing love, and we are moving in together so we can have more."

As Mey burst out laughing, Yamanu joined her, clapping his hands on his thighs.

"Close enough." Jin smiled. "Now, that wasn't so hard, right?" She kissed him, ignoring her sister and Yamanu, who were still clapping and laughing.

Soaking up the waves of joy coming at him from everyone in the room, Arwel no longer minded the embarrassment in the slightest.

It had been well worth it, and given a chance, he would gladly do it again.

DARK SPY'S MISSION

1

KIAN

Kian turned his office chair around and looked out the window at the wet pavement below. The rain had started about an hour ago, chasing away the café's customers and whoever else had been enjoying the village square.

The gloomy atmosphere was not conducive to work.

Instead of analyzing the file that Shai had put on top of the stack, he would have much preferred to go home to Syssi. The sticky note his assistant had attached to the file said 'read first,' and he'd been right about the property having great potential for development. But it didn't excite Kian as it normally would.

The problem was not with the deal, it was with the lack of motivation that had been plaguing him since he'd come back from vacation.

Kian wondered whether the rain was affecting his mood, or his mood was making everything seem glum.

The truth was that he was tired.

He should have felt energized after the vacation, but the break in routine only made it harder to get back to it.

Not that anything about his days was routine.

There was always something going on, and it usually had absolutely nothing to do with the business conglomerate he was running.

Like the three new potential Dormants hiding in the keep, who might also be spies for the government program he'd freed them from. Then there were the ten paranormal talents that he'd left behind, which bothered his conscience.

Kian hoped to someday free them as well, but that wasn't a sure thing.

Then there was Kalugal to worry about, a powerful immortal who might become either an ally or a foe.

Jin was the perfect spy to send after him, but she was young and inexperienced, and Kian worried about the thousand and one things that might go wrong with that plan.

That was why instead of calling it a day and going home to his wife, Kian was still in the office, waiting for Turner to arrive so they could brainstorm the plan.

Just another ordinary day in his hectic life.

How the hell was he going to add fatherhood to the mix?

Kian didn't want to be the kind of dad whose only interactions with his child would be a good morning and a goodnight kiss.

"Good evening." Turner walked into the office, put his briefcase down, and removed his dripping jacket.

"Thank you for coming." Kian pulled out a box of cigarillos from the drawer. "Do you mind accompanying me to the roof?"

"It's raining." Turner smoothed his hand over his wet hair. "I still expect to find a bald head when I do that. When I got out of the pavilion, I braced for my scalp to get hit by the rain. I was pleasantly surprised when my hair got soaked instead."

"You were human and bald for much longer than you've been an immortal with a full head of hair. Don't worry about getting wet, though. I have a big-ass umbrella up there."

"Then lead the way." Turner lifted his briefcase and put it under the chair. "I'll leave it here."

That was out of character for the guy. Turner was the definition of paranoid.

"I can put it in a drawer if you wish. Or hide it in the fridge." Kian walked over to the minibar and pulled out four miniature bottles of whiskey.

Turner chuckled. "You would need to make more room in there. And what's the deal with those miniatures? Did you pilfer them from the plane?"

"I have better taste than that. Shai got them for me. He's always coming up with ways to make my life easier. Instead of carrying a large bottle and a couple of glasses to the roof, I can just slip several of those into my pocket. But if you want, I can move things around and stick your briefcase in the fridge."

Turner shrugged. "I'm not worried. The only people who might be able to hack into my laptop are William and Roni, and I trust those two to stay out of my business."

"That's good to know. I thought that you didn't trust anyone."

Turner followed him out of the office. "I trust you."

"Thank you. I'm touched."

As Kian opened the rooftop door at the top of the stairs, he got pelted with raindrops, not because it was raining more heavily, but because it had become windy. Rushing, he and Turner took cover under the umbrella, and Kian turned on the outdoor heater.

"Every time I come up here, there is an additional improvement to the setup." Turner sat on one of the rockers. "Did you find out who is doing this?"

"Anandur promised to snoop around, but so far no one is taking credit. The prime suspect is Shai."

"A smart way to get a promotion or a raise."

"Not if he does it anonymously." Kian handed Turner one of the bottles. "Shai is just looking out for me."

Turner unscrewed the cap and took a sip. "Are you ready to brainstorm?"

Kian nodded. "I told Jin about Kalugal, and she agreed to do it. She suggested taking Jacki along because the girl is an immune, but I don't trust any of the three newcomers."

"You shouldn't. But do you have a concrete reason to mistrust them?"

"Just my gut feeling."

Turner cradled the bottle between his palms and leaned closer to the heater. "Jin is a smart girl. We haven't made any plans about her actually approaching Kalugal, but we need to take into consideration that he can thrall or compel her and get any information he wants out of her. I hope that you followed the same protocol with Jin as you did with the other three."

Kian frowned. "She is Mey's sister and a sure Dormant. It didn't occur to me to hide the keep's location from her. But I don't think it's a problem. We got there in the middle of the night, and she was half asleep. I don't think she paid attention to where we were going."

Turner shook his head. "You should have considered who you wanted to send her after. She knows that the keep is in downtown Los Angeles, and she knows it's a high-rise. Kalugal could show her an aerial map, and she might be able to narrow it down for him to just several buildings."

"You're right. I wasn't thinking. It was late, and the other three were sleeping, so I didn't even bother with going to the building across the street first and using the tunnel. I told Okidu to go straight to the clan's parking level in the keep." Kian pulled out a cigarillo and lit it. "You are worried about the worst-case scenario that is not going to happen. All Jin needs to do is touch Kalugal once. He'll think nothing of it. Just a random human girl touching his arm for a brief moment won't even register."

Turner chuckled. "And how long do you think she is going to stay human?"

"That's a good point. I think something is going on between her and Arwel. I need to have a talk with him."

That wasn't a conversation Kian was looking forward to. The Guardian's sex life shouldn't be anyone else's business. Except, it was when it could induce Jin's transition prematurely.

Perhaps Bridget could do that? Coming from the doctor, it would be less embarrassing.

"I hope that you are not too late." Turner crossed his legs. "The rumor machine has it that they are already together."

"They only met two days ago."

Turner arched a brow. "And your point is?"

"What have you heard?"

"Bridget was gushing about how happy she is that Arwel has found a mate, and how deserving he is. I guess she heard something. Don't forget that Jin is a millennial, Kian. She is not a damsel of yesteryear who expects her first time to be on her wedding night."

"Right."

The current generation of young humans was as casual about sex as the immortals had always been.

"I will talk to him."

Turner nodded. "When you send Jin after Kalugal, you should give her a substantial Guardian backup. The problem is that they can't be anywhere near her when she approaches him. I wish I could go with her, but, unfortunately, this is not going to be a quick one-day mission, and I have several projects I'm working on that require my presence. Weeks might pass before Kalugal is spotted in a place appropriate for Jin's tethering."

Kian hadn't considered Turner accompanying Jin, but he was starting to realize that he should have. Not only was the guy a blank as far as projecting emotions, but he was also an immune. The question was whether he was immune to Kalugal's mind tricks as well.

Annani was the only one who could test immortals for immunity, and he should have asked her to check Turner's.

Taking another puff, Kian leaned closer to the heater. "If Kalugal realizes that Jin has information he can use and decides to take her, Guardians are going to be useless because he can thrall and compel other immortals. Our only chance is her tethering the guy without him noticing it."

Turner put the empty miniature bottle on the side table. "I don't like depending on luck."

"Neither do I. Regrettably, you can't go with Jin. Still, I should have asked Annani to test your immunity to mind manipulation as an immortal. Other than Navuh and Kalugal, she is the only one who can do it to other immortals."

"I'm pretty sure that I'm still immune. I wasn't susceptible as a human, so there is no reason to think that I am as an immortal. What about Jacki?"

Kian shrugged. "I don't see how she could be helpful. Even if she is immune to Kalugal's compulsion, it's not like she could prevent him from abducting Jin. She could raise the alarm, but Kalugal would just compel the Guardians to do nothing about it."

"You could put a tracker on her."

"What for? We know where he would take her. What would we do? Storm the place?"

"As a last resort, yes."

2

KALUGAL

"Welcome home, Professor Gunter." The immigration officer returned Kalugal's passport.

"Thank you, young man." Kalugal pushed his wire-rimmed glasses up his nose and smiled. "Have a pleasant rest of your day."

When disguising himself to look like an old man, the thing to remember was to talk and walk accordingly. He affected a heavy German accent, hunched his shoulders, and walked slowly.

Unfortunately, when traveling through airports a shroud was not enough. He had to put on the old, distinguished gentleman disguise as well. There were cameras everywhere, and the security personnel was actually watching, especially those travelers returning from places like Egypt and Iraq, both of which Kalugal visited often.

The cameras saw what was really there, not what he was projecting into the minds of the humans around him. Those sitting in the security office might be miles away, which was too far for his mind to reach.

He was continually working on improving the range, as well as the precision, but the skill was far from perfected. And then there were the rare immunes whose minds were not susceptible to manipulation.

"Professor Gunter, over here!" Rufsur waved at him.

His second-in-command was standing among the other limousine drivers, holding up a cardboard sign, and trying hard not to laugh.

Pushing the cart with his luggage, Kalugal ambled up to him. "After all these years, you still find this funny?"

Rufsur shook his head, took the cart from him, and started walking toward the exit. "I think that, while you are wearing the disguise, you actually turn into the old professor. You've developed a split personality."

"It's called good acting. But you are not entirely wrong. After two full weeks of this, it becomes second nature, especially since it's my third archeological dig this year. Sometimes I catch myself thinking with a German accent."

"Did you find anything interesting this time around?"

Kalugal shrugged. "I always find something, but regrettably not what I'm looking for."

"You know what I think." Rufsur stopped at the pedestrian crossing. "Everything was destroyed when Mortdh dropped the bomb on the gods' assembly. The entire city was wiped out of existence."

"Those gods didn't all live in one place. Most of them had their own homes and temples in other cities, and some of their possessions must have survived. I just need to keep on looking. The problem is that Professor Gunter is getting old." Kalugal stuck out his fake belly and patted it in a grandfatherly gesture. "In a few years, I will have to switch to Gunter Junior. I'll have the old man die and his son take over the research."

As they reached Rufsur's car, he popped the trunk and hefted one of Kalugal's suitcases.

"Careful with that!"

"Don't worry. By how heavy it is, I figured that you brought artifacts back with you again."

"Naturally. I love seeing my collection grow."

After Rufsur had loaded the suitcases, Kalugal added his leather satchel and closed the trunk. "I probably have the largest collection of Sumerian artifacts outside of a museum."

It had started as a curiosity some twenty years ago and had quickly turned into an obsession. Kalugal's fortune allowed him to finance private archeological digs and, thanks to his thralling and shrouding, he could get the artifacts out of the country with ease. His original goal had been to find more information about the gods and their technology, but it was no longer just about that. He loved discovering new things about the past. With many of the pieces missing, putting the puzzle together was an intellectual challenge, and it fed Kalugal's thirst for knowledge.

Besides, if he ever decided to sell his collection, it could also be highly profitable. Not that he had any intention of doing that.

It was priceless.

It was his passion.

"I still don't know what you are hoping to find." Rufsur drove toward the exit and stopped to pay the parking fee. "If the gods had advanced technology, it has turned to dust by now. All you are going to find are clay tablets that humans wrote their impressions of the gods on. It might be interesting, but it's not worth the effort and time that you are putting into it."

His deputy was a pragmatic male, and seeking knowledge for its own sake seemed pointless to him. Unless there was a profit to be made or power to be gained, he considered it a waste of time.

"One of their tablets must have survived. My father used to rant about Annani and how she and her clan had an unfair advantage over the Brotherhood. He was convinced that she must have taken one of those tablets with her when she escaped."

Rufsur arched a brow. "With all due and undue respect, Navuh is unhinged.

Annani and her clan probably have nothing to do with the humans developing new technologies. If the knowledge came from her, the industrial and technological revolutions would have happened much sooner. Why would she wait so long to give the technology to humans?"

Kalugal shrugged. "Maybe she thought that they weren't ready. Or maybe she didn't understand the technical information contained in the tablet and had to wait until one of her descendants managed to decipher it much later. My father is a power-hungry despot, but he is not crazy. I believe him about the tablet. He said that Mortdh had one and that he used it to communicate with Ahn and to record his thoughts and plans. Given that Navuh told me about it many years before iPads and other tablets were invented, he couldn't have made it up. Mortdh's tablet was just such a device or maybe something even more advanced."

Rufsur waved a hand. "That only reinforces my opinion that you are not going to find anything in those digs. The tablets of today are not designed to survive a decade, let alone thousands of years. If Annani indeed has one, she must guard it like a precious treasure and take excellent care of it. That wouldn't be the case with a device that was left to disintegrate in the ground. After so many years, there would be nothing left of it. Not even a scrap."

"You are probably right. But that's not the only reason I keep digging for artifacts. I find it exhilarating."

Rufsur shook his head. "I don't get it. Working in the dust and the heat while wearing the professor's disguise cannot be pleasant."

Kalugal smiled. "But then I get to go home with my loot, deposit it in my perfectly air-conditioned underground bunker, and work on putting the puzzle pieces together. That's my hobby. It gives me a pleasant respite from my day job of taking over the world." He lifted his chin and affected a haughty expression. "Mwahaha."

"Speaking of conquering the world, did you hear the news about your main competitor for the position?"

His levity gone, Kalugal grimaced. "I thought that I had more time, but it's like someone in the Chinese government is reading my mind and implementing my ideas before I even have time to think them through." He shrugged. "Then again, they might be unwittingly putting my plan into action for me. I just need to figure out a way to hijack it from them and improve upon it."

Rufsur smirked. "Payback is a bitch. I would love for them to get a taste of their own medicine. They've been stealing technology for decades. Now it's their turn to develop a brilliant plan to take complete control of their population and have it stolen from them."

3

JIN

"Is everyone here?" Amanda looked around Mey and Yamanu's living room.

The place seemed to be bursting at the seams with people, but not because there were so many of them. The dungeon apartment was small, and it felt even smaller after Amanda and the makeup artist had put down the two huge trunks they'd wheeled in.

Since there weren't enough seats for everyone, Jin vacated her spot on the couch and sat in Arwel's lap. She had expected some raised eyebrows or snarky remarks, but everyone ignored it as if she and Arwel becoming a couple was old news.

The question was how had they heard about it so soon?

This morning, when she'd made Arwel recite the proclamation about them hooking up to Mey and Yamanu, none of her new friends had been there. So, unless her sister and her fiancé had been calling everyone in the village to tell them the news, Jin couldn't figure out how they'd learned about it.

Since she was quite sure that Mey and Yamanu hadn't been the culprits, Jin lifted her eyes to the surveillance camera mounted near the ceiling and wondered whether the security personnel were behind this.

That was just as unlikely, but she couldn't come up with anything else.

Still, the fact remained that no one had batted an eyelid when she had plopped onto Arwel's lap.

Except for Richard, who seemed uncomfortable and was doing his damnedest to avoid eye contact with her.

It was a weird situation.

Up until two days ago, Jin and Richard had been a couple. And even though they had both realized that their feelings for each other had been the result of compulsion, they had some history together. Thankfully, Jin had held off on the sex. It would have been doubly awkward for everyone involved if she and Richard had done the deed.

Especially for Arwel, who was showing possessive caveman tendencies.

Richard's life would have been in danger, or at least the integrity of his face would have been.

The surprising part was that she didn't mind Arwel's attitude. In her former life, Jin would have dumped a guy for acting like that faster than he could blink. But for some reason, she liked Arwel's possessiveness.

Maybe because with him it went both ways. She felt just as possessive about her guy as he felt about her.

Amanda put her arm around the makeup artist's shoulders. "Let me introduce Eva. She is going to do your makeup."

Eva dipped her head.

"And this is Jin, Mey's sister, and over there at the table are Jacki, Wendy, and Richard."

Eva waved. "Hello, everyone."

Amanda continued. "You all know Callie, so I don't need to introduce her. I will be in charge of cutting the hair, and Callie will style it."

Callie lifted a blow-dryer and a brush. "I'm armed and ready."

Yamanu got up. "I'll leave you ladies to have your fun."

"Stay!" Amanda pointed at him. "The guys are getting makeovers too."

Stifling a chuckle, Yamanu bowed his head. "I don't need a makeover. I'm perfect the way I am."

"I agree." Mey crossed her arms over her chest. "It's crowded in here. I think the guys should go hang out somewhere else."

"I want a makeover," Richard said. "I'm staying."

"No one needs to leave," Eva said. "We can use the bedroom for the makeovers, and the living room for those waiting their turn."

"I still don't want anyone touching this." Yamanu flipped his long hair back. "It's the source of my power." He winked at Mey.

"You can watch," Eva said. "Who wants to go first?"

"I do." Jin lifted her hand. "I want to look like a completely different person. Nothing permanent, though. I'm fine with wigs and makeup, but I don't want you to cut my hair."

Per Kian's instructions, Jin hadn't told any of her friends about her upcoming mission, so they wouldn't understand why Eva was changing her looks so drastically.

"Why do you want to look different?" Wendy asked. "You're beautiful."

"Thank you. But this is for fun. Eva is a professional makeup artist, and I'm curious to see what she can do."

Wendy shook her head. "I don't want to look like someone else. I just want to look pretty and glamorous."

"No problem." Eva patted the girl's arm. "I promise that you will be happy with the results."

"I'm going to put the trunk in the bedroom."

Yamanu lifted Eva's trunk, but when Richard grabbed the other one, he almost keeled over. Gritting his teeth, he braced it on his chest and followed Yamanu.

"Poor guy." Amanda cast Arwel an accusing glance. "You should have grabbed it before he had a chance. He saw me lift it off the cart, so he thought that it wasn't heavy."

Chuckling, Arwel tightened his arms around Jin. "I couldn't get up without dropping my precious cargo."

Jin kissed his forehead. "Your precious cargo needs to get up anyway."

Reluctantly, he loosened his arms and let her go.

Pulling out a chair from the dinette, Eva took it to the bedroom and put it in front of the bed. "Come and sit over here." She motioned to Jin.

Amanda closed the door. "What look are we going for?"

"Can you make me look not Asian?" Jin asked. "My height and ethnic features give me away."

Eva snorted. "Easily. I can do it just with makeup. I don't even need prosthetics."

"What about the hair? A blond wig would look weird on me."

"An Afro?" Amanda suggested.

Both Jin and Eva grimaced.

"It was just a suggestion. What about dreadlocks?"

Eva shook her head. "They would attract too much attention to Jin. We don't want to make her look pretty, she already is. We want to make her look drab and not as noticeable."

"That's no fun." Amanda plopped on the bed. "Makeovers are supposed to be about making people look better, not worse. Ella looked adorable when we changed her looks. The disguise didn't make her ugly."

Jin frowned. "Why did Ella wear a disguise?"

"It's a long story." Eva pulled out a fluffy brush from her case. "But since this makeover is not going to be quick, we have time."

4

ARWEL

"How about a game of cards while we wait?" Mey put a deck on the coffee table.

Lifting it, Wendy examined the design. "I don't know any card games that are played with real cards. Do you have Uno?"

Mey shook her head. "That's all I have."

"Can we play charades instead?" Wendy put the cards down.

"That's a great idea." Mey smiled. "I haven't done that since Jin and I were kids."

The last thing Arwel wanted was to play silly games, but some form of distraction was needed.

Richard was casting him accusing glances, and the guy's emotional grid was all over the place. He appeared to mourn the loss of his relationship with Jin, even though it hadn't been love, but he also lusted after Jacki, who was ignoring him.

In fact, she was acting strangely.

Staring into the distance, she seemed to be somewhere else. If Jacki were the quiet type, her behavior wouldn't have attracted Arwel's attention, but normally she had an opinion on everything and wasn't shy about voicing it.

Was she having a vision?

The only other clairvoyant Arwel knew was Syssi. Her visions were sporadic, and when they happened, they were hard to miss. She looked like an epileptic having a seizure.

Jacki just stared with unfocused eyes. But when he tried to tune into her feelings, he couldn't get a read on her because she was sitting next to Richard, whose strong emotions overwhelmed her muted ones. Later, when there weren't so many people around, he could ask what was bothering her. Was she scared? Worried about her future?

Since he couldn't tell her anything about immortality yet, assuaging her fears would be difficult, but he could at least reassure her that she would be taken care of.

When the bedroom door opened before his turn for charades arrived, Arwel counted himself lucky. It had been almost an hour since Jin had entered the bedroom with the self-appointed makeover specialists, and except for him and Jacki, everyone else had already had their turn at playing charades.

"Attention, everyone." Amanda clapped her hands. "Get ready to be wowed."

When Jin made her entrance, Arwel's eyes widened. How the hell had Eva accomplished such a transformation?

As the rest of the makeover crew came out, Yamanu started clapping, and then everyone joined him.

A chin-length auburn-colored wig covered Jin's long hair, and heavy makeup obscured her Asian features while making her look a decade older. The baggy, shapeless dress added to the illusion of a thirty-something suburban mom.

Arwel didn't like the new look, but it was one hell of a disguise.

"Amazing," Jacki murmured. "I wouldn't have recognized you on the street."

Richard grimaced. "It's unattractive."

Arwel seconded that opinion, but he was smart enough to keep his mouth shut. No woman wanted to hear that even when she was making herself look worse on purpose.

"I agree," Mey said. "But as a disguise, it's perfect." She got up and walked over to Jin. "The makeup is fantastic. But I doubt you can do it without Eva's help."

Eva shook her head. "Jin doesn't need to go that far when she does it herself, and I can teach her how to do a simplified version. Thankfully, her disguise doesn't have to be as complicated as the one I did for Areana."

"Who is Areana?" Jacki asked.

Eva cast her a suspicious glance. "Someone who also needed to change her looks."

Anyone else would have been intimidated, but not Jacki. "You must be doing a lot of those to be so amazingly good at it."

"I'm a private detective. My work often necessitates elaborate disguises. This is nothing compared to what I do for myself."

"Cool. Is there a school for that? Or are you self-taught?"

Eva narrowed her eyes at the girl. "Why do you want to know?"

Jacki shrugged. "At some point, I will need a job, and this seems like fun. I wondered if I can go to school for it and how much it costs."

Evidently, he'd been right about what had been troubling her. Jacki had been thinking about her future.

"I'm self-taught," Eva said. "But there are schools for stage makeup and costume design. I have no idea how much they cost, though."

Jin tapped Eva's shoulder. "Can we take it off now and make me look pretty?"

"Sure." Eva smiled. "Unlike this, making you pretty won't take long because you already are."

Just as promised, ten minutes later Jin walked out looking like herself again, with just a little color on her lips and barely-there eye makeup.

"That's much better." Arwel got up and pulled her into his arms for a quick hug.

Amanda tapped his shoulder. "Your turn."

"Are you going to make me look like a grandpa?" he joked to cover his embarrassment.

Fates forbid that anyone should find out about him asking Amanda to help him out with his looks. The Guardians would never let it rest.

"No, silly. I have something different in mind for you."

5

JIN

After Arwel left with the makeover crew, Jin sat next to Jacki. "Do you have a new career in mind?"

She shrugged. "There aren't many job openings for unreliable clairvoyants, and I don't have any other skills."

"What did you do before joining the program?"

"Mostly waitressing and some other occasional gigs. Basically, I did what I could to scrape together enough money for rent and other necessities."

Jin had a feeling that Jacki didn't want to talk about her past before the program. Every time she'd asked her about it, Jacki would answer in generalities and change the subject.

"I'm sure you made good money in tips."

"The tips were good, but not good enough. Besides, I want to do more with my life."

"Have you considered college?"

Jacki shook her head. "I can't afford it, not even with a full scholarship. I need to support myself."

It was so difficult to keep quiet and not tell Jacki about the possibility of her being a Dormant. When she turned immortal and joined the clan, all of the concerns that were troubling her so much would become irrelevant.

Instead, Jin patted her arm. "Don't worry. The solution will present itself."

"I'm in the same boat," Richard said. "I hope the organization will find jobs for us."

Wendy didn't contribute her opinion, but she didn't have to. Her troubled expression said it all.

The thing was, even if her three friends turned immortal, that didn't solve the problem of them earning a living. It wasn't like clan membership came with a free ride. Every member Jin had met so far had a job.

She and Mey should start working on the business proposal that Kian had promised to look over. If he decided to invest the clan's money in their business, they could offer jobs to her friends.

Doing what, though?

Richard was a hustler, so he could be the sales manager. Wendy could be the secretary, and Jacki could model. At five foot nine, she was tall enough for their fashion line, and even though she was much curvier than what models were supposed to be, that wasn't a problem either. The clothing line Jin and Mey had in mind was meant for real women who didn't wear size zero or two. The average was more like size twelve. And that was especially true for tall females.

Except, she couldn't even tell Jacki that. Her friend's lack of a college education wasn't the result of a low IQ. Jacki was smart, and she would wonder why Kian was making Jin and Mey such a generous offer.

It was better to bite her tongue and say as little as possible.

Then again, she could lie and say that Yamanu had money and was investing in Mey's dream. But to do so, she had to coordinate it with them first.

"I'm bored." Wendy got up. "Can I turn on the television?"

"Don't you want to play some more charades?" Mey asked.

"I'm too good at it, and it's not fun when I can guess it right away. I kept quiet not to spoil your fun."

Jin had been under the impression that Wendy had suggested the game. Why had she done it if she didn't like playing it?

The girl was weird.

"How about something to drink?" Yamanu asked. "There is enough left over to make several margaritas."

The bedroom door opened, and Amanda walked in. "Did I hear margaritas? Because I would love one. But first, let me introduce the new and improved Arwel." She waved both arms toward the door. "Please give him a round of applause."

As everyone started clapping, Arwel walked out with a shy smile on his handsome face.

Talk about a transformation.

He looked like a freaking GQ model.

His hair was trimmed and slicked back, which made his gorgeous eyes pop, and he was clean-shaven, which made him look even more kissable than usual.

But the best part was the change of wardrobe.

Gone were the baggy cargo pants and the oversized checkered shirt over a plain white T-shirt. Instead, Arwel had a pair of slim jeans on and an elegant button-down shirt, both fitting him perfectly and showing off his fantastic body instead of hiding it.

The man was mouthwateringly handsome, and he was all hers.

"You cleaned up nicely," Yamanu said.

"Thank you." Arwel wasn't looking at his friend when he thanked him. He was looking at Jin, waiting for her to say something.

"Wow," was all she could come up with.

What she wanted to do was take Arwel's hand, lead him out of Mey's room, take him to hers, and lock the door.

He wasn't going to stay dressed for long.

6

ARWEL

Some might have scoffed at Arwel's efforts to look good for his mate as unmanly, but he didn't care what others thought. If he did, he would have taken care of his schlumpy appearance a long time ago.

The only person whose opinion mattered was Jin, and she seemed very happy with his new haircut and the well-fitting, elegant clothes Amanda had given him.

It was so worth it.

Smiling suggestively, she got up, walked up to him, and took his hand. "I'm tired of playing charades. I think I'm ready to call it a night."

"It's not even eight yet," Mey said.

Jin cast her an amused glance. "I didn't say that I was going to sleep."

Pulling on Arwel's hand, she led him out of the room to the sounds of snorts and chuckles.

"You look good enough to eat," she whispered in his ear. "I promise to be careful when I remove your beautiful new clothes."

Fates, he loved how bold she was.

"You know that most of them can hear you, right?" He used his phone to open her door.

"I don't care." Jin pulled him inside and pushed him against the wall. "Kiss me."

He pressed on the close icon, tossed the phone on the bed, and closed his arms around her body, palming her ass.

"Why don't you kiss me?"

"You are better at it." She touched a finger to his fang, sending a pulse of heat straight to his shaft. "Because of these."

Smirking, he turned them around and pressed his body to hers. "Happy to oblige." He took her mouth.

Soon, the kissing got frenzied, with both of them fumbling for buttons and zippers in their rush to remove the barriers between them.

And then his damn phone started ringing.

Ignoring it, Arwel pulled Jin's blouse over her head and cupped her breasts over her bra.

As she moaned into his mouth and attacked his shirt buttons with renewed fervor, he helped, shrugging the shirt off as soon as she popped the last button and pressing his bare chest to hers.

With the skin to skin sending another bolt of lightning down into his straining shaft, he kicked his boots off and was ready to push his pants down when the damn phone started ringing again.

"You'd better answer it," Jin murmured. "It might be an emergency."

"Someone else can take care of it." He reached behind her back to unclasp her bra.

The phone kept ringing.

With a curse, Arwel let go of Jin and walked over to the bed. His intention was to bark at whoever was calling and tell them to get lost, but luckily he stopped for a split second to check who it was.

"Fuck! It's Kian." He accepted the call. "What's going on?"

"I apologize for the interruption and for what I'm about to ask of you, but regrettably, I have no choice. You need to use condoms, Arwel. Jin can't enter transition before she tethers Kalugal."

"Noted."

"Goodnight."

Damn. He should have thought of that. Not only had they had unprotected sex already, but he hadn't gone out to buy condoms. Perhaps there were some left over in the old clinic?

"What's the matter?" Jin hugged him from behind, pressing her naked breasts to his back.

He put his hands over hers and turned his head to kiss her cheek. "Kian reminded me that we need to use condoms to prevent you from entering transition before you tether Kalugal."

She chuckled. "It might be too late. We didn't use them last night."

"Still, we need them now, and I don't have any."

"That's a bummer." She rubbed herself against him. "But as I said before, you look good enough to eat, and that's what I want to do. I don't think you can induce my transition like that." She nipped his ear.

His eyes rolling back, Arwel pulled Jin's arms tighter around him. "There might be some condoms left in the clinic. I can go check."

"You are not going anywhere." Turning him around to face her, she pushed him onto the bed. "Not right now, anyway."

When she kneeled on the floor and started tugging on his socks, he tried to stop her and do it himself, but she batted his hands away.

"Let me. This is my treat to you."

Leaning back, he groaned. "Fates, woman. What are you doing to me?"

She took a sock off and tossed it aside. "Pampering you." She pulled the other sock off and dropped it on the floor. "And pleasuring you."

Bracing on his arms, he lifted his ass and pushed his jeans and boxer shorts down his thighs.

Jin pulled them the rest of the way. "Oh, my." She licked her lips. "Now, that's a treat." She touched his erection.

His hips shot up. It was an involuntary action, but it seemed to please her.

"Excited to meet me, aren't you?" She flicked the head with her tongue. "I'm excited too." She licked all around it.

"Fates," he groaned.

"Jin would suffice." She smiled up at him and then opened her mouth and took him deep inside it.

His head dropped back, and he arched up into her mouth.

She took him even deeper.

Damn. He had to see that.

Lifting on his forearms, he looked at Jin's lips wrapped around his shaft. The dual sensation of feeling and seeing was enough to trigger his climax.

Sensing it, she tightened her hand and pulled back. "Not yet. I'm not done having fun with you."

7

KALUGAL

After a shower and a short nap, Kalugal headed down to the bunker. Not trusting anyone else to handle his treasures, he hadn't allowed his men to unpack the trip's loot and was excited about doing that himself. There was nothing like coming home and going over his latest finds before putting them on display.

His best one was a small statue of a beautiful woman that was nearly intact. What fascinated him most about it, though, was that it looked a lot like a woman he'd seen on one of his trips to Egypt.

On the way back from one of his digs, Kalugal had passed the Colossi of Memnon, but even though he'd visited the statues several times over the years, something had prompted him to stop at the tourist attraction and have another look.

When he'd noticed the female, it was because of her height and her most unusual jade eyes. He'd been intrigued, but he'd had no intention of flirting with her while in his Professor Gunter disguise. Still, if she had been alone, he could've shrouded himself in a more appealing form and approached her, but since she hadn't been, he had just walked over to take a better look.

Something about her was different.

When he'd gotten closer, that elusive something had turned into a most interesting discovery. The woman was an immortal. His reaction to her had been much subtler than the one he'd had to her man, but both of them had caused the hair on the back of his neck to tingle in alarm.

As her senses had picked up on him as well, she'd turned to look at him.

Instinctively, Kalugal had shrouded himself in thin air, disappearing from sight. Since she could sense his otherness, even his Professor Gunter disguise wouldn't have been enough. The female would have wanted to check out who he was and why he'd triggered that particular response, or worse, send her formidable mate to investigate.

Then he had bumped into the two of them again at the airport.

Who were they?

If he had met the male alone, Kalugal would have assumed that he was a member of the Brotherhood sent by Navuh to search for him. But the presence of the immortal female precluded that. The two couldn't have belonged to the Devout Order of Mortdh.

They either belonged to Annani's clan or were an unaffiliated couple. In either case, he had no wish to engage, and not just because the male looked dangerous.

Kalugal's curiosity had been piqued, though, more on a personal level than anything strategic.

The clan played no part in his future plans, and they could do nothing to stop him, so he was perfectly okay with leaving them alone. But ever since he'd seen that couple and the loving way they had interacted with each other, he'd been having thoughts about finding an immortal female to share his life with, and the clan was the only community that had them.

"I knew that I'd find you here." Rufsur walked over to the worktable. "Pretty." He leaned to look at the small statue.

"Don't touch it." Kalugal cast him a warning glare.

"I know better than to breathe on your artifacts." Clasping his hands behind his back, Rufsur peered over the fragments of a stone tablet that Kalugal was carefully spreading over the table.

"Anything interesting happen while I was gone?"

Rufsur rubbed the back of his neck. "There was a small incident that I forgot to mention."

Straightening up, Kalugal narrowed his eyes at his number two. "What is it, and why didn't you call me right when it happened?"

"Relax, it's nothing. We had a woman stop by the gate and ask to see the grounds. She and her husband were looking for a house in the neighborhood, and she wanted to see the landscaping. Just in case, I had them followed and checked them out. They seemed to be precisely who they claimed to be. They were staying at a posh hotel, looking at properties during the day, and enjoying their evenings in nearby restaurants and bars."

"It could be nothing, and it could be something." Kalugal took his gloves off and started walking toward the security office. "I want to see the footage from when that woman stopped by the gate. Was she alone?"

"The husband stayed in the car."

That made it less suspicious. A woman alone wouldn't ring the bell on a stranger's estate and ask to come in. But a pushy one who had her husband as backup might.

"Hello, boss." Gabe turned his swivel chair around. "What brings you into my humble office?"

"I want to see the footage." Kalugal looked at Rufsur. "When did the woman stop by?"

"Twelve days ago. I think it was Thursday."

"I remember her." Gabe turned back to his monitor array. "A hot little number. I hope they find a house in the neighborhood and that her husband leaves on many business trips." He typed on his keypad, bringing up the gate footage from that day and then scanning it on fast forward to the right moment.

Kalugal leaned over Gabe's shoulder. "Freeze it and zoom in on her face."

She was petite and too skinny for his taste, but her face was beautiful. Her hair and the gentle expression on her face reminded Kalugal of his mother, and as always, the memory made his gut clench with sorrow.

Keeping him away from her was a sin for which he was never going to forgive his father.

"That's indeed a gorgeous woman. A trophy wife," he said to cover up for his momentary slip into sentimentality. "Let it play with the audio on."

Without consciously admitting it to himself, and for no reason whatsoever, he hoped that the woman also sounded like his mother, but she didn't. No woman ever had.

His mother was one of a kind. A gentle soul trapped by a despot whom she for some reason loved.

Was this woman who called herself Viv also married to a control freak?

"Can you show me the husband?"

Gabe switched to another camera. "Here he is. Nice car."

"Mercedes' finest," Kalugal said.

The top of the convertible was down, and the husband was clearly visible. The man was immaculately groomed and elegantly dressed. While his wife conversed with the guard, the guy was busy typing a message on his phone.

So far, everything had fit with who the couple claimed to be, but they also could have been well-prepared spies. People were curious about the mysterious owner of the estate, and ambitious journalists might have devised a plan to find out more.

"Can you zoom in on the phone? I wonder if I could read what he is typing."

"I can try."

The camera angle was such that it was impossible to read the message, but the phone itself was interesting. At first glance, it looked like the latest iPhone model, but upon closer examination, it didn't look like any of the major brands.

"Are either of you familiar with that phone?"

Rufsur leaned closer. "It looks like one of those cheap Chinese copies of an iPhone."

That was what had crossed Kalugal's mind as well, except it didn't fit the rest of the picture. The couple seemed rich. Why would the husband use a non-brand phone?

There were two possibilities Kalugal could think of.

One was that the couple had been journalists in disguise, using a rented Mercedes and expensive clothing as disguises, but not bothering with a small detail like a phone.

The other possibility was that the phone wasn't a cheap replica, but rather a special issue of breakthrough technology or powerful encryption, or both, like the ones he and his men were using.

"I want security increased, and I want you to report anything suspicious to me right away. And I mean everything, no matter how trivial you might think it is."

"Yes, boss." Gabe saluted. "Code red?"

"Code yellow will do."

Rufsur frowned. "Why? What did you see?"

"The phone. A guy wouldn't be driving a Mercedes and at the same time using a cheap Chinese counterfeit. I have a feeling that this device is a special issue, encrypted like ours."

8

SYSSI

*A*manda walked out of her office and stopped at Syssi's desk. "Let's have lunch at Gino's."

Syssi looked up. "We haven't been there in ages, and Gino is going to give us the look."

"What look?"

"The guilt-inducing sad one because we've stopped coming."

Amanda frowned. "We are there at least once a week."

"Precisely. But the last time was three weeks ago."

"We need to plan Kian's birthday, and that's the best place for it. I'll just give Gino a hug and all will be forgiven."

"Be careful." Syssi pulled her purse out of the drawer and pushed to her feet. "A hug from you might give him a heart attack. The old lecher has the hots for you."

Amanda shrugged. "And so do ninety percent of my male students and ten percent of the female."

"Yeah, but they are young. Gino is in his sixties, and he is about fifty pounds overweight."

"You've got a point. I'll just air kiss his ruddy cheeks and leave a big tip."

"That's better."

As usual, when they got to Gino's it was packed. The excellent home-style Italian food, combined with reasonable prices and big portions, attracted customers from as far as the university. Which meant that there was a chance that Amanda would bump into one of her students, something she tried to avoid on her lunch break.

Thankfully, Gino wasn't there to give them the look, but since all of his staff knew them, they still got the royal treatment.

"Follow me, ladies." Gino's nephew headed toward the back of the restaurant. "The only table I have available is in the private room on the second floor. I hope you don't mind. Otherwise, you'll have to wait."

"That's perfect." Amanda started up the rickety stairs. "Syssi and I need to plan my brother's birthday."

He turned around with a big grin on his face. "We could cater it. How many people are you inviting?"

"That's what we are about to figure out."

"Let me know when you have a number, and we can go over menu options."

"I will do that."

After he took their order and headed back down, Syssi leaned and whispered, "We can't have Gino cater the birthday."

"Why not?"

"Because after the party is over, we would have to thrall all the waiters."

Amanda shrugged. "I don't think it will be necessary. They won't notice anything. It's not like our guys are going to get aggressive or horny and start flashing fangs. They will get drunk and sing in Gaelic but that's fine. Just a bunch of guys having fun."

Syssi nodded. "I hope you are right."

"The question is where to do it and who to invite. I vote for the banquet hall in the keep. If we invite the Scottish arm of the clan and they all come, bringing them to the village would be a hassle, and housing them would be a problem as well. Also, the increased traffic to the village might get noticed. The keep, on the other hand, is close to several high-end hotels, and it's in the middle of downtown."

Amanda's mention of hotels lit up a bulb in Syssi's head.

Leaning back, she crossed her arms over her chest and smiled. "I have a better idea. Let's do it in the clan's hotel in Hawaii."

Amanda's eyes brightened. "You are a genius. Why didn't I think of that? It's perfect. Everyone loves Hawaii, and that way we won't risk exposing the village or the keep."

"That's just one of the benefits. Think about the weather and the beaches. It's going to be so much more fun than hanging around Los Angeles in the winter." Syssi looked out the window. "It's drizzling again."

Tapping her finger over her lower lip, Amanda squinted. "What about a cruise ship? We could rent one exclusively for the clan."

Syssi sighed. "The problem with that is the same as with my idea. Someone would have to stay behind and guard the village here and the castle over in Scotland, which means that not everyone will take part in the celebration, and that sucks. I want everyone to be there."

"Not everyone came to your wedding, or to Nathalie and Andrew's. That's just how it is."

"Maybe we could have two parties instead of one? That way everyone can participate."

"True, but then it's not going to be a clan-wide celebration."

"Right. There must be a solution; we are just not thinking creatively enough."

Amanda chuckled. "If the Perfect Match studios had enough devices, we could hook up everyone and have a virtual party."

"Maybe by Kian's third millennial party there will be one in every home."

Amanda laughed. "No one would ever leave. People would spend their lives inside virtual realities."

It was a scary thought, but Syssi doubted it would ever happen. "Real life brings endless scenarios and possibilities. The virtual world is limited by the designers' imaginations. Eventually, people would get bored."

"You think?" Amanda arched her brows. "For most people, real life is boredom and tedium. They get up in the morning, go to work, come back home, eat dinner with the family, watch some television, and go to sleep. Rinse and repeat. It's the same for us. It's not like every day brings new and exciting things, and when it does, they are rarely good."

Syssi nodded. "Kian would agree with you a hundred percent. There is always something going on, and it's usually trouble."

When the sound of footsteps announced their waiter's arrival, they paused the conversation and waited until the guy left.

"We've gotten sidetracked," Amanda said. "Back to Kian's birthday. Are we holding it in Hawaii, or are we renting a cruise ship?"

"I prefer Hawaii. Having most of the clan on one boat is dangerous. If word somehow got out, it would be very easy for our enemies to get rid of us with one freaking missile."

"Or a torpedo. And it's not like we can hire an escort of battleships to protect us." Amanda tapped her palm on the table. "So, it's decided. We are having the party in Hawaii."

"Yes."

"Now to the next item on the agenda. Do we tell Kian? Or are we going to surprise him?"

"Let me think about it. If we coordinate it well and get everyone to cooperate, we might be able to surprise Kian. I can tell him that I want to celebrate his birthday by going on a vacation to Hawaii. We will go first, and then everyone else will follow. I'm pretty sure Onegus can take care of the village's security. Except, Kian doesn't like surprises. I think he would enjoy the event more if he knew about it ahead of time."

9

KIAN

"Good afternoon." Kian got up and pulled out a chair for Vivian.

When Magnus had walked into the office with his wife, Kian hadn't been surprised even though he hadn't invited her. Vivian had been an integral part of the operation in the Bay Area, providing cover for her husband. Her idea to walk up to the gate and ask to see the grounds hadn't been sanctioned, but it seemed as if no harm had been done. The tail that had followed them around for a couple of days had eventually given up.

"Thank you." She sat down. "I hope you don't mind me joining the meeting."

"Not at all. You were an unofficial team member, and your contribution was appreciated."

"That's so kind of you to say, but in retrospect, I regret going up to the gate and pressing that button. I thought that we could learn something by courting a tail, but you didn't want me to engage the guy following us. Then to keep our cover, we had to pretend to show interest in nearby properties. I enjoyed the house walkthroughs, but Magnus not so much."

Kian stifled a chuckle. That had been an accusation cloaked in an apology.

"We've found what we were after anyway, and you two got to see some nice houses for sale."

She smiled at her husband. "Magnus was bored out of his mind."

"I wasn't." The Guardian took her hand. "I just couldn't stand the realtor's endless prattle. Besides, it wasn't a total waste of time. One of the houses we saw has potential."

Kian frowned. Surely, Magnus wasn't thinking about buying it for his family or even as an investment. Unless he'd meant it had potential for the clan.

"How so? I typically invest only in hotels and office buildings, not in private houses."

"I meant as a stakeout house," Magnus clarified. "It's located at the end of the street Kalugal's mansion is on, but because it's a corner house, its front and its driveway face the other street."

Kian's curiosity was piqued. "Go on."

"The good part is that Kalugal's gate is visible from the home's second floor balcony. The bad part is that the property costs a fortune to lease. The quoted price was twenty-seven grand a month, and the minimum lease term was one year."

"We can thrall the owner to agree to a month-to-month."

"That occurred to me. But the owner lives abroad. Regrettably, we can't thrall humans over the phone."

Kian leaned back and smiled. "You are right about that. But Lokan can compel him. He proved that he could do it when he compelled his island manservant to send him Navuh's portrait even though it was not allowed."

Vivian shook her head. "Still, twenty-seven grand a month is a lot of money."

"It is. But that would be the best cover possible for our operation. Especially if you two moved in. Since Kalugal's men have already checked your story and found no holes in it, they won't find it suspicious that you rented or bought a property nearby."

Magnus didn't look convinced. "They might go for a more thorough investigation if we become their neighbors. Besides, we've been away from home for too long already. We can't leave Parker alone again."

"Can you take him with you?"

Vivian and Magnus exchanged glances, and then Vivian shook her head. "I don't want to expose Parker to even a whiff of danger. But if you think this will be helpful for the mission, I'm willing to accompany Magnus again. Ella is back, so she can take care of Parker in our absence." Vivian chuckled. "Not that he is thrilled about living with his sister. Parker prefers spending time with Merlin. If the doctor ever wants an apprentice, our son would jump on that."

Magnus grimaced. "Merlin fills Parker's mind with useless information instead of teaching him actual biology and physiology, things the kid could actually use in school."

"It's not useless." Vivian smiled shyly. "Merlin's potion is helping us to conceive."

Magnus's eyes softened. "I like the guy, and I want to believe that his potions actually work, but Syssi and Kian's success might have been coincidental. None of the other couples who have started the treatments have been successful yet."

"Give it time, love. It will happen."

"Fates willing."

Kian waited impatiently for the discussion between the mates to be done. It wasn't that he lacked sympathy for their cause, but it was irrelevant to what the meeting was about.

"Give me the house's details, and I'll arrange the lease. Get ready to go back on Thursday."

Vivian's eyes widened. "So soon? You can't close the deal so quickly."

"With Lokan's help, I can. Kri and Michael are going to join you there, and once Jin is ready, she and Arwel will stay with you as well. I haven't decided how many additional Guardians I'm going to send with her, but they are also going to stay at that house, provided that it's big enough."

Magnus nodded. "Six bedrooms and eight bathrooms. I think that should do it."

"Indeed. Given the cost of hotel rooms in the Bay Area and how many I would have had to rent for the mission, the house is probably a better deal."

10

JIN

"How did you enjoy the lesson with Dalhu?" Arwel looked at Jin's sketchbook expectantly.

She put it on the coffee table. "It was fun. You should have stayed."

Showing up mid-morning with a bunch of artists' sketchbooks and charcoals, Dalhu had surprised everyone, including Arwel. He'd murmured something about doing it because Amanda had demanded it of him and apologized for not calling ahead of time.

Arwel had arranged for them to use one of the classrooms, stayed for a little while to watch, and then left ten minutes into the lesson.

"I draw like a six-year-old." He glanced at her closed sketchbook again. "Can I see what you have in there?"

Jin shook her head. "I'm not much better than you. Mey is the talented one." She pulled a bottle of water from the fridge and joined Arwel on the couch. "Richard can't even draw a stick figure, and yet he stayed. Dalhu was very patient with him."

Snaking an arm under her, Arwel lifted her onto his lap. "Good for him. But I don't have the patience for it. My next chosen career is not going to be anything artsy."

He kissed her softly, his arms skimming over her sides and brushing lightly against her breasts.

It didn't take much for Jin to get excited. Turning in Arwel's arms, she straddled him. "Did you get condoms?"

It was a mood killer to talk about rubber, but she had to ask. For some reason, they had to use condoms until she tethered Kalugal. Arwel hadn't explained why, just saying that it was necessary.

Was Kian afraid she'd get pregnant and that it would interfere with her ability to tether people? Or maybe it was about the immortals' superior sense of smell. If they didn't use protection, could Kalugal smell Arwel on her?

Talk about gross.

Arwel smirked. "I did. There is an entire commercial-sized box of them in the clinic. Someone was very thoughtful."

The thought of having sex with a barrier between them was far from exciting, and using up an entire box before they could stop was depressing.

"Yeah, remind me to thank whoever left it there for us later." She looked down to hide the involuntary grimace.

Arwel hooked a finger under her chin. "You look upset."

"I don't want to make love to you with those things on. They take away from the pleasure. Besides, I don't understand how they will prevent me from entering transition. I was tested when I entered the program, and I'm clean, my birth control shot is good for another month, and after that Bridget can give me another one."

"It's not about preventing pregnancy or catching diseases. Immortals don't get infected, and we don't transmit either. Our bodies eliminate viruses and bacteria. But in order for you to transition, I need to bite you and to come inside you at the same time. It has nothing to do with getting you pregnant. It would be a miracle if I did."

Maybe for him, but not for her. Jin wasn't ready to start a family.

"I don't get it. You said that for guys to transition it's enough for them to get bitten during a fight. How come females need semen in addition to the venom?"

He shrugged. "I'm not a doctor, but I suspect that the venom's different composition has something to do with it. Maybe it's not as concentrated when used during sex, and to transition the extra chemical boost from semen is needed. Bottom line, experience has taught us that this is how it works, and as long as condoms are used, transition doesn't happen. And since it is important that you approach Kalugal as a human, you can't transition until you tether him."

"Then I don't want to wait. I want to do it as soon as possible and be done with it. I want us to make love with nothing to diminish the experience, and I want to transition."

He nodded. "I want that too, but I don't want to rush things. Kalugal is a dangerous man, and we should plan the operation carefully. I don't know whether Kian and Turner have finalized the details yet."

"What's to finalize? Their part is to locate him in a place where I will have access to him. Once I'm there, it can be all done in five minutes. Bada bing bada boom."

Arwel laughed. "Suddenly, you are enthusiastic about going out on a spying mission?"

She undulated, rubbing her center over his erection. "I have strong motivation. I want that bad boy in me without a raincoat. Call Kian and tell him that I'm ready to go."

Arwel arched a brow. "Now?"

"Yes. If he knows that I'm ready, he will finalize those details you are so concerned with."

Arwel frowned. "You are taking this way too lightly. So many things can go wrong. We need to use every precaution possible to ensure your safety. If anything happens to you..." He trailed off.

Jin cupped his cheeks. "I'm not stupid. I'm not going to rush into it or go in without backup. But this is not some dangerous mission that involves walking into the lion's den or crossing enemy lines. What's the worst that could happen? Kalugal walks away without me having a chance to tether him? Then we will do it again."

"What if he grabs you and runs? No one will be able to stop him because he can compel other immortals, and he can certainly compel you to go with him without a struggle."

"Why would he do that, though? Has he kidnapped random girls from clubs before?"

"Not that we know of."

"So he is not going to start with me." She reached into his pocket and pulled out his phone. "Call Kian. The sooner you do that, the sooner we can make love."

He chuckled. "Is that supposed to motivate me to make the call?"

"You betcha."

11

ARWEL

Arwel dropped the phone on the couch beside him and put his hands on Jin's waist.

"What are you doing?" She batted them away.

"You told me to call Kian, and I can't do that with you sitting on me." He gripped her waist again and started to lift her.

She put her hands on his forearms to stop him. "Why not?"

"Because I can't concentrate when you are rubbing all over me."

Smiling evilly, Jin leaned to the side and picked up the phone. "Call." She handed it to him. "Let's test your self-control." She emphasized by twisting her hips and grinding against the club pushing on his zipper.

"You are evil."

"I'm a challenge."

That she was, and Arwel loved every moment of it. She was like no other female he had ever been with, and that was saying something when coming from an immortal who'd been sexually active for more than three centuries.

With an exaggerated groan, Arwel chose Kian's contact and then waited for the line to connect.

"He is not picking up." He disconnected the call.

"Give him a moment. Maybe he's in the restroom and is just zipping up."

Arwel shook his head. "I really don't want you thinking about Kian and zippers in the same context."

She chuckled. "Sorry. I just thought that if he was on the line with someone else, he could have paused, switched over to you, and told you to wait. But since he didn't do that, I figured he couldn't get to the phone."

As his phone started ringing, he arched a brow. "Maybe you were right." Planting a quick kiss on the tip of her cute nose, he answered. "Hi, Kian. Thanks for calling back."

"I was on another call."

Jin shrugged and made the zipping motion.

He mouthed, *naughty girl*. "I have Jin here with me. Do you mind if I put you on speaker? I'm calling on her behalf, and the door to her room is closed, so the others can't hear us. We can talk freely"

"Go ahead."

She leaned into the phone even though it wasn't necessary. "Hi, Kian. How is your day going?"

"Very well. And yours?" He sounded amused.

"I'm ready to go after Kalugal."

"Don't you need to rest a little longer?"

"She is impatient to start her transition," Arwel interjected before Jin had a chance to blurt something about the damn condoms.

The girl really had no filter.

"I see," Kian said. "Can you be ready to leave for the Bay Area by Thursday?"

Arwel frowned. He hadn't expected Kian to be ready so soon. "That's only two days from now. Are there any new developments that I'm not aware of?"

"I spoke to Vivian and Magnus earlier, and they told me about a house for lease down the street from Kalugal's mansion. We are renting it starting Thursday. The place is fully furnished, so you can move right in. Since Vivian and Magnus have been pretending to look for a property in the area and Kalugal's men have investigated them already, they are going to be the official renters."

"How many Guardians are you sending with us?"

Arwel took it for granted that he was going, and if Kian objected, they would have a problem, because he wasn't letting Jin go without him.

"Kri and Michael are already there. I'm thinking of sending four more, but that might be overkill. You, Magnus, and Kri, that's already three, and you can count Michael as half."

"What's half a Guardian?" Jin asked.

"Michael is still in training, but he is very good," Arwel explained.

Jin pursed her lips. "Then that's more than enough. You don't need to send any more people to guard me. Once you locate Kalugal and I get to him, the whole thing is going to be over in five minutes."

"The problem is that none of the men can go in with you because Kalugal would sense them. They can only guard the exits. If there is more than one, they will need to split up. Also, he is probably not going to be alone. A guy like him doesn't leave the house without a bodyguard or two. I need to add at least two more Guardians to your team."

"You are the boss." She shrugged. "What about Jacki? Is she coming with me?"

"Yes."

Jin pumped her fist in the air. "Awesome." But then her expression turned serious again. "What about Richard and Wendy? They will feel abandoned here. Especially since it could take a long time until Kalugal is spotted somewhere nearby and in a place that I'll have access to him."

"I'm sorry, but you can't take them with you. They would be a liability."

"Not really. Wendy is an empath, and Richard is a touch telepath, and they are both human. They can be part of my backup."

"Does either of them have military training?"

"Only what we were taught in the program. We had firearm training and some hand-to-hand fighting. But that wasn't much. Still, that's all Jacki and I have to work with."

"Let me think about it, but it's probably a no. Jacki is an immune, so she is too valuable not to be used in this situation, but the other two are basically untrained civilians."

Jin nodded. "I understand. I don't like it, but I get it."

"Do you still think you can be ready by Thursday?" Kian asked.

"Nothing has changed about that. I'm ready to be done with this."

"Did you have a chance to tether your friends?"

Jin grimaced. "Not yet."

"Make sure to do it before Thursday."

"I really don't think it's a good idea. It's not like I can follow the tethers all at once. I can do it only one at a time, and when I have several connected to me, it takes a lot of concentration."

"I understand. Like everything else, there is a learning curve, and I'm sure that with practice it will become easier for you to handle."

"Maybe. But it's still uncomfortable. Morally, I mean. I would hate it if anyone did it to me."

"Think of it as a temporary measure."

"Do I have a choice?"

"I'm afraid not."

12

JIN

*A*rwel ended the call and dropped the phone on the couch again. "So, where were we?" He palmed the back of her neck and pulled her in for a kiss.

Things were just starting to heat up again when Jin's phone rang.

Arwel groaned. "What now?"

"It's Mey's ringtone." Jin reached into her back pocket. "What's up?"

"Dinner. We are all heading to the kitchen. Kian's butler delivered groceries, and Ingrid brought four extra-large pizzas and a cake for dessert. I say we make a salad to go with the pizzas and leave the cooking for tomorrow."

"Aren't we lucky. I totally forgot that we planned on making dinner for everyone tonight. We need to thank Ingrid for saving us the trouble."

"I already did. So, are you two coming?"

Jin chuckled. "Yeah, in a bit." They were about to, but Mey's phone call had ruined those plans.

"Don't wait too long. The pizzas are getting cold."

Arwel groaned. "I knew that we should have waited with calling Kian."

"It actually worked out better this way. We can eat dinner with everyone, tell them the sad news about us leaving, and then go back and make love for as long as we want. No interruptions."

"Let's get it over with, then." Arwel lifted her off his lap and then adjusted himself. "I'm not going to be comfortable."

"Sweet torture." She winked at him. "I'll make it up to you."

When they got to the kitchen, Mey waved Jin over. "Can you grate the Parmesan? I'm almost done."

"Sure thing." Jin grabbed the thick chunk of cheese and went to work. "Just like old times in Mom's kitchen. It makes me feel nostalgic."

Mey nodded. "I miss Mom and Dad. Maybe after this thing with Kalugal is over, we can go visit them?"

"That's an awesome idea. Except, you forget that I'm a wanted woman. How am I going to fly over there?"

Mey stole a quick glance around to make sure none of the humans were within earshot. "The clan can arrange for fake documents. And if, after you tether Kalugal, Kian feels generous, he might let us use the private jet." She leaned closer to Jin's ear. "Naturally, we won't go until you transition, and then we can take Arwel and Yamanu with us." She smiled. "We can introduce our fiancés to our parents."

"Arwel is not my fiancé. And besides, they are not going to be happy with our choices." Jin leaned closer. "Our guys are pagans who believe in Fates. Mom and Dad are going to have a conniption over us not marrying Jewish boys."

Mey grimaced. "Do you think there is a chance that they will agree to convert?"

Jin arched a brow. "You are an optimist, aren't you?"

From over at the center island, Yamanu cleared his throat. "Not going to happen."

Jin waved a hand. "That's what I thought."

"I think that's enough Parmesan." Mey put a hand on Jin's.

There wasn't much left of the big hunk of cheese. Without paying attention, she'd grated a mountain.

Mey took a plate and emptied half of it into her salad, tossed it, and carried it to the kitchen island that served as their dining table. "Enjoy, everyone."

Sitting between Mey and Arwel, Jin munched on a slice of pizza while watching Ingrid flirting with Richard.

He seemed to be enjoying the attention, and Jin wondered whether the two of them had already had sex. She hoped so, and not only because she felt guilty for moving on so quickly. If things got serious between Ingrid and Richard, he would be too busy to feel abandoned when Jin and Jacki left for San Francisco.

But that still left Wendy.

Right now, she was talking with Jacki, and the two were laughing about something, but Jacki was leaving too.

Then another thought occurred to her. Mey and Yamanu were staying at the keep only because of her. As soon as she left, they would probably go back to their house in the village.

Damn, she hadn't thought things through. Maybe she should have waited another week?

"You are atypically quiet," Mey said. "What gives?"

"Arwel and I spoke with Kian, and I told him that I'm ready to go after Kalugal. Naturally, he was happy to hear that, and he told us to be ready by Thursday. Jacki is coming with us too, but I didn't tell her yet. I'm worried about leaving Wendy and Richard alone here. You and Yamanu are probably not going to hang around once I'm gone, right?"

Mey glanced at her guy, who shrugged.

"We can stay a little longer, but eventually, everyone has to move on. Richard seems to be in good hands. So that leaves only Wendy."

"I can introduce her to a very nice young man," Yamanu said.

Mey lifted a brow. "Who do you have in mind?"

"You don't know him, but he is Wendy's age."

The girl looked their way. "Are you talking about me?"

Jin nodded. "Yamanu wants to introduce you to a guy he knows."

Wendy blushed. "I don't want a boyfriend."

"Who said anything about a boyfriend? I was thinking about a boy who can be your friend. Vlad is one of the nicest guys I know, he is your age, and he could really use a friend as well."

"Why?" Wendy narrowed her eyes. "What's wrong with him?"

Yamanu shrugged. "He's a bit odd, but he is also very sweet. He attends college in the area, so it's not a problem for him to stop by."

Wendy seemed to warm to the idea. "What's his talent? Is he part of your organization?"

"He's a shrouder like me. Not nearly as powerful, but then he is still young. He might become stronger when he gets older."

That sounded like an awesome solution, provided that the kid wasn't some kind of a freak. For the match to work, Wendy needed to be attracted to him, and if he was odd-looking, or behaved strangely, that might not happen.

Before Yamanu made a big mistake and exposed the poor kid to unnecessary heartache, she needed to ask Arwel what he knew about Vlad.

13

ARWEL

When Jin and he returned to her room, Arwel wanted to pick up where they'd left off before Mey had called, but Jin seemed troubled.

"What do you know about that kid?" she asked.

Arwel pulled her into his arms. "I really don't want to talk about Vlad now." He picked her up and carried her to the bed.

"Just tell me if he is really as nice as Yamanu claims. I worry about Wendy, and Yamanu also said that the kid was odd. In what way? And why is he lonely? Is he socially awkward? And is he good at keeping secrets? Because he will have to keep his immortality from Wendy."

Arwel put a finger on Jin's lips. "Slow down. I can only answer one question at a time. I don't know Vlad well, but those who do say that he has a heart of gold. The thing is, the kid looks like a vampire, and not the sexy Hollywood kind. For some reason, his fangs are more pronounced in their resting state than those of other immortal males. On top of that, each of his eyes is a different color, he is about six feet four inches tall and skinny like a twig."

Jin's eyes softened. "Poor kid. College must be hell for him. How does he manage?"

"He wears black clothes, covers one eye with his bangs, and fronts the Goth rocker image. People assume that the teeth are glue-on, and the different colored eyes are contact lenses."

"Is he a rocker?"

Arwel nodded. "He plays bass guitar and has a good voice. But right now, he is missing the rest of his band. Jackson, who is the lead guitarist and vocalist, is busy running his sandwich and pastry empire, and Gordon, that's the drummer, is away at college. So that's why he is lonely."

Seeming satisfied with his answer, Jin smiled. "Two lonely hearts. It could work. But I thought that the plan was to bring in Guardians for the girls to choose from."

"It will have to wait. Jacki is coming with us to the Bay Area, and after what Edna said about Wendy, I don't think the girl is ready for a Guardian. None of them are young lads, and I think that Yamanu made a great choice with Vlad. I hope that the kid is not too shy to befriend a girl."

Jin lifted a brow. "Is he a virgin?"

"I don't know for sure, but I suspect that he is. What about Wendy?"

"I don't think so."

"She blushed when you told her about Yamanu's idea."

"So what? A lot of people blush when they are embarrassed. It doesn't mean a thing." Jin sighed. "I just want all three of them to move on, so they can leave this freaking underground and join the living. But I'm still trying to figure out how it's going to work. I understand that inducing Richard is not a problem because he only needs to fight one of your men. Maybe this can be done while Jacki is away? If it doesn't work, his memory of it can be erased, right? But if she is here, we will need to isolate Richard until he either transitions and moves into the village, or gets his memories wiped and you give him a new identity and send him somewhere safe."

"It's not that simple. If he bonds with an immortal female, we can be pretty sure of his loyalty. Without it, he could betray us even if he turns immortal. And after he turns, we won't be able to thrall him at all. That only affects humans."

"Then I really hope Richard and Ingrid fall in love. But if they don't, Kian should send more females down here. They can pretend to volunteer giving classes on this or that like Dalhu did."

"That's smart. We should suggest it to him. But first, let's give Ingrid a chance. She called dibs on Richard, and she'd be majorly pissed if he slipped through her fingers."

"True." Jin plopped back on the bed. "I wish that by the time we come back, Wendy and that kid are in love, and so are Richard and Ingrid. That would leave only Jacki to take care of."

Lying on his side next to Jin, Arwel brushed his fingertips over her cheek. "You are such a mother hen. You want to make sure that everyone is okay before you allow yourself to be happy. They are all adults, Jin, and they knew what they were getting into when they asked to join the escape. You are not responsible for them."

She threw her arm over her eyes. "I can't help it. That's how I'm wired."

He lifted her arm and dipped his head to kiss her lips. "For tonight, none of that matters. It's just you and me. Can you do that? Can you clear your mind of all the noise and concentrate on us?"

A smile tugging on one corner of her mouth, Jin shifted to her side. "I know how you can help me do that. When you make love to me, I can't think of anything at all, especially when I'm orgasming."

"I can definitely help with that."

14

JIN

All during breakfast, Jin tried to come up with something to say to her friends other than *Kian told me to do it*. To claim that tethering them was for their own safety would insult their intelligence. They were in an underground facility that no outsiders had access to, and they couldn't leave even if they wanted to because the elevator was programmed to prevent them from reaching the exit.

Tethering them was purely a spying device and a terrible invasion of privacy.

When she and Arwel returned to her room, he pulled her into his arms. "You were frowning all throughout breakfast, and you've barely said a word to me. Did I do something wrong last night?"

She chuckled. "You should know better than that. I lost count of the number of times I climaxed." She kissed him lightly. "You were amazing."

"So what's the bad mood about?"

"I don't want to tether my friends." Jin pulled out of his arms and walked over to the mini fridge. "Why can't Kian put trackers on them instead?" She took out a bottle of water.

Taking it out of her hand, he unscrewed the top as if she couldn't handle the task. Usually she didn't mind his over-the-top chivalry, but this morning it annoyed her.

Jin shook her head. She'd known the guy for a total of four days, and she was talking about usual. Except, it felt as if they'd been together for much longer. Maybe it had to do with how intense those four days had been.

Since the first time she'd seen Arwel, they hadn't been apart for more than an hour.

Or maybe it felt right simply because they belonged together, and that was why it seemed so natural, even easy, to be with Arwel. Two pieces of a whole finding each other and sticking together to form something better and stronger than the sum of its parts.

Talk about getting carried away.

"You've tethered them before." Arwel handed her the bottle. "So they shouldn't make too big of a fuss over it."

Jin rolled her eyes. He hadn't seen the resentful looks she'd gotten after tethering the other trainees. And that had been done only as an experiment, not because the director had wanted her to keep tabs on them.

The other problem was holding on to several tethers at once. It was a mental burden, and finding the right tether to follow wasn't easy. She'd had to concentrate hard to figure out which of her friends had been at the end of what string.

"They didn't make a fuss the first time, but it was a big deal." She took a sip from the water bottle. "The stinky eye looks they gave me are still fresh in my mind."

Arwel shook his head, but she didn't give him a chance to respond.

"Why should I have to tether them when they are right here? Especially since Kian wants them to know that they are tethered. I don't get the advantage of my metaphysical spying over that of a physical device attached to them in a way they can't remove. I'm sure your boy-genius William can come up with something."

"Do you want to talk to Kian?"

She wasn't looking forward to it and doubted she could convince him to change his mind, but it was worth a try.

"Can you call him and ask if he is willing to hear me out? I feel odd about calling him directly, especially since I will have to use your phone."

Arwel chuckled. "I get it. Whenever I want to talk to Kian, I prefer to text him first. With everything he has to do, the guy is so busy and short-tempered that it's better to let him answer at his convenience."

Pulling out his phone, Arwel typed up a short message and sent it.

As several long moments passed without a response, Jin concluded that Kian wasn't going to bother acknowledging her request. After all, she was a nobody, not even a member of his clan.

Not yet.

Or was she?

As Arwel's mate, she probably would have been granted membership. According to Mey, no official ceremony was needed to establish them as a couple, so what determined her status? Did Arwel have to make an official announcement?

Jin stifled a chuckle. He could use the one she'd come up with.

When Arwel's phone buzzed, she hoped it was Kian.

"Yeah, she is right here with me." Arwel handed it to her.

Taking a deep breath, Jin closed her eyes for a moment. "Hi, Kian. Thanks for calling back."

"Arwel said that you wanted to talk to me about tethering your friends. I assume that there is a problem?"

"It's not that I can't do it, but I don't think it's the best way to keep tabs on them. It's not like I follow that tether all of the time. That's impossible to do, especially when I have several attached. Besides, if they do something while I'm not watching, I wouldn't know about it. A physical tracker of some sort would do a much better job."

"I see your point. I'll have William put tracking cuffs on Richard and Wendy, but you still need to tether Jacki because she is going with you, and the cuff is not going to do us much good. You can also tell her that it's for her own safety while on the mission."

Jin exhaled a relieved breath. "Thank you. That's going to be much easier to explain and not as creepy. Also, I forgot to mention something about my talent when I was talking to you and Edna. It's really difficult for me to hold several tethers at once, and even more difficult to follow a particular one to the right person. I guess it's a cognitive load that gets heavier the more people I tether. I think it would be best to leave my mind as unencumbered as possible while I'm connected to Kalugal. Keep the connection uncluttered, so to speak."

Which meant that she would have to release Mey's tether. Most of the time, Jin didn't think of it or even feel it, but that was because she wasn't tethering anyone else at the moment, and the load was light.

"Absolutely. I didn't know that it burdens you like that. Did the program director know about it?"

"Yes. That was the purpose of the experiment. I tethered all of my teammates to test how many I could hold at once, and whether I could follow the tethers to the right people. After three, it got messy. The director told me that when I got an assignment, it would be to tether one person only, and that whenever possible, I would get notified when to follow it, like during important meetings."

"I'm starting to get a better picture of how it works," Kian said. "To know what your target is doing, you need to actively follow the string and listen and watch. You need to suspend whatever you are doing at that moment to concentrate on that."

"Correct."

"Then it's not a good tool to keep tabs on someone. It's only good for emergencies and for spying on people at particular times, not on an ongoing basis."

"That about sums it up."

"Let me think about what to do with Jacki. I'm not sure your tether is the right tool for keeping tabs on her either."

"You are right about it not being good for that, but I think I should tether her, especially when we go after Kalugal. If he messes with my mind and makes me see things, my tether to Jacki might help me see what's really there because she is immune to his mind tricks. Or at least we hope that she is. If he is as powerful as you say, he might be able to compel her as well."

15

ARWEL

"You are good." Arwel took the phone from Jin and put it in his pocket. "Kian accepted your explanation without argument."

"I'm just as surprised as you are. Maybe I have some compulsion power too?"

"You just speak in a language he understands. Logic."

Jin sighed dramatically. "You have no idea how hard it is to find people who are fluent in it. Most have no clue."

"How about me?"

She pursed her lips. "You are an empath, so naturally, your thought process is influenced by your emotions and those of others. You are no Spock, that's for sure."

"And neither are you and Kian. You are both motivated by feelings, and doing the right thing is more important to you than doing the smart thing. Turner, on the other hand, is the most Spock-like person I've ever met. I can't remember if I've mentioned it before, but he is the strategic mastermind behind our most daring missions, and he's also Bridget's mate."

"I would like to meet him."

"You'll get your chance when you move into the village. Or maybe even before that. Turner's curiosity might bring him over here sooner."

"Is he curious about me, or is it my spying talent that interests him?"

"Neither. I bet he wants to hear every detail about that facility and the people in charge of it."

"I'll tell him everything I know, but I'm afraid it's not much."

"Nevertheless, he'll want to know every little detail and store it in his big brain for later."

Jin finished the last of her water and tossed the empty bottle into the trashcan. "I need to tell Jacki about the tether."

"Do you want me to come with you?"

"Yes, please. You can back me up if she gets snappish."

Since it was no longer Kian who wanted Jacki tethered, Arwel wondered how he was supposed to do that. But if Jin needed him to come with her, he would.

They found Jacki in Mey and Yamanu's place, which had become the central hub for the dungeon inhabitants.

"I need to talk to you." Jin sat next to her friend on the couch.

Arching a brow, Jacki crossed her legs. "About?"

"Tethering you."

Arwel stifled a chuckle. Jin was no diplomat, that was for sure. She rivaled Kian in her no-nonsense, get-straight-to-the-point attitude.

Walking over to the dining table, he pulled out a chair and joined Yamanu. "This should be good," he said in a whisper inaudible to humans.

"I thought that you'd removed the tether." Jacki narrowed her eyes at Jin. "Did you put out a new one without telling me?"

Jin huffed. "Do you always jump to conclusions without hearing the explanation first?"

"Just say yes or no."

"No, I didn't tether you without your knowledge, but I want to explain why I think tethering you is a good idea." She glanced at the open door. "Can you please close it? I don't know how much I'm allowed to say around the others."

"It's better that they don't know too much about your target." Yamanu pulled out his phone and activated the door's mechanism.

When it clicked into place, Jin continued. "I don't have to do it now, but definitely before we go after that guy. Since you are immune to his mind tricks, I might be able to see the real him through your eyes."

Jacki shook her head. "I don't think so. He is not manipulating your eyesight. Your eyes see one thing, but your brain translates it into what he wants you to see. So even though your connection to me doesn't pass through your eyes, it still needs to enter your brain. Your brain will turn what you get from me into whatever Kalugal wants everyone to see."

That sounded logical, and given Yamanu's nodding, he thought so as well.

Mey, on the other hand, seemed to disagree. "Not necessarily. I'm not a neuroscientist, and maybe you should consult Amanda about it, but even as a layperson I know that the brain has many regions and processing centers. It's not straightforward like a computer. Kalugal might be affecting the visual and auditory perceptions, but the feed from the tether may rely on a different mechanism and get processed by a different region in the brain."

That made sense too.

Yamanu nodded proudly. "My lady is smart."

Jacki cast him an amused glance. "And you are not at all biased."

He shrugged. "I am. But I'm also right. You are smart too."

"Thank you." Jacki rewarded him with a happy smile.

It seemed important to her that other people regarded her as smart. Did she feel insecure because of her lack of a college education?

That was nonsense, of course. Should he mention that the formidable Kian had never received any formal education? And that neither he nor Yamanu had gone to school either?

Nah, that would open up a whole can of worms, with a lot of why questions he couldn't answer truthfully.

"So, what do you say? Are you okay with me tethering you?"

"On one condition." Jacki lifted a finger.

"Name it."

"You have to promise to remove it as soon as you tether Kalugal."

"Of course. I don't want to have you tied to me indefinitely. As much as I like you, that's a mental burden I can do without."

Jacki's lips twisted in a half-smile, half-grimace. "That didn't sound very friendly to me, but it will do."

Arwel cleared his throat. "Maybe you shouldn't remove the tether right away. Wait until we get back."

"I don't want Jin in my head for a moment longer than absolutely necessary. It's a creepy feeling. Would you like it if she tethered you?"

He hadn't thought about that before, but Jin having a tether to him might open up very interesting possibilities. When they were making love, she could see herself through his eyes.

Damn. Just thinking about it got him stiff as a baseball bat.

Shifting in his chair, Arwel affected an innocent expression. "I would love it. In fact, I'm going to insist on it."

"Really?" Jin regarded him with a frown. "You don't mind me seeing everything that you do?"

"I have no secrets from you." He pushed to his feet, walked over to her, and offered her a hand up. "Let's go to your place, and I'll explain the benefits."

His lady was smart, getting his meaning right away.

Letting him pull her up, she wrapped her arm around his middle and smiled at the others. "Excuse us, but Arwel and I have some private matters to discuss."

Mey stifled a giggle, Yamanu rubbed a hand over his jaw, and Jacki rolled her eyes.

"Will we see you two at lunch?" Mey asked.

Shrugging, Jin winked. "Maybe."

16

KIAN

"Turner is already here." Anandur pulled into the restaurant's parking lot. "That's his Tesla." He pointed at the car.

"Did you memorize his license plate?" Kian asked. "Turner's black Tesla is a popular model."

Anandur turned the ignition off. "Did you forget that I followed him around after he'd asked you to turn him immortal?"

"I had assumed he'd gotten a new one since then."

"Nah. It's the same one."

Stepping out of the SUV, Kian glanced at his watch. "We are not late. He always gets to the meeting place first."

"That's because his office is less than a five-minute drive away from here. He doesn't have to deal with traffic."

What Anandur had hinted at was that Kian, as the head of the clan, shouldn't have to drive forty minutes to meet Turner. It should be the other way around.

There was something to that, but it wasn't about a power play. He and Turner were both super busy, but since it was Kian who needed a favor from Turner, it was only fair that he meet the guy where it was convenient for him.

"I'm just glad that the place has a good selection of excellent vegan dishes for me. I don't mind the drive."

As usual, they found Turner sitting in the restaurant's most private booth. It was close to the kitchen, which was the main downside, but it was also the farthest from the other tables and booths.

"Good afternoon." Kian slid into the bench across from Turner and offered him his hand. "Thanks for meeting me."

Anandur sat next to him and Brundar next to Turner, which was another habit they'd adopted. Turner didn't like to be crowded, which couldn't be helped with Anandur's bulk, but he was fine with Brundar sitting next to him. It had probably more to do with how quiet the guy was and how still he sat than with his slim build.

"I'm sorry I couldn't make it to the village for a lunch meeting. I'm in the middle of planning a complicated rescue mission, and I want to be done with the initial framework by the end of the day."

Kian unfurled the napkin and put it over his knees. "The downside to meeting here is that I can't smoke my cigarillos. The upside is the food. I need to bring Okidu here to sample them. Perhaps he can figure out what goes into the vegan dishes."

"I'll bring Callie here," Brundar offered. "She can analyze your favorites and write a recipe for Okidu."

"Thanks. That's a better idea." The task might be too complicated for Okidu.

Turner reached for the breadbasket, looked at it, and then pushed it toward Kian without taking anything. "What did you want to talk to me about?"

Kian lifted a slice of bread. "The other recruits. Those we've left behind."

Turner arched a brow. "I thought we decided to leave them be for now."

"My conscience is not letting me do that, especially the kids. I've been thinking about their families, and that they might be at risk too. What if those kids have siblings? Even if they don't manifest special abilities, the program's director might go after them as well. He might even go after the parents and test them to figure out the genetic combination that produced their special children. Given what Jin told me about the super-babies he was pushing for, that's not a farfetched scenario."

Turner leaned back. "They could do that to the families of the adults too. Do you want to rescue them all?"

It was a rhetorical question, but Kian nodded. "If I can."

Turner sighed. "That is not your job, Kian. Shit is happening all around the world that is much worse than this, and you can't do anything about it. You are already going above and beyond by fighting trafficking."

"This is different. These might be my people. The adults, the kids, and their families are all likely Dormants."

When the waitress arrived to take their orders, Turner seemed relieved to hit pause on the conversation. His opinion on the matter was clear, but despite his opposition to taking action, Kian needed the guy's big brain to come up with a creative idea for getting the rest of the recruits out of the program.

Once the waitress left, Turner shook his head. "Give it a rest, Kian. You don't want the government breathing down your neck. You can't ask for a worse enemy. The Doomers will seem like annoying mosquitoes next to the big gorilla that would come after you."

Raking his fingers through his hair, Kian sighed. "I know that. I was hoping that you could come up with a brilliant solution. So far, it seems that they are not making too much of a fuss over the missing talents, right?"

Turner nodded. "There is an APB on Richard. He is accused of kidnapping the three ladies, and photos are included. It's important for all four to stay in hiding or use good disguises when they venture out. Later, those who do not transition should consider either plastic surgery or moving out of the country."

"I've seen the APB. Roni showed it to me. Doesn't it strike you as odd, though, that that is the extent of it? Roni did some snooping around, and apparently there were no airport searches either."

The lack of serious pursuit only reinforced Kian's gut feeling that one of Jin's friends was a mole.

"I know what you're thinking," Turner said. "But there might be another explanation for why their escape didn't get more attention. The program is top secret, and they want to keep it that way. Making too much of a fuss about the four escapees might attract unwanted attention to what they are doing. Especially if some of it is not sanctioned by the higher-ups. I would be very surprised if the program for breeding super-babies had gotten official approval."

Kian snorted. "The government has done much worse in the past. Like exposing soldiers to toxic materials and later covering it up. I wouldn't put it past them to approve a fucking breeding program."

Turner's lips narrowed. "That was a long time ago. Things have changed."

Kian snorted. "Take it from someone who's been around for a very long time. The more things change, the more they stay the same. But if you are right, and the program's director or directors are not interested in anyone finding out what they are doing there, it gives us an advantage. We can snatch people with impunity. They will be more interested in keeping their activities secret than finding out who is stealing the paranormals and their families."

Reaching for a bread roll, Turner tore it in half. "I can assure you of one thing. After the escape, there will be no more outings for the recruits, not without them being implanted with serious tracking devices. And if they do get to go anywhere, it will be with a strong security detail."

That was regrettably true.

"I hoped that we could take them out sooner, but it seems like we will have to wait for the program to end and for the recruits to go home to their families. We can snatch them then."

Turner arched a brow. "What if they don't want to come? And what if they get a tail?"

"We can thrall the tail. I doubt they have immune snoops on staff, other than Eleanor, aka Marisol. And as to willingness, we will need to approach the families first and explain what's going on. If they don't believe us or prefer to ignore what we have to say, we can thrall them to forget about us or compel them to silence. If they agree, we can just compel them to silence to ensure their discretion."

"I see that you already have a plan of action. What do you need me for?"

That was another rhetorical question, but Kian answered it anyway. "I want you to point out all the pitfalls and suggest safeguards."

Turner nodded. "The most important thing is to avoid the government's notice. We need to come up with a decoy, or rather a scapegoat. Someone we can cast suspicion on that would divert attention from us."

"The Chinese," Anandur offered. "They wanted Jin and took whoever was with her."

Kian chuckled. "And then they decided to go back for the others?"

Anandur shrugged. "Why not? They are good at spotting opportunities and even better at stealing ideas from others."

"You might be onto something," Turner said. "The question is how to implicate the Chinese."

Grinning, Anandur spread his arms. "I provided the idea. It's your specialty to turn it into an actionable plan."

17

JIN

"That's awesome." Mey ended the call and grinned. "Eva is coming to teach you two how to put on your disguises, and she is bringing little Ethan with her." Mey danced a happy dance. "I'm so excited. I can't wait to hold him in my arms and kiss his soft little cheeks."

Jacki smiled. "Someone needs her baby fix."

Jin shook her head. "You and Yamanu should start working on it." She regretted the words as soon as they'd left her mouth. Damn, she really didn't know when to keep it shut.

Way to spoil Mey's good mood.

Her smile melting away, Mey cast Jin a reproachful look. "We need to get married first. You know how Mom and Dad are. They like things to happen in the right order."

The real reason for Mey's sad face was the low fertility rate immortals suffered from. She'd shared the information with Jin on one of the rare occasions that they'd been alone, but she'd also mentioned something about an elixir the other clan doctor had developed that was supposed to help with that. Mey would be miserable if she had to wait centuries to have a baby.

Glad that her sister had brought up wedding plans, Jin jumped at the opportunity to change the subject. "Speaking of nuptials, are you going to design your own wedding dress?"

That brought the smile back to Mey's face. "I have a couple of ideas, but I think I should have a professional work with them instead of doing the whole thing myself. I'm not confident enough in my skills yet."

"If you need someone to sew it, I know how," Jacki offered. "You can get some inexpensive fabric for a trial run or two. I'll need a sewing machine, though."

Jin and Mey exchanged glances. Jacki was full of surprises.

"Where did you learn how to sew, and why?"

Jacki shrugged. "One of my foster moms was creative. She made Halloween costumes for the kids from leftover fabric pieces and altered things that needed fixing."

"That's nice." Jin smirked. "I'm curious to see what Eva has in mind for our disguises. The other time she made me look so different, but I don't think I can pull that off on my own." She waved at Jacki. "You have it easy. A wig and glasses will do the trick."

Jacki shrugged. "The same is true for you. I don't think you should change your ethnicity. There are more than a billion Chinese people in the world. I'm sure many of them are tall. You just need to look a little different, that's all."

"I hear Ethan." Mey jumped up and rushed out into the corridor.

"Your sister must have bat ears," Jacki said. "I didn't hear a thing."

It seemed like Mey's hearing was improving by the day without her realizing it. She should be more careful to hide it from the other humans.

Jin scrambled for an explanation. "I think she has a baby radar."

As the sounds of Mey's baby talk and Ethan's cooing got closer, Jin got up and walked out into the corridor.

"Hi." She offered her hand to the mother, kissed the top of the baby's head, and waved at Bhathian, who was carrying Eva's big trunk.

Holding Ethan, Mey looked in love, and the baby responded with sweet smiles.

Eva shook Jin's hand. "Are you and Jacki ready for your transformation? Kian told me to do my best."

"Your best is not something that Jacki or I can do on our own. We need something just good enough."

"That's what I told Kian. He suggested that I go with you to the Bay Area, but I said that won't be necessary. I can teach you what to do."

"Awesome."

As they walked inside the apartment, Bhathian lowered the trunk to the floor and glanced around. "Where is Yamanu?"

"He is with Arwel in the gym," Mey said.

"I'm going to join them." He kissed his wife's cheek. "Do you want me to take Ethan?"

Mey hugged the baby closer to her chest. "He is perfectly fine with me. Go have fun with the guys."

"Okay." Smiling, he kissed his son's cheek as well. "Be a good boy, Ethan, and don't give Mey any trouble." He leaned closer and pretended to whisper in the baby's ear. "If you behave, she might decide to have a baby of her own, and you'll have someone to play with."

"God willing," Mey said. "I want one just like that. Well, almost. I want my baby to look like his daddy."

"Naturally." Bhathian patted her arm.

"Who goes first?" Eva asked.

"Me." Jacki lifted her hand. "Last time you gave me a makeover but not a changeover. I'm curious to see myself turning into someone else."

Eva pulled out a chair and put it in the middle of the living room. "Take a seat."

"Yes, ma'am."

Popping the lid of her trunk, Eva looked inside, moved a section over, and pulled out four different wigs. "Let's start with the hair. Since your magnificent blond mane is your most striking feature, that is going to be the biggest change."

After pinning Jacki's hair around her head and securing it with a net, Eva fitted her with a shoulder-length brown wig.

"How do I look?" Jacki asked.

She looked plainer and paler. "Twenty percent less sexy." Jin pursed her lips. "Make it twenty-five."

Jacki smiled. "Good. The less attention I attract, the better."

"Put these on." Eva handed her a pair of reading glasses. "Those are the special kind that fool facial recognition software."

"How about now?" Jacki asked.

"Another ten percent reduction in sexiness."

"Does it change me enough, though?" She turned to Mey. "Would you recognize me?"

"Yeah, I would, but only if I looked closely. But if you don't want to attract attention, you should wear a minimizer bra. That cleavage is like a magnet to male eyes."

Jacki looked down at her chest. "Tell me about it. Most guys don't even notice that I have blue eyes."

"About that." Eva pulled out a small box from her trunk. "Have you ever worn contact lenses?"

"Nope."

"These are brown colored. But you might be uncomfortable wearing them."

"I'll give it a try. I'd rather be uncomfortable than get caught."

"Is there anything else Jacki should do?" Jin glanced at the chest. "As drab as the wig makes her look, she is still pretty."

"We don't need to make her look ugly."

"I don't want to attract any attention," Jacki said. "And guys tend to ignore ugly chicks."

"I can do that with makeup." Eva hooked a finger under Jacki's chin and lifted her face. "Put the contacts in first. If you can tolerate them, you'll need less makeup."

Jacki opened the box and looked at the lenses. "What do I do?"

"First, you need to wash your hands. You don't want any dust getting in your eyes."

After several tries the contacts were in, and Jacki looked so different that Jin doubted anything else was needed. "How are you doing? Do you think you can tolerate them for a couple of hours?"

Jacki shrugged. "I can't even feel them. I guess my eyes are not that sensitive."

"That's good." Eva pulled out several jars of foundation from her trunk. "Let's make you look even drabber. I'm going for the grayish, sickly look."

"Awesome." Jacki rubbed her hands. "The uglier I look, the more invisible I become."

18

ARWEL

"Hey, Bhathian, what's doing?" Yamanu called from the bench. "Are you in for some heavy lifting?"

The Guardian grinned. "I'm trying to cut down." He flexed a muscle, straining the seams of his T-shirt. "I keep running out of clothes that fit."

"Show off," Arwel murmured.

Bhathian was a mountain of muscle, and he worked hard for it, but he was also naturally predisposed to gain them faster and with less effort than most immortal males.

"I can spot you guys." He walked over to Yamanu's station.

Arwel could use help with spotting as well. The problem was the ease with which Bhathian could lift what he had to strain for. But those were petty thoughts, unbecoming of a Guardian. They each had their areas of strength, and Arwel had never been on a muscle squad.

"It's good that you came," Yamanu said. "I wanted to talk to you about Vlad. I don't know him well, but you had him in your sex education class together with Jackson and Gordon."

"That was years ago." Bhathian shook his head. "It's hard to believe that Jackson is happily mated and running a successful business of his own. He was such a know-it-all, a real ladies' man, which was what had gotten him in trouble. Someone got jealous of his success with the fairer sex, and that someone was probably Gordon, but he's never admitted it."

"What about Vlad?"

"Vlad is a pure soul. He would have never played such a nasty prank on a friend. Jackson could've been sentenced to whipping."

"Nah." Arwel sat up and reached for a towel. "Not without iron-clad proof. But still, Gordon should have been punished for causing all that brouhaha. Accusing a clan member of thralling a girl into having sex with him is a grave offense."

Bhathian chuckled. "I think Kian decided that suffering through the sex-ed class with me was punishment enough. I scared the living daylights out of those boys. After that, they knew to ask permission for every move they made."

"As it should be," Yamanu said. "But most young guys, whether human or immortal, have no idea how to do that. You should write an instruction manual. It would sell like crazy."

"No one would buy it." Bhathian took the bar from Yamanu and put it on the rack. "The other thing most young guys suffer from is thinking that they know better than their elders. Unless it's coming from the mouth of some idol, or influencer as they call them today, they won't listen to advice."

"We sound like a couple of old farts, bemoaning the shortcomings of a younger generation." Yamanu waved a dismissive hand. "But back to Vlad. I want to introduce him to Wendy. She is lonely. He is lonely. And they are about the same age. What do you think?"

Bhathian rubbed the back of his neck. "Vlad is painfully shy. He wouldn't know how to talk to a girl."

"Wendy seems shy too," Yamanu said.

Arwel dropped the towel on his thighs. "I think that they might work. Usually, I would have advised against putting two timid people together, but you are right about Vlad being the best candidate for Wendy. I can't think of any other male that won't scare her. She's so young."

"Wonder was nineteen when Anandur met her," Bhathian pointed out.

Arwel shook his head. "You can't compare Wonder to Wendy. Wonder entered stasis five thousand years ago. Back then, an eighteen-year-old woman was considered a grownup in every sense of the word. Most had a couple of kids by that age. Nowadays, eighteen is still a child."

Bhathian lifted a weight and started bicep curls. "I assume that you want me to ask the kid?"

Yamanu joined him next to the free weights. "You know him better than I do. He will feel less awkward if you do it."

"I doubt that he will agree, but I can ask."

"Is he that bad?" Yamanu moved the weight to his other hand. "The boy is nineteen, for Fates' sake. At his age, I'd already been active for years." He grimaced. "And had gotten into shitloads of trouble, so maybe Vlad is right about keeping it in his pants."

"I'm sure he is not happy about it," Arwel said. "Show me a nineteen-year-old who wants to be a virgin."

"The boy is a romantic." Bhathian put the weight back on the rack and lifted a heavier one. "He's not the type who would go for a casual hookup."

Yamanu snorted. "I'm a romantic too, but at that age... well, chasing women was a hobby. Hell, it was an obsession. I couldn't think about anything else."

"Is it the same for the lasses?" Bhathian asked. "As an empath, you have the advantage of knowing how they really feel. Do they get boy obsessed?"

"They sure do." Arwel smiled. "When we were setting a trap for Lokan in Georgetown, thoughts of sex were what I was picking up the most, from males and females alike."

"I'm glad I have a boy this time," Bhathian said. "I would have gone nuts if I had been around Nathalie when she was a teenage girl." His face saddened.

"Don't get me wrong. My greatest regret is not being there for her when she was growing up. It's just that I know it would have been difficult."

"You didn't mind when Andrew went after her," Arwel pointed out.

"That's because she was a thirty-year-old woman by then, not a teenager. And Andrew is a standup guy. I couldn't have asked for a better son-in-law."

Arwel shrugged. "Same difference. If you trust your daughter and you like the guy she chooses, it shouldn't be a hardship. On the contrary. If I have a daughter, and if she finds a decent guy who is close to her age and who I approve of, I would be happy for her, even if she was still a teenager."

A knowing smirk lifted one corner of Bhathian's lips. "Let's have this talk again when you actually have a daughter, and she is the most precious person in the world to you. No guy will do for your princess. I'm willing to bet on it."

Arwel offered Bhathian his hand. "How much are we betting on it?"

"A hundred bucks." Bhathian clasped his hand. "Adjusted for inflation."

"Deal."

19

JIN

Undecided about what to take with her, Jin had spent the morning packing and unpacking her few belongings. In the end, she just stuffed everything into the duffle bag Arwel had given her and walked over to Mey's place.

"Are you done packing?" Mey asked.

Jin nodded. "I couldn't decide what to take, so I took everything."

"You're welcome to dive into my closet and take whatever you want."

"Thank you. But I don't need nice things. I need ugly ones, and that's what I'm short on."

Mey pulled her into a hug. "I'm going to miss you. I wish you weren't leaving so soon."

Jin hugged her back. "Thank you for agreeing to stay for a little bit longer. I hope this mission will be over quickly, and I'll return before you have to go back to the village."

Mey smiled. "I wish it was so, but I doubt it. Your target is careful and elusive, and the stakeout will probably be long. They usually are."

"Great." Jin plopped down on the couch. "What am I going to do with myself while the Guardians are trying to locate the *target?*" She smirked. "You sounded like such a pro when you said *target*, like a spy from the movies."

Ignoring her comment, Mey walked over to the media cabinet. "I have a going-away present for you." She opened it and pulled out a flat box.

Jin perked up. "Is that what I think it is?"

"If you think that it's a new laptop, then yes." Mey sat down next to her and handed her the box. "Instead of being bored, you can start working on that business proposal for Kian."

"Thank you." Jin leaned and kissed Mey's cheek. "You are the best. When did you get it? Did you sneak out of here without telling me?"

"I didn't, but Yamanu did."

"Where is he? I want to thank him too." Jin started carefully peeling the cellophane wrapping off. "This is such a nice box."

"He is in the gym, but he said he will be back before it is time for you to leave. He wants to say goodbye."

"What about Vlad? When is he bringing him over?"

"Tomorrow. I hope."

"Why? Doesn't he want to come?"

"He told Yamanu that he has a big project to finish, but Yamanu thinks that Vlad is stalling because he is scared of meeting Wendy."

"Her in particular, or any girl?"

"Any girl."

Jin nodded. "The poor kid has probably never dated before."

"Most likely."

"Maybe they can play William's game together. Wendy gave it another try yesterday, and she's been obsessed with it ever since. She says it's one of the best computer games she's ever played."

"That's a good idea. Maybe Yamanu and I can join them at the beginning, just until they warm to each other, and then leave them to play alone. I can prepare snacks, maybe even dinner."

"Sounds like a plan. Instead of a date, it would be a friendly get-together. That should be less scary for the dude."

Mey chuckled. "I feel like Yamanu and I are the den mother and father."

"Admit it. You are enjoying this." Jin opened the box and pulled out the shiny new laptop. "This is so nice."

"Yamanu also got me a present. But it hasn't arrived yet."

"Oh, yeah? What is it?"

"A tablet and a stylus to draw on it. I'm going to start working on the designs. I haven't done it in so long that I'm out of practice."

Jin hugged the laptop to her chest. "I've been thinking. Since my friends have no job prospects at the moment, maybe we can employ them in our business?"

"We don't have a business yet, and by the time we do, they will probably be doing something else already. Richard is going bonkers from having nothing to do."

"What about him and Ingrid?"

Mey shrugged. "I know just as much or as little as you do. She comes every day, and they hover around each other, but I don't know whether she's stayed the night yet or not."

"I'm sure she has. Ingrid doesn't strike me as the shy type, and I know that Richard is more than ready. The poor guy didn't get any for over a month."

"Right, well." Mey shifted. "That's not the end of the world."

"For us it isn't, but guys are different. I read somewhere that men think about sex constantly."

Mey regarded her with a frown. "Don't you crave Arwel all the time?"

"I do. But that doesn't mean that I'd go crazy if I didn't get him into bed every day."

"Interesting. I was the same way before I met Yamanu, but since then, I crave him quite obsessively. Apparently, it's part of the bond between immortal mates. I wonder why you don't feel the same way."

What was Mey suggesting?

If her sister was wondering whether Arwel was Jin's fated mate, then she wasn't the only one. Jin wasn't sure about it either. In her gut, she felt that he was, but they had just met, and it was too early to make such big decisions.

They liked each other a lot, the sex was phenomenal, and for now, it was enough. Love, commitment, and all that jazz would come later.

Still, it bugged her that Mey doubted their relationship. "Maybe the enhanced libido will come after I transition. Besides, I can talk a big talk, but I might be totally wrong. So far, Arwel and I have been making love at every opportunity, so I didn't have a chance to test my boasting about being able to do without."

Letting out a breath, Mey seemed relieved. "I hope it works out between you two. Arwel is an awesome guy."

"I agree." Tucking the laptop under her arm, Jin pushed to her feet. "I should check on Jacki and see if she needs anything."

"Does she have a suitcase? I can lend her mine," Mey offered.

"Thanks, but Arwel is getting her a bag." Jin leaned and kissed Mey's cheek. "Thank you again for this amazing present. You are the best sister ever."

Mey waved a hand. "Think of it as Yamanu's first investment in our business. That's how he convinced me not to pay him back for the laptop and the tablet."

Smart guy. He might have used it as a persuasion tactic, but Jin was going to take it seriously.

"Ask him for the receipts and write the expense down. That will make it official."

Mey nodded. "Good idea."

20

ARWEL

Jacki's door was open when Arwel walked in with the duffle bag. He'd gotten it from one of the Guardians on rotation in the keep, but it hadn't been given without strings attached. The guy had jokingly conditioned lending it on an introduction to Jacki upon her return, and Arwel had gladly given it.

The sooner Jin's friends found mates, the sooner he could take her to the village and the new home he'd applied for.

He hadn't told Jin about it, first of all because he wanted to surprise her, and secondly, because he didn't want to freak her out by going too fast.

After all, they'd known each other for all of five days, and getting them a house was premature. Jin might think that he was taking her for granted and assuming things he shouldn't.

"Is this big enough?" He handed Jacki the bag.

She put it on the bed next to the small pile of clothes and other stuff. "I don't have much, so that's enough with room to spare."

A minute later, Jin walked in. "Is that all you are taking?" She looked at what Jacki had prepared. "Where is all of Amanda's fabulous stuff?"

"I'm saving it."

"What for?"

Jacki shrugged. "To sell it. I don't know how long I'm going to be stuck in here, or what my prospects are once I can leave. What I'll get for that designer stuff might help me start a new life."

Jin looked at Arwel with sad eyes.

He knew what she wanted, but he couldn't allow it. Until Jacki found an immortal male to bond with, she couldn't know that all of her troubles were most likely over.

"When are we leaving?" Jin asked.

"Kian sent his driver with the limousine. Okidu should be here in about half an hour." Arwel looked at Jacki and rubbed a hand over his jaw. "Once you are done packing and everything is ready, I will need to put you to sleep."

She nodded. "I figured that you would do that."

"Unfortunately, it's necessary," Jin said. "If Kalugal can force you to talk, he can get the location of this hideout from you. But if you don't know where it is, you can't tell him."

Jacki lifted her head and pinned Jin with a hard look. "It's even truer in your case. I'm immune. You are not."

"I'm going to sleep too."

Arwel arched a brow. That wasn't part of the plan. Jin already knew where the keep was.

"I don't understand why blindfolding us is not enough." Jacki started arranging her things in the duffle bag.

"Because we don't want Kalugal to know what city it is in, and since we are flying over to the Bay Area, you might figure it out by the time it takes us to get there."

Jacki looked at him. "Are you that scared of him?"

"He is a dangerous man."

"And yet you are okay with sending your girlfriend after him?"

Arwel pushed his hair back from his forehead. "I'm not okay with her getting anywhere near him, but that's just because I'm overprotective. Kalugal is dangerous to our organization in the sense that he might expose us. But as far as we know, he is not a violent man. He is not going to hurt Jin for just touching him."

"What if he can sense her motives? Maybe in addition to his other powers, he is also an empath?"

Areana hadn't said anything about that, but then the last time she saw her son, he was a little boy. In adulthood, Kalugal might have developed additional powers.

"We will have Guardians securing the perimeter. Worst case scenario, we will muscle Jin and you out."

Jacki snorted. "I was under the impression that Kalugal can compel people. He can tell them to stay away, and they will, including you. Since I'm the only one he can't do it to, I should have a weapon on me. Non-lethal, of course. I don't want to kill him or miss him and kill an innocent bystander. Maybe a taser? Or even mace?"

"That's actually not a bad idea. I'll have to run it by Kian."

That got a smile out of her. "I'm glad that you would trust me with a weapon. I'm sick of being treated like the enemy."

"I'm sorry that you feel that way, but we need to protect ourselves. You should have a pretty good idea about how many people are interested in paranormals and to what lengths they are willing to go to get us."

"I get it. Doesn't mean that I like it." She sat on the bed. "Give me the sleeping pill."

"Are you all done packing?"

She nodded.

"Anything other than the duffle bag that you want to take with you?"

"No, everything is in there, including my purse." She snorted. "That has lipstick and eyeliner in it. I don't have any money or even an identification card."

"Actually, you do." He pulled out an envelope from his back pocket and handed it to her.

Curiosity shining in her eyes, Jacki opened it and pulled out a driver's license. "Charlotte McNamara? Who came up with that name?"

"The guy who made these documents chose it from a list. I think that Charlotte is a nice name."

"I'm Debra Wang," Jin said. "That's not any better."

"It's okay." Jacki looked at the card. "When did you take that picture?"

"Do you remember when Mey was taking photos of your teammates? She took some of you as well. But if you look closely, it's not actually you. The artist created a composite from a stock photo and one of those that Mey snapped."

"Amazing." She reached into the envelope and pulled out a wad of cash and a credit card with the same name. "You guys are thorough. I'll give you that." She riffled through the money. "And generous. Thank you."

There were only three hundred bucks in there, but Jacki regarded the money as if it was a fortune.

Unzipping the duffle bag, she pulled out the purse, put everything he'd given her inside, and then zipped the bag closed. "Now, you can put me to sleep."

Reaching into his shirt pocket, Arwel pulled out a packet with two pills in it. "Julian said these will knock you out for at least six hours."

Jin handed Jacki a bottle of water. "You're gonna have a nice long nap on the plane."

21

JIN

After saying goodbye to her sister and friends, Jin and Arwel returned to Jacki's room together with Yamanu.

"Come on, sleeping beauty." Yamanu snaked his arms under Jacki and lifted her gently.

Jin appreciated him handling her friend with such care, but she wasn't sure Mey would have approved. "I'm glad Mey stayed in your room. She would have been jealous."

"Nah, my mate knows that I'm hers one hundred percent."

Mey might know it logically, but seeing a beautiful woman in her boyfriend's arms would provoke an instinctive response, especially since he was cradling her like a sleeping princess.

Arwel took Jacki's duffle and added it to the two he was already carrying.

"Give me that." Jin reached for the bag. "You don't have to be such a macho man."

He shook his head. "That's nothing for me. Just make sure that Yamanu doesn't bang Jacki's head into something."

Yamanu cast him a haughty look. "She is perfectly safe in my care. I wouldn't let anything happen to her."

Arwel called the elevator down, and the three of them walked in. "You should at least blindfold me," Jin said. "I feel bad about telling Jacki that I would be asleep too and not doing it."

"What's the point? You already know where the keep is."

"All I know is that it's in Los Angeles. I was half asleep when we got here, and it was dark. I have no idea where in the city we are."

Arwel shook his head. "I trust you. Closing your eyes will have the same effect."

Yamanu's shoulders heaved with suppressed laughter.

"What's so funny?" Arwel asked.

"Your lady asks for a blindfold, and you say no? Shame on you."

Arwel's brows shot up.

Jin shook her head. "You have a dirty mind, Yamanu, but I like the way you think."

The elevator doors opened, and Yamanu walked out first, with Jin and Arwel following several steps behind him.

Arwel leaned close to her ear. "If you want to play kinky games, I'm all for it, just not in company."

It hadn't been Jin's intention, but now that Yamanu had brought it up, the thought excited her. Mindful of the immortals' excellent hearing, Jin brought her mouth close to Arwel's ear and covered it with her hand for good measure. "Jacki is asleep, and she is not going to wake up for a long time. And since we are riding in a limousine, we can raise the partition so the driver can't see what we are doing."

The more Jin talked about it, the more turned on she got. There was something very exciting about the idea of sitting blindfolded in the limo while Arwel did all kinds of naughty things to her.

Where had that come from?

Jin had never played games like that, or even fantasized about them.

"I wish," Arwel whispered back. "But three additional Guardians are waiting for us in the limousine, and if you keep broadcasting pheromones like that, it's going to be a very awkward ride."

Talk about a cold shower.

"I thought they were going to meet us at the airstrip."

"That was the plan. They were supposed to share a ride with Magnus and Vivian, but the guys couldn't wait to see Jacki." He snorted. "All the bachelors wanted to be chosen for the mission. The chief had them draw straws to determine the three lucky ones."

Yamanu stopped in front of a door that was marked as storage and looked over his shoulder at Arwel. "Can you get it?"

Arwel punched in the code, and after they walked in, he closed the door behind them and opened the one on the other side.

A long tunnel stretched in front of them.

"Where is the limo waiting for us?" Jin asked.

"The tunnel leads to the lowest parking level at the building across the street. It's a safety precaution."

"I assume that it also belongs to the clan?"

"Kian built most of the high rises on this street." Arwel glanced at Yamanu. "Are you sure you don't want to use the golf cart? I can jog over and bring it."

"I don't want to wait. It's just a short walk."

The tunnel was wide enough for a car to pass through it, and it had dim lights spaced out every twenty feet or so, but it still made Jin uneasy. The echoes of their footsteps and their conversation, together with the long shadows they were casting on the concrete floor, reminded her of scenes from a horror film.

When they finally got to the end of the tunnel, there was another storage room with doors on both sides, and when Arwel opened the last one, Jin let out a relieved sigh.

"Thank God that's over. I really don't like tunnels."

The limousine was parked right next to the door, and the moment they exited, both the driver and the passenger's door opened at the same time.

A big guy jumped out from the passenger side. "Hello, I'm Duncan." He offered his hand to Jin, shook it briefly, and then turned to Yamanu. "Let me relieve you of your beautiful cargo."

As he took Jacki into his arms and brought her close against his chest, Jin cringed. If her friend was awake, she would not like that.

Very carefully, Duncan folded himself into the limo with Jacki.

Kian's butler bowed to Arwel. "May I take the luggage, sir?"

Arwel handed him the bags and followed Jin into the limousine.

Inside, two more Guardians were looking at Jacki like a pair of hungry wolves, their eyes blazing inner light. Duncan, who was holding her and grinning as if he had just won the lottery, didn't look like he was about to part with his prize anytime soon.

"Hello." Jin leaned forward. "I'm Jin. Mey's sister."

"Nice to meet you. I'm Gregor." The one on the right offered his hand.

The one on the left leaned forward and shook her hand as well. "Ewan. A pleasure to make your acquaintance, ma'am."

"Same here. Duncan, do you mind putting Jacki down on the seat? I don't think she would appreciate being held by a stranger."

The shocked expression on the guy's face was comical. He hugged Jacki even closer to his chest, then sighed and motioned for his two friends to move over. "Jin is right."

Carefully, as if he was handling a Jacki-sized china doll, he put her down and then sat on the floor next to her.

Jin stifled a chuckle. "There is plenty of room. You don't need to sit on the floor."

He shook his head. "It's not safe for her. Jacki is still human, and she could get hurt if we get into an accident. If anything happens, I'll catch her."

Arwel shook his head. "You three better start practicing pretending to be humans. Jacki thinks we are an organization of people with paranormal talents, and it's important that she keep thinking that until she finds a mate."

Duncan smirked. "She doesn't have to look far. I'm right here."

"Hey," Ewan protested. "I'm here too. She's asleep, so it's not like she has chosen you."

"We each get a shot," Gregor said.

"May the best man win," Duncan agreed, but given his grin, he'd already assumed the win.

Oh, boy. Jacki was in for a big surprise when she woke up.

"Goldilocks and the three big bears," Jin murmured.

22

ARWEL

"That's the house?" Jin gawked as Arwel pulled the rented van into the driveway. "It's a freaking mansion." She glanced at her sleeping friend. "Jacki is going to flip out when she sees it."

Julian had been right about the two little pills knocking Jacki out. She hadn't stirred once, not when they put her in the limo, not when Ewan had carried her into the clan's aircraft, and not when Gregor had carried her out and into the van.

The upside of Jacki passing the entire trip sleeping had been that no one needed to pretend to be human, and Vivian had told Jin about her and Ella's adventures and how they had ended up with the clan.

Listening to her tell the story, Arwel couldn't help thinking that Ella and her mother were very gracious about forgiving Lokan for what he had planned for them.

Jin had been appalled, calling him a self-centered jerk with little regard for others. She was convinced that Lokan's selfish interest was the only reason he'd helped Kian get her and her friends out of the program. He wanted to find out what his brother was up to, and Jin was the only one who could do that for him.

Arwel had to agree. Kian and Lokan cooperated because it benefitted them both, not because they liked each other, and not because they were cousins.

"It's easy to get used to luxury," Vivian said. "Magnus and I have been pretending to be rich for a couple of weeks, and I can't say that I didn't enjoy it." She sighed. "I miss my home, though. It was hard to get on the plane and leave my kids behind again. But I owe Kian, and he needs Magnus and me to go on keeping up appearances."

Michael opened the front door. "Do you need help carrying things inside?"

"We've got it covered." Ewan got out of the van.

Without verbally agreeing on it, everyone knew that it was Duncan's turn to carry Jacki again, while the others took care of the luggage.

"Welcome to Chateau Kri." The Guardian spread her arms and turned in a circle. "What do you think?"

"It's impressive." Jin looked at the high ceiling with the exposed wooden beams crisscrossing it. "Are those real?"

Kri shook her head. "It's not structural, if that's what you're asking. It's just a decoration, but the wood is real." She smiled and offered Jin her hand. "I'm Kri." She waved her hand at Michael. "And this is my mate, Michael."

"Nice to meet you." Jin appraised Kri from top to bottom and up again. "You are the perfect customer for the fashion line my sister and I want to launch. Have you ever considered modeling?"

Kri's jaw dropped, and then she started laughing. "Do I look like a model to you?"

"Why not? You are tall and pretty. Our fashion line is going to be for tall women who can't find flattering stuff in department stores."

Kri shrugged her leather jacket off and flexed her biceps. "Do you still think I can model for you?"

"Sure. You'll be perfect for the sports line." Jin didn't sound as sure as she pretended to be, but it was a good save.

"In that case, count me in." Kri smiled happily. "I mean, as much as I can. I work full time as a Guardian, and I volunteer many hours a week teaching girls self-defense."

Jin put her hand over her heart and tipped an invisible hat to Kri. "That's so incredibly admirable."

The Guardian waved a dismissive hand. "It's nothing. I'm good at just one thing, so I make the most of it." She glanced at Duncan, who was still standing with Jacki in his arms. "Let me show you to her bedroom. Follow me." She started walking toward the stairs and then stopped and turned around. "In fact, you can all come, and I'll show you your rooms."

As they all headed for the grand staircase, William walked in. "Hello, everyone. How was your trip?" He looked at Jacki and then lifted his head to Duncan. "Has she been asleep the entire time?"

"Yes," Arwel answered for the Guardian. "Are you done securing the property?"

"I installed the disrupters and they are already working, so everyone can talk freely without fear of being overheard." He looked at Jacki again. "As much as it's possible with our guest."

"Come on," Kri beckoned. "You can go over the security protocol later. Let's get everyone settled first."

When they got to the second-floor hallway, Kri opened the door to what looked like a little girl's room. "You can put Jacki on the bed. Don't blame me for the decor because it was like that when we got here. I tried to make it look more grown up with the bedding."

"Jacki won't mind." Jin walked over to the bed and folded the comforter. "Put her down, Duncan. I'll tuck her in."

Reluctantly, he let go of his cargo.

"Let's keep moving," Kri said once Jin was done taking Jacki's shoes off and covering her with the blanket. "The master bedroom is next."

The Guardian opened the double doors to a big room with a massive king-sized bed. "This is where the three of you are going to stay." She waved at the men.

Jin frowned. "Shouldn't Vivian and Magnus take the master?"

Kri opened the French doors, showing everyone the balcony, and then closed them. "This is the stakeout room. And since it should be accessible at all times, I figured that it would be best for the bachelors to stay in it." She winked at Vivian.

That made sense, but only if there weren't enough bedrooms in the house. They could leave the master unoccupied and use it only for observation.

"How many bedrooms are there?" Arwel asked.

"Six," Vivian said.

The house looked larger. Arwel made a quick calculation in his head. There were three couples and five bachelors. The three Guardians would have to stay in the master bedroom.

Apparently, Gregor had just arrived at the same conclusion. "We can't all sleep in one bed."

"Two in the bed, and one on the couch." Kri chuckled. "Unless one of you prefers to sleep in the bathtub to sharing a bed with a friend. Or, you can run tomorrow to a store and buy an inflatable mattress." She kept on walking. "This is Vivian and Magnus's room. Luckily for us, all the secondary bedrooms have queen-sized beds."

"Lucky indeed." Vivian stepped inside. "This is lovely. And the bedding looks very nice. Thank you, Kri."

"You are welcome."

"When did you and Michael have time to do all this prep work?" Jin asked. "Arwel told me that you got the keys yesterday evening."

"There wasn't that much to be done, and we hustled. We got bedding, towels, food, and some pantry stuff. Whatever is missing, we can get tomorrow."

As Kri assigned the fifth bedroom to Jin and him, Arwel looked out into the corridor, where William was patiently waiting for the tour to be over.

"What about you? Where are you sleeping?"

"The maid's room downstairs. I've set up my command post in the home office, and the maid's room is the closest to it."

23

JIN

*J*in sat on her friend's bed and put her hand on her shoulder. "Come on, Jacki, wake up. It's been five and a half hours since you took the sleeping pills." When that didn't help, she added, "It's dinner time."

Jacki's eyes popped open. "I'm starving."

"I thought so. The last meal you had was breakfast."

Throwing off the comforter, Jacki looked at the room. "Someone likes pink."

"This must have been the daughter's room."

"I don't really mind. I need to use the bathroom."

"It's over there." Jin pointed.

Five minutes later, Jacki was ready, and they headed out.

"This is one hell of a place. It's like a freaking palace." Jacki put her hand on the curving banister. "I've never been in a house like this. This alone was worth the headache." She rubbed her temple. "I don't know how people can take sleeping pills every night. I feel so groggy."

Jin wrapped her arm around Jacki's shoulders. "Did you have nice dreams?"

"If I did, I don't remember. Why are you smiling like that?"

Jin leaned to whisper in her ear. "Three hunky guys were fighting over the right to carry you from place to place, and William is here too. So, from Goldilocks and the three burly bears, the cast expanded to four."

Jacki grimaced. "Yay me. Can you get me a fly swatter? Or better yet, a bear spray?"

"Wait until you see them and then ask me. Come on, I promised Vivian that we will help her make dinner."

"Who is Vivian?"

"Ella's mother. She's very nice."

"Oh, right. She donated some of the clothes for Wendy."

"Yeah, that's the one."

"Where is everyone?" Jacki asked as they passed the family room.

"The three bears are upstairs, setting up the stakeout room. They brought an old-fashioned, non-electronic scope."

"Much good it is going to do them at night."

"Yeah. I don't know what they are going to do about that. Maybe they just want to collect the license plate numbers. Anyway, Arwel and William are in the home office, where William has set up shop. And Kri and Michael are in the home gym."

"Are they nice?"

"I didn't get to talk to Michael much, but Kri is awesome." Jin smiled. "She is as tall as I am, but her shoulders are twice as big as mine. The girl is a serious bodybuilder."

In the kitchen, they found Vivian standing next to a big pot of pasta sauce.

"Hello, Jacki." She smiled. "I'm Vivian. Ella's mom."

Jacki walked up to the petite woman. "You look more like her sister than her mom."

"Thank you. I was eighteen when I had Ella."

"Still, good for you. You must be taking good care of yourself."

"I try." Vivian looked at the pot and grimaced. "I don't know how to cook for so many people. Can you taste this and tell me if it's any good?" She handed Jacki the stirring spoon.

Scooping some on her finger, Jacki tasted the sauce. "It needs some spicing up. I'll tell you what. I'll take over the pasta and you two chop vegetables for the salad."

"Thank you." Looking grateful, Vivian took the mittens off and handed them to Jacki.

Turned out that Jacki knew her way around a kitchen. Bossing them around like a military chef, she managed to produce a big meal with something for everyone.

"Where did you learn to cook like that?" Jin asked as they carried the stuff to the dining room.

"Did you forget that I was a foster kid? Usually, the foster parents took in as many kids as they could get because it was good money. We all had our chores, and that included kitchen duty. I've always cooked for many people."

"Thank you for saving the day," Vivian said. "I'm going to call everyone to the table."

She started walking away.

"Don't go. I'll do that," Jacki said. "Yo! Everyone! Dinner is ready!"

Vivian clapped her hands over her ears. "Did you also serve as a drill sergeant in the military?"

Jacki chuckled. "My skills were honed at the foster homes."

"How many have you been in?" Jin asked.

"A few. It's a common thing to switch homes." Jacki's expression closed up, indicating that the topic was no longer open for discussion.

Grabbing a serving tray, she headed to the dining room. Exchanging glances, Vivian and Jin each grabbed something and followed her out of the kitchen.

William, Magnus, and Arwel were already there, with Gregor and Ewan arriving a moment later. Kri and Michael were the last.

"Where is Duncan?" Jin asked.

"It's his turn on watch." Gregor walked up to Jacki. "I'm Gregor. It's a pleasure to meet you."

"Yeah, same here." She offered him her hand.

He lifted it up to his lips and kissed the back of it.

Jacki pulled it out of his grasp. "Let's do the introductions while we eat. I don't want the food to get cold. Who is bringing a plate for the guy upstairs?"

"I'll do it." Ewan, who looked disappointed at missing his chance to kiss Jacki's hand, lifted a plate and started loading it with food. "I'll need two. One will not be enough for Duncan."

Jacki shook her head. "Take him this one, and once you are done eating, switch places with him so he can eat his second serving with everyone."

"Yes, ma'am." Ewan saluted.

As Jin watched Jacki take over and boss everyone around, it occurred to her that she didn't know her friend as well as she thought she did. This was a whole new facet of her that she hadn't seen before.

Jacki was assertive, but in the program, she had never demonstrated any aspirations towards leadership and had been happy to hang back and watch the others. It seemed, though, that she was a natural at it.

Who knew?

24

ARWEL

"That was excellent." Ewan put his fork down and looked at Jacki. "Thank you to all the cooks."

"You're welcome. Are you going to switch places with Duncan now?"

"Yes, ma'am."

"Thank you." Jacki rewarded him with a smile. "And because you are so nice, I'll bring you coffee and dessert upstairs."

Ewan looked as if he'd just won the lottery. "That would be much appreciated."

Watching the guys compete for Jacki's attention was better than any reality show on the dumb box. So far, the Guardians and William were all acting quite gentlemanly, but that was because she wasn't showing interest in any of them. Once she picked a favorite, the competition could get vicious.

The question was, why wasn't she responding to any of them?

All four men were good-looking, each in his own way. William could still lose some weight and get in shape, but what he lacked in big muscles he compensated for with big brains.

Jacki wasn't into women either. If she were, Amanda and Carol would have gotten some reaction from her, but they hadn't. So that wasn't the issue either.

Perhaps she just wasn't sexual, and what a waste that would be.

Jacki was a knockout, the typical all-American girl, with long blond hair, blue eyes, and a tall, curvy figure that was just right.

Duncan walked into the dining room and sat in the chair that Ewan had vacated. "I saw someone leave the mansion in a fancy-ass car. I got excited, thinking I was going to spot Kalugal, but it was someone else." He turned to Jacki and flashed her his most charming smile. "Hi, I'm Duncan."

"Nice to meet you." She smiled but didn't put her utensils down. Probably to forestall any ideas he might have about kissing her hand. "I don't get how you could see inside the car. Was the light on?"

"It was a Ferrari convertible. I could see the driver perfectly." Duncan started loading a plate. "That's one hell of an expensive car. I wonder if Kalugal lets his men borrow his toys, because I doubt that anyone else has one."

"Maybe they are all loaded," Gregor said. "And since they don't have housing expenses, they can afford fancy-ass cars."

"We don't pay rent either." Duncan scooped up spaghetti on his fork. "Do any of us drive a three-hundred-thousand-dollar car?"

As Arwel nudged his foot under the table, the guy arched a brow. "What?"

Idiot. He shouldn't be talking about having no rent expense. Jacki might ask how come, and then they would have to make up a story.

"We could if we wanted to." Gregor crossed his arms over his chest.

Jacki frowned. "How much are you guys getting paid that you can afford a luxury like that?"

"Not that much," Arwel jumped in before the guys could blurt out more incriminating details. "Gregor is talking hypothetically."

"Did you write down the license plate?" William asked.

"Naturally."

"Text it to me. I want to check something."

Duncan pulled out his phone. "It's done."

"If I ever buy a fancy car, it's going to be a Lamborghini. Those are damn sexy." Duncan looked at Jacki, but she didn't react.

Apparently, fancy cars were not her thing.

While the other Guardians kept the discussion going about which car was best, William got busy texting.

"What is it?" Arwel asked.

"I have a hunch that I want Roni to check up on. I'm having him run the license plate through a program we designed. It's comparing the footage from the parking lots of restaurants, cafés, and bars in the area. Once he gets a match. I want him to look at the feed from inside the place that the car is parked next to."

Several moments and texts later, William grinned. "Bingo. Just as I thought. It was him."

Arwel leaned forward. "Kalugal?"

"The program found the car parked in the valet parking lot of Dorothea's, and Roni identified Kalugal on the feed coming from inside the restaurant."

"Did one of his men drive over to pick him up?" Vivian asked.

"No. He was the dude behind the wheel. Apparently, he doesn't leave the house without shrouding himself, and that was what Duncan saw. Except, his shroud only works on brains, it doesn't work on equipment."

Magnus waved a hand. "Then we should take snapshots of everyone leaving that house."

"That won't be enough," William said. "Apparently, his shroud extends over a large area. It can't fool the camera, but it can fool the observers, unless they are too far away from him to be affected. Because we are within Kalugal's range of mind manipulation, we will see what he wants us to see even when looking at a snapshot. The effect will be lost when he gets far enough, but by then we would have lost his trail anyway. The only thing that will work is sending the picture to Roni right away, and him telling us who's really in the car. Besides, at night, we won't be able to see the driver inside the vehicle, and Roni will need to locate him for us like he did just now."

Jacki rubbed her temples. "This is all so complicated and bizarre that following your logic brought my headache back. Perhaps I should be the one watching the gate. He can't fool me because I am immune to his tricks."

"Right, I forgot about that." William pushed his glasses up his nose. "You can look at the photos taken during daylight."

"What about clubs?" Jacki asked. "He is a young guy, right? Is he single?"

"He is." William put the phone on the table. "But we haven't caught him in a club yet. Actually, this is only the second time that we've gotten him on camera at all, which is odd. He must leave the house more often than that."

"Maybe he has a tunnel leading out somewhere else," Jin suggested.

She was probably thinking about the keep and the tunnel leading to the building across the street.

Arwel took her hand and gave it a little squeeze, reminding her not to say anything about it in front of Jacki. "That's possible, but Kalugal doesn't need it. He is confident that his shrouds are camouflaging his comings and goings."

"Maybe he goes to clubs that you are not monitoring," Jacki suggested. "He might be partying in San Francisco, and if he is, then you are screwed because there are probably hundreds of them."

"Or he takes care of the camera feed." William took his phone and started texting. "I'll ask Roni to watch the feed and see if it disappears at some point. Kalugal might erase it before he leaves the place."

"Why does he go to so much trouble to hide?" Jacki asked. "And why is he so important to your organization?"

Anticipating the questions, Arwel had prepared the answers. "He uses the shrouding to get inside information about stocks. And it's crucial for him to keep his identity hidden or he'd get caught. He also might pose a threat to our organization. We would rather have him as an ally than a foe, but we need to find out the extent of his illegal activity."

Leaning back, Jacki crossed her arms over her chest and narrowed her eyes at Arwel. "I don't buy your explanation, and frankly, I don't care what your real reason is. Just tell me one thing. Are you planning on killing him?"

"No."

"You sure about that?"

"Positive."

"How so? Because you are the good guys?" Her tone was mocking.

"We are, and also because he is Kian's cousin, and Kian's mother would be majorly pissed if we killed her nephew."

Arwel figured the information would be meaningless to Jacki, but because it was the truth, it would sound convincing.

Her eyes widened. "But if he is family, why doesn't Kian just call him and talk to him?"

"Kalugal doesn't know that Kian is his cousin. In fact, he doesn't know anything about his mother's side of the family because he hasn't seen her since he was a boy."

Jacki's eyes softened. "Are his parents divorced?"

"Worse. His father is a dangerous man, and Kalugal is hiding from him." As

Jin kicked Arwel under the table, he put his hand over hers and gave it a little squeeze, reassuring her that it was okay before continuing. "That's another reason he is so careful. He probably fears his father more than the authorities and definitely more than us."

Naturally, that answer prompted Jacki to ask more questions. "Why? What would his father do to him if he finds him?"

Jin pulled her hand out of Arwel's clasp. "Force Kalugal to come home and join his crime syndicate," she said. "Or kill him." She pushed to her feet. "I'm ready for coffee and dessert. Are you coming to help me?"

"Yeah." Jacki got up. "Let's divide the chores. The guys can clear the table and load the dishwasher while we take care of the coffee and cake."

"There is a cake?" Kri asked. "Because Michael and I didn't buy any. We only got cookies."

"Cookies will do," Jacki said.

25

JIN

Jin sat down on the bed and crossed her arms over her chest. "Kian said that this was supposed to be top secret, and yet you just blurted it to Jacki. What's the deal with that? And you also promised to tell me more about Annani and Areana and never did."

She hadn't wanted to ask him in front of Jacki because Arwel would have given her a censored version, and the truth was probably fascinating.

He sat next to her on the bed. "It's a long story, and it doesn't really matter. Kalugal and Kian could be enemies or allies, depending on Kalugal's agenda. Even Lokan doesn't know the guy, and he is his full-blood brother."

After kicking her shoes off, Jin swung her legs onto the bed and pushed up against the headboard. "We have time. Tell me the whole story."

He followed her, wrapping his arm around her middle. "I would rather spend the time doing something else."

Jin wanted that too, but later. Right now, her curiosity had been whetted and she wanted to hear about the two sister goddesses. "Tell me an abbreviated version. Or is it a story I'm not supposed to know?"

"Frankly, I'm not sure." Snaking his hand under her shirt, he drew small circles on her belly. "Kian said that you shouldn't be told too much, not because he didn't trust you, but because there is a slight chance that Kalugal could capture you. He could get any information out of you."

"But he can do that to anyone, right?"

Arwel nodded. "Except for Jacki, but she doesn't know anything. You and she are the only ones who will get close to him, and if he is also a strong empath, he might feel your anxiety or your intention to attach a tether to him. It's very unlikely, but it's always better to err on the side of caution."

"So, tell me only the things that Kalugal already knows."

"I can't. He will wonder how you found out. You already know too much because Kian didn't think it through when he told you Kalugal's background. If he compels you to tell him everything you know, he might realize the clan's weaknesses and how to exploit them."

When the hand that had been drawing lazy circles around her belly button inched higher, it became harder to think.

"You are distracting me."

He smirked. "Do you want me to take my hand away?"

"No. Keep going but keep talking too."

"You think I can?" He cupped her breast over her bra.

"Give it a try. We can call it the focus and endurance test."

"Are you challenging me?" He tweaked her nipple.

"Yes. Let's see who can keep up a coherent conversation longer." She wasn't sure who was going to win that game, but even though it was going to be torturous, it would be fun to try. It was a challenge, and Jin loved pushing herself to the limit.

Besides, she was a spy in training, and spies should be able to extract information from their targets even during sex. Heck, especially then.

Oh, damn. Now she really had to win.

"Any rules?" Arwel pushed her shirt up and the bra cups down, and then dipped his head to lick her nipple.

Jin shut her eyes. He wasn't going to make it easy on her. But then she was planning on doing the same to him.

"No rules. Anything goes."

"Oh, lass, you should never say that to a guy."

He nipped her nipple, sending a zing of pain straight into her core, the tiny current turning the dial on her burner from simmer to high.

"I trust you."

Raking her fingers through Arwel's long hair, Jin was glad that Amanda had only trimmed it a little instead of giving him a full haircut. Fisting his silky hair, she held him to her breast.

He lifted a pair of glowing eyes to her. "That means a lot to me."

The adoration in his gaze was enough to melt her resolve, but she wasn't going to let him distract her. "That look is not going to work. Start talking."

He looked at her breasts with longing. "I can't talk and kiss these at the same time."

"Yes, you can. Alternate."

"Okay." He sucked on her other nipple, then let it go and cupped both breasts. "Annani and Areana are half-sisters. They shared a father but had different mothers. In the gods' culture, that wasn't considered a close blood relation. A half-brother and a half-sister who shared only a father could mate."

"Gross," Jin murmured.

"Yeah, I agree. According to their beliefs, the hereditary material passed through the mother, not the father, but we know it's not entirely true. It seems that the immortality gene passes through the mother, but paranormal talents can pass through the father as well. Lokan and Kalugal are proof of that. They inherited their powers from Navuh."

"Can't you check it? I'm sure that the clan doctor could examine the goddess's blood."

"Even if Annani allowed it, which I don't think she would, we don't have Areana's blood to compare, and we can't get it."

"Do they look alike?"

"Not at all. Annani is a tiny redhead with a strong and fiery personality to match that wild hair of hers. Areana is a tall blonde, who is mellow and timid and so lacking in power that she is supposedly weaker than most immortals."

"So, maybe they were right about the genetics. Heck, one of Kian's single sisters could marry Kalugal and bring peace to the two factions like they used to do in the olden days. They are only second cousins, and that's not a problem genetically even for humans. Second cousins marrying each other is common in many cultures."

26

ARWEL

"Not a bad idea, but I doubt that Sari or Alena would be game for that, and not because Kalugal is a second cousin. He is an ex-Doomer of questionable morality, and even though he is of even purer blood than they are, Annani's daughters would look down on him."

Jin frowned. "What about Amanda? You told me that Dalhu is an ex-Doomer too, and that he was just a lowly commander."

"That's different. The Fates brought those two together. They were destined for each other. No one wanted Dalhu to be Amanda's mate, not even Amanda. She went away for a while, hoping she could get over him, but the pull to come back was too strong. Fated mates can't stay away from each other."

All that talk about the goddesses and their children had distracted them from getting on with the business of making love, and Arwel wasn't happy about it. Apparently, they had both failed at the focus test, but not in the way they'd thought they would.

Instead of necking, they were talking.

Staring into his eyes, Jin caressed his cheek. "Mey says that the pull is very strong. But since we've been together from the moment we met, we haven't had a chance to test it."

"I don't want to test it. I want to be with you always."

"That's sweet, but after this assignment is over, you will have to go back to your everyday work, which I assume is rescuing girls and boys from traffickers, and I'll have to focus on building my business. We will have to be apart."

"We will manage just like the other couples. From what I hear, the first two weeks are the most intense. I guess it's our physiology at work. The insatiable pull lasts until the addiction sets in. Once that happens, it is possible to stretch the rubber band a little further."

Jin's hand on his cheek stilled. "Addiction? What are you talking about?"

Damn. Mey hadn't told Jin about it. Did Mey even know?

"I thought your sister explained."

"She didn't."

"The venom is addictive. The time it takes differs for every couple, but after a while you will crave only me."

"What about you?"

"Same thing. But it takes longer for the males to get addicted to their females."

"Figures. The guys always have it better. Will it work on human males as well?"

"I suppose so. So far, no one has tested it. All the clan couples are happily mated."

"I wonder what came first, the chicken or the egg. That's an awesome way to ensure fidelity."

Arwel groaned. He really didn't want to talk about that while staring at Jin's magnificent, bare breasts. But if he kept the information from her, she would think that he had an ulterior motive for doing so.

"When the mating is fated, the couple doesn't mind the addiction. But in the goddess's times arranged matings were common, and the partners didn't want to limit themselves to the official mate. The way to circumvent it was basically the opposite of fidelity. The more males the female was with, the less chance there was she would get addicted to just one venom. And if she didn't get addicted to her mate, he didn't get addicted to her because her scent didn't change to match his."

Winding a lock of his hair around her finger, Jin smiled. "For an advanced species, immortals have a lot of animalistic traits."

"You don't know the half of it." He climbed up and covered her body with his. "The time for talking is over."

As he took her mouth in a careful kiss, Jin grabbed his T-shirt and pulled it up, bringing them skin to skin. It bunched under his arms and neck, and Arwel wanted to take it off and expose more of his skin to Jin's silky smoothness, but he didn't want to stop kissing her. With the soft mounds of her breasts pressing against his chest, and her hard nipples rubbing against its sparse hairs, it felt too good to interrupt.

Eventually though, he had to let her come up for air.

"What about the others?" Jin whispered in his ear. "You said that they can hear us."

"I don't care. Besides, they are all downstairs watching television. I can hear it blaring from here."

"I'll be quiet. Did you bring condoms?"

"You betcha." They were still in his duffle bag and going for them was a mood killer. "I'll get them." He rolled out of bed.

Well, that was an exaggeration. Nothing short of a fire or some other disaster could kill his mood for sex, but it certainly detracted from the experience.

Taking two packets out, he put them on the nightstand and then pulled his T-shirt over his head.

"I'll never get tired of seeing you like that." Jin pushed her leggings down. "You are made beautifully."

"Thank you." He looked at her long legs. "But you are perfection. When we move into our own house, I want you naked all the time. We will keep the shutters closed so the neighbors won't see anything."

"Same for you." She laughed. "We will live in a nudist colony of two."

Luckily, Jin thought he was joking or talking in the hypothetical. For now, he would leave it at that. There was plenty of time to discuss living arrangements after the mission's completion.

He climbed on the bed and covered her body with his. "I accept your terms."

27

KIAN

As Kian opened the door to his office, his phone buzzed. Glancing at the display, he accepted the call.

"Good morning, William."

"Good morning. I hope it's not too early for our daily update."

Kian put his thermos down. "You have perfect timing. I just walked into my office. What do you have for me?"

"We started watching the mansion shortly before lunch, but Kalugal's gate didn't open until evening. After that, four left the premises and later returned. The first was a Ferrari convertible, so it was relatively easy to see the driver, but Ewan said that it wasn't Kalugal. I had a hunch that only he would be driving a car like that, so I had Roni check surveillance feeds from parking lots of nearby restaurants and clubs. We got lucky, and Roni found it parked outside a restaurant. When he checked the feed from inside the place, Kalugal was there. Apparently, the guy doesn't leave the house without shrouding himself first."

"That complicates things."

"It does. Whenever they can, the guys will snap photos of the driver and show them to Jacki. But the solution might be simpler than that. If Kalugal is into fancy cars, we can narrow it down to just checking those."

"He might have many of them. You'll need more Guardians to follow the vehicles to their destinations. Besides, I wouldn't mind getting snapshots of his men as well. In time, we can collect all of them, provided that they leave the compound during our stakeout."

"That won't solve our Kalugal problem, though. The Guardians won't be able to see past his shroud."

"That's true, but they can report the location to Roni and have him check. That would save him time searching for Kalugal's car in parking lots. Those minutes could make all the difference between Jin getting to him on time or missing the opportunity. And given that not every place has surveillance cameras that Roni can hack into, we won't have that many opportunities to get Kalugal."

"That's true. But managing more Guardians complicates the logistics. We can't fit more people in here unless you want them sleeping on the floor in the living room."

"We'll figure it out. I'll talk with Onegus and let you know."

"What do you want us to do in the meantime?"

"Keep doing it the way you suggested until I get you reinforcements."

After ending the call with William, Kian called the chief. "Good morning, Onegus. Can you come up to my office?"

"I'm on my way."

Less than ten minutes later, the chief knocked on the door.

"Come in."

"Is it about the Bay Area mission?" He took a seat in front of Kian's desk.

"Yes. I just got off the phone with William. We need the cars leaving Kalugal's estate followed. Only four cars have left the gate since they arrived, so that could have been handled by the team already there. But it would have left fewer Guardians in the house to watch over Jin and the gate."

Onegus frowned. "I thought that you didn't want to risk alerting Kalugal to the fact that he's being watched. Following him and his men around would do that. Isn't it better to rely on Roni and William's virtual surveillance?"

"It has limits. Not every place has cameras, and out of those a significant percentage are closed-circuit and not hackable remotely. What can we do to follow him around discreetly?"

"Keep switching cars and drivers, but that requires many more Guardians. We will have to reschedule rescue missions, and I know that you don't want to do that either."

No, he didn't. Every day that passed meant more suffering for the victims, but as Turner had pointed out, the clan could not save all of those who needed saving.

"You are right about that, and I hate postponing even one rescue, but I have a strong gut feeling that the team I've sent after Kalugal is not big enough. It's good for what Jin needs to do, but not if things go wrong." He raked his fingers through his hair. "And we know that nothing ever works as planned."

Onegus nodded. "We don't even know how many men Kalugal has with him. But if we wait patiently, we can get a good estimate. A week of watching that gate will give us that."

"A week is a long time to wait."

Onegus arched a brow. "What's the hurry?"

"Jin has to wait to transition until after this is done. Naturally, she and Arwel are impatient to start."

"Yeah, I can see how that could be a problem. Still, Arwel is a Guardian, so he will understand the importance of good intel. And from what I've heard, Jin is a sensible woman, so she's not going to protest too much either."

"Possibly. But I don't want to wait."

"Aha." Onegus smirked. "So you are the impatient one, not them."

"Nothing new there. Besides, as you pointed out, we need the men to get back to rescuing people. Why waste a week?"

Sighing, Onegus accepted defeat. "How many do you want to send, and where are you going to put them up? Sleeping bags on the living room floor?"

"They've lived through worse. But no. I don't want them coming and going from the rented house. Ideally, they would sit in their cars and wait for the team to give them a signal to follow. The problem is that fucking fancy neighborhood. No one parks on the streets, so it's not like they can wait a couple of streets over and then pull behind the car they are following. That could work once. After that they will get noticed."

"During the day, it shouldn't be a problem. But at night they would have to stay in the house and leave from there. Its front faces another street, so it's not like Kalugal and his men would notice the gate closing and opening." Onegus rubbed his jaw. "We will have to rent high-end cars for them. The more expensive, the less suspicious they will look."

"True. In that city, only the help drives Hondas and Toyotas. But if we put them in the house, we can't send more than four additional Guardians, and I have a feeling that it's not going to be enough."

Onegus arched a brow. "Did you catch the paranoia bug from Turner? Even four additional Guardians is overkill."

"I have a gut feeling, and at my age, I know better than to doubt it. If I could, I would have liked to have a force of at least twenty-five men there."

"Definitely paranoia." Onegus leaned back and crossed his arms over his chest. "I'll tell you what we can do. Since it's Friday, and we have no rescues scheduled for Saturday and Sunday, I can send several later today and a larger group tomorrow and have them return Monday evening. That way, we will lose only one working day."

"Do it. Put them up in a nice hotel and rent them some fancy cars. If I'm just being paranoid and nothing happens, they'll get to enjoy a long weekend off. But I'll feel better knowing that we have enough men on standby if needed."

Onegus smirked. "They can take turns in the house, which will make the guys super eager to go. They all want a shot at the new Dormant."

"Possible Dormant. We won't know for sure until Jacki attempts transition."

28

JIN

*J*in had expected to get some smirking looks at breakfast, but everyone was pretending as if they had heard nothing last night.

The house they were staying in was super fancy, and she was sure it had great insulation, but it had been built with human hearing in mind, not immortal. Those sleeping in the adjoining bedrooms for sure had heard the sounds of lovemaking she and Arwel had made, but they were acting maturely about it.

Besides, the three single Guardians were busy trying to charm Jacki out of her pants, and William was looking at her with longing in his eyes while letting the three hungry bears do the hovering.

Magnus and Vivian probably had been busy last night as well, so they'd made noises of their own.

"Would you like fresh coffee?" Arwel got up. "I'm going to brew some more."

"Sure." She handed him her mug. "I didn't get much sleep last night."

That got a smile out of Vivian. She leaned closer to Jin and whispered in her ear, "There is nothing as magnificent as new love's bloom."

Grinning happily, Magnus took his wife's hand. "There is. The maturing of that love is just as wonderful if not better. When the craziness is over, you can really learn to appreciate your mate."

Jin cast him a polite smile.

She and Arwel were great together, but it wasn't frantic like the other couples were describing. Perhaps the difference was the freaking condoms' fault, and as long as they had to use them, the bond couldn't form.

Or at least that was the explanation she had arrived at.

Arwel wasn't saying anything, but she knew he was bothered by it as well.

"We should get ready," Jacki said. "We need to practice putting the makeup and disguises on."

Jin waved a hand. "It's still morning. It will be hours before Kalugal goes somewhere that I can get to him."

"Maybe. But when he does, we will need to move out right away. There will be no time to get into the disguises."

"You are right." Jin sighed. "Can I at least have my second cup of coffee? I need the energy boost to put all that gunk on."

"Eva said that we don't need much. The wigs, the glasses, and the baggy clothes should do it. Add a little foundation in the wrong color, and we are done."

"Yay, us." Jin waved a pretend flag. "I've never thought I would choose clothes and put on makeup to make myself look worse, not better."

"That's mission impossible." Arwel put the fresh mug in front of her. "No matter what you put on, you will always be beautiful."

"You wanna bet?"

Chuckling, he leaned down and kissed the top of her head. "My girl is a gambling woman."

"That's right. Whoever loses does the lunch dishes."

"Deal."

Mug in hand, Jin pushed to her feet. "Let's go, Jacki. We have a bet to win."

"Your room or mine?"

"Yours."

As Jacki started lifting dishes off the table, Duncan put a hand on her arm. "We will take care of it."

As they climbed the stairs to the second floor, Jin leaned into Jacki's ear. "I don't think you will get to touch the dishes for the rest of this mission. The three burly bears want to pamper their Goldilocks."

Scrunching her nose, Jacki looked over her shoulder down into the dining room. "I don't want to offend any of them, but I wish they'd stop it." She opened the door to her room. "I feel like a prize horse they all want to buy."

Jin patted her arm. "I'll get my stuff and be right back."

There was something to that. Naturally, Jacki didn't know what a rare find she was, and Jin couldn't tell her. Maybe she should ask Arwel to talk to his fellow Guardians and ask them to tone it down. They were making Jacki uncomfortable.

Grabbing the duffle bag with her costume and makeup, she got back to Jacki's room and closed the door behind her.

"What's their deal anyway?" Jacki continued. "They are good-looking guys. Why are they acting so desperate?"

"You are gorgeous. The guys in the program were like that too."

"They weren't as persistent. Those three don't get hints, and I really don't want to be rude, especially since I depend on them to keep me safe."

Jin put the duffle on the dresser and sat next to Jacki on the bed. "Why don't you pick one? If you do, the others will stop."

"I don't feel it for any of them."

"What about William?"

Jacki shrugged. "He is nice and mellow, so I can be nicer to him without him interpreting it as an invitation."

"Talk about picky. What are you waiting for, Prince Charming?"

"Maybe."

For some time now, Jin had been suspecting that Jacki wasn't into men, but she'd been too embarrassed to ask. But heck, they were not only friends, they were also going on a mission together. Perhaps it was time to put their cards on the table.

"Are you into girls? Because it's fine if you are. I won't be offended that you didn't pay me any attention." Jin affected a sniffle.

Jacki laughed. "I'm not into girls. But I'm not too hot for guys either." She grimaced. "Growing up the way I did, and looking the way I do, I had to stave off unwanted advances left, right and center. It got to the point that I feel nauseated when a guy looks at me like I'm a piece of meat."

Jin was taken aback. "The Guardians don't look at you like that. Sure, they want you. But they are not leering."

"Maybe not, but that's what I'm used to."

Jin arched a brow. "You don't like sex?"

"I can do without. I decided a long time ago that I'm not going to do hookups. If a man wants me, he will have to make me fall in love with him first, and of course he will have to love me too. I don't mind waiting for marriage."

"Is it a religious thing?"

Jacki laughed. "No. But I often lie, using it as an excuse. Nothing gets rid of a guy faster than telling him I won't have sex outside of marriage."

As what Jacki was saying sank in, Jin's eyes widened. "Are you a virgin?"

The outspoken, rough around the edges Jacki was a freaking virgin? It was inconceivable.

Jacki snorted. "Of course not. I'm just not hung up on sex. There is more to life than that."

Was she telling the truth?

For some reason, Jin doubted it. Then again, it was hard to believe that Jacki had never been with a man. She could believe it about Wendy, but not Jacki.

29

KALUGAL

"Which car do you want to take?" Rufsur asked.

"The Mercedes. I need to appear rich but not frivolous." Kalugal closed his eyes and imagined the way he wanted the world to see him.

To get the features right, he usually planned ahead, going over magazines and picking several prominent figures. He created a montage by mashing their features together, and after studying the picture he'd created, he would practice the shroud on his men.

There were several advantages to the method he'd developed. First of all, the shroud looked realistic. Secondly, he could pull the montage from memory and reinforce the shroud when it wavered, which happened when he had to maintain it for a prolonged time. Thirdly, he seemed vaguely familiar to whoever he was meeting with, and because his montage was based on well-known businesspeople and politicians, his appearance usually also inspired respect.

"Hello, Mr. Wang Huateng," Rufsur said.

Kalugal inclined his head. "Good morning to you, Rufsur."

"Good accent."

"Of course. I'm fluent in Mandarin."

After English, that was the second most important language to learn, and even though it had been a pain in the rear to do so, Kalugal had made sure to master it, including reading and writing. He was also fluent in most Western languages, as well as Russian, Arabic, and Japanese.

His real passion, though, was the ancient languages: Sumerian, Egyptian, Mayan, Quechua, and several lesser known ones. There was a wealth of knowledge to explore, and doing it without relying on iffy translations was the only way to go.

Regrettably, his hobby wasn't going to bring him closer to his goal of world domination.

Technology would.

As the car lift settled on the ground level, Rufsur opened the gate and drove out. "Who am I supposed to be?"

On rare occasions, Kalugal shrouded his men as well, but today it wasn't required.

"My secretary and translator. From time to time, I'll ask you something in Chinese, and you will lean toward me, pretending to whisper the translation in my ear."

"Can't I just come as your bodyguard?"

"Mr. Wang Huateng is not the caliber of businessman who travels with bodyguards."

Rufsur stopped at a traffic light. "I wish I understood why you are doing things this way. You are just buying startups. Many investors are doing that. Why the elaborate charades?"

"When the time comes, and I put all of these technologies together, it will take everyone by surprise. I don't want Jeff, Larry, and Sergei to know that their empires are at risk. Let them bask in their glass towers and think that they are invincible."

"What about Mark?"

"Facebook is already on its way out. My vision of a social network is one that will emerge from my commerce and internet conglomerates. You know what I have in mind."

"Yes, I do." Rufsur shook his head. "You, my friend, are the most dangerous man in the world, and no one realizes it."

"Which is exactly how I want it. They won't know it even when I control each and every individual on this planet."

That was an exaggeration, but only a slight one.

He was going to control all the humans. The immortals, he was going to leave alone, mainly because they were irrelevant. Except for one. When he was in power, Kalugal was going to get his mother to visit him. Regrettably, Areana loved Navuh, and she had made Kalugal swear never to go after his father, not even when he grew up and became more powerful than Navuh.

He'd only been a little boy when he'd given her his word, but he had no intention of breaking it.

"So, what's the point? Aren't you after the glory?"

"No. That's not my motivation. I don't seek fame. I just want the control." Kalugal smiled. "I'll be a god. Invisible, indescribable, and yet feared and revered."

Rufsur laughed. "No one can accuse you of aiming low. But for now, you can be a god only over half the world's population. China is a whole separate market to conquer. Perhaps you should have started there."

"I have time, and I like it here. After I establish my power base in the West, I'll go after the rest of the world."

His second-in-command didn't say a thing, but Kalugal knew what his friend was thinking.

Rufsur was doubting his sanity, and from his perspective, he wasn't entirely wrong. For a guy of average intelligence, it was difficult to see ten thousand moves ahead and understand how the pieces of the puzzle aligned to form the tapestry of the future.

And that was good.

Only a handful of people around the world could do that, but since there were so many variables, none of them could imagine what Kalugal was planning.

His only real concern was the advancement in artificial intelligence.

At some point, a computer could spit out a picture of the future that Kalugal saw in his imagination.

But even if that happened, no one was going to take it seriously or take steps to prevent it.

30

ARWEL

"The chief is sending more Guardians." Magnus walked into the office, which aside from serving as William's lab had become their command center as well.

Arwel looked up. "What for?"

Hopefully, it wasn't because he wanted more Guardians to meet Jacki. The girl already had more admirers than she could handle. If additional suitors arrived, she might decide to run away, and Arwel wouldn't blame her.

"Kian wants us to follow every car that leaves Kalugal's place," William said. "He told me that when I called him this morning."

That was a one-eighty deviation from the original plan. Not only that, why was the chief calling Magnus and not him? Arwel was a head Guardian. Magnus was not. He was on his way, but the chief hadn't made an official announcement yet.

Besides, Arwel was under the impression that he was heading this operation. It was his mate's safety on the line, and he wasn't about to let anyone else call the shots.

He glared at Magnus. "Turner advised against it, and I agreed with him. Kalugal and his men are too alert and careful not to notice a tail. The whole idea was to keep him unaware that his location was compromised."

Pulling out a chair, Magnus parked it and crossed his legs. "Kian is the boss. I'm only the messenger. Most of the guys are going to stay in a hotel, and only three or four at a time will come over here. In case something goes wrong, Kian wants to have a sizable force on standby."

That sounded better. It was still overkill, but where Jin was concerned, Arwel welcomed any and all safety measures.

"How many are coming?"

"Twenty-five."

Arwel whistled. "That's a lot."

"Onegus said that they were fighting over who gets to come. Kian approved a five-star hotel for their accommodations, as well as fancy car rentals, so they would blend in at this neighborhood."

Arwel had a feeling that the hotel and cars had nothing to do with the guys' enthusiasm.

"Someone is leaving the gate," William said.

Whenever the guys upstairs had something to report, they shot a text message to William. Arwel had suggested mounting one of their phones on a stand and leaving the camera recording function on, but William had shot it down.

Eyes on the gate was the only method that was a hundred percent safe and guaranteed not to get noticed, especially since the men were sitting behind a closed balcony door.

The glass had a reflective coating on it. During the day, it was impossible to see anything inside, even for immortals, and during the night, they kept the lights off. Except, the only information readily accessible was the license plate numbers. It was hard to see who was leaving Kalugal's mansion without either following the car to its destination or checking where it was parked by locating its license plate number.

So far, the method had worked, and Roni had found all four vehicles that had left the place last night. But not all parking lots had hackable surveillance cameras.

"I've alerted Roni," William said. "I just hope that the Mercedes will park somewhere public, and that the parking lot has cameras."

Magnus put his hands on his thighs and leaned forward. "Did the guys see who was inside?"

"The windows were tinted. They saw the driver, but not clearly, and the passenger had his head down, so they couldn't see his face."

That was probably Kalugal. It seemed that the guy had a collection of expensive cars. Last night it had been a Ferrari, and now a Mercedes, which Arwel was willing to bet was the flagship model.

"When are the reinforcements arriving?" he asked.

"Some of them this afternoon and the rest tomorrow." Magnus shifted in his chair. "The good news is that they are not going to be sleeping here. They will work in shifts and return to the hotel to sleep."

William turned around. "Someone needs to tell them not to harass Jacki. The resident Three Stooges are already making her uncomfortable. She doesn't need more admirers."

"I'll do that," Magnus said. "As the father of a young woman, I can speak with authority."

The guy was taking his role as Ella's stepfather very seriously. As a mated woman, she had little need of his parenting, but the girl humored him. Or maybe she liked having him as a father figure in her life.

Magnus was a standup guy, or a mensch as Eva would say, and he loved his stepchildren. Whenever he talked about Parker or Ella, his eyes shone with pride.

31

JIN

"I hate this makeup." Jin started down the stairs with Jacki right behind her. "It feels like I'm wearing a mask."

Jacki chuckled. "You are. But that's nothing compared to me. I look like a hag."

"No, you don't. Nothing could make you look ugly. Not even this drab getup."

Despite planning for a simple disguise, Jacki had ended up going all out and turning herself into someone else. She either enjoyed it or was really concerned about being discovered.

The brown wig was best described as mousy, the black-rimmed thick glasses were the uglier of the two pairs Eva had given them, and the clothes Jacki had chosen made her look thirty pounds heavier and fifteen years older.

And that was before the makeup.

She'd smeared on a foundation that was two shades darker than her natural, peachy color, and a lipstick that was a shade lighter than her lips. The effect was a sickly-looking woman whom no one was going to spare a second glance. Not ugly, but not attractive either.

"Jacki, can you come to the office for a moment?" William said without looking directly at them.

"Sure. What do you need me for?"

"A..." He stopped and gaped. "What have you done?" He sounded as if she'd run over his favorite pet.

"It's called a disguise."

The guy looked horrified. "For what? The zombie apocalypse?"

Jin laughed. "I told you that you'd gone too far."

"Nah, it's good." Jacki leaned to whisper in Jin's ear. "The three burly bears are not going to drool over Brownilocks."

"Aha, now I get it. This is your version of bear spray."

"Precisely."

Head held high, Jacki sauntered into the office as if she was a participant in a beauty pageant making her grand entry. "What can I help you with, gentlemen?"

Arwel took one look at her and started laughing. "Jacklin, you've outdone yourself." He then looked at Jin. "You too. But at least yours is not as bad as hers."

"You mean as good," Jacki said. "Who is going to recognize me like that, huh?"

"No one."

William cleared his throat. "Can you come over here and look at the screen?"

Jacki got closer and leaned in. "It's him."

"Are you sure?"

"The picture is grainy, but I'm ninety-nine point nine percent sure."

Peeking over Jacki's shoulder, Jin looked at the still photo of two guys sitting at a restaurant table, but neither of the men looked like Kalugal. One was an older Chinese gentleman, and the other a thirty-something geeky-looking guy.

"That's bad news." William pushed his glasses up his nose. "The restaurant is seventeen miles away from here, and Kalugal's shroud is still affecting us. Which one is he?"

Jacki pointed at the Chinese guy. "That's him. Do you see that smirk?"

The guy was indeed smirking, which looked somewhat out of place on the face of a distinguished older gentleman wearing a suit and tie.

"I see it," William said. "What about it?"

"That's Kalugal's signature smirk." Jacki straightened up. "He had the same expression on the picture you showed me. The one the forensic artist sketched. When in doubt, wait for it. I bet that smirk looks the same no matter what face he is shrouding himself in."

"Shouldn't we get going?" Jin asked.

"We are not going to make it in time," Arwel said. "Besides, it's not the right environment. We need a crowded place, like a bar or a club."

Jin leaned against the desk and crossed her arms over her minimizer-bra-flattened chest. "I don't think we will get another chance today. I put all of this on for nothing." She waved a hand at her face.

"Not for nothing," Jacki said. "We needed practice, and I also wanted to ask the guys if it's obvious that we are wearing ugly-looking makeup."

William, who up until now had been doing his damnedest not to look at Jacki, lifted his head from the computer screen and then got up and walked closer to her. "I can see that you are wearing makeup, but I would have assumed that you look even worse without it, and that it's meant to make you look good."

She smiled, and the radiance of those pearly whites obliterated the ugliness in a flash. "That's awesome. Thank you."

"You are welcome." William pushed his glasses up his nose and returned to his seat.

"When we are out, try not to smile," Jin said. "Even with all this gunk you look gorgeous when you do that."

"Right." Jacki nodded. "I wish there was makeup for teeth. Some yellow tint could have been useful."

"I heard there was a sighting." Kri walked into the office and then stopped.

"Damn. That's one hell of a transformation. Both of you. But Jacki, wow." She shook her head. "It takes guts to make yourself look that bad."

"Thank you." Jacki smiled. "Whenever you want to look ugly, I'm your girl."

Kri nodded. "I wanted to show you two some self-defense moves. But I guess that's out of the question with all the makeup you have on. You don't want to sweat it off."

"I don't," Jacki said. "It took over an hour to put on."

Jin pushed away from the desk. "I need something to distract me from feeling this gunk on my face. I'm going upstairs to start working on my business plan."

"Can I help?" Jacki asked.

"Sure."

"I have a few ideas," Kri said. "If you are interested in hearing them."

"Of course." Jin threaded one arm through Kri's and the other through Jacki's. "Three brains are better than one."

"For what?" Vivian walked in.

"We are going upstairs to create a business plan. Do you want to join us?"

Vivian chuckled. "What would I know about clothing for tall women? I have the opposite problem." She leaned closer and whispered. "Don't tell anyone, but sometimes I shop for clothes in the teen department."

"I have an idea," Jacki said. "Perhaps you should design two fashion lines. One for tall women and the other for short ones."

32

MEY

"How are we going to fit everyone into this small living room?" Yamanu dropped the groceries on the kitchen counter. "Maybe we should have the party here."

Mey glanced around the commercial kitchen with its stainless-steel appliances and counters, white cabinets, and concrete floor. They had gotten used to having meals around that long central island, but the place definitely didn't have the right atmosphere for romance to flourish.

Which was the entire point of arranging the get-together.

"There won't be that many people. Bhathian and Eva are going to bring Vlad. And Ingrid is coming. We can squeeze eight people in there."

Regrettably, Eva was going to leave Ethan with her daughter. A couples get-together was not the place for a baby, but Mey would have loved to cuddle him some more.

That was another reason for getting out of the keep as soon as possible. In the village, she would have plenty of opportunities to hold Ethan, and maybe Eva would even let her babysit him from time to time.

"I don't know what to do about the Guardians that Kian sent over." Mey leaned against the counter. "The evening is supposed to be about Wendy and Vlad getting to know each other, and Ingrid and Richard to come out and admit that they are a couple. Bringing two bachelors into the mix is going to be counterproductive to what we are trying to achieve."

Smiling, Yamanu leaned against the counter next to her and wrapped his arm around her shoulders. "And what is that exactly?"

She rolled her eyes. "Getting those two out of our hair so we can go home. I'm tired of living here. I need sunshine, and I want to hang out with my new friends in the village café and go out for walks and have some privacy in my own home."

an optimist. Wendy and Vlad haven't even met yet, and they might ⟨nd as for Ingrid and Richard, in my opinion, they are just scratching ⟨r's itch."

⟨ettably, that was Mey's impression as well. Ingrid was showing up every ⟨nd the two were spending a lot of time in Richard's room, but there had ⟨ no public displays of affection other than fond glances.

"They seem to like each other, but it's not like it was for us."

Yamanu arched a brow. "Was?"

Mey chuckled. "Is. But I'm talking about the falling in love part. That was so fast and intense. A whirlwind romance."

He pulled her around, so she was wedged between his thighs. "I'm still falling in love with you. As impossible as it seems, I love you more with every passing day."

Richard walked into the kitchen. "Should I come back later?"

Reluctantly, Mey pushed away from Yamanu's hard chest. "We need to start working on dinner."

"That's why I'm here." Richard peeked inside one of the grocery bags. "What are we making?" He moved to the next.

"Nothing fancy." Mey walked over to the center island and started pulling things out. "Dips, cheeses, crackers, salads and finger food. Unless we want to dine here, we can't have a proper sit-down dinner. Our place is too small."

Richard lifted a head of lettuce. "What's wrong with eating here? This counter is big enough for twenty people to dine comfortably, and there will be only ten of us."

"Eight. I'm not inviting the Guardians." She looked at Yamanu. "Can you come up with a good excuse? I feel bad about excluding them."

Yamanu shrugged. "I could tell them the truth."

Mey tensed. Had he forgotten about keeping Richard and Wendy in the dark about the matchmaking and the reasons for it?

"You can't just tell them that it's a couples' evening. They'll feel offended."

She cast Richard a sidelong glance, checking to see if he would react. He and Ingrid had made no official announcement, and in public they acted more like friends than lovers.

But all he did was take the lettuce to the sink. "It's their job to guard us, right?" He opened the faucet and started rinsing the lettuce leaves one at a time.

Yamanu shook his head. "What I'm going to tell them is that we are introducing Wendy to a nice young man. And since she seems intimidated by big guys with lots of muscles, with them around she might not open up to Vlad."

"That's good," Richard said. "And it's also true. I usually don't notice things like that, but you are right. Wendy shies away from big men. It took her a long time to get comfortable around me, and I'm not nearly as big as those two." He snorted. "They look like they live in the gym."

"It's part of their job." Yamanu flexed. "You want the people guarding you to have muscles."

"Absolutely." Richard pulled out a chopping board and a knife. "But it's not just about the muscles. You are a big guy, and yet Wendy is not intimidated by you."

Mey put her hand on Yamanu's arm. "That's because Yamanu is a sweetheart. Everyone can see how kind he is."

Richard paused with the chopping knife. "What about me? Do I look kind?"

Mey chuckled. "To me, you seem harmless. But you are not overflowing with kindness."

"Hey, I'm chopping lettuce for the get-together. That's nice of me."

33

VLAD

Vlad stood next to Bhathian's car, his hand hesitating on the handle of the back passenger door. "I don't know about this."

"Just get in." Bhathian opened the door for Eva. "You know how the saying goes. No guts, no glory."

There wasn't going to be any glory regardless of him having the guts to talk to the girl or not.

Girls didn't like him. They didn't look at him, and they didn't talk to him. He was invisible.

"Wendy is a nice girl," Eva said before getting in. "You'll like her."

That wasn't the problem, but it was too late to back down now.

Stupidly, he'd let Bhathian convince him to meet the girl. The Guardian had played on all of his strings, saying that Wendy was lonely and that she was shy, and the other village males were all too old for her. Maybe even intimidating. And then he'd pulled the trump card of her possibly being a Dormant and perhaps even Vlad's fated love.

As if that was ever going to happen for him.

He wasn't lucky like Jackson, and his mate was not waiting for him in the old keep. But he wanted to believe in the fairytale Bhathian had sold him on.

The truth was that he was lonely too.

It was difficult to make friends with humans, especially for someone who looked like him, and his immortal friends were busy living their lives.

Chase had moved to Scotland more than two years ago, Jackson had Tessa and a business to run, and Gordon was away at college.

With a sigh, Vlad opened the door and slid into the back seat.

Eva turned around and smiled at him. "You are not going to be alone with Wendy. Bhathian and I are going to be there, Mey and Yamanu, and Richard and Ingrid. So, if you don't like her, you don't even have to talk to her."

He nodded.

That was good. Not because he expected not to like Wendy, but because he never knew what to talk about with girls.

As Bhathian pulled out of the parking garage, he glanced at him through the rearview mirror. "Do you still remember what I taught you and your buddies in my sex-ed class?"

Vlad felt his ears heat up. Luckily, his long black hair was covering them, as well as half of his face, so no one would notice. "How could I forget? But why do you bring it up now?"

Hopefully, Bhathian didn't think that Vlad still needed instruction in that area.

He was twenty, for Fates' sakes. Most guys his age had been sexually active for years. But then they didn't look like lanky vampires. He was six foot five, but most people thought he was shorter because he walked hunched over, he weighed a hundred and forty-two pounds, had paper-white skin, fangs that were elongated even when he wasn't excited, and eyes that were different colors.

Bhathian chuckled. "I don't mean the sexual stuff, which is obviously what you were thinking about. Do you remember the relationship advice I gave you and your three clueless buddies?"

Vlad frowned.

The emphasis of the class had been on consent and how important it was not to make assumptions. He'd internalized that, and not because of the horrifying consequences Bhathian had threatened them with. There had been a lot of advice on how to approach kissing a girl, which he had hoped to put into practice.

Regrettably, he hadn't had a chance to try it out yet.

"Well?" Bhathian prompted.

"I remember the stuff about kissing a girl, and how I was supposed to stop an inch away from her lips and wait for her to close the rest of the distance. That was good advice. It was all about consent and making sure to get it, not assume it."

"True. But I also spoke about the importance of communication and respect. As long as you communicate clearly and show Wendy that you respect her, everything is going to be fine. Provided of course that she does the same. If she doesn't, just walk away."

Vlad nodded. "Now, I remember. You also said that confidence makes a man seem more attractive to women. Especially when he also has a job because no girl wants a penniless loser."

He was good on the job front. Jackson was paying him well for the part-time baking gig he did at nights, but his confidence was still nonexistent.

Bhathian grinned. "Good memory. So, let's see what you've got. You are a nice guy, so I know you will treat Wendy with respect, you have a job, and you are attending college. You have most of the requirements covered. Now all that's left is confidence and communication skills."

"Yeah. Tell me something I don't know. I don't have either."

Eva turned around. "You can fake confidence. Most guys do."

Bhathian nodded. "It takes courage to approach a girl, and no one likes rejection. Just remember that you are not the only one feeling like that."

"Did you?" Vlad asked. "I mean before you met Eva?"

Bhathian shook his head. "It was different for me than it is for you. I wasn't expecting to find my mate, so I didn't care about rejection."

Vlad stifled a snort.

Looking like he did, Bhathian had probably never encountered that problem unless the lady was taken. And perhaps not even then.

Looking at him as if she could read his mind, Eva smiled reassuringly. "Don't build up too many expectations and try to relax. Pretend that Wendy is just a girl who needs a friend, and don't expect anything romantic. That will make the entire thing less stressful for you. Probably for Wendy as well, since she is also shy."

"Just remember," Bhathian said. "Wendy, Richard, and Jacki think that we are an organization of humans with paranormal talents, who try to stay under the government's radar and watch each other's backs. Don't mention anything about immortals, the clan, or the village. They don't even know where the keep is, so don't say anything about Los Angeles or the college you attend. If you have to, make up some name she won't recognize and say that it's a private institution."

"Got it. What talent am I supposed to have?"

"Yamanu told her that you are a shrouder like him."

Vlad chuckled. "I'm nothing like him. I can shroud a room, not an entire city."

Bhathian shrugged. "It's still better than most of us can do. I can only shroud myself for several minutes. You have a unique talent, which is another point in your favor."

Eva turned around. "You are a real catch, Vlad. Try to remember that."

34

WENDY

As the last episode of her anime ended, Wendy glanced at the open door and switched to another one, hoping that the loud Japanese voices would keep visitors away.

That was why she preferred to watch anime in its native language and read the subtitles instead of watching those with English dubbing.

In the Japanese original, there was always one obnoxiously excitable character who screamed a lot.

It gave her a headache, but it was worth it. The screaming was her shield.

Since everyone left their doors open during the day, Wendy couldn't close hers without getting looks and questions, but she didn't want anyone coming in either.

They were all so freakishly nice.

Even Richard, who'd been somewhat of a jerk in the program, was acting all goodie two-shoes. He'd even volunteered to help Mey in the kitchen, which he would have never done back in the program.

Was he falling in love with that interior designer? Was love making him suddenly soft? Or was he trying to win over their hosts?

Probably the last one.

If he loved Ingrid, Wendy would have felt it. He liked the woman and lusted after her, but Richard was too self-absorbed to love anyone other than himself.

Oh well, it wasn't as if she cared one way or another.

Flicking through the offerings, Wendy searched for something new to watch. She was all caught up on her favorite shows, but she needed to fill the time with something, and it wasn't with the guy Yamanu had invited to meet her.

Why the hell were they playing matchmakers?

Wendy didn't want to meet anyone, or date, or even to go through the torture of making small talk. Guys only did that to get into her pants, and she had no intention of allowing anyone in there.

She was perfectly fine with staying celibate for the rest of her life. If she believed in God, joining a convent would have been a perfect solution.

But she didn't.

If there was a God, Wendy was majorly pissed at Him. So, it was better to believe that her life didn't suck because God was punishing her for something and wanted her to suffer. Life was just unfair, and shit happened to good people for no good reason.

What could she possibly have done as a baby to deserve abandonment by her mother?

Had she pooped and cried too much?

Her father had claimed that it had been all her fault, and he'd used it as an excuse to torment her. Countless times he had called her a curse, a plague, a good-for-nothing worthless shit, blaming her for driving her mother into drug addiction and into leaving and never coming back.

Wendy suspected that he had abused her mother as well, and that was what had driven her away. But after hearing that same crap for most of her life, she sometimes wondered whether there was something to it.

Maybe she'd been a hellish baby, one of those who never slept and who had cried all the time?

Nah. That was no reason to leave a child behind. Her father was full of shit, a jerk, an abuser, and a liar.

The thing was, everyone thought that he was a charming guy, and people admired him for raising his daughter on his own. No one knew the monster he'd become when there was no one there to watch.

He'd always been careful not to hit her face or her arms, and he'd never beaten her up badly enough for her to miss school or need medical attention.

On the face of things, he'd looked like a great dad. She had nice clothes, a good laptop, two gaming systems, and a room kitted out for a princess.

It had been a great cover for the constant abuse.

Wendy had kept quiet because she'd been ashamed to admit that her life had been hell. She still was. Part of it was because she knew he would have convinced people that she was making it up, that she was a disturbed teenager, and that her bruises had been self-inflicted.

They would have believed him too, because how could a charming guy like that abuse his own daughter?

Besides, even if anyone had listened to her, she had nowhere to go. She would have been sent to a foster home, and that might have been even worse.

The lesson had been learned, though.

No men for Wendy.

No matter how nice and charming they appeared on the outside, some had monsters living inside of them that even her empathic ability couldn't detect. A guy could seem and feel perfectly normal, until some trigger awakened the sleeping beast lurking below the surface, and he lashed out.

She wasn't going to become anyone's punching bag ever again.

"Wendy? Can I come in?" Mey poked her head into her room. "Everyone is here already."

With a sigh, Wendy swung her legs over the side of the bed. "I'm coming. But don't expect me to be nice to that guy. I told you that I didn't want to meet anyone."

Shaking her head, Mey walked up to her. "Don't think of Vlad as a potential boyfriend. Think of him as a possible friend who happens to be a boy."

That, she could do.

"Fine. I'll try to act friendly."

Mey smiled. "That's all I'm asking."

35

VLAD

As soon as Vlad walked in with Bhathian and Eva, Yamanu got up and wrapped his huge arm around his shoulders.

"Vlad, let me introduce you to Wendy." He turned him around to face the couch, where a girl sat huddled between Mey and Ingrid, looking as if she was trying to hide.

"Wendy, this is Vlad."

She lifted a pair of eyes that were sad and annoyed at the same time.

Great, her response was exactly like that of all the other girls he'd met in college. No one wanted to get to know the freak boy.

Vlad tried to take a step back, but Yamanu's arm around his shoulders kept him from moving an inch.

Wendy's eyes softened. "Hi," she murmured. "Nice to meet you, Vlad." She extended her hand.

For a moment, he just stared at it, but then Yamanu squeezed his shoulder, reminding him to move.

"Yes, nice to meet you too." He took her hand gently, mindful of his strength.

On top of his weird appearance, he was also freakishly strong and had to remember to be careful when interacting with humans.

Mey rose to her feet. "Come sit next to Wendy, Vlad. I'm going to check on the food in the kitchen."

"I'll help you." Ingrid got up as well.

Damn, why wasn't he a telepath? He could have projected a *no way* straight into Mey and Ingrid's heads. But since he wasn't, he had to sit next to the girl who was obviously not interested in him.

Richard and Yamanu pushed to their feet as well and followed the ladies out.

Now he was stuck alone with Wendy.

There was one good thing about being built like a twig, though, his butt didn't take up much space, and if he squeezed all the way to the left, he could leave at least three feet between him and Wendy.

She smiled. "I don't bite, you know."

Yeah, but I do. Hell. Where did that thought come from? He'd never bitten anyone in his life. Not in a fight and definitely not sexually.

Frowning, she narrowed her eyes at him. "Did I offend you? I'm sorry if I did. I'm just not good at talking with people."

Her admission helped him ease up a bit. "I'm not good at it either. Usually, I just don't say anything."

"Same here. The best way not to put a foot in your mouth is not to open it in the first place, right?"

He nodded. "That's my philosophy as well."

Well, at least they had that in common but nothing else.

Wendy was pretty, soft, and feminine, and there was nothing strange about her. He wondered why she felt awkward around people.

She glanced at him from under lowered lashes. "Yamanu told me that you are a shrouder like him."

"Not like him, but yeah. I can shroud a small place for a short time."

"That's awesome. No one in the program had an ability like that. I didn't even know that it existed."

Wanting to change the subject, he asked, "What's yours?"

"I'm an empath, like Arwel. Not as strong as he is, though. Not even close."

Great, she was a freaking empath, and no one had bothered to tell him?

Most likely intentionally.

So, that's why Wendy was suddenly being nice to him. She'd felt how hurt he'd been by the look she'd given him.

"What's wrong?" She leaned to try to see his eyes under his bangs. "Why did you get upset?"

Remembering what Bhathian had told him about the importance of open communication, Vlad decided to go with the truth. "Girls usually don't talk to me. And the only reason you are doing it is that you felt me getting upset when you gave me the look."

She arched a brow. "What look?"

"Annoyance. Like you really didn't want to be where you were, and you were mad at the others for inviting me and introducing us."

As the guilty look in Wendy's eyes confirmed his suspicion, Vlad started to get up, but she put her hand on his arm to stop him.

"It's not what you think."

Goosebumps popping all over his arms, he sat back down. "How so?"

"You are right about me being annoyed at Mey and Yamanu for doing this, but it had nothing to do with you personally. I just didn't want to meet any guys. But they were right about you. You are really nice."

He couldn't help the blush that heated his skin. "You don't know me well enough to know whether I'm nice or not."

Smiling, she tapped her temple with two fingers. "Empath, remember? I can feel you, and you feel safe. I don't often get that from people."

It was an odd thing to say. "Everyone here is safe. I don't know Richard, but I know Yamanu and Bhathian. Both are awesome men, and superb Guardians. With them around, you are as safe as a baby bird under its mother's wing."

She laughed. "That's a cute analogy. I didn't mean to say that they are not safe. And Richard, with all his faults, is not a bad guy either. But you are different."

"You think? Different is my middle name."

Shaking her head, Wendy put a hand over her heart. "I didn't mean your Goth getup or your multicolored eyes, which I think are super cool." She took in a deep breath. "I don't know how to describe it, so I'll use your mother bird analogy, but with a twist. You are like a hawk, with huge wings that you want to spread over others to protect them, but because you look different, they run away instead of getting under those wings and seeking shelter." She chuckled. "Maybe you should become a Guardian like Yamanu and Bhathian. It's in your blood."

Embarrassed, Vlad laughed. She'd nailed it about him wanting to shield others, but he wasn't Guardian material.

"You think anyone is going to accept my application for Guardian training with these sticks?" He waved his spindly arms.

"Hey, you might fill out. You are still young. How old are you? They told me that you are nineteen, but you look younger."

"I've recently turned twenty."

She shrugged. "It's good to look younger than you really are. When you are in your thirties or even forties, you are going to look like you are in your twenties."

"True."

He was probably stuck with looking like a walking twig for eternity, but it wasn't as if he could or wanted to tell her that. Maybe if she thought that one day he would look like a man, she would take a chance on him.

36

WENDY

Vlad was indeed a sweet guy, just as Yamanu had described him.

Even though he was reserved and anxious and generally uncomfortable in his own skin, his emotional makeup was beautiful, and it was as clear to her as if she was able to see his aura, which of course she couldn't.

She wondered what Spencer would have said about Vlad.

There was a fierceness in him, but it was warm and kind and completely nonaggressive. She doubted he could swat a fly.

It was rare to meet someone who was an open book like that. Only to an empath like her, though. Regular people couldn't even see his eyes, which he was hiding under long bangs. She wondered if he colored his hair, which was raven black, glossy and smooth.

And those teeth, they must have been filed to look that sharp. He was rocking the vampire look, and even had the name to match. Was it his real name, though?

And why would a nice guy like him put so much effort into looking menacing? Was it to protect himself from bullies?

Probably.

Kids were mean, especially to those who were different in some way. Maybe by putting on the vampire costume, Vlad was making himself look more dangerous so no one would mess with him.

"What are you studying?" she asked. "Yamanu said that you are going to college."

"Graphic design."

She smiled. "With that getup, I figured that you must be the creative type."

He looked down at his black jeans and his black boots with the metal buckles, then back up at her. Except, it was only with one eye because the other was covered by his bangs. "I play bass guitar in a band. It's part of the image."

He wasn't telling her the truth, and she could tell that he felt bad about it.

That was probably the answer he gave everybody who asked about his fashion choices.

Poor guy. It wasn't easy to be different.

Wendy had been different her entire life, in part because of her empathic ability, and in part because of her home situation. But at least she looked normal to strangers.

Vlad probably got stinky looks from everyone.

Not from her, though.

For some reason, Wendy wanted him to feel comfortable with her. She wanted to be his friend, for real, not just pretend it so the others would leave her alone.

It was a shame that their friendship had to be temporary, though. She wasn't going to stay any longer than she absolutely had to. The first opportunity that presented itself, Wendy was going to run.

But maybe in the meantime, she could boost Vlad's confidence a little.

One small good deed to compensate for the betrayal of these kind people who had taken her in and were trying to help her.

"You can tell me the truth, Vlad. It's okay to like dressing in black. It simplifies life. When you get up in the morning, you don't have to think about what pants go with what shirt because everything matches. And if impersonating a vampire makes you look tough, so other guys don't mess with you, then go for it."

"That's not why I do it."

"Oh yeah? Then why?"

He shrugged. "This is the only look that works for me. Can you imagine me in blue jeans and a white T-shirt? Talk about a dorky geek. Like this, I at least look cool."

It was a legitimate answer, and this time Vlad wasn't covering up the real reason. He believed it to be true, and perhaps he was right.

Looking weird but cool certainly beat looking weird and dorky.

Except, he was going too far with it.

Tilting her head, she tried to see under his bangs, then reached with her hand and pushed them back. "You have beautiful eyes. Don't hide them."

He pulled the bangs back down. "They freak people out."

"Only the idiots. I think they are beautiful, and I'm sure that I'm not the only one." She pushed his bangs back again. "You also have amazing lashes. They are so long that they look fake."

Taking her seriously, he frowned. "They are not."

"I know that. But anyway, don't hide your eyes. At least not from me."

He nodded, and the bangs fell back down, but this time he pushed them back himself, tucking the long strands behind his ears.

Wendy smiled. "You have a handsome face."

"Thank you."

"You're welcome."

As he looked down at his hands, she noticed how long and elegant his fingers were, like a pianist's. Except, his nails were long and painted black. Another detail to add to the vampire look. Or maybe to the rocker image?

"I've never gotten so many compliments. It feels strange."

"But you believe me, right? I'm not just saying it to make you feel good. You really have a handsome face and beautiful eyes and gorgeous eyelashes."

Vlad's pale cheeks reddened, and he looked away. "I wonder what's keeping the others. Do you think they decided to eat in the kitchen?"

"I think they wanted to give us privacy."

The blush deepened. "I'm sorry about that."

"Don't be. They must have roped you into coming just as they roped me. But now I'm glad that they did."

"Yeah, me too."

37

ARWEL

"Are you clear on what you need to do?" Arwel looked at the four new arrivals.

Douglas nodded. "We wait in the cars until we get the go signal from William."

"We are going to do it in four-hour shifts." Arwel clapped the Guardian on the back. "I know that's a long time to sit on your ass, but since you don't have to be alert until the signal arrives, you can take a nap or watch something while you wait."

"No worries. We are on it."

After the Guardians left, Arwel headed back to William's office. Jin was upstairs, working on her business plan, the new team members had been assigned their tasks, and Arwel had nothing to do but wait for a fancy car to exit Kalugal's gate.

"I have them on the screen." William pointed. "Do you see those four dots moving? Those are our guys."

Arwel watched them until they stopped in various spots next to the major streets crossing the neighborhood.

Whenever a car left Kalugal's mansion, they would get the model and license plate, and once it passed by one of the Guardians, he was going to follow it while the others remained in place for the next one.

It was risky, but hopefully with enough cars to switch around, Kalugal and his men would not notice the tails.

"And now we wait." He pulled out a chair, sat down, and fired an update text to Onegus.

"We should give the girls earpieces," William said. "I don't like the idea of them going in with nothing."

"Kian doesn't want anything about them to arouse Kalugal's suspicions, and even a small earpiece might get noticed from up close."

"Not if it's covered by hair. They could braid the wigs over their ears to hide the devices."

Arwel chuckled. "True. It will match the dorky look they are going for."

William leaned down and pulled two devices from a box he had stashed under the desk. "Do you want to call them?"

"Not yet. They are brainstorming Jin's business plan."

William put the earpieces next to his keyboard. "I would feel better knowing that they have them and know how to use them before we next spot Kalugal."

"You are right." With a sigh, Arwel pulled out his phone and texted Jin.

She replied a moment later. *Give us five minutes.*

"They'll be down shortly." He put his phone down.

Not surprisingly, Arwel could feel William's excitement rising, and it wasn't because of the earpieces.

"You like Jacki."

William shrugged. "She's beautiful, and I like her assertiveness, but she is not interested in me."

"She is nicer to you than she is to the other guys."

"That's because she doesn't view me as a threat." He grimaced. "I'm the cuddly teddy bear, not one of the wolves."

Arwel chuckled. "Jin calls Jacki Goldilocks, and the Guardians the three burly bears."

William smiled. "Good one."

"I think that Jacki is not interested in anyone. Jin says that she was the same way in the program. She might be asexual."

"Or she might be waiting for the right guy. It's uncommon these days, and especially for a knockout like her, but it's possible."

They both fell silent at the sounds of footsteps coming down the stairs.

"You wanted to show us something?" Jin asked.

William held out the two earpieces. "I know that we agreed on no communication devices, but I feel uneasy about it. I want you to try hiding it under your hair. I mean the wig's hair. Maybe braid it over it to hide the earpieces."

Jacki took one and pushed it into her ear. "I don't think it's a big deal even if he notices the thing. People wear earplugs to clubs, and many have earphones on. I thought you were concerned about him somehow picking up on the transmissions."

William shook his head. "If he can do that, it's another talent I've never heard of. To monitor transmissions the conventional way, he would have to travel with a van full of equipment, and we didn't see one following him the few times that he left the compound."

Jin took the other piece and put it in her ear. "Can you see it? It's really small."

Arwel nodded. "But that's because your ear is showing. Try pulling your hair over it."

She shook her head, letting the wig's thick waves cover her ears and half of her face. "Better?"

"It's invisible."

"Good." William walked up to her. "I'll show you how to work them."

When he was done, Jacki tried it first. "How come there is no wire coming out of it? I thought it was needed to talk back."

"These are special," William said. "Tap once to connect just to me and tap twice to connect to everyone in the loop."

Jin took the piece out and examined it closely. "So, the moment I tap it once, you hear everything that's going on around me?"

William nodded. "That's correct."

"And I hear what you are saying?"

"Only if I open a talking channel to you. I can talk to everyone in the loop at once, or I can select one or more people at the same time."

"But I have only two options, right? I can talk either to you or to everyone. I can't choose just Arwel if I want to."

"Correct. But I can do that for you. I'm like a switchboard."

"Who do I hear? Do I hear everyone, or just you?"

"Normally, just me. But if, for example, Arwel wants to talk to you, he can tell me, and I can connect the two of you."

Jin nodded. "Got it. So basically, the moment I walk into wherever Kalugal is, I tap the earpiece once and leave it open."

"That's right."

"Shouldn't Jacki and I be connected?"

"Of course."

"What about Arwel?"

"You'll have to ask me. Arwel needs to communicate with the other Guardians, so he can't be connected to you the entire time."

38

KALUGAL

Kalugal peered over the crumbling fragments of an ancient tablet and snapped a photo. Piecing the puzzle together was his favorite part, and the best way to do that was to upload the pictures to a large-screen computer and move them around until things started to make sense.

A lot of guesswork went into filling in the blanks, and sometimes he would go to bed frustrated with the results because he knew he hadn't done it right. Oddly, the answer would often come to him in a dream.

The mind was a curious thing, and little was known about its functioning. Should he invest in research in the field? Doing so would not provide any immediate benefits for him, or even long-term ones, and it would cost a lot of money. But then Kalugal didn't have to justify his actions to anyone, and not everything he did was motivated by financial gain.

He was spending most of his free time deciphering ancient texts and piecing together fragments of the past, and he could hardly claim that it was good for anything other than stimulating his intellect and satisfying his curiosity. Even if he discovered more clues about the gods, those probably weren't going to give him anything tangible either.

"We were supposed to leave by now," Rufsur said as he walked into the room.

"I know." Kalugal straightened up. "I needed to take more photos of the tablet I'm working on." He walked past Rufsur and put the camera on his desk. "I'm ready."

Rufsur looked him up and down. "You've got dust on your pants."

"No one is going to see them anyway."

"You are, and it's going to bother the hell out of you."

His number two knew him well. Kalugal slapped his thighs, clearing some of it.

"Phinas is coming with us," Rufsur said.

That was a surprise. The guy liked to go hunting alone.

"I'm glad. The more, the merrier."

They were going out to celebrate the successful acquisition from that morning. No documents had been signed yet, but he'd shook on it with the human. If for some reason the guy went back on his word, Kalugal could compel him to go through with it.

As a rule, he didn't use compulsion or thralling to convince people to sell their businesses to him. It wasn't because he was such a straight-up guy, but because it tended to backfire.

He needed the owners to keep working on the new technologies he was acquiring, and if they'd been coerced, their reluctant subconscious would sabotage progress.

In the bunker's sprawling car garage, they found Phinas leaning on the wall next to the door.

"I didn't know which car you wanted to take."

Kalugal glanced at the rows of cars, and as always, his eyes were drawn to the Ferrari.

It was a forty-five-minute drive to San Francisco, long enough to enjoy his favorite toy.

"The Ferrari, and I'm driving."

39

JIN

"Take a look, is that Kalugal?" Arwel handed Jacki his phone.

She nodded. "That's him. He's wearing aviator glasses, but I recognize that mustache. What does he look like to you?"

"A handsome young dude in his mid to late twenties. His shroud is wearing aviators as well."

"Does yours also have a small mustache?"

Arwel shook his head. "No. He's clean-shaven."

While they were talking about glasses and mustaches, Kalugal was getting farther away. Jin put her hand on Arwel's shoulder. "So, do we go after him?"

"Let's see where he is going first."

"He is going out to party," Jacki said.

Arwel looked up at her. "How do you know that?"

"He is shrouding himself as a young, handsome guy. When he goes out to business meetings, he put on an older man's shroud. We should get in the car and drive in whatever direction he is going, so when he gets there, it won't take us long to reach him. And if he is not going anywhere public, we'll go home."

"Let's do it." Jin pulled out the earpiece from her pocket and put it in. "I just need to get my purse."

"Yeah, me too." Jacki rushed after her. "I wish I could see what he looks like while he's shrouding himself. I can't even tell you it's the guy in the white button-down because he can project whatever clothes he fancies. I can only describe whoever he is standing next to."

"It's still possible that I could see the real him through the tether. Which reminds me that I need to do that."

"You can tether me on the way," Jacki said. "You can't do it while rushing out. It requires concentration."

"Yeah, you're right." Jin slung the strap of her purse across her body. "I'm so nervous that my hands are shaking. I'm actually going to do this."

Jacki looked her over. "Take your puffer coat. It's freezing outside."

"Right. I forgot about that."

Jacki shook her head. "You need to relax, girl."

Easier said than done. Up until now Jin had thought of herself as such a badass. She was going to attach a tether to a very dangerous man and spy on him. But when it was actually time to do it, she was scared like a little mouse.

Down in the house's garage, Arwel was waiting for them next to one of the cars, while two of the three burly bears were sitting inside another.

"Who's driving?" Arwel asked.

Jacki lifted her hand. "I am."

He tossed her the keys. "Tap the earpieces open as soon as you get into the car and test them."

Jin nodded.

Arwel pulled her into a quick hug. "We will be right behind you. You have nothing to worry about." He kissed her hard before letting her go.

Planting a smile on her face, Jin waved goodbye before getting in the car with Jacki.

"Arwel said to tap the earpieces open."

"I heard him. Mine is on."

Jin tapped hers. "Testing. Can you hear me, William?"

"Loud and clear."

Letting out a breath, Jin leaned back and closed her eyes.

"Don't forget to tether me."

"Right. Let's do it now."

She put her hand on Jacki's arm and imagined attaching a hook to her mind and tying a string of her consciousness around it.

"Is it done?" Jacki asked.

"Yup."

The whole thing had taken no longer than a couple of seconds, but Jin wondered whether it was too long for the brief contact she would have with Kalugal. The way she envisioned the encounter, she would bump into him and then clutch his arm as if to stabilize herself.

She would have to buy time by apologizing. The thing was, she'd never tried tethering anyone while talking. Hopefully, it wouldn't be a problem.

It hadn't occurred to her to test it before, and now she considered releasing the tether from Jacki and then reattaching it while talking.

Yeah, she should definitely test it.

"I want to release the tether and reattach it while talking to you. I need to find out if I can do that."

Jacki shrugged. "Go for it."

"Okay." Jin put her hand on Jacki's arm. "I'm releasing it now." She checked the connection. "It's done. That wasn't hard to do while talking."

"Talk about something else while you are tethering me again. You need to find out if you can concentrate on two separate things."

"Good idea. So, what do you think about dyeing my wig red? I think I would look good as a redhead."

"Horrible. But I'm willing to do it." She cast Jin a sidelong glance. "Did it work?"

"Yup. You are tethered."

That was a relief. "My plan is to fall onto Kalugal and apologize while holding on to him. I need about two seconds to latch on to his mind."

"Good plan. I can push you."

"Yeah, that will look more natural."

40

KALUGAL

"There's no selection here." Kalugal emptied the whiskey down his throat and signaled for the waitress to bring him another.

Rufsur frowned. "What are you talking about? They have the best whiskeys from all around the world. That's why we come here. And for the Cuban cigars."

The Cubans were illegal, but for the right price the owner was willing to sell them, sans the label, of course. He only sold them to regulars he knew well, and the transactions took place inside the humidor. Cash only.

It was a good place to celebrate successful business deals, but it was probably the worst for hunting. After a good drink and a great cigar, the only thing missing was good sex.

Kalugal waved a hand at the mostly male clientele. "No gazelles."

Phinas arched a brow. "Did you expect to find any here?"

"So far, it's been a lucky day. I hoped my luck would hold, and we would find a trio of hotties here. I had this image of slender fingers with long nails holding on to thick cigars, red lips curling around them as my imaginary seductresses puffed out smoke, cloaking themselves in mystery."

Rufsur laughed. "I didn't know you had such an active imagination."

"How do you think I come up with all my world domination schemes?"

"I guess that requires a creative mind."

"Of course it does." He leaned back in his chair and contemplated buying another Cuban.

Rufsur puffed on his cigar. "We can go after I finish this." He looked at Kalugal. "Unless you'll allow me to smoke in your precious Ferrari. Then we can leave right now."

"You know the rules. No one smokes in my cars. Not even me."

They were more than vehicles of transportation. They were a collection, and Kalugal took good care of the things he collected.

When the door opened and two lovelies walked in, he smiled. "Perhaps I'll get another cigar."

"They are not going to stay," Rufsur said. "And besides, there are only two of them and they are nothing special."

Kalugal shrugged. "Up to you, gentlemen. But I think they have potential." He pushed to his feet. "I'm going to get another thick one and see if either of them would like to take a puff."

It was true that the young women were plain-looking, and they were brunettes, which wasn't his favorite. But the one with the long hair had a very nice butt, and the other one had lush lips that would look amazing wrapped around a thick cigar.

As the owner opened the door to the humidor, and the two went in, Kalugal followed them inside.

"Are you ladies buying for yourselves or for someone else?" he asked, to start a conversation.

The one with the lush lips smiled seductively and flipped her hair back. "We are getting a birthday present for our father." She leaned closer to him. "Cubans are his favorite. But I hear that they are quite pricey."

Sisters.

That could have been fun if his men weren't there and he didn't have to share.

"They are," the owner said. "For a present, I would suggest a box of superb Dominicans. They are almost as good, and you can get the entire box for the price of one Cuban."

Apparently, they were new to the store, and he didn't trust them with his illegal stuff.

Smart man.

He'd offered Kalugal the first Cuban only after they had become pals.

"I agree with John." He clapped the owner on the back. "You can trust his recommendations." He offered his hand to the one who was doing all the talking. "I'm Kenny."

She put her hand in his. "Nice to meet you, Kenny. I'm Bella, and this is my sister Victoria, but everyone calls her Vicky."

Vicky smiled shyly. "Hi." She offered him her hand as well.

As the owner went to retrieve the box for the sisters, Kalugal affected a hesitant smile. "My friends and I are heading to a club later. Would you ladies care to join us?"

"Which club?" Bella asked.

Vicky shook her head. "We need to get up early tomorrow. Did you forget?"

Bella rolled her eyes. "We are driving home to Arizona, but we can leave whenever we want."

"Have you ever been to the Magnet?"

It wasn't one of Kalugal's favorites, but it was trendy and incredibly hard to get into, which would whet the sisters' appetites.

Bella snorted. "It's impossible to get into. Especially on a Friday night."

"The owner is a good friend of mine. I can get us in."

That was no problem for Kalugal and his men. A little thrall could get them in anywhere they pleased.

"Fine," Vicky relented. "But we are taking our own car."

He dipped his head. "Of course. It's the prudent thing to do. But it's also a shame. I could have offered you a ride in my Ferrari."

Bella's eyes widened. "No way? You drive a Ferrari?"

"Here is your box, ladies." John came back and opened it for them. "It's two-hundred and ninety-nine dollars before tax, which is a bargain for these."

Bella looked at Kalugal for confirmation.

He nodded. "It's a good price. I've seen those sell for double at an airport duty-free shop."

"We'll take it," Vicky said.

"Excellent choice." John smiled and opened the humidor's door.

While the owner rang up the sale, Kalugal motioned for his men to get up and join them at the counter. "These are my friends, Rufus and Phillip. Guys, meet Bella and Victoria."

After the handshakes and small talk were done, the five of them headed out.

"Can we at least see your Ferrari?" Bella asked.

"You can even sit in the driver's seat. I paid the valet to keep it close."

"Smart move." Bella zipped up her puffer jacket. "A car like that is a magnet for thieves."

41

JIN

"Should we leave the car with the valet?" Jacki asked.

Jin glanced at the street stretching out in front of them. Cars were parked on both sides, and there was no vacant spot in sight. "We don't have time to look for parking. Kalugal might leave the bar before we get there."

There had been an accident on the freeway, and they had been stuck in stop-and-go traffic for an hour. What should have taken forty-five minutes had ended up taking twice as long.

Jin's earpiece crackled a moment before William came through. "Park in the valet. The Guardians are going to watch the entrance from across the street."

"Did you hear that?" she asked.

Jacki nodded and pulled into the bar's long driveway.

When she saw a guy outside puffing on a thick cigar, her confidence took another nosedive. "It's not a bar. It's a freaking cigar lounge with a bar. How are we going to stage it? I bet there are no women inside, or just a few."

Jacki stopped in front of the valet booth. "Do you want to turn around? This is definitely not the optimal environment for what you need to do."

The truth was that Jin wanted nothing more than to grab on to the out that Jacki had given her and go home.

She was scared.

On the other hand, if she succeeded tonight, the mission would be over, and she could start her transition process. Putting an end to the limbo she and Arwel were hanging in was worth the risk.

"I want to be done with it. We can pretend to be buying a gift for someone. You know, like a box of fancy cigars. During the holidays, I bet a lot of women come in to buy presents for their husbands and fathers, right?"

Jacki shrugged. "Maybe. Besides, some women might be into cigars." She snorted. "There is something erotic about sucking on a thick one."

The naughty comment managed to ease some of Jin's anxiety, and she laughed. "You're so bad."

As the valet opened the door for her, a blast of cold air hit her face, and she hurried to zip up her puffer jacket before getting out of the car. San Francisco was at least ten degrees colder than where they'd come from, and the humidity made it feel even colder.

"I should have worn a scarf." Jacki threaded her arm through Jin's, and they huddled closer. "Let's get inside before we freeze."

They took two steps toward the door when it opened, and a group of people spilled out.

Jacki jerked on Jin's arm, pulling her back. "It's him," she whispered in her ear.

There could be only one *him*, but Jin didn't know which one of the three men was Kalugal.

Jin could've followed the string of consciousness to Jacki and seen him through her eyes, but she was too terrified to move. Like a deer caught in the headlights of an oncoming semitrailer, she could do nothing other than stare.

"The one talking to the girl," Jacki whispered.

He must've have heard her and turned to look at them. Appraising them with his intense eyes, he frowned. "Do I know you, ladies?"

"Aren't you Barry's brother?" Jacki asked.

It was a good save, and even though the arm holding on to Jin's was shaking, Jacki's voice didn't waver.

He smiled, or rather smirked. It was what Jacki had called his signature smirk, which gave him away no matter who he shrouded himself as.

"I'm sorry to disappoint you, but I don't have a brother named Barry."

"My bad," Jacki said. "You look just like him."

She gave Jin a little push, but Jin's legs refused to move.

"I must have a generic-looking face because I get that a lot." He took the elbow of the girl standing next to him. "Good night, ladies." He walked toward the valet, who was waiting with the Ferrari's door open.

"Go," Jacki urged in a whisper.

Jin shook her head. "I can't."

Her feet felt like they were embedded in the pavement, and she couldn't force them to move.

Trying to save the situation, Jacki turned and waved at the group.

As one of the girls got behind the wheel and sat in the luxury car for a few moments, all Jin could do was keep on staring.

Jacki, bless her heart, pretended to admire the Ferrari so Jin's imitation of a statue wouldn't look strange.

Once the men drove off, leaving the two girls behind, the shorter one turned to her friend. "You are insane. Going to a club with three guys we just met in a bar? How stupid can you be? I'm going home."

The other one put her hands on her hips. "He can get us into the Magnet, Vicky. And besides, what are you so scared of? Serial killers don't drive Ferraris."

"Maybe not. But rapists might. And I don't care about the club. I want to go home."

"I could skip the club, but not the opportunity to hang out with three super hot guys. Come on, Vicky, don't be such a scaredy-cat."

As the two kept arguing, the valet pulled up with their car. They got in, drove away, and only then did Jin manage to move her shaky legs.

"Fuck!" Jacki cursed. "He was right there. If you had followed my lead, we could've introduced ourselves, and you could have shaken his hand while I talked about going with them to that club."

"I'm so sorry. I froze."

42

ARWEL

"Do you want me to follow the Ferrari?" Douglas said in Arwel's earpiece.

"There is no need. We know where he is going."

For some reason Jin had hesitated, but maybe it wasn't a total loss, and they could follow Kalugal to the club the girl had mentioned.

But first, he had to check up on Jin.

She was still rooted to the same spot, distraught despite Jacki's attempts to console her.

Arwel could feel her distress all the way from across the street.

Turning the earpiece off, he got out of the car and walked over to her. "Let's get inside. It's freezing out here."

The valet was watching them, and Arwel didn't want the guy to get suspicious. The incident might prompt Kalugal to come back and ask the valet about the two women.

No empathic ability was required to see how agitated they both still were, especially Jin, who seemed badly shaken.

He found them a table in the back and signaled for the waitress. They all could use a drink. After ordering, he leaned closer to Jin. "What happened?"

"I froze. I just couldn't move a muscle."

"Kalugal must have done something to you," Jacki whispered. "He might have given you a subliminal command or something."

"I wish it was so." Jin closed her eyes and took in a deep breath. "I got scared. That's all. And then he looked right at me, and I couldn't move. I'm not ready for this."

Jacki groaned. "We are screwed. He's seen us up close and he is going to recognize us. We need to come up with new, more elaborate disguises, and we don't have Eva to do it for us."

It seemed like following Kalugal to the club was a no-go, and that was a pity. After overhearing the conversation between Vicky and the other one, Jin and Jacki could have shown up there with the perfect excuse. They could have pretended to want to get into that club as well.

But Jin was too distraught for that.

When the drinks arrived, she finished hers in two gulps.

His heart going out to her, Arwel wrapped his arm around her shoulders. "Don't beat yourself up over it. You are a newbie, and it's perfectly understandable for you to freeze on your first go."

Her badass attitude and assertive character had blinded everyone to the fact that Jin was a twenty-four-year-old girl who had just graduated from college. The month of training she'd gotten at the government program was not enough to teach her any real skills, and she had no field experience.

She shook her head. "I was so sure that I was ready." She cast an accusing look at Jacki. "Where is your precognition when I need it? How come you didn't see this coming?"

Jacki shrugged. "As I've said many times before, it's a useless talent. I didn't get any glimpses lately, not even the random stuff I occasionally get. It's like there is a power outage up there." She tapped her temple.

"Is there a way to jump-start it?" Jin asked.

Jacki leaned back and crossed her arms over her chest. "I'm not going on drugs again, if that's what you are suggesting."

Jin gaped at her. "I would never do such a thing. How can you even think that?"

"That's what they did in the program to jump-start my visions."

"I'm not them. I was thinking about things like meditation. It helps Mey when she does her thing."

"Even if that helped, my visions are about random things. I'm surprised they showed me your sister coming for you."

Jin rolled her eyes. "That's why I thought that they might tell us something about Kalugal and when it is best for me to approach him."

"I'm sorry to disappoint you."

"It's not Jacki's fault," Arwel said. "If you are looking for someone to blame, Kian and I are guilty of thinking that an inexperienced girl could pull off such a difficult task on her first go. Before going on this assignment, you should have had months of practice on easier targets."

Jin sighed. "Should have, could have. It's water under the bridge. What do we do now? Follow him to that club?"

"You are in no shape to go after him tonight. We will have to wait for the next opportunity."

"I still think that he compelled you," Jacki said. "You are not the type who crumbles under pressure. I've never seen you act like that."

"I wish that was true." Jin slumped in her chair. "I would feel like less of a failure."

"You are not a failure." He squeezed her shoulder. "I think you were terrified of him compelling you, and that was why you froze."

"Maybe subconsciously."

"I have an idea that I should have thought of before. Lokan could compel you to resist Kalugal's compulsion."

If nothing else, it would boost her confidence.

She turned hopeful eyes to him. "You think it will work?"

"It's worth a try."

43

KALUGAL

"Even with the damn shroud you are a chick magnet," Rufsur grumbled. "Did you see how those girls gaped at you like you were a movie star?"

That had been an odd experience on several levels.

The shroud Kalugal used was of a handsome young man, but not a striking one. He'd purposely chosen a composite of features that made him look like the average American guy. Brown hair, brown eyes, a strong chin. He'd kept the height and physique the same as his because it was easier to maintain, especially when getting naked with a woman. But at six foot two he wasn't overly tall, neither was he overly muscled, so that didn't stand out either.

"They stared at me because they thought I was someone else. Barry's brother. That composite I use as a shroud makes me look like a lot of guys."

"Yeah, maybe." Rufsur shifted in his chair. "If they were better looking, we could've invited them to the club. I have a feeling that the sisters are not going to show up."

"They weren't ugly," Phinas said. "And both had decent figures under those puffy jackets and loose pants. The Asian was too tall, but the other one was just right."

Rufsur shook his head. "You have low standards, my friend."

For a change, Kalugal agreed with Phinas. At first glance, both girls had been nothing special, and yet something in him responded to them.

What was it, though?

He didn't recognize the feeling. It was as if he knew them from somewhere, but he was pretty sure he'd never met them before.

Except, they could be students at Stanford, and since it was his favorite hunting ground, he might have bumped into them but not committed them to memory. Neither was his type, and Rufsur was right about them being nothing special.

He liked tall blonds with kind, smart eyes, and from those he chose the ones who were prettier than average.

Kalugal could afford to be picky. With so many to choose from, he didn't have to compromise his preferences unless there was a good reason to do so.

A particularly bright mind could compensate for less than average looks, and not only in terms of exchanging ideas and interesting conversations. Experience had taught him that smart females were also better sex partners. It probably had something to do with having thriving imaginations and being open to new experiences.

Or maybe it was about having someone to talk to that was interested in the same things they were. Stimulating conversations stirred more than just the mind. If he got excited by just talking, it was reasonable to assume that his partners experienced the same.

Still, Kalugal was sure that he had never engaged with those two, sexually or otherwise. He would have remembered them.

The likeliest explanation was that he'd passed them by, or that they had been around someone he had engaged with.

That could also explain why the girls had stared at him as if they knew him.

"No response?" Rufsur asked.

"What do you want me to say?"

"Would you have taken either of them to bed?"

"I don't know. I didn't get the chance to talk to them."

Rufsur shook his head. "Sex and talking are two separate things. If you want to talk, you can make appointments with top professors in the university that you admire so much. That way you'll know for sure that they are smart. No guesswork involved."

"And where's the fun in that?" Kalugal cast him an amused glance. "Sex and talk go together like cheese and wine. Both are good on their own but even better when put together."

Phinas nodded. "The problem is finding women who want to talk about interesting stuff. You know, like politics, or economics, or philosophy, or even books. But most girls today want to talk about this or that blogger and this or that celebrity. I have no patience for that, so I prefer to go straight to the business of getting them naked and shutting them up."

"That's why I like hunting at Stanford."

Except, it seemed that Kalugal hadn't been changing his shrouds as often as he should. The problem was keeping track of which ones he'd used where. That was why he had them organized by activities.

Going for more than the five or six that he usually employed would require keeping a log, and that was a hassle. Unless Rufsur did that for him.

After all, his job was to assist Kalugal in any way he could.

He turned to his deputy. "Since being recognized is becoming an issue, I need you to start a log of which disguise I use when and with whom. I'll give each shroud a different name, which you will notate next to the activity."

Rufsur smirked. "Does that mean that you won't be sneaking out alone anymore? Because if you do, you'll have to keep the damn log yourself."

"Not really. When I travel abroad for my archeological digs, it's always as

Professor Gunter. And when I venture out alone while I'm here, I'll let you know who I am going as."

"That's good enough. At least you'll let me know, so I won't have to find out that you have left the compound from whoever is in charge of monitoring the gate on that day."

"I don't need a babysitter, Rufsur. I've told you that often enough."

Phinas shook his head. "I'm with Rufsur on that. You are too valuable to lose. If something happens to you, none of us would be able to continue your work. You keep those world domination plans of yours all in your head."

"Unless disaster strikes and a plane explodes while I'm on it, you have nothing to worry about. With my compulsion, shrouding, and thralling abilities, I'm invincible."

Rufsur cast him a sidelong glance. "So why are you still worried about your father finding you?"

"I'd rather avoid conflict if I can. My plans don't involve any outward struggle. One day, I'll just be the one pulling all the strings with no one any the wiser. A peaceful, non-hostile takeover."

Phinas let out a long-suffering sigh. "If no one will know, why bother?"

Kalugal chuckled. "Because I'll be a god."

44

KIAN

"Fuck!" Kian pushed to his feet and started pacing. "What do you mean, she froze?" he barked into the phone.

Syssi looked up at him. "Calm down. It's not Jin's fault. She wasn't ready."

Taking a deep breath, he tried to do as his wife suggested while listening to Arwel explain.

"Jacki thinks that Kalugal compelled Jin, but Jin says that she just got scared. We didn't prepare her well enough."

If the Guardian was implying that Kian had sent Jin after Kalugal without proper training, he wasn't wrong.

Except, it was supposed to be simple. How hard could it be to bump into a guy and touch him?

Girls sometimes did that just to get a guy's attention, and Jin wasn't the shy type. She'd projected a badass attitude, but apparently, it had been all bluster.

Kian raked his fingers through his hair. "Now Kalugal knows what she looks like."

"He does, but that isn't really a problem. So what if he sees her in another club or bar and recognizes her? It's not like San Francisco is a huge metropolitan area with thousands of places for young people to party. She could go up to him and say hi, and he wouldn't suspect a thing unless she panics again."

"How do we ensure that it doesn't happen again?"

"We get Lokan to help. He can compel her not to respond to Kalugal's compulsion. I think that was the main source of her fear. If that's no longer an issue, she will regard him as just any other guy and won't be afraid to approach him."

"I'm not sure Lokan can do that. In fact, I'm pretty sure that he can't. His compulsion works only on humans, not on immortals. Kalugal can manipulate both."

"True, and there is no doubt that Kalugal is more powerful, but since Jin is still human, Lokan might be just as effective in compelling her as Kalugal."

Kian stopped in front of the sliding door to the back yard. "I assume that Jin is not within earshot."

"No. I'm in the car by myself. I was sent to get ice cream. Apparently, that's what women medicate with when they are upset."

"I can call Lokan and arrange a conference call with Jin."

"Please. Even if it ends up not working, it's worthwhile just as a confidence booster. She needs it."

Kian opened the slider and stepped out. "I should send Parker to join his parents. Having a compeller in the house would make her feel even safer."

"Vivian and Magnus would never agree to that. We are about two hundred feet away from the lion's den, so to speak. It's too dangerous to bring a kid in here."

They were all overestimating how dangerous Kalugal was, including him. True, the guy was a powerful immortal, but he didn't seem inclined to commit acts of violence.

Then again, when cornered, even a peaceful gorilla could tear a human to shreds.

"I've already suggested it, and they've already declined. But I thought that under the circumstances they might relent."

"They won't, and I agree with them." Arwel sighed. "Putting Jin in danger is killing me, especially since I have to pretend that it's not a big deal for her sake. Is there a chance I could convince you to call the whole thing off? We can tell Areana that we found her son but that it's too dangerous for us to approach him."

"I'm not doing it just for her." Kian lifted the box of cigarillos from the side table and pulled one out. "Kalugal might be a threat to us, and now that he is in our neighborhood, we need to safeguard ourselves. Jin's tethering ability could give us the only advantage over him to be had."

"That's not the only advantage. We also have more people. From what we have seen so far, he has about a dozen men with him. Maybe even less."

"Our numbers are meaningless when Kalugal can blanket compel everyone other than Turner and Jacki. And we are not even sure about that. If he can compel immortals, he might be able to compel even the immunes."

It was a scary thought, but Kian was right. Which meant that they couldn't afford to cancel the mission.

"When are you going to call Lokan?"

"Right after I hang up with you."

"I'll be back in the house in about ten minutes. I'll tell Jin to get ready."

Syssi shook her head. "The girl needs to rest and unwind. It can wait until tomorrow."

As usual, his wife was the voice of reason.

"I'll call him tonight, but I'll have him do it tomorrow, and not only to Jin. I want him to compel each of the Guardians as well. I'm pretty sure that's a futile exercise, but what do we have to lose?"

"True. As you said, we need every advantage we can think of."

When he ended the call, Kian lit up his cigarillo and called Lokan.

"Hello, Kian. If you are calling me this late, there is trouble. Bad news from the Bay?"

"You might say so. I need your help."

45

JIN

"Don't sweat it," Kri said. "You'll get him next time."

Everyone was being so freaking nice, and it was annoying the hell out of Jin.

She wished someone other than herself would berate her and tell her that she couldn't do it, so she could get mad, double down, and stubbornly prove that she could.

That had always worked for her. Whenever a teacher had told her that she wasn't good at this or that and should choose another subject, she had studied her ass off and had proven them wrong.

That was how she'd ended as a business major. Math had been a struggle in middle school, and not her favorite subject, but after a teacher had made a disparaging comment about her inability to keep up, Jin had asked her parents to hire her a tutor.

Unlike her schoolteacher, the retired professor had been excellent at explaining and simplifying all those concepts she'd had trouble with, and after two months with him she'd gotten her first perfect score on a math test and had never looked back.

Jin needed someone to challenge her now, to tell her that she wasn't good enough and make her so angry that she would forget about her fears.

But even Jacki, who she'd expected to be tough on her, was being uncharacteristically quiet.

Maybe she was shaken up as well?

Probably.

Except, Jacki was putting up a calm façade, while Jin was letting it all out. "Where is Arwel? I need that freaking ice cream."

She didn't like keeping things boiling up inside. It was better to let it go and move on.

"Do you need to spar?" Kri asked. "When I'm frustrated or angry, that usually helps."

Michael nodded. "All that negative energy needs an outlet. If you are not into sparring, you can run on the treadmill."

"Thank you, but that's not how it works for me. I need the anger to fuel my resolve. I operate best when I have something to prove."

"You do have something to prove," Jacki said. "Next time we go after Kalugal, don't freeze. Imagine that he is a big ice cream cone and that you need to get it."

Vivian laughed. "I don't think Arwel would appreciate that imagery."

Jacki waved a hand. "I didn't mean it like that. It's just that Jin is so desperate for Arwel to come back with that ice cream. She needs to feel just as strongly about tethering Kalugal."

Kri snorted. "Hey, he could shroud himself as an ice cream cone. That could be fun for his lover."

As Jacki's expression turned dreamy, Jin wondered whether it had anything to do with Kalugal. After all, she'd gotten to see what he looked like without the shroud.

"How hot is he?" Jin blurted.

"Hot." Jacki fanned herself. "He has that bad boy vibe that women find irresistible. I wonder why he shrouds himself as a less attractive guy."

Jin cast a quick glance at William. As she'd expected, he had a pained look on his face.

Damn, Jacki was so obtuse.

"Maybe he doesn't want to attract too much attention," Vivian said.

"Then he shouldn't drive a Ferrari." Jacki rose to her feet and stretched. "I'm beat. I think I'm going to skip the ice cream and hit the sack."

"Me too." Vivian got up. "Doing nothing is very tiring."

Naturally, Magnus followed. "Good night, everyone." He looked at Jin. "Don't agonize over what happened. We've all been rookies and have made our share of mistakes. Tomorrow is a new day."

"Thanks. I'll try."

When they were gone, she turned to the three burly bears. "Did you make mistakes when you were newbies?"

Ewan chuckled. "I was fifteen the first time I had to fight off invaders. I didn't only freeze, I pissed myself."

Jin's eyes widened. "Fifteen? You were just a kid!"

"Back then, fifteen was old enough. I wasn't even the youngest."

Shaking her head, she crossed her arms over her chest. "I can't believe that. Who sends kids into battle?"

"It's obvious that you are not a history buff," Gregor said. "When needed, anyone who could swing a sword joined the defending force. Don't forget that we were post transition immortals, and we were much stronger than the human males we fought."

"Yeah, I forgot about that. Still, mentally you were boys."

"They still are." Kri chuckled. "I'm the youngest Guardian, and when they start goofing around, I feel like I'm their mother."

Michael wrapped his arm around his mate's broad shoulders. "You are not the youngest, I am."

"You are not a Guardian yet. You are a Guardian in training."

"Semantics."

"How old are you, Michael? If it's okay to ask. I don't know what the immortal etiquette on age questions is."

"It's okay to ask, but not everyone will answer. I'm twenty-two."

Jin looked at Kri, who looked about the same age as Michael, but that didn't mean that she was.

"If you are wondering about me, I'm fifty." Kri flipped her long braid back. "But just for your information, I'm considered a very young immortal. Gregor here is over three hundred years old, Ewan is pushing five centuries, and Duncan is a youngling at two hundred and something."

"Wow. Is there a way to tell?"

Kri smiled. "Nope. Unless you are told, there is no way you can guess. We just don't age physically, and the men don't age mentally either. I think their brains stop developing at fourteen." She cast Michael a fond look. "Except for my mate, who is incredibly mature at twenty-two."

It occurred to Jin that she didn't know how old Kalugal was, and whether it had anything to do with how powerful he was.

"How old is Kalugal?"

"He is young," Kri said. "I don't know his exact age, but I know that he is less than a hundred."

"Does age have anything to do with an increase in power?"

Kri nodded. "It's scary to think that he is already so powerful. He is going to surpass his father as the strongest immortal ever born."

Jin lifted a brow. "Stronger than Kian?"

"Definitely."

Damn. And that was who they were sending her up against?

"Suddenly, I feel like a sacrificial lamb. What chance do I have against him?"

Kri leaned forward and braced her arms on her thighs. "None. But you are not going up against him. Your only job is to touch him briefly. Try to think of it as touching a fully armed jet fighter. It's much bigger and stronger than you, but you are not fighting it. You are just walking up to it and putting a hand on the metal. That's it."

46

ARWEL

"I have a stomachache." Jin walked into the bedroom with a towel wrapped around her head and another one around her body. "But at least I washed the gunk off my face, and that feels wonderful."

Sitting on the bed, Arwel spread his legs. "Come here, gorgeous."

She sauntered toward him, sat on his thigh, and wound her arms around his neck. "I like hearing you say that. I know you mean it, and it makes me feel sexy." She dipped her head and kissed him softly.

Delving into her mouth, he could still taste the ice cream even though she'd brushed her teeth. "Sweet," he murmured.

"I should be after all that sugar."

"You are sweet no matter what you eat."

"And a little prickly."

"That's what makes you so exciting." He put his hand on her belly. "How is that stomach ache?"

"If you rub my tummy, it will go away."

"I can do that. I can also rub you all over and massage the bad tension away while arousing the good kind."

"I could go for that."

He lifted her off his lap and put her on the bed. "I'll get the lotion."

Just imagining Arwel's big hands all over her body made Jin purr like a kitten. "I'll be waiting right here."

She pulled the towel off and lay on her tummy.

"Now I can't go. I have to kiss that beautiful ass first."

She wiggled it. "Be my guest."

Cupping both cheeks, he kissed one and then the other. Then went back for another round. It was a struggle to tear himself away, but he'd promised her a massage.

"Don't move."

Grabbing the lotion from the bathroom counter, Arwel rushed back into the bedroom.

He found Jin in the exact position he'd left her, which was what he had hoped for. That gorgeous ass of hers needed a lot more attention.

"That was fast," she murmured.

"I didn't want you to fall asleep before I got back."

"No chance of that. I'm still buzzing with nervous energy, and I'd rather spend it playing with you than sparring with Kri." She chuckled. "If she were standing next to Kalugal, I would have been less afraid of him than her. Kri's shoulders are broader than his."

"She's a helluva fighter. Excellent instincts and the muscle power to back them up."

Arwel squeezed a generous amount of lotion into his palm and then rubbed his hands together to warm them up.

"I like her. But her offer to spar with me wasn't smart. Even if she does her best not to hurt me, she's going to."

Arwel put his hands on the small of Jin's back and fanned out from there.

"She won't. Kri teaches self-defense at the sanctuary and also at the halfway house. She knows how to handle fragile human girls."

"I'm not fragile."

Arwel smiled. Jin still thought of herself as a badass, which was good. It meant that her confidence had been shaken but not broken.

"Of course not. I meant the rescued girls."

Her hair was still wrapped in the towel, which gave him free access to her shoulders and neck. "Your muscles are all knotted up here." He applied gentle pressure.

As Jin moaned in pleasure, the sound sent a bolt straight to his shaft.

"That feels so good. You have magic hands."

Suddenly, Jin lifted her head. "Crap, I forgot to untether Jacki."

He gently pushed her head back down. "Good. Then we don't have to worry about her running off on William."

"No, wait. I did untether her. I did it in the car on the way back. I just forgot." She put her head down. "They are probably back already. Jacki only needed to buy dye for the wigs."

"I didn't hear them coming in. But I'm sure William would have called me if she gave him the slip."

"Jacki is not going to run. But I wish she'd give William a chance. He's such a nice man, and so smart."

"Maybe the outing is his chance, and this day isn't going to be a total loss." Arwel regretted the words as soon as they'd left his mouth.

Jin groaned. "Now that you mention it, I remembered what my mom used to say. Bad things come in threes. Maybe I shouldn't have untethered Jacki."

He'd heard about that superstition. "Only one bad thing happened, not two. So, you have nothing to worry about."

"Not true. Two bad things happened. I froze and didn't tether Kalugal, and then I ate too much ice cream and got a stomachache."

"I don't think the stomachache counts. Just relax. Jacki isn't going anywhere. I would have sensed if she was planning something."

"I'm not worried. I was speaking hypothetically." Jin turned her head and looked at him. "Can you sense how I feel when we make love?"

Arwel nodded. "I know when you get impatient and want to rush forward but don't say anything because you trust me to bring you pleasure." He leaned forward and took her lips in a gentle kiss. "And I know when you are about to come."

"That's not fair. You have insider information. No wonder you are such an exceptional lover." She smirked. "But there is a downside. I can't fake orgasms with you."

Even though he knew she was teasing, Arwel arched a brow. "Did you ever do that?"

"No. There was no need."

He paused with his hands on her shoulder blades. "Do you always climax?"

"With you, yes."

That was a smart answer to a question he shouldn't have asked. The past and other partners were inconsequential.

"Good to know. But then I knew that already." He cupped her ass cheeks and gave them a squeeze.

"I wish I could feel you the way you can feel me."

"You can if you tether me."

Jin flipped around, her perky breasts mesmerizing him for a moment.

"That would be amazing. I could actually see myself through your eyes, and experience what you are experiencing. That's going to be surreal. Are you sure you don't mind?"

"Mind? I think it's sexy as hell."

47

JIN

What a surreal trip that could be. She could actually experience sex as a man. Or rather as both a man and a woman.

Double the pleasure. Or double the confusion.

For a woman, climaxing required a certain level of mental focus. It wasn't a purely physical thing like it was for a man. Seeing herself through Arwel's eyes might be distracting.

Still, the intimacy would be at a whole different level, and she just had to give it a try.

As Arwel's hands traveled up her torso and cupped the undersides of her breasts, Jin clasped his wrists and closed her eyes.

Attaching her tether had never been easier. The string of consciousness floated toward Arwel's mind without her having to direct it, as if it belonged there.

The moment she switched to watching through his eyes, Jin gasped. "Is that how you see me?" She opened hers to look at him.

His answer was a fanged smile.

As she'd expected, the experience was confusing. She couldn't look at Arwel and at herself at the same time, and since she was fascinated by what she saw through his eyes, Jin closed hers.

The face she saw wasn't the same one that stared back at her from the mirror. Arwel's perception colored her in a much more flattering light. If only she could look like that for real—radiant, sexy, every feature perfectly chiseled, skin smooth like silk.

Jin was stunned to discover that she could actually feel the texture of it under Arwel's hands. That had never happened before with the other tethers, which had been limited to transferring only visual and auditory signals.

But that wasn't the half of it.

Through the tether, she could also feel Arwel's emotions, desires, needs, which was no less shocking. She wasn't an empath, and thoughts and emotions normally didn't travel along the strings of consciousness she'd attached to others before.

It was an entirely different experience with Arwel.

Jin felt his desire for her as if it was her own, and she was stunned by the level of aggression he was keeping in check because he was afraid of hurting her.

Arwel's need to possess her was so overwhelming that it was scary.

Damn, she hadn't expected that.

Arwel seemed so mellow, so accommodating. Where was that intensity coming from?

She'd tasted some of it the other times they had sex, but he'd been holding back more than she'd realized.

Surprisingly, Jin didn't feel threatened by Arwel's caveman urges, or offended. All of the feminist objections that she should have felt were overshadowed by a resounding *Hell yeah! Bring it on!*

The primitive female in her responded to the primitive male in him, and letting her cave-girl out felt liberating.

What a curious contradiction it was.

Jin could never have imagined submission could feel so liberating.

But then she'd never been with anyone whom she trusted as completely as she trusted Arwel. The direct mind connection he'd allowed her to form proved what she'd already known. Arwel was her safe haven, and as much as he yearned to possess her, he also yearned to be possessed by her.

"The intensity is electrifying. The overwhelming need. I don't know how you are holding back and taking your time with me." She opened her eyes and smiled. "Actually, I do know. You care for me, and I'm precious to you. You are fighting your urges in order to protect me."

As he dipped his head and kissed her, she tasted him and herself at the same time, got excited and sensed his arousal flare as well, much hotter than hers.

Was it because he was male and his higher testosterone level made him more sexed up? Or was it the difference between a human and an immortal?

She felt dizzy with the wealth of emotions ricocheting between them. Her feelings sensed by him and then transmitted back to her, augmented by his.

It was too much.

She had to let go of the string, leaving it in place but not following it to Arwel's mind.

Somehow, he felt it. "Why did you stop?"

"It was too much. Too intense. The feelings, I mean. Your need is so savage."

"It doesn't frighten you?"

"No. I welcome it."

Lacing his fingers with hers, he pulled her arms over her head. "I can't wait for you to transition."

She knew what he meant. There was no way he could let go while she was still human.

"Me neither. I want all of your unleashed ferocity, and I want to be just as ferocious back."

He smiled, his fangs gleaming white in the dim light. "I have a feeling that you will be."

"I think I am pretty wild already."

Was it Arwel's aggression that was spurring hers on?

Because suddenly she felt like fighting him, not because she didn't want him, but because she wanted him to prove that he could subdue her.

Since she had no fighting chance, it was an utterly stupid reflex, but the instinct was so strong that she couldn't help the urge to scratch, to bite…

Damn. It must be coming from him.

"I like it when you get feisty."

His hands still clasping hers over her head, he slid down her body and licked her nipple before sucking it into his mouth.

Jin ground. "Arwel.' His name left her mouth on a breath.

He lifted his head, his elongated fangs gleaming like twin daggers. "What do you need, love? Tell me."

"I need you to take your pants off."

His tongue curled out and he licked his fangs, looking more predatory than she'd ever seen him.

"With pleasure."

48

ARWEL

The self-feeding loop Jin had created with her tether had been a revelation.

His mate was a fighter, and she craved his dominance. Which in turn, had spurred on his aggression.

He wanted to take her savagely while she fought him, thrust into her and keep on pounding until they both climaxed and he sank his fangs into her long neck.

Regrettably, for now he could only give her a symbolic taste of it, which would leave them both unsatisfied.

Getting rid of his pants in one fluid move, he tossed them on the floor and gripped Jin's legs.

She tried to close them. But he pulled them apart, spreading her wide for his hungry eyes.

Panting, she fought his grip, but his unrelenting hold only added to her rapidly rising arousal.

As the sight and scent of the moisture coating her folds wrested a hungry growl from deep in his throat, Arwel tasted venom on his tongue.

He was dangerously close to losing control.

First, though, he was going to make sure that Jin could take the pounding he was about to treat her to.

Lifting her legs over his shoulders, he went after that sweet nectar like a man possessed. He latched his mouth onto her silky folds, sucking, licking, nipping...

The urge to turn his head slightly to the right and bite her inner thigh was so strong that he had to summon all of his willpower to keep his touch gentle.

As Jin's breathing became labored and her legs started trembling, she lifted her head to look at what he was doing. "Even without following the tether to you, I can feel the echoes of your thoughts. I know that you want to bite me."

"I'm not going to. Not yet."

As he licked into her, she let her head drop back on the pillows.

Her petals were swollen, like ripe peaches for him to lick and suck on, and as he did just that, her hands clutched his shoulders, her fingernails digging into his skin.

The little pain Jin was causing was like pouring gasoline on an already raging fire.

He had to be in her, but first, he was going to make her come.

Pushing two fingers inside her, he closed his lips around her clit and sucked.

It was like detonating an explosion, and the sound Jin made as her body arched up was probably heard all the way to Kalugal's complex.

In a heartbeat, Arwel was on top of her.

His mouth latching on to Jin's to muffle her screams, his shaft breached her entrance, and he surged inside her.

Glorious.

Gripping her hips, he pulled back and shoved in again, then ducked his head and sucked on a nipple.

But when his shafting became too frenzied, he had to let go.

As Jin's arms closed around him, she lifted her long legs and wrapped them around the back of his thighs. Holding on to him as he pounded into her, her fingers were clutching his back muscles, and her nails were digging into his skin.

Then she bit his shoulder, and he nearly came.

She moaned. Arching up and sliding her hands down to grip his ass, she was meeting him thrust for thrust.

Their lovemaking was beautifully synchronized.

Was Jin following the tether to his mind? Was she feeling what he was?

Arwel was too far gone to differentiate between his feelings and Jin's, his need and hers, his desire and hers.

They were one entity, moving, pulsing, throbbing.

The connection was phenomenal.

"Please," she whispered. "I need to come."

Arwel needed that too, but he didn't want this to end yet. It was too good to cut short.

Shifting sideways, he drove into her in a corkscrew motion, rubbing against the center of her desire with every stroke.

As Jin's second orgasm blasted out, shaking her body violently, he shook along with her, and when her spasming sheath tightened around his shaft, he could no longer hold back.

Latching his lips on to her neck, he licked the sweet spot and then hissed before striking with his fangs.

Jin screamed, but it wasn't in pain. She was coming again, milking him as he shot into her.

Only when he was spent, and she lay limp under him, did he remember that they had forgotten to use a condom.

"Fuck," he murmured into Jin's neck.

When she didn't respond, he lifted his head and looked at her beautiful face and the blissed-out expression that he'd helped put on it.

What a pity that bliss was going to dissipate once she floated back down and realized what they had done.

49

JIN

"Oh, my God." Jin draped her arms over her eyes. "We are in so much trouble. Kian is going to excommunicate us."

Arwel groaned. "He just might."

Pulling her arm over her head, she smiled at him. "I'm not sorry, though. First of all, this was the best sex ever, and I mean in the entire history of humans and immortals alike. And secondly, I want to transition." She lifted on her elbows. "Worst case scenario, we will leave the clan and establish a new community. You and me and the ten kids we are going to have together."

She was just teasing, trying to bring a smile to Arwel's worried face. Having a bunch of kids was Mey's dream, not hers. Jin was in no hurry to start a family, and when she was ready, two or three would do.

Arwel arched a brow. "Is that a proposal? Because I heard you telling Mey that she and Yamanu should get married before having kids."

Winding her arms around his neck, she pulled him over her. "You are mine, Arwel. And I am yours. I'm taking it for granted that we are getting married."

He kissed the tip of her nose. "Don't you think something is missing?"

She frowned. "Like what? The bond you keep obsessing about? I don't care about that."

His expression turned serious. "That too, but there is another, more crucial component missing. Do you love me?"

Jin's eyes widened.

They had never said the love word. There hadn't been time for mushy feelings. Since her escape, things had been moving fast, and stress levels were high. It wasn't the most conducive environment for love.

Did she love Arwel?

What was love?

With a sigh, he rolled off her and lay on his back. "That's what I thought."

"Don't do that." She turned on her side and faced him. "I've never been in love, so I don't know if what I feel is that. I was trying to think, but you immediately jumped to conclusions." She huffed. "Talk about insecurity."

He turned to look at her, his turquoise eyes still glowing from the lovemaking. "What were you thinking?"

"That I want to be with you, like all of the time. I can't imagine being separated from you for more than a few hours. I need you in my bed, and I don't ever want to go to sleep without you right next to me. Is that love?"

His eyes softening, he put an arm around her and pulled her closer to him. "Sounds like love to me."

"What about you? Do you love me?"

"I'm in the same situation that you are. I've never been in love either. My reaction to seeing just your picture was so powerful that it confused the hell out of me. Rationally, I realized that a photo is not enough to fall in love with someone, and yet the moment I saw you, I knew you were destined for me. My problem is that I'm not a believer in the Fates or some other power like Yamanu is. I'm still trying to analyze and rationalize how I feel and why."

Jin nodded. "We just met a week ago. Can people fall in love so quickly? Or is it just lust and like? It is so confusing." She scrunched her nose. "Mey told me that it happened just as fast for her and Yamanu. So maybe it is the Fates' work."

He caressed her cheek with two fingers. "That's how it happened for all the couples I know. Or at least those who shared their experiences with me." He chuckled. "Lokan and Carol bonded their first night together. I was right there on the other side of the wall, feeling what they felt, and it was phenomenal."

So that was why Arwel was obsessing about the bond. He'd felt it form between Lokan and Carol and he was expecting the same to happen between them.

"Lokan and Carol were both immortal when they bonded, correct?"

He nodded.

"So that's why it happened so fast for them. And they probably didn't use freaking condoms either because they had no need for them. You can't compare us to them. I'm still human, and this is only the second time we've made love without protection."

He grimaced. "We've messed up. You could enter transition tomorrow and Kian would probably fire me."

"So let him. You can help me with my business." She clapped her hand on her forehead. "I'm so stupid. If we fail Kian, he is not going to invest clan money in us. Both of us are going to be out of a job."

Arwel smiled. "I've known Kian my entire life. He is going to be majorly pissed, and he will berate us both for our carelessness. He might even put me on suspension, but eventually he will get over it."

Jin plopped onto her back and draped her arm over her eyes again. "He needs you, so he will reinstate you. But he doesn't need a fashion line. I can kiss that idea goodbye."

"You might still get Kalugal before you enter transition. It took Mey two weeks, and that was while she and Yamanu were going for it full speed ahead. As much as I don't want to, I'll make sure that we use protection until this mission is over."

Letting out a relieved breath, Jin turned toward him. "You are right. There is no way my transition has started on an unlucky day like this."

He gathered her into his arms. "We don't know whether it was a lucky or unlucky day. Perhaps by not tethering Kalugal today, you saved yourself and Jacki. And maybe our lovemaking was fruitful, and we've created a child." Arwel put his hand on her belly.

He looked so wistful that Jin felt bad about delivering a dose of reality. "Did you forget that I'm on the pill?"

"Yeah, I did. And anyway, that was just wishful thinking."

50

YAMANU

"Anyone want more coffee?" Mey asked.

Wendy shook her head. "No thanks. I'm going back to my room." She picked up her plate and took it to the sink to rinse. "Thanks for breakfast. Call me when you are ready to make lunch. I want to help."

"Sure thing."

Yamanu and Mey exchanged glances. The girl was a recluse, preferring to spend her time alone rather than interact with them and Richard.

Not that they were such great company for a young woman.

The truth was that since Jin, Arwel, and Jacki had left, it was damn boring in the keep.

Yamanu was spending most of his time with Mey, which was great. But since she was busy working on her fashion designs, he was also putting in many hours in the gym and the swimming pool, getting back into the shape he'd been in before leaving for New York.

But other than that, there was nothing to do.

He used to spend a lot of time meditating every day, but the main purpose of that had been managing his celibacy. Thankfully, that stage of his life was over, and his meditation routine had shrunk to twenty minutes a day.

Yamanu was very happy to substitute all those hours of solitude with making love to his incredible mate.

Instead of the cravings subsiding over time, they were only getting stronger, and they were making love for breakfast, lunch, dinner, and a midnight snack.

Nevertheless, it still left many hours of nothing.

"I'll have some." Richard lifted his mug for Mey to refill, and then turned to Yamanu. "When are you heading to the gym?"

"In an hour. Are you joining?"

Richard shrugged. "It's not like I have anything better to do. By the time Kian lets me out of this hole in the ground, I'll be in fantastic shape."

The trouble with the guy using the gym was that Yamanu couldn't train with the Guardians on rotation in the keep or use his full strength. They were too strong and too fast, and watching them spar, Richard would have figured out that something was up.

Yamanu had toyed with the idea of telling him that they were all on some experimental steroids, but Richard was just the type who would ask to have some of that for himself.

"Are you sure? Yesterday you said that you were going to take a break today. You whined about being sore all over."

"Ingrid brought me Motrin from the clinic."

It was still unclear whether there was more than just sex going on between the two, and Yamanu decided to just come out and ask.

"What's the deal with you and Ingrid? Are you dating?"

Richard snorted. "Dating? Where am I going to take her out on a date? To the kitchen? Or the home theater? No, we are not dating. And even if I could take Ingrid out of here, I don't have any money. I'm a pauper with nothing to offer a woman other than my fabulous body." He flexed his arms.

Could that be the problem?

"I meant, are you serious about her, or is it just sex?"

"I don't know." Richard ran a hand over the back of his neck. "She is a fine woman, but we don't have a lot in common."

Lifting both brows, Mey gave Yamanu a barely perceptible shrug.

It seemed like Ingrid and Richard were not a fated match. The question was how to introduce the guy to some other clan females while Ingrid was still spending every night with him.

A conundrum.

It wasn't the kind of talk Yamanu was comfortable having with Ingrid, and Mey wasn't a good candidate for that either. Perhaps he should ask Amanda to intervene?

Things couldn't go on like this forever. He and Mey needed to go home, which meant finding potential mates for Richard and Wendy.

Yesterday's get-together had been a success in that regard. Vlad and Wendy had warmed to each other, but because they were both shy, things hadn't progressed beyond a friendly conversation.

It was a good start, though. Given the rebellious expression she'd had on her face prior to Vlad's arrival, Yamanu had been afraid that Wendy wouldn't give the kid a chance.

The question was how to move things along.

As his phone rang, he lifted it and looked at the display but didn't recognize the number.

"This is Yamanu," he answered.

"Hi, it's Vlad. I was wondering if it's okay for me to come over. I have a bunch of video games for Wendy."

Yamanu grinned. "When should I tell her you are coming?"

"Are you sure it's okay? Maybe she doesn't want to see me."

"I'm sure she does."

"Then I'll be there in an hour."

"Good deal. See you here."

Yamanu lifted his face to the ceiling and offered his thanks to the Fates. They must have been tuning into his thought stream.

Mey rose to her feet. "I'd better tell Wendy to get ready. I just hope that you are right, and she wants to see him."

"Who is coming?" Richard asked.

They'd forgotten that he couldn't hear the person on the other end of Yamanu's phone.

"Vlad. He has some video games and books for Wendy."

Richard nodded. "That's good. He is a nice kid, and she needs to get out of that room. This must be really hard on her."

"Wasn't she like that in the program as well?"

"I have no idea what Wendy did after hours, but during the class sessions, she was much friendlier than she is here. She must be stressing over what's in store for her."

51

JIN

Jin opened her eyes to find Arwel staring at her.

His handsome face and those kissable lips of his was the best view to wake up to.

"Good morning, love." He kissed her cheek. "How are you feeling?"

Hearing Arwel calling her his love warmed Jin from the inside. Their love was just in its infancy, they still had so much to learn about each other, and so much was happening that had nothing to do with them as a couple.

But Jin had no doubt that their love would grow and flourish and that its roots would thicken, wrapping around their souls and connecting them at the very essence of their being.

That was what she imagined the bond that Arwel was so desperately hoping for would feel like. The seeds were already there, but it needed time to grow.

It was morning, though, and much too early for sharing her philosophical musings with him. Maybe he wouldn't like her tree analogy, thinking that it was too simplistic.

For now, exploring their physical connection was enough. After only one week together, it would be premature to talk about them being soulmates or fated mates.

Stretching her arms over her head, Jin smiled. "I feel fabulous. Sex with you is like an injection of vitality. I'm ready to conquer the world."

He seemed relieved. "That's good. It means that your transition didn't start yet."

"Does it usually start in the morning?"

"I'm not sure. I'll have to ask Bridget, but then I'll have to admit to our mess up, and I'd rather not say anything unless I have to."

Jin nodded. Them using or not using protection should be nobody's business. "It's bad enough that Kian butted into our sex life and told you to use condoms."

"Yeah." Arwel grimaced. "That wasn't a comfortable conversation. I should've realized it first and saved him the trouble."

"I can't wait to be done with this stupid mission. If I weren't so damn chicken, it could have been over and done with, and we wouldn't be having this conversation."

She flung the comforter off and slung her legs over the side of the bed. "I'm starving." Her stomach rumbled in agreement. "What time is it?"

"Ten-twenty." Arwel sounded slurred.

She glanced at him over her shoulder and smiled. His gorgeous eyes were glowing, and his fangs were showing.

"Are you randy again, my love?"

It felt just as nice to say it as it did to hear it.

"You can't expect me to remain indifferent when you reveal your beautiful nude body to me."

He'd only seen her back, and that was enough to excite him?

Sweet.

"You've only gotten a glimpse." Pushing up to her feet, she turned around and struck a pose. "How about now?"

"Dangerous. If you don't hurry into the bathroom, you might not make it there for another hour or two."

With the hunger in his eyes and his husky tone awakening her desire, Jin decided that breakfast could wait. But she really needed to use the bathroom first. "Would you like to join me in the shower?"

His fangs punched down even lower. "I would never refuse such an invitation."

It was a full hour later when they finally made their way to the kitchen.

"Good morning." Vivian looked up from her book. "You're late, but I managed to save some eggs and hash browns for you. Just stick the plates into the microwave."

"Thank you."

While Arwel took care of the food, Jin walked over to the coffeemaker and put two cups under the twin nozzles. She put a new packet in, pressed the button, and leaned against the counter.

"Where is everyone?" she asked.

Vivian turned sideways in her chair. "Douglas is upstairs watching Kalugal's gate, and the other Guardians are waiting in their cars for a signal from him. William is in his office with Magnus."

"What about Kri and Michael?" Arwel put two plates on the table.

"In the gym."

"And Jacki?" Jin asked.

"I think she is still sleeping. I haven't seen her this morning."

Jin and Arwel exchanged glances. Had Jacki and William gotten busy last night?

That would be awesome.

"I'd better check on her." Jin pushed away from the counter.

Arwel waved her over. "Eat your breakfast first. You said you were starving an hour ago."

That was true, but her curiosity was stronger than her hunger.

"I guess I can let Jacki sleep a few more minutes."

Stifling a smirk, Jin pulled out the coffee mugs from the device and brought them over to the table. What she'd really wanted to say was that Arwel hadn't been all that concerned about her empty belly when they'd been making love in the shower.

Vivian closed her book and got up. "I'll leave you two alone to enjoy your breakfast."

After they were done eating, Jin took their plates to the sink. "I'm going to check on Jacki." Holding a plate under running water, she looked over her shoulder at Arwel. "Your job is to coax information out of William."

He handed her the coffee mugs to rinse. "Guys don't talk about things like that."

"Right." Jin rolled her eyes. "I don't mean getting him to reveal details. Just general stuff. Does he like her? Does she like him back?"

"I'm just going to join him in the office. It's up to him if he wants to talk about it."

"Fair enough." Jin dried her hands on the dish towel. "But I'm crossing my fingers."

52

VLAD

Vlad stuffed his entire collection of video games into a duffle bag, added several fantasy books that he had read and enjoyed, and some romance novels that he'd borrowed from his mother.

Was it too much?

Maybe he should leave some of it behind so he would have more excuses to visit Wendy?

Yeah, that was a better plan.

He pulled out all of the romance novels except for one. Perhaps she wasn't into that genre. He knew she liked fantasy, though, so he took out only two of his books. They were part of a series, so once she was done reading the first three, she would want the other two and would have no choice but to invite him over.

Except, he wanted her to do it because she liked him and wanted to see him, not because she needed the books. Then again, if she was as shy as he was, Wendy would need an excuse as well.

Vlad smiled.

It was a good plan.

Zipping up the duffle bag, he wondered whether he should buy some chocolates on the way. Everyone knew that girls loved them. Then again, it would imply that he had romantic expectations, while Wendy hadn't given him any indication that she was interested in him that way.

With a sigh, he slung the strap over his shoulder and headed out of the house.

It wasn't a big surprise that she wasn't attracted to him. But at least she'd been friendly, and that was more than he'd gotten from other girls, or guys for that matter.

Even if all he gained was a new friend, it was worth the effort.

On the way to the pavilion, he stopped by the café and bought coffee and several pastries. That wasn't the same as chocolates, and he was bringing enough for everyone, so it couldn't be construed as a romantic gesture.

"Good morning, Vlad." Anandur clapped him on the back. "Heading out for a study session with friends?"

For a moment, he was tempted to lie. It would have been so simple to just nod in agreement and keep on walking. Not a biggie.

And then there was Anandur's proclivity for gossip. If he told him about Wendy, the entire village would know about it in less than an hour.

Except, Anandur could learn the truth from Yamanu or Bhathian or from the Guardians on rotation in the keep.

Maybe he could get away with partial truth.

"Bhathian asked me to befriend one of the newcomers. She is about my age, and she has no one to talk to. I'm bringing her books and video games."

"That's kind of you." Anandur smirked. "Is she pretty?"

"She is okay." *Beautiful.* "But we are just friends. Or rather acquaintances at this point. I've only met her once, and today is going to be the second time."

"Good luck." Anandur clapped him on the back again. "Friendship is a good start for a relationship. Just don't let her put you in the friend zone. Keep your options open."

Vlad didn't want to ask, but he couldn't help it. "How am I supposed to do that?"

Wrapping his massive arm around Vlad's slim shoulders, Anandur led him to a table. "Sit."

"I don't have time. I told Yamanu that I'd be there in an hour, and that was fifteen minutes ago."

"It's Saturday, so the traffic isn't bad, and this will only take a minute or two."

Perhaps Anandur's advice was worth a short delay. If he was late, he could always blame traffic.

"Okay." Vlad planted his ass in the chair.

The Guardian pulled one out for himself and sat down. "I'm not an expert on dating, but I know a thing or two about women. The thing they find most desirable in a guy is confidence. That's why assholes have such great success with them. Contrary to popular belief, women are not attracted to the jerkiness, they are attracted to the confidence those guys exude."

Vlad grimaced. "It's easy for good-looking dudes to be confident. I'm a walking scarecrow with fangs and mismatched eyes."

Anandur leaned closer. "That's where you are wrong. I've seen ugly dudes score with the hottest girls just because they were confident or faked it well. And you are not ugly, Vlad. You are not ordinary looking, and you can use that to your advantage. You are an awesome guitarist and vocalist, I hear that you are also a talented graphic artist, and you make good money working for Jackson. Don't be shy; tell her about your passions and your accomplishments."

"I don't want to boast."

"It's not boasting when it's true, and if you don't tell her, how will she know?"

"Maybe I can show her instead?"

"Even better. Show her your art, sing for her, bake her some goodies. You have a lot to offer, my friend."

"Thanks, Anandur." Vlad rose to his feet and offered the Guardian his hand. "That was good advice."

"Any time."

53

JIN

*J*in knocked on Jacki's door. "Can I come in?"

When there was no answer, she tried the handle. It wasn't locked, and the door opened.

Jacki's bed was made, and through the open bathroom door, Jin could see that she wasn't there either.

Smelling a strong chemical scent, she went inside and followed her nose to the shower, where the two wigs were draped over clothes hangers, still dripping.

It was hard to tell their color while wet, but it looked like one got a deep reddish hue, while the other was light brown.

Maybe the strong smell had chased Jacki out of her room, and she went out to the back yard for some fresh air?

Why hadn't she come into the kitchen, though?

Feeling a little apprehensive, Jin walked over to the window and looked out into the yard. There was no one there, but with the screen preventing her sticking her head out, she could only see a part of the area.

Wait, maybe Jacki went straight to William's office? If the two had spent a night of passion together, she would want to give him a good morning kiss.

Or better yet, what if she'd spent the night in his bedroom downstairs?

The wigs were wet, though, which meant that she'd dyed them this morning. Still, she could've come upstairs to do that, and then gone back down to cuddle with William in bed.

Not a likely scenario, but it was worth checking out.

After rushing down the stairs, Jin slowed down before entering the office. "Good morning, William. Have either of you seen Jacki? She is not in her room."

William shook his head. "The last time I saw her was yesterday."

Arwel frowned. "Did you come home straight from the store? I didn't hear her door open."

"We did some grocery shopping, so it took longer than we originally planned, but not by much. We were back before midnight, unloaded the stuff in the kitchen, and said our goodnights."

That was disappointing and a little worrisome.

"Where could she be?"

"Let's check the gym." Arwel pushed to his feet. "Maybe she took Kri up on her offer to teach her self-defense moves."

Jacki wasn't in the gym, and Kri and Michael hadn't seen her that morning. Checking the back yard didn't produce her either.

"Maybe she is in the master bedroom with the guys." Jin started up the stairs. "It would be odd if she is, though. She tries to stay away from them as much as possible."

"The outing with William might have changed her mind." Arwel followed her up. "Perhaps she realized that he wasn't who she wanted, and she decided to give the others a try."

Again, that wasn't likely, but they had run out of places to check.

Jacki wasn't in the master bedroom either.

"Have any of you seen her this morning?" Arwel asked.

Ewan shook his head. "No. I thought she was still sleeping."

"I assume that you didn't see or hear her leave the house either?"

"How is this possible?" Jin put a hand on her hip. "You guys are supposed to have superior hearing, and as far as I know, Jacki can't fly or levitate. You would have heard her open the door and go down the stairs."

"There are a lot of people in the house." Duncan ran an agitated hand through his short hair. "Our job is to watch Kalugal's gate. We don't pay attention to doors opening or closing or check who is going down or up the stairs."

The Guardian's nervousness and slight blush had finally clued Jin in.

Freaking hell. They had been too busy listening to her and Arwel making love to notice Jacki giving them the slip.

Embarrassed, Jin turned toward the door. "We need to go look for her."

"Wait." Arwel stopped her with a hand on her shoulder. "Let's check her bedroom first. I need to know if she slept in her bed at all, or if she snuck out last night after she and William returned from the store."

"Her bed is made, but she didn't leave last night. I know that she dyed the wigs this morning because they are still wet."

If she could get Arwel alone, Jin could tell him what she suspected about the Guardians listening in on their lovemaking instead of paying attention to Jacki's comings and goings.

"Let's check the garage." Arwel turned to the three men. "Duncan, you stay here. Ewan and Gregor, you come with us. If she's on foot, we still have a chance to find her."

54

ARWEL

Arwel scanned the garage. "All the cars are here, which means that she's walking. She couldn't have gotten far."

He turned to the Guardians. "Ewan, you go west. Gregor, you head north. Magnus, you are going south. I'm going to take the east."

"I'm coming with you," Jin said.

"Of course." He opened the passenger door for her.

"I don't think Jacki ran away." Jin buckled up. "She wouldn't have bothered dyeing the wigs if that was her plan. She's probably out jogging."

Arwel arched a brow. "Is she a jogger?"

"Not as far as I know. But it's a nice day, and her room is stinky from the hair dye, so she might have decided to go out for some fresh air."

"She could have waited for the right opportunity." He cast Jin a sidelong glance. "We gave her the perfect cover this morning."

"So you figured it out, huh? The perverts were too busy listening to us making love to hear Jacki leave the house."

"It's not like they could help it. This house has standard insulation, and we didn't bother to keep quiet."

Jin had been loud, thinking that the running water would mask the sounds she'd been making. On his part, Arwel was just as guilty for not saying anything. He'd enjoyed hearing her sounds of pleasure too much to do anything to stop them.

"It's so damn embarrassing. Maybe the noises we made were the reason Jacki left. She doesn't have immortal hearing, but she's in the room right next to ours. It's not fun listening to other people making love." She grimaced. "Although it seems like your fellow Guardians enjoyed it very much."

"Don't let it bother you."

"I can't help it." Jin crossed her arms over her chest. "I think your freaking

Fates are messing with us. Do they want us to abstain? Because it seems that our sex life is endangering the mission."

"At least we were good and used a condom this morning."

Jin huffed. "Yeah, like it's a good thing."

Arwel decided not to respond. It seemed like Jin needed to vent her frustration, so it didn't matter what he said.

"Look." She pointed at a woman walking stooped over with her hands stuffed in the pockets of her hoodie. "That's her. I recognize those sweatpants."

As Arwel pulled up to the woman, she turned to look at them. "What are you doing here?"

Jin lowered the window. "Looking for you. Everyone is worried sick about you. Get in the car."

"I'm just taking a walk. What's the big deal?"

Arwel threw the gearshift in park and got out of the car. "You are not supposed to be alone on the street." He opened the back passenger door for her. "Did you forget that you are a wanted woman?"

Letting out an indignant huff, Jacki got in the car. "I have the hoodie up, and I'm wearing the special glasses. That's good enough to fool surveillance cameras if there were any out here. But there are none. Do you see any? Because I don't."

Jin turned around to look at her friend. "Still. You should have at least told someone that you were going out."

"Why? So they could tell me that I can't? I'm sick of being treated like a freaking prisoner and at the same time being expected to help your organization."

Arwel looked at her through the rearview mirror. "You are not a prisoner. Do you think that you would have been allowed more freedom in a witness protection program?"

Shrugging, she looked out the window. "I've never been in one, so I don't know."

"Next time tell someone. There is also the issue of Kalugal and his men. It's not smart for you to be walking around his neighborhood, and especially not after last night. What if you were recognized? It's not like there are many people out on the streets for you to go unnoticed. In fact, we haven't seen anyone else walking around."

Jin nodded. "You should have taken one of the guys with you."

It wouldn't have helped Jacki if she was discovered by Kalugal or his men, but the immortals were not the only threat to a woman walking alone on a deserted street. Human males were dangerous too, even in broad daylight.

Jacki ignored Jin. Looking out the window, she appeared just as pissed as Arwel felt she was. Usually, he didn't pick up on her emotions, either because they weren't strong or because she was good at erecting walls around them.

Still, Jacki knew that he was an empath, and anger was a strong emotion that easily overshadowed other, more subtle ones like anxiety over plotting an escape.

This whole episode could have been designed to test the waters and see if she could get away with sneaking out of the house unnoticed. Even dyeing the wigs and leaving them to dry could have been part of the setup.

Was he giving her too much credit?

On the contrary. He probably wasn't giving her enough.

Arwel had a feeling that the girl was much smarter than she appeared and way more devious.

55

WENDY

Wendy checked the time on the television screen. She still had a few minutes until Vlad got there.

She'd hoped he wouldn't come over again. He was such a nice guy and leading him on was wrong.

Not that she had done it intentionally, it just happened. Yesterday, she'd planned to act indifferent so he would get the hint and not bother coming back. But she'd found it impossible to be mean to Vlad. He was so sensitive, so unsure of himself, that she'd felt compelled to help him out.

No, not compelled. She shouldn't use that nasty word when she knew what it really meant.

How could the director have allowed Marisol to use it on her?

Eh, who was she kidding? He probably told the bitch to do it. The guy didn't trust anyone, not even his own niece.

Still, she owed him. If not for Director Edgar Simmons, she would have still been in her father's grip.

Literally.

Wendy hadn't known anyone on her mother's side of the family until one day the director had knocked on her father's door, introduced himself, and offered her a lifeline.

Her father had been more than happy to get rid of her, but only after negotiating with her uncle that half of her pay would go to him, supposedly to compensate for the expenses he'd incurred raising her alone.

There hadn't been any warm fuzzies between Wendy and her uncle. He'd claimed that he hadn't known about her existence and that as soon as he'd found out, he'd come for her. Not because he'd wanted to get to know his niece, but because as his blood relative, she was likely to possess some paranormal talent. And if not talent, then at least an immunity to mind manipulation like his.

Hopefully, he knew that she'd joined the escape group only to gather intel for him.

That had been the task he'd assigned her to. She'd been his ears, eyes, and sensor to anything out of the ordinary going on in the trainee group.

She'd failed to detect Jin and Jacki's plotting an escape, but she had salvaged the situation by going with them.

Except, she was stuck with no means of communication, and she couldn't leave. Perhaps she could use Vlad to do that.

He was so sweet and naive that it shouldn't be difficult. First of all, she could find out from him where she was. He'd been told to keep quiet about it, but she could trick him by asking him the name of the college he attended or to tell her about his favorite hangout places.

Maybe she could even get him to sneak her out.

The worst part was that she really liked Jacki and Jin, and Mey and Yamanu and Arwel and everyone else. Betraying them wasn't easy.

She even liked Edna, whom she'd been terrified of but had managed to fool just like everyone else, despite her probing ability.

There were advantages to having been so well-practiced in disassociation. Only this time, she'd done it in reverse, stepping back into her real life instead of the one she'd created as a substitute and was living so comfortably in.

First, Wendy had swamped her mind with memories of the abuse she'd suffered throughout the years. With that filling every brain cell and nerve in her body, there had been little else for Edna to latch onto. But then Wendy had added a twist, imagining the director making advances towards her.

It wasn't hard to do since there was some truth to it. He had never actually done anything, but she'd felt his perverted desire for her.

Having an empathic ability was both a gift and a curse. Without it, she probably would never have known her uncle had the hots for her because he wouldn't have acted on it.

At least she hoped he wouldn't have.

Men could never be trusted.

Nevertheless, she owed him and was dependent on him for her future. The lifeline he'd offered her had been the first stroke of luck she'd had in her entire life. It got her out of the house and provided her with a great income for skills she'd been born with and didn't have to work on acquiring.

It was a chance of a lifetime. Heck, it was her only chance.

Hopefully, Edna had forgotten all about her promise of cupcakes and girl talk and wasn't going to show up anytime soon. Wendy wasn't sure she could pull off the same trick again, and if possible, she would rather avoid immersing herself in memories of pain and insults.

It had been hard enough when she'd forced herself back into her real life. In fact, she was still reeling from the aftershocks. Usually, the catalyst for entering her alternate reality had been her father's abuse. Without it, she was struggling to go back to the better place she'd created for herself.

56

JIN

The drive back to the house lasted less than five minutes, but those minutes were tense. As soon as Arwel parked the car in the garage, Jacki opened the back passenger door, got out, and then slammed it behind her.

"Someone is in a bad mood," Jin muttered. "I'd better go talk to her."

She got out of the car and followed Jacki inside.

"Wait up," she called after her. "Are you hungry? You left the house without eating breakfast."

"I'm going to my room." Jacki continued up the stairs.

Arwel put a hand on Jin's shoulder. "I'm going to the office."

"Coward."

"She is your friend. You deal with her tantrum."

Jacki was already at the top of the stairs, and Jin had no intention of going up after her.

"Don't be an idiot, Jacki. Are you punishing me by going hungry?"

Jacki stopped and turned around. "I did nothing wrong, and yet you and your boyfriend treated me like a criminal."

Rolling her eyes, Jin beckoned with her hand. "Come on. You can yell at me over eggs and toast. I'll even make them for you. Together with hot chocolate." That was an offer her friend couldn't refuse.

One corner of Jacki's mouth twitched with a ghost of a smile, and then it bloomed into a full one. "How can I stay mad at you when you offer to make me food and hot cocoa?"

"That's the idea."

In the kitchen, they found Vivian waiting for them with fresh coffee.

"I heard you coming in and made two cups. Would you like some?"

"Yes, please." Jacki sat at the table. "Aren't you going to berate me as well?"

Vivian shook her head. "I'm sure you've gotten an earful already. We were worried about you. That's all."

Jacki took the mug Vivian handed her. "I'm a grown woman, and I wasn't abducted by humans or aliens through my second-floor bedroom window. The logical assumption should have been that I'd gone for a walk."

The fact that they'd thought she had run away hung in the air unspoken.

"I actually considered the alien theory," Jin said to break the silence. "They'd taken you during the night but were nice enough to make your bed and dye the wigs."

She pulled a tray of eggs out of the fridge and cracked three into the pan.

"The stinky hair dye was the reason I went out for a walk. How did they come out?"

"I don't know." Jin popped four slices of bread into the toaster. "They were still wet when I saw them. You should have blow-dried them."

"I thought about doing that, but then I figured that we should ask Eva if that was okay. It didn't occur to me until after I'd applied the color that maybe the wigs were not meant to be dyed."

"I'd better call her while you eat your breakfast. We need to ask her how to change our appearance with what we have. We might have to buy some new stuff."

When the eggs were ready and the toast popped up, Jin put everything on a plate and brought it to the table. "Enjoy."

"Thank you."

As Jacki dove in, she placed the call.

"Jin. I was waiting for your call."

"Why? Have you already heard about what happened?"

"Kian called me and asked me to design a new disguise for you. I'm waiting for Ella to come over so I can demonstrate on her. We can do a Skype session, and you can do Jacki's makeup while following what I'm demonstrating on Ella, and then you can switch."

"Awesome. By the way, Jacki dyed the wigs. I hope that's okay."

"That's fine. What colors did she use?"

"Let me put you on speaker." She turned to Jacki. "Eva is asking what colors you used for the wigs."

Jacki wiped her mouth with a napkin. "I used L'Oréal. One was cayenne red and the other deep golden brown. After I washed the color off, I left them to air dry. Any styling ideas?"

"We will do the makeup first, and then check on the wigs. You didn't alter the colors by much."

"I was afraid to go with something too bold. We are supposed to blend in, not stand out."

"True. Most of the work will have to be done with makeup and hairstyles rather than color. I'll call you as soon as Ella is here."

"Thank you, Eva." Jin took the call off the speaker. "And I'm sorry for bothering you on the weekend."

"No problem. As a stay-at-home mom, weekdays or weekends makes no difference to me."

"Nevertheless, I'm sure you would rather have spent the day with your family."

"I'm glad to help, Jin. In any way I can. Besides, nowadays, that's the only excitement I get. I'm living vicariously through your and Jacki's adventure."

Jin chuckled. "I could have done with much less excitement. I don't think that the spy lifestyle is for me."

57

VLAD

"Hello, Vlad." Mey welcomed him with a hug.

When she let go, Yamanu clapped him on the back. "I'm glad you came." He slung a towel around his neck. "I'm heading to the gym. You don't need me here, right?"

Vlad glanced at the couch where Wendy was patiently waiting for her turn to say hello.

"I hope you are not leaving because of me."

Yamanu laughed. "It's not you. It's me." He winked. "I have a date with Richard at the weights station." He looked Vlad over. "You should come with me sometime. I'll show you the proper way to build up muscle."

From the corner of his eye, Vlad saw Mey glaring at Yamanu.

She probably thought that Vlad had been offended by the suggestion, but the truth was that he didn't need the training. He was already freakishly strong. To develop muscles, he would probably need to push up semitrailers.

"I'll take you up on your offer once you and Mey go back to the village."

Now it was Yamanu's turn to glare. "You mean the neighborhood gym."

"Yeah, that's what I meant."

"Good deal." Yamanu clapped him on the back again. "Have fun, kids."

Vlad rolled his eyes. Yamanu looked to be in his late twenties or early thirties. Calling Vlad and Wendy kids was telling.

When he left, Mey ducked into the bedroom but left the door open as if they needed a chaperone.

"What's all that?" Wendy pointed at the duffle bag slung over one shoulder and the guitar case slung over the other.

He dropped the bag on the floor and put the case on a chair. "You said you were bored, so I brought you video games and books…"

"Thanks. And what's that?" She pointed at the case.

"I brought my guitar, thinking that you might want to hear some of the songs my band used to play. We wrote them ourselves."

"I would love that."

He clicked the fasteners open. "I play the bass and Jackson plays the lead guitar, but for a solo performance, I figured an acoustic would be best." He pulled it out.

Wendy sat up straight. "I've always wanted to play an instrument."

"Why didn't you?"

She grimaced. "My father didn't think it was necessary."

"I can teach you if you want."

"That would be nice. Although I would have preferred to play the piano."

"I can teach you that as well, but we don't have one down here."

Her eyes brightened with admiration. "You play three instruments? That's amazing."

Remembering Anandur's advice, Vlad decided to boast a little. "Six. I can also play the flute, the clarinet, and the saxophone."

"Wow. That's impressive."

He strummed a chord. "Ready?"

"Yes."

He chose one of the quieter songs, and when the first notes left his throat, Wendy gaped a little.

Mey came out of the bedroom and joined Wendy on the couch.

Feeling shy, he watched his fingers on the guitar even though he didn't need to. But looking at Wendy while he was playing would have been too nerve-racking.

He was a good singer, but she might not like his style, or the lyrics, or whatever.

Once he was done, Wendy and Mey started clapping, and Vlad took a bow. "Thank you."

"You are an amazing vocalist, Vlad," Mey said. "Your voice is unique, and you have perfect pitch."

"It was beautiful." Wendy crossed her arms over her chest.

Was she suddenly feeling shy? Had he gone overboard showing off?

"Did you go to music school?" Wendy asked.

"I had tutors that I went to."

"That's nice."

She sounded sad, maybe a little envious, which was a first for him. What he got most from people was either pity or wariness.

Perhaps showing Wendy his artwork could wait for another time.

He lifted the duffle bag, put it on the coffee table, and unzipped it. "Check out the games I brought for you. If you find one that you like, we can take it to the theater. Playing a video game on the big screen is an experience. You have to try it."

She pulled out several and looked them over. "I like them all, but I'm not in the mood for playing. Maybe we can just watch a movie?"

That was even better. Perhaps while watching, he'd gather the nerve to put his arm around her shoulders.

"Sure. We have all the latest movies on the server."

Wendy rose to her feet and turned to Mey. "Would you like to join us?"

Mey waved a hand. "You two go and enjoy yourselves. I could use the time to work on my designs."

Vlad held his breath. Was Wendy going to find an excuse not to go?

He wanted to be alone with her again, but what if she'd asked Mey to hang around because she didn't want that?

"We even have an antique movie popcorn machine," he murmured.

"I know. And it's the best ever."

"So you've been there already?" He started for the door.

Thankfully, she followed. "There is not much to do here."

As Wendy walked next to him, Vlad was very aware of the difference in their heights. She was so small, and he had an intense urge to protect her, to wrap his arm around her shoulders and bring her close to him so he could shield her.

It was a silly thought because, despite his freakish strength, he wasn't a fighter. Not in skill and not in inclination. The only times he'd felt violent was when witnessing injustices, the strong preying on the weak. But he'd never acted on those impulses, and he wasn't sure that he could.

"I get a weird vibe from you." Wendy looked up at him. "What's going on?"

He'd forgotten about her empathic ability. But wasn't she supposed to touch someone to get a read on them?

"I was thinking about Yamanu's invitation to train with him in the gym. He is a Guardian, so I assume that some hand-to-hand combat training would be part of it. The thing is, I'm not sure I can strike someone even in self-defense. But I probably could do that to defend someone else."

She smiled. "You are really a nice guy, Vlad. Too nice. Training could be good for you. If someone attacks you, your training will take over, and you'll defend yourself without even thinking."

"Did you experience that?"

She shrugged. "We had a self-defense class in the program, and that was what the instructor said. She said that it was important to practice a lot so the response would be instinctive. If you have to think about your next move, you are already too late."

"That sounds reasonable. Maybe you can come with me and Yamanu can train us together?"

She looked up at him, examining his skinny arms and probably thinking that he was a weakling.

"Is Yamanu a good teacher?"

"I don't know. I've never attended any of his self-defense classes. I guess we will have to find out."

58

WENDY

"Which movie would you like to watch?" Vlad scrolled through the selection on the tablet that served as the remote for the theater.

"Have you seen *Ready Player One*?"

She'd watched it on Netflix in her room, but she wanted to watch it again. Living inside a virtual game world appealed to her on so many levels. She could choose an avatar that was beautiful and strong, and she could do things that were impossible in the real world.

The possibilities were endless.

"I did. But I don't mind watching it again." Vlad selected the movie. "Would you like some popcorn?"

"Yes, please."

"I'll be right back."

Vlad had surprised her today. It seemed like her pep talk from the day before had done him good. He was less timid, and he'd even sung for her.

His voice was as beautiful as his soul.

She sighed, wondering whether growing up in a loving home had made him a good person, or was it genetic? Did children of decent, loving people inherit their parents' genes, which made them good as well?

What did it say about her, though? Was she destined to be bad?

Neither of her parents were good. Her father was a nasty man with a drinking problem who had taken out his frustrations on his daughter, and her mother was a drug addict who'd left her baby to be raised by a monster.

That was probably another good reason to never get into a relationship. With the example she had, what kind of a mother could she possibly be?

Perhaps people with her genetic makeup should never have children.

"Here you go." Vlad handed her a paper bag filled to the brim with popcorn.

"Is it all for me?" she teased.

"I'm going to help." He took a fistful. "And we can always make more."

"I don't think we will be able to finish this one."

Vlad shrugged and pretended to drape his arm nonchalantly over the back of her seat.

It was cute for a twenty-year-old guy to make a middle-schooler move, and she was glad that he was so reserved. If he had put his arm on her shoulders, she would have removed it. They weren't on a date, and she shouldn't encourage him.

Except, if she wanted to get out of this basement prison, perhaps she should pretend that she wanted to be more than friends. Using Vlad like that would be a nasty thing to do, but then she wasn't a good person, so why would she care?

Her objective was to stay in her uncle's good graces, and giving him a cache of paranormal talents would earn her a permanent position as his favorite person. She could have a good future in the program, helping her uncle run the secret paranormal division.

She would just have to make it clear that making babies, normal or super, was not part of the deal. She was never going to get married or become a mother. Her life would be about her work and nothing else.

Wendy grimaced.

She'd just described Marisol.

Did she want to be like that heartless bitch?

Thankfully, Vlad hadn't gathered the courage to move his arm from the back of her chair to her shoulders. But he was thinking about it while nervously shoving popcorn into his mouth until it was all gone long before the movie was over.

Wendy felt the battle he was waging with himself and was glad that the timid side was winning.

When the movie ended, she lifted the empty paper bag and shook it. "I think I would like some more after all."

"Do you want to watch another movie?"

"No, I just want more popcorn. We can take it to my room and play one of your video games."

Vlad's eyes sparkled with excitement, or rather the one she could see. The other one was covered by his long bangs.

Wendy reached up and swiped it aside. "You will ruin your eyesight like that."

"Not much chance of that." He climbed the stairs to the back of the theater.

"Yeah, right. You think that you are invincible because you are still young, but it's all downhill from here."

He smiled, his long canines gleaming white in the dark theater. "Not for me."

Wendy rolled her eyes. "Pretending to be a vampire doesn't make you one."

That seemed to amuse him, but he didn't respond. Instead, he loaded the machine with more corn kernels and pressed a button.

Nothing happened.

"Is there a power outage?" She looked at the dim lights illuminating the back of the theater. Those could be powered by backup batteries.

Vlad shook his head. "We have generators that come online automatically when it happens. Something must be wrong with the machine."

"Usually, it's as simple as the plug getting loose."

Wendy crouched and looked under the antique popcorn maker. She could see the cord and part of the socket. If she flattened herself on the floor, she could reach it.

"What are you doing?" Vlad sounded alarmed.

"I can see part of the plug, and it looks loose. I think I can reach it." She pushed herself forward on her tummy, but her arm was still too short.

"Let me do it. I have longer arms."

"I almost got it."

She pushed a little further, stretching her arm as far as it would go, and made contact with the socket, as well as something furry that moved.

"Yikes!" Jerking back, Wendy bumped her head against the underside of the machine, and the whole thing started listing.

Closing her eyes, she expected to get crushed under its weight, but it never happened. Instead, she felt the whole thing vanish.

A split second later, Vlad was crouching next to her. "Are you okay? What happened?"

Turning around, she wondered where the popcorn machine had gone. She saw it behind Vlad, resting innocently on its spindly legs as if nothing had happened.

"I bumped my head on the underside of that thing. How did it get there? Did I black out or something?"

"I hope not. I caught it before it fell on top of you and moved it there."

Wendy looked at the machine again. It was about five feet tall, two feet wide, and four feet long, and it looked heavy.

"How did you manage that? That thing must weigh a ton."

"It doesn't. It just looks heavy. How is your head?"

She rubbed the spot. "It's okay." Then remembering what had caused the incident, she jumped to her feet and shook out her hands.

"What are you doing?"

"There was a spider on the socket. That's what freaked me out."

Vlad shook his head. "You could've been killed because of a harmless spider."

"Hey, you just said that the machine wasn't that heavy, so it couldn't have killed me."

Curious, she put her hands on it and tried to push it. "It doesn't even budge."

"That's because its legs are wedged in the carpet."

"Okay, then I'll try to lift it."

She grabbed a bar on one side and tried to just tip it, but barely managed to lift it an inch before letting it drop back.

Narrowing her eyes at Vlad, she put her hands on her hips. "Is telekinesis one of your talents?"

He laughed. "No. I lifted it with my arms, not my mind. I was so scared for you, and the adrenaline rush must have added strength to my muscles."

What muscles? He didn't have any.

Then again, she'd heard about impossible feats that had been fueled by adrenaline, so maybe Vlad was right.

"I think I'll skip another serving of popcorn. Let's grab a beer from the kitchen instead."

He frowned. "You're nineteen. You are not supposed to drink."

"Who is going to tell me no? Come on. I'm sure that after all this excitement, you can use one yourself."

59

KIAN

Syssi walked into Kian's home office with a guilty expression on her beautiful face. "I'm heading out to the café to have lunch with Amanda. Are you going to be okay here by yourself?"

He knew that the guilt was not over leaving him in the house to eat his lunch alone. It was over keeping secrets from him. Syssi and Amanda were planning a surprise birthday party for him, and that's what the lunch was about.

"I'll miss you, of course. But don't worry about me. I still have a lot of work to do, and I also need to call Lokan and arrange a conference call between him and the Bay Area team."

"Should I tell Okidu to bring your lunch in here?"

Kian nodded.

Rounding the desk, Syssi leaned over to give him a kiss, but he wasn't satisfied with the quick peck on the lips and pulled her onto his lap for a proper one.

When she came up for air, they were both panting and ready for more.

"Do you have time for a quickie?"

Her eyes were glazed with desire, but she shook her head. "I wish I did. But Amanda is waiting for me." She pushed up.

"That's a shame."

She smiled coyly. "I'll be back in about two hours. Try to be done by then, and I'll take you up on your offer."

"Deal. Only it's not going to be a quickie then. I'm going to take my time with you." He adjusted himself.

As always, the mention of sexual play made his wife blush, her pale cheeks flushing with the most beautiful pink hue. Which had him thinking about turning her other pale cheeks pink.

No doubt the same thought, or something along those lines, had caused the blush and the sudden flare in the scent of her arousal.

Syssi loved their kinky games.

"I'd better get out of here while I still can." She blew him an air kiss and walked out the door.

For a long moment, Kian stared at the open file on his desk, trying to read but comprehending none of it. With images of what he and Syssi would do in a couple of hours dancing in front of his eyes, it was impossible to get his mind back on track.

It could wait for later.

He had phone calls to make, and those could be done outside the house in the back yard while enjoying a cigarillo. Maybe a shot of whiskey as well? Or was it too early for that?

Beer would be better.

Pulling the sliding door open, he stepped out, closed it behind him, and sat down on one of the easy chairs right outside of his home office.

After lighting up, he called Lokan first. "Are you ready for the conference call?"

"Give me five minutes. Carol and I are just about done with lunch."

"No problem. I'll get everyone ready for you and call you back."

"Good deal."

Arwel was next. "How are things going, is everyone ready for Lokan?"

"I have everyone here in the living room, and the others are waiting for his call in the hotel. Three of the guys are on watch duty, but he can do them last."

"Good plan. Anything else?"

"Yeah." He heard Arwel get up and start walking. "We had an incident this morning that might be nothing or might be something. Jacki gave everyone the slip and went out for a walk around the neighborhood."

Kian frowned. "How could that have happened? Did no one hear her leave?"

"It's a big house, and people go in and out of rooms and the front door all of the time. Besides, the Guardians on duty were not aware that they were supposed to keep an eye on Jacki."

"I assume that you found her, and everything is okay?"

"We drove around the neighborhood and found her walking several streets over. She had her hood up and was wearing the special glasses."

"Do you think she was planning to escape?"

"It crossed my mind that it might have been a test run to see if she could get away."

"Keep an eye on her."

"Of course. I told the Guardians to do the same and report to me if she leaves again. I don't want them to stop her because we are trying to maintain the illusion that she's not a prisoner."

"Technically, she is not. If she really wants to leave, we will have to let her go. But unless she is very clever and knows how to stay under the radar, that would mean an immediate capture for her."

"Unless we give her fake documents and drop her off in another country."

"That would increase her chances of evading capture, but not eliminate them. The government is investing a lot of resources into finding paranormal talents. They want them back."

"Any new developments on that front?"

Kian took a puff of his cigarillo. "Surprisingly, very little is being done. Which reinforces my suspicion that one of the three is an informant."

"Who's at the top of your suspect list, Jacki?"

Kian chuckled. "That position keeps rotating every few hours. Each of them has something to gain or lose, and they all passed Edna and Andrew's tests."

"That's what makes Jacki the most likely suspect. She has the strongest protective walls, and as far as she knows, she has a lot to lose and little to gain by staying with us."

"True. On the other hand, she was the one who convinced Jin to run."

"Jacki is a seer. She might have seen more in her vision than what she told Jin. She could have realized that it was a great opportunity for bringing a bunch of new talents into the program."

60

JIN

"Jin, is that you?" Lokan leaned closer to the screen. "If I saw you on the street, I wouldn't have recognized you."

Eva's online tutorial had worked out great. With tons of makeup and new-colored and styled wigs, Jin and Jacki were hardly recognizable. They were also wearing layers of clothing to make themselves look fatter.

Luckily for them, it was cold outside. Unluckily for the rest of the house's occupants, they had to go without heating.

"That's because you can see only my face and it's a small screen. I can't hide my height, and that's what people notice first about me."

"You look fifteen years older. Can I see Jacki?"

Her friend popped her head next to Jin's. "What do you think?"

"Same for you. Fantastic job."

Jacki grinned. "I never thought that I would be so happy about looking old and ugly."

"You're not ugly. Not even with that on."

Jacki waved a dismissive hand. "You're such a charmer, Lokan. But let's get down to business. Tell Jin not to listen to anything Kalugal tells her to do, and just in case I'm not immune to him, do the same for me."

He chuckled. "Compulsion needs more precise wording. If I do what you suggest, neither of you would hear a word he says."

"Yes, master." Jacki mock bowed. "Whatever you say."

"Refuse to obey Kalugal's commands. It's as simple as that."

Jin frowned. "That's it? What if he asks nicely?"

"Jin, you must refuse Kalugal's commands and requests no matter how politely he phrases them."

"That's better. Is that all?"

"Yes. You can give the tablet to Jacki."

As Jin listened to Lokan give each of them the same command, she wondered whether it would do any good.

Logically, the answer was no. Given that Kalugal was much more powerful than his brother, he could most likely override Lokan's compulsion.

And yet, combined with the new disguise, it helped her feel a little more confident and a little less scared.

When he was done with the last Guardian in the room, Arwel took the tablet, thanked him, and ended the call.

"How are you feeling?" he asked.

"Even though it's probably a placebo effect, I feel more confident."

Kri walked over and put her hand on Jin's shoulder. "Your problem is not enough practice. When you saw Kalugal, you started to think about how you were going to touch him and about everything that could go wrong. The trick is to just do it. Move forward without thinking, and that can be achieved only with a lot of training."

"Who am I going to practice on?"

Kri waved a hand around the room. "Everyone here. We will put music on and pretend the living room is a club. All of us will dance while you walk around with a drink in your hand, bump into people and tether them. Then you are going to release the tethers and start all over again."

Arwel shook his head. "If Jin expends all of her mental energy on practice, she will have nothing left by the end of the day. And since it's Saturday, there is a good chance Kalugal will go out hunting tonight."

Jacki grimaced. "Why do you call clubbing hunting? It sounds like a safari."

Kri snorted. "Because that's exactly what it is. But back to Jin. She has to practice no matter what. Worst case, she will get Kalugal some other day or even next Saturday. It's better than blowing another disguise."

"I agree with Kri," Jin said. "The draining part is not attaching the mental hook or removing it, it's holding on to several strings at once."

"Then let's party." Vivian clapped her hands. "Guys, start moving furniture. We need to clear an area for a dance floor."

When the living room was ready, Arwel put on music, and everyone other than Jin started dancing. It was fun to watch, especially William, who had surprising moves.

Even Jacki looked impressed.

Two of the three burly bears just swayed in place, holding their beers and pretending to be scanning for girls.

Hunting, as Arwel called it.

Wine glass in hand, Jin concentrated on the loud music instead of looking at the people she knew well. Letting her vision blur, she started a meandering path.

She bumped into one person and then another and caught the arm of the third as if to steady herself.

"I'm so sorry." She wiped nonexistent wine drops from Ewan's sleeve while tethering him. "I spilled some on you."

"That's okay," the Guardian said. "No harm done."

And so it went on.

After she'd tethered and released everyone twice, Arwel turned the music off. "I think that's enough."

"For now," Kri said. "We will take a break for lunch and then do another round."

Arwel looked at Jin. "How are you holding up?"

"I'm good. Kri is right. After the third or the fourth tether, I stopped thinking and just did it on autopilot. Another round of tethering after lunch is a good idea."

Arwel didn't seem convinced. "Did it become harder the more people you tethered?"

"Not if I released the tether right away. If I kept more than three at the same time, I felt fatigued."

Kri clapped her on the back. "Good job, girl. Your act was very convincing. You looked a little tipsy but not stupidly drunk, and your apologies didn't sound fake."

Jin let out a breath. "Thanks. I was worried about that."

To her, the act seemed forced and her apologies sounded insincere. She was glad Kri thought otherwise, but she wanted another opinion. The one person she knew wouldn't try to be nice and would give it to her straight was Jacki.

"What do you think?" she asked her.

"It was good. But more practice wouldn't hurt. And don't look at the person you are apologizing to. Pretend to be embarrassed and focus on the spilled drink."

Jin nodded. "If I don't look at Kalugal's face, I can pretend that it's not him."

"That too," Jacki said. "But I was thinking more along the lines of him not getting a good look at you. He might recognize you from before."

61

KALUGAL

Rufsur walked into Kalugal's study. "Are we going out tonight?"

"I'm not in the mood." He didn't even lift his head from the book.

The Inca were much more fascinating than chasing tail in clubs.

Last night had been meh. The sisters had been a no show, and the girl he'd picked up had been a bore. She'd seemed so promising but had turned out disappointing on all accounts.

As an English major who loved literature, she should have been well-read and interesting to talk to. But after twenty minutes or so he'd found himself carrying on a monologue because she had nothing to say.

Perhaps he'd intimidated her into silence. That happened sometimes. Not because he was overbearing or condescending, but because he was so knowledgeable.

And the sex had been meh as well. The girl had no spirit.

"You are never in the mood. That's why you have me to drag you away from your musty books and your dusty artifacts. You need to interact with people, and you need to get laid."

Kalugal lifted his head. "I really hate that expression. Getting laid implies passiveness. I'm anything but."

Rufsur bowed low. "My apologies, supreme ruler. Let me rephrase. You need to hunt."

Despite his best efforts to keep a straight face, Kalugal's lips lifted in a smile. One of the main reasons he'd chosen Rufsur as his second-in-command was that the guy refused to take any crap from him and was immune to his bullshit.

"Where do you want to go?"

"I liked the Magnet. Plenty of quality females to choose from, not too loud, and the bar doesn't serve diluted drinks."

Kalugal grimaced. "Let's agree to disagree about what qualifies as quality.

Our tastes are different. If I am to abandon this fascinating book, it would be for fascinating company."

Rufsur didn't look happy. "Stanford. That's where you want to go."

"Obviously. Why do you think I chose to live fifteen minutes away from the campus?"

"The startups?"

"That too. You'd be surprised how much more interesting the sex is with a smart woman."

Rufsur shook his head. "I have a rule against schtupping women smarter than me, and I'm not into the mind games that you like to play."

"Not every smart woman is into them either, but I find that the higher the IQ, the more the lady is willing to experiment."

"And the less appealing she is. Brainiacs don't put as much effort into primping."

That was true, but Kalugal didn't like overly done-up females either. "To each his own. But since I compromised yesterday, it's your turn to do so today."

"Can't argue with that. Do you want to include Phinas in our outing?"

"Ask him if he wants to join."

Ideally, Kalugal would have preferred to go out by himself, but his men wouldn't have it, which was quite absurd given that he routinely traveled alone to troubled areas around the world.

They weren't happy about that either, but he'd put his foot down.

After Navuh, Kalugal was the most powerful man in the world, and no one could mess with him. Besides, old Professor Gunter didn't attract attention. And if the unthinkable happened and his plane went down or a bomb exploded right over him, his men would perish with him. He didn't need them for protection.

Still, he needed at least one to accompany him to clubs and bars and such. His shrouds worked only locally. If anyone unaffected by his shroud checked the footage from the surveillance cameras later, or the checkers were in a distant location, they would see his real face, and donning a disguise was not practical for hookups.

Naturally, Kalugal could have taken care of the recordings himself, but it was more efficient to have Rufsur or one of his other men do it for him.

That way, he could concentrate on having fun.

"Phinas is going out with Dandor and Welgost. So, it's only the two of us."

"As it usually is."

On the weekends, Kalugal kept only a minimal guard on the premises, and the rest of the men went out to hunt. On weekdays, they each had two evenings out.

Some complained that it wasn't enough, but Kalugal figured that if it was enough for him, it should suffice for them. After all, he and his older brother were the most pure-blooded immortals out there, and from what he had learned, the more pure-blooded the immortal was, the stronger his libido.

Did it work the same way for immortal females?

Kalugal had been too young to think about sex when he'd snuck into the harem to see his mother.

As always, thinking of her brought about a sharp pang, and he rubbed his chest as if the motion could relieve it.

If only he could talk to her again, see her beautiful face, have her hold him in her arms...

Shaking his head, Kalugal put his book away and rose to his feet. It was absurd for a grown man to long for his mother's embrace.

62

ARWEL

"It's busy at Kalugal's today," William muttered. "More people are living in that mansion than we estimated. I counted eight cars so far."

Each time a car left the gate, Jin and Jacki would be on high alert. Since none of them had been a convertible, they couldn't see who was inside until the car reached its destination and the Guardian following it snapped photos of those getting out.

None had been Kalugal, but they were collecting valuable information about his men. So far, it seemed like there were no females in the compound. Not a single woman had left the place or had gotten in.

Which was odd.

Arwel had expected housekeeping staff, but it seemed that Kalugal's men were responsible for the upkeep. Either that or they kept a bunch of enslaved women in his bunker. Given what Sharim had done in the basement of the monastery, it wasn't such a farfetched scenario.

Arwel flipped through the photos that the watchers had snapped. "Even without following them, it's obvious that none of these was driven by Kalugal. He likes fancy cars."

"We can't be sure of that. A careful guy like him is probably aware of how noticeable those are."

"In this neighborhood, he is not the only one driving an expensive vehicle. Living here, he can get away with it."

"Still, if it were me, I would keep a lower profile. Mercedes and BMW are fine automobiles and don't attract as much attention."

When Jin walked into the office looking like someone else, all Arwel had to do was close his eyes and inhale her familiar essence to reassure himself that everything was as it should be.

The poor girl had been stuck in the costume the entire day, but he'd convinced her to at least take off the layers of clothing. Putting them back on would take a minute, and there was no sense in her and Jacki sweating buckets while waiting for the right car to leave the gate.

"Dinner is ready," she said.

William shook his head. "I'll eat here if you don't mind. I don't want to miss Kalugal."

Jin put her hand on her hip and struck a pose. "You can't sit in this chair all day long and not move. We have watchers upstairs, and they take turns. They will alert us when a car leaves that gate."

"Yes, ma'am." He rolled his chair back and got up.

In the dining room, everyone other than the Guardian on duty was already seated at the table.

"Who cooked?" Arwel pulled out a chair for Jin.

Vivian waved a hand. "Magnus, Kri, and Michael. I only made the salad."

"Thank you."

Regrettably, none of them was a good cook, but Jacki couldn't perform her culinary magic while wearing an itchy wig and tons of makeup. Both girls were uncomfortable, but it was unavoidable.

"I hope this ends tonight," Jin said. "I don't want to spend another day like this. I'm a nervous wreck." She bit into a piece of dry toast.

"Aren't you going to eat the spaghetti?"

She shook her head. "I'm nauseous, and toast is the only thing I can stomach right now."

He took her hand and brought it up to his lips. Her hands and the back of her neck were the only spots not covered in makeup and safe to kiss. "Try to relax."

Jin chuckled. "That's the best I can do."

Jacki had no such problem. She was slurping the spaghetti up one noodle at a time, oblivious to what it was doing to the bachelors watching her.

"Can you stop that?" Jin made a face. "The slurping sounds make me even more nauseous."

Jacki frowned. "Sorry. I didn't realize it was so loud." She looked around the table, finally noticing the men's eyes on her. "Am I grossing you out?"

"Not at all," William said. "I've just never seen anyone eating spaghetti like that."

The discussion that started about the best way to eat noodles was interrupted by William's phone buzzing with an incoming message.

"The Ferrari just left the gate. I'm sure it's Kalugal behind the wheel, but you'd better verify." He passed the phone to Jacki.

"It's him." She handed the phone back. "What face is he shrouding himself in this time?"

"It's the same one from yesterday," William said while texting the info to the Guardians waiting to follow the car. "Apparently, he has several shrouds that he uses for different activities. This one is his hunting face. He needs to look handsome for that."

Jacki pushed away from the table. "We should get in the cars and wait for directions."

Arwel motioned for the others to do the same. "I want everyone in the garage in five minutes. Kri, you are going with Jin and Jacki. Michael and Ewan, you are with me. Magnus and Gregor, you are in the third car."

They hadn't planned on Kri accompanying the girls, but suddenly it seemed like a good idea to him.

Jin would feel safer with Kri around, and if shit went down for some unforeseeable reason, the Guardian was a force to be reckoned with.

63

JIN

*A*rwel poked his head through the passenger side window. "He is heading to Stanford. You can start driving in that direction, and as soon as he arrives at his destination, the guys will text you the address."

"You're going to follow close behind us, right?" Jin knew that, but she needed reassurance.

"That's right. And you have Kri with you. She can kick ass just as well as any of the guys."

Jin smiled. "I've seen her in action, and I'm glad she is coming with us."

Behind the wheel, Kri snorted. "You've seen nothing. That was just friendly sparring. I'm a killing machine in a real fight."

Jin leaned away. "Have you ever killed anyone?"

"Not yet. Humans are too easy to kill to bother, and Kian would not let me fight Doomers."

Arwel growled.

Kri had just blurted stuff she wasn't supposed to next to Jacki.

Thinking quickly, Jin lifted her finger. "I've heard about those gangs. The Humans are not nearly as vicious as the Doomers. No wonder Kian keeps you away from the fights. I've heard they do ritual killings, really gruesome, horrible stuff."

Luckily for them, Jacki wasn't an empath. "I've never heard about those gangs. Where are they operating, Chicago?"

"They are all over." Jin turned around. "They are quickly becoming the two largest drug cartels in the States. And there have been rumors about the Doomers getting into trafficking as well."

Jacki shook her head. "I really need to pay more attention to the news."

"You'd better get moving." Arwel leaned and kissed the top of Jin's head. "Good luck."

"Thanks."

As Kri eased out of the garage, a ghost of a smile lifted the corners of her lips. "You are going to be fine."

Jin slumped in her seat. "I hope so."

"Don't think. Just do. Pretend that you are back at the house, training. Do exactly what you did this morning. You were perfect."

"How are we going to do it?" Jacki asked. "We can't go in together because we are all tall and we will attract attention. Especially you, Kri. You are pretty, and with those boots and that leather jacket, you look like a badass. Guys will look at you. Jin and I look like a couple of suburban housewives."

Kri didn't bother to deny it. "We can use that to our advantage. I'll go in first and strut around, maybe flirt loudly with some guys, make a scene and start a fight. Everyone will be looking at me while Jacki enters quietly. Jin, you will come in last."

Imagining Kri knocking guys over and making a scene, Jin shook her head. "Isn't a bar fight too much?"

Kri shrugged. "I'll play it by ear."

"You need to tether me," Jacki said.

"We have earpieces. You can just tell me who he is and where he is standing. That way Kri will know as well."

"I know what he looks like because I saw the picture of who he shrouds himself as." Kri glanced at Jacki through the rearview mirror. "But he might decide to change the shroud for some reason, and then we will need you to find him."

Jin nodded. "That could easily happen if Kalugal sees someone he's been with already and doesn't want her to recognize him while he is hitting on someone else."

"You know what I find really bizarre?" Jacki said.

"What?" Jin tensed, hoping it wasn't about the two gangs she'd made up to cover for Kri's mistake.

"The pictures the guys snap of Kalugal. If he is not in the area, actively manipulating your minds, how come you still see his shroud in those and not his real face?"

"Good question." Jin glanced at Kri. "Maybe the suggestion he plants in our heads stays there. That makes him even more powerful than what we've suspected."

Kri nodded. "Compulsion is a very rare talent. Kalugal must combine it with his shrouds. That's why they hold. I don't know Lokan well, so I'm not sure if he can do that as well, but I would be very surprised if he can."

"I still think that you need to tether me. Shit can happen, the earpieces can malfunction, the reception in the club might be lousy, and Kalugal's men might invade the house and take William hostage. Even a power outage can mess things up. The tether is the most secure connection."

"As unlikely as those scenarios are, you are right about the tether." Jin turned toward the backseat. "Give me your hand."

Jacki shook it. "Done?"

"Yes."

Ten minutes into the drive, Arwel spoke in their earpieces. "Kalugal and his guy just parked at a club. I'm sending you the address."

As the churning in Jin's belly turned from mild to intense, she rubbed a hand over it. "How do I keep from throwing up?"

Kri put a hand on her thigh. "You are not going to puke. You are going to get in there, get a drink, zero in on our boy, and bump into him. He'll be too busy watching me to notice you approach him."

"Are you still planning on starting a fight?"

"I'll wait to see how you are doing. If you hesitate, I'll go up to a random chick and start accusing her of stealing my boyfriend."

Jacki chuckled. "A catfight will attract everyone's attention."

"Yeah, I'll pretend to be drunk. As soon as you tether Kalugal, let me know and I'll apologize, saying that it was a case of mistaken identity."

"Who will leave the club first?" Jacki asked.

"Jin, then you, and lastly, me. I'm not going to leave until I know that both of you are safe."

64

ARWEL

As Kri turned into the club's parking lot, Magnus entered behind her, while Arwel continued driving to the nearest intersection and turned around.

After parking across the street from the club's entrance, he called the Guardians who'd followed Kalugal to the club. "You can leave."

"Good luck," Chester said. "If you need us, we will be in a pub five minutes away from here."

"Thanks. I won't say no to additional backup."

"We are too close," Michael said. "And this is a loading zone. Maybe you should park a little farther down the street."

"I want to be where I can see the door."

"Then backtrack a little. Everyone going in will wonder about three dudes who are just sitting in their car."

"It's fine. The windows are tinted, and even if they can see us, people will assume that we are waiting for someone."

Michael shrugged. "You're the boss."

The club had two egress points. One in the front and one in the back.

To get in, club-goers had to go through the front door and get cleared by the bouncer. But to leave, they could also use the back door to the parking lot, which Magnus and Gregor were watching.

The additional three Guardians Arwel had requested would be arriving shortly, and he debated whether to assign them to guard the back or park farther down the street like Michael had suggested. They were a precaution, so maybe it was better for them to stay out of sight. Together with the two at the pub, Jin had a total of ten Guardians ready to jump in if needed.

The problem was that all of them were useless against Kalugal's compulsion.

As Kri rounded the corner and sauntered toward the entrance, the bouncer gave her a thorough once-over and opened the door with a slight dip of his head.

A few minutes later, Jacki came around, but instead of walking straight in, she glanced around, probably to check where they were parked.

Arwel groaned. That was such an amateur move. He'd thought that not acknowledging their escorts was self-explanatory, so he hadn't bothered warning the girls against it.

The mistake was his, not Jacki's. She was a newbie with no training, and what was obvious to him was not necessarily obvious to her.

When she saw the car, Jacki smiled but thankfully didn't wave, and only then headed toward the club's entrance.

More than ten minutes passed before Jin rounded the corner, huddling into her coat and not looking left or right while hurrying toward the door.

Was it an act? Or was she really cold?

If it was an act, it was a good one because he had the urge to grab his coat and rush to cover her with it.

When the door closed behind her, Arwel's gut twisted with worry.

He tried to reason with himself that Kalugal had only one man with him, and if needed, Kri could take care of the guy, but the problem was Kalugal himself.

They were all defenseless against his compulsion. If anything went wrong and he became aware of Jin and her intentions, they were all royally screwed.

Even if every Guardian on the force was there as backup, it would not make a difference. Kalugal could walk out of there with Jin in tow and no one would be able to stop him.

Given his powers, it was a wonder that the guy had only used them to make money. He could've taken over the damn White House if he wanted.

Thank the merciful Fates for immunes. That was probably the only reason Kalugal hadn't done anything crazy. He must have encountered some over the years and figured that he shouldn't risk it. With the right kind of bullet and a carefully aimed shot to the head or the heart, one immune sharpshooter could incapacitate Kalugal long enough for his teammates to finish the job by either decapitating him or removing his heart.

"You are stressing the hell out of me," Michael murmured. "Relax."

"My mate is in there."

"So is mine, but I know Kri can handle any situation. I've only seen her in action once, and it was awe-inspiring. She took out seven armed humans in seconds."

"I'm not worried about humans. I just wish we had several immune Guardians. As it is, we are defenseless against Kalugal. He could walk right past us or command us to follow him into his bunker."

"Maybe some of the Guardians are immune," Ewan said. "We were never tested."

"We should have been." Arwel turned to the Guardian. "Annani could have tested us."

"Too late for that," Michael said. "Besides, I think you are all worrying too much. Worst case scenario, we can negotiate with him. After all, we have an ace up our sleeve."

Arwel arched a brow. "What?"

"His brother."

"We don't actually have him. He is his own man."

"Semantics. He is not going to refuse to help. Carol would castrate him."

Arwel's lips twitched in an involuntary smile. "I'm not sure about the castrating part, but she might threaten him with bodily harm. The question is whether Lokan can override Kalugal's compulsion. If he can, we have nothing to worry about because he compelled us to refuse Kalugal's commands."

Michael shrugged. "What we can be pretty sure of is that Lokan is immune. If Navuh's compulsion didn't affect him, Kalugal's most likely will not either, and he can negotiate for us."

It wasn't much, but it was better than nothing. Arwel had kept up a confident façade in front of Jin, but the truth was that he was terrified for her.

Closing his eyes, he let his awareness spread wide. If anything went wrong, he would feel it.

65

JIN

As Jin entered the club, she didn't try to find Kalugal right away. Her eyes went searching for Kri first. The Guardian was her safety net, and just knowing that she was there, watching over her, diminished her anxiety by at least half.

She found her leaning against one of the supporting pillars and holding a bottle of beer in her hand.

No glass for the badass.

The woman was formidable, and not only physically. She had a warrior's attitude, which meant that she wouldn't hesitate to jump in and do whatever she could to help Jin.

"Look to your right," Jacki said in her earpiece. "Do you see the girl with the pink miniskirt?"

Afraid to move her lips, Jin nodded, hoping Jacki could see her.

"The guy she is plastered against is Kalugal."

Closing her eyes, Jin followed the tether to Jacki and looked at the couple through her friend's eyes.

Still, all she saw was the shroud and not Kalugal's real face.

"Can you see the real him?" Jacki asked.

It was weird to hear her in the earpiece and through the tether at the same time.

Jin shook her head.

"So Kri was right. He manipulates everyone around him to see only his shroud, and it sticks no matter what medium is used to look at him."

Jin nodded, then searched for Jacki, figuring her likely position by her viewing angle.

She was sitting on a barstool, holding a large drink in front of her face to hide her moving lips as best she could.

With so many people crowding the space getting to the bar wasn't easy, especially since Jin didn't want to shove people out of the way and attract attention.

It took her what seemed like forever to get there, and then she had to wait for the barman to take her order.

Everything was taking too long. What if Kalugal left, and she missed her opportunity once more?

The thing was, she had a script to follow, one that she'd rehearsed over and over again. If she deviated from it, she might freeze again.

When the barman finally handed her the large mojito she'd ordered, Jin took it and turned around, fearing that Kalugal would no longer be where she'd last seen him on the dance floor.

Thank God, he was in the same spot with the same blonde girl clinging to him.

Drink in hand, Jin ambled toward the couple. Swaying to the music, she inched toward them the same way she'd practiced at home.

Kri was right. With enough repetition, it almost felt natural, and Jin managed to keep her anxiety at a low simmer, not letting it flare up.

She didn't go straight at them. Instead, she went a little to the left, then a little to the right, never facing them but keeping track of them in her peripheral vision.

Even though she looked very different from what Kalugal saw the day before, he still might recognize her face or her smell.

She'd sprayed herself with enough perfume to knock out an elephant, but then she wasn't dealing with an ordinary immortal. He might be able to smell her real scent under the artificial one.

Stop it!

Those thoughts were needlessly stressing her out. She was very close to him now, and he hadn't even turned his head in her direction.

The blonde with the pink skirt must have been sent by the Fates. With her hands roaming all over Kalugal's back, her big boobs pressed against his chest, and her ass filling his hands, she had his full attention.

As it turned out, Jin didn't even need to fake stumbling into him.

As someone bumped into her from behind, she pitched forward, spilling her mojito all over Kalugal and the blonde and then catching his arm to stop herself from falling.

The training kicked in.

Holding on for a moment longer, she inserted a hook into his mind and attached her tether to it.

It was done in under two seconds.

"You idiot!" the blonde yelled. "Look what you have done!"

"I'm so sorry." Jin patted Kalugal's sleeve. "I'll pay to have it dry cleaned. Someone bumped into me, and I lost my balance. I'm so sorry."

"Don't worry about it," Kalugal said. "Alcohol dries fast."

Pretending to obsess about his ruined shirt, Jin kept her face down. "Are you sure? Let me at least pay for the dry cleaning."

"Forget it. No harm done."

"What about me?" the blonde whined. "She spilled her drink all over my new skirt."

"It will dry out. And if not, I'll buy you a new one."

"Really?" Her tone turned sugary and she put her hands over his chest. "You look sexy with your shirt all wet."

And just like that Jin was forgotten and the couple went back to necking on the dance floor.

Mission accomplished.

Almost. She still needed to check whether the tether worked, and she also couldn't leave right after the incident.

If it had been real, she would have ordered another drink to calm her nerves, as would most girls in her situation.

As she made her way toward the bar, Jacki spoke in her earpiece, "Did you get him?"

Jin nodded.

"Then let's get out of here."

Jin ignored the suggestion until she reached Jacki, who was still sitting on the same stool. Squeezing between her and the guy sitting next to her, she ordered another drink.

"I have to check it out," she said without looking at her friend. "And it would look suspicious if I leave right away."

"You can go toward the bathrooms and continue to the back door," Kri said in the earpiece.

Jin looked at the barman. "I'm waiting for my drink."

"Coming right up. You're next in line."

Leaning against the bar, Jin closed her eyes and followed the tether to Kalugal.

The connection was loud and clear.

"You told me that your ex-boyfriend was working on something interesting," Kalugal said.

"Yeah, he had an idea for an Alexa type device, but then Google came up with something better."

"Did he drop it?"

"I don't know. Why are we talking about him?"

"I'm curious about new technologies."

"Then maybe you should hook up with him instead."

Jin could feel a little of what Kalugal was feeling, which was annoyance and contempt.

Apparently, he wasn't even attracted to Blondie. He only wanted to pump her for information about her ex-boyfriend.

Except, she might have been projecting her own feelings on him. It was rare for Jin to feel her targets' emotions at all.

Except for Arwel.

The connection with him had been amazing, but then what he'd been feeling at the time was intense.

"Let's go," Jacki said in her earpiece.

"I'm still waiting for that drink." Jin smiled at the bartender so he wouldn't get mad at her for pestering him.

Her words were meant for Jacki and Kri.

What Jin really wanted was to hear more about Blondie's ex-boyfriend and his invention. She could try to listen while walking out, but if someone talked to her she might lose concentration and miss some of what was being said. If Kalugal was interested in the technology, then it must be something important, and it might give Kian a clue about Kalugal's future plans.

66

ARWEL

"How long has it been?" Michael lifted his phone to check the time. "Damn, not long at all. Jin only went in thirteen minutes ago. Time moves slowly when the stakes are high."

Arwel nodded.

It felt as if he'd been spreading his mental feelers for at least an hour. Regrettably, he couldn't get a read on any of the three women.

Kri was an immortal, Jacki had thick protective walls, and Jin didn't project her feelings as strongly as other humans did.

Which was excellent for the mission.

Even if she got nervous, Kalugal wouldn't pick up on the intensity. To him, it would feel like the normal emotions of a woman alone in a club. A little apprehensive and a lot hopeful.

His thoughts were interrupted when something dark and nasty registered on the edge of his awareness. Arwel opened his eyes and looked out the window.

The strength of the emotions indicated that the source was human, not immortal, but where was it coming from?

There was no one in front of the car, and the only person at the entrance to the club was the bouncer.

The darkness wasn't coming from his direction.

As Arwel glanced at the rearview mirror, he saw a man walking toward them. His head was bowed, and he was huddled in a heavy coat, holding his arms over its front.

Was he hiding a weapon under there?

The closer the man got, the stronger Arwel felt the turmoil raging inside him. The pain and the hatred were almost too much to bear, and Arwel was only getting it secondhand.

The source was about to explode.

Was he heading toward the club? Arwel waited to see if the guy would cross to the other side.

Even if he had dark deeds on his mind, there wasn't much Arwel could do about it. Intentions, even murderous ones, were not a crime.

Only acting upon them was.

"I feel nefarious intentions," Michael muttered. "Someone is planning to do harm. A human male."

"He is right behind us."

"Should we do something about it?"

"Only if he goes into the club. Intentions don't qualify as a crime, and we are not the police."

Except, when the guy got off the sidewalk and started for the other side of the street, legal or even moral considerations went out the window.

His mate was in that club, and Arwel wasn't going to wait for this bomb to explode anywhere near Jin.

As the guy handed the bouncer what was probably a cash bribe, Arwel opened the driver's side door. "Wait here."

"I'm coming with you," Ewan said.

He didn't need help to handle one human. And if the guy had a bomb under his coat and was planning to murder countless people while committing suicide, Arwel didn't want anyone else to get hurt.

"Both of you stay in the car, and that's an order."

Sensing the human's determination, Arwel yelled into the earpiece, "Take cover. A gunman just came in."

Running toward the entrance, he didn't bother with thralling. Arwel barreled past the bouncer, threw the door open, and leaped just as the guy pulled out a gun.

Sailing over people's heads, he landed on the shooter, tackling him to the ground.

Except, he wasn't fast enough.

The gun fired.

The panic gripping Arwel was like nothing he had experienced before, and if not for his training dictating his moves, he might have first looked up to check on his mate.

Instead, he went for the gun, wrenched it out of the guy's hand, at the same time delivering a blow to his head and knocking him out cold or possibly killing him.

The screaming started a split second later, followed by a stampede.

He couldn't see Jin from where he was, and with the panicked humans all around him, there was no chance of him feeling her either.

It took him another split second to remember that he had an earpiece. "Is everyone okay?"

"Jacki and I are hiding behind the bar."

Arwel felt faint with relief.

"I'm trying to get to you," Kri said. "Damn humans are like a stampeding herd of scared buffalos."

67

KALUGAL

Kalugal hadn't seen the shooter come in, and he hadn't felt his intentions either. He wasn't close enough. Besides, with so many humans around, lusting, envying, plotting, it would have been impossible to isolate one who was crazier than the rest even if he was standing right next to him.

What had alerted Kalugal and made him look over his shoulder, were the blonde's widening eyes and her sudden flare of fear.

He watched the scene unfolding before his eyes as if it was going in slow motion.

One second the shooter was pulling out his gun, and the next a man was sailing in the air over the crowd, his trajectory on a collision course with the guy.

As he landed on the shooter, the gun went off, but not into any of the humans. Somehow the flyboy had managed to knock the gunman's hand up, and the bullet hit the ceiling and went right through the plaster, getting lodged in it.

The screaming started a heartbeat after the shot, which was about how long it had taken the flyboy to get the gun away from the nutcase and knock him out cold.

Unless the guy was an Olympic champion, his speed and power were inhuman.

With people screaming and rushing out, Kalugal could no longer see him, but he was almost certain that Flyboy was an immortal.

Was he one of his father's men?

Sent to protect him?

For a brief moment, Kalugal entertained the absurd notion that his father had known where he had been the entire time and had men watching over him.

Right. More like watching him and reporting back. And the only reason they hadn't attempted to capture him yet was that they were waiting for an opportune moment to catch him by surprise and knock him out before he had a chance to compel them.

Then again, his father might have sent immune warriors after him. Just as there were immune humans, Kalugal had no doubt that there were immune immortals.

Except, Navuh wasn't supposed to know that Kalugal could compel immortals, not unless his mother had revealed his secret.

Was it possible that she had betrayed him?

Regrettably, he couldn't discount that possibility. Areana loved Navuh and thinking that Kalugal was safely out of his reach, she might have told him about his son inheriting the ability to compel immortals.

Whatever the case was, he had to find out. Which meant interrogating that immortal.

"Freeze!" Kalugal shouted over the crowd, infusing his voice with compulsion. "No one move! And no one utter a sound."

The ruckus stopped as if it had never begun.

Moving the blonde aside, Kalugal glanced at Rufsur. His second, who had been on the dance floor right next to him when it had all started, was now frozen like everyone else. "Except for you, Rufsur. You can move."

As Kalugal headed toward where he'd seen Flyboy land, he noticed a woman standing behind the bar who wasn't frozen like the others. Her eyes peeled wide, she gaped at him, and then ducked behind the bar again.

Damn immune.

She looked familiar. Had he seen her before? Perhaps he'd noticed her in his peripheral vision. But why she would register at all baffled him. From one to ten, she was barely a six, and he was being generous.

It didn't matter. No one was going to believe her anyway. They'd think the shock had made her see things.

As Kalugal crouched next to Flyboy, the small hairs on the back of his neck tingled, confirming what he'd suspected. The guy was an immortal.

"Did my father send you? You can answer yes or no."

"No."

Noticing something sticking out of the guy's ear, Kalugal leaned closer and moved his hair aside, exposing it.

"What do we have here?"

He pulled the earpiece out. Obviously, Flyboy wasn't alone, and damage control was required.

Kalugal needed to buy himself time to get away without anyone following him. Activating the device, he put it in his own ear. "Everyone listening, stop talking, texting and any other form of communication. Don't move unless you are driving. If you are, pull to the side of the road and then sit in the vehicle until I tell you to move."

That should do it without causing too much trouble.

For a moment, he debated whether to unfreeze the immortal and tell him to follow, or just lift him up and carry him to the car.

In case the guy tried to resist the compulsion or work around it by dragging his feet, it was better to just carry him.

"Rufsur. Pick him up and carry him to the car. Put him in the trunk."

"He's not going to fit. It's too small."

"Then put him in the back seat."

"Yes, boss."

As his second-in-command heaved the dead weight over his shoulder, Kalugal checked the shooter. The nutcase was still out cold, but regrettably not dead.

He might wake up and start shooting again. Kalugal could take the gun, but the dude might have more hidden under his clothes. It would be quicker to tie him up than search him for more weapons.

Pulling out his belt, Kalugal tied the guy's hands behind his back.

With that done, he got up and looked in the direction he'd seen the immune, but she was still hiding behind the bar.

Good.

He took out the earpiece and put it in his pocket.

"Listen up, everyone," Kalugal yelled to be heard over the music that was still blaring from the loudspeakers. "You are going to forget what you've seen, and in half an hour, you will resume dancing. You'll remember watching a Coldplay concert on the screen in the back."

At the start of the evening, Rufsur had fixed the surveillance cameras, putting them on a loop, so none of what had happened was going to show up on the recording.

With the thrall taking care of the humans' memories of the incident, the only remaining evidence other than the gunman would be the bullet lodged in the ceiling, which no one was going to notice.

Looking down at the shooter, he wondered what to do with him. The best thing would be to throw him into the dumpster out back, but Kalugal had sent Rufsur with the immortal, which meant that he would have to take the trash out himself.

The things he had to do to protect a bunch of insignificant humans.

With a sigh, he wrapped his hand in his shirttail, picked up the gun, and put it in his pocket.

Grabbing the gunman by the belt he'd tied around his wrists, he dragged the piece of human trash out the back door, where he encountered two more males frozen mid-stride.

When the small hairs on the back of his neck started tingling, he took another look at the males. The males could only move their eyes, and the expression in them was more angry than terrified.

They knew what was going on.

He smiled at them. "I apologize for the temporary inconvenience, but don't worry. I'm going to release you as soon as I'm safely away with your friend."

If looks could kill, he would already be dead. Thankfully, he'd never heard of an immortal possessing that power.

Had any of the gods?

His father was the only one who could answer that question, but since he couldn't call Navuh and ask, it was another mystery Kalugal hoped he could solve through research into the past.

Heaving the shooter up, he tossed him in the dumpster. The gun was next. Pulling it out of his pocket using his shirt again, he tossed it inside as well.

With that done, Kalugal turned to assess the two immortals. They didn't look like his father's men. Fair-skinned and light-haired, they looked European. But then many years had gone by since he'd left the island, and his father might have been breeding the Dormants with European men, producing warriors who could more easily blend into the population in the Western countries.

But Flyboy had said that he hadn't been sent by Navuh. Maybe they were Annani's men?

And if so, had they been looking for him, or had it been a coincidence?

He would soon find out.

68

JIN

The moment Arwel had shouted in their earpieces, Jacki climbed on top of the bar and pulled Jin behind her.

"What are you doing?" the barman yelled at them. "Get down."

"That is what we are doing," Jin yelled back. "Everyone, duck!"

She and Jacki jumped behind the counter and crouched down.

The two barmen did the same. "What's going on?" the closest one asked.

"A shooter," Jacki said.

A moment later, a gun went off and then the screaming started.

As Jin lifted her head to check if anyone had gotten hurt, Jacki grabbed her shirt and pulled her back down. "It might not be safe yet."

"I disabled the gunman," Arwel said in their earpieces.

Jin started pushing to her feet again when she was stopped by one shouted word.

"Freeze!" Somehow the voice overpowered the screaming and the music. It was loud, clear, and infused with command. "No one move! And no one utter a sound."

Immediately, the screaming stopped as if someone had waved a magic wand. Not the music, though. It kept blasting from the loudspeakers.

But that wasn't all. As Jin tried to get back down, she realized that she couldn't move and was stuck in a mid-crouch.

She couldn't talk either.

As the implications sank in, an involuntary shiver seized her. The command had been a compulsion, issued by Kalugal.

Thankfully, Jacki wasn't affected, and she pulled Jin down, making her land unceremoniously on her ass. "We are majorly screwed," she whispered. "I'm the only one the compulsion doesn't work on."

Panic seizing her lungs, Jin wanted to tell Jacki to check on Arwel, but all she could do was blink, which she did rapidly, hoping her friend would understand.

The tether worked only one way, and Jacki wasn't an empath. But she got the message.

Slowly, she pushed up to her feet and then immediately ducked back down. "Damn. He looked right at me. He's crouching next to Arwel, who is lying on top of the gunman, immobilized just like everyone else."

Where were the other Guardians? Were they affected by the compulsion as well?

Her answer came a moment later, delivered by Kalugal's calm voice straight into her earpiece. "Everyone listening, stop talking, texting, and any other form of communication. Don't move unless you are driving. If you are, pull over to the side of the road and then sit in the vehicle until I tell you to move."

Kalugal had just eliminated her last hope.

Help was not coming.

But at least he'd made sure they wouldn't cause accidents by freezing inside moving vehicles.

Trying to force her hand to move, Jin struggled against the compulsion, but disobeying the command proved impossible.

As hot tears started rolling down her cheeks, Jacki wiped them away with her sleeve. "Don't cry," she said quietly. "You won't be able to blow your nose. I can wipe the snot but not blow for you."

She was trying to cheer Jin up, but it wasn't working.

The situation was desperate.

Arwel was at Kalugal's mercy, and no one was coming to help them.

"Wait, maybe you can blow your nose. He just said not to move. Smart guy. He must have a lot of experience with compulsion to make his wording so precise."

Jin didn't want to hear about Kalugal's brilliance. She wanted Jacki to do something, anything.

"Rufsur," Jin heard him call his man. "Pick him up and carry him to the car. Put him in the trunk."

"He's not going to fit. It's too small."

"Then put him in the back seat."

"Yes, boss."

The him could only be Arwel.

Blinking rapidly, she signaled her distress to Jacki the only way she could.

"Okay, I got it. I'll take another look."

Jacki pushed up slowly, only as much as she needed to peek over the bar. "The other guy is carrying Arwel out, and Kal is tying up the gunman." She ducked back down. "I don't know what to do. The pepper spray is in my purse and I dropped it when I climbed on the bar. Maybe I can use a big bottle to hurl at his head?"

Since Jin could see through Jacki's eyes, the spoken update wasn't necessary, but she had no way of reminding Jacki of the tether. The only response she could give her was to widen her eyes.

"I guess it's no. I didn't think so."

"Listen up, everyone," Kalugal said. "You are going to forget what you've seen, and in half an hour, you will resume dancing. You'll remember watching a Coldplay concert on the screen in the back."

"He is so smart." Jacki started pushing up again. "Maybe I can somehow get the shooter's gun."

Through her friend's eyes, Jin saw Kalugal drag the gunman toward the back exit.

He was leaving.

If Jacki didn't do something soon, Kalugal would drive away with Arwel.

Communicating the urgency by darting her eyes from side to side, she hoped Jacki would understand.

Except, how could she possibly overpower two immortal males and free Arwel?

It was hopeless.

69

ARWEL

As Arwel was lifted and swung over the immortal's shoulder, he had never in his entire life felt so helpless.

They passed by Magnus and Gregor, who had been frozen mid-stride. Only their eyes moved, and they reflected the same desperation that Arwel felt.

He was at Kalugal's mercy, his fellow Guardians were just as frozen as he was, and his only possible savior was Jacki, a human girl who could do nothing to help him.

He was screwed, and so was the entire clan.

Arwel was privy to almost everything there was to know, including the village's location. Hopefully, Kian would immediately implement the lockdown protocol to secure the place.

The one good thing was that Arwel didn't know the override codes. They were computer-generated daily, one set going to Onegus and the other to Kian. Both were needed to override the shutdown and access the village.

If only he had a suicide capsule in his tooth like the spies in the movies, he could have killed himself to save the clan. But no one had imagined a scenario in which a head Guardian would be captured by an immortal who could compel him to do anything he wanted.

"Look on the bright side," Rufsur said. "You are getting a ride in a Ferrari. I'm afraid it's going to be a little cramped in the back seat, but at least I don't have to stuff you in the trunk."

He opened the door with a key, moved the chair forward, and dumped Arwel on the tiny back seat. It took some maneuvering, and the guy had to fold Arwel's legs all the way up to his chin before dropping the driver's seat back down.

"I keep telling Kalugal that this car is a joke, but he loves his expensive toys."

Sitting on the driver's seat with his legs outside the car, Rufsur looked at Arwel. "I hope you are not in pain, my friend."

What a surprisingly amiable fellow.

Except, Arwel was under no illusions. When it came time for torture, Rufsur would not hesitate for a moment.

There would be no need for that because Kalugal could compel him to talk, but he might decide to do it for the fun of it.

Where was he?

Why hadn't he come out yet?

Hopefully, he wasn't looking for Jin. Had he connected the two incidents?

Kalugal had asked him if he'd been sent by Navuh, so that was where his mind was going, and Navuh would never have used a woman for his schemes. So, if Kalugal still thought that Arwel was connected to his father, it wouldn't occur to him that the girl who'd bumped into him was with Arwel. She would be just another face in the crowd of frozen humans.

Was he ever going to see her again?

Their story couldn't end like this.

The Fates had not brought them together only to break them apart.

Furthermore, they wouldn't have been arranging matings left, right and center if they knew about the clan's imminent demise.

It was ridiculous to base his hopes on the elusive Fates, but as the saying went, there are no atheists in foxholes, and even a nonbeliever like Arwel found himself praying to a higher power.

Please don't let it end like this. But if you need a sacrifice for your boon, take it out of me, and spare Jin.

70

WILLIAM

As soon as Arwel yelled, *take cover*, William opened his channel to the other Guardians so they could hear what was going on.

The problem was that William was operating on blind, and the only information he was getting was through Arwel and the girls' earpieces.

The cameras inside the club had been tampered with, most likely by Kalugal or his guy. William couldn't see the girls going in, nor could he see the shrouded Kalugal.

The same was true for the camera in the parking lot.

By the time he'd hacked into the feed, it hadn't shown the Ferrari or Magnus's car, when he knew that it should.

"Everyone, go in," William shouted as he heard the gunshot through Arwel's earpiece.

"Arwel ordered us to stay in the car," Michael said.

"He didn't say anything to Gregor and me," Magnus said. "We are going in."

"So are we," the Guardian in the backup car announced.

"I'm trying to get to Arwel," Kri yelled. "Everyone is screaming and pushing to get out."

"Are Jacki and Jin safe?"

"They are hiding behind the bar."

A few tense seconds passed, and then William heard another voice coming through Arwel's earpiece. "Freeze! No one move, and no one utter a sound."

William froze with his hand on the control screen, the command affecting him even though he was nowhere near Kalugal.

The air silence from the Guardians meant that the same had happened to them.

The only one he could hear was Jacki, who was talking to Jin. "We are majorly screwed. I'm the only one the compulsion doesn't work on."

William strained, trying to move his hand to open a channel to Onegus, but it refused to cooperate. On second thought, it was a good thing that he hadn't succeeded. Kalugal could have compelled Onegus to freeze as well.

And if he had any doubts, a moment later they were dispelled when Kalugal spoke directly into the earpiece. "Everyone listening, stop talking, texting, and any other form of communication. Don't move unless you are driving. If you are, pull over to the side of the road and then sit in the vehicle until I tell you to move."

Arwel's device went silent, but William could still hear some of what was going on through Kri's earpiece. It was muffled, drowned out by the loud music still blasting as if nothing had happened.

If not for his immortal hearing, he wouldn't have heard Kalugal order his man.

"Rufsur. Pick him up and carry him to the car. Put him in the trunk."

"He's not going to fit. It's too small."

"Then put him in the back seat."

"Yes, boss."

A drop of sweat detached from William's forehead and landed on his desk.

Jacki was right. They were all majorly screwed.

71

JIN

"Crap." Jacki's eyes darted around. "It's now or never. I need a weapon." She grabbed a stainless-steel cocktail shaker. "Not heavy enough." She tossed it aside and grabbed a large bottle of vodka. "That's good. I need another one." She skirted the barman who was frozen in a crouch next to Jin and went for a second bottle. "I need that damn pepper spray." Jacki left the bottle on the counter, pulled herself on top of the bar, and jumped down on the other side. "Where is my damn purse?"

Through the tether, Jin saw Jacki crawling between people's legs, searching for her purse and the pepper spray. She was wasting time, and in the meantime, Kalugal could be driving off with Arwel.

Jin switched to Kalugal's tether.

Through his eyes, she saw him throw the gunman into a dumpster. Kalugal wrapped his hand in his shirttail and pulled the gun out of his pocket, wiped it, and then tossed it into the dumpster as well.

What was he going to do next? Drive away? Come back and look for her?

Pepper spray in one hand and a vodka bottle in the other, Jacki leaned over the bar. "Wish me luck."

Jin blinked and then closed her eyes to follow the tether to Jacki.

As her friend ran out the back door at full speed, Kalugal looked over his shoulder.

Without a moment's hesitation, Jacki hurled the bottle at his head. If not for his inhuman reflexes, she would have made it.

But he snatched the bottle before it could hit him and smiled at Jacki. "Nice try. Now, be a good girl, turn around, and go back inside."

"Like hell!" She ran at him with the pepper spray aimed at his eyes.

What the hell was she doing? He was going to kill her or tie her up and throw her into the dumpster together with the gunman.

But before Jacki could reach Kalugal, his guy intercepted her, catching her from behind with an arm around her waist, and at the same time wrenching the pepper spray out of her hand and tossing it away.

As he threw her over his shoulder, Jin got just as dizzy as Jacki from seeing things upside down.

"What do you want me to do with her?" Rufsur asked.

Jacki struggled, pounding on his back and kicking her legs.

The guy didn't even grimace. It was as if a child was wriggling to get out of her father's grip. He wasn't hurting her, but he wasn't letting go of her either.

Kalugal looked at Jacki's struggles dispassionately. "Will she fit in the trunk?"

"I think so. She's not as chubby as she looks. It's all clothing."

"Stop!" Jacki yelled at the top of her lungs. "Rape!"

As if that was going to help her.

"You'd better tie her up and gag her." Kalugal gripped Jacki's chin and squeezed. "Is the immortal your boyfriend?" He lifted her face. "You must love him very much to take a stupid risk like that.

Jacki stopped struggling. "Immortal?"

Kalugal smiled indulgently. "You didn't know. He must have liked the challenge of an immune. A woman he couldn't thrall into sleeping with him."

"Let me go. I won't make any trouble."

"I'm sorry, but I can't do that. You are not just a random human who happens to be immune to mind manipulation. You are connected to immortals, and you've seen my real face."

"The clock is ticking," Rufsur said.

"Load her up." Kalugal looked at Jacki, who started struggling again. "It's not a long drive, and you have nothing to fear. No one is going to rape you. You have my word."

72

KALUGAL

"Call security and tell them to move everyone into the bunker," Kalugal said as he pulled out of the club's parking lot.

"Are you going to lock down the bunker?"

Kalugal nodded. "Until we know what we are dealing with. If this was a random coincidence, then a lockdown is not necessary, but if they were after me, it is, and that's the more likely possibility. If he was there alone, I would have been inclined to believe that it was random. But he had backup."

Rufsur glanced at the back seat. "Why don't you ask him?"

"First, I want to get back to the bunker and secure it. His questioning can wait."

Kalugal was worried about the woman in the trunk. She was too quiet. Even though she was tied up and gagged, he'd expected her to kick and thrash.

Maybe there wasn't enough air in there for her to breathe? What if she suffocated?

Humans were so damn fragile, and he didn't want her death on his conscience.

When he heard a thump and then another one, Kalugal let out a relieved breath.

Apparently, she'd been stunned by the revelation that her boyfriend was an immortal and only now had gotten over the shock.

"You'll have to sell the Ferrari," Rufsur said. "The buddies of the guy in the back probably saw us put him inside."

The car was registered to one of Kalugal's subsidiary corporations at a different address, but it was too easy to spot.

Regrettably, Rufsur was right.

"I'll replace it with a different model."

"You should go for a different make. The Aston Martin Valhalla is going to be a sweet ride."

Kalugal chuckled. "You keep complaining about the Ferrari having a joke of a backseat and a small trunk. The Valhalla is a true sports car. Besides, it's not offered for sale yet."

"Aha. So, you were thinking about it."

"Of course. I'm a collector."

And now he was adding an immortal of uncertain origins and an immune human to the rare treasures stored in his bunker.

If the immortal was part of Annani's clan, then he could be used as a bargaining chip. The question was how much the goddess cared about her people. If it were Navuh, he wouldn't even negotiate, not unless the immortal had knowledge that could endanger the island or Navuh himself.

Was the male in the back someone important in the clan?

Kalugal doubted it. An important member of the clan would not rush to save a bunch of humans at the risk of exposing himself. But then his girlfriend was inside, and he'd probably acted on instinct.

He would soon find out, though, so there was no point in speculating.

After the car lift descended into the underground garage, Kalugal parked the Ferrari in its designated spot and killed the engine.

"What do you want to do with the immortal?" Rufsur asked.

"Pick him up and carry him to a holding cell. I'll carry the immune."

Rufsur grimaced. "I'll get one of the men to do it. She's a feisty wench. She'll bite and scratch you."

Normally, Kalugal didn't mind a little rough play, but only if it was in a sexual context and consensual. The woman's heart belonged to another, and he had other things to take care of.

"Make it so."

"Do you want me to put them in the same cell?"

"Yeah. Why not. She was so desperate to save him, I'm sure she'll appreciate being locked up together with him."

It was possible that the two were just teammates, but lovers was more likely. The immortal had exposed himself to protect the immune, and she'd run out to help him with no regard for her own safety.

"Do you want to unfreeze him?"

"He will be released at the same time as the humans in the club. I'm sure he heard the command."

"In case he didn't, maybe you should do it again. If he pisses in his pants because he can't use the toilet, I don't want to have to clean him up."

"Very well." Kalugal turned to the immortal. "Ten minutes from now you can move and talk."

He got out of the car and headed to the security office.

"Has everyone made it back already?" he asked.

Dammal shook his head. "Phinas is five minutes away, and he has Dandor and Welgost with him. But Ruvon and Hivak are all the way in San Francisco. I told them to stay there and get a hotel room. The rest are down here."

"Very well. As soon as Phinas is back, lock the place down and initiate the perimeter's code red security protocol."

"Yes, boss."

"I'll be in my office."

Pushing his hand into his pocket, Kalugal closed it around the earpiece.

Once the lockdown was executed, he would unfreeze the rest of the immortals connected to the listening device.

In the short term, it would be safer for him to leave them frozen. But leaving them in that state guaranteed their exposure, and that was an undesirable outcome that would make his life more difficult in the long term.

Humans should not be allowed to discover the existence of immortals. If they ever did, a witch hunt would start, the scope of which the world had not seen before.

Not only would they feel threatened by a superior race of people living among them, they would also want to get their hands on the secret to immortality.

73

WILLIAM

"Hello," Kalugal's voice sounded in William's earpiece. "Everyone listening can move and talk now. Good night."

"Wait!" William called. "What have you done with Arwel?"

He had to act fast and keep the guy talking. Which meant that he had to start the negotiations before Kalugal disconnected the earpiece.

Sweating profusely, William forced himself to concentrate. His fingers flying over the keyboard, he typed up a message to Kian to get his earpiece in and get online.

"Oh, so that's Flyboy's name. I haven't had the opportunity to chat with him and his girlfriend yet."

William's heart skipped a beat. If Kalugal had Jin, they were flying blind. He'd hoped she could tell them what was going on.

The problem was that he couldn't check with her as long as he had Kalugal in his ear.

"Flyboy? And what girlfriend are you talking about?"

His phone pinged with a text message from Jin. *He has Jacki. She and Arwel are locked in a cell in his bunker. He initiated a lockdown of the entire place.*

William had never been more glad of his ability to do several things at once.

He texted back. *Call Kian.*

Magnus already did.

So why the hell hadn't he come on the line yet?

William wasn't a military man, and he knew nothing about negotiating a hostage situation.

Then it dawned on him that Jin and the rest of the team were still connected to Arwel's channel and could hear Kalugal. What if he decided to compel them again?

William cursed soundlessly.

He was no good at handling a critical situation like this. His first action should have been to isolate Arwel's channel.

"Your man sailed over the crowd to knock out the shooter, which was very impressive, but it also gave him away. Then Flyboy's immune girlfriend rushed to save him and fought like a hellcat. But don't worry, we handled them both with care. As you are aware, I don't need to use force to extract information from people."

Brave, stupid girl. What had she been thinking?

"She is not his girlfriend, and we know where you've taken them. As we speak, your place is being surrounded."

He was bluffing, but it was going to be true in a minute or two.

The door to his office burst open and Vivian rushed in in her pajamas. William lifted a hand to stop whatever questions she might have.

"Kri just called me..." She stopped when he pointed to his earpiece.

Kalugal chuckled. "I can just command them to freeze again. Should I do it now?"

"They are no longer connected to this channel. It's just you and me."

"Who am I talking to?" Kalugal asked. "Are you the head of this operation?"

"I'm just the communications guy. The head of the operation is going to join us in a moment."

"Wonderful. I can't wait."

Damn. Maybe it wasn't a good idea for Kian to come on the line. Kalugal could command him to do whatever he pleased.

His fingers flew over the keyboard. *Don't open the channel without Turner next to you. I'll connect Turner's earpiece to Arwel's in a second.*

"If you are planning to compel him as well, it's not going to help you. His second-in-command is an immune."

William hoped that he wasn't revealing the ace up Kian's proverbial sleeve too soon. The trouble was that he had no experience in crisis management, and he was just doing everything he could to keep Kalugal talking.

"How fascinating. I can't wait to hear who your boss is and what he wants with me."

74

JIN

*J*in used the hem of her dirty T-shirt to wipe her tear-stained cheeks for the hundredth time since Kalugal had unfrozen everyone connected to Arwel's channel. "Wasn't that the right turn?" she asked Kri.

The Guardian had been talking on the phone, and she might have missed it.

"We are not going back to the house." Kri put her phone down. "My instructions are to keep you safe. You are our bargaining chip." The Guardian lifted her hand off the steering wheel. "Not to trade you for Arwel, of course. Just letting Kalugal know that we can see and hear everything he is doing should be a good enough motivator for him to cooperate."

"I don't mind getting traded if it will keep everyone safe. I don't know anything useful, while Arwel knows everything."

"That's very brave of you. But I don't think it will come to that."

"Just let Kian know that it's on the table. Okay?"

If she could save Arwel and the rest of the clan by sacrificing herself, Jin would take it with both hands.

"Where are we going?"

She didn't care what happened to her next, but changing into a clean shirt qualified as public service. Hers was covered with tears and snot that she hadn't been able to wipe off while frozen.

Gross. But who cared about that?

Kalugal had Arwel, and she had no idea how Kian was going to free him.

It had felt awful to drive away without Arwel and Jacki, but it had made no sense to stay in the club either. Kalugal's release was going to kick in in a few minutes, and all those humans wouldn't remember anything from what had happened. About forty-five minutes would be missing from their lives, but they would be under the impression that they'd been watching a concert on the club's big screen.

If not for Magnus filling in the blanks for her and Kri, they wouldn't have remembered any of it either. Luckily, Kalugal had deactivated the earpiece he'd taken from Arwel before issuing his command to forget what had transpired inside the club, so the compulsion hadn't affected the Guardians. Curiously, Magnus's input had triggered the return of their memories, but Kri's were not the same as Jin's. While Jin had been hiding behind the counter and hadn't seen much, Kri had seen everything.

None of the other club goers would remember the gunman, though, or the bullet that had by some miracle missed its target.

Well, not by a miracle. By Arwel. The hero who had saved who knew how many lives tonight and by doing so had sacrificed himself.

She should have left the tether attached to him.

Damn, she should have refused the mission and then none of this would be happening.

She and Arwel would be in the village, working on her transition and planning a wedding.

The one thing keeping Jin from falling into despair was the tethers she had to Jacki and to Kalugal. That was enough to give her a good picture of what was going on. Thinking that Jacki and Arwel were a couple, Kalugal had them thrown into the same cell.

So far, no one had questioned either of them, but that was only because Kalugal was busy talking to William. Hopefully, Kian would take over soon and negotiate something.

What she worried about, though, was that Kalugal would assign one of his men to interrogate Arwel away from Jacki, and he would be tortured. But that didn't make much sense. Kalugal was the only one who could compel Arwel to tell him whatever he wanted, and he could do that without resorting to torture.

He didn't seem like the mean type. So far, the only nasty thing the brute had done was to lock poor Jacki in the trunk of his car. Some other guy had taken her out and carried her tied up to a cell that wasn't as nice as the ones at the keep.

Stopping at a red light, Kri glanced at the rearview mirror for the thousandth time. "Magnus told me to keep driving until he gives me further instructions. He is moving everyone out of the house."

"If they leave, who will watch Kalugal's gate?"

"All the other Guardians who are on their way to surround his compound. In a few minutes, the bastard will be under siege."

"That bastard can walk out of there, and no one will be able to stop him."

"That's true. It's a fucked-up situation. I don't know how Kian is going to handle it."

"He should trade me for Arwel. Once he tells Kalugal that he is tethered, the guy will do anything to get rid of it."

Kri cast her a sidelong glance. "Yeah, and that includes killing you. That's the easiest way to get rid of the tether."

"He is not a killer."

"What makes you think that? Kalugal is an ex-Doomer. Don't think that all of them are like Dalhu. Amanda is his fated mate, and she is the only reason he switched sides and reformed. Before that he was a killer like the rest of them."

Jin passed a shaking hand over her mouth. "Kalugal escaped, which means that he didn't agree with his father's agenda. And his actions so far prove that he is not heartless. Besides, I don't care what happens to me as long as I can free Arwel and Jacki and save everyone else in the village."

"No one is going to trade you, so you can forget about that crazy idea."

Jin had no such intention.

Holding the phone in her pocket, she thought about calling Kian directly and convincing him that this was his best option. Except, right now he was in the midst of managing a crisis, and her call would only distract him.

But maybe she could send him a text?

The moment Jin took the phone out, Kri put a hand on her arm. "Don't."

"Don't what?"

"Text Kian."

"He needs to know that trading me for Arwel and Jacki is an option."

"Wait until he calls you."

"What if he doesn't?"

"He will need you to tell him what Kalugal is doing."

"Right."

Waiting for Kian to call her was better. That way, she wasn't going to distract him. Jin put the phone away.

As the light changed to green, Kri glanced at the rearview mirror before pulling out of the intersection. "You have guts. I admire that."

Jin chuckled. "I'm terrified, and when Kian trades me, I'm probably going to pee in my pants."

Kri cast her a knowing glance. "You must really love Arwel to be willing to do that."

Jin nodded. "I would do anything for him. But this is so much bigger than just the two of us. Even if he wasn't my fated mate, this is the right thing to do."

75

KIAN

As Kian's phone rang, he had a feeling bad news was coming his way, and when he saw Magnus's contact information on the screen, he was sure of it.

"What happened?"

"Kalugal has Arwel and Jacki. You need to lock down the village and evacuate the keep."

Kian's blood ran cold in his veins. This was worse than the worst scenario he'd imagined.

Syssi's panicked expression reflected his own feelings. The only difference was that he was better at hiding them.

"Hold on. I'm going to put Onegus and Turner on a four-way call." He got up from the couch and started walking toward the door while arranging it. "This is an emergency," he said once he had them on the line. "I'm on my way to the war room. Head there while Magnus tells us what happened."

By the time the Guardian finished his report, Kian was halfway to the pavilion, and as he entered the elevator, a text from William arrived.

Kalugal has Arwel's earpiece and he is talking to me. Put yours in. I already have your channel connected. I'll try to keep him on the line for as long as I can.

Kian didn't answer. That would only break William's concentration, and after hearing Magnus's account of what had happened, he had no intention of putting the earpiece in without Turner right next to him.

The motion-activated lights turned on as soon as he entered the war room, and as he booted up the computer, Turner and Onegus rushed in.

"Onegus. We need to lock down the village and evacuate the keep. Whoever is not here will have to find a room in a hotel. Everyone in the Bay Area has to relocate. Find them accommodations. Everyone other than William needs to leave now. All the Guardians are to get in their cars and surround Kalugal's compound."

"I'm on it."

"Do it in your office, and don't listen to the channel."

"Got it." The chief rushed out.

"Turner. If Kalugal compels me, take over." He wrote his override codes on a post-it. "Mine aren't going to work without Onegus putting his in. If I'm compromised, go to his office and lock the door."

Turner took the note and stuffed it in his pocket.

"Get Lokan on the line and tell him what's going on. Call Ella and have her bring Parker over here."

"Good move."

Kian wasn't sure that it was, but he had no choice.

His phone pinged with another text. *Don't open the channel without Turner next to you. I've connected his earpiece to Arwel's as well.*

Way ahead of you, buddy. Kian pulled out his earpiece from his pocket and put it in.

Turner did the same, connecting his to Arwel's channel as well.

"His second-in-command is an immune," Kian heard William say.

"How fascinating." Kalugal sounded like a smug son of a bitch. "I can't wait to hear who your boss is and what he wants with me."

He was in for one hell of a surprise.

"Hello, cousin."

William's sigh of relief was the first response.

The second was Kalugal's. "Who is this?" His tone was no longer smug.

"I am Kian, son of Annani, your mother's sister."

DARK SPY'S RESOLUTION

1

KALUGAL

Kalugal watched the monitor, following the steps as the program ran through the lockdown protocol. Once the bunker was secure, he pulled his immortal captive's earpiece out of his pocket, put it in his ear, and tapped it to activate.

"Everyone listening can move and talk now. Good night."

"Wait! What have you done with Arwel?"

Kalugal paused with his finger a fraction of an inch away from the device.

Should he disconnect? Or should he engage?

A dilemma.

On the one hand, he was eager to start questioning his captive, but on the other hand, this was an opportunity to talk with the team's commander and learn what he had in mind as far as escalating things.

Was the guy on the other side of the connection in charge of the operation?

His quick recovery from compulsion indicated that he had a good head on his shoulders and a strong personality, which were both prerequisites for a command position. Most people would have needed several moments to collect their wits.

This should be an interesting conversation.

Leaning back in his chair, Kalugal crossed his legs at the ankles. "So that's Flyboy's name. I haven't had the opportunity to chat with him and his girlfriend yet."

"Flyboy? And what girlfriend are you talking about?"

Kalugal sighed. He hated it when people played dumb.

"Your man sailed over the crowd to knock out the shooter, which was very impressive, but it also gave him away. Then Flyboy's immune girlfriend rushed to save him and fought like a hellcat. But don't worry, we handled them both with care. As you are aware, I don't need to use force to extract information from people."

"She is not his girlfriend, and we know where you've taken them. As we speak, your place is being surrounded."

Even if the guy wasn't bluffing about knowing the location of Kalugal's compound, there was no way Arwel's pals had made it there so fast. Except, he might have had additional warriors stationed nearby or some that hadn't been connected to Arwel's channel when Kalugal had compelled them to freeze.

His immediate safety was not an issue.

While locked down, the bunker was nearly impenetrable, and they had enough supplies stored to last them for months. The problem would be getting out of there while a large force was surrounding the place.

Two tunnels led in and out of the bunker, but one went into the house, which wasn't going to be helpful as an escape route, and the other led to a grate in the sidewalk on the other side of his property, which wasn't very useful either.

That was the trouble with building a bunker inside an established and affluent community. Digging under existing houses had not been possible.

If the force outside wasn't large, he could just walk out and compel the men surrounding his property to let him through, but there was a limit to how many immortals he could compel at once.

Kalugal wasn't as powerful as his father. Not yet. Twenty or so warriors were the most he could handle at the same time.

With a few quick taps on the keyboard, he flipped through the feeds from the perimeter's cameras and was relieved to find no one outside the compound or on its grounds. That meant that his initial assessment had been correct. The team that had been sent after him wasn't large, and they were all still in the vicinity of the club. Or so he hoped. Whoever had organized this operation might be sending reinforcements.

It was time to issue some threats of his own. "I can just command them to freeze again. Should I do it now?"

"They are no longer connected to this channel. It's just you and me."

Smart move, which Kalugal had anticipated.

"Who am I talking to? Are you the head of this operation?"

"I'm just the communications guy. The head of the operation is going to join us in a moment."

That wasn't good. A small unit didn't need a dedicated communications person, which implied that he was dealing with a large force after all.

The most logical conclusion was that it belonged to Annani's clan. Except, what did they want with him?

He had never bothered them or tried to find them, and they had left him alone as well. Kalugal was surprised that they even knew of his existence.

He was supposed to be dead.

Why the sudden interest? Perhaps they sought his cooperation against his father?

If that was why Annani had sent men to follow him around, she would be disappointed. Kalugal had no such intentions.

He lifted his legs and put his feet on the desk. "Wonderful. I can't wait."

"If you are planning to compel him as well, it's not going to help you. His second-in-command is an immune."

The possibility of compelling the commander hadn't even crossed Kalugal's mind. At this point, all he wanted was to find out why Annani's clan was after him, and then to get them off his back as soon as possible. Which probably meant releasing the warrior and his girlfriend.

He would gladly do that, but only after interrogating them. There was little chance that an opportunity to learn about Annani's clan and what they were up to would present itself again.

Regrettably, once this was over he would have to relocate, and that was a damn shame. Kalugal liked the neighborhood and its proximity to Stanford, and the bunker had cost him a fortune to build, not to mention the hassle it had been. But his location had been compromised, and he couldn't allow the clan to breathe down his neck and interfere with his plans.

"How fascinating. I can't wait to hear who your boss is, and to find out what he wants with me."

"Hello, cousin."

Cousin?

All immortals had common ancestry, but to call him cousin was a stretch.

"Who is this?"

"I am Kian, son of Annani, your mother's sister."

What?

"You heard me right. Areana, your mother, is my mother's sister, which makes us cousins."

Kalugal wasn't aware that he'd voiced his astonishment.

It took a brief moment for the shock to subside and for the gears in his mind to start spinning again. The guy couldn't be talking about Annani the goddess. Many of the clan's daughters were probably named after her.

Had Navuh stolen Annani's sister from the clan?

Was that why they had been stalking him? To get her back?

His mother hadn't said anything about the clan. But then Kalugal had been a young boy the last time he'd seen her, and the subject of the clan and how she'd come to be in Navuh's possession hadn't come up in their conversations.

"Are you still there?" Kian asked.

"I can't help you recover your clanswoman. If I could have, I would have freed my mother a long time ago. Regrettably, she loves my father, and even though I must assume that he kidnapped her and forced her to mate him, she wants to stay with him. I guess Areana is suffering from prolonged Stockholm syndrome."

2

KIAN

*K*ian felt like scratching his head.

What the hell was Kalugal talking about? Could it be that he didn't know who Annani was?

Navuh had kept Annani's survival secret from her sister, but not from the Brotherhood. Since the very beginning of the conflict, he'd been using her and the supposed evils she and her clan were committing to unify his men behind his so-called cause.

Perhaps Kalugal was suffering from amnesia?

Could it be that he hadn't escaped during WWII but had been buried in stasis for decades, only to revive recently?

It had happened to Wonder, so it wasn't an implausible scenario.

"Do you know who Annani is?"

"I know who *the Annani* is, but naturally, I don't know any of her namesake descendants. If memory serves me correctly, and I'm quite sure that it does, my mother has never mentioned her sister, by name or otherwise."

That explained it.

Kalugal assumed that Kian's mother was an immortal named after Annani, not the goddess herself. And given that Areana hadn't revealed her true identity to her son, Kalugal's assumption made sense.

Unfortunately, the wind had already been knocked out from under the bombastic proclamation that Kian had hoped would have such a profound impact on Kalugal.

How disappointing.

On the other hand, lengthy explanations were precisely what Kian was after. The longer he kept Kalugal talking, the more time he would buy Kri and Jin to get out of the area, and the Guardians to surround the complex.

"No clan females are named after Annani. My mother is the goddess, and your mother is her half-sister."

There was a long moment of silence before Kalugal responded. "What you are saying is impossible. If my mother were a goddess, she would be more powerful than my father, and she obviously is not."

"Areana is a very weak goddess, and Navuh is a very powerful immortal. Still, Navuh doesn't want anyone to know that his mate is a goddess who outranks him in the gene hierarchy. That's the reason he's hiding her in the harem, and that's also the reason he didn't allow her sons to grow up with her."

"He doesn't allow any of his children to be raised in the harem. He thinks that by preventing his sons from being raised in the harem he is protecting them from killing each other over succession rights. If we don't know who our mothers are, we also don't know the hierarchy of who was born to a wife and who was born to a concubine, and Navuh does not play favorites. No one knows who he is going to choose."

Kian shook his head. He'd assumed that Kalugal knew so much more than he actually did, but he should have realized that Areana couldn't have told all that to a five-year-old boy. He'd been too young to understand harem politics and the web of lies and deceit that Navuh had created.

"Navuh has only two sons. You and Lokan. The others were fathered by human males who look like him. I loathe saying anything positive about your father, but he loves your mother and has been loyal to her throughout the years."

As Kalugal processed that nugget of information, there was another long moment of silence.

"Are you saying that the other women in my father's harem are having relations with the human male servants? That means that other than Lokan, my other so-called brothers are not related to me at all."

"That's right."

"I'll be damned. My father actually cares. That's an ingenious way to protect Lokan's and my identity. With numerous fake sons, no one suspects who Navuh's real successors are, or rather is. I have no intention of taking over. Lokan can have it all."

That hadn't been the take-home value Kian had hoped for, but it didn't matter. His main goal was to keep Kalugal talking and asking questions until Turner confirmed that Jin was safe and that the Guardians were in position.

"I'm not sure that you've got it right. Whatever Navuh does serves him and no one else. Technically, you and your brother outrank him as far as godly genes go. While Navuh is the son of a god with a mortal, and therefore only half a god, you and your brother are three-quarter gods. It's just as important for him to keep that information from you as it is to hide his mate's godly identity."

Kalugal chuckled. "Following that logic, unless Annani found a first-generation immortal to mate with, my brother and I outrank you as well."

That was regrettably true, but Kian wasn't going to provide Kalugal with any more information than he absolutely had to.

"You, Lokan, and I are not competing for positions."

"That's true. I'm not interested in your job any more than I'm interested in my father's. So, if that's why you sought me out and sent your warriors after me, rest assured that your clan is of no interest to me. You are not my enemy, and you are not my friend either. Can we leave it at that?"

Albeit mistaken, that was another logical conclusion on Kalugal's part.

The guy was level-headed, smart, and he wasn't easily shaken either. His cousin was a worthy opponent, of whom Kian would be wise to be wary.

"I have no reason to fear you, Kalugal. I sought you out because your mother asked mine to find you. She is worried about you, and she misses you."

3

JIN

Kri tapped her fingers on the steering wheel. "What if the Guardians surrounding Kalugal's place are given really good earplugs so they can't hear him?"

Jin's heart fluttered with renewed hope. "That's a very good question. His shrouds and his compulsion don't work the same way. It seems that he needs to be heard in order for the compulsion to work. Otherwise, he wouldn't have bothered with Arwel's earpiece. But he can shroud himself without being heard."

Kri nodded. "That's no less problematic than his compulsion. Even if he can't compel them because they have earplugs in, he can shroud himself and his men to be invisible and waltz out of there. The Guardians are not going to see them leave."

"True. But if there is a camera pointed at his gate, and the watchers are all the way back in the village, his shroud is not going to affect them. They will see him and can tell the Guardians."

Kri cast Jin a sidelong glance. "Very clever. I need to call Magnus and have him get everyone the best earplugs he can find. Roni, our hacker, can tell Magnus what to do about installing a surveillance camera." Kri pulled to the side and parked. "Damn. We forgot about Arwel's phone. He has everyone's numbers on it, and Kalugal can start calling people and compel them to do all kinds of shit."

"I can check if he has the phone." Jin closed her eyes and followed the tether to Kalugal. "He is still talking with Kian. I'll check on Jacki." She followed the tether to her friend. "She and Arwel are whispering in each other's ears. They are in a prison cell, but it's not nice like the ones in the keep. It has bars instead of a door, and I can see the toilet. Gross. It doesn't have a privacy wall or anything. It's just there, sitting against the back wall."

Kri grimaced. "It's just getting better and better, isn't it?" She turned to her phone and scrolled through her contacts until she found the right one and placed the call. "Roni. Can you erase Arwel's phone remotely?" A brief moment passed. "Good. I wasn't sure he would think of it."

Disconnecting, Kri huffed out a breath. "Onegus has already told Roni to do that. This is a nightmare. No one's come up with an SOP for dealing with a compeller. We are so unprepared."

The clan had known about Kalugal's ability for a while, and someone should have come up with a protocol before poking the bear. In hindsight, the entire operation appeared amateurish and gung-ho.

"You said that you are going to call Magnus about my idea."

"Right." This time Kri put the call on speaker. "Magnus, Jin and I have some ideas that we would like to run by you."

"Shoot."

"The Guardians surrounding Kalugal's place should have earplugs in, maybe the noise-canceling ones, so he can't compel them to do things. But since he can shroud himself and probably anyone else that he wants to, we need a camera installed somewhere to watch the gate, with the feed going to the village. That's too far for his shroud to reach."

"Good thinking," Magnus said. "I just need to figure out a way to communicate with my men while they are deaf."

"That's easy." Jin waved a hand. "Tell them to put their phones on vibrate and communicate via text messages."

"Excellent solution. Except, I'll have to find a store that sells quality earplugs and rob it, because I can't wait for it to open in the morning."

"You can leave money on the counter with a note," Jin said.

"I can do that. Thank you both for the excellent suggestions. You were thinking outside the box."

Kri lifted her hand for a high five, and Jin slapped it.

"That's why you need women on the force," Kri said.

"You won't hear me arguing against that. But there are no candidates for the position."

Kri nodded. "Wonder would have made a great Guardian, but her heart is not in it."

Jin had no wish to become a Guardian either, but that didn't mean that she couldn't help in other ways. "Please tell Kian that I'm fine with him trading me for Arwel."

"That's not going to happen."

"Please, just tell him that. Trading me for Arwel before Kalugal has a chance to get him to talk will solve the most urgent problem. Later, Kian can figure out a way to get me out, either by negotiating and bargaining or by threatening."

The more she talked, the more convinced Jin became that this was the only solution to the clusterfuck they found themselves in. "Kalugal is not a bad man. He made sure to get the gunman out of the club so he wouldn't shoot people when he woke up, and he told everyone who was listening to pull over before freezing them, so they wouldn't cause accidents. He's not heartless, and he's not going to hurt me. I'm sure of that. Please, Magnus. I appreciate the chivalry, but it would be really stupid on Kian's part not to use me to get Arwel and Jacki out. I beg you to convince him that this is the best option for everyone."

There was a long moment of silence before Magnus replied. "I'll convey your message to Onegus and have him explain the pros and cons to Kian. But just so you know, if we do that, Arwel is never going to forgive any of us."

"Once this is all over, I'll deal with Arwel. Right now, the future of everyone in the village is in jeopardy. That should be our first priority."

"I can't argue with that."

Jin let out a relieved breath. "Thank you."

When Magnus ended the call, she closed her eyes and followed the tether to Jacki. Everything was still the same as it had been the last time she'd checked. They were still alone in the cell, talking in hushed voices. She listened for a few moments, but it felt awkward to spy on them, so she moved to Kalugal.

Jin had no qualms about spying on him, not after he had taken her man and her friend and put them in a freaking prison cell with a damn toilet that was in full view of everyone passing by in the hallway outside.

4

ARWEL

*J*acki glanced at the toilet at the back of the cell. "If you need to use the loo, I will look away," she whispered.

"I'm good. You go first." Arwel closed his eyes and leaned against the wall.

"Can you also put your hands over your ears?"

"No problem."

Kalugal's underground bunker was no keep, and the cell they were in looked like what the name implied.

It was a prison.

The front wall was made of bars, two narrow bunk beds were the only furniture, and the toilet had no privacy wall. There was a sink, but no shower, and there were no towels.

Kalugal's men had dumped him and Jacki on the bottom bunk without bothering to untie her. She had to wait for him to unfreeze first so he could release her.

It had been cruel and unnecessary.

Jacki was human, and being tied up for an extended length of time messed up her circulation and caused muscle spasms.

Curiously, Jacki hadn't asked him any questions yet. Since he'd freed her from her bindings, she'd been quietly massaging the stiff muscles in her arms and legs, and other than thanking him, she hadn't spoken at all.

Not typical behavior for someone who had just discovered that she'd gone down the rabbit hole into a world she hadn't known existed.

Could it be that she'd forgotten Kalugal's comment about Arwel being an immortal?

Getting tied up and stuffed in the trunk of a car could mess with anyone's head. Still, even if Jacki didn't remember that, Kalugal almost certainly was going to repeat it at some point, which meant that he probably had no intention of ever letting Jacki go.

No matter on which side of the divide immortals were, they had one thing in common. Keeping their existence secret from humans was necessary for their survival, and since Kalugal couldn't thrall Jacki's memories away, he must either plan to kill her or to keep her imprisoned for life.

The only way things could have been worse was if Kalugal had also captured Jin.

Thank the merciful Fates that the guy hadn't made the connection between the girl bumping into him with what had happened shortly after that.

Jin's tether to Kalugal might help Kian with storming the place. If he had access to everything Kalugal said and did, he might even get from her the override code to unlock the bunker.

As the bed sank under Jacki's weight, Arwel opened his eyes and removed his hands from his ears. "You know that they can see you, right?" He motioned with his head toward the camera mounted near the ceiling.

"I can't do anything about it, so screw them." She flipped a finger at the camera.

"Antagonizing your captors is not a good strategy."

"It doesn't matter." Jacki kicked her shoes off, lifted her feet onto the bed, and wrapped her arms around her knees. "They are going to kill me anyway. Probably you too."

So, she'd figured it out.

Smart girl.

Except, it would have been better for her not to be so clever. As the saying went, ignorance was bliss.

He moved closer to her and whispered in her ear. "The boss is going to get us out."

She arched a brow. "How?"

"I don't know. But between him and his brilliant right-hand man, I'm sure they will figure out something."

Hopefully not by bombing the place, but Arwel couldn't discount the possibility. To keep the clan safe, Kian might decide to sacrifice them. It wouldn't be his first choice, but if everything else failed, this might be a last resort move.

Jacki leaned closer. "I still have Jin's thing, so if you want to say something to her, you can pretend that you are talking to me. Anyway, they assume that we are a couple."

The ability to talk to Jin was the one bright spot illuminating their bleak circumstances. He just wished that the communication went both ways.

Looking into Jacki's blue eyes, Arwel pretended that they were Jin's big brown ones. "I love you. Please don't do anything stupid. Stay safe."

Jacki put her head on his shoulder, probably to maintain the illusion of them being a couple. "What do you think she is going to do?"

He wrapped his arm around her shoulders. "Offer to trade for us."

"Yeah, she might do that. If I were in her shoes, that's what I would do."

That was bad. Jacki had known Jin longer than he had, and if she thought that Jin would offer to sacrifice herself, then she was probably right.

"The boss would never agree to that."

"He might have no choice." She lifted her head off his shoulder and looked at him. "Is Kalugal really his cousin?"

"It doesn't mean much to either of them."

"Are they also immortals like you?"

Damn, she hadn't forgotten.

Arwel nodded.

"Enemies?"

He nodded again, but then tilted his head. "Kalugal's father is our enemy. We don't know whether Kalugal counts himself as one too. I guess we will find out soon."

Jacki leaned against the wall. "You've come up with a good cover story. An organization of paranormally talented people made sense to me." She shook her head. "If you'd told me that you were immortal, I wouldn't have believed you. Is Jin also immortal?"

"No. But I'd rather not talk about it in here."

Even though they were whispering in each other's ears, with the proper equipment their whispers could be amplified.

"Do all immortals have paranormal talents?"

He could answer that. "To some extent. Some are stronger than others. But our mind tricks usually work only on humans. Kalugal and his father are the only immortals we know of who can affect other immortals. That's what makes them so powerful."

Annani could do that too, but that was because she was a goddess, and a powerful one.

Jacki closed her eyes. "We are so screwed. What chance does your boss have against that?"

"There are more of us than there are of them, and we have better weapons." Or so he hoped. "Kalugal can't hide inside this bunker forever, and if he thinks that this place is impenetrable, he is wrong. With the right equipment, any structure can be penetrated."

That had been meant for Kalugal's ears.

There was little chance of Kian launching a massive ordnance penetrator into a bunker located in a suburban neighborhood, but Kalugal wouldn't know that.

5

TURNER

While Kian kept Kalugal busy talking, Turner went into hyper mode, the gears in his brain picking up speed as he evaluated the situation, projected outcomes, and set things in motion.

His first priority was to get Jin to a safe location.

She, or rather the tether she had attached to Kalugal, was the best leverage they had over him. The Guardians, who in a few moments would surround his property, were more a show of strength than a tactical tool.

Once Magnus delivered the new earplugs and had cameras installed across from the compound's gate, they might prevent Kalugal and his men from leaving. But Turner had no doubt that the bunker they were in was well-stocked and could sustain them through a long siege.

Except, the clan couldn't keep the blockade up for long. They were in one of the most expensive neighborhoods in the country, and even with every immortal trick in their proverbial bag, there was no way they could maintain it for more than twenty-four hours.

In the meantime, Kalugal would learn everything there was to know about the clan.

Jin was the key to preventing that from happening. More than Kalugal wanted to learn the clan's secrets, he wanted to keep his.

Jin's tether would paralyze him, preventing Kalugal from doing anything he didn't want the clan to know.

To get rid of that, the guy would do anything, which meant that the moment Kian pulled out that trump card, Kalugal was going to divert every resource at his disposal to locating Jin.

Except, he wasn't going to find her, because Turner was going to stash her in the safest and most secret location on the globe.

The goddess's sanctuary in Alaska.

Since no one knew how to get there other than Annani and her Odus, Kalugal couldn't compel anyone to reveal the sanctuary's location.

Turner had already arranged for a private jet to pick up Jin and Kri. The airfield was ten minutes away from their current location, and the flight to Alaska would take about four and a half hours. From there, he had no clue how long it would take them to get to Annani's place.

Alaska was a big state.

It would be preferable to hold back on issuing the threat until Jin was in the sanctuary, but Turner figured that as soon as she was in the air, she would be safe from Kalugal and whoever he might deploy after her.

Kian seemed to be doing fine, and Turner had no doubt that he could keep Kalugal talking for twenty more minutes or so before the guy lost his patience and demanded that the real negotiations start.

After giving Kri the location of the airfield, Turner still had to arrange for one of Annani's Odus to pick them up from the private airfield outside of Anchorage.

Thankfully, he had Alena's phone number, which Kian had given him when she'd left for her modeling stint in New York.

Not wanting Kian to know where he was sending Jin, Turner typed a text. He would have preferred to speak to Alena, which would have been the proper thing to do, but he didn't want to chance Kian overhearing the conversation, and he couldn't leave the room as long as Kalugal was on the line.

It's an emergency, and I don't have time to explain. I need you to send a jet to pick up Kri and Jin from Sky airfield in Anchorage and take them to the sanctuary. They are leaving San Francisco in about fifteen minutes and will get there in about four and a half or five hours. One more thing. Don't text or call Kian about it until I tell you it's okay to do so. I'll explain once I can spare a moment.

Her return text arrived a few seconds later. *Consider it done. Let us know what's going on as soon as possible.*

He erased the exchange from his phone and typed a new message for Kian.

Keep Kalugal talking for at least fifteen more minutes before telling him about Jin's tether.

After reading it, Kian nodded and gave him the thumbs up.

Next order of business was to evacuate the keep and send Yamanu to San Francisco.

To maintain the siege, they needed to shroud the Guardians' presence from the human neighbors, or better yet, have Yamanu thrall them into leaving their homes for the entire day.

He also needed to get offensive weapons for the Guardians that could penetrate an underground bunker. The delivery of a mobile command center for William and attack drones for the force had already been arranged.

Hopefully they would never get deployed, but when engaged in negotiations, it was advisable to have as much leverage as possible.

Onegus could handle the evacuation, but Turner needed to take care of supplying the force and finding places for the evacuees that Arwel and Kian didn't know about.

After several back-and-forth texts with his subcontractors and friends, he texted Onegus the address of a cabin in Big Bear along with the code for the lock pad.

He also added a note about sending Yamanu to the Bay Area.

The chief might have thought of that already, but Turner didn't leave anything to chance, and he wasn't concerned with stepping on anyone's toes either.

When lives were at stake, everything else became irrelevant.

Onegus texted back. *Charlie is in the hangar, and I notified Yamanu. How many bedrooms are in that cabin? Other than Mey, Wendy, and Richard, we need room for the two Guardians watching over them and for Vlad and Ingrid, who happened to be in the keep.*

Turner shook his head. Sleeping arrangements were the least of his concerns at the moment.

It has five bedrooms and three baths. I don't know how many beds. They will have to figure it out. How many Guardians do you have stuck outside the village?

As he waited for Onegus's response, Turner shot a text to William. *A mobile command van is on its way to the house. Get ready to transfer your equipment.*

In the meantime, the return text from Onegus had arrived. *Fifteen.*

I want you to send them with Yamanu to the Bay Area. I also arranged for a mobile command center and attack drones to be delivered to the Guardians.

Onegus texted back. *I can send them to the airfield, but I'm worried about leaving the village with a skeleton force. I counted on them as backup.*

Turner typed. *The village is securely locked. The more men we have around Kalugal's compound, the better chance we have of defusing the situation before he learns anything from Arwel. And the stronger show of force we manage, the more willing Kalugal will be to negotiate.*

6

KALUGAL

Kalugal rubbed the spot over his heart.
His mother was worried about him, and she missed him.
If only the fantastic tale Kian had been weaving was true, but he was most likely making the entire story up.

Kalugal had no way of proving or disproving the information, but it made no sense for Kian to know all that. Areana was locked up in the harem and could tell her story to no one on the outside. And since no one ever left the harem, she couldn't send a message out either.

There were only two ways Kian could have obtained that information, and both were highly unlikely.

One was that someone had managed to escape the harem and deliver Areana's story to her sister. The other was that the clan had an extraordinarily talented remote viewer who could see what went on in the harem, and a powerful telepath who could converse remotely with Areana.

"With all due respect, I find your story hard to believe. I admire your imagination, though. Are you in the film industry?"

Kian chuckled. "Even if I was the creative type, which I'm not, I would never have come up with an unbelievable story like that. I would have thought of something that made more sense."

As Rufsur entered the room, Kalugal motioned for him to keep quiet and turned his chair around. "I'm sure that you can understand why I'm skeptical of your claims. What do you really want from me, Kian?"

"I told you the truth. Your mother asked mine to locate you, but I didn't want to approach you before investigating what you were up to. I don't know whether you have contact with your father or not, and with him seeking my clan's extinction, I'm not taking any chances."

"I'm curious to hear what you have learned."

Rufsur got up and waved his hand in front of Kalugal's face to get his attention. "Several cars are parked on the street, and more are arriving," he mouthed.

So, the communications guy hadn't been bluffing about that. Obviously, Kian's intention was to keep Kalugal talking long enough for his warriors to surround the property, but it didn't matter.

Kalugal was ready for a prolonged siege.

"I know that you made a fortune on the stock market, and I also know that you faked your own death and that of your entire platoon during WWII. You are very careful, never leaving the house without first shrouding yourself, and you keep a low profile. Still, that doesn't tell me what you are up to."

It seemed that Kian had been observing him for a while now. The question was how.

The compound's sophisticated monitoring equipment hadn't picked up any new signals from surveillance cameras, and what was there before belonged to their neighbors. It had to be boots on the ground.

"How did you find me?"

"It was purely coincidental. I like to believe that fate had something to do with it."

"Fate? You don't strike me as the kind of guy who believes in a mystical higher power. Please don't insult my intelligence, Kian. What do you want? And I mean other than buying time for your men to surround my property."

Kian chuckled. "Every word I said was true. But it's also true that I was buying time for my men to get in position. I want you to release the warrior and the woman you've abducted."

"And why would I do that? Your men are of no consequence to me. I can compel them to do anything I want."

"You said that my clan is of no interest to you, and that you are neither my enemy nor my friend. I hold the same position. If you release my people, I'll take it as a sign of good faith and remove the blockade. After that, you and I can continue our conversation and come to an agreement of peaceful coexistence, or maybe even cooperation."

"That's what you want now. But what did you want before I took the warrior and his girlfriend?"

"Precisely what I have already told you. Your mother wanted to find you, and my mother promised her help."

Kalugal turned back toward the monitor and checked the feed from the perimeter cameras. He counted seven vehicles parked along the street, which didn't tell him much about the number of men surrounding his property. If there were three immortals in each car or less, he could compel them all. But if there were four in each, it would be a stretch for him.

Kian didn't know that, though.

If the story he'd told was true, and Areana was indeed a goddess, then Kian must have assumed that Kalugal was as powerful as Navuh or more.

Naturally, he was going to reinforce that misconception and keep on bluffing.

Kian's objective was to get the warrior out before Kalugal had a chance to interrogate him, but Kalugal had no intention of allowing that. He had to find out what Kian's real agenda was, as well as every clan secret the captured warrior had ever been privy to.

Knowledge equaled power.

7

JIN

No more than an hour had passed since Kri had dragged Jin into the car and driven her away from the club, but it seemed like they had been in that freaking car forever.

At some point, Kri had left the surface streets and had gotten on the freeway. She was obeying the speed limit, but they were getting further and further away from the city. By the time Magnus let them know where they were supposed to go, they could be all the way to Oregon for all she knew.

Were they even heading north?

Since Kri had turned the GPS off, Jin had no clue. Navigating by the stars had never been her strong suit. Heck, she could get lost leaving the mall.

Besides, Jin had been busy listening to Kalugal talking to Kian. She could barely hear Kian because he was speaking into Kalugal's ear using Arwel's earpiece, but even if she missed parts of it, she could still figure out what he'd said by Kalugal's responses.

So far, the negotiations hadn't started yet, and it seemed like Kian's main objective was to keep Kalugal talking. As long as he was on the line, he couldn't interrogate Arwel.

She'd also checked on Arwel and Jacki several times, but only for a couple of seconds to make sure that they were still in the cell together and neither was being tortured.

As much as she would have liked to gaze at Arwel's amazing eyes through Jacki's, Jin decided that keeping tabs on the conversation between Kian and Kalugal was more important.

"Turner gave me instructions." Kri's voice pulled Jin away from the tether. "We are going to the sanctuary."

"What's that?"

Kri glanced at her and smiled. "Annani's place. You are about to meet the goddess. Are you excited?"

Under different circumstances, Jin would have been thrilled, but meeting the goddess was not at the top of her priority list.

"Where is it?"

"No one other than her and her trusted servants know how to get there, but I know that it's somewhere in Alaska."

Jin's gut twisted in a knot. "How is Kian going to trade me if I'm so far away?"

"I told you that he's not going to do it. The most important thing right now is to get you to safety, and there is no safer place than the sanctuary. Kalugal can't get information about its location from Arwel or anyone else because no one has it."

"Can I talk to Turner?"

"Sure. He's going to call you as soon as we are on the plane." Kri turned on the GPS. "We are five minutes away from the airfield."

Looking down at her dirty T-shirt, Jin shook her head. "Is that a country airstrip?"

"Yup."

"So, on top of everything else, I'm going to meet the goddess in a snot-covered T-shirt."

Kri glanced at Jin's middle and grimaced. "I'm sure that Annani is not going to wait for us in the hangar. I can ask Alena to have someone prepare a change of clothes for you."

As the tears started leaking out of her eyes again, Jin whispered, "It's such a silly thing to be concerned with at a time like this."

Reaching over the center console, Kri took her hand. "It's going to be alright. Kian and Turner are going to negotiate Arwel and Jacki's release."

"With what? They need something to bargain with, but they are sending their best chip to freaking Alaska." She looked down at her shirt again. "I'm going to freeze."

In all the commotion, she'd left her coat at the club. Luckily, she still had her purse, but that was only because Kri had noticed it and shoved it into her hands before dragging her out of there.

Jin had left her purse on top of the bar before ducking behind it to hide, but the coat must have slipped down to the floor and then got kicked somewhere by the panicked people who'd been trying to get away.

"I'll give you my jacket," Kri offered. "You can take off the T-shirt, put the jacket on, and zip it all the way up."

"But then you'll be cold."

"I'm an immortal and a Guardian. I'll survive. You, on the other hand, are still a human and might get sick." Kri cast Jin a crooked smile. "Arwel will kick my butt if I let that happen."

She shrugged the leather jacket off and handed it to Jin. "Do it now. I don't want you getting out of the car without it."

Since there were no vehicles on the rural road Kri had turned onto, Jin pulled the T-shirt over her head, tossed it on the floor at her feet, and pulled Kri's jacket on.

"It's so warm. Thank you." She zipped it all the way up.

"The airstrip is over there." Kri pointed. "And our ride is already waiting for us. Turner is a freaking miracle worker."

It took another minute for Jin to see the lone aircraft waiting on what looked like just another country road. "I really don't want to go. I want to stay here, close to Arwel."

Kri patted her arm. "You need to do what Turner tells you because he knows what he's doing. He has a lot of experience in crisis management, while you have none."

8

TURNER

Turner missed his yellow pad.

Without it, he had to keep all the details in his head, which wasn't a huge issue, but he didn't have the satisfaction of marking items as done.

While Kalugal was on the line with Kian and could compel him to do anything he wanted, Turner couldn't risk writing anything down.

Regrettably, despite his new immortal physical strength, Kian could still overpower him with ease and take his notes. First of all, the guy was about half a foot taller. Also, he was Annani's son. That alone made him more powerful than immortals with blood that had been diluted over many generations of breeding with humans.

What Kian couldn't do, though, was take the information from Turner's head. He could try to beat it out of him, but Turner had been trained to withstand torture.

He'd never been captured, so his training hadn't been put to the test, but he was pretty sure that it would kick in when needed.

Being stuck in the village was a sort of captivity, but he wasn't helpless. Like a chess master, he was moving the pieces around while trying to anticipate his opponent's moves.

He shouldn't be enjoying this so much, but it was incredible how much he'd managed to achieve in under half an hour. It was impressive, even in light of his usual high standards.

There were two things that he still needed to do. One was to verify that Jin was in the air, and the other was to contact Lokan.

Since Kian had asked him to contact Lokan, Turner didn't need to be secretive about it and decided to call instead of texting. It was the middle of the night in Washington, and Lokan was probably asleep, so he might not hear the incoming text.

When Lokan answered, he sounded alarmed and fully alert. "What's going on?"

"Your brother has Arwel and Jacki, and we need you to get on the plane and fly to San Francisco as soon as you can."

In the background, Turner heard Carol gasp. "I'm getting dressed," she informed Lokan.

"Wait. What exactly are you expecting me to do? Kalugal is not going to listen to me. He doesn't even know me."

"He might, or he might not, but we need all the ammunition we can get. Besides, we are in this mess because your mother asked Kian to help you find your brother. You can't stay home snuggled in your bed with your mate while we are dealing with him."

Lokan uttered a long-suffering sigh. "You're right. I'll be there as soon as I can. Damn. I have two important meetings scheduled for tomorrow that I will need to move."

The guy's priorities were skewed.

"You can claim to have fallen ill. That would reinforce your human cover."

Lokan huffed out a breath. "Where do you want me to go once I get there?"

"I'll let you know. Call me when you are about to land."

"It's going to be early morning your time."

"I'm not going to sleep anytime soon." Turner ended the call.

A couple of moments later, he got the text he'd been waiting for from Kri. *We are in the air.*

He was about to give Kian the thumbs up when another text came from Kri.

Jin wants me to tell you that she is offering herself to be traded for Arwel and Jacki. She wants you to tell Kian.

The girl was in love and not thinking straight. *That's the worst thing we can do. As long as Kalugal knows that he's being watched, he is practically paralyzed. We will negotiate Arwel and Jacki's release in exchange for the tether's removal, not the tetherer herself.*

Kri texted back. *She says that he will want to see proof of the tether's removal.*

Turner frowned. *I was under the impression that the tethered can be told what to pay attention to, and that once released, he can feel the difference. Kian told me that Edna even managed to detach the tether on her end.*

A long moment passed before the return text came in. *Jin says that it's impossible to demonstrate without removing the tether and reattaching it. She can remove it remotely, but she needs to touch Kalugal again to reattach it to him.*

That was a complication he hadn't foreseen.

He texted back. *We will try to work around it and tell Kalugal that he will feel the difference. Can Jin describe it to me?*

Jin says that from her side, releasing the tether feels like a mental weight was lifted. She says that you should call Edna and ask her how it felt to her.

I'll do that. Don't fall asleep. After Kian tells Kalugal about the tether, he will want proof. I'll call Jin and ask her to report what she sees.

9

ARWEL

"I'm cold." Jacki pulled the blanket from the top bunk. "Do you want some?" She sat back down. "We can share."

"I'm not as sensitive to the cold as you are."

She wrapped the blanket around her shoulders. "Is it because you are immortal?"

He nodded.

"Can you tell me more? I mean things that are not top secret."

"Our very existence is a secret, but the cat is out of the bag on that."

Jacki put her feet up and tucked her legs under the blanket. "If I ever get out of here, no one is going to believe me anyway. It's like those poor folks who report alien encounters. They are ridiculed and dismissed." She cast him a sidelong glance. "Do you guys have anything to do with that?"

He shook his head. "None of us have ever met an alien."

"Really? I thought that you and the others like you were aliens."

"Maybe our ancestors were. We are the descendants of the mythological gods. The result of them taking human partners."

"Like in the Bible? And the sons of the gods saw that the daughters of men were fair and took them as wives?"

"Not only the sons of gods. The daughters did that as well. Except, they didn't take them as wives or husbands because they were considered too lowly for that. They took them as lovers, or if they were really fond of them as concubines and paramours. The reason behind the practice was the gods' low fertility rate and limited gene pool. Without the infusion of human genes, they would have died out. Even the gods couldn't live forever."

Jacki lifted a brow. "Isn't that the definition of immortal?"

"The gods could live hundreds of thousands of years. That's as immortal as it gets."

"What about you? The descendants are hybrids, so their genes are diluted. Does it go down to tens of thousands? Single-digit thousands?"

He chuckled. "I don't know. The longest living immortal is only five thousand years old, give or take a few centuries, and he is still in his prime. He is also Kalugal's father and our clan's arch-nemesis."

"I don't understand. If Kalugal is the son of your enemy, what made you think he could be a friend? Or was that just the story you told me?"

"Kalugal escaped his father and has lived in hiding ever since. What we don't know is whether he considers his father an enemy. If he does, that could make him our ally by default. The enemy of my enemy is my friend sort of thing."

Jacki leaned her chin on her upturned knees. "What happened to the gods?"

"Kalugal's grandfather dropped a bomb on their assembly, killing them all. What he hadn't expected was getting caught in the blast and dying with them."

"Why did he do that?"

"Jealousy or greed or a combination of both prompted him to kill another god by beheading him. When the assembly of gods sentenced him to entombment for his crime, Mortdh's solution was to kill them all."

Jacki sighed. "I wonder how Kalugal deals with a heritage like that. It must be difficult."

Since in Arwel's mind all Doomers were predisposed to evil, it hadn't occurred to him that Lokan and Kalugal were less so than others. They were the grandsons of Mortdh and the sons of Navuh.

It didn't get any worse than that.

Except, they were also the grandsons of Ahn and the sons of Areana.

Arwel didn't know much about Annani's father, but from what the goddess had shared about her half-sister, Areana was a gentle and benevolent soul. Carol's impression of her had been the same.

The question was which side was dominant.

Arwel had a feeling it was the paternal side. "Kalugal seems like a conceited bastard. He probably wears his murderous godly heritage like a badge of honor."

Jacki chuckled. "He's like a very handsome version of Doctor Evil from *Austin Powers*." She waved a hand. "He's polite, soft-spoken, and extremely intelligent."

Arwel arched a brow. "Isn't it a bit early for Stockholm syndrome to set in? You've been a captive for less than an hour, and you had contact with your captor for less than a minute."

Jacki huffed. "I'm not crushing on him if that's what you're thinking. I'm just stating the facts."

10

KIAN

"As fun as it was chatting with you, cousin, it is late. Perhaps we could continue our fascinating conversation tomorrow?"
Like hell.

Kalugal was eager to start questioning Arwel, and Kian was not about to allow it. To keep him on the line, he would tell Kalugal the entire history of the clan if necessary, or rather the version of it he saw fit to share.

He glanced in Turner's direction, but the guy was in the back of the room, still talking to Lokan. Evidently, he hadn't gotten confirmation from Kri and Jin that they were in the air.

It was imperative to keep Kalugal talking.

"Using the earpiece is not very convenient. We should exchange phone numbers. Would you like to write mine down?"

"Certainly. Go ahead."

After dictating the numbers, Kian asked Kalugal to repeat them. It was an obvious ploy to buy time, but he only needed a couple of minutes.

"Is that your direct line?" Kalugal asked.

"Yes. You can call me day or night. My phone is always with me."

"I feel so privileged." Kalugal's tone was mocking. "And now I feel obliged to do the same. Here is mine." He rattled out the numbers.

"Let me read it back to you."

As Kian enunciated each number, he glanced at Turner again and finally got the thumbs up he'd been waiting for.

"That's correct. Good night, Kian," Kalugal said.

Kian leaned back in his chair. "Before we call it a night, there is something you should know."

Kalugal chuckled. "I'm well aware of your men surrounding my property. They are of no consequence to me."

"I'm sure you are. But what you are not aware of is that one of ours has a direct mental connection to you, and she can see and hear everything you do. There is no hiding from her, and there is no way to circumvent her tether. Everything you say, hear, or see is no longer private. I'm informed of your every move."

There was a long moment of silence as Kalugal processed the information.

"You are contradicting yourself, Kian. You said that you wanted to find out what I was up to. If you had such a fantastic spy working for you, you would have no need to send men to follow me."

"To attach the tether, she had to touch you. And for that to happen, we needed to get her to you. The plan was to do it without you noticing a thing, but as often happens, the best of plans go awry. We couldn't have anticipated a human psychopath showing up at the club and pulling out a gun."

This time the moment of silence was longer.

As the door to the war room opened, Kian turned his swivel chair around and lifted his hand to motion for whoever entered to stay quiet.

Ella came in with her arm wrapped around Parker, who was wearing his pajamas with a coat draped over his shoulders.

Kian had forgotten about asking for Parker to be brought over, and seeing the anxious expression on the kid's face, he felt guilty.

It seemed that there would be no need for Parker's compulsion removal services, but it wasn't a sure thing. So, even though he hated to involve the kid in the drama, he needed him to hang around until it was over.

Okidu entered right behind the siblings, pushing a rolling cart with food and drinks, and the last arrival was Syssi, who sent him an air kiss and then joined Ella and Parker at the back of the war room.

"I assume that you can prove this?" Kalugal asked.

"Naturally." Kian motioned for Turner to get closer. "What proof would you like? I'll have my second-in-command ask her. And just in case you forgot, he is an immune."

"I didn't forget. I want to know how she did it."

Kian repeated the question out loud. "It will take him a couple of moments to communicate with her."

"I'll wait."

As Turner got busy texting, Kian pushed to his feet and walked to the back of the room. Taking Syssi's hand, he mouthed, "You shouldn't have come."

She kissed his cheek and handed him a bottle of water from Okidu's cart.

He nodded and then examined the cart's contents.

Syssi chuckled, and then whispered, "If you are looking for beer, it's in the cooler on the bottom." She pulled one out for him.

"You are the best," he mouthed.

He had time for two heavenly gulps before Turner lifted his phone and motioned for Kian to pull out his right as it buzzed with an incoming message.

It was a copy of the one Turner had received from Jin, detailing in length her encounter with Kalugal.

"Let me read you her answer."

11

KALUGAL

As Kalugal listened to Kian read the story from the girl's perspective, he closed his eyes and replayed in his mind the events preceding the appearance of the shooter.

In the excitement that had followed Flyboy's amazing display of acrobatics, Kalugal had forgotten all about the girl who'd spilled her drink over him and his dance partner.

Apparently, he hadn't been as indifferent to Blondie's charms as he'd thought he was. Between her ample cleavage and his irritation over her response to the spilled drink incident, he hadn't paid much attention to the girl who'd clung on to his arm for a couple of seconds too long.

Or maybe it had been his arrogance at play, assuming that the girl didn't want to let go of him because of his magnetic masculinity, which even his shroud couldn't hide.

She was tall, he remembered that, and not because she had high-heeled shoes on. Assuming footwear was the cause of her stumble, he'd glanced at her feet. She'd also had a lot of badly-applied cheap makeup on, but for some reason, he'd found her attractive despite her below-average looks.

The immune was tall as well, and she too had similarly done heavy makeup on...

Two tall females with bad hair and bad makeup.

Damn. How had he missed that?

They were the same two he'd encountered the night before outside the cigar lounge.

The tall Asian had stared at him looking stunned, and her friend had done all the talking. In hindsight, their behavior made perfect sense. The Asian was the one with the tethering talent, and the immune was there as a precaution against his compulsion.

After failing to tether him outside the lounge, they'd changed their appearance and completed their mission in the club. If not for the shooter, he wouldn't have noticed that anything was amiss.

Even though recounting the events was no proof of the tether's existence, the effort the woman had invested into putting her hand on him was convincing enough.

Still, before starting negotiations, he needed indisputable proof.

"Everything you are telling me could have been witnessed by hidden cameras or your spies. I need something more conclusive."

"Hold on. I'll ask."

As Kalugal waited, he tried to imagine what proof the spy could provide. Maybe describe the room he was in?

First, he turned his chair around, so he wasn't facing the monitor. That really wasn't necessary since she couldn't figure out anything from what was on the screen, but if she'd been watching earlier, she could have seen his entire lockdown protocol.

Thankfully, no codes had been displayed, and he hadn't been the one who had entered them. Phinas had done that.

"She asks that you write something on a note," Kian said. "After that, look at the note long enough to read it, but don't show it to anyone. She will tell you what you've written."

"Does she have a name? Or are we just going to call her the spy?"

"Her name is Jin."

Kalugal opened a drawer, pulled out a sheet of computer paper, and clicked on his pen. "I'm writing the note."

Hello, Jin. I wonder what you look like under all that ugly makeup. You looked prettier last night outside the cigar lounge.

Holding the page in front of him for several seconds, Kalugal read the note twice and then put it down. "Well?"

"Let me read it to you." Kian recited word for word exactly what he had written. "Need more convincing?"

As the last of his doubts was quashed, Kalugal felt chilled. His mind working quickly, he tried to come up with ways of working around the tether, but there were none. Regrettably, his talents didn't include telepathy, and he had never bothered to learn Morse code, which was the only other method of communication he could think of. While his auditory and visuals were compromised, the only thing left was touch. Except, the spy's talents might include that as well, and Kian had just failed to mention it, intentionally or not.

"No, that will do. What do you want in exchange for removing the tether?"

"That's obvious. I want you to release my people."

Kalugal had expected that. "They must be very important for you to give up an asset like that."

Either that or they had information that Kian could not afford to fall into Kalugal's hands. The immune hadn't even known about her boyfriend's immortality, so she probably held no value other than her immunity. The warrior was the important one. Maybe he was related to Kian?

A brother, perhaps?

No one knew who Annani's children were, and how many she had, but given the gods' low fertility rate, she couldn't have more than two. Since she had most likely mated with humans, she must have had at least one daughter to continue her line, and Kian had proclaimed himself as her son.

"Every member of my clan is important. Unlike your father, who doesn't care about the individual cogs in his war machine, I value each and every one of my people. We are a family."

They were a tight-knit community because there weren't as many of them, but Kalugal saw no reason to point it out. At this stage of the game, Kian had the winning card, and antagonizing him was not going to work in Kalugal's favor.

"That's admirable. Unlike my father, I also value my men. You and I have that in common." Pointing out similarities was always a good strategy. People, humans and immortals alike, were more positively predisposed toward those who they thought were like them. "What about the immune, though? Is she a member of your clan?"

With the love the clan had been showing humanity from its very start, it was possible that they had some living among them.

"She is not a member of my clan, but after she has graciously agreed to help us, I'm not going to abandon her."

Kalugal had a feeling that Kian was not just spouting those things to flaunt his benevolence. The guy believed in what he was saying.

Nevertheless, the sanctimonious verbiage grated on Kalugal's nerves because its purpose was to demonstrate Kian's moral superiority.

"So, her immunity has no bearing on her value to you?"

"Of course it does. But I would do the same for any human who risked herself to save one of mine."

"I must admit that I was impressed by her heroics. She must truly love your clansman to do something as stupid as that. Then again, he must love her too. He exposed his inhuman abilities to protect her."

"My warrior protected his team members, which is his job. And I assume that the immune acted out of desperation because she was the only one who was able to move."

"Then I'm even more impressed. The woman fought like a wildcat."

"Did you hurt her?" Kian's voice turned into a growl.

"Relax. She is fine. We handled her with utmost care."

"I was told that you stuffed her into the trunk of your car, bound and gagged."

"Regrettably, I had no choice. She was screaming rape, scratching and kicking, and there was nowhere else I could put her in my Ferrari. Your warrior was too big to fit in the trunk."

12

KIAN

$\mathcal{K}$ian stifled a chuckle. As critical as the situation was, it lifted his mood to imagine Jacki raising hell and fighting two immortals who were doing their best to subdue her without hurting her.

Even though she wasn't a member of the clan, not yet, he was damn proud of the girl. If she transitioned, Jacki should join the Guardian training program. She sure had the right spirit.

"Do we have a deal then? You will release my people, and I'll tell Jin to release the tether."

"I'll sleep on it."

Right, as if Kian was going to buy that.

"If you're thinking about sending one of your guys to interrogate either of the two, you should know that Jin has them both tethered. If either is questioned, I will know, and the deal will be off. You'll be forever stuck with me as your shadow, and I'll do my damndest to thwart your every move."

"Let's assume for a moment that I believe you, but naturally, I would like proof of that as well. I wonder, though. What does your warrior know that you are so afraid of me discovering? Were you planning on capturing me and selling me to my father? Maybe in exchange for one of yours that he's holding prisoner?"

Kian could understand Kalugal's suspicions.

He was imagining the worst possible scenarios from his perspective, which was the prudent thing to do.

"You have one hell of an imagination. But my reason is simpler than that. My clan's survival depends on our ability to hide. Your father's army outnumbers ours, and we can't afford him discovering our location. That's the big secret that I'm trying to protect, not any plot against you. In fact, I'm okay with you asking my guy whether we had any plans to capture you, or sell you, or harm you in any way. But I'm not okay with you asking about anything of strategic importance to my clan."

"I believe you because I'm in the same situation. After we solve our little problem, I'll be forced to relocate." Kalugal sighed. "It will be a shame. I like it here."

"We don't mean you harm, Kalugal. As long as you don't engage in trafficking, we won't bother you."

"Trafficking? What on earth makes you think I would ever do something as despicable as that?"

"That's your father's latest business endeavor."

"I don't believe that. Navuh wouldn't stoop so low."

"You'd be surprised. There isn't much work left in the world for his mercenary army, and he's looking for other sources of revenue. It also gives his men something to do. Restless soldiers might start thinking, and he can't allow that."

For a long moment, Kalugal was silent. Out of all the fascinating new things he had learned from Kian, his father's involvement in trafficking seemed to rattle him the most.

Should Kian mention the drugs as well?

"That's regrettable," Kalugal said. "I don't have much love for my father, nor do I approve of his methods, but until now, I respected him. I can no longer do that."

That was somewhat hypocritical of Kalugal. Even before his escape, he must have been aware of the influx of females to the island who had been conscripted into prostitution. Navuh had been paying traffickers to deliver the women. The only difference was that now the middlemen had been cut out, and the warriors had taken their place.

Nevertheless, Kalugal had just provided him with an excellent opening, and Kian wasn't going to ruin the opportunity by pointing out the hypocrisy.

"I'm glad we see eye to eye on this issue. Perhaps it is time for you to take over. The island needs a new leader, and you are the only one who can do that. As long as Navuh compels everyone's loyalty, no change is possible."

"I have no intention of going after Navuh's position. I made a promise to my mother to never go against my father, and I won't break that promise. But I wouldn't have done it regardless. I'm not interested in the island."

"What are you interested in?"

"Making money. I like my peaceful anonymity, and I intend to keep it. My brother can take over if he has such aspirations. For now, he can only compel humans, but perhaps in time, his power will grow."

"Your mother had him make a similar promise. He vowed never to kill his father."

"How do you know all that? Is my father suddenly letting my mother out of the harem? Has she told someone who delivered the news to her sister?"

"Areana is still locked in the harem, but we managed to smuggle a communication device to her. She talks with my mother almost every day. This little piece of technology was a life-changer for her. With my mother filling her in on what's happening in the world, Areana is no longer as isolated. She didn't even know that Annani or any of her people had survived."

"How did you manage to get anything to her? I've thought about doing just that for many years, and I've never come up with anything that was doable."

It was tempting to tell Kalugal about Lokan, and that it had been his idea that had made contact with Areana possible, but it was too early for that. Kalugal was still an enigma, and although Kian was quite sure that the son had no contact with the father, he wasn't willing to bet Lokan's safety on that.

Kalugal might use the information to gain leverage.

Telling him about Areana communicating with the outside world and how she was doing it was risky enough.

"I can't tell you the details because we are not friends yet. Once we are, and you prove your trustworthiness to me, I'll let you talk with your mother. I'm sure you are eager for the chance to speak with her again after so many years."

13

KALUGAL

Kalugal's heart skipped a beat. Contact with his mother was a dream he had almost given up on. He'd been tempted by many fantasies of clever ways to achieve it, but none of them had ever passed a reality check.

His life and that of his men depended on him staying as far from the island as possible and not attracting any attention to themselves.

It grated that Kian had figured a way to make contact with Areana while Kalugal had failed to do so, but he wasn't going to hold it against his cousin, especially given what Kian had just offered.

Kalugal had about a thousand questions he wanted to ask his mother, but the first and most important one was about her lineage, and through her, his. In the heat of the conversation and the bombs his cousin had been dropping one after the other, Kalugal had almost forgotten about that.

His mother was a goddess.

But even that was not as exciting as the possibility of actually talking to her. Would her voice be as lovely as he remembered it? Was she as angelically beautiful as he saw her in his mind's eye?

"I don't suppose the communication device you've smuggled into the harem has video as well as audio."

"Regrettably, no. But I can give you a copy of her portrait. We had a gifted forensic artist draw her from Annani's memory. It's a very accurate depiction."

Kalugal's heart missed another beat. "I would love to see it."

"As a gesture of goodwill, I'll send it to your phone, and I'll send you a full-sized replica at another time."

"What do you want for it?"

"Consider it a gift, a proof that what I've been telling you is true."

Kian didn't strike him as the sort of man who did something for nothing, but a moment later, Kalugal's phone pinged with an incoming text.

His hands shook only slightly as he opened the attachment, but when he saw the picture, he almost dropped the phone.

Sad, blue eyes looked at him from the most beautiful, pale face, framed by blond wavy hair that was almost white.

It was his mother. Exactly as he remembered her.

"Did you get it?" Kian asked.

Kalugal cleared his throat. "Yes."

"Is that how you remember your mother?"

"You were right about it being a very accurate depiction. Thank you. What do you want in exchange?"

"As I told you, it's a gesture of goodwill and proof of my claims. But since you are offering, you might consider moving my people to better accommodations as a gesture of your goodwill. My second-in-command has just shown me a text from Jin, and she is appalled by the prison cell you've thrown them in. She says it doesn't even have a modesty wall separating the toilet from the rest of the room, and the blankets on the bunk beds are so thin that her friend is shivering from cold."

If Kalugal wanted proof of the spy's tether to her friends, he'd just gotten it.

"I can do that."

"Also, Jin is requesting that you put them in a room with two good beds that have proper blankets, and a bathroom that has a shower. She also asks that you provide them both with a change of clothes."

"I'll see what I can do. This is a bunker, not a hotel."

"I'm sure you can manage something. I've seen the blueprints for your underground facility, and you have plenty of rooms with en-suite bathrooms. Jin also says that your men haven't fed her friends since their arrival or given them anything to drink."

To dig out the blueprints for the bunker, Kian must have been planning this for a long time. If not for the random interference from the shooter, he would have pulled it off without a hitch.

That deserved respect, but Kalugal didn't appreciate Kian's insinuation that he was mistreating his prisoners. "It hasn't been that long. It's not like they've been starving for days."

"Still, you might want to be a good host. Or, you can release them and save yourself the trouble. Once this is done, we can meet as friends, and I'll arrange for you to speak with your mother."

As much as Kalugal wanted to end this fiasco, he wasn't about to capitulate so quickly. Besides, he needed to figure out how to verify the tether's removal. He hadn't felt it being attached, and he still didn't feel anything different, but the proof Jin had provided had left no doubt as to its existence.

"Your spy is a demanding woman."

Kian chuckled. "Indeed. If I were you, I would play nice with the person who's privy to all my secrets."

"Noted." He lifted his phone and looked at his mother's picture. "Have your spy release the tether, and I'll let your people go."

"That's what I offered an hour ago, and I will sweeten the deal by letting you talk with Areana."

"I will need proof of the tether's removal."

A long moment passed until Kian answered. "I'll have to check with Jin whether she can describe the feeling of having it removed. I will also ask those who she tethered and then released what they felt."

"I'm sure you can understand why I can't agree to any deal without definite proof. And describing a feeling is too vague to prove anything."

Kian sighed. "We will work something out."

"I hope so. While you do that, I suggest that we take a break for the night. As a gesture of my goodwill, I will not question your people and will move them to a better room. I'll also send food and a change of clothing. You can have your spy verify that I'm good at keeping my promises."

14

YAMANU

As Yamanu walked into the bedroom, it wasn't to follow his original plan to make love to his mate.

It was to deliver bad news.

"Kalugal's captured Arwel and Jacki, and we need to leave the keep because its location might already be compromised."

Clutching the blanket to her breasts, Mey sat up. "What about Jin?"

"She is fine. She managed to tether him before everything went to shit. Kri has her, and she is driving out of the city. Turner is going to stash them somewhere safe."

"What happened?"

"Onegus didn't have time to give me the details, so I called Magnus. A gunman entered the club, and when Arwel felt his intention to kill, he ran in to stop him. His speed and strength gave him away, and when Kalugal realized that Arwel must be an immortal, he compelled everyone to freeze. When he took Arwel, Jacki ran after them, trying to save him, which resulted in her getting taken as well."

"That's so brave of her. But stupid. What did she hope to achieve?"

Yamanu rubbed the back of his neck. "That was my reaction as well, but Magnus pointed out that Jacki didn't know that she was going after immortals. If they had been a couple of human males, her bear-spray attack might have worked."

Mey ran a shaky hand over her mouth. "What's going to happen to Arwel and Jacki?"

"Kian is negotiating for their release." Yamanu pulled out his duffle bag from the closet and started shoving his clothes inside. "You should get dressed. We need to get going."

"Where?" As Mey flung the comforter off, her beautiful nude body momentarily distracted Yamanu from his task. She padded to the bathroom but left the door open. "Are we bringing Wendy and Richard to the village?"

He forced his eyes away and leaned to pick up his boots. "The village is locked down, which means that no one is getting in or out. Onegus gave me the address of a cabin in Big Bear. It belongs to a friend of Turner's, so Arwel doesn't know about it. You'll be safe there."

"You mean we, right?"

"I'm not coming with you." He walked into the bathroom and gathered her into his arms. "I'm needed in the Bay Area. The Guardians are surrounding Kalugal's compound, and I have to shroud them from the human neighbors. It's an upscale community, and with so many cars parked on the street at night, someone is bound to call the police."

He didn't want to worry her, but his shrouding might be needed to hide more than just parked cars. If they were forced to attack the compound, he would have to shroud the sounds, sights, and even smells of gunfire and explosions.

Mey clung to him. "I don't want to be separated from you."

"I know." He kissed the top of her head. "I don't want that either. But this is an emergency, and we have to play our respective parts."

"What's mine?"

"Taking care of Wendy and Richard. The Guardians will join you, of course, so you don't have to worry about security, but you'll be in charge of the household until the crisis is over."

"I think that Vlad is still here, and probably Ingrid as well. Since they can't go back to the village, do they come with us?"

Yamanu nodded. "They could rent rooms in a hotel, but it's probably better if they join you. They'll keep Wendy and Richard occupied."

"Don't you have another secret clan location? Like a safe house? A cabin in Big Bear is not secluded, and our guests will know where they are. I can demand that they wear blindfolds on the way up there, but once we are at the cabin, they will have to come off. What do I do then?"

"We have another location that could have been perfect, but Arwel knows about it."

"Damn." Mey rested her forehead on his chest. "What am I supposed to do if they decide to leave the cabin?

"We can no longer play this game with them. They will know where they are, and if they want to walk away, there isn't much you or the Guardians can do about it. The only way to prevent it is to make them terrified of getting discovered. I'll leave it up to you to get creative with all the possible scenarios. The more horrible, the better."

"I hope there is no landline in that cabin. It would be really difficult to explain why they can't use the phone."

"When you get there, Leon and Bowen will go in first and take care of the phones. Big Bear is about two hours away. Use that time to scare Richard and Wendy into compliance."

"I'll do what I can." Pulling out of his arms, Mey walked into the closet and took out a sweater and a pair of warm leggings. "What excuse am I going to give them for the rushed escape?"

"Tell them that Arwel and Jacki were captured by Kalugal, the head of a rival organization, and that he is planning to attack and capture all the talents he can find. That should scare them into cooperating. Make him sound really evil."

Mey paused with the leggings halfway up her thighs. "What if he really is? Kalugal's father is a heartless dictator who had no problem causing the deaths of millions of humans, and his grandfather was a god who had singlehandedly killed all the other gods except for Annani and Areana, ending their era."

"True. But Lokan shares the same genes as Kalugal, and he is a decent guy."

"Lokan might take after his mother, and we have no idea what kind of a man Kalugal is. Finding what he's about was the entire purpose of Jin's mission."

Yamanu zipped up his duffle bag. "So far, the only thing we know about him is that he is using his powers to make money. It's dishonest and immoral, but it's not in the same league as what his father is responsible for. I hope he's a reasonable man and that he'll agree to a deal. This whole thing might be over by tomorrow."

"From your lips to God's ears."

Yamanu smiled. "I'll beseech the merciful Fates to help us reach a peaceful agreement. But if that is not to be, we can overpower Kalugal despite his abilities. Right now, twenty-eight Guardians are positioned outside his estate, and I'm bringing fifteen more with me. That's more than half of the Guardian force. We can take him and his men."

"I hope it won't come to that. I don't want to even think about an all-out war between immortals in the middle of a human neighborhood. People could get caught in the crossfire."

15

MEY

Mey had kept up a brave face for Yamanu, but the truth was that she was scared and overwhelmed. She was only a baby immortal, and suddenly she was put in charge.

Saying goodbye to him had been hard, but there was no time to fall apart and cry. She had to ignore the heaviness in her chest, get herself into operational mode, and get everyone moving.

Thankfully, the two Guardians were there to help.

"Leon, can you get Ingrid and Vlad and explain what's going on? I will deal with Wendy and Richard."

The Guardian scratched his short stubble. "Vlad is in Wendy's room, and Ingrid is in Richard's. How am I going to excuse taking them aside?"

He had a point. "Can you text them?"

"That should work. I'll do it right now."

She lifted a hand to stop him. "Wait. I prepared a story to tell our guests, and I want to deliver it first. You can tell Vlad and Ingrid the truth later. Is Wendy's door open?"

Leon nodded. "They are playing William's video game."

"I'll start with her."

Mey rushed out, walking briskly toward Wendy's room.

She wanted to check on Jin, but first, she had to get everyone moving. Once they were on their way to Big Bear, she would text Jin and ask her how she was holding up.

Her sister was a strong woman, but with her mate taken by the enemy, she was probably freaking out. In fact, Mey was surprised that Jin hadn't called her yet. When they were younger and Jin got in trouble, she'd called Mey, not their parents.

But Jin was all grown up now, and apparently it hadn't crossed her mind to call her older sister.

Then again, Jin was probably following the tether to Kalugal and reporting to Kian what she was seeing. And if she had Jacki tethered as well, she was following that string too.

Poor Jin. She could use some handholding right now.

Slowing down right before she reached the door, Mey schooled her facial expression and affected a mask of calm. She rapped her fingers on the doorjamb. "Wendy, you need to pack up your things, sweetheart. We are moving to a different location."

The girl lifted a pair of frightened eyes to her. "What happened? Did they find us?"

"If by they you mean the government, then no. But Arwel was captured by a rival organization, and this location might be compromised. We need to get out of here fast."

"What are you talking about? What rival organization?"

"I don't have time to explain. I'll tell you more on the way." Mey looked at Vlad. "Are you coming with us?"

"I guess that going home is not an option, right?"

Smart kid. Mey nodded.

Wendy put her hand on his arm. "What's going on, Vlad? You are scared."

"Arwel's capture is bad. But Mey is right. We need to hurry up and get out of here. We can talk on the way." He got up and started shoving video games into his duffel bag. "I hope there is a games console where we are going."

"I don't know," Mey admitted. "All I have is an address. We will figure things out when we get there. I need to check on Richard and Ingrid."

"Wait." Wendy stopped her. "Do I take everything with me? And where am I going to put it? I don't have a suitcase."

"You can pull the sheet off the bed, pile everything on top of it, and then tie it up like a sack. Vlad can help you."

"Okay." Wendy's chin quivered.

Poor girl, she was frightened, and Mey didn't have time to handhold her through this. Heck, she needed some handholding herself.

When Mey walked out into the corridor, she saw that the door to Richard's room was open, and she could hear Ingrid cussing up a storm, with Richard trying to calm her down.

"What's going on?" Mey asked as she walked in.

"I can't go home! That's what's going on."

Apparently, Ingrid had learned about the village lockdown.

"You can't stay either. We need to get out of here."

"Where are we going?"

"To a safe location Turner has found for us. Think of it as a mini-vacation in the mountains."

"Are we going to the cabin?" Ingrid asked.

"Yes, but I don't think it's the same one you are referring to. Turner found a place for us to hide out in until this is over. But if you wish, you can stay in a hotel in the city. You don't have to come with us."

"Are Bowen and Leon going with you?"

Mey nodded.

"Then I'm coming too. There is safety in numbers."

Richard looked at Mey. "Are we under attack?"

"Not yet. But we might be. Arwel was captured by a rival organization, whose head can compel him to reveal everything he knows. They would like nothing more than to collect all the paranormal talents they can find, and that includes you and Wendy. Please hurry up and pack your things. You can use the bed sheet to create a carrying sack."

"You said that we are going to a cabin in the mountains. Does that imply snow?"

"I guess so. It's winter."

"We don't have warm clothing or proper shoes. I know it's not urgent right now, but I'm being practical."

Mey hadn't considered that. She still had her snow attire from the trip, but the others didn't have even warm coats. Richard and Wendy's coats had been burned, and Ingrid and Vlad didn't need them in Los Angeles's mild winter. Vlad had a hoodie on, and Ingrid probably had a sweater, but she wasn't wearing it now.

"We will get everything we need once we get there."

"Wendy and I don't have any money."

"Don't worry about it. I'll get you everything you need."

16

LOKAN

"An hour is fine. Thank you." Lokan ended the call. "I need to pack." Arranging for his private jet to be ready for takeoff this late at night had taken some maneuvering, but for the right sum of money, it wasn't hard to get people to cooperate.

"I'm going with you." Carol walked into the closet.

Stifling a groan, Lokan rubbed the back of his head. He didn't want Carol anywhere near Kalugal and his powers of compulsion, but convincing her to stay behind would start a major argument.

"We have proof now that I can't shield immortals from Kalugal. If he compels you, I would be powerless to do anything about it."

She walked out of the closet with a stack of clothes and dumped them on the bed. "Why would he do that?" She went back in and came out with a carry-on. "And how? I'm not going to be anywhere near him."

"Really? Are you going to stay behind in the hotel?"

He knew her better than that. Carol would want to take an active part in whatever was going on.

"Hopefully, I can stay with the others wherever they moved everyone to. I'm sure Turner's found them a safe house." She looked at him over her shoulder. "You need me there for moral support."

He stifled a snort. "So, if I have to negotiate with Kalugal face to face, you are going to keep away?"

Carol put the luggage on the bed. "I'm not stupid. If I come with you, he can use me as leverage against you. He can't compel you directly, but he could do it by compelling me." She chuckled. "If he told me to strip naked, you would freak out."

"Hmm." Lokan rubbed his hand over his chin. "If he does that, it will backfire. He'll be mesmerized by your beauty, and then you can compel him to do anything you want."

He was teasing, of course, but he'd done it with a straight face to see if she'd take the bait.

Given the spike in her excitement, she had. "You'd actually let me do that? You wouldn't mind your brother seeing me nude?"

Wrapping an arm around Carol's waist, Lokan pulled her close. "We are mated, love, and that means you are mine, and I trust you. I have no fear of my brother's charms winning you over, but I don't trust him. I don't want his eyes on you, neither nude nor fully dressed."

Carol shook her head. "This could be an opportunity for you and Kalugal to get closer, to become real brothers, a family. Don't go into it expecting the worst. He might surprise you."

"I'd rather expect the worst and get surprised for the better than the other way around." He dipped his head and kissed her lightly. "You are my family, Carol."

She smiled. "You are so sweet. But I'm not your only family. In a small way, you have your mother back, and you are getting to know her a little better with each phone call. Wouldn't it be nice to have the same connection with Kalugal?"

"That's different. I can trust Areana because she is my mother, and she has as much to lose as I do if my father discovers our clandestine communications. Kalugal is an unknown. I don't know what his agenda is."

"Whatever it is, it's not about the island." Carol put the stack of clothes in the carry-on. "Do you want me to pack for you?"

"I'll do it." Lokan walked into the closet. "Kalugal could've been building up his power base and waiting until he's strong enough to take our father on."

Carol followed him inside. "Isn't that what you want?" She pulled a pair of boots off the shoe rack. "Without Kalugal's help, your dreams and aspirations for the island will remain just that. With him, you have a chance of making them a reality."

"It all depends on what kind of man Kalugal is, and what he wants. He might want nothing to do with the island, or he might want to take over without me because he doesn't need me."

And that was what bothered Lokan the most. On the one hand he needed Kalugal, but on the other hand he feared him.

Lokan's plans to take over the island had never been concrete, so even if Kalugal was willing to cooperate, Lokan had nothing to show him yet. His brother would realize right away that he didn't need Lokan to take over from Navuh if he so wished. And if he had no such aspirations, he definitely didn't need Lokan for anything else.

Brotherly love was a foreign concept to both of them.

Other than their genes and the unique powers that they had inherited from Navuh, he and Kalugal had very little in common.

Some would argue that blood-ties were enough, and that their shared genetics manifested in more than similar body build and facial features.

Their personalities were determined by their genes as well.

Given who his father was, however, Lokan preferred to think that wasn't the case. Because if everything was determined by biology, free will was an illusion, and no one should be held responsible for their actions.

Except, this was not the time to ponder a philosophical conundrum.

Right now, there was a private jet waiting for him and Carol at the airport, and they had to hurry up. The six-hour flight to San Francisco would be better utilized by coming up with a strategy for dealing with his brother and organizing his thoughts regarding the island's future. Perhaps if he could get Kalugal excited about the possibilities, his brother would feel more inclined to join forces with him.

17

MAGNUS

"A motel?" Magnus checked the address Turner had sent him. "That can't be right."

Vivian opened the window and looked up. "The lights in the sign are off, and there are no cars parked in front. The place seems deserted."

"Before we go in, I want to double check." Magnus placed the call to Turner. "Did you send us to a motel?"

"I should have mentioned it, but as you can imagine, I was in a rush. The owner is the brother-in-law of a buddy of mine, and he closed escrow on it less than a week ago. That's why it's vacant. He knows it's a covert operation and he's not going to ask any questions."

"What about the staff?"

"There isn't any. You'll have to make your own beds. The linens and everything else is in the housekeeping supply room. The code I sent you will open that too."

"Not a problem. How are things going with the negotiations?"

"They ended for tonight and will resume tomorrow. Kalugal promised not to interrogate Arwel and Jacki and to move them to a better room. Jin is verifying that he is keeping his promise."

"At some point, she will need to go to sleep."

If she were an immortal, she could get away with a short nap, but as a human she needed more than that.

"I'm aware of that, but Kalugal doesn't know when she's watching him and when she is not. He wouldn't risk it. Kian told him that if he questions Arwel, he's going to be stuck with her tether forever. He wants to get rid of that more than he wants to know the clan's secrets."

"Have you told Kian about her offer?"

"No, and I'm not going to unless I think there is no other way. What about the blockade, did you get decent earplugs for everyone?"

"I got the best, but don't ask me how because you'd become an accomplice to a crime. William's equipment is all in the van, and he is right here behind me. I'm going to leave Vivian and him in the motel and go back to the blockade."

Magnus had never been in charge of such a large force, but he knew each of the men well, and they were all capable fighters.

In fact, he was glad of the opportunity to show Onegus and Kian that he and the other old-timers were just as good as the head Guardians, and that they could be entrusted with more than rescuing trafficking victims.

It didn't matter that some of the men were still better with a sword than a rifle. Being a warrior was not about the mastery of a particular weapon, it was about grit and attitude, and after centuries of service, they all still had it despite their temporary retirement.

"Who did you leave in charge?"

"Gregor. He is an experienced and capable Guardian who has proven himself many times over."

"You don't have to defend your choices. You are the field commander, and you call the shots. Good thinking with the earplugs."

"It was Kri's idea. Or maybe Jin's. Are they safely hidden?"

Magnus didn't expect Turner to tell him where he had stashed them. Even with the earplugs, it was better that those who could be compelled didn't know where Jin was. Finding her would be Kalugal's top priority, and the guy would stop at nothing to get her.

"Rest assured, they are out of his reach."

"Good. That's one less thing to worry about."

"Yamanu should be arriving with the reinforcements shortly. I told him to head straight to Kalugal's complex. He needs to shroud the vehicles and take care of the neighbors. Lokan is on his way as well, and I gave him the motel's address. I don't know if he will be needed, but just in case, I want him nearby."

"Is that a smart thing to do? He can't do anything about Kalugal's compulsion. His preventive measures didn't work."

"That's true, but since Lokan is immune to his father's compulsion, we can be pretty sure that Kalugal can't compel him either. If needed, he could do the negotiating for us."

"Or against us. Do you trust him?"

"We have no choice. I have to stay here to guard Kian. In case Kalugal takes control of him, I will have to take over command. Lokan is the only other immune we have, and you might need him on location. Besides, this is his chance to prove his loyalty, and if we want Lokan's help against his brother, we can't keep treating him as an outsider."

Magnus smoothed his hand over his goatee. "I understand your reasoning. But I'm not convinced that testing Lokan's loyalty during a crisis that involves his brother is a good idea."

"I'll use him only as a last resort. If possible, I don't want Kalugal to know that his brother is working with us. It's better not to expose the connection before we know what Kalugal's intentions are. But I want Lokan in the area in case all else fails."

"Got it. Are you calling it a night, or are you going to stay in the command center?"

"I'm not going anywhere until this is over. By the way, your son is here. Kian brought him to the war room."

Vivian grimaced. "I know. Ella called me. But Parker can't help remove Kalugal's compulsion. Lokan, who is more powerful than my son, failed to safeguard us against it."

"We don't know that for sure. But in any case, since the negotiations are done for tonight, Kian is sending Parker and Ella home."

"Can you tell Ella to call me once she is out of the war room?"

"No problem. Good night, Vivian."

After Turner ended the call, Magnus put the phone away and took Vivian's hand. "Parker is tough, and I'm sure that he feels two feet taller because Kian asked for his help."

Vivian shook her head. "The village is locked down, everyone is terrified of Kalugal and what he might do, and Parker is just a boy. He's probably scared and shaking in his pajama pants."

Magnus chuckled. "I know that you don't want to hear this, but at his age, I was already wielding a sword."

"Yeah, but this is now, and a thirteen-year-old is not equipped to deal with a situation like that. Kian shouldn't have asked him to come."

18

KIAN

After ending the conversation with Kalugal, Kian leaned back in his chair, closed his eyes, and let out a long breath.

"That was intense." Turner walked over. "Ready for updates?"

"Let me grab another beer first." He pushed to his feet and walked to the back of the room where Syssi was waiting for him.

The beer was an excuse.

What he really wanted was to hold his wife in his arms and absorb the positive energy she emitted. Syssi was his rock, his foundation, his life.

"How are you doing?" she asked.

"I'm drained, but I'm relieved that Kalugal and I were able to reach an agreement."

She chuckled. "You didn't leave him much choice."

"Negotiation at its best is holding a big stick in one hand and offering a treat with the other. Some people respond better to the promise of a reward, while others are more afraid of sustaining a loss than they are eager for a profit. I like to cover both bases."

From the corner of his eye, Kian caught Parker nodding sagely.

The kid no longer looked shell-shocked. A good meal combined with Syssi's calming presence had done the trick.

He turned toward the boy and offered him his hand. "Thanks for coming, Parker. I really appreciate it."

Parker shook it. "I didn't do anything."

"But you were here in case I needed you. It must've been stressful."

Parker nodded. "I didn't know what was going on, and when Syssi explained that you were talking with someone who could compel immortals, I got really scared because I don't think I can override a compeller that powerful. But I listened to you negotiate with him, and you seemed to have things under control." The kid smiled. "It was interesting, and I'm glad I got to be here. I even learned something I can use. I liked your stick and treat negotiation method."

Kian clapped him on the back. "You are a smart fellow, Parker. And who knows? Maybe your powers have grown since the last time you used them. If we manage to bring Kalugal to our side, I might ask him to help us test you."

Parker's eyes widened. "Do you think he'd agree?"

"It all depends on what he will gain by it. I have a feeling that Kalugal is an opportunist, not an idealist. Which is good. It makes him much easier to negotiate with."

"Why is that?"

"People are seldom willing to compromise on ideology, and beliefs are almost impossible to bend, let alone change. But Kalugal is a smart fellow who thinks logically, which makes him a good partner for the negotiation table." Kian leaned closer to Parker's ear. "Here's another lesson you should internalize. Not everyone can be reasoned with, and bullies respond best to a show of force."

"Is Kalugal a bully?"

"He might be. But he proved that he can at least listen to reason. That's the mark of an intelligent man."

Kian lifted his eyes to Ella, who was sitting on Parker's other side. "Thank you for bringing your brother here. It must have been difficult for you as well."

She waved a dismissive hand. "It was much scarier on the outside. When the lockdown was announced, Parker and I freaked out. We thought that the village was under attack. Then when Onegus called and told me to bring Parker, it was a relief to know that the lockdown was only a precaution because the location might have been compromised. Being here and knowing what is going on was less stressful than staying home and wondering when the explosions would start."

"God forbid." Syssi put a hand over her heart. "We would have been forced to move everyone into the underground facility." She lifted her eyes to Kian. "After this is over, I'm going to enlist Ingrid, and we will figure out how to house everyone down here. I know that we have emergency rations, but we don't have beds and blankets and everything else that's needed for a prolonged stay."

Turning the underground into an emergency shelter was a good idea, but the place hadn't been designed for that.

"We don't have enough room down here. And besides, aerial shelling is the last thing I'm worried about. The Doomers wouldn't dare attract that much attention. What I'm worried about is a siege. Our emergency rations will not last indefinitely."

"You need an escape tunnel," Turner said. "Or several of them. If the Doomers discover one, we can collapse it and use another."

Syssi waved a hand. "We've all gotten carried away, imagining doomsday scenarios. Can Parker and Ella go home now?"

Kian nodded. "But please keep the phone nearby in case I need Parker again."

The kid saluted. "Yes, sir."

After the two left, Syssi shook her head. "We were scaring Parker with all that talk about escape tunnels."

"I think he was more fascinated than scared," Turner said. "I'm not in favor of coddling children. Ignorance is bliss, but it's also dangerous."

"I agree." Kian pulled a beer out of the cooler. "You said that you had updates for me."

"William and his equipment are safe in the van, the Guardians surrounding Kalugal's estate are all wearing earplugs and communicating by texting. They have their phones set on vibrate."

"That's brilliant since Kalugal's compulsion is obviously delivered by auditory means. But I worry that no earplugs are good enough to block it completely. We need to test it, and there is no way to do it."

"I had the same reservations." Turner tossed his empty water bottle into the trash bin. "I figured that it's worth a try. Lokan is on his way to San Francisco, so we can have him test the earplugs' effectiveness on a human. Not that it matters at this point. We need the men there whether the earplugs work or not."

Syssi sighed. "There must be something in the sound waves compellers produce that has a hypnotic effect. I wish we could test it."

Turner nodded. "If it can be measured, it can be reproduced. Imagine having a weapon like that. It would trump all other nonlethal measures."

"It reminds me of *Dune*." Syssi lifted the thermos and poured coffee into three paper cups. "I was fascinated by the Order of the Bene Gesserit, women who could control others by modulating their voices."

Turner cracked a smile. "And I was fascinated by Kwisatz Haderach. I fantasized that it was me, the super-being that the sisterhood produced after thousands of years of careful genetic breeding."

Kian chuckled. "That would explain your god complex. It seems to me that you still believe you are that super-being."

"We are all entitled to our fantasies." Turner took one of the cups Syssi poured and took a sip. "I later learned that Kwisatz Haderach meant a leap of distance in Hebrew, and that Bene Gesserit meant the daughters who bridge. Frank Herbert didn't invent those names, he borrowed them from another language."

Syssi handed Kian a cup. "When I call Mey to check how they are doing, I'll ask her if she read *Dune* and noticed that."

He lifted a hand to stop her. "Don't tell me where they are. I don't want to know. And don't tell me where Jin is either."

"I couldn't even if I wanted to. I don't know where Turner sent them."

"They are safe from Kalugal," Turner said. "That's all you need to know."

19

KALUGAL

"What are you going to do?" Rufsur got up and started pacing. "Capturing the immortal was not worth all this trouble."

Kalugal crossed his arms over his chest. "Taking him was the best thing in this fucked-up situation. Otherwise, I would have nothing to bargain with to get rid of the spy and her tether. I wouldn't even know that I was being spied on."

Rufsur nodded. "Then we got lucky."

"Yes, we did." Kalugal pushed to his feet. "I promised to give them better accommodations. Do we have a vacant room that can be locked from the outside? I don't want them to wander around."

"We don't, but I'll station a guard outside their door. The thing is, we don't have cameras inside the rooms in the residential side of the bunker. Do you want me to put one in before we move them?"

"That's a good idea. I want to know what those two are talking about. Kian and his communications guy both claim that the immune is not the warrior's girlfriend, but I don't believe them. She wouldn't have done a stupid thing like chasing after us to save a teammate. That was a desperate act of a woman in love."

Rufsur nodded. "They are also sitting huddled under one blanket on the lower bunk. I haven't seen them kissing, but they've been whispering in each other's ears like a couple of lovebirds."

Kalugal walked over to his desk and brought up the camera feed from the prison cell. "They are probably plotting an escape."

"From what I managed to hear, he was telling her about immortals."

"That should be interesting." Kalugal sat back down. "I wonder what Annani's people know about our history. It's probably more than my father bothered to share with us."

"Why would you think that? For all we know, Annani is just as bad as Navuh. A female despot."

Kalugal glanced at Rufsur over his shoulder. "That's what my father wanted us to believe. Given that she is my mother's sister, Annani must have good in her."

Rufsur nodded, but he didn't say anything.

Kalugal knew what his lieutenant was thinking. A five-year-old boy's memory of his mother was not reliable, and Areana was probably not the benevolent angel Kalugal remembered.

He waved a hand in dismissal. "Put a bug somewhere they won't notice."

"Yes, sir." Rufsur turned around and walked out.

His friend could think whatever he wanted, but even as a young boy Kalugal hadn't been naive, and as an adult he was basing his opinion on facts and not just speculation.

If Annani was indeed Areana's half-sister, then she couldn't be an evil dictator. His mother was the gentlest soul that Kalugal had ever encountered, and if Annani was only half as good, she was leaps and bounds better than Navuh.

Besides, if Annani was behind humanity's technological advancements, which was what Navuh accused her of, then her intentions were at least good.

Misguided, but not evil.

Humans were too susceptible to brainwashing and too violent to be entrusted with the future of the planet and their own survival. If not monitored and controlled by a strong and capable hand, they would destroy each other and the planet, which they unknowingly shared with immortals.

Kalugal was not going to let it happen. The humans might not care whether their descendants survived, but since Kalugal was still going to be around thousands of years from now, he had to ensure that he had a habitable planet and enough humans on it to keep the machine working.

Apparently, Annani wasn't smart enough to see the trajectory humanity was on, or maybe she naively hoped that her influence would change their doomed future.

Without him taking over, they would eventually nuke each other and every living thing out of existence.

It would only take one crazed fanatic to start the chain reaction.

Putting the earphones on, he listened to the recording, but the sound amplification distorted whatever his prisoners had been whispering to each other. He managed to catch a few words here and there, enough to confirm what Rufsur had said about the topic of their conversation, but not enough to piece together the story Arwel had been sharing with the immune.

Getting the warrior to talk and tell him everything he wanted to know could have been extremely satisfying. But Kalugal had made a promise, which he wasn't going to break regardless of the spy's tether.

He wasn't an honest man or even a good one, but he held himself to certain standards.

Going back on a promise was the mark of a lesser man.

Besides, now that the channel of communication was open between him and his cousin, he could just ask Kian to tell him what he knew about their shared ancestry.

It wasn't as if the information would provide Kalugal with a strategic advantage, so there was no reason for Kian to keep it from him.

In fact, if Kalugal played his hand well and pretended to want an alliance with his cousin, he might even get to meet the mother goddess herself.

According to Kian, Areana had asked her sister to search for him, but he didn't believe Annani would have agreed to do it unless she sought to gain some benefit from it. At the very least, she was probably curious about her nephew.

He was definitely curious about his aunt, and specifically whether she was susceptible to his compulsion.

If she was, that would open up some interesting possibilities.

20

WENDY

*W*endy knew where she was, which was a big improvement. The guards hadn't bothered to blindfold her or Richard, and as they left their underground prison, she'd seen high rises. But since she'd never been to Los Angeles before, it had taken several road signs until she'd figured it out. Then they had gone up and up, through narrow, serpentine roads that had snow piled up on the shoulders. When Bowen finally parked the car in the driveway of a fancy cabin, Wendy let out a relieved breath. Some of the narrower spots had been scary.

"Everyone stay in the car. I'm going to open the garage and park inside, so you don't have to brave the elements."

She wasn't going to argue with that.

The clothes she had on were not warm enough for snow. The heating in the car was on, and she was in no hurry to get out into the cold night.

Mey turned to look at her and Vlad. "Tomorrow, I'm going to get you proper clothing. Tonight, we are just going to blast the heat in the cabin."

As Bowen opened the garage doors, Wendy's eyes widened at the two snowmobiles parked in the smallest of the three bays. "Can we ride those?" She pointed.

"I'll have to check," Mey said. "I don't know if they are part of the package."

"I've never ridden a snowmobile. I really want to try it."

"Do you have a driving license?" Vlad asked.

"Of course. I didn't grow up in the boonies, you know."

He lifted his hands in the peace sign. "Not everyone gets a license right away, and not everyone owns a car."

"I didn't have a car of my own, but I got my driver's license as soon as I was eligible."

Her father would have never gotten her a car, and not because he couldn't afford it. It was just another way for him to control her every move.

After Bowen parked his car inside, the other guard drove in, and Bowen closed the garage doors. "It's freezing in there. I turned on the heating, but it will take time for the place to warm up. Until it does, I suggest that you grab blankets from the beds."

Bowen was wearing a light jacket like the rest of them, but the guy didn't seem bothered by the cold. Neither did Leon, the other guard.

In a surprising gesture, Vlad wrapped his thin arm around her. "I'll try to keep you warm until we get a blanket."

"Thanks." She let him pull her against his body, and it didn't even gross her out.

Maybe she was just too cold to care.

As they rushed inside, Vlad immediately zeroed in on the throw blanket draped over the couch's arm. "This one is for you." He wrapped it around her.

"Don't be silly. We can share it." She lifted one end for him to get in.

He looked at it longingly, but then shook his head. "I'll get the fireplace going first."

The guy was too nice for his own good.

"I like it." Ingrid walked into the middle of the room and turned in a circle. "Not to my standards, but with a few tweaks, I could make this place spectacular."

Richard headed for the stairs. "I'll get us blankets."

He seemed chilled to the bone, while Ingrid appeared as impervious to the cold as the two guards.

"Aren't you freezing?" Wendy asked.

Ingrid smiled and waved a dismissive hand. "I was born in Scotland. This is a warm day for me."

Well, that explained it. Bowen and Leon had slight Scottish accents too, so it must have felt warm to them as well.

Once Vlad had the fire crackling, he joined her on the couch. Too shy to take her up on her offer to share the blanket, he sat several inches away from her and wrapped his arms around himself to keep warm.

"Come here." Wendy lifted the blanket. "I'll warm you up."

"Thanks." He slid over, trying to get under the blanket while keeping a couple of inches between them.

"Get closer. I'm cold."

It wasn't as if he had enough body mass to warm her, but she had enough for both of them. The padding that she normally resented would finally be good for something.

"Okay."

When his hip touched hers, it was trembling, and at first, she thought that it was because he was cold. But tuning into his emotions revealed the real reason. Vlad was excited, and he was trying to hide it.

Strangely, though, his arousal didn't repulse her.

Maybe the reason it didn't bother her was that she knew Vlad would never act upon it without massive encouragement from her, which he wasn't going to get. He was safe, and that was something that Wendy had never felt around a male older than twelve.

They were all predators, and they all wanted sex. Not all of them wanted it from her, some wanted it from other guys, but this was what they were all thinking about.

Her father was an abuser and a liar, but he was right about that.

Except, Vlad's need had a different flavor to it. Maybe because he didn't believe that he had any chance of ever fulfilling it, his longing felt more sad than aggressive, and it touched on the dormant nurturer in her.

She wanted to take care of Vlad, to bring a smile to his sad, handsome face, to show him that he was wonderful and worthy, and that he was selling himself short.

But that wasn't going to happen. Instead, she was going to use him, and he was going to end up even less confident and more hurt.

Maybe it would teach him not to be so nice.

Good people were losers. Like sheep, they were just waiting for the big bad wolves to devour them.

For better or worse, Wendy had vowed a long time ago never to be a sheep.

She was a short, chubby wolf cub, but her bite was just as vicious as that of her big, bad compatriots.

21

VLAD

It took almost an hour for the cabin to get warm enough for Wendy to put down the blanket, and it was the best and also the most torturous hour Vlad had ever suffered through.

He'd never been so physically close to a girl. Huddling under one blanket, their thighs and their arms touching, he couldn't help but get excited. And since Wendy was an empath, she must have known what he was going through.

Talk about embarrassing.

Still, if given the opportunity again, he would seize it without hesitation.

Wendy was so soft, so feminine, and being close to her made him feel like a man. He could protect her, shield her from all threats.

Provided she'd let him.

Did he make her feel safe?

She was hard to read, and he wasn't an empath, but he was quite certain that she wasn't repulsed by him or afraid of him. That was already better than what most girls projected at him.

He should be grateful for that.

Mey leaned back in her armchair, cradling a hot mug of cocoa in her palms. "I didn't expect to find a 7-Eleven that was open twenty-four hours in such a small town. It would have been pretty miserable to have to wait until morning to get something to eat and drink."

Wendy lifted her own mug and saluted Mey with it. "This was a life saver. It warmed me from the inside."

Ingrid grimaced. "The sandwiches were terrible, but I was so hungry that I didn't care. I forgot that cold weather makes people hungrier."

Vlad wondered whether that was why he had wolfed down more than half a bag of Oreo cookies and had chugged down three full mugs of hot cocoa.

Not really. It had been warm under the blanket with Wendy, but it had made him nervous, and that was why he had eaten so much. It had given him something to do other than think about Wendy's soft thigh that was pressed against his.

Not that it had helped.

He was still acutely aware of it and savoring every moment.

"I love hot cocoa in the winter. Jin and I used to drink it while watching *Doctor Who*." Mey crossed her legs. "We need to figure out the sleeping arrangements. There are five bedrooms and three bathrooms in the cabin. The master bedroom has its own bathroom, and I think it should go to Richard and Ingrid." She glanced at the two, who were squeezed together in one armchair. "Is that okay with you?"

"We'll take it," Richard said.

Mey nodded. "That leaves four bedrooms and two bathrooms. We can divide them in two ways. Wendy and I can share the bedroom that has two beds, while Vlad, Bowen, and Leon each get their own room. Or, Bowen and Leon can share the bedroom, and the rest of us each get a room."

"Bowen and I will share," Leon said. "Since we are going to take turns guarding the place, we won't be sleeping at the same time anyway."

"Then it's settled." Mey pushed to her feet. "I don't know about you, but I want to take a hot shower and crawl into bed."

"Yeah, me too." Wendy put her mug down. "I hope there are televisions in the bedrooms." She folded the blanket and put it over the back of the couch. "Can I choose my room?"

"Of course."

As Mey walked over to the front door and lifted her suitcase, Wendy got up as well, depriving Vlad of her warmth.

"I'll get your stuff." He followed her.

Taking Wendy's bundle in one hand, he slung the strap of his guitar case over his arm and lifted the duffle bag full of video games and books with the other.

Regrettably, he didn't have a change of clothes in there, and anything he could borrow from Bowen or Leon would be six sizes too big.

"I can take that." Wendy reached for her bundle.

Vlad shook his head. "It's okay. I've got it."

Following Mey upstairs, they walked into the first bedroom.

Wendy eyed the television. "Can this one be mine?"

"Yes." Mey opened the door to a bathroom. "I'll take the room on the other side, so we can share the bathroom. The boys can use the bigger one that has a door to the hallway."

Vlad put Wendy's bundle on the bed and then stood there unsure of what to do next. "Do you want to maybe watch something together before going to sleep?"

He didn't expect her to say yes, but he loathed parting with her so soon.

"Yeah, that would be nice. But I want to shower first. Can you come back in half an hour?"

His heart started beating so fast that he was afraid she could hear it. "Of course. If Bowen and Leon don't hog the shower, I'll grab one myself." He was proud of managing a casual tone.

Wendy sat on the bed and started working on untying the knot on her bundle. "Do you have anything to change into?"

"I don't, but maybe one of the guys can lend me a pair of sweatpants. If not, I'll just sleep with nothing on." The moment the words left his mouth, Vlad felt his ears catch fire. "I have a room to myself, so it won't bother anyone." He pushed the strap of his duffle bag higher on his shoulder. "Have fun showering."

Damn. That was another wrong thing to say.

Imagining Wendy's curvy nude body as she stood under the spray, her long brown hair cascading down her back, Vlad felt the flame from his ears spread to the rest of his face, and not all of it was covered by his long bangs.

"I'll be back in half an hour." He turned around and rushed out the door.

22

KIAN

Syssi glanced at her watch. "It's one o'clock in the morning. Is it too late to call Mey?"

Turner shook his head. "They arrived at their destination not too long ago. She is probably still awake."

"I'll send her a text first."

Kian doubted that anyone involved in the crisis was going to sleep anytime soon, and that included Kalugal. His cousin's claim that it was late and he was tired had been an excuse to get off the line and do some thinking.

He wondered what clever scheme the son of a despot would come up with.

There was no way out of his predicament, so no matter how much the guy strained his noggin, he wasn't going to come up with anything other than doing exactly what Kian wanted him to do.

The problem was arranging the exchange.

Kalugal would not give up Arwel and Jacki unless he was convinced that the tether was removed, and that was going to be a problem. And the same went for Kian. He wasn't going to let Jin remove the tether until Arwel and Jacki were released.

Hopefully, Turner could come up with a solution that would be acceptable to both sides because Kian had nothing.

Well, that wasn't entirely true. The easiest way to do it was to trade Jin for Arwel and Jacki, but Kian wasn't going to do that no matter what.

Kalugal might decide that the best way to get rid of the tether was to kill the one holding it. Or he might decide to keep Jin and never let her go. In either of those scenarios, not only would the clan lose a valuable asset and an almost certain Dormant, but they also might lose Arwel, who would never forgive Kian for allowing that to happen.

"Yamanu just texted me," Turner said. "He is on his way to the blockade, and he plans on thralling the neighbors to have a strong urge to leave early in the morning and not come back until nightfall. Do you want to talk to him?"

"Tell him that I like his plan. I need to call my mother and give her an update."

Turner nodded. "Do you want me to leave?"

"There is no need. You know everything that I'm going to tell her."

"I thought that you would like privacy."

Normally he would, but not tonight. Turner was indispensable, and having him near made the entire situation more tolerable.

Things would have been a lot scarier without an immune who Kian trusted to take over and run things as well, if not better than he could.

"This is still a crisis situation. I need you here." He pulled out his phone and checked the time in Alaska.

It was after midnight there, but he doubted his mother and sister were sleeping. In fact, they might not be there at all. Annani liked to travel, and she might be in Paris or London for all he knew.

Placing the call, he didn't expect her to answer before it even rang once.

"Kian. I was waiting for your call."

He'd forgotten about the grapevine. His mother always knew what was going on mere moments after it happened.

"I guess you heard about the village's lockdown."

"I did. What happened?"

"Do you remember the saying I'm so fond of?"

She chuckled. "There are many of them. Which one are you referring to?"

"The one about no good deed going unpunished. We found Kalugal, but things have gotten out of hand, and he captured Arwel and a human woman who is an immune and a possible Dormant. With his power of compulsion, Kalugal can get Arwel to tell him where the village is as well as everything else Arwel knows, which as head Guardian is basically everything."

"That is very troubling. What are you going to do?"

"I'm negotiating for their release. We were lucky that Jin managed to tether Kalugal before things went south, so I at least have a big stick to threaten him with. The carrot is Areana. If he releases our people, I'll let him talk to his mother."

"Did you tell him about her?"

"I did. Apparently, she never told him that she is a goddess. He thought that she was an immortal who Navuh stole from the clan."

"Why would he think that?"

Kian smiled. "That's actually a funny story. When I introduced myself as his cousin and Annani's son, he thought I was talking about a clan female who was named after you. He even apologized for not being able to help me retrieve my clanswoman. As you can imagine, I was very disappointed to have my thunder turned into a hiccup."

Annani laughed. "How uncooperative of Kalugal. He should have at least pretended to be stunned."

"He was. But it was too much for him to swallow, so he tried to rationalize it."

"Given that he did not know that his mother is a goddess, that is understandable. Can I tell Areana that she is about to hear her son's voice for the first time since he was a small boy? Or should I wait until the negotiations are done and the conflict is resolved?"

"You can tell her. After all, I'm using Areana as a bargaining chip. I need all the ammunition I have to dissuade Kalugal from trying to compel me. I have Turner with me, so if Kalugal tries anything, Turner will take over, but I'd rather stay in control."

In the moment of silence that followed, Kian braced for his mother's response.

"I should be there with you to protect you. Kalugal cannot compel me."

It was precisely what he'd expected her to say. "That would be the worst move we could make. Did you forget that the village is locked down because I fear the location might get compromised? You have no idea how glad I am that no one knows where you are, including me, so there is no one who can be compelled to reveal that information. Your safety is my number one priority."

Glancing at Syssi and her slightly rounded belly, Kian was no longer sure that his mother still held that position. At least not exclusively. Her safety was the number one priority as far as the world was concerned, but Syssi and their daughter were his top priority.

"I understand. Tell me, what is your impression of Kalugal?"

"He is full of himself, smart, eloquent, and not easily shaken."

"What about his morality? Is he good or bad?"

Kian raked his fingers through his hair. "I don't know. It's not the kind of thing that can be determined after one conversation, or even a thousand. People are complicated, and they might be good on one front and bad on another."

"What does your gut tell you?"

His mother was big on letting her subconscious answer difficult questions, which was what gut feelings were.

Not that she was wrong, sometimes the gut made a quicker and better assessment than the brain, but oftentimes it also got it all wrong. Emotions, prejudices, beliefs—they all contributed to the smorgasbord from which the subconscious gathered its data and processed it to produce gut feelings.

"My gut tells me to tread carefully. It would be a mistake to underestimate Kalugal and allow his amicable attitude and soft tone to lull me into a false sense of security."

23

ARWEL

When Rufsur showed up with two more ex-Doomers, Arwel braced for the worst. And when the cell's bars started sliding aside, he was sure that it was interrogation time.

His only hope was that they wouldn't harm Jacki.

Rufsur grinned and motioned for them both to get up. "You are being moved to better accommodations. Please, follow me."

Arwel let out a soft breath.

"That's nice," Jacki said. "Do we get a toilet with a door?"

"Better. You are getting a nice room with an en-suite bathroom, a meal, and a change of clothes." He gave Jacki a once-over. "I apologize for not having any female clothing for you. The smallest I found are still going to be too big, but they are clean."

Jacki narrowed her eyes at him. "Why are you being so nice to us all of a sudden?"

One of the guards walking behind them coughed to cover up a chuckle.

"A gesture of goodwill. My boss is negotiating with yours, and certain concessions have been made."

Arwel hoped that those concessions didn't include giving up Jin, but he didn't want to ask questions that might reveal things Kalugal didn't know.

Jacki cast Rufsur a sidelong glance. "I hope that includes no cameras in the bathroom. I've given you perverts enough of a show already."

If he could, Arwel would have kicked her to shut her up. Antagonizing their captors wasn't smart, especially since she was the only female in the bunker. They might get ideas, and there was nothing he could do to prevent them from doing whatever they wanted to her.

Rufsur dipped his head. "My apologies, little lady. The cell was designed with males in mind. We never expected to have a female guest in there."

"I'm not little. And why do you have a prison cell to start with? Who do you bring down here?"

The Doomer gave her a lopsided smile. "Do you really expect me to answer that, or do you just like to hear yourself talk?"

"You are being rude."

Arwel lifted his eyes heavenward. *Fates, help us.*

Rufsur shrugged. "You called us perverts. That wasn't nice either." He stopped in front of a door marked number 31 and opened it. "Your new room."

It was a big improvement on the prison cell, but it was a far cry from the luxury of the keep. Apparently, none of Kalugal's men had a degree in interior design.

The room was utilitarian, but the bed looked comfortable, the blanket was thick, and there was even a couch he could sleep on.

Apparently, their captors had realized that he and Jacki were not a couple. Next to the stack of clothing on the couch, there was also a pillow and a folded blanket.

"This is so much better." Jacki opened the door to the en-suite. "Awesome. Tell your boss that he's forgiven for stuffing me in the trunk of his tiny car."

"I will." Rufsur turned to Arwel. "The door is not locked, but there will be a guard posted outside, so don't get ideas about snooping around. If you need anything, you can poke your head out the door and ask him, but don't step outside. Understood?"

Arwel nodded.

"And the same goes for you, little lady. I don't want any trouble from you."

Jacki rolled her eyes. "Stop calling me little, give us something to eat and drink, and I promise to behave."

"Your offer is accepted." He opened the door and motioned for a guy with a rolling cart to enter. "Enjoy your dinner."

"Thank you." Arwel spoke for the first time.

"You are welcome." Rufsur and the guy who'd delivered the food stepped out. "Good night."

Jacki lifted the covers off the two plates. "Not bad." She brought them over to the coffee table and then went back for two bottles of water.

"Are you just going to stand there? Come eat. With what their boss can do, they have no reason to drug us."

It hadn't even crossed his mind, but it was a legitimate concern. "They might."

She twisted the cap off the water bottle. "I'm willing to risk it."

When he sat next to her, Jacki leaned to whisper in his ear. "Kalugal knows about the tether. He moved us to a better room because Jin demanded it."

That had occurred to him as well, but he wasn't a hundred percent certain. "I'd rather not mention it in case we are wrong."

She leaned toward him again. "I'm certain of it, but you are right that it's better to keep quiet about it."

Arwel took the other bottle of water and opened it. "What makes you so sure?"

"Rufsur was trying to be polite despite the way I talked to him. He wouldn't have been so reserved if no one was watching." Jacki cut a piece of chicken and stuffed it in her mouth.

So that was why she'd acted so foolishly. Or rather smartly.

"My impression of Rufsur is that he's an amiable fellow. He wasn't rude or unnecessarily cruel when he apprehended you. I couldn't see much from where I was stuck frozen on the back seat, but from what I heard, you were fighting him with everything you had, and yet he was careful not to hurt you."

Jacki nodded. "True. Still, I insulted him and his comrades, calling them perverts. With no one watching, he would have done worse than the one slightly snide remark."

24

JIN

"Wake up, Jin." Kri nudged her shoulder. "You don't want to miss this."

"Miss what?" Jin cracked one eye open.

The shades on the jet's window were locked in the down position, so there was nothing to see outside, but the pressure in her ears told Jin that they were landing.

"The sanctuary, the goddess. You are the first human to ever set foot inside of it."

"Have you ever been there?"

"As a baby, and I don't remember anything, but I've heard stories, and the place sounds magical."

"I bet. Where else would a goddess reside?"

Kri smirked. "Wherever the goddess wished to."

"Is that supposed to be a joke? Because I don't get it."

After less than an hour of sleep, Jin's brain was sluggish.

Kri shrugged. "It's like the joke about where does the 800-pound gorilla sit? Anywhere it wants."

"Oh."

"You don't seem excited."

"I'm too tired and worried for that, and I want to check on Jacki and Arwel. Give me a moment."

When she found Jacki asleep, Jin followed the tether to Kalugal. He was awake, but he was alone and staring at the wall, so there wasn't much to see there either. Regrettably, her tether didn't give her access to his thoughts.

Since Arwel and Jacki had been taken, Jin had been wondering about that. Her hook was mental, so it was strange that she only had access to the visual and auditory parts of her targets' brains and not their thoughts.

"Anything interesting?" Kri asked.

"Jacki is asleep, and Kalugal is staring at a wall."

"No news is good news."

"True. How do I address the goddess? Do I bow? Curtsy? What's the protocol?"

"You can bow if you want to, but it's not required. You should address her as Clan Mother, but if she asks you to call her by her given name, don't argue and do as she says. Just be polite and don't use cuss words. Annani does not tolerate crude language."

Jin snorted. "Kian must have a real hard time with that. He likes his expletives."

"He has a hard time with her in general. He can't boss her around, and Annani is not as careful with her safety as he would like her to be. There are also some other issues that they disagree on, and it's difficult for him when she puts her foot down, and he has no choice but to obey."

Jin yawned and stretched her arms. "Does it happen a lot? Is she bossy?"

"She is definitely bossy, but she lets Kian and Sari run things as they see fit and only intervenes on rare occasions. Sari is Kian's counterpart in Europe."

"I know. Mey told me. She talked a lot about Alena and how nice she is. I'm glad of the opportunity to meet her, but I wish it was under different circumstances."

As the jet's wheels touched down, Jin released her seatbelt. "I'm going to brush my teeth."

"Hurry up. It's not a long runway."

In the jet's tiny bathroom, Jin used the toilet, brushed her teeth and her hair, and then adjusted the sweater that Alena had kindly sent for her with the pilot. It was warm and cozy, but most importantly, it made her look more presentable. She would have hated meeting the goddess wearing Kri's leather jacket with only a bra underneath.

Taking a deep breath, she opened the door and stepped out just as the plane came to a full stop.

"Ready?" Kri asked.

"Is anyone ever ready to meet a goddess?"

"I don't know if Annani will be there to greet us. We will probably be taken to our suite first."

"I hope that they put us together. I don't want to be alone."

In the short time that she had spent with Kri, Jin had come to depend on her. The Guardian was so strong, so confident, that it felt natural to do so.

Kri wrapped her arm around Jin's shoulders. "If they don't, I'll ask that they do."

"Thanks."

When the pilot opened the door, Jin expected a blast of cold air, but instead of snowy vistas, she saw the interior of a large hangar, and a tall blonde woman smiling and waving at her and Kri.

"Welcome to the sanctuary." She waited for Jin to come down and offered her hand. "I'm Alena."

Jin shook it. "Mey told me a lot about you. I just wish we'd met under more pleasant circumstances."

"Oh, sweetheart." Alena pulled her into her arms and hugged her fiercely. "Everything is going to be fine. The Fates work in mysterious ways, but so far, they have been kind to us. I'm sure they had a good reason for allowing this to happen."

"Like what?"

Alena let go of her. "I guess we will find out soon enough. Let me take you to your room." She looked at Kri. "I figured that you would want to be near your charge, so I put you in a two-bedroom suite."

"That's perfect. Thank you."

Apparently Jin wasn't going to meet the goddess tonight. On the one hand it was a little disappointing, but on the other hand, it would be better to meet Annani when she wasn't as tired, and her brain was functioning properly.

There was just one more thing Jin needed to do, and that was to let Mey know that she'd landed in the sanctuary. Since it was four in the morning in Los Angeles, a text would be better than a phone call. After all, they had talked only a few hours ago, covering everything that had happened, and she had nothing new to report other than her safe arrival.

I'm in the sanctuary, and I met Alena. I'll get to meet the goddess tomorrow.

Mey replied almost immediately, which meant that she couldn't sleep. *Give Alena and Annani my best regards.*

Any pointers on how to talk to a freaking goddess?

Just be yourself. Annani is friendly, and once you get over the glowing skin, it will be like talking to a girlfriend, but one who happens to be a queen.

25

KALUGAL

Kalugal had spent the night sitting in his armchair and thinking. He might have dozed off a couple of times, but for no longer than several minutes at a time. His mind was too troubled for a peaceful sleep.

It had been ages since he'd been so perturbed by anything. Since escaping his father's control, his life had been uneventful.

Even boring.

He'd been busy amassing his fortune, which had been exciting at the beginning, but had quickly become just another routine. There was no challenge to it, and the money was just a means to an end. However, for the longest time, he couldn't decide what that elusive end was.

Freeing his mother could have been a worthy goal, but she didn't want to be freed. For better or worse, she loved Navuh.

It was one of the few things that grated on Kalugal's psyche and soured his mood whenever he thought about it. There was no solution that would make him and his mother happy at the same time.

Unless his father miraculously changed his entire outlook on the world, Kalugal was never going to see Areana, because to do so he would have to conquer the island and take Navuh down, which he'd promised his mother never to do.

During the negotiations with Kian, Kalugal had kept his cool, not letting his cousin know how tantalizing the prospect of talking to Areana was to him, but the truth was that it was on an almost equal footing with wanting the damn tether gone.

Perhaps since he'd last seen her, his mother had grown disillusioned with her mate and was willing to leave him?

That would be a game-changer for Kalugal.

He would divert his efforts from gaining global control to first taking over the island and getting his mother out.

His world domination plans could wait a few years longer.

Or maybe not.

If the Chinese beat him to it, which they were actively pursuing, wresting control from them would be a much tougher mission than gaining it before they managed to spread their tentacles over the entire world.

Kalugal might not be the most benevolent ruler imaginable, but he would be better than them. He at least would give humans the illusion of democracy and personal freedom. Under his control, most of humanity wouldn't even know about the puppet master who was running the show, and their elected officials would want to keep it that way.

The Chinese wouldn't bother with such niceties.

As a knock on the door interrupted his thoughts, Kalugal glanced at his watch. At five in the morning, only one person could be standing behind the door to his private suite.

"Come in, Rufsur."

His second-in-command walked in and closed the door behind him. "Did you spend all night sitting in this armchair?"

"Most of it. What brings you here so early in the morning?"

"I couldn't sleep, and I figured that you'd be awake too. We need a strategy."

Kalugal shook his head. "Have you forgotten that none of what is said in front of me is private?"

"I thought you would figure a way around it."

"If you and I could have learned Braille overnight, we could have done it that way. But neither of us is that talented."

"True. But it could be a long-term solution."

"It could. Right now, I'm more concerned with finding a way to confirm the tether's removal without demanding the spy be delivered to me."

Rufsur sat in the other armchair and crossed his legs at the ankles. "There is no other way. Besides, if she is here, it doesn't matter that she has you tethered. She can't tell anyone what she sees and hears."

"That's what Kian wants me to believe. What if she can? They might have staged the entire thing to create the perfect setup for a Trojan horse maneuver."

Rufsur arched a brow. "Do you really believe that?"

"No, but it's possible."

It all depended on the kind of man his cousin was. If he was indeed such a caring ruler who would do anything to free his people, he wouldn't sacrifice the spy. He must realize that the easiest way to get rid of her tether and the risk she represented would be to kill her.

But if his posturing was just for show, Kian might have orchestrated the entire thing to get the spy into the bunker. And if she was also very beautiful, he might have hoped that Kalugal would want to keep her at least for a little while.

Except, she wasn't even close.

All he could remember from their first encounter was that she was Asian, or maybe of mixed heritage, had a nice figure, and was pleasant-looking but not strikingly beautiful. Then again, her heavy makeup had been designed to obscure her features and not to make her look pretty. Perhaps she was beautiful under all that gunk.

He wondered if that was true of the immune as well. She was a feisty one, and he liked that in a woman.

"How are our guests doing?"

"The immune is snoring in the bed, and the warrior is lying on the couch, awake and looking worried."

"So, they really aren't a couple."

"They are not, but they seem to be either close friends or just at the beginning of their relationship. Until she fell asleep, they were whispering in each other's ears and it looked pretty damn intimate."

"Do you have it on tape?"

"Naturally. Do you want to listen to the recording?"

Kalugal shook his head. "Kian might view it as a breach of our agreement." He pushed to his feet. "I need a good cup of coffee before I call him."

"What are you going to offer him?"

"The better question is what is he going to offer me."

26

KIAN

Syssi opened the sliding door and walked out, huddling inside her thick night robe. "Did you get any sleep at all?"

Kian extinguished his cigarillo and pushed to his feet. "You shouldn't be outside. It's too cold." He wrapped his arm around her and led her back inside. "And to answer your question, I slept for about two hours. That's enough to keep me going."

Leaning her head against his arm, she sighed. "Any news from the front, so to speak?"

He walked over to the couch, sat down, and pulled her onto his lap. "The Guardians are still surrounding the complex. Magnus had them take turns sleeping for a couple of hours each, so they are good to go. Yamanu thralled the neighbors to have an irresistible urge for a day trip, and some are leaving already. That's about it. I know that Jin has arrived safely at her destination, but I don't know where it is, and I'm not asking."

He had a feeling that Turner had sent her to the sanctuary. That would have been Kian's first choice because even he didn't know how to get there. But on the flip side, he could call his mother and ask her to send one of her Odus to pick him up, which he might do if Kalugal compelled him to do that.

It was better that he didn't know for sure that Jin was there. If Kalugal compelled him to reveal her location, he could truthfully answer that he didn't know where she was.

"What about Turner? Did he go to sleep?"

Sweet Syssi. Always thinking about everyone else.

"He stayed in the war room, so I don't know. He might have caught a catnap on the couch in my office." Kian leaned and kissed her soft lips. "Now that you have all the updates, how about you go back to bed? You need your rest." He put his hand on her rounded belly.

Syssi smiled. "I've heard of eating for two, but not sleeping for two. Since I turned, four hours is enough for me."

He arched a brow. "Could've fooled me. You never want to get out of bed before seven in the morning."

"That's because I like to cuddle and make love to you when I wake up, and after that, I'm too languid to get up."

"I love our mornings." He kissed her again. "And our evenings." Another kiss. "And our nights. But I don't like everything in between because you are not there with me."

Syssi rested her head against his chest. "Absence makes the heart grow fonder."

"My heart is fond of you twenty-four-seven."

"Mine too." She pushed up from his lap. "Would you like some coffee? I can make us cappuccinos."

"I can do that. I want you to go back to bed. All this stress is not good for the baby."

Syssi snorted. "She'd better get used to it. If she wants to hang around her daddy, stress is going to be an integral part of her life."

"That doesn't make me happy."

"I know, my love. I'm sure you didn't have it easy growing up as Annani's son. You told me that she'd never coddled you and expected you to shoulder many responsibilities from a young age."

"That is true. But I want my daughter to have a normal, carefree childhood."

Syssi lifted a brow. "Did you suffer so greatly growing up?"

"I can't say that I did. I was quite proud to be entrusted with important tasks as a boy. But it wasn't a normal childhood."

"What is normal?" She walked over to the cappuccino machine and turned it on. "Normalcy is subjective. What's normal for a child in urban suburbia is not normal for a child growing up in the jungle. The parents' job is to teach their children survival skills that are appropriate for their environment. Our Allegra will have to learn to function in stressful situations and make hard decisions."

"That doesn't make me happy either. I don't want her to take over my job."

Syssi chuckled. "You are immortal, my love. You can keep your job indefinitely. But maybe she could assist you and ease your burden. Wouldn't it be nice to work together with your daughter?"

"How about we let her decide what she wants to do with her life?"

"Of course. But first, we need to give her all the tools we are able to and let her try things out, so she can choose wisely." Syssi handed him a cappuccino. "Besides, we have time to figure it all out."

He was about to answer that they needed to have a plan when his phone rang. Pulling it out of his pocket, he looked at the display.

"It's Kalugal." He hadn't expected the guy to call him this early, and talking to him without Turner right there next to him was dangerous.

He let the call go to voicemail.

"I have to leave."

Syssi nodded. "Call Turner and make sure that he is still in the war room. I'll bring you both breakfast."

"You are the best." He pulled her in for a quick kiss.

27

KALUGAL

"Voicemail." Kalugal disconnected and put his phone down. "Kian is either sleeping or decided not to answer."

"It's early." Rufsur rose to his feet and walked over to the wet bar. "Do you want coffee?" He dropped a fresh packet in the coffeemaker.

"Yes."

"Did you eat anything?" Rufsur poured water into the machine and turned it on.

Kalugal shook his head. "I was too preoccupied to think of food, but now that you mention it, I'm hungry."

"Do you want breakfast brought over here, or do you want to go to the dining room?"

"I'd rather eat here. Kian is going to call me back soon."

"You didn't leave a message. He might not."

"He will. I'm sure he wasn't sleeping. He might have been in the bathroom, but what's more likely is that he didn't have his immune lieutenant next to him. Kian wouldn't risk talking to me without safeguards."

"I'll get you a tray."

"Thank you."

Rufsur could have called for one of the other men to bring the food in, but it wasn't in his nature. He liked doing things himself, mostly because he didn't trust anyone to do it as well as he could or as quickly.

If Kalugal's force ever grew substantially, Rufsur would no longer be the right man for the position of second-in-command. He was loyal to a fault, and Kalugal enjoyed his company, but leadership required the ability to delegate, and Rufsur had a problem with that.

Not that his friend had anything to worry about. Kalugal didn't plan on recruiting more men. The only way to get more immortal warriors was to steal them from his father, but that was too complicated and the quality of the men would be questionable. Kalugal didn't need a bunch of brainless yes-men. When he'd planned his escape during WWII, he'd carefully selected the warriors, handpicking them one at a time.

Regrettably he and his men didn't have access to Dormants or immortal females, so increasing their ranks the natural way was not going to happen either.

When the coffeemaker finished brewing, Kalugal poured himself a cup and went back to his armchair. The phone call he was waiting for came in a few minutes later.

Leaning back, he answered. "Good morning, cousin. Did you have a good night's sleep?"

"It was probably as good as yours."

Kalugal smiled. Talking with Kian was like playing a game of chess. "Did you decide on how you would like to proceed?"

"I believe that when we decided to break for the night, the ball was in your court."

"You are mistaken. You were supposed to check with your spy about her ability to provide conclusive proof of the tether's removal."

"It's not even six in the morning, and I haven't had a chance to talk to Jin yet. You called, so I assumed that you had come up with something."

He was right of course, and Kalugal had come up with the only viable solution, but he hadn't wanted to open with that.

"My solution is simple. You hand over the spy, and I hand over the warrior and the immune. We can do a middle of the road exchange."

Kian chuckled. "Nice try. I'm not handing her over."

"Then we are stuck. I doubt she can prove the removal of something I didn't feel her attaching. I still don't feel anything different. For all I know, the reading of the note I wrote could have been done by telepathy, and she might have access to me and my men anytime she wants."

"If that was the case, she wouldn't have to touch you. Why would we go to all the effort of getting her to you if that wasn't necessary?"

"She might need to touch a person to create the telepathic connection with him or her, but there is no tether and nothing to remove. Once it's done, it's there forever."

Kian sighed. "I understand your concern but think about it logically. If the connection was permanent, do you think I would have allowed her to do that to my Guardian? Or to the immune?"

"If you trust the spy, then why not?"

"They wouldn't have agreed to that. No one wants to be an open book to someone else, not even a loved one. It's crippling."

"That had occurred to me. If not for the spy's accurate description of the cell your people were originally in, I would have doubted her connection to them. In fact, I'm going to have my men check the two for hidden recording devices. Since it doesn't involve questioning, you can't view it as a breach of our agreement."

"It depends on how your men conduct the search. If you subject my people to anything humiliating or painful, I will consider it a breach. Do you have a female in your bunker who can search the immune?"

Unless Kian was one hell of an actor, his concern sounded genuine.

"I don't. But the woman doesn't need to be fully nude for the search. I can allow her to keep her underwear on."

"No patting down," Kian growled.

"There is no need. She can't record any visuals with clothes covering the camera. But her hair is a different story. My man will have to comb through it."

"That's acceptable."

"When will you talk to your spy?"

"Soon."

"Make it so. The neighbors are probably starting to wake up, and when they see all the cars parked along the street, they will call the police."

"Your neighbors are leaving their homes as we speak. I have a powerful thraller who is urging every human in your neighborhood to go on a day trip."

Kalugal doubted that was true. Even the most powerful thrallers couldn't cover an entire neighborhood. Kian's guy was probably going from house to house and convincing the closest neighbors to leave. Still, that might be enough for what Kian and his Guardians needed.

"That's an impressive skill."

"It's one of a kind. No one on your side of the fence has it."

Kalugal chuckled. "I'm not on either side of the fence or even anywhere near it. I'm an unaffiliated party, and I wish to stay that way."

28

JIN

"Are you awake?" Kri walked into Jin's bedroom.

"Yeah, I can't sleep." She scooted aside, making room for Kri to sit on the bed. "What are you doing awake?"

"I slept enough." The Guardian sat on the edge of the bed. "Immortal, remember?"

It was more than that. Kri was a tough cookie. Jin could imagine her sleeping in the trenches, bombs exploding all around her, and then waking up two hours later refreshed and ready to fight. She doubted other immortals were as resilient.

"It wouldn't have helped me even if I was post-transition. I kept waking up and immediately panicking that I might have missed something. I kept checking on Jacki and Arwel and on Kalugal."

"Anything interesting?"

"Jacki was still asleep, so no news from that front, and Kalugal just finished talking with Kian." Jin pushed up on the pillows. "Kian is under the impression that I have a tether to Arwel as well, or he might be bluffing so Kalugal doesn't separate them. The guy is seriously paranoid. He thinks that I'm a powerful telepath and that's how I knew what he wrote. He's going to have Jacki and Arwel checked for hidden cameras. But that's the small stuff. Just as I thought, he wants Kian to trade me for them."

"Did Kian agree?"

"No, but he will have no choice."

Kri shook her head. "He can't do that. Kalugal will kill you. That's the surest way to get rid of your tether or any other form of reporting he imagines you have."

Jin shivered. "No, he won't. Kalugal wants to be left alone. He doesn't want to start a war with the clan, and if he kills me, that's exactly what he'll get."

"I'm sorry for being so blunt." Kri gathered the blanket and pulled it all the way up to Jin's chin, tucking it around her shoulders. "Are you cold, or did I scare you that badly?"

"I'm cold, and scared, and tired. I don't feel so good." As another shiver rocked her body, Jin turned on her side and brought her knees up against her chest. "Do you think we can get some hot tea in here?"

"I'll get it. I'll also turn the heating up a notch."

"Thank you. For everything." A tear slid down Jin's cheek, but thankfully Kri didn't notice it.

Jin had done her best not to fall apart, but for some reason Kri's kindness had undone her. Maybe because she didn't think she deserved it?

"You're welcome. But I'm just doing my job." The Guardian got up and walked out of the bedroom.

Kri was so nice, and she was taking such good care of her, but that was no reason for tearing up.

Everything else was.

Talking with Mey would help, but it was too early to call her. Thinking about her sister alone in the mountains with a bunch of strangers added to Jin's stockpile of guilt. If not for her botching the assignment, Yamanu would be right there with Mey, sleeping or cuddling with her in bed.

Another salty tear made its way to Jin's lips.

She missed Arwel, she was worried sick about him and Jacki, and she felt responsible for the entire freaking mess. If she'd only left the club when Jacki had told her to, none of this would be happening.

But she hadn't been thinking straight. She had worried that Kalugal would see her leaving the club, and she'd wanted to listen to his conversation with his dance partner, but both reasons had been stupid. She could have used the back exit, and even if Kalugal had noticed, he would have assumed that she went to the ladies' room. And as for the conversation, she could have followed the tether from anywhere.

God. Why had she been so dumb?

When her phone rang, Jin reached for it with a shaky hand, hoping it was Mey.

But it was Kian.

Jin wasn't surprised that he was calling her after the talk he had with Kalugal, but she hadn't expected him to do it so soon.

"Hi, Kian."

"I hope I didn't wake you up."

"You didn't. I followed the tether to Kalugal before, so I know what you are calling about. You want to know how I can prove the tether's removal."

"Correct. Is there a way of doing it without you having to be there?"

"I can't do it remotely. When I tethered Edna, she didn't feel it at first. But after I removed it and then reattached it, she noticed the difference and was able to cut it from her end. Except, none of the others I've tethered were able to do that. Most didn't feel it being attached or removed, but then they weren't trying. I think that if I release and reattach it several times, Kalugal will be able to feel the difference. The problem is that I can remove the tether remotely, but I can't reattach it without touching him, which means that it will have to be done in person. You have to trade me, Kian."

"I can't do that. He will have no reason to let you go."

Kian wasn't as blunt as Kri, but he was probably thinking the same thing.

"You can keep something of his in exchange for me. He seems to really like his assistant, a guy named Rufsur. You could hold him hostage until I convince Kalugal that the tether is off."

"I'm afraid that he might sacrifice his right-hand man to free himself from your tether. I'll talk it over with Turner and let you know."

Jin bunched the comforter in her fist. "I just want you to know that I'm more than willing to be traded. This whole mess is my fault, and it's on me to get it resolved."

"How did you arrive at that conclusion? No one could have foreseen a crazy human gunman entering the club right when you were there. It was a freak coincidence."

"If I'd left five minutes earlier, which I could have done because I already had Kalugal tethered, none of this would be happening."

"Not necessarily. If Arwel wasn't there to stop the shooter, people would have died. Because you stayed five minutes longer than was necessary, those lives have been saved. I think that the Fates had something to do with that."

That was another way to look at it, and it eased her conscience a little, but not entirely.

Now she felt guilty for not thinking about the people whose lives Arwel had saved, and for still preferring to save Arwel and Jacki over strangers.

29

ANNANI

Alena walked into Annani's suite, a steaming mug in each hand. "I thought you could use some calming tea before calling Areana."

Annani smiled. "I am not nervous."

"It's a precaution."

"I don't know whether I should mention that Jin is here. I do not think it is risky to confide in Areana, but Kian might not second that opinion."

"He probably won't. Just in case, don't say anything about Jin's whereabouts, only that she is in hiding. I doubt Areana would ask where. And if she does, tell her that you don't know."

"But I do know."

"No, you don't. I didn't tell you which suite I put her and Kri in. Focus on that, and you won't be lying."

Annani took a sip of the tea and then put it down on the side table. "You have developed interesting skills during your New York adventure."

Alena chuckled. "It was the exposure to Eva. Jin should have trained with her before going after Kalugal."

"Indeed." Annani pulled her phone out of the hidden pocket in her gown. "I feel guilty for pushing Kian. Because of me, he rushed things and did not prepare Jin well enough."

Sitting down, Alena sighed. "It's everyone's and no one's fault. It is what it is." She glanced at her watch. "It's time."

At seven o'clock sharp, Annani's phone rang, but instead of William handling the call, it was Roni.

"Hello, Clan Mother. I have your sister on the line."

"Please connect her, Roni."

"Right away."

"Good morning." Areana opened with her regular greeting.

It had taken her a while to switch from saying good evening. Theoretically, she had been aware of the different time zones around the earth, but as someone who had never traveled, it was a foreign concept to her.

"Hello, Areana. I have good and bad news for you. The good news is that we have made contact with Kalugal. The bad news is that he took two of our people and is holding them hostage."

Areana gasped. "Why did he do that?"

After Annani finished telling her an abbreviated version of what had happened, Areana released a long, suffering breath. "I need to talk to Kalugal and explain the situation. He would believe me when I tell him that the clan means him no harm."

"I am afraid that is out of the question at the moment. Kian is dangling communication with you as a reward for releasing our people. If he lets you talk to Kalugal without him making any concessions first, we will lose an important negotiating chip."

"I do not know how important that chip is. Kalugal is a grown man, and re-establishing contact with his mother might not be a top priority for him. He might not even remember me."

"I am sure he remembers, and I am also sure that he longs for contact with you, but he will most likely pretend that he does not care about you. It is all part of the negotiations. Besides, given how suspicious he is, Kalugal might not believe that it is you on the phone. I do not think you can persuade him to do or believe anything."

"He will know it is me. I remember every word we spoke to each other in those brief encounters when he snuck into the harem. He was only a little boy, so he might have forgotten, but I will remind him."

"That gladdens my heart. I was worried that you would have no proof other than your voice, which he might have forgotten as well."

Alena chuckled. "If Areana's laugh is anything like yours, that would be proof enough. No human or immortal female can make a sound like that."

"Your daughter is correct, which is why I never laugh out loud around anyone other than my mate and Tula."

Annani grimaced. She would never get used to hearing Areana talk lovingly about Navuh. How could her sister be so blind to what a monster her mate was?

Even if Navuh treated her like a queen in closed quarters, the fact remained that he kept her isolated from her children and the rest of the world.

Areana was willingly living in a gilded cage.

Even if she lacked the means to get free, she could at least feel resentful about the way he was treating her.

Annani was a big believer in love and its power to heal and unite. She also believed that the Fates required great sacrifices to grant the boon of great love, but this was taking it too far.

"I did not perceive Navuh as the humorous type," she said sarcastically and immediately regretted her tone. Making Areana feel bad had not been her intention. "Does he tell you funny stories to make you laugh?"

Annani did not imagine that Navuh did anything of the kind, but she tried to sound genuinely curious.

"On occasion. I am the only person he can let go around. With me, Navuh is not the iron-fisted ruler of the Brotherhood. He is only my mate."

Annani shook her head but bit her tongue to prevent herself from saying another thing she would regret. Instead, she changed the topic. "If Kian and Kalugal reach an agreement later today, your next scheduled call could be with your son."

"I cannot wait. Being able to talk to Lokan has given me so much. When I can do the same with Kalugal, my life will be complete."

This time, Annani could no longer hold her tongue. "What about holding your sons in your arms? And later your sons' children? How can your life be complete without that?"

Areana sighed. "None of us gets everything she or he wants. Life is about compromise and sacrifice. I accepted that truth a long time ago."

30

ARWEL

As Jacki came out of the bathroom, dressed in the simple sweats Rufsur had given her, Arwel was startled by how beautiful she was. He'd seen her like that many times before, but he'd gotten used to her looking much less attractive, with the heavy makeup dulling her complexion and the mousy-brown wig covering her lustrous blonde hair.

She'd showered and changed last night, but since he'd given her as much privacy as he could by closing his eyes and pretending to be asleep, he hadn't seen the transformation.

Right now, she looked like her old self, with her long blonde hair cascading down her back and her peach-toned skin glowing with health.

The ex-Doomers might get ideas.

"You should put the wig back on. You look too good."

"Thank you." She sat next to him on the couch. "Without the makeup, the wig is not going to make much difference, and it would look very obvious that it's not my natural hair."

Regrettably, she was right. Besides, the Doomers had already seen her through the surveillance camera that he was sure was somewhere in the room. He'd tried to locate it without it being obvious, but the device must be very small and well hidden.

In his imagination, Arwel could see the guy in security calling his friends to take a look at the bombshell they had in their bunker.

This was bad.

"Prepare to stave off unwanted advances."

She shrugged. "What else is new. I've been doing that since I was twelve."

He arched a brow. "That young?"

"I was tall for my age, and my boobs started growing when I was eleven. I hated it. Old men were always giving me leering looks, and I felt disgusted." She chuckled. "At twelve, I thought that any guy over twenty was an old man."

At the sounds of footsteps out in the corridor, Arwel turned to look at the door. "Our first visitor of the day is approaching."

"Rufsur?"

"I think so."

Following a quick knock, Rufsur pushed the door open and walked in with a large tray in his arms. "Good morning. I brought your breakfast."

His lack of surprise at Jacki's new look confirmed Arwel's suspicion that there was a hidden camera somewhere in the room.

Rufsur put the tray on the coffee table. "Enjoy."

"Thank you." Jacki poured herself a cup of coffee from the thermos and added cream and sugar. "Do you want me to fix yours, Arwel?"

"Sure." He looked at their host, who didn't seem to be in a rush to leave. "Any news that you can share with us?"

Rufsur pushed the ottoman to the other side of the coffee table and sat down. "I'm afraid so. I was instructed to search you for hidden communication devices." He cast an apologetic glance at Jacki. "We don't have any ladies down here to search you, but I promise to be as gentlemanly as I can about it."

She put her cup down and crossed her arms over her chest. "I knew you guys were perverts. This is just an excuse to get me naked."

Rufsur shook his head. "I wouldn't ask that of you. If you can hand me the old clothes you arrived in, I will hand them to the men outside to search. After you are done with breakfast, I will kindly ask you to remove your outer clothing and leave only your undergarments on. I will have my men search the clothing you have on now, and promptly return them." He looked at her hair. "I won't put my hands on any part of you other than your hair. It's so thick that you could hide several devices in it."

"Why the sudden suspicion?" Arwel asked. "You didn't bother searching us last night."

Rufsur spread his arms. "We weren't prepared, and we didn't think things through. When your spy described your cell to your boss, and he repeated the description to mine, we didn't stop to think that there might be another, more mundane explanation for her being able to see where you were. This morning we realized that it might have been a clever hoax."

Arwel leaned back and crossed his legs. "Your boss must have demanded more than one proof."

"Correct. The spy also had my boss write a note and then repeated it word for word, but that can be achieved by strong telepathy. None of us have ever heard about a talent like hers, so naturally, we are skeptical."

"Makes sense for you to doubt it," Jacki said. "But the tether is real. You are not going to find any hidden cameras on us."

"I believe you. But I have my orders. If your spy has indeed tethered my boss, that's good news for you two. He is willing to trade you for her."

Arwel stifled the growl that threatened to escape his throat.

If Kian agreed to the trade and anything happened to Jin, Arwel was going to quit the force and dedicate his life to revenge. He would kill Kalugal and make Kian regret his decision for the rest of his immortal life. He wasn't sure how he was going to do that, but he would make Kian suffer. And after that was done, he was going to find a way to end his own life because living without her would be too painful.

The powerful response and the conviction behind it took Arwel by surprise.

Evidently, the bond between Jin and him had solidified after all, just without the fireworks that had accompanied Carol and Lokan's. Arwel had been waiting to experience exactly what they had, but apparently every couple was different, and for some the bonding happened quietly in the background, thickening and sprouting more and more roots until separation became impossible.

He couldn't wait to tell Jin. He could do that through her tether to Jacki, but it didn't feel right. This realization was as significant as realizing that he loved Jin, and telling her about it had to be done face to face.

Arwel had to believe that they would both come out in one piece on the other side of this crisis, and that he could take Jin in his arms and whisper in her ear that they were going to spend eternity together.

"Let's get it over with." Jacki pushed to her feet and glared at Rufsur. "Do you want me to undress here, or can I do it in the bathroom?"

Avoiding her eyes, Rufsur rubbed his jaw. "Here, if you don't mind. That will save me the trouble of searching the bathroom as well."

"I'll go first," Arwel offered. "Do I get to keep my underwear on? I'd rather not give Jacki a show."

She chuckled. "I'll turn around to give you privacy."

Rufsur nodded.

After he was done with Arwel and handed his clothes to the guy waiting outside the room, he turned to Jacki. "Arwel and I can turn our backs to you while you undress."

She huffed. "Yeah, as if that is going to do me any good. I know that there is a camera hidden somewhere in here and that the rest of your pervert friends are going to watch me strip." She waved a hand. "You might as well enjoy the show."

And a show she gave them. Removing the sweatshirt, she swung it around and tossed it on the bed, and then repeated the performance with the sweatpants.

The whole thing took less than a minute, but by the end of it Rufsur was breathing hard.

Nevertheless, he conducted the search just as he had promised, treating Jacki as if she were made from highly breakable glass and apologizing every couple of moments for having to comb his fingers through her hair.

In return, Arwel hadn't said anything about the guy's acute arousal. If Jacki didn't notice the boner he was sporting, Arwel wasn't going to mention it.

When Rufsur left, Jacki let out a breath. "That could have been so much worse."

"It will get much worse if Kian trades Jin for us."

She looked at him with a pair of sad eyes. "What choice does he have?"

"He can bomb the damn place. Invade it. Kalugal is outnumbered and outclassed. We have a much larger force, and the weapons at our disposal are the kind he can only dream about."

His words weren't meant for Jacki.

Arwel was talking to the hidden recording device, and also to Jin in case she was tuning in.

"Yeah, I know that." Jacki played along. "But that might kill us as well. Or just me, the accidental human."

31

KIAN

His mood somber, Kian poked his fork at the blueberry pancakes Okidu had put on his plate.

It seemed like he had two choices. One was to trade Jin for Arwel and Jacki, and the other was to attack the bunker. Both were bad, but as much as he strained to come up with a third option, every idea he'd come up with had big holes in it.

"These are excellent." Turner put two more pancakes on his plate. "Can I get the recipe?"

Syssi smiled. "Okidu's waffles and pancakes are the best. I'll ask him to write the recipes down for you."

"Much appreciated."

Kian pushed the plate away. "What do you think of Jin's idea?"

"What idea?" Syssi asked.

Addressing the question to Turner, he'd forgotten that Syssi hadn't been there when he'd talked with Jin.

"She suggested that we trade her for Arwel and Jacki but also demand Kalugal's second-in-command as hostage. Once she convinces Kalugal that the tether is gone and he lets her go, we will release his guy."

"That's good." Syssi put her fork down and reached for her coffee cup. "But I think you should also hold off contact with Areana until he releases Jin. Give him double the incentive."

Turner shook his head. "Both might not be enough. If Jin can't prove the tether's removal, or if Kalugal doesn't believe that she can remove it, he could sacrifice his lieutenant as well as access to his mother to get rid of it, either by keeping Jin locked up or killing her."

Syssi put her cup down in the middle of her plate. "But we have his place surrounded." Using her finger, she drew an imaginary line around the cup. "If he does either of those things, we can attack, right? I'm sure he would rather avoid an all-out war with the clan."

"He might have an escape tunnel." Kian got up and started pacing. "We didn't find any, but that doesn't mean that there are none. He could have a tunnel leading into one of the neighbors' houses. Even one that's a couple of streets over. We can't post guards to cover the entire area. He could grab Jin and run or kill her and run. I can't risk that."

"I can bring in more drones and monitor the neighboring houses," Turner suggested. "But it's a temporary measure that can work only while Yamanu's thrall is keeping them out of their homes."

"Yamanu can thrall the neighbors to pay no attention to the drones," Syssi said. "The other option is to have Kalugal come to Jin instead of sending her to him. That way we control the situation." She looked at Turner. "You will need to be there."

Kian and Turner exchanged glances.

That would mean lifting the lockdown to allow Turner out of the village, and possibly Kian as well. Right now, it didn't seem like the village was in any danger, but things could quickly change if Kalugal decided to break his promise and interrogate Arwel.

He might figure out that by doing so he would gain even greater leverage over the clan. Like threatening to bomb the village in retaliation for them attacking his bunker.

Pulling out a chair, Kian sat back down. "Kalugal would agree to come to us only if I am held by his men at the same time. And that's too risky."

"Right. We can't have that." Syssi leaned back and crossed her arms over her chest. "What about Lokan? Can we use him in any capacity? We can threaten to do him harm if Kalugal harms Jin. Naturally we won't, but Kalugal doesn't know that."

Turner sighed. "He might not care about his brother either."

"Then let's wait," Syssi said. "Let him stew and chafe knowing that he can't make a move without us knowing about it. After a day or two, I bet he'll be willing to leave the safety of his bunker and come to us if it means getting rid of the tether."

As a contemplative silence stretched across the conference table, Kian ran through the various options. So far, taking Kalugal's second-in-command seemed like the best one, but it wasn't good enough.

"How long did it take Jin to demonstrate to Edna how it feels with and without the tether?" Turner asked.

"Not long." Kian remembered Jin walking out into the corridor a couple of times. "The entire experiment lasted about twenty minutes."

"Then we have another option. Kalugal will not take Jin into the bunker. Instead, they will meet outside in the yard, where we will have snipers ready to take him out if he tries to harm her or compel her to come with him. Naturally, he would have snipers aiming at her at the same time, but they wouldn't do anything as long as we have him in the crosshairs."

"A Mexican standoff," Syssi muttered. "That could work."

Kian took a deep breath. "Only if Kalugal is as attuned to his psyche as Edna is. If he is not, Jin won't be able to convince him that the tether is gone."

32

JIN

Jin finished her tea and put it on the nightstand. "I think I'm getting sick." She sneezed. "Damn. Do they have any tissues in this place?"

"I doubt it." Kri got up. "I'll get you toilet paper."

"Thanks."

A moment later, the Guardian came back and tossed the roll at Jin. "What exactly are you feeling?"

Jin put her hand on her forehead. "I think I have a fever, but it's not very high. My throat hurts, and I have a runny nose."

"Are those normal symptoms for a human?"

Jin chuckled. "It's like any other flu or cold. Why?"

Kri shrugged. "Transition usually starts with a fever. We should have the sanctuary's doctor check you out."

It had crossed Jin's mind, but unfortunately her symptoms were typical of a simple cold.

Except, as much as she wanted to transition, now was the worst time for it to start. How was Kian going to trade her if she was unconscious?

And even if he didn't trade her, she needed to be conscious to follow the tethers to Jacki and Kalugal.

"I'm not transitioning. Arwel told me what to expect, and it didn't include sneezing and coughing."

"When Michael's started, he thought that it was just a toothache. Everyone experiences it differently. I'm going to find the doctor."

That reminded Jin that Mey's symptoms had also started with a toothache, and that her gums had been swollen.

Was she growing fangs like Mey's?

The first thing Jin did after Kri left was to pat her gums with her fingers. It was a huge relief to find that everything was normal. No swollen gums and no wiggly canines.

With a sigh, she let her head drop back on the pillows.

Getting sick at a time like this was inconvenient, but it was better than entering transition. What if the loss of consciousness caused her to drop the tethers?

That didn't happen during sleep, so maybe it wouldn't happen then either, but she couldn't be sure of that, and losing the connection would have catastrophic consequences.

Ever since Jin had woken up, she'd been checking the connection every half an hour or so, and the last time was mere minutes ago, but she felt the urge to check again.

Closing her eyes, she followed the tether to Jacki, catching a fragment of a sentence. "…kill us as well. Or just me, the accidental human."

The sound of the bedroom door opening broke her concentration and Jin opened her eyes.

"The doctor is coming." Kri rushed into the room. "But so are Annani and Alena. Do you want to get dressed?"

"Oh my God." Jin flung the blanket off. "I can't meet the goddess in a sheer nightgown."

"You can put the robe on." Kri held the equally sheer garment out to her.

Both items were Alena's, but thankfully those weren't the only ones Kri and Jin had found waiting in the closet for them. Kian's sister had prepared outfits to last them several days.

Jin shook her head. "I'll get dressed."

As she pushed to her feet, her head spun, but she ignored the dizziness and padded to the closet.

A long, loose skirt wouldn't have been her first choice for a meeting with the goddess, but it looked comfy and elegant and it was hanging together with a matching loose sweater.

At least she would be color coordinated.

"They are here!" Kri called out just as Jin pulled the sweater over her head.

Damn. There was no time to duck into the bathroom to brush her hair. Combing it with her fingers, she pushed her feet into her boots and walked out of the closet as steadily as she could.

Kri opened the suite's door and bowed. "Good morning, Clan Mother."

As Kri stepped aside, Jin held her breath in anticipation of her first glimpse of the goddess.

Everything Mey had told her about Annani was true, and at the same time it wasn't.

She'd expected the glow, and she'd expected the beauty, she'd even expected the goddess's petite frame, but she hadn't expected to feel as overwhelmed by her otherworldliness.

There was no mistaking Annani for a stunningly beautiful human. She was clearly an alien, and an extremely powerful one.

For the first time, Jin understood what Spencer saw when he described people's auras. She didn't see Annani's Aura, but she felt it. It was like a force field of power, except it wasn't oppressive or terrifying. It was warm and welcoming.

Remembering her manners, Jin bowed. "Thank you for inviting me to your sanctuary, Clan Mother."

The goddess glided toward her. "You are most welcome, child." She reached for Jin's hand. "Let us sit down. I heard that you were not feeling well."

It was the oddest thing to have the goddess lead her by the hand to the couch.

When they were both seated, Annani smiled. "That is much better. You are so tall that I had to crane my neck to look into your beautiful eyes."

"They are just like Mey's." Alena walked in.

Jin had been so absorbed in Annani's awesome presence that she hadn't noticed the goddess's daughter enter behind her.

She took Alena's hand. "Mey sends her regards." She glanced at Annani. "To both of you."

Damn, it was hard to look at the goddess, but it was just as hard not to. Her beauty and power were mesmerizing, but they were too much to handle.

"Your sister is a lovely woman." Alena sat in an armchair facing the couch. "My mother and I are very fond of her."

"Such unique talents you both have." Annani patted Jin's knee. "When you feel better, I would like to see a demonstration of your tethering."

Jin swallowed. Hopefully, the goddess didn't mean for Jin to tether her. It would be like trying to tether the sun.

Alena laughed. "Don't look so terrified. My mother is not suggesting that you tether her. You can use me for your demonstration." She spread her arms wide. "I am an open book with nothing to hide."

"Your secrets are safe because I don't read thoughts. I will only hear what you hear and see what you see." Jin glanced at Annani. "I'm just afraid of creating a mental link with a goddess. I imagine it would be like connecting a battery-operated device to a high-voltage power line."

As Annani let out a melodic string of laughs, the sound was so beautiful that it sent shivers running down Jin's spine. The laughter was just as otherworldly as the female producing it. If she had to describe it, the best analogy Jin could come up with was crystal music, but that wasn't even close.

"We would not want that. What ails you, Jin? What do you feel?"

Jin waved a dismissive hand. "It's a simple cold. In the rush to get out of the club, I left my sweater and my coat behind and went out into the cold night with just a thin T-shirt on. My mother would have had a conniption."

Annani tilted her head. "This is a word I am not familiar with. What does it mean?"

"It means a fit," Alena said. "It's in Yiddish, but like many words from other languages, it was incorporated into English."

The goddess nodded sagely. "That is the fate of all tongues. My native one no longer exists in its original form, but many words have survived by being adopted into others. It gladdens my heart to hear them on occasion."

"The doctor is here." Kri got up and walked over to the door.

Jin hadn't heard anyone knock. Apparently the sanctuary's doors were soundproof just like the ones in the keep.

"Hello." A pretty brunette with a friendly smile walked in. "I apologize for the delay, Clan Mother." She dipped her head. "I misplaced my thermometer." She smiled apologetically at Jin. "No one ever gets fevers here."

Jin wondered if the doctor even knew how to examine a human. Except, if she had a real medical degree, she must have at least interned in a human hospital.

"I'm Doctor Rebecca." She offered Jin her hand. "Let's start with taking your temperature."

It was super weird to get examined while the goddess and her daughter were watching, but thankfully the doctor didn't ask her to remove her sweater but only to lift it a little so she could listen to her lungs and her heart.

After that, she checked Jin's throat and measured her blood pressure.

"It's just a cold." The doctor folded the pressure cuff and put it back in her bag. "I'd be very surprised if it's anything else. Your throat is a little red, but that's all." She pulled an unlabeled container of pills from her bag. "This is for the fever and should make you more comfortable." She chuckled. "I was lucky to find some that were not expired. As I mentioned before, no one gets fevers in here, but some suffer from the occasional headache."

"Thank you." Jin took the small bottle. "Should I take them only if I feel feverish?"

"And if you feel achy. Also drink lots of liquids and try to rest."

33

KIAN

"So, this is how we are going to do it." Kian got up and started pacing. "First, we will demand Arwel and Jacki's release and Kalugal's second-in-command as a hostage. Kalugal will come out, deliver the three to his driveway, and open the gate. The exchange will happen outside with sharpshooters aiming at Kalugal, and he will no doubt have sharpshooters aiming at Arwel, Jacki, and Jin. Ours will have earplugs in, so he won't be able to compel them. The removal of the tether will happen outside, while our sharpshooters are aiming at Kalugal's head. Once he is convinced the tether is removed, he will exchange Jin for his guy."

Kian looked at Turner. "Feel free to poke holes in my plan. I need your brain to flag the pitfalls."

Releasing a long breath, Turner leaned back in his chair. "The biggest possible pitfall is Jin's inability to prove the tether's removal. We need a contingency for that."

"If she weren't Arwel's mate," Onegus said, "a possible solution could have been for Kalugal to marry her. Maybe that's what the Fates had in mind all along."

Kian glared at the chief. "How can you even suggest that? After all that Arwel has sacrificed for the clan, the Fates wouldn't be so cruel to him. Jin is his mate."

Onegus shrugged. "Maybe there is a better one for him out there."

"Remember Robert and Carol?" Syssi asked. "He sacrificed everything for her, and yet she wasn't his fated mate. Sharon was his, and Lokan was Carol's."

Could that be possible?

As a headache started pulsating behind his eye sockets, Kian pushed his hair back and rubbed his temples. "We can't base our strategy on a hypothetical like that. I need a concrete contingency. If Kalugal refuses to release Jin, do we take him out? Do we attack the bunker? What do we do?"

"You threaten to expose his mother," Turner said. "And if that's not enough, threaten to kill her. We have the means to do that. We know when she is outside, and we can launch a missile from a boat at her." He looked at Kian. "All he needs to know is that we can, and you will have to convince him that you are heartless enough to do that. Make him believe that it's a matter of pride for you."

"He knows I would never do that because Annani wouldn't allow it."

"He doesn't know who runs the show. Kalugal is the product of a patriarchal society. It should be easy for you to convince him that you are in charge and that your mother is just the figurehead."

"I'm not sure that I'm that good of an actor."

"I can do that for you if you wish."

"Won't work. Up until now, Kalugal has been dealing exclusively with me, so if you suddenly take over the negotiations, he would immediately suspect that something is up."

Turner nodded. "I can coach you."

"How? By practicing on you?"

"You can do that if you wish. But what I have in mind is teaching you how to lie convincingly, or rather how to become a better actor. It starts with imagining the kind of asshole who wouldn't hesitate to kill his aunt to prove a point, and then becoming that person until Jin is safely back."

"It's called method acting," Syssi said. "But actors train for years to be able to immerse themselves fully into a role. Kian has hours."

"It will have to do," Turner said. "After all, you are not a novice. You have two thousand years of experience pretending to be human. That should be worth something."

"I'm not very good at it."

"And yet you pulled it off. Who will be your role model, so to speak?"

"Navuh," Onegus suggested. "I'm sure he would kill his own mother if it benefited him in any way."

"I don't know him well enough to emulate his act."

"How about Alex?" Syssi suggested. "Anyone who deals in trafficking is exactly that kind of monster."

"Not him. I could never immerse myself in a role like that."

"What about the Russian?" Turner offered. "Gorchenco is a cruel, emotionless son of a bitch, but he takes care of his people."

Kian grimaced. "He is also a rapist."

Turner shook his head. "I'm out of ideas. Immersing yourself in Mother Teresa's character is not going to help you achieve your objective."

"I'll create a fictional character. Or better yet, I'll pretend that Jin is my sister. If one of my sisters was captured by Kalugal, and killing Areana was the only way to save her, I might give it serious consideration."

"So, it's settled." Turner tapped the table. "When you talk with Kalugal, take into account that it will take Jin about six hours to get back to San Francisco. Perhaps I should tell her to get going already. If it's a no, she can always turn around and head back."

Now Kian was convinced that Jin was at Annani's sanctuary, but as long as Turner didn't verify it, he could claim ignorance. "There is no need to rush her back. I want the exchange to take place at night, and I prefer for her to stay out of reach until it's time."

"The neighbors will be back by then," Syssi pointed out.

"Yamanu will have to shroud the area. Those types of things are better handled in the dark."

34

KALUGAL

"Did you look at the feed from the guest room this morning?" Given Rufsur's smirk, he was referring to the immune having to strip for him.

"What did I miss?"

"Miss Jacqueline the immune is a knockout. The makeup and the wig were designed to make her look plain, and the clothes made her look chunky, but she is perfectly shaped and beautiful. No wonder the warrior risked exposure to save her."

"You said that they are not a couple. They didn't share the bed."

Rufsur shrugged. "Not yet. But he's probably hopeful."

"How did he react to you searching her?"

"He watched me closely, making sure that I was professional about it."

"Were you?"

"Of course. The spy might have been watching. I'm also not into putting my hands on a woman who doesn't want them on her. There are more than enough willing females for me to choose from, and even if there weren't any, I would not debase myself like that. I'm an honorable male."

Kalugal nodded. The men under his command knew his position on proper seduction etiquette. Getting consent without the help of thralling was not negotiable.

"I assume that no recording devices have been found on our guests?"

"None."

"That's actually good news. It means that the tether is removable. Otherwise, those two would have never agreed to it."

Rufsur rubbed his hand over his jaw. "That's true only if the spy bothered to ask their permission. She might be forming a connection with everyone she touches, and it might not even be intentional. It just happens whether she wants it or not."

"That would make her life very difficult. She would be treated as a pariah by her own people."

Kalugal hadn't asked Kian whether Jin the spy was a clan member or just another talented human like the immune. When she'd touched him in the club, he hadn't felt anything different about her, but then immortal females didn't trigger an alarm like the males did, so there was no way to differentiate them from humans. Not unless they demonstrated unusual strength or enhanced senses.

But he wasn't sure about that either.

What if immortal females didn't have the same advantages as the males?

When he'd visited his mother all those years ago, Kalugal had been too young to ponder such questions, and his father was not forthcoming with information on the subject.

If the spy was an immortal, it would open up some interesting possibilities, though. If he married her, Kalugal would gain several advantages for himself, while Kian could not view that as a move against the clan. In fact, if Jin was an outcast because of her ability, he would be doing her and the clan a favor by taking her for himself.

Having an immortal mate could provide him with immortal children, or dormant children that could be later induced into immortality. And he would also have her special ability at his disposal.

As for her looks, just like the immune, she was probably much prettier without the makeup and the wig. But it wasn't a deal-breaker if she wasn't. Jin the spy was a great asset even if she was no beauty queen.

The more Kalugal thought about it, the more he liked the idea. By mating a clan member, he could not only defuse the situation, but also form an alliance with Kian.

That would be the best solution for everyone.

Kalugal wasn't interested in cooperation with the clan, but he wasn't interested in a conflict either. A non-interference agreement would suffice.

Rufsur frowned. "You're smirking, which means that you're plotting something. What devious plan have you concocted in that brilliant mind of yours?"

"A change in strategy. When Kian brings Jin the spy to me, I'm going to be the most gracious of hosts and lay on the charm. This troublesome situation could provide me with the most unexpected boon."

"You want to keep the spy?"

"Indeed."

"That would start a war."

"Not if I marry her."

Rufsur gaped, and then dropped onto the nearest chair. "Why didn't we think of that before? The clan has immortal females. If we play nice with Kian, we could get some for ourselves."

Kalugal lifted a hand. "Don't get carried away. I'll dangle the possibility of an alliance in front of Kian and see how he reacts to that. He might view us as not worthy of his clanswomen."

Rufsur grimaced. "If he judges us based on the Brotherhood's conduct toward females, that might be the case."

"He has no reason to think differently. He knows nothing about us."

Which was exactly what Kian used as an excuse for sending the spy after Kalugal in the first place.

Before initiating contact, Kian had wanted to know who he was dealing with. Or at least that was what he claimed.

What else could he have wanted, though?

The clan was not looking for a confrontation any more than Kalugal was, and both wished to fly under the Brotherhood's radar and remain hidden from Navuh.

Perhaps showing Kian that he and his men were nothing like his father and his organization was precisely what Kalugal needed to do.

Except, how could he prove that?

In Kian's eyes, he was guilty until proven innocent, and innocence was always harder to prove than guilt.

35

WENDY

"Can Vlad and I take out a snowmobile for a ride?" Wendy looked hopefully at Mey.

"I have to get everyone warm clothing first. And then I need to ask if that's okay. I don't think the snowmobiles are included in the rental."

That wasn't a no. Mey not shooting down the idea right away was an encouraging sign.

"I hope they are. I've never ridden one." Wendy looked at Vlad. "Have you?"

He shook his head. "My mom took me skiing a few times, and I've ridden a jet ski but not a snowmobile."

That was more than Wendy had ever gotten to do. But then Vlad's parents were normal people who loved their son. Except, he'd only mentioned his mom.

"What about your dad? Did he go skiing with you?"

"I don't have a dad. I mean, I don't know who he is." Vlad looked into his cereal bowl and fished out the one remaining cornflake.

"Would you like more?" Mey asked.

"Yes, please."

It was his third serving, and that was in addition to two pieces of toast smothered with peanut butter and jam.

Wendy shook her head. "You are so lucky. If I ate as much as you do, I would turn into a ball. Where is all of that going?"

"I wish I knew. I try to gain weight, but no matter how much I eat, nothing sticks to my bones." He smiled shyly. "That's what my mother says."

"Your mom sounds nice."

"She is."

"I'm done." Bowen pushed away from the table. "Are you ready to go, Mey?"

"I need to write down everyone's sizes first." She pulled out her phone. "Ingrid, what's your shoe size?"

"Eight and a half. I wish I could go with you. I'm choosy about my footwear and my clothing."

"I'll send you pictures. You can't go out wearing a thin sweater and yoga pants. Besides, I'm only going to get basic stuff. Snowshoes, puffer coats, gloves, scarfs, hats, and warm socks. You and Vlad also need underwear and pajamas."

"Get me a swimsuit," Ingrid said. "I want to get into that hot tub out on the back patio."

"I must have some clairvoyant talent because I packed my swim shorts." Richard waggled his brows. "Although if the others promise not to peek, we can enjoy the hot tub in the nude."

"Ooh, you naughty boy. I like how you think."

Things seemed to be heating up between those two, and Wendy was happy for them. She was even happier about Richard's idea to share the hot tub with Ingrid in the nude. If they were busy with each other while Mey and Bowen went shopping, that would leave only Vlad and Leon to pay attention to her.

Perhaps that was her opportunity to sneak out?

Except, without a coat and proper shoes, she would probably freeze to death before reaching the town on foot.

Damn.

"I also brought mine," Mey said. "How about you, Wendy?"

"I have it. I was in a rush, so I just dumped everything I had on the bedsheet and brought it with me. I left nothing in the underground."

Mey glanced at Vlad. "Should I get you swimming trunks?"

He shook his head. "I'm not a fan of hot tubs."

Poor guy. He was probably embarrassed about being seen without clothes on.

As guilt assailed her once again, Wendy's gut twisted. It would have been so much easier to use Vlad if he were a jerk. Well, not easier because he would have been less trusting, but her conscience wouldn't have bothered her as much.

Every time he showed vulnerability, Wendy's resolve to betray him and the others faltered. But what choice did she have?

They couldn't offer her the safe future her uncle had arranged for her, and without his help, she wouldn't make it a week on the outside.

Maybe if she were a fighter like Jacki, she could've managed, but she wasn't. She had no skills, and no family to support her. All Wendy had was a paranormal talent that was mostly useless.

On her own, she would probably end up homeless. Or dead. A young girl alone on the streets had no chance of survival. She'd get raped on the first night.

The sad truth was that she couldn't afford to take the moral high ground. As sweet as Vlad was, and as nice as the others were, her life was more important than their hurt feelings.

Except, more than their feelings would get hurt.

If she managed to contact her uncle, all these nice people would end up in the paranormal program whether they wanted to or not. But even that wasn't worth giving her life up for. There were much worse fates than getting conscripted into a government program that paid extremely well and using their special talents to serve their country.

A small voice in the back of her head reminded Wendy of her uncle's super-babies breeding program, but she stifled it.

So what if the director and Marisol were compelling people to sleep with each other? There were much worse things than that too. And when she delivered a bunch of new paranormal talents to him, Wendy was going to demand to be excluded from that as her reward.

"Wendy, what's your shoe size?"

"Seven. And I wear a medium in some clothes and a large in others. It depends on the cut."

"Okay." Mey closed her phone. "I've got everything I need. Any special requests?"

"Meat," Leon said. "And lots of it." He glanced at Vlad. "And also potatoes. We are going to fatten this boy up."

"You can try," Vlad said. "But it's not going to work."

Leon cocked a brow. "Do you object to eating steak, ribs, and potatoes?"

"Not at all."

"That's what I thought."

36

VLAD

"I want to see the jacuzzi." As Wendy opened the sliding door to the back yard, a cold gust of wind swept through the cabin's living room.

Vlad grabbed the throw blanket from the back of the couch and rushed to wrap it around her. "You should have waited for Mey to come back with the coats."

She smiled up at him. "Thank you, but I only want to take a peek."

"I turned it on before breakfast," Richard said. "Check if it's warmed up yet."

"Okay." Vlad followed Wendy outside and closed the sliding door behind them.

Lifting her face toward the sunshine, she closed her eyes and took a deep breath. "It's so peaceful up here. And the air is so crisp. I wish I could live in a place like this."

Vlad commanded his heart to stop pounding like a locomotive. It was beating so hard that even a human could hear it, and if not that, then his labored breathing for sure.

The friendlier Wendy was toward him, the more he wanted her. His arousal had become almost constant, and he was thankful that his dark clothing and the long hoodie hid the erection that wouldn't let up. So far, his fangs hadn't elongated yet, but Vlad was afraid that the smallest touch would trigger that as well.

He'd never had that problem before.

Knowing what most girls thought of him stifled any attraction he might have felt. Perhaps it was the smidgen of hope that allowed him to feel things he'd been suppressing since puberty.

Wendy turned to look at him and smiled, her ruddy cheeks making her look even more beautiful than usual. "I love being surrounded by nature. Do you want to go for a hike later?"

"Sure. After Mey gets here with the clothes, though. I don't want you to get sick."

Vlad was cold, but he could tolerate it better than Wendy and he was not going to get sick.

"Of course." She lifted her foot to show him her sneakers. "These would get wet right away, and my toes would freeze." She walked to the side of the deck where the hot tub was. "But until Mey returns, we can sit here and keep our feet warm in the jacuzzi, or I can get into my swimsuit."

He would love to see Wendy in it, but he didn't want her to see him. If she felt even a little attraction toward him, that would be gone the moment she saw his scarecrow-like body.

"I'll check if the water is warm enough."

The hot tub was built into the deck, and Richard had left the cover on, but it wasn't tight, and steam was escaping through the sides. Crouching next to it, Vlad lifted the cover and dipped his fingers in the water. "I think it's good to go."

"For now, I'm just going to dip my feet in." Wendy sat on the deck and started taking her shoes off, but then stopped. "I can let Ingrid borrow my swimsuit." She pushed up. "Wait here. I'm just going to give it to her and come back. And put your feet in the water, that will warm you up."

He nodded.

His feet were okay looking, so there was no harm in Wendy seeing those. His calves, however, were just as skinny as the rest of him.

With a sigh, Vlad sat on the deck, removed his boots and socks, folded his black jeans up all the way above his knobby knees, and put his feet in the tub.

Wendy was right. The heat from the water spread from his toes all the way up, and the warm vapor heated the air. It would have been pleasant if he weren't so self-conscious about his knees.

When Wendy opened the sliding door, he quickly covered them with his hands. "Are Richard and Ingrid coming out?"

"Ingrid is trying on the swimsuit." Wendy kicked her shoes off and sat on the deck. "She is taller than me, so it might not fit. It's a one-piece."

Wendy took her socks off, pulled her leggings above her perfectly shaped knees, and swung her legs into the water. "Hot!" She pulled them back up. "Why didn't you warn me?" She cast him an accusing look.

"It wasn't hot for me, and it only feels hot to you because your feet were probably cold before. You'll get used to it."

She eyed the water suspiciously. "Yeah, and they are getting even colder now."

In a surprise move, she scooted closer to him, lifted the blanket that served as her coat, and wrapped it around his shoulders, cocooning them inside the same way they had done last night. "You don't have to act all macho and pretend the cold is not bothering you."

"Thank you," he managed to say through his rapidly elongating fangs.

37

WENDY

*V*lad was aroused.

Wendy felt it every time she got close to him. Outwardly he acted like they were just friends, not making advances, not casting her suggestive looks or saying suggestive things, but that was only because he totally lacked confidence.

Which was probably the only reason she had the courage to continue with the charade. If he made a move, she would most likely run away as fast as her short legs could carry her.

Liar.

The truth was that the more time she was spending with Vlad, the more he appealed to her. She no longer saw the skinny, hunched-over guy who hid his face behind a mop of black, glossy hair. Instead, she saw a very tall young man, who was handsome in his own unique way, and who was also kind, intelligent, and oddly protective of her.

In daylight, he appeared even more vampiric than in the underground's artificial lighting, but Wendy found that kind of sexy too. She liked that he was different in just about every possible way.

The question was whether she was attracted to him enough to kiss him.

Maybe.

The turning point had been when Vlad had sung for her. His voice was deep, soothing, and beautiful. There was a softness to it, but also strength, and for the first time in her life, Wendy had felt a stirring. Listening to his voice had transported her to a different place, and in those moments, she could have imagined herself kissing him.

"Can you sing for me?" she blurted.

He arched a brow. "Here?"

"Why not? Do you need your guitar to sing?"

"No, but we are outside."

"So what? There is no one around to hear you."

"Richard and Ingrid are about to come out."

"So they'll get a treat too. You are very good."

Vlad shook his head. "I can't. Maybe later."

Oddly, the emotion she picked up from him was fear, not embarrassment.

What was he afraid of? Wild animals coming closer to hear him sing? She was about to tease him with that, when the sliding door opened and Richard rushed out, wearing only swim shorts and a towel draped around his shivering shoulders.

Anticipating his next move, Wendy scooted back. "He's going to jump!" she warned Vlad.

Since the hot tub wasn't big, it ended up being more of a hop than a jump, but they still got sprayed with hot water.

"Richard!" Wendy admonished. "You've got us wet."

"I'm sorry." He didn't even affect an apologetic expression. "It's so damn cold out here, and we don't have robes."

He crouched, submerging his body all the way up to his nose.

A moment later, Ingrid came out wearing similar attire, but instead of running, she sauntered casually, displaying her hot body in Wendy's swimsuit. The thing looked enviably better on the interior designer.

Richard lifted a couple of inches out of the water. "Aren't you freezing?"

"It's nothing." She waved a dismissive hand. "This is like summertime in the Highlands."

After dropping the towel on the deck, Ingrid gracefully sat on the hot tub's edge, swung her legs over, and slid inside.

Wendy had expected Vlad to steal glances at Ingrid, but even though the woman was hot and moved like a ballet dancer, he paid her no attention. His sole focus was on Wendy, and that felt nice.

Leaning closer to him, she whispered in his ear, "We should go inside. They probably want to be alone out here."

Ingrid smirked as if she'd heard that, which was not likely given the noise the jets were making. Maybe she'd guessed.

Richard was oblivious, and he also didn't care about having spectators. Pulling Ingrid down to join him under the water, he wrapped his arms around her and started kissing her.

"You are right." Vlad pushed to his feet and offered Wendy a hand up.

When they got inside, they found Leon sitting in an armchair that he'd dragged next to the front window. Other than them, he was the only one in the house, but he was watchful. Even if she had a coat and snowshoes, Wendy doubted she could have snuck past him.

"Do you want hot cocoa?" Vlad asked.

"Sure. There isn't much else left in the cabin. Mey is going to bring supplies, but until then, it's either cocoa, coffee, or tea."

"I could eat," Leon grumbled.

Vlad nodded in agreement. "Me too, but all I can offer you is a hot drink."

"I'll take it."

Leon seemed friendly, and so did Bowen, but getting past those two would be impossible. They were professionals. Wendy's only hope was to go on a hike alone with Vlad and then give him the slip. The question was whether the guards would let him take her out. And even if they did, what was she going to do? Bash him over the head and run?

She was a wolf in sheep's clothing, but she wasn't a mean one. It was semi-okay to trick Vlad, but not to hurt him.

The town wasn't far, and she could convince him to walk all the way there. Then she would suggest a coffee break, go into the ladies' room, and ask someone to use her phone. It would take her only a couple of seconds to tell her uncle where she was, and since she had his private cellphone number, she knew he would answer right away.

Once that was done, she would go out and join Vlad as if nothing had happened.

Easy.

He might never find out that she was responsible for his capture. In fact, she was going to tell her uncle to keep it a secret. No one needed to know how he found them. And once they were in the program, perhaps they could continue their friendship.

Dream on.

This story was not going to have a happy ending, not for Vlad, and not for the others, and perhaps not even for her.

Her heart heavy, Wendy forced a smile when Vlad came back with the hot cocoa. She motioned at his guitar case. "How about you sing Leon and me a song? It will take his mind off the subject of food."

38

VLAD

After giving Wendy and Leon a singing performance, Vlad picked up the remote and clicked the television on. "Any preferences?"

"Anime, if you can find any," Wendy said.

Leon didn't respond, so Vlad searched through the offerings until he found a show Wendy approved of.

As long as he got to sit cuddled with her on the couch, he didn't care what he was staring at.

An hour passed with Wendy engrossed in the show and him engrossed in her. At some point, Ingrid and Richard came in and went upstairs, supposedly to shower and change. But given the sounds coming from the master bedroom, they were busy doing something else.

He tried not to listen, but it was difficult to ignore. Luckily, Wendy's human hearing spared her the embarrassment.

When Mey's car pulled into the driveway, Vlad sighed. "I should help them carry the stuff in."

"Yeah, me too." Wendy started to rise.

"It's okay. Bowen and I can manage. You can stay and finish watching your show."

She smiled. "Thanks. There are only a few minutes left."

In the garage, Vlad waited for Mey to pop the trunk. It was full to capacity, as was the back seat.

When everything had been brought in, Mey handed him one of the bags. "That's yours."

It had his name written on it with a marker.

"And that's yours, Wendy." She handed her a bag with her name.

"What did you get?" Wendy asked.

He pulled out a puffer coat, a pair of snow boots size fourteen, a hat, a scarf, and a pair of gloves. He left a pack of underwear and a pajama set inside the bag.

"Put them on." Wendy waved a hand. "I want to see how you look in them."

Modeling outfits was girly but saying that would probably make Wendy think that he was a chauvinist, so he'd better not.

"How about you go first?"

"Okay." Wendy pulled out a pair of thick socks. "I love these." She smiled at Mey. "Thank you."

"You are welcome."

When Ingrid and Richard came down the stairs, Mey handed them both their bags.

"Let's see what you've got." Ingrid peeked into hers. "The colors are nice." She pulled out a long scarf.

"The fashion show can wait for after lunch, people." Bowen dug into one of the bags that he'd put on the kitchen counter. "Let's eat first. Mey and I were hungry, and we got hamburgers and fries for everyone."

"Bless your hearts." Leon left his station by the window and walked over to the counter.

Sniffing, he dove into one of the other bags. "I hope you brought enough."

"I second that." Vlad joined him in the shopping bags attack and helped bring it all to the dining table.

Fifteen minutes later, he was done with two hamburgers, his and Wendy's fries, and was still a little hungry.

"That was only to tide us over," Bowen said. "I've got a big, juicy tri-tip roast, and I'm going to put it in the oven. It will be ready in an hour."

"I'm going to check out my new things," Ingrid said.

Once everyone was done going over Mey's purchases, she looked from one person to the next. "Did I forget anything?"

"I got everything I need," Wendy said. "Thank you." She pulled her new hat over her hair and wrapped the scarf around her neck. "I'm ready for a hike."

"Are the shoes okay?" Mey looked at the snow boots she'd gotten Wendy. "Nothing pinches?"

"No, they are great. And the socks are so cozy. Thank you."

Richard got up and turned in a circle. "How do I look?"

Apparently, the guy didn't think it was girly.

"Awesome," Ingrid said.

Wendy got up and repeated Richard's performance. "I want to try this stuff out. Come on." She offered Vlad a hand up. "Let's take a walk."

"Don't go too far," Mey cautioned. "I didn't see any of our neighbors walking outside, but I suggest that you keep that scarf ready. If you see anyone, wrap it around your nose and mouth."

"I will." Wendy's excitement was palpable.

Looping the long scarf around her neck twice, she pulled Vlad behind her and headed for the door.

Given the circumstances, it was surprising that Mey was letting Wendy out of the cabin. The government was searching for the escapees from the paranormal program, the village was under lockdown, and Fates only knew what was going on that had necessitated it. Other than the one-sentence explanation Bowen had given them in the keep, Mey and the Guardians were being tight-lipped about it, probably not because they wanted to keep things from him and Ingrid, but because of Richard and Wendy.

Nevertheless, he was glad that Wendy was getting her wish. After being cooped up in the Keep's underground for days, it was no wonder that she was so eager to get outdoors.

As they started down the road with an easy stroll, all Vlad could think about was Wendy's hand, which she hadn't pulled out of his. They were both wearing gloves, so it wasn't as if he was actually touching her, but he was acutely aware of the delicate bone structure of her small hand, and its warmth that was seeping through the double layers and warming much more than his hand.

Wendy took a deep breath and then let it out slowly. "I love the cold air. It's as if my lungs are getting more oxygen, and I feel more energized."

He smiled. "I think that you are just happy to be outdoors."

"I am, especially in a beautiful place like this, surrounded by nature. Do you want to walk along the road, or do you want to cut through the woods?"

"There might be wild animals in there."

Wendy grimaced. "Yeah, I guess it's called Big Bear for a reason. Are there many bears out here?"

"I don't know if there are a lot of them, but one is enough if it thinks that you smell tasty. Then there are the coyotes, mountain lions, and bobcats. The cats are rare, so I'm not too worried about encountering one of those, but coyotes are plentiful, and they run in packs. They can be just as dangerous."

"Then we should stick to the road." She sounded disappointed.

"If you want, we can venture in a little bit. I doubt the animals would get close to the road in the middle of the day when cars are passing by."

Except, so far they hadn't seen any.

"I would like that."

They stepped off the asphalt, but Vlad kept to a parallel path. The snow cover wasn't deep, and in some places only patches of it remained, but the ground was wet and spongy, which slowed them down.

"Are you okay?" He glanced at Wendy's pink cheeks. "Are you cold?"

"A little, but I don't mind. It's so nice out here."

Was that his cue to put his arm around her? How would she react if he did that?

"I can keep you warm." He tugged on her hand and brought her closer against his body.

When she didn't object, he let go of her hand and wrapped his arm around her. "Better?" His voice quivered only a little.

"Yes. Thank you." She leaned her head against his arm.

Vlad lifted his face heavenward and offered a silent thanks to the Fates.

He was walking with his arm around a pretty girl, and she liked it. That was better than anything he'd dared to hope for.

Except that wasn't entirely true. A kiss was as far as he was daring to dream, but that was probably going too far. He didn't know how to initiate it, or when was the right time to do so, or how was it done.

Bhathian's lesson had covered the consent part, but not the mechanics of the kiss itself. Even if Vlad gathered the courage and initiated it, his lack of experience would be painfully evident and embarrassing as hell. He didn't want Wendy to know that at twenty he had never kissed a girl before.

39

KIAN

"Thank you, Okidu." Kian took the box of cigarillos his butler had delivered and sat at the far end of the war room.

"Whiskey or beer?" Onegus asked.

"Whiskey."

"Coming right up."

Turner smiled. "Getting into character for the call?"

"Yeah, my own." Kian lit a cigarillo and leaned back in the chair. "This is just another business deal with a particularly sharp adversary. Been there, done that."

Kian wasn't a stranger to negotiations, and if he approached this one with the same attitude and confidence that he'd approached a thousand other deals he'd made over the years, he should be fine.

After all, these days Kalugal was a businessman, and his Brotherhood days were long gone. Deal-making was a game he knew how to play and he was familiar with its rules. And since they were both comfortable in that arena, it shouldn't be too difficult to negotiate a deal that would make both sides happy.

The trick was to stay emotionally neutral and not blink first. Appearing nonchalant and making the other side sweat the final offer always resulted in better terms.

"Here you go." Onegus handed him a full tumbler and put the bottle on the table next to him. "Good luck."

"No worries. I got it." Kian placed the call.

He wasn't surprised when Kalugal didn't answer until the fifth ring. His cousin was playing the same game.

"Hello, Kian."

"I spoke with Jin earlier, and she told me that you had my people searched." Putting his adversary in a defensive mode was a good opening strategy.

"Then she must have also told you that it was done respectfully, just as I promised it would be."

Jin hadn't actually witnessed the search. She'd heard Jacki and Arwel talking about it later, but Kalugal didn't need to know that. Kian wanted him to have the impression that Jin was on him every moment of the day.

"She did. Are you convinced now?"

"We found no recording equipment on either of your people. I assume that you and your spy have thought of a solution?"

"I've talked it over with Jin, and there is only one way she can prove the tether's removal. She will have to release and reattach it a couple of times for you to notice the difference."

"What if I don't?"

"Then you'll have to take her word for it."

"You must understand that it's not possible for me to agree to that."

"That's the best offer I can make you. Besides, Jin assures me that you'll feel the difference, and that it will take her no longer than half an hour to convince you."

"I'm not worried about her trying to trick me into believing that she released me while keeping me tethered. If it's at all possible, then I can simply compel her to do that. Her inability to remove the tether is what worries me."

"Jin has tethered and un-tethered many of my people. I know she can do it, and those who paid attention felt the difference. What I worry about is you trying to deny it in order to detain her."

His claim was an exaggeration, but it wasn't a complete lie. Only Edna had felt the difference. The others had taken Jin's word for it.

"Trust me. If the spy upholds her part of the deal, I'll uphold mine."

Kian smiled. "I'm sure you can understand why I can't take your word for it. I've devised an exchange plan that will ensure Jin's release."

"Why do I have a feeling that I'm not going to like it?"

"I don't like bringing her to you either. A workable solution requires compromise on both sides."

"What's your plan?"

"We will meet on your driveway. You will bring out my people together with your second-in-command, who Jin tells me you seem very fond of. I'll hold him hostage until you release Jin. You are not going to take her into your bunker. Instead, she is going to demonstrate the tether's removal and reattachment out in the open on your front lawn. I'll have snipers pointing at you, and you will no doubt have snipers pointing at Jin. Once she is done, you open the gate, she walks out, and your guy walks back in."

For a long moment, Kalugal didn't respond, and Kian imagined him mulling over his offer. He wondered what counter the guy was going to come up with.

Obviously, Kalugal wasn't just going to agree to all of Kian's terms.

"If you want me to risk my own safety and to keep my second-in-command as a hostage, then I want to keep your people until I'm safely back inside. When you return him, I'll release your people."

"No deal."

"Then we are back to the starting point. Your offer is extremely one-sided, and I can't accept it. We can do it the way I suggested it or your way, but without me coming out into the open. Jin will have to do her demonstration in the bunker."

"I can't risk her like that. Her safety is not negotiable."

"I'm not going to harm her. If she can't prove the tether's removal, she will have to stay with me as my honored guest."

Kian chuckled. "The cat hosting the mouse. I don't think the arrangement bodes well for the mouse." He lifted the glass and took a sip of whiskey.

"That's not a good analogy. I prefer to think of it as a king hosting the daughter of a rival monarch. That story could end in an alliance."

As what Kalugal was implying sank in, Kian snorted. "Are you asking for her hand in marriage?"

"Not yet. I haven't had a chance to talk with the lady and see if she is agreeable. But this could be an excellent solution to our problem. Don't you agree?"

This was what Onegus had suggested, but Kian was still convinced that Jin was Arwel's fated mate.

Nevertheless, the fact that Kalugal was thinking along those lines was encouraging. The guy was willing to mate a woman he'd never met to defuse the situation and form an alliance with the clan.

"I appreciate the offer, but I doubt the lady in question would."

40

KALUGAL

Kalugal chuckled. "Let me worry about winning Jin over. I can be quite charming, and the ladies find me very appealing."

He was a good-looking man, but that wasn't why he was confident in his ability to win over every woman he set his sights on.

Kalugal could change his appearance to precisely match the lady's taste in men, and as to his personality, he had enough experience to woo and charm even the most resistant. In fact, he enjoyed himself more when females didn't just drop into his lap.

What was the fun in that?

For the win to be meaningful, it needed to be challenging.

Regrettably, these days most young women had lost their natural instincts and succumbed much too easily. Not only that, many fancied themselves pursuers instead of embracing their traditional role of seductresses.

"I have no doubt. Especially when you compel them to feel that way."

"You insult me, cousin. I never compel women into my bed. I might compel them to reveal information relevant to my business interests, but only if more mundane methods of coaxing it out of them fail, which rarely happens."

In the spy's case, though, he might have to break that rule. If she couldn't prove the tether's removal, and if she was resistant to his charms, he would have no choice but to compel her to mate him. After all, rules were meant to be broken, and pragmatism demanded that he set his moral code aside.

"Let's leave matchmaking out of the deal, Kalugal. You'll have half an hour with her, and it's going to be in full view of my people and yours. Even as skilled as you claim you are in the arts of seduction, I'm sure you can't convince a woman to marry you under those conditions. Not without using underhanded tricks like compulsion or thralling."

Kalugal huffed. "You are one to talk about underhanded tricks. You sent a spy after me, who inserted a mental camera and voice recorder into my brain. How is that better than compelling or thralling someone?"

"It's not the same. You might not be free to do anything in secret, but you still have your free will. The only times I sanction thralling or compelling is when it's necessary to hide who we are or to save lives, immortal and human."

"I didn't know that you had compellers among your clansmen."

"You don't know many things about us."

"Same here. But if I marry your clanswoman, we can become allies and share information. Maybe even cooperate on some projects."

Kalugal had no intention of getting the clan involved in his dealings, but he would love to know what they were doing. As far as he knew, their goals were to stay alive and to stop Navuh and the Brotherhood from enslaving humanity. For some reason, the clan believed in humanity's ability to govern itself in a democratic and peaceful way, which was an absurd notion. Most of the world was governed by dictatorships of this or that kind, and humans had been at war with each other throughout history. The only way to stop them from destroying themselves and the planet was to make wars impossible.

Under Kalugal's watchful rule, wars and the senseless slaughter of millions would be a thing of the past. Nevertheless, Kian would probably not approve of Kalugal's method of achieving global peace.

"This is the twenty-first century, and political marriages are no longer used to ensure cooperation. After we overcome this impasse, we can sit down and negotiate like two civilized men."

"Agreed. But I still don't like how one-sided your proposal is. I suggest a compromise. I'll release one of your people and keep the other until I'm convinced that the tether is gone. You can have the warrior, whose return you consider vital to your safety. I'll keep the immune."

"Getting Jin is enough. You don't need another hostage."

"But I'm not really getting her. You want her to do the demonstration out in the open while you have snipers aiming at my head. That's not the same as the simple exchange I had in mind. In fact, I assumed that you would trade the spy for your people and withhold communication with my mother until after the spy's release."

"That was my original plan, but I then realized that communicating with your mother might not be as important to you as getting rid of the tether in any way you could. I'm not about to chance Jin's life on your eagerness to talk to your mother. But just so we are clear, if you harm Jin in any way or refuse to return her, I will retaliate by harming your mother. We know where she is each evening, and we can kill her with one well-aimed missile."

Kalugal's blood chilled in his veins. "You wouldn't do that. If any of what you've told me is true, your mother would have your head if you killed her sister."

"My mother is not in charge. I am. I humor her when I can, but I'm not obligated to do so. Don't get me wrong, I'm not looking forward to killing my own aunt, but don't think for a moment that I won't do it if you harm Jin. This is not a warning. This is a promise."

Kalugal chuckled. "I know that you are bluffing, cousin, but you have nothing to worry about. I give you my word that I will not harm the spy. The worst that can happen to her is marriage to me, which in itself is an excellent deal. As my wife, Jin would live like a queen."

Kian let out a breath. "You think that you are so different from your father, but you are not. Navuh keeps your mother in a gilded cage, but at least he loves her. You plan to do the same to Jin, but without the love. That makes you worse than Navuh."

As the truth of Kian's words hit Kalugal, his first instinct was to abandon the plan to marry the spy. But that was a knee-jerk response, and letting Kian's accusation affect him was precisely what Kian wanted.

"You threaten to kill your mother's beloved sister. How does that make you any better than my father? And besides, what makes you think that Navuh loves her? I know that she loves him, but I don't think he is capable of loving anyone."

"If Navuh didn't love Areana, he would have killed her a long time ago. Your father doesn't want anyone to know that Annani is not the only surviving goddess, and that her sister is sequestered in his harem. She could potentially undermine his authority, and so could you and your brother. Provided that your real maternal lineage is discovered, that is. Your blood is purer than his."

"Blood purity is irrelevant in today's world. Navuh is a charismatic leader, and his compulsion ability is incredible. He is in no danger from my gentle mother or from me. Perhaps Lokan poses a threat to him. How is my brother, by the way?"

Kalugal had the feeling that Kian had approached Lokan on behalf of Areana first. Had the spy tethered him as well?

"As far as I know, he is well."

Which meant that Lokan hadn't been tethered. If he were, Kian would have known everything there was to know about him.

Perhaps they hadn't gotten to Lokan yet?

He was curious about his brother and what he was up to, but Kian wasn't going to volunteer any information without getting something in return.

"We need to finalize the terms of the exchange. You get your warrior and my lieutenant, Jin and I meet out in the open, and once the tether is removed, I let her go in exchange for my man. Later, I'll trade the immune for communication privileges with my mother."

Kalugal sighed dramatically. "This is my final offer, Kian. I can't sweeten the deal any more than I've already done. And if she can't convince me of the tether's removal, we will have to negotiate for her to remain with me. I don't have to marry her, but she will have to join my organization and stay by my side. I can't afford to release her and have her report everything I do to you. I'm sure you can understand that. I promise you that other than her freedom, she would lack for nothing."

"How would I know that you won't kill her or keep her locked up in a cell?"

"Simple. She will call you every day, under supervision of course, and report how she's being treated. As you've indicated, you hold my mother's life in your hand. If I break my promise, you have the means to retaliate."

"I don't know how important your mother is to you."

Kalugal rubbed his chest. "Even villains love their mothers, and I'm not a villain. When are we going to do this?"

"Midnight."

Kalugal let out a silent breath.
Without stating it explicitly, Kian had accepted his terms.
"Agreed."

41

JIN

Jin's heart was beating so fast that she was sure Kri could hear it from across the room. Kian had actually listened to her plea and arranged for the swap. She was going to save Arwel, Jacki, and everyone in the village, and also prevent a war between the clan and Kalugal.

Except, everything depended on her ability to convince Kalugal that the tether was off.

No pressure.

"You can still change your mind," Kian said. "I can call Kalugal and tell him that the deal is off."

He didn't sound like he meant it, but Jin appreciated him leaving the final choice up to her.

"Not only will I not change my mind, but I am adamant about doing this. And thank you for using my idea to hold Kalugal's second-in-command as a hostage."

"I did much worse than that. I threatened to kill Areana if he harms you."

Jin gasped. "You didn't."

"I had no choice. Your life is on the line, Jin, and I'm not taking it lightly. Kalugal's best option is to kill you. I need a powerful deterrent to ensure that he won't dare do it."

She sighed. "I don't know what's worse. If I can't prove the tether's removal, and the only way to defuse the standoff is for Kalugal to marry me, it would kill Arwel. So maybe it's better for Kalugal to kill me instead."

"Don't talk like that. Do you think Arwel could live without you?"

"Yeah, you are right. I guess I'll just have to convince Kalugal. No one else has doubted it before. Not my teammates in the program and not Edna. It should be okay."

Jin wasn't sure who she was trying to reassure, Kian or herself.

"Let's hope so. Turner is going to arrange your transport back to San Francisco."

"Thank you."

Across the suite's living room, Kri smiled. "I don't know about you, but I'm glad to go home. I miss Michael."

"And I miss Arwel. If everything goes well, I'll have him in my arms tonight."

Just thinking about it made her heart flutter like a happy butterfly. In twelve hours or so, this nightmare was going to be over.

Kian still wouldn't know much about Kalugal, but Jin was sure that during their negotiations, Kian was gaining valuable insight into the guy's character. Maybe when it was over, they could meet somewhere neutral and talk.

Except Kalugal's compulsion ability complicated everything. Kian would have to take Turner with him.

"You didn't tell Kian that you were sick."

Jin waved a dismissive hand. "It's just a stupid cold. I'll load up on fever reducers, and I'll be fine. Do you think that he knows where we are?"

Kri chuckled. "I'm sure of it. Where else could Turner have sent you that is five hours away by plane?"

"Many places. I could be back in New York."

Kri shrugged. "Plausible deniability is good enough. If Kalugal compels Kian to tell him where you are, he can honestly say that he doesn't know."

Jin cradled the cup of tea in her hands. "It's weird to get ready for a flight and not have anything to pack."

Kri nodded. "I'll ask Alena to give you a warm coat to put over the sweater."

Jin was about to decline the offer, but then she thought better of it. She didn't feel well, and a warm coat sounded too good to say no to.

As Kri left the room, it occurred to Jin that the Guardian could have used a phone to communicate with Alena, but she had chosen to do everything in person instead. Was it because she thought it was more respectful to do it this way?

Alena was the goddess's daughter, but so was Amanda, and Kian was her son. Was Kri as polite with them as well?

Thinking back to her conversations with Kian, Jin realized that she could have addressed him more formally, and probably should have. She needed to remember it when dealing with Kalugal. He might not be as forgiving as Kian.

She blamed her Israeli upbringing. Even in the army, her commanders hadn't expected to be treated formally unless it was on official business or a ceremony. On a day-to-day basis, the atmosphere had been informal and friendly.

In that respect, American society was very different, and the hierarchy was still observed in schools and in the workplace. Things were changing, though, and informal camaraderie was slowly replacing the older, more rigid models.

When the door opened, Jin half expected Alena and the goddess to enter, but it was only Kri, and she had a long, wool coat draped over her arm.

It was pink, but Jin didn't mind. It looked cozy.

"Alena says she and Annani will see us off. The Odu is preparing the goddess's jet. And he's going to fly us all the way back to San Francisco. That way, you can sleep comfortably during the flight."

"Awesome. I loved the fully reclining seat."

Pushing to her feet, Jin held on to the couch's armrest, but it didn't mitigate the dizziness that assailed her every time she changed positions.

What a lousy time to get sick.

Kri was next to her in a blink of an eye. "Why didn't you wait for me? Falling down and breaking something would really screw everything up." She wrapped her arm around Jin's middle, propping her up. "Perhaps I should carry you. That would be the safest."

Jin glared at her. "Don't you dare."

"You wouldn't have objected if a male Guardian suggested it."

"Yes, I would. Unless I'm nearly dead, the only one who is allowed to carry me is Arwel, and only under special circumstances."

Kri snorted. "Like when? Over the threshold while you are wearing your wedding gown?"

"I was thinking more along the lines of him carrying me to bed, but I like the threshold idea too. I can't wait for this to be over so we can move into the village and start our lives together. Unfortunately, I need to wait until Wendy, Richard, and Jacki find their mates."

The Guardian slanted her a glance. "I heard rumors about Ingrid calling dibs on the guy."

"She did. But from what Mey is telling me, they are just fooling around. Vlad and Wendy, on the other hand, seem to like each other a lot. The one I'm worried the most about is Jacki. She doesn't seem interested in anyone."

"Is she into girls?"

"It had occurred to me that she might be, so I asked her. Jacki said that she's just waiting for the right guy, and that she's not going to hook up with anyone just for sex. It's either the real deal for her or nothing."

"It might be a convenient excuse for someone who is not ready to come out, so to speak. Not everyone has the guts to do that."

"Maybe." Jin shrugged. "Or she might be telling the truth. Not everyone is into hookups either."

Kri nodded. "I can understand that. Before Michael, I was quite sick of meaningless sex, and I'm a young immortal, so it's not like I had centuries of it. I'm so glad that that part of my life is over, and I feel sorry for those who still have to hunt. Sometimes I feel guilty for getting lucky."

That was an unexpected confession. "Don't you believe in the Fates? From what I understand, immortals credit them with happy matings."

"Not all immortals are believers. I doubt the Doomers even know about the Fates. They worship Navuh's father, the god Mortdh." Kri's lips twisted in a smile that was more of a grimace. "It fits for an evil organization to worship a murderer who singlehandedly ended the gods' era." She pinned Jin with a hard look. "You should remember that when you deal with Kalugal. That's what he carries in his genes, and I bet it's the dominant part."

42

ARWEL

Following a quick rap on the door, Rufsur entered together with another guy carrying a tray, and Arwel immediately picked up on his agitation.

Normally, Rufsur reminded Arwel of Anandur. He was easygoing, positive, and difficult to rattle. Even the club fiasco hadn't affected his pleasant demeanor.

Not that Arwel had any illusions as to how deadly the guy could be. There was a reason that Kalugal had chosen him as his second-in-command, and it wasn't his amiable personality. Like Anandur, the guy probably turned into a killing machine when it came to protecting his boss.

But that wasn't the reason Arwel hadn't tried to overpower him and make a run for it. The place was locked down tightly, and Kalugal's men who had been too far away to get back in time were locked out.

Which led Arwel to believe that there were no escape tunnels.

If there was a secret way into the bunker when it was locked down, Kalugal would have ordered those men to return and not stay away in the city. He didn't have a large force, and every one of his warriors was needed.

"Enjoy your lunch." Rufsur opened the door and let the other guy out.

"What's going on?" Arwel asked, stopping Rufsur with his hand on the handle. "You seem agitated."

The guy turned around. "Our bosses reached an agreement. You and I will be traded for the spy. When she removes the tether, your boss is going to release me, and mine is going to release the spy."

Arwel's gut twisted. "When is that going to happen?"

"Tonight."

Fuck. Was there any way he could prevent the trade from happening? Maybe he could talk to Kalugal?

Except since the abduction, Areana's son didn't seem interested in them.

"Is your boss going to visit us at all? I find it curious that he hasn't bothered to do so after going to all the trouble of kidnapping Jacki and me."

"Kalugal promised Kian not to interrogate you, so he has no reason to come here. If the spy sees him talking with you or Jacki and reports it to your boss, he might reach the wrong conclusion."

That explained it. Since it seemed like he would get traded without ever talking to Kalugal, Arwel's only chance was to convince Jin not to do that. And the only way to communicate with her was to keep talking to Jacki about it over and over again.

"I'll come again with your dinner." Rufsur looked at Jacki and cracked a lopsided smile. "Which will probably be the last time we see each other." He ran a hand over the back of his neck. "Unless you are willing to go out on a date with me once this is all over."

"I'll give it some thought."

Even without engaging his empathic ability, Arwel knew that she had no such intention. Rufsur was a good-looking fellow, and he had treated them both well, but Jacki wasn't attracted to him.

It was easy to sense the guy's disappointment, but that wasn't the emotion Arwel was interested in. What he wanted to know was the reason for Rufsur's agitation. Since he should have a good idea about Kalugal's plans for Jin, he might be afraid for his life.

Then again, he was probably expecting treatment similar to what he would have gotten at Navuh's camp, and that was reason enough to worry.

Arwel could alleviate his concerns, and if Rufsur was still nervous after that, it wouldn't bode well for Jin's prospects of survival.

"You have nothing to worry about from my people." Arwel pushed to his feet and offered Rufsur his hand. "You've been cordial to Jacki and me, and I'm going to make sure that you're treated just as well by my friends."

It could be that the only reason for Rufsur's exemplary behavior was Jin's tether to Jacki, but Arwel could at least pretend to believe that Rufsur's gentlemanly act hadn't been for Jin and Kian's benefit. "The clan is not like the Brotherhood. No one is going to beat you up or torture you for information."

As Rufsur took Arwel's offered hand, his relief was palpable. "I'd appreciate you putting in a good word for me, but I want you to know that I didn't expect anything in return for treating you right. Even though I was raised in the Brotherhood, I'm not like them. I left with Kalugal for a reason."

"He didn't compel you?"

"He only compelled our silence. We were free to choose."

"How many chose to join him?"

Smiling, Rufsur shook his head. "You sly dog. I was being nice, and you are trying to get strategic information out of me."

"That wasn't my intention. I'm curious about the percentage of Doomers who decided to stay behind. I don't need to know the numbers. Just the ratio."

"Doomers?" Rufsur arched a brow. "Are you referring to Brothers?"

Arwel stifled a smirk. "Doom is the acronym of Navuh's organization. We nicknamed the members, Doomers."

"I see." Rufsur chuckled. "Kalugal will have a good laugh when he hears that."

The fondness in Rufsur's tone helped Arwel relax a little further. The guy liked his boss, and hopefully the feeling was reciprocated. Kalugal wouldn't sacrifice a man who he considered a friend.

"I hope your boss has a good sense of humor."

"He does." Rufsur rubbed the back of his neck. "Kalugal handpicked each of his men. We were not the average Brothers, and when he decided to run, most of us followed him. On our own in the big world, we have become like real brothers. You might think that Kalugal runs a military organization, but that's not how it is. We are a family. But don't think we would be easy to take down. We are all warriors as well, and we've kept up with our training."

"I have no doubt."

In that regard, Kalugal's people were not that different from Arwel's. Annani's clan was a family first and an organization second. The difference was that clan members were related to each other either by blood or by mating, while Kalugal's men were not.

Still, Arwel chose to believe that their bonds of friendship were just as strong as those of blood, and that if Kalugal could help it, he wouldn't let harm come to his second-in-command.

43

WENDY

*W*endy kicked at a patch of snow. "Do you know how far it is to the town center?"

"It's far, and we can't go there. You need to stay hidden."

She huffed out a breath. "No one is looking for me in Big Bear. It's not like my wanted poster is plastered on every utility pole." She leaned on his arm. "Imagine how nice it would be to get a cup of coffee and maybe even a piece of cake."

She didn't have any money, but Vlad did. He wouldn't mind paying for her. "Can you check on your phone? The map application can tell us how far it is on foot."

Reluctantly, Vlad reached into his pocket and pulled out his phone. Wendy had seen him use it before, but she hadn't noticed whether it was one of those new models that were unlocked by scanning his face or a fingerprint. If she were lucky, it would be a simple phone that required a numerical code, and she could memorize it.

Her prayers were answered when Vlad punched in a series of six numbers that were surprisingly easy to remember.

Why would he use a stupid code like that?

The guy was too naive for his own good. Naturally, she wasn't going to comment on it and let him know that she now knew how to unlock his phone.

"The town center is on the other side of the lake. It would take an hour and a half for us to get there." He showed her their location on the map.

"That's not too bad. We can make it there and back before nightfall."

"I'm not taking you there. If we are gone for more than an hour, Mey is going to send Bowen or Leon after us."

"Bummer." She let her chin drop.

Since the coffee shop plan wasn't going to happen, she needed to come up with a different one.

Could she take Vlad's phone without him noticing it?

She could pretend to need to pee, which wouldn't be a lie, go hide behind some rocks and make the call. Vlad might notice the outgoing call she'd placed to a number he didn't know, but by then, Director Simmons would have sent people for them.

Perhaps she could ask Vlad to give her the phone while she went to take care of business because she needed the flashlight feature?

Peeing in nature was a potentially dangerous endeavor, and he knew how scared she was of spiders and other creepy crawlies that might be lurking between the rocks.

But what if he refused?

This might be her only chance, and she didn't want to risk blowing it. The best thing would be to steal the phone, and to do so, she would have to kiss the boy.

He would be too stunned to pay attention to anything other than her lips on his. And if she used her tongue, he was probably going to faint.

The problem was that Wendy had never kissed a boy, and her knowledge of kissing was based on movies and romance books. Still, it shouldn't be too difficult, especially since she was quite sure Vlad was just as inexperienced as she was. Even if she was a bad kisser, he probably wouldn't know if he had no one to compare her to.

"Vlad?"

He looked down at her. "Yes?"

"Did you ever kiss a girl?"

His cheeks reddened. "Of course."

"I mean a romantic kiss, not a kiss you give your cousin or your aunt."

His cheeks turned crimson. "No," he admitted.

"Neither did I. I mean kiss a boy, not a girl."

"Really?" He smiled shyly. "I was sure that a pretty girl like you must've gotten plenty of kisses."

The guy was just too sweet.

"I've never wanted to kiss anyone before."

Vlad stumbled, but managed to stop himself from falling and turned to her. "And now you do?"

Wendy nodded. "I like you, and I feel safe with you. I haven't felt that way about any other guy."

She wasn't lying. Not about that.

What a pity that after he discovered her betrayal, Vlad was going to hate her guts.

But it was for the best.

Her future had no place for a boyfriend, but Wendy wasn't sure that she was strong enough to push Vlad away. The betrayal would do that for her. She might cry a few tears, but she'd get over it.

Lifting to her toes, she wrapped her arms around his neck and pulled him down. "Let's be each other's firsts."

With a pained sigh, Vlad closed his eyes, but he didn't bring his mouth any closer to hers, probably waiting for her to close the distance. Which was fine by her.

Wendy the seductress was about to be born.

Lowering her hands to his shoulders, she kept going down until she reached his lower back. He'd put his phone in the back pocket of his jeans, which meant that she would have to cup his ass to get it.

That would shock him for sure.

His lips were a mere inch away from hers, but closing that distance took a monumental effort. With butterflies flapping frantic wings in her stomach, partially in excited anticipation of her first kiss and partially in fear, Wendy put her mouth on Vlad's.

As her body got hit by a thousand volts of electricity, it was a miracle that she retained the presence of mind to pull the phone out of his pocket and slip it into the sleeve of her puffer coat.

Once her mission was accomplished, though, her mind did what it had always done in times of extreme stress. It disassociated from the deceit and immersed itself in the incredible experience of her first kiss.

44

VLAD

As Wendy's lips touched his, Vlad felt like he was getting zapped with a high-voltage current. The overload of sensations short-circuited his brain, and there was a brief moment of blackout, but then his neural system rebooted, reawakening completely rewired.

Suddenly, there was something primal and feral inside him that was utterly new and yet familiar. It felt real, it was still him, but different.

That ferocity that had lain dormant until now burst into existence, and he welcomed it like the first breath of truly fresh air after a lifetime of staleness.

Vlad felt invincible.

His arms, which had been hanging by his sides, shot around Wendy, and he lifted her up, crushing her against his chest and taking over the kiss.

With a husky moan, she melted into him, and as his tongue darted experimentally to lick at the seam of her lips, she opened up for him. At the first taste of her, Vlad got light-headed and nearly lost his footing, but he wasn't going to let her fall no matter what.

Somehow, he knew what to do, and nothing about the kiss felt awkward, but it was sure as hell overwhelming. He wanted to consume Wendy, to become one with her and never let go.

Hell, he wanted to strip them both naked and make love to her right there on the ground.

As frantic as the kissing was, Vlad was aware of how crazy those thoughts were. He couldn't act on them, mainly because Wendy was human, and the ground was too cold and too rough for her, but also because she wasn't ready for that.

Her humanity became painfully obvious when her small hands pushed on his chest, and he realized that she'd run out of breath.

As Vlad let go of her mouth, Wendy sucked in a long gulp of air. "Oh, wow.

That was one hell of a kiss. Are you sure it was your first? You are a natural." She touched her lips with two trembling fingers. "Wow."

He couldn't answer because his damn fangs were fully elongated. Instead, he nodded and lowered her gently until her feet touched the ground.

They were out in the daylight, so Vlad could get away with the glow in his eyes, but the fangs were another story. He needed a few moments to beat them into submission.

"I need to pee." Wendy started shifting from foot to foot. "It must be because of all the excitement." She giggled as she glanced around. "I need to find a bush or rock to hide behind."

He just nodded again.

"I'll be right back." She jogged toward an outcropping of rocks.

"Slow down!" he called after her while shielding his mouth with his hand. "You don't want to fall and break something!"

Wendy waved a dismissive hand in his direction, but she did as he asked and switched to a fast walk.

He expected her to stop by the rocks, but she kept on going toward a larger outcropping further away. Was she that concerned about him hearing her pee?

For a human, the first hiding place would have been far enough, and Wendy didn't know about his super-hearing, but perhaps she needed a few more moments to collect herself as well.

He was still panting like a locomotive, his shaft felt like it had grown to the size of a baseball bat, and his fangs were refusing to retreat.

Regrettably, Bhathian's class hadn't covered what happened after the kiss. In Jackson's case, the kiss had usually led to other stuff, which had resulted in biting the girl and then thralling her to forget the bite. But was thralling allowed after only a kiss?

Bhathian had said that it was okay to erase the memory of the bite, and to change what the human female remembered about the immortal male who she'd had sex with, but not the sex itself.

Still, hiding who he was should be the overriding factor, right? If he couldn't retract his fangs, he would have to thrall Wendy to forget what she'd seen.

How did other immortal males deal with that?

Their fangs probably retreated much faster than his, so they didn't need to worry about them showing. Or maybe a mere kiss didn't trigger venom production and their fangs remained dormant.

Vlad was a freak even among his own people, with fangs that were too long even in a resting position and elongated in response to the slightest of triggers.

Not that Wendy's kiss could qualify as such.

It had been earth-shattering, mind-blowing, brain-altering...

He wasn't the same guy he'd been before. From now on, he would think of his life as having two stages. The one before the awakening, and the one after.

Except, what was he supposed to do next?

How would the new Vlad act? What kind of a man was he going to be?

The answer to that was simple. He was going to be Wendy's man. He was going to take care of her, protect her, and make her happy.

45

WENDY

Wendy's plan had worked without a hitch, but it had also misfired big time.

She had the phone, Vlad was dazed and confused, but so was she. The kiss was supposed to be a diversion for the pickpocketing, but it had turned out to be so much more.

Wendy was still reeling from it.

Instead of Wendy the seductress, she was Wendy the seduced, or Wendy the confused, or Wendy the hot and bothered, or all of the above.

Who would have thought that Vlad was such an amazing kisser? Or that he would take over with such confidence?

Something inside him had snapped, banishing the shy boy and bringing out the man. And it wasn't just the kiss. It was the whole experience. The way he'd effortlessly picked her up and crushed her against his chest, the way his tongue felt and tasted inside her mouth, the way his male scent had intensified, scrambling her senses and making her go limp in his arms.

Wendy had loved every moment of it, and if she were a braver soul, she wouldn't have stopped at the kiss. She would have gone all the way to having sex with Vlad right there and then.

And how crazy was that?

They were both virgins, it was too freaking cold to get naked outside, and she was about to betray Vlad and break his heart.

Maybe she shouldn't?

What if she gave up on her uncle and her cushy future in his organization? What if she married Vlad and had a bunch of babies with him?

Yeah, talk about crazy.

Thinking about a future with a boy because of one hot kiss was even worse than the disassociation she used to employ to escape her crappy life. This was pure la-la land.

Wake up, Wendy! You are not in Kansas, and Vlad is not the wizard.

The only real wizard in her life was Director Simmons. He'd saved her from her abusive father and had given her a fantastic job with even more fantastic pay and a promise of a life she could've never dreamt of.

She wasn't going to let her hormones derail her future.

That was probably what had happened to her mother. When she'd met Wendy's father, she'd probably felt the same way her daughter was feeling now, but unlike Wendy, she hadn't had the wisdom to shake it off.

That one wrong decision had ruined her mother's life, turning her into a drug addict and making her abandon her only child.

Her resolve reinforced, Wendy quickened her step. When she got to the large rock outcropping, she circled to its back and peeked to check on Vlad.

Head hung low, his hands stuffed in his pockets, he was pacing in circles, still looking lost and confused.

Good. She had him exactly where she wanted him.

Crouching behind the rocks, she shook her arm and dropped his phone from her sleeve into her hand.

Quickly entering the six-digit code, she held her breath, and then nearly choked on her own saliva when the screen flashed with access denied. She must have gone too fast and clicked a wrong digit. The second time around, Wendy forced herself to slow down and make sure she hit the right numbers.

Her uncle answered almost immediately. "This is Director Simmons. Please leave a message, and I will call you back as soon as I can. Have a pleasant day."

Damn. He'd probably let the call go to voicemail because he didn't recognize the number.

"Hi, this is Wendy," she whispered into the phone. "I'm in Big Bear, California, with a bunch of people who have paranormal talents. They came to get Jin out of the program, and Jacki and Richard begged them to take them too. I went along so I could tell you where to find them. We are in a cabin on Faulkner Road. The number is 227. I have to go now. Don't return my call. I stole the phone, and I need to give it back."

Disconnecting, she debated what to do with the device. Maybe she should leave it there?

Vlad would think that he lost it.

But what if it had the find-my-phone feature? She should destroy it somehow. Except, if she bashed it with a rock, Vlad would hear it. Would turning the power off do the trick?

46

MEY

When all the groceries and other supplies were put away, Mey made herself a cup of tea and sat on the couch.

Ingrid and Richard were back outside in the hot tub, Vlad and Wendy were on their hike, and Bowen was sitting next to the front window. He had switched places with Leon, so his buddy could catch a few hours of sleep.

Looking at her, he smiled. "Enjoying a few peaceful moments?"

"I have nothing better to do. You are making a roast, and I already peeled the potatoes and put them in a pot to cook. Ingrid said that she would make the salad."

"You can join Ingrid and Richard in the jacuzzi."

She grimaced. "No, thank you. I think they are very happy to be alone out there. Besides, I need to call my sister."

Mey pulled out her phone and sent a text to Jin. *Can you talk?*

Her phone rang a moment later. "I'm on the plane heading back to San Francisco."

Mey sat up straight. "Why?"

"Kian is trading me for Arwel, but don't worry. We have everything figured out. Kalugal is going to send his second-in-command to be held as hostage until my safe return. That was actually my idea, and I'm so glad that Kian listened to me. Maybe I have what it takes to be an undercover operative after all."

"Thinking outside the box is good for anything that you choose to do. The question is what you will enjoy doing the most. But back to the trade. Having a hostage still doesn't guarantee your safety. Kalugal might decide to sacrifice his guy."

"I didn't finish telling you the whole plan. We are going to do it out on his front yard, with Guardians pointing guns with special bullets at his head. I'm going to show him how it feels without the tether and then with it, and once he is convinced that it's off, I will just walk out of there."

"What about Jacki?"

"Kalugal will trade her for the privilege of talking with his mother. Kian is going to arrange that."

"What if he talks with his mother and then doesn't release Jacki?"

"Then he doesn't get to talk to Areana again. I don't think it will be a problem. Jacki is not important to him. Arwel is the valuable one as far as Kalugal is concerned."

"And you."

"Naturally. Although I want Jacki out of there as well. She is being treated well, and so is Arwel, but that's because they know I'm watching."

"You'll still be watching even after you release Kalugal. No one is demanding that you release Jacki as well."

"That's so true. It didn't occur to me, but you are right. Except, if Kalugal or his men mistreat Jacki, we won't have anything to retaliate with other than withholding contact with Areana."

Mey sighed. "I hope that's enough."

"Kalugal is not a bad guy, but I don't know his men other than the one he talks with the most. That's the guy we demanded as hostage, and he is okay too. If the others are like Kalugal and Rufsur, Jacki will be treated well."

As smart as Jin was, she was still naive. People had many layers, and what they showed on the outside was their best. The ugly usually came out when they thought no one was watching.

"You don't know that. Kalugal might be polite, soft-spoken, but totally emotionless. But then I've never met him, while you've been observing him since yesterday. That's not much to go by, but it's more than any of us have."

"What I saw and heard was mainly his negotiations with Kian, so obviously he was putting on a show. I'm actually basing my impression of him on his interactions with his lieutenant, and on that guy's behavior. Rufsur was never cruel or even unkind to Arwel and Jacki, and that was even before he knew about the tether."

"You told me that he put them in a prison cell."

"Yeah, that's true, but that's because the other rooms inside the bunker don't lock from the outside. I just wonder what Kalugal needs the cell for."

"Maybe he uses it as a brig. You know, for when one of his men does something he shouldn't. Every military organization needs to have disciplinary measures."

Jin sighed. "I guess I'll find out soon."

The knot in Mey's gut twisted tighter. "I'm worried about you."

"I'm worried too," Jin admitted. "But there is no other way. I have to do this."

"When is the exchange going to happen?"

"Tonight. Kian wants to do it after midnight. I want to get some sleep on the plane so I won't be dead when I get there. This freaking cold couldn't have come at a worse time."

Mey switched the phone to her other ear. "Are you certain it's a cold? The symptoms are very similar to transition."

"I'm sure. The doctor checked me, and she said it's a cold. I have low fever, runny nose, and I'm nauseous and dizzy. Those are not transition symptoms."

"The doctor up there has no experience with adult Dormants transitioning. So far, only Kian's part of the clan has found any."

"I've had colds before. It feels exactly the same. By the way, how come you are talking so freely? Are you alone in your bedroom?"

"I'm in the living room, but only Bowen is here. He's one of the two Guardians who have joined us. Richard is out back with Ingrid, playing footsie in the hot tub, and Wendy went on a hike with Vlad."

"Alone?"

"With each other."

"Vlad is not a Guardian in training, is he?"

Mey chuckled. "The kid is so skinny that a strong gust of wind could blow him away. But even if he were as buff as Bowen, Vlad is not Guardian material. He has the gentle soul of an artist. You should hear him sing. And he studies graphic design."

From the corner of her eye, she saw Bowen grinning as he crossed his thick arms over his chest.

Show-off.

"So basically, Wendy is out there with no protection. I don't like it."

"No one is looking for her out here. It's just trees and snow and there is barely any traffic on the street. I think most of the cabins are unoccupied."

"How far is the town? Is it walking distance?"

"Not really. It's on the other side of the lake."

"That's good. It means that they are not likely to encounter many people on their hike."

"My thoughts exactly. Get some sleep, Jin. And call me when you wake up."

"I will."

"Please, don't forget. I want to hear from you before you go into the lion's den."

"I love you too."

When Jin ended the call, Mey put her phone on the coffee table and leaned back. It had been more than an hour since Vlad and Wendy had left.

Maybe she should call Vlad to make sure that they were all right?

"Call him," Bowen said. "For your own peace of mind."

"Do you read minds?"

"It's written all over your face."

Mey lifted the phone. "I would hate to interrupt a romantic moment."

Bowen chuckled. "I doubt it. Those two are so shy that neither would have the courage to initiate anything. Observing them together, I can see the wisdom of old-fashioned matchmaking and arranged marriages. They are perfect for each other, but unless someone gives them a push, nothing is going to happen."

47

WENDY

Wendy turned the device around, looking for the off button, but it was like no other phone she'd handled before. There were no visible buttons on the sides or on the back. The screen came to life when it was lifted, and a code was needed to unlock it. That was all.

What if it needed a fingerprint or Vlad's face to turn on and off? Or maybe a voice command?

It seemed like she had no choice but to destroy it. The question was how to do that without making a noise. If there was a brook or a pond anywhere near, she could drop the phone into it and hope it wasn't waterproof.

Maybe snow would do it?

Or perhaps she could pee on it? Would that be enough to destroy the blasted thing?

The seconds were ticking away, and she was running out of time. Soon, Vlad would overcome his stupor and come looking for her.

Glancing around, she caught the glint of water several feet away. It was only melted snow, but it was her only option.

Wendy made two steps in its direction when the phone rang, the sound piercing the quiet and making her heart leap out of her chest.

Panic choking her throat, she started running. And when she heard Vlad's boots pounding on the ground behind her, she hurled the device away from her with all the force she could muster.

Hitting a rock with a crunching sound, the phone bounced and landed somewhere she couldn't see.

As Wendy prayed that it was destroyed and wouldn't turn on, Vlad's arms shot around her from behind.

He lifted her up in the air and turned her to face him. His expression a mask of fury mixed with hurt, he held her suspended above the ground and away from him, her legs pedaling in the air. "What have you done?"

"Nothing." Tears started streaming down her cheeks. "I did nothing."

"Why did you steal my phone?"

"I wanted to call my father. I'm sorry. But I missed him, and I wanted to let him know that I was okay. He must be so worried about me."

Vlad's face twisted in a disgusted grimace. "You are lying." He dropped her carelessly and headed toward where the phone had landed.

Crumpling down to the ground, Wendy wept. She was so stupid. What had she thought would happen a moment after she'd succeeded in making the call?

What was Vlad going to do to her?

He picked up the broken device, but since his back was turned to her, she couldn't see what he was doing. Was the thing still functioning?

If she were smart, she would get herself off the ground and start running. Except, Vlad was incredibly fast. How had he managed to get to her so quickly?

He must have crossed a distance of at least two hundred feet in less than ten seconds. Her time perception must have gotten distorted because that wasn't humanly possible. Or perhaps he'd been much closer to her than she'd thought when the phone started ringing, and she hadn't heard him approach.

Except, that wasn't possible either unless he'd hovered above the ground. It was too quiet for her not to hear his boots crunching on the snow and the fallen twigs and leaves under it.

"It's still working." Vlad's words shattered the last of her hopes.

He turned around while returning the call. "Mey, we have a problem. Wendy stole my phone and called someone. She says she called her father, but I think she is lying."

Listening to him talk chilled her to the bone. He sounded so cold, so remote.

She'd expected hurt, anger, accusations, but this was much worse. Vlad had simply shut down. His face was expressionless as he looked down at her. "Mey is on her way to pick us up."

She nodded. "I'm sorry. It was a stupid thing to do."

He arched a brow. "Stupid? I wouldn't call it that. How long have you been planning to betray us, Wendy?"

48

VLAD

*A*s Wendy looked up at Vlad with a pair of teary eyes, his conviction of her guilt wavered.

Perhaps she'd really called her father because she missed him?

That would have been stupid, but not criminal.

Except, he'd clearly smelled the lie on her, and he wasn't even a good sniffer of emotions, which was painfully evident by the ease with which she'd managed to fool him.

Wendy had no feelings for him, and the reality-bending kiss they had shared was nothing more than his pheromones in action. He was so desperately attracted to her that some of it must have rubbed off on her, and that residual had been enough to evoke her passionate response.

And it had been passionate.

Wendy could have faked her feelings, but she couldn't have faked the flaring of her arousal. It had started as just a whiff, and when the kissing had gotten more intense, that scent had bloomed.

"I'm sorry," she whispered. "I had to."

He was about to ask why, and who she'd had to call so desperately, when the sound of a car engine diverted his attention.

They were about two hundred feet downhill from the road, so he couldn't see who it belonged to, but as it slowed down and then stopped, he figured it was Mey. All clan phones were equipped with excellent location trackers.

Vlad heard two doors open, and a moment later saw Mey and Bowen coming down the hill toward them.

Bowen cast Wendy a glare that could chill lava. "Did you find out who she called?"

Vlad shook his head and handed him the phone. "You can check the outgoing calls." The screen and the back cover were broken, but the device still worked.

As a Guardian, Bowen knew the override code to unlock every clan phone and didn't need Vlad's. Finding the outgoing call, he redialed it.

From the corner of his eye, Vlad saw Wendy drop her head between her knees and start shaking all over. Resisting the impulse to crouch next to her and take her into his arms, he looked away.

As Bowen put the call on speakerphone, it rang once, twice, and then it was answered by a recording. "This is Director Simmons. Please leave a message, and I will call you back as soon as I can. Have a pleasant day."

Was there a chance that the voice on the recorded message belonged to Wendy's father?

Given Mey and Bowen's angry expressions, it didn't seem so.

Her hands on her hips, Mey glared at Wendy. "You called the program's director? What possessed you to do that?"

Rocking back and forth, Wendy didn't look up and didn't answer either.

"Isn't it obvious?" Bowen sounded pissed. "She is a spy. We need to get out of here pronto." He handed Vlad his phone back and pulled out his own. "Leon. Put Richard and Ingrid in the car and drive down to Redlands. Wendy is a mole, and she ratted us out. They know our location."

"Aren't we going back to pack?" Mey asked.

"No time." Bowen lifted Wendy off the ground as if she was a sack of potatoes and threw her over his shoulder. "Damn." He shook his head. "I was looking forward to eating that roast." He started up the hill.

The Guardian was going to miss out on a tasty meal, but Vlad was going to miss so much more.

He'd been looking forward to a relationship with a girl that he'd thought liked him. Instead, he was left with an empty cavity where his feelings and hopes for Wendy had been.

Mey put her arm around him. "I'm so sorry, Vlad. She had us all fooled, including Edna."

He shook his head. "That's impossible. Edna is our judge, and everyone knows it's impossible to hide malevolent intentions from her."

With her arm still wrapped around him, Mey urged Vlad to keep going. "Wendy must have an additional talent she was hiding from us. She can mask her true emotions somehow."

"Edna's probe goes deep. I can't believe that she didn't sense anything."

"The best liars are those who believe in their own lies. Maybe that's Wendy's trick. She might have a split personality that she can control."

Vlad hadn't studied psychology, so he couldn't comment on Mey's hypothesis.

Explaining Wendy's actions away as a psychological problem could have eased the terrible sense of betrayal he felt, but it didn't help with the numbness that was spreading from his heart to the rest of his body.

Was that how grief felt?

What did humans do when they lost someone they cared about?

The only thing that came to mind was immersing himself in his art and his music or even baking. Anything that could take his mind off the pain would do.

"Can you tell Leon to grab my guitar? I don't care about the rest of the stuff. But I've had it for years, and I would hate to lose it."

49

KIAN

"You were right about the mole." Onegus walked into the war room with a grim expression on his face. "Wendy stole Vlad's phone and called the program's director. They left the cabin and are heading to Redlands."

Kian shook his head. "How the hell did she manage to fool Edna? I thought that her probe was infallible."

"That's not good," Turner muttered. "That cabin belongs to a friend of mine. I don't want him implicated." He pulled out his phone. "If you'll excuse me, I have damage control to take care of."

As Turner walked to the far corner of the room, Kian got up and started pacing. "Who called you? Was it Mey?"

"It was Bowen. He's asking what to do with Wendy."

"I think it's safe for them to get back to the keep. So far, Kalugal is keeping his promise not to interrogate Arwel, and Jin is verifying that no one else attempts to do so either. Once we trade her for Arwel, the threat to the village and the keep will be gone."

Onegus rubbed a hand over the back of his neck. "Let me check with Bowen first. It's not likely, but she might have given the director the keep's location as well. I'm not sure whether he and Leon bothered to blindfold the two humans when they left the keep."

"Tell Bowen that I authorize thralling her. He needs to know for sure whether the keep is safe." Kian raked his fingers through his hair. "I should have thought of that before. The Guardians should have thralled Richard and Wendy to forget where they've been."

"There was a lot going on."

"There still is." Kian walked over to the cooler and pulled out another bottle of beer.

It was his third that day, and it wasn't going to be the last. He and Turner were still working out the details of the exchange, and he planned on calling Kalugal again and continuing their negotiations.

They had settled the prisoner and hostage exchange, but there was so much more they needed to figure out going forward.

Naturally, now that they knew of each other's existence, things could never go back to the way they'd been. Rules of conduct had to be figured out, and safeguards had to be put in place on both sides.

If only there was a way to counteract Kalugal's compulsion, Kian would have felt much better about dealing with the guy. Kian hated the feeling of vulnerability and the fact that every conversation with his cousin required Turner's presence.

Dalhu had mentioned something about learning to resist Navuh's compulsion. But he'd been able to do that only after he'd been away from the island for a while. Navuh's daily devotions were designed to reinforce his hold over his people, and Dalhu remembered that his thought process had become clearer only after he'd been away for about six weeks.

It seemed that compulsion needed tending to, or its power dissipated over time. Generally speaking that was good news, but it wouldn't help Kian when he was face to face with Kalugal.

Onegus ended the call and walked over to Kian. "Bowen says that Wendy only told the director about the cabin and its location. She didn't even speak with him and only left a message on his voicemail."

"Give the director's number to Roni. Maybe he can do something about that voicemail. If we are lucky, the director hasn't had the chance to listen to his messages yet."

Onegus glanced at his watch. "She called him twenty minutes ago, so that's possible."

"Tell Roni to be careful. We don't want any breadcrumbs trail leading back to us."

"I will."

As the chief talked to Roni, Kian reached into his pocket and pulled out the box of cigarillos. Since Arwel had been taken, he was breaking every rule he'd made about smoking and was excusing his weakness as temporary. What made him feel even worse about it was his relief every time Syssi left the war room. It was the mark of a real addiction when he preferred the ability to light up to the company of his wife.

"Roni is on it," Onegus said. "If the director hasn't heard it yet, he's not going to."

"Tell Bowen to blindfold Wendy on the way back and lock her inside her room."

"What for? She can't go anywhere."

"Punishment. I want her to stew until I can talk to her." Kian lit up his cigarillo and took a puff. "I need to figure out what to do with her next, but I can't dedicate mental bandwidth to her issue while I'm dealing with Kalugal."

"We will need to get rid of her." Turner joined them next to the cooler. "We will give her some pocket change and dump her someplace. She can go back to the program."

Kian nodded. "It will be a shame to lose a potential Dormant, but just like

Eleanor, Wendy is a rotten apple, and there is no place for her kind in the clan. Naturally, we will have to thrall away her memory of us, and it is going to be a deep scrub. I hope she doesn't end up with brain damage, but I wouldn't get too worked up over it if she does."

Onegus leaned down and pulled out a bottle of water from the cooler. "There is no rush. We can let her stay in the keep for a little while and have her talk to Vanessa. Maybe the girl has issues that can be fixed. We shouldn't give up on a potential Dormant so quickly."

"Once a rotten apple, always a rotten apple." Turner pulled out a chair and straddled it. "I'm not a great believer in redemption. Then again, we need to investigate Wendy's reasons for doing what she has done. They might have been compelling. It reminds me of Sandoval's nephew. The kid had a legitimate reason for betraying his uncle, and after they ironed out their grievances, the two found a way to work together."

Kian lifted a brow. "So, what is your recommendation? You sound undecided, which is atypical for you."

"I want to hear her out first and then decide. In Eleanor's case, there were no redeeming qualities or extenuating circumstances, but there might be in Wendy's."

50

ARWEL

"You know what pisses me off?" Jacki sat on the couch and crossed her arms over her chest.

Arwel could have made a long list of things, but he wondered which item Jacki was choosing to focus on.

"How come my freaking foretelling didn't warn me about any of this? Before, when I got glimpses of things that were about to happen to other people, I assumed it was because their events were more interesting than mine. But I should have known it wasn't true. I didn't see the program in my future, and I definitely didn't see this." She waved her hand at the room. "It's not fair."

Arwel suspected that Jacki's motive for revealing her paranormal talent was to make herself seem more valuable to her captors. Was she worried about what would happen to her when she was left alone with Kalugal and his men?

He sat close to her on the couch and whispered in her ear, "If we can convince Jin not to do it, you won't be left alone in here."

Jacki wrapped her arm around him and put her head on his shoulder. "We don't know that she wants to do it. Your boss might be pressuring her."

"You know Jin. It's probably her idea, and it's a bad one."

"She loves you."

"And I love her, but she must realize that I can't have her sacrificing herself for me. If anything happens to her, I'm not going to survive it, so her sacrifice will be wasted." Hoping that Jin would hear him, Arwel intended to repeat the same thing over and over again. "Without her, I have no reason to go on."

Jacki sighed. "It's neither here nor there. We can't influence her decision."

"I can. If she tunes in and hears what I have to say, she might reconsider."

Looking up at where they suspected the hidden camera was, Jacki shook her head. "I don't think letting our jailers know how much you care for her is a good idea. You should pretend that she's nothing to you." She smirked. "Maybe we should pretend to be warming up to each other to confuse them."

"At this stage of the negotiations, it doesn't matter if they know that Jin is my mate. Her own freedom depends on her ability to release Kalugal, so it's not like they need to threaten to hurt me to make her do that."

"Yeah, I guess I've seen too many spy movies."

"I just want her to know that she is making a mistake. Once she walks in here, she might never come out." His gut twisted on itself, making him nauseous. "I'm never going to forgive Kian or her for doing this. What the hell are they thinking? Kalugal will not believe that she removed the tether, not even if he feels its absence. His best option is to keep her."

"But then he's not going to get Rufsur back, and he seems to like the guy."

Arwel glared at Jacki even though none of this was her fault. "If you were in his shoes, what would you do?"

"I wouldn't abandon my right-hand man."

Naturally, Jacki wasn't thinking strategically. She was thinking with her heart. Getting to know her better, Arwel realized that her rough exterior was a cover for a soft interior. Jacki was loyal, selfless, and she cared deeply about Jin and even about him.

"Kalugal is a calculating fellow. He will make his choice based on what serves him best, and he will choose Jin because she is a greater asset than Rufsur."

"Would you do that? Would you trade a good friend for a talented paranormal?"

"No, but I'm not Kalugal. The quest for wealth and power is not as important to me as it is to him."

"Let me translate it into terms that are more relevant to you. What if the paranormal was someone who could shield your people from Kalugal's compulsion? Would you trade your friend to gain that protection?"

"I might. But you are only reinforcing my point. Kalugal is going to keep Jin even if it means losing Rufsur. That's why the exchange is such a monumental mistake." He looked into Jacki's eyes, but saw Jin's instead. "Don't do that." And to emphasize, he added, "You think that you are doing this for me, but I don't want to lose you. I'm as good as dead without you. So, if you are hearing this, think again before doing something that I'm never going to forgive you for."

Jacki rolled her eyes. "How many times are you going to repeat the same thing in different words?"

"As many times as it takes. I don't know when she's following the tether to you, so I need to keep saying this like a gif on a loop."

"I should just write it on your T-shirt so she can see it through my eyes. Do you think the guard outside will bring us a pen if we ask for it?"

"I doubt it. He'd probably think that we want to use it as a weapon. Besides, Jin would not be the only one who would see the message." Arwel motioned at the camera. "I don't think Kalugal would allow me to keep the shirt if he saw what was written on it."

"You can turn around and sit on the bed facing the wall and your back to the camera."

Jacki's silly idea was meant to cheer him up, but he was too irate to even smile.

"Perhaps you can write the message on my back."

"Nah, then I won't be able to look at your beautiful eyes. They really are gorgeous. There was a guy in the program that had a similar eye color, but his looked dull compared to yours." She looked him up and down. "And the rest of him also paled in comparison to you. When you dress in clothes that actually fit you, you are one hell of a hunk." She waggled her eyebrows.

Jacki wasn't attracted to him. It was all an act, and not even a very convincing one, but it managed to amuse him despite his bad mood.

"I'm glad you approve."

"Oh, I do." She winked. "I think that you and Jin are perfect for each other."

"Good, for a moment there I thought that you were flirting with me."

"I was." She leaned back. "I need to relearn how to do that. I haven't flirted with anyone in ages."

"Your beauty does the work for you. All you need to do is be there, and guys will flock to you. Magnus had to tell the Guardians to ease up because you seemed bothered by all the attention."

"That was because I wasn't interested in any of them. It's never the guy I actually want to pay attention to me."

He arched a brow. "And who might that be?"

She waved a hand in dismissal. "I haven't met him yet, but if I do, I want to make sure that he notices me."

51

JIN

As Jin followed the tether to Jacki, Arwel looked straight at her through her friend's eyes, his own blazing with barely suppressed anger. "So, if you are hearing this, think again before doing something that I'm never going to forgive you for."

Gasping, she dropped the connection, and the waterworks started in earnest.

He'd sounded so vehement. What if he really wasn't going to forgive her? What if he dumped her?

It could happen.

Their bond hadn't solidified yet, which meant that they were not mated, and Arwel was free to leave her if he wanted.

Maybe he didn't mean it, and it was only worrying that had made him say that?

Perhaps if she kept on listening, she would hear him say something nice about her, like how much he loved her and appreciated what she was doing for him and his clan.

Instead, she heard Jacki tell him how beautiful his eyes were. Was her so-called friend trying to steal her man?

And what was even worse, Arwel seemed to be responding to Jacki's flirting.

"What's wrong?" Kri leaned over.

"Arwel is angry at me for agreeing to the exchange, and he says that he's never going to forgive me." Jin's chin quivered as more tears spilled out of her eyes. She wiped them off with the sleeve of Alena's sweater. "I don't know why I'm such a cry baby all of a sudden. I'm usually not like that."

"It's the stress." Kri patted her knee. "You are also tired. You should get some sleep."

"I tried. I'm too hyped for that." Jin took a shuddering breath.

She hated to admit her fears, but she needed to talk to someone who had insider information about immortal matings and how they worked from the immortal's point of view.

What was the bond supposed to feel like? How would she know that it was there?

Except, it might be different for a female immortal, and Kri's perspective might not explain what Arwel was or wasn't feeling.

Jin cast her a sidelong glance. The girl, or rather female, acted tough and had the muscles to back her swagger, but despite the breadth of her shoulders, Kri wasn't butch. She wore no makeup, and her clothing was appropriate for her Guardian job, but she softened the look with long hair that was kept in a tight braid, and a light-gray Henley shirt with sparkly buttons that she kept hidden under her leather jacket. Those small touches of femininity made a big difference.

"Arwel and Jacki seem to be getting very close," Jin said in a near whisper. "What if he chooses her over me? He said that our bond didn't solidify yet. Jacki is much prettier than me, and now that they are stuck together, he's definitely noticing her."

Kri shook her head. "Arwel is in love with you. He might like Jacki, he might even show appreciation for her good looks and her misguided heroics, but that's as far as it goes. You have nothing to worry about."

"You don't see them together as I do. They often sit with their arms around each other, and they whisper in each other's ears. I know it's necessary so they are not overheard, but still, they don't need to act so familiarly with one another. I wouldn't put my arm around my cousin and whisper in his ear so intimately, let alone a guy who I know is in a relationship with another woman."

Nodding, Kri twisted the end of her braid around her finger. "I get why you are upset. I would be too. But I'm certain that there is nothing romantic going on between them. I watched Arwel with you. His entire expression changed every time you entered the room."

"Really?" Jin grabbed a tissue and blew her nose.

Kri smiled. "Really. I'm not one to make things up even for a good cause. While all the unmated males were flirting with Jacki, Arwel hardly spared her a glance."

"Things might have changed in captivity. They only have each other, and as you've pointed out, she also tried to save him, which he is surely grateful for. That's enough to spark something that wasn't there before."

The Guardian shook her head. "I've known Arwel for many years, and he is like a brother to me. Most of my Guardian training was with him, and after that, we served together. Since meeting you, he is not the same man that he was before. He's smiling more, and that damn perpetually suffering expression is gone from his face. I haven't seen him get drunk even once, while before he met you the guy was sober only when going out on missions. Do you really think that anything short of falling in love could have made such a change?"

"Mey made a similar comment. She said that Arwel had the tormented artist look."

"You see? Your sister noticed the same thing." Kri let go of her braid and leaned back in the seat. "Feeling better?"

"Much. Thank you."

"Any time. Now try to get some sleep." The Guardian closed her eyes.

Following Kri's example, Jin lowered the back of her seat and closed her eyes, but instead of dozing off, she followed the tether to Jacki once more.

"I'm scared." Arwel looked into Jacki's eyes. "We haven't seen Kalugal even once since he brought us here, and I can't access his emotional grid without him being close. I don't know what his intentions are."

"It's obvious. He wants to get rid of the tether."

"The question is how far is he willing to go to accomplish that. He might decide that killing Jin is the most expedient way to do so, and there is nothing I can do to stop him."

"You can't, but your friends can. You heard what Rufsur said."

Arwel rubbed his temples between two fingers. "As we've seen, the best plans can go to shit. There are no guarantees."

"That's life. As an immortal, you are not as vulnerable, so you don't experience it as acutely as I do as a human, but I know that my life can get snuffed out in an instant. Except, I don't dwell on it because that would be paralyzing. I just do what I can to survive and hope for the best."

"If I lose Jin, I don't want to survive. I can't go on without her."

The sheen of tears in his eyes cut into Jin's heart, and if she could, she would have used Jacki's arms to embrace him and comfort him.

But Jacki didn't need her to animate her arms. Reaching for Arwel, she wrapped them around him. "Have faith. Everything will turn out okay. I promise."

"How can you promise that?" He leaned his forehead against hers. "Did you have a vision?"

"No, but I have a good gut feeling, and I don't get those often. I'm a glass-half-empty kind of girl, and I usually brace for the worst."

52

KIAN

Unease churning in his stomach, Kian paced the length of the war room. Ever since he'd laid out the exchange plan for Kalugal, he had a niggling feeling that they were forgetting something important.

With Turner there, Kian should have felt more confident, but no one was infallible, and they were dealing with an unknown.

Given the circumstances, Kalugal had been a reasonable and agreeable negotiation partner, but that didn't mean that he was a good guy, or that he had nothing sinister and underhanded planned.

After all, Kalugal was Navuh's son, which meant that he was smart, ruthless, and had questionable morals at best, none at worst.

Lokan was Navuh's son as well, and he wasn't all bad, but he wasn't good either. He'd had no qualms about sacrificing Ella and Vivian to achieve his objective, and Kian was certain that Kalugal wouldn't hesitate to sacrifice Jin as well as his lieutenant to achieve his.

They had put in place every safeguard imaginable, but the trade was not as fail-proof as Kian would have liked it to be.

"Do you have any plans to use Lokan?" Syssi asked.

"I'm keeping him as backup. I'd rather not expose his involvement with the clan yet."

Syssi shook her head. "Lokan is playing a dangerous game. He is living with an immortal female. How long does he think he can keep it a secret? We need to bring him and Carol in."

"Not yet." Kian pulled out a chair next to his wife. "When it gets hot for him, and there is no other choice, I'll do that. But in the meantime, he is our ears and eyes on the island. The sense of security it gives me is too precious to give up. If Navuh ever plans something big against the clan, I want to know about it ahead of time. This could make the difference between surviving an attack and not."

"We could pretend to have captured Lokan," Turner said. "Which isn't a lie because we did. You can tell Kalugal that you are holding his brother prisoner. That should be a better deterrent than holding his second-in-command hostage."

"I'm not sure about that." Kian crossed his arms over his chest. "Kalugal's lieutenant has been by his side since the very beginning, and Jin says that he seems fond of him. Lokan might as well be a stranger, and they have never interacted before as brothers or even as members of the Brotherhood. Back then, Kalugal was a young and unimportant commander, while Lokan was already at the top of the Brotherhood's hierarchy."

Turner looked skeptical. "Still, Lokan is his one real brother, son of Kalugal's mother. That carries a lot of weight. I think Lokan would be as important to Kalugal as Rufsur, and having two hostages is better than one."

If Turner thought it was a good idea, Kian wasn't going to argue against it. "Let's see what Lokan thinks about it." He pulled out his phone and placed the call.

"Hello, Kian. I was wondering when you were going to call me with instructions. Carol and I are sitting in the hotel room and biting our nails."

"No, we are not." Carol laughed. "We've been busy doing other things."

Lokan cleared his throat. "Magnus told us that the trade is happening tonight."

"How can we help?" Carol asked.

"That's what I'm calling about. We had an idea to use you as a fake hostage. We can claim that we captured you, and if your brother kills Jin, we will kill you. We won't do that, of course, but Kalugal doesn't know that."

"He won't care. I doubt that he even remembers what I look like."

"You are still his one and only brother, and you are the son of his mother. Part of the deal was to let Kalugal talk with Areana after the trade was made, and even though he tried to hide it, he seemed eager for that. He cares about her, and he wouldn't want to be responsible for the anguish your death would bring her."

"Frankly, I can't predict what Kalugal would do because I don't know him. But I'm willing to put on an act in exchange for another foundation stone for my home in the village."

At his core Lokan was an opportunist, who always looked for his angle in the game, but at least he was upfront about it, and so far he'd helped whenever Kian had asked him to.

"At this rate, you'll have your house ready in no time. But you can't move in until you move out from your island home, and neither of us is interested in that. Not yet."

"I'm playing the long game. But that's not my only motivation. If my mother knows what's going on, which I'm sure she does because Annani keeps her updated, she is probably worried, and she'd appreciate it if I help in any way I can. If you want to offer me in exchange for Arwel, I will gladly do that."

Carol gasped. "No way."

"Relax, darling. Kalugal is not going to harm me. Why would he?"

"Because you are first in line for the throne, so to speak. You are the first-born son."

"Kalugal claims that he is not interested in the island," Kian said. "He says that it's Lokan's for the taking."

"And you believe him?" Carol asked.

"I do. I have a feeling that Kalugal has bigger plans than the island, and I would love to find out what they are."

"If you trade me for Arwel and Jacki, I can get Kalugal talking."

"I appreciate the offer, but Kalugal's top priority is to get rid of the tether."

"Or the spy who holds it," Lokan said.

"He offered to mate her."

"What?" Carol grabbed the phone from Lokan. "Jin is already mated."

"Kalugal doesn't know that, and I didn't volunteer the information. As long as he believes that it's a possibility, he won't do anything rash. I don't want him to feel cornered."

"But you didn't agree to that, right?"

Kian smiled as he imagined the ferocious expression on Carol's cherubic face. "I told him that it wasn't going to happen and that political marriages are a thing of the past. But he might still think of it as an option, and I prefer to leave it at that."

"It's actually not a bad idea," Lokan said.

"How can you say such a thing?" Carol seethed. "What if Kian offered me as a political bride. Would you be okay with that too?"

"No, but that's different."

"How so?"

"Arwel isn't me, and Jin isn't you. Maybe they are not fated mates."

Kian cleared his throat. "You can keep arguing after we end the call. Just be ready to get picked up."

"Carol is not coming with me." Lokan's tone no longer sounded amused.

"Of course not. She can stay at the hotel."

"Like hell!" Carol exploded. "I'm going with you."

53

JIN

"Can you turn the heat on?" Jin huddled inside Alena's coat.

Gregor glanced at her in the rearview mirror. "It's boiling in here."

Jin had expected the weather to be more forgiving in San Francisco, but as soon as the pilot had opened the jet's door, she'd been blasted with a cold gust that had taken her breath away. Luckily, crossing the distance to Gregor's car had taken only a couple of minutes, but unluckily, he hadn't turned the heat on, or rather not enough to keep her warm.

"Jin is sick." Kri reached for the control and turned up the heat. "Take your coat off if you're too hot." She shrugged her leather jacket off and tossed it on the back seat.

Jin pulled it over her knees. "Can we stop at a CVS? I need to load up on meds."

Gregor shook his head. "I'd rather not. Turner gave me instructions to drive through the mall, but that's only to make sure we don't have a tail. I don't want to stop."

Kri turned around to face Jin. "Call Vivian and tell her what you need. She can get it for you."

"That's a great idea. I'll text her the list."

Thanks to Kri, Jin hadn't left her purse behind in the club and could pay Vivian back. She hadn't spent any of the pocket money Kian had given her before the mission.

"How are you going to use Turner's maneuver?" Kri asked. "Did you leave another car in the mall?"

"Turner arranged everything. He had a rental car delivered to the mall's parking lot. It has a coded lock, and I have the numbers."

"Cool." Kri leaned back. "Don't you love modern technology? Next thing we know, there will be services delivering driverless cars to us that we can activate from our phones. Like Uber or Lyft, but without the driver."

"I think they already have those in Europe," Jin said. "Personally, though, I don't trust machines that much. Computers malfunction, and I don't want to be stuck inside a driverless car when that happens."

Kri turned around and smiled. "Then you're not going to like living in the village. Our cars take over a few miles before we get home, and the windows automatically turn opaque. It's a safety precaution so if a clan member gets captured he or she can't reveal the village's location."

"So how come Arwel knows it?"

"He is a head Guardian," Gregor said. "And so is Kri. They and the council members are the only ones who know the exact location of the village and the codes to open the underground tunnel. They should have never been allowed anywhere near Kalugal. That was one hell of a costly mistake."

Kri nodded. "He is right."

It was comforting to realize that the mess wasn't entirely her fault, and that Kian and Turner shared in the blame. Then again, nothing could have kept Arwel away from her while she'd tethered Kalugal, so it was back on her. Or was it on Arwel?

Heck, it was everyone's and no one's fault.

"Yamanu is a head Guardian too," Kri said, "but in his case Kian didn't have a choice. We don't have anyone else who can shroud such a large area and thrall so many humans at once."

"Yamanu is careful," Gregor said. "He is staying as far as he can from Kalugal's place while maintaining the shroud, and he has earplugs in."

After changing cars in the mall's parking lot, they continued out of the city for another half an hour or so, and when Gregor parked in front of the motel, it was after seven in the evening.

The place looked like it wasn't ready to receive guests yet, but all Jin cared about was crawling under the blanket and putting her head on a pillow. She was sleep-deprived, sick, and she had a long night in front of her.

Talk about bad timing.

Maybe Kalugal could wait until morning?

Except, even if he did, Kian wanted to make the trade at night. Besides, despite how exhausted she was, Jin doubted that she could sleep.

When Kri opened the back door and offered her a hand up, she reluctantly accepted it. "I feel like an old woman." She didn't object when the Guardian wrapped her arm around her middle and propped her up.

"I don't know how an old woman feels, but the doctor said that you'll be fine in a day or two."

Poor Kri. She was trying to be supportive, and she was incredibly helpful, but she had no idea what it felt like to be so weak and helpless. Immortals never got sick, and Kri was in top physical shape.

"After this is all over, I want to join your self-defense class. I need to get stronger."

Kri grinned. "Awesome."

The door to one of the ground floor rooms opened, and Vivian stepped out. "Welcome to our home away from home." She waved them over.

As soon as they reached her, Vivian lifted her hand and put it on Jin's forehead. "I got you the NyQuil and DayQuil that you asked for, and I also got you chicken soup."

"Thank you." Jin offered her a placid smile.

Inside, the room was much nicer than the exterior of the motel had suggested. There were two full beds, a table with three chairs, and a door that was opened to the adjacent room.

"Magnus and I are right over there." Vivian pointed. "As soon as I heard that you were coming back, I moved the Guardians who were staying here into another room." She took Jin's hand and led her to the dining table. "Eat your soup before it gets cold."

"Thank you for warming the room up." Jin took her coat off and draped it over the back of the chair. "And for everything else."

Vivian patted her arm. "I haven't been immortal long enough to forget how it feels to have a damn cold."

As Jin sat down, the door opened, and Carol came in. "Miss me?" She walked over and gave Jin a hug and a kiss on the cheek. "I heard that you were sick."

Jin nodded. "I'm so glad to see you, but what are you doing here?"

Carol pulled out a chair and sat down. "Kian, or rather Turner, wanted Lokan to be on standby in case his compulsion ability was needed. We flew overnight and stayed at a nice hotel." She looked around the room. "Much nicer than this place. But anyway, Kian came up with the idea to use Lokan as an additional hostage. Not for real, of course, but just as more leverage on Kalugal."

"Eat your soup." Vivian pointed at the takeout container and then turned to Kri. "There is enough for you too."

"Bleh." Kri took her leather jacket off and dropped it on one of the beds. "I hate the stuff."

Jin wasn't crazy about chicken soup either. Her mother, who also believed in its supposed healing power, had fed it to Jin and Mey not only when they'd gotten sick, but also as a preemptive measure nearly every winter day.

Needless to say, they both grew to hate it.

"I'll have some." Carol reached for the second container. "Does it come with noodles or matzo balls?"

"Noodles," Vivian said.

Jin removed the lid from the container and picked up the plastic spoon that came with the meal.

Fighting nausea, she put a spoonful in her mouth and tried not to gag. It wasn't the soup's fault. The broth was only a little too salty, and the noodles were quite good, but her stomach's churning had little to do with the food.

She was worried, stressed and tired, but she didn't want to repay Vivian's kindness with rudeness. She could force down a few spoonfuls before excusing herself, getting into one of the beds, and crawling under the blanket.

54

KALUGAL

Kalugal brought up the feed from the camera scanning the front yard. "What do you think about the gazebo for my meeting with the spy?"

Rufsur leaned over his shoulder. "Your cranky cousin might object because of the roof. His snipers wouldn't have a clear shot at your head."

Kalugal turned and smiled at his friend. "So, it occurred to you too that he is likely to use drones?"

"They are not going to sit on top of our fence where we can take them out easily, and other than that, there is no conveniently available spot. There are no utility poles or even street lamps to perch on top of. So, unless he brings in a crane or two, drones are his best option."

Kalugal leaned back in his chair and gazed at his front yard, following the surveillance camera as it swiveled around. It was beautifully done, and the landscaping was perfect. There were no tall trees for anyone to hide in, only flowers and bushes that were artfully arranged.

Regrettably, he wasn't set up for offense, and he didn't have drones. His men were stationed on the roof of the house, exposed to Kian's remote-controlled equipment.

He was at a disadvantage, and they both knew that.

His setup was defensive, with state-of-the-art security systems, a bunker that could withstand bombing, and a couple of short escape routes. His men had the best rifles money could buy and an assortment of cold weapons, but that was the extent of it.

Was Kian better equipped?

He could only speculate, but it made sense that the clan would be better armed than he was, even if it was only to defend themselves. Kalugal doubted that his father had eased up on his efforts to eliminate his archnemesis and her progeny.

They needed to be prepared.

Kalugal, on the other hand, had managed to fly under his father's radar. Or so he hoped. Evidently, his mother didn't believe that he had perished during WWII, and she'd probably shared her thoughts with her mate, which made Kalugal wonder why Navuh had never come after him or at least tried to find him.

If Kian had located him, then Navuh could have done so as well.

"What do you want to do with the gazebo?" Rufsur asked.

"I want it to be set up nicely as if it's a romantic date. I'll call Kian to finalize the details of the trade and to let him know that my men are going to venture outside to prepare the gazebo for the meeting. I want the spy to be comfortable and relaxed. I don't know much about her ability, but she will have an easier time if she isn't stressed."

"Got it." Rufsur winked. "A tablecloth for the table, soft cushions for the chairs, candles, wine, a fancy midnight snack. The works."

The bunker was accessible through a tunnel from inside the house, and that was how his men were going to leave the bunker and come back.

The access was set up with a double door system that was controlled from inside the bunker during a lockdown, so getting in without invitation was nearly impossible. The foot-thick reinforced doors could withstand explosives, and the mechanism operating them was just as secure.

With the right equipment, Kian could potentially blow up the first door or the walls around it, but that would be as far as he would get.

The moment the first barrier was breached, all hell would rain down on those trying to cross the distance to the other door. They would be buried alive, and then burned to a crisp. Not even immortals could survive that.

"What about the lights?" Rufsur asked. "We can put on strong ones so the entire front yard is bright and Kian is happy or soft ones that will make the mood more romantic."

"Even if he uses drones, he has no need for strong lights, or any. They are equipped with night vision."

"Just in case, ask him. I don't want a trigger-happy immortal to freak out and activate the drone's guns. Especially since they will be aimed at your head."

Kalugal nodded. "I'll do that." He pulled his phone out and placed the call to Kian.

"Good evening, cousin." As usual, Kian's voice was gruff, but by now Kalugal realized that it didn't mean that he was angry. That was his normal speaking voice.

A charmer, he was not.

"I want to iron out all the small details. Looking at my front yard, I decided that the gazebo would be a nice place to conduct my meeting with Jin. I need to send my men out to set the place up, so don't shoot at them."

"I'll let the field commander know. What else?"

This confirmed Kalugal's suspicion that Kian wasn't in the area and was managing everything from the clan's central location, wherever that might be.

That was not so good, but Kalugal could work with that. The good news was that Kian hadn't objected to the gazebo idea.

"The lighting. Do you want me to turn on the floodlights, or will soft illumination suffice?"

Kian chuckled. "Are you planning a romantic dinner?"

"I want Jin to feel comfortable. If she is stressed, she might not be able to access her talent. We all know that paranormal abilities require a calm mind and concentration. I have heaters in the gazebo, so she'll be warm, and I'll have the table set up for a midnight snack. I'm just being a gracious host."

"I bet. Do whatever you want with the lights. It doesn't make a difference to us."

"I figured that your drones were equipped with night vision."

"Good guess. But what would immortal warriors need with night vision equipment? We can see perfectly well in starlight."

"You've just confirmed my suspicion that you're not in the area. It's cloudy here tonight, and visibility is minimal, even for immortals."

"It will do."

"Of course. Your drones will be equipped with night vision."

55

KIAN

Kian cast a quick glance at Turner, who shrugged and mouthed, "Smart guy."

"What makes you think we will be using drones?"

"It's obvious. Where are you going to hide your snipers? The trees in the neighbors' houses are not tall enough or strong enough to provide support for a grown man or even a slight woman, and sitting on top of my fence would leave your men exposed. If I were you, I would employ drones."

Kian wondered if Kalugal even had them. He didn't engage in offensive or recon operations, so he had no use for such sophisticated equipment. Still, given the guy's penchant for expensive toys, he might have invested in a drone or two just because he had the money to throw around.

"For someone who is engaged mainly in accumulating wealth, you are very well informed about the latest in weaponry. Are you dealing in that as well?"

Kalugal chuckled. "No, cousin. I don't deal in weapons, or drugs, or prostitution, or anything else you might sneer at."

"If you were dealing only in stocks and shares, you wouldn't have needed a bunker."

"Did you forget that I am a fugitive? My father is most likely still looking for me, and I need to protect myself."

"That seems like a waste of resources. I know what it costs to build a bunker that size. What else are you doing in there?"

"That's my business, Kian."

"As long as you don't keep slaves down there or produce meth, I don't really care."

"I can assure you that I don't engage in either of those activities. I'm a collector, and I like to keep my treasures in a controlled environment and safe from theft and vandalism. Does that satisfy your curiosity?"

"Partly. It's good to know that you're not doing anything illegal."

Kalugal chuckled. "I wouldn't go that far. Some of the things I have in here should be in a museum, and the countries they've been collected from don't allow their extraction, but since I paid for their discovery, I think they belong to me."

"That's an interesting hobby."

"You have no idea."

So far, the things Kian was slowly discovering about Kalugal were encouraging.

The guy wanted to make Jin comfortable, which meant that he wasn't planning on killing her. It seemed like he was still entertaining the idea of charming her into mating him.

His cousin was a dishonest businessman, gaining an unfair advantage by getting insider information about mergers and acquisitions before they were publicly announced, but he wasn't a murderer, a drug dealer, or a trafficker. His artifact hobby was of no interest to Kian, and he didn't care which laws Kalugal was breaking to smuggle them out of the countries he'd collected them in.

If that was all the case, and there were no hidden skeletons in the guy's closet, Kian would have no problem forging an alliance with him.

"When we can talk more leisurely, I would love to hear more about your hobby. I bet you have many fascinating stories about the things you've found."

"With pleasure."

Was it Kian's imagination or had Kalugal sounded eager for a meeting that had nothing to do with the crisis they were dealing with?

Time would tell.

For now, they had to discuss the details of the exchange. "We need to decide on the exact sequence of who comes out first and with whom."

Kalugal chuckled. "I'm sure you have it all figured out."

"Obviously. You will send your lieutenant out first, on his own. When we have him in our custody, the field commander will escort Jin to your gate, where you and Arwel will be waiting. Arwel and Jin will exchange places, you escort Jin to your pavilion, and hopefully the whole fiasco will be over in less than an hour."

Kian hadn't mentioned Lokan yet, and he was wondering if he should do that now or right before the exchange took place.

Truth be told, he was reluctant to issue the threat. It had been difficult to pretend that he would hurt Areana if any harm befell Jin, not only because it was a lie, but because so far Kalugal had acted in a very civilized way. Kian didn't want to burn the tenuous bridge they had built between them by also threatening to kill the guy's brother.

Perhaps he should discuss it with Turner and Syssi first. Turner's talent was clarity as to the advantages and disadvantages of such a step, while Syssi's talent was understanding the emotional impact such a threat might have on Kalugal, and how it could affect his decisions.

Kalugal snorted. "This situation reminds me of the riddle about the farmer who has a goat, a cabbage, and a wolf, and needs to cross the river with all three but can only take one at a time. If he takes the cabbage and leaves the wolf and the goat behind, the wolf is going to eat the goat. If the goat and the cabbage are left alone, the goat will eat the cabbage. How does he do it?"

"I know the solution to the riddle, but who is the wolf, the cabbage, and the goat in our story, and how does the analogy fit?"

"If I send out Rufsur together with Arwel, Rufsur might be armed and kill Jin in passing, that's why you want me to send him out first. You don't want him anywhere near her until your men have searched him and made sure that he is unarmed. So, he is the wolf, and Jin is the goat. I guess that makes Arwel the cabbage."

"I don't think he would appreciate the analogy. But you are right about my motive for requesting that your man come out first."

"I'm not going to kill your spy. But we've already covered that, and I don't like repeating myself."

56

JIN

"Once we get out of the car, put these in." Magnus handed Jin a set of high-quality earplugs. "Keep them in until you pass Arwel."

She nodded. "This is so Kalugal can't compel me to come to him before releasing Arwel."

"Precisely." He put his hand on her shoulder. "How are you holding up?"

Jin had taken four Motrins before leaving the motel, and she was wearing Alena's warm coat over a thick sweater, but she was still shivering.

"I think that the sanctuary's doctor has no experience in treating humans. The last time I ran a high fever that Motrin couldn't take care of, it was a case of strep throat. I might need antibiotics." She huddled inside the coat. "I can't stop shivering."

Magnus cast her a worried glance. "Why didn't you say so before? We need to postpone the trade."

Jin shook her head. "I want this to be over already. Then I'll see a human doctor, get the medication I need, and spend a week in bed. Since this nightmare began, I haven't slept for more than one hour straight. I'm exhausted, but I can't fall asleep."

"The adrenaline is keeping you going." Magnus reached for the pack of bottled water he'd put on the back seat. "Vivian told me to keep you hydrated."

"Thank you."

Sweet Vivian. She'd fussed around Jin, trying to get her to rest and relax. She'd also fed her chicken soup until Jin refused to take another spoonful. Not only had it not done any good, it had made things worse.

She felt as if there was a gallon of soup sloshing around in her stomach, and it was a struggle to keep it down. If she didn't hate barfing as much as she did, she would have excused herself to the bathroom and puked it all out in the toilet.

"Can you take a deep breath, or are you too congested?"

"Too congested." She smiled at him. "Were you going to suggest a relaxation technique?"

"It works." He demonstrated. "Breathe in as deeply as you can, hold it for a couple of seconds, and then release the air through your mouth." He produced a whoosh sound while doing just that.

"I'll give it a try."

They were parked outside the house they'd stayed in before, waiting for the show to begin.

Precisely at midnight, Kalugal was going to send out his right-hand man, and once the guy was in the Guardians' custody, they were going to bring him into the house to search him more thoroughly before taking him to the motel. After that was done, Magnus would drive up to Kalugal's gate and wait for it to open.

When Kalugal showed up with Arwel, Magnus was going to escort Jin to the midpoint, and then walk back together with Arwel.

After that, she would be on her own.

Jin wasn't sure what she dreaded more, seeing the angry look in Arwel's eyes or being left alone with Kalugal and his compulsion power. After experiencing its effects once, she never wanted to be in that helpless and hopeless situation again.

Having someone else take control of her body had been awful, and that was when all she'd suffered through was being stuck in a crouch and unable to move or talk.

If Kalugal was the vindictive type, he could compel her to strip naked in front of his men, and she would do that. Except, right now, what bothered her most about that scenario was not the nudity but the cold.

Just thinking about being naked made her shiver.

"What's wrong?" Magnus looked at her with worried eyes. "Are you feeling worse?"

"No." She sighed. "I'm just having silly thoughts that are not helping me to calm down. Do you know any jokes? I need something to distract me."

He chuckled. "As of late, my arsenal is comprised solely of lame dad jokes."

The funny thing was that Magnus sounded more proud of it than embarrassed.

"Perfect. That's exactly what I need."

"Okay." He grinned. "Tell me something, how does a penguin build its house?"

"Makes a hole in the snow?"

"Igloos it together."

Jin's laughter opened the floodgates to Magnus's store of lame jokes.

"Why is Peter Pan always flying?"

"Because he can?"

"He never lands."

57

ARWEL

Jacki looked at her watch. "It's almost time."

Arwel took her hand and clasped it between his two. "I hate leaving you alone here."

She gave him an unconvincing smile. "I'll be fine for the one hour tops that it will take Jin to convince Kalugal that the tether is gone. He's going to release me right after that."

They both knew that it was the best-case scenario and that not everything was going to work as planned. Hopefully, it would be limited to small bumps in the road, like Jin taking longer than they thought it would, or Kalugal coming up with more demands at the last moment.

Arwel didn't even want to contemplate the worst case scenario.

When the door opened, he was surprised to see Rufsur walk in. "Aren't you supposed to get ready to leave?"

Was Kalugal planning to trick them and send another man? That hadn't occurred to him, but if Kalugal planned on killing Jin, he might have decided to send someone he considered disposable.

"I'm leaving in a few minutes." He rubbed his hand over the back of his neck. "I came to say goodbye to Jacki." He took a step toward her. "After this is over, we are not going to see each other again. Not unless we want to, that is. I was wondering whether you'd had time to consider my proposition to meet me for a dinner or a drink somewhere."

Jacki shook her head. "I'm afraid that won't be possible for reasons that have nothing to do with you."

The smile evaporated from Rufsur's face. "I see. Well, it was worth a try."

Jacki got up and put a hand on his arm. "I'm not giving you an excuse. I'm not from around here, and right now, my life is one big mess. I don't have a job or a place to stay, and until that is taken care of, I can't afford to date. If I could, I would have said yes."

"Then say yes. I can help you solve all of those problems. With me, you wouldn't need to pay for anything. I'm old school."

Jacki smiled sadly. "I like that about you, and I hope that it will help you understand the main reason why I can't date you. You are an immortal, and I am human. If I were the kind of girl who is fine with short-term flings, I would have taken you up on your offer in a heartbeat. But I'm the type who is only interested in a life-long commitment, and that's impossible for us."

"I understand." Rufsur turned to Arwel. "What are you going to do with Jacki? She knows about immortals, but she can't be thralled or compelled to forget what she knows."

The guy sounded worried for her, which was touching. Maybe after Jacki was free, he would tell the guy that she was a possible Dormant and might turn immortal. But not as long as she was still a captive. Her chances of release would turn to zero.

"We trust her. Jacki has proved herself as a valuable member of our team."

Rufsur lifted a brow. "You didn't tell her what you were."

"No, but she also tried to save me. Don't worry about her." Arwel looked at Jacki. "Your future is secure with the clan."

"Do you have other humans living with you?" Rufsur still sounded doubtful, and rightfully so.

"One, and he was an immune as well."

"Was?"

The guy didn't miss much. No wonder Kalugal had made him his right-hand man.

"He still is. I meant to say that we let him in on the secret even though we knew he was immune. The guy is a strategic genius, and he is very good at keeping secrets. He's been an invaluable addition to the clan."

Turner was also immortal now, but he had known their secret long before approaching Kian and asking to attempt transition.

Rufsur frowned. "Don't tell me that Kian appointed a human as his second-in-command."

Kian must have told Kalugal that Turner was on standby, ready to take over for Kian if Kalugal attempted to compel him.

"Kian doesn't have a second-in-command. The guy I'm talking about is an outside contractor. We've used his services many times in the past, and apparently Kian asked for his help in this. He is definitely capable of taking over for Kian if needed."

Rufsur shook his head. "I can't believe that you let a human reach such a vital position in your organization." He glanced at his watch. "But that's a conversation for another time." He smiled at Arwel. "If your friends are not going to lock me up in a cellar, we can continue our talk while the spy does her thing."

Arwel offered Rufsur his hand. "Gladly."

58

KALUGAL

In a rare display of affection, Kalugal embraced Rufsur and clapped him on the back. "I owe you for this."

Rufsur chuckled. "You bet. I get to choose next month's hunting grounds."

"You've got it."

"It's five minutes to midnight." Phinas punched in the code to open the first door leading to the tunnel.

"Good luck with the spy," Rufsur said as he walked out.

"You too."

Kalugal waited until Phinas closed the door and then headed back to his office. Bringing up the camera feeds, he watched Rufsur make his way into the house, then walk out the side door and stride toward the gate.

"Now?" Phinas asked.

"Open the gate."

Two men were on the roof, and three more were out in the gazebo, preparing the place for his meeting with the spy. The two on the roof had their rifles aimed at the gate, and those in the gazebo carried an assortment of cold and hot weapons.

It was more for show than anything else.

Kian's drones were hovering over the grounds and could take out any of them in an instant.

The truth was that they were outclassed, and the only real advantage they had was the bunker, where they could hole up for months if needed. Except Kian didn't know that, and it was crucial that he remain ignorant as to Kalugal's real military power.

As per their agreement, Kian's men waited for Rufsur across the street, and the first thing they did when he reached them was to frisk him.

That had been expected, and Rufsur had nothing on him aside from a phone, which they examined as well.

One of the men lifted it in the air and then made a show of putting it on the sidewalk.

Careful bastards. But then Kalugal would have done the same. Aside from providing its location, which was damaging enough on its own, all kinds of damage could be done with something as small as a cellphone. Its electronics could be replaced with powerful explosives, which Rufsur could have potentially activated once he reached their headquarters.

A van pulled up to the curb, blocking the view, but when it pulled out, Rufsur and Kian's men were gone.

"Time for stage two." Kalugal swiveled his chair to face Phinas. "Get Arwel and put restraints on him. I'll meet you at the entrance to the tunnel."

"What about the blindfold?"

"Wait for me to get there before you put it on him. I want to talk to him first."

"Won't it be a violation of your agreement with Kian?"

"I just want to say goodbye and apologize for the inconvenience."

Phinas arched a brow. "Regardless of your good intentions, it might be seen as a breach."

Kalugal clapped him on the back. "Don't worry about it."

"Yes, sir."

That was the good thing about Phinas. He knew when to quit arguing and just do as he was told.

Shrugging on his wool jacket, Kalugal took a quick glance at his hazy reflection in the monitor. It had been a very long time since anyone other than his men had seen his real face, and it felt odd to proceed without shrouding himself in one of his guises. It was like going out naked in public, exposed, even vulnerable.

He shook his head.

Habits were stronger than willpower, hijacking a person's brain, or rather circumventing it. Sometimes it was beneficial, like always putting his car keys in the same place so he didn't need to dedicate any cognitive bandwidth to locating them. But the habit of always wearing a shroud made him anxious about being seen, and that was detrimental to his self-perception.

When Kalugal got to the tunnel's door, Phinas had already put handcuffs on Arwel's wrists and was now attaching shackles to his ankles.

Looking at Kalugal, Arwel lifted his hands. "Is this really necessary?"

"I don't want you to run for it the moment we open the gate. But if you are uncomfortable with the restrains, I can compel you to move only when I say so."

Arwel dropped his hands. "I prefer the shackles."

"That's what I thought. I will also need to blindfold you."

"How am I going to walk out like that?"

"I'll lead you, and once we are outside, I'll remove the blindfold. You can walk with the shackles, and once the spy is inside my property, I'll toss the keys to your friends."

Arwel let out a breath. "It's not like I have a choice in the matter." He pinned Kalugal with a hard stare. "A word of warning. If you harm a hair on Jin's head, I will come after you. I don't care how long it takes, or what I have to do, but I'll have my vengeance."

Kalugal had expected a warning regarding the immune who stayed behind, but not regarding the spy, and certainly not the vehemence with which it had been delivered.

Suddenly, the pieces of the puzzle fell into place.

Jacki wasn't Arwel's girlfriend, or even someone he was interested in. The spy was. He had risked exposure and jumped the shooter not to protect Jacki, but to protect Jin, which meant that she wasn't immortal. Otherwise, Arwel would not have been so desperate to protect her because even if she got shot, nothing serious would have happened to her.

Kalugal shook his head. "Loving a human female is a mistake, my friend. You shouldn't have allowed yourself to fall for her. I will not harm her, you have my word, but she will get old and eventually die, leaving you heartbroken."

"I'll treasure every moment I have with her."

The man was a fool, but supposedly love did that to people. Kalugal had never experienced it, so he couldn't judge Arwel.

"Best of luck with that." He clapped the guy on his back. "Before Phinas puts the blindfold on you, I just wanted to offer my apologies for your brief imprisonment. No hard feelings, eh?"

"That depends on whether Jin comes back unharmed. If all I suffer at your hands is a short rest in your bunker, then we are good."

59

JIN

As Jin waited for the gate to open, the adrenaline in her system kept her legs from turning into jelly, but it also made her heart thud loudly in her chest. If she weren't so young, she would have feared heart failure.

Then again, young people died from heart problems, and she might have an undiagnosed condition.

Stop it.

The last thing she needed was to pile on more stress. She was at the end of her rope, operating on fumes and holding on by a thread.

Finally, the gate started moving, and Jin held her breath, only to release it in a whoosh when it opened all the way. "Why is Arwel shackled?"

Magnus shrugged and pointed to his ear.

How could she have forgotten that both of them were wearing earplugs? No outside sounds filtered through them, but apparently her inner turmoil was enough to fill the void.

As Arwel started walking toward them, Magnus put his hand on her shoulder, gave it a little squeeze, nodded, and pointed at her ear.

His expression combined with that small gesture conveyed everything he wanted to tell her. Good luck, it's time to go, and a reminder to take out her earplugs.

Walking toward Arwel, Jin dreaded what she might see on his face when he got closer. Would he be angry? Indifferent? What was he going to say to her?

With shaking hands, she took out the earplugs and put them in the pocket of Alena's coat.

But she should have known him better.

The first thing she saw clearly were his eyes, which were two glowing turquoise beacons of light, and the next were his lips, which were mouthing, "I love you."

Unable to resist the urge to hold him, she ran up to Arwel and put her arms around him. "I love you so much. Please don't be angry at me for doing this."

He couldn't return the embrace because his hands were shackled, and the handcuffs chained to his ankle restraints. Instead, he leaned his head on her shoulder. "I'm not angry. I'm terrified."

"Please keep moving," Kalugal commanded, but he didn't infuse his voice with compulsion.

"I love you." Jin quickly kissed Arwel's lips and then let go of him. "See you in an hour."

Putting one foot in front of the other, Jin forced herself to keep going. The simple act of ambulating consumed all of her willpower, and there was nothing left to keep her tears at bay. By the time she reached Kalugal, Jin was sobbing quietly.

He looked at her with concern in his eyes and took her elbow. "There is no need for tears." He led her to a gazebo that looked like it was set up for a romantic dinner. "Your boyfriend is fine, and you have nothing to worry about. As soon as the tether is off, and I can verify it, you are free to go."

When he motioned for her to sit, Jin's legs practically folded under her. "I'm sorry. I'm usually not such a cry baby. It's just that I've gotten sick at the worst possible time, and I can barely hold it together."

Kalugal sat right next to her. "Let me pour you some tea."

"Thank you."

He was treating her like delicate china. Every move was slow and calculated as if not to spook her, and his tone was soft and caring.

It was all an act, of course, designed to help her relax so she could do what she was there for, but it was working. The anxiety was still spinning the contents of her stomach like a bunch of wet clothes in a dryer, but at least it wasn't on the turbo spin cycle.

"Careful. It's hot." He handed her a small porcelain cup with a matching saucer.

"Thank you." She sniffed at the cup he handed her. "What kind of tea is this? It smells woodsy."

He smiled, his perfect lips curving in that signature smirk that Jacki had talked about. "It's not poisoned if that's what you are worried about."

"It didn't even cross my mind. I've just never had tea like it."

The smell wasn't unpleasant, but it wasn't enticing either, and it was still too hot to drink.

"It's a special Chinese tea."

She narrowed her eyes at him. "Is that why you got it? I don't know what a Chinese tea even tastes like."

He chuckled. "How could I have known I would be entertaining an Asian lady when I purchased this tea? I've been drinking it for years. I like it for the unique taste, but it also has many health benefits for humans. Which is most fortunate, don't you think? It might help you feel better."

After taking another sniff, Jin put the cup on the table. "I need it to cool a little." She turned to Kalugal. "May I touch you?"

"Anytime." He flashed her that smirk again.

If she weren't in love with someone else and sick as a dog, she might have found it sexy. The guy had a bad-boy charm that girls went wild for, but it was softened by his good manners and his lighthearted attitude.

Jin had to acknowledge that Kalugal was super sexy, but she was indifferent to his charms. They had no effect on her. It was like admiring a beautiful picture without lusting after it or even wanting to hang it in her living room.

"I need to touch you to remove the tether. And you need to concentrate on feeling its removal."

He offered her his arm. "I'm ready when you are."

60

ARWEL

His mind in a haze, Arwel trudged over to the other side of the street. Twice he stumbled on the chain connecting his ankles, and Magnus caught his elbow before it happened for the third time.

"Let me get you out of these." Magnus crouched and fiddled with the key Kalugal had tossed. "Quit swaying on your feet. You are distracting me."

"I wasn't aware that I was doing that." Arwel stood as still as he could.

Jin had looked haggard as if she hadn't slept for days. There had been dark circles under her eyes, and the spark was gone from them, or maybe they had just been misted with a sheen of tears.

When Magnus was done with the ankle restraints, he straightened up and examined the handcuffs. "Those are weird. They must be custom made." He turned them around until he found the keyhole.

Arwel was about to comment when he noticed the earpiece sticking out from Magnus's ear. Except, it didn't look like the ones William had given them. Was it a new model?

Magnus removed the handcuffs as well.

"New earpiece?"

Ignoring the question, Magnus waved a hand, and a moment later Gregor pulled up next to them. "Let's get out of here."

"Where are we going?"

When neither of the guys responded, Arwel leaned toward Magnus and took a closer look at the device stuck in his ear, and then pulled it out.

"I was wondering why you guys didn't answer me. What's the deal with the plugs?"

Magnus took the other one out. "It was Kri's idea. If we can't hear Kalugal, he can't compel us."

"Did he try?"

"He might have." Gregor chuckled. "We didn't hear him. We wear these when we are within hearing distance of him and use texting to communicate. Our phones are set on vibrate."

"Smart. So where are we going?"

"Get out of your clothes and put these on." Magnus pointed to the paper bag on the seat next to Arwel. "When you are done, put everything in the bag. After we get out, Gregor is going to drive away and drop them in a dumpster at the nearest shopping strip."

It had occurred to Arwel that the *search* Rufsur had done on him and Jacki was not meant to find bugs but to plant them.

"Good idea." He started stripping. "Jin looks terrible. What's wrong with her?"

"She caught a cold," Magnus said. "Poor girl. I don't know much about human illnesses, but I assume that the stress weakened her body and made her vulnerable to viruses."

Arwel's heart skipped a beat. "She might be transitioning."

"She is not. The sanctuary's doctor checked her and said it's just a cold."

"The sanctuary?" He paused with the sweatshirt hovering over his head.

Magnus nodded. "Turner decided that it was the most secure place for her, so he sent her there without telling Kian about it. There was always a chance that Kalugal would compel Kian through the phone and get him to reveal things. That's why he doesn't talk with Kalugal unless Turner is right there beside him. He can take over if needed."

"What a damn clusterfuck. Whose idea was it to trade Jin?"

"Hers. She insisted we do it from the very start. Believe me, Kian tried every possible angle before finally agreeing to the trade. There was no other way. She also came up with the idea of taking Kalugal's second-in-command hostage."

"Jin has a good head on her shoulders. Rufsur and Kalugal are good friends, and Kalugal is not going to forfeit Rufsur's life lightly. Where did you take him?"

"First, we took him to the house, stripped him, and searched him for bugs. After that, we took him to our new location."

"And where is that?"

"One of Turner's many acquaintances has a motel that isn't open for business yet. We've got the entire place to ourselves."

"How has he been behaving?"

"He's complaining about being tied up and claims that you promised he would be treated well."

"I did. But what I meant was that no one was going to beat him up. I didn't promise him a five-star hotel and gourmet meals if that's what he's been expecting. Who is watching him?"

"We have several Guardians there, and Vivian is keeping him company, even though I would have preferred for her to stay away from him."

Arwel wasn't sure how smart that was. Rufsur was an okay fellow, but if he was presented with an opportunity to get free or take Vivian hostage, he'd most likely take it.

"I hope that he is properly restrained and guarded, and that the guys are at least cordial to him." Arwel pulled up the sweatpants and reached into the bag for socks.

Magnus cast him an amused glance. "With Vivian keeping watch they are going to be on their best behavior. Lokan is there as well, but we are keeping him away from Rufsur because Kian is not sure he wants to reveal the connection yet. If needed though, he's going to use Lokan as an additional hostage."

"When did Lokan get here?"

"Yesterday, and naturally Carol couldn't stay away from the action and came with him."

"That's Carol. Even a direct order from Kian wouldn't have kept her away." Arwel pulled the new pair of boots out of the bag and leaned to put them on.

Magnus shrugged. "He's too busy with managing the crisis to care about that."

"I'm ready." Arwel put the clothes he'd taken off into the bag.

"Then let's go." Magnus opened the door and got out.

At the door Arwel was greeted by Kri, who pulled him into a fierce hug. "I'm glad to have you back."

He returned the embrace. "I wish I could say that I'm glad to be back, but I can't while Kalugal has my mate."

"Jin campaigned hard for it. She knew that Kalugal wouldn't agree to anything else and she was right. I know that it's hard for you to accept, but she did the right thing. Now that you are out, the village's location is safe, and Kian has lifted the lockdown. People can go back to work, and those who were caught outside during the lockdown can come back home."

He hung his head. "It's my fault. I should have stopped that shooter before he got into the club. I felt the darkness eating at him, and I knew he was up to no good. But we are not supposed to interfere based on intentions, only actions. Except, it seems that following the rules is not always the right thing to do."

Kri put her hand on his arm. "We can't live our lives agonizing over should've and could've. In hindsight, disarming that man before he reached the club was the right thing to do, but you couldn't have known it. The rules are not infallible, but they keep us from making many more mistakes than what we would have committed in their absence."

"Words of wisdom." Magnus clapped Kri on the back. "I didn't know you were so deep."

Flipping him a finger, Kri smiled and sauntered off.

61

JIN

Jin let go of Kalugal's arm. "Did you feel it?"

She could've released the tether on her side without touching him, but she wasn't sure he would notice the difference if she did it that way. It was better to remove the hook from his brain than just let go of the tether.

He shook his head. "I'm sorry. I didn't notice any change."

Leaning back, Jin sighed. "I feel like a mental weight lifted off me. Letting go of the tether always feels liberating." She looked at him. "Don't you feel freer? Lighter?"

He smiled. "I didn't feel oppressed or weighed down before."

"When I reattach it, focus inwardly. When you know it's coming, you should be able to feel it. Others did."

"Maybe it's a placebo effect. People expect to feel a difference, so they do."

Jin closed her eyes. "I need a few moments to rest."

"No problem. Take your time. If it were up to me, I would have taken you to a guest room where you could sleep, and we could have continued this the next morning. It was Kian who insisted on doing it so late at night and outside in the yard." He looked her over. "I don't know much about human illnesses, but I don't think you should be out in the cold."

"Thank you for turning up the heaters. I would've been really miserable without them."

"You're welcome." He lifted his teacup and took a small sip. "Tell me something. How come the clan is working with humans? If there is one thing both sides of the divide agree upon, it is that humans shouldn't find out about the existence of immortals."

Crap. Jin didn't know if she was allowed to tell Kalugal about being a Dormant. Mey had said that the Doomers didn't know how to find Dormants in the human population or that paranormal abilities were a good indicator of a person having the immortal gene.

"They are very selective about who they let in on the secret." That wasn't a lie, so it should be okay.

But given the change in Kalugal's expression, it wasn't. In an instant, it turned from easygoing charm to hard determination.

How could someone so handsome suddenly look so terrifying?

"Tell me the truth, Jin." His voice was imbued with compulsion. "I don't appreciate evasive answers any more than I appreciate lies."

"I'm not human," she heard herself say. "Not entirely."

He arched a brow. "How so? Are you the daughter of an immortal mother?"

"I was adopted, so I don't know who my mother was. But she must have been a Dormant, and so am I."

"I see." The smirk was back. "So, you can turn immortal. How come you didn't yet? Has your relationship with Arwel been platonic?"

Embarrassed, Jin reached for her teacup. "Condoms," she muttered under her breath.

"What about them?"

She shook her head. "How come you guys don't know basic stuff like that? To induce a Dormant, it's not enough to have sex with her and bite her. The immortal male's sperm has to actually get inside her and not into a condom."

"Interesting." Kalugal sipped on his tea. "It would appear that my father doesn't know that. He never permitted immortal males to have sex with the Dormants because he wanted to keep them human so they could produce more children. But if condoms are enough to prevent transition, it's not necessary to segregate them."

"He might know about that but doesn't trust the men to use protection."

Kalugal nodded. "That's possible. Navuh is highly paranoid."

"Can I reattach the tether now? I really want to be done with this."

"Not yet. I have many more questions for you."

"That wasn't part of the deal."

He smiled. "But it wasn't explicitly excluded either. I like finding loopholes that I can use to my advantage."

"I bet." Jin grimaced.

"How did they find you? Or did you find them? Are they actively searching for Dormants?"

"They found my sister first, and it was purely by chance. But once she was confirmed as a Dormant, so was I. I don't know how they found the others."

"So, there are more?"

Jin nodded.

"How many?"

"I don't know. I'm new to all this, and I haven't even visited the clan's village yet." She slapped her hand over her mouth. "Crap. I really hate this. But before you ask, I don't know where it is. They kept me in the dark, so to speak."

To buy herself a short reprieve, she took an experimental sip from the tea. "Interesting flavor. What's in it?" She took another sip. It tasted odd, but not unpleasant.

"It's called the Poo Poo Pu-Erh tea, and it was the drink of emperors."

"Poo Poo? That's funny. What does it mean? I know very little Chinese."

"It means exactly what it sounds like. It's made from the droppings of insects that have fed on tea leaves. It's considered a delicacy and costs accordingly."

As Jin's stomach heaved, she only had enough time to turn her head away from Kalugal before everything she'd eaten that day came up geysering out of her throat.

She was dimly aware of Kalugal jumping up and saying something to her, but she couldn't understand what it was. It felt as if she was puking out her brains together with the contents of her stomach, and with every new spasm, her vision blurred further, until she could no longer hold on to consciousness.

Tipping over, Jin's last thought was that falling onto the puddle of puke she'd made was just the perfect ending to the most miserable day of her life.

62

KALUGAL

For the first time in a very long time, Kalugal panicked. Something was very wrong with the pretty spy, and he didn't know how to help her.

Should he offer her a napkin?

He unfurled one and held it out for her, but she was too busy spilling out the contents of her stomach all over the gazebo's floor to pay any attention to the napkin hanging right in front of her face.

"Tell me what I can do for you."

Oblivious to his presence, she pitched forward, and if not for his quick reflexes, she would have landed right on the pile of vomit.

Catching her by gripping the back of her coat, Kalugal swung her into his arms and started walking. "Bring a doctor!" He yelled loud enough for the warriors outside his gate to hear. "The girl passed out, and I'm taking her inside the house!"

His men gathered around him, forming a wall of bodies to protect him. It wasn't going to help if whoever was controlling the drones decided to shoot, but he hoped Kian's men were aware of Jin's sickness and would not assume that he had done something to her. All it would take to end him was one trigger-happy moron and the right kind of bullet.

"Any of you know how to resuscitate a human?"

The response he got was head shaking all around.

"Bring the immune to the house. She might know what to do."

"Yes, sir."

"I'm taking the girl to my bedroom."

This was no time to think about propriety or what her boyfriend would think.

Taking the stairs two at a time, he held on tight, making sure to clear the banister on one side and the wall on the other. Humans were so damn fragile, and any impact would leave a bruise on the girl that he would have to explain to Kian.

When his phone went off in his pocket, Kalugal cursed under his breath. He had a good idea who was calling him, but he couldn't answer it without dropping Jin.

The damn thing kept ringing all the way to his bedroom and stopped just as he laid the girl on his bed.

"Get me some wet washcloths," he barked at the men who followed him into the bedroom.

"Yes, sir." Shamash rushed into the bathroom.

Kalugal pulled out his phone and clicked return on the last incoming call.

"What's going on?" Kian growled.

"Your spy is sick. She threw up and then passed out. What should I do? I have no experience in taking care of humans."

"I'm getting our clan doctor on the line so she can walk you through it. I'm also sending another doctor to your place, but it will take him about an hour and a half to get there. You might have to take Jin to a hospital."

"That's the best idea you've had so far. I should take her right away."

"Wait. Let the doctor decide if it's necessary."

"If she dies because you made me wait, it's on you."

"She is not going to die. Hold on, I'm connecting you to the doctor. Her name is Bridget."

"Hello, Kalugal." The female sounded calm as if nothing major was happening. "Is Jin breathing?"

"She is."

"Check her pulse. Do you know how to do it?"

Who did she think she was dealing with? An ignoramus?

"Of course. Hang on."

As he took Jin's limp wrist and counted the beats, Shamash returned with the washcloths and started cleaning her up.

"Eighty-six beats per minute."

"That's fine. Since she threw up, you need to lay her on her side. Put a pillow or two under her legs, so they are elevated about twelve inches over her heart."

"Done. What now?"

"Is the room warm?"

"No. But I can turn the heating on."

"Do that, but make sure that she doesn't get overheated. What is she wearing?"

"A coat over a thick sweater and a long skirt that doesn't look too warm. Should I remove the coat? I can cover her with a thick comforter."

"You can do that. Tell me how it happened. Did you give her something to eat or drink that might not have agreed with her stomach?"

"She arrived already sick and said that she had a cold. I gave her tea, which she enjoyed, but when she asked about the tea, and I explained how it was made, she started vomiting. My explanation must have disgusted her."

"What kind of tea was it?"

"It's a Chinese delicacy, which I thought she would appreciate. It's called the

Poo Poo Pu-Erh tea, and it's made from the droppings of insects that digest the tea leaves."

"I see." The doctor chuckled. "Poor Jin. She must have been queasy because of the cold, and then you exacerbated the situation with that gross tea."

"It's not gross. It has a unique flavor, is purported to have many health benefits for humans, and it costs over five hundred dollars per pound."

"I'm sure it does, but that's neither here nor there. Stay with Jin and watch her closely. If anything changes, like her pulse accelerates or drops or her breathing becomes labored, give me a call."

"Are you sure that's wise? I'd rather take her to the human hospital. I don't want to be responsible for her demise."

"That's not advisable. She might be transitioning, and they wouldn't know what to do with her. A clan doctor is on his way, and he knows what to do in case she is."

63

ARWEL

*J*in threw up and fainted. Kalugal took her inside the house, and Kian is sending Julian over. Bridget thinks she is transitioning.

As Arwel read the text from Magnus for the second time, he wanted to scream in frustration.

Next to him, Kri was reading the same text and cursing quietly. "The damn sanctuary doctor said it was a cold. Maybe she should go back to medical school."

"It still might be just that." Arwel pushed his fingers through his hair. "I need to call Bridget and ask her why she thinks Jin is transitioning."

He placed the call and started walking toward the door.

Kri stopped him with a hand on his shoulder. "Where are you going?"

He cast her an incredulous glance. "Back where I came from. I need to be near my mate when she transitions."

"Don't be an idiot. You are not going anywhere. We just went to all this trouble to get you out."

"Other Guardians are surrounding Kalugal's mansion. I can at least be out there."

"No, you can't. You and I are not allowed anywhere near Kalugal because we are head Guardians, and we know the village's location as well as shitloads of other stuff that the other Guardians don't. If either of us gets captured, it's back to square one."

"I can wear earplugs."

As his call to Bridget went to voicemail, Arwel was ready to throw his phone at the wall. "Why isn't she answering?"

Kri's hand on his shoulder tightened. "You are not going to help Jin by standing outside Kalugal's gate with earplugs in."

"I can't stay here and do nothing either."

"You have no choice. Call Bridget again or call Kian and get an update."

Seething, Arwel redialed Bridget's number.

This time the doctor answered. "I was expecting your call. First of all, don't panic. Jin was under a lot of stress, hasn't slept much, and has gotten sick on top of that. I talked with the sanctuary's doctor, and Rebecca assured me that Jin's symptoms are classic cold and a mild one at that. Then I got a call from Vivian, who told me that she fed Jin lots of chicken soup, which is good for congestion, but it might not have agreed with her stomach."

"So, she is not transitioning?"

Bridget sighed. "She might be, but it's unlikely. From my limited experience with adult Dormants transitioning, they need to be healthy for it to start. Remember Roni? He couldn't transition because his body was weakened after being sick with pneumonia. But just in case she is or in case she's suffering from something more serious, I'm sending Julian over with a bunch of medical equipment."

"If you think she might have a more serious illness, perhaps it's best to take her to a human hospital."

"We can bring in a local doctor, but since Julian will be there in less than an hour and a half, I think it's more prudent to wait for him and have all the possibilities checked out."

"Isn't it dangerous for her to stay unconscious for so long?"

"I was about to call Kian and check whether she still was when your call came in. She might have woken up already."

"When you find out, let me know."

"Of course."

Arwel ended the call and let out a breath. "Jin is probably not transitioning."

"That's what I thought." Kri flipped her braid back. "Come on. You need a drink." She started walking toward the kitchen. "I hope there is some beer left in the fridge."

"A moment ago you were ranting about the sanctuary's doctor not knowing what she was doing, and now you claim to have known that Jin is not transitioning?"

"I thought that Bridget had already spoken with Dr. Rebeca and found fault with her diagnosis. To me, it looked like the flu or a cold. Jin was sneezing and blowing her nose every two minutes, which none of the other Dormants have done while transitioning." Kri opened the fridge and pulled out two beers.

Handing one to Arwel, she leaned against the counter. "If it swims like a duck and quacks like a duck, it's probably not a chicken, even though they look a lot alike." She popped the cap and took a long swig.

"Ducks and chickens look nothing alike, but growing up in the city you wouldn't know that because you've only seen them in the supermarket, cut up and neatly packaged."

Kri waved with her bottle. "Whatever, country boy. You get my meaning."

64

KALUGAL

"Oh my God. What happened?" The immune rushed into Kalugal's bedroom.

For a moment, he was lost for words. If she weren't the only female on his estate, he wouldn't have recognized her.

The mousy brown wig was gone, as well as the makeup that had made her skin look sallow.

Her complexion was a healthy peach color, her hair was a magnificent mane of blond strands that were waist long and lushly wavy, and it flew behind her like a golden halo as she ran through the room.

Bending over Jin, she checked her breathing and then put her hand on her forehead. "She is burning up." Jacki pinned him with a stare so intense that it penetrated the thick layers of rust around his heart. "Do you have any Advil or Tylenol, or do immortals have no need for painkillers?"

He affected a calm expression. "Jin told me that she had a cold and then threw up and fainted. Your boss is sending a doctor."

"If you mean Kian, he is not my boss," Jacki muttered.

"Shamash, check the first aid kit. Maybe it contains some painkillers."

"Yes, sir."

Sitting on the bed next to Jin, Jacki took one of the washcloths that Shamash had left on the nightstand and continued what he had started. "Jin, honey, wake up. I need you to talk to me."

The faint groan Jin uttered in response was music to Kalugal's ears. Why hadn't he thought about coaxing the girl to talk? He could've compelled her to answer him.

But the doctor hadn't said anything about talking. She'd said to watch Jin, which was exactly what he'd been doing. Sitting on a chair next to the bed, he watched the girl's chest rising and falling to make sure that she was still breathing.

"That's a good start, honey." Jacki caressed Jin's cheek. "Can you tell me what's wrong?"

Jin opened her eyes a crack. "Mommy?"

"It's Jacki, sweetheart. Does anything hurt?"

Jin lifted her hand to her throat. "It hurts here."

Jacki turned to Kalugal. "Can you bring her a glass of water?"

"Of course." He pushed to his feet.

"And a bowl with ice water and a couple of fresh washcloths."

"What for?"

She rolled her eyes. "I know that you are an immortal, but living among humans, you should've learned a few basic things about us. I need to reduce her fever, and since I don't have any medication that I can give her, I'll wet the cloths in ice water and put it on her forehead to cool her a bit. It will make her feel better."

"I see."

Kalugal dipped his head before marching to the wet bar in the master suite's sitting room.

Why the hell had he felt the need to do that?

As far as he knew, Jacki was a nobody, but her authoritative tone and lack of fear implied otherwise. She'd also said that Kian was not her boss.

Who was she? And what was her connection to the clan?

Had Kian lied about her not being important? But then he would have asked to trade her first and not the warrior. Except, he might have done it on purpose, so Kalugal wouldn't suspect her real value.

Regrettably, he couldn't compel Jacki to reveal her secrets, and it seemed like she was also immune to his charms, which was no less disconcerting.

Even the spy had looked at him appreciatively, and she was in love with another man.

His curiosity demanded that he find out who Jacki was and what she was hiding, but it was more than that. She knew who he was, knew where he lived, and was immune to thralling. If he let her go, she would walk away with knowledge that no human should ever be privy to.

After scooping cubes from the freezer into an ice bucket, he put some in a tall glass and filled both containers with water.

"Thank you." Jacki took the bucket and put it on the nightstand.

"You're welcome." He handed her the glass. "I'll get the washcloths."

In the bathroom, he took out the whole stack of them from the closet and headed back.

"I need your help." Jacki handed him a pillow. "When I turn Jin on her back and lift her, stuff the pillow behind her. I want her to drink the water."

He put the washcloths on the nightstand. "The doctor said to put her on her side and to keep her legs elevated over her heart."

"Yeah, but that was for when she was unconscious. She is awake now. Sort of."

Bending at the waist, Kalugal put his face a few inches away from Jacki's. "Are you a doctor?"

"I'm not, but everyone other than clueless immortals knows that."

No one talked to Kalugal like that, and he should have felt offended, but instead, he was amused. Hell, he was delighted.

For the first time since he could remember, he was being treated like a regular guy. Even while shrouded, most people sensed his power and trod cautiously around him.

Could Jacki's immunity make her obtuse?

Or was she used to having powerful people around her, and that's why she wasn't impressed by him?

Kalugal was practically salivating with curiosity. Especially since it came with a heavy dose of attraction.

Before this was over and he let Jacki go, he was going to seduce her, and since she was immune to his compulsion as well as to his charms, conquering her would be doubly fun.

"Why are you smirking? It's the truth. For a smart guy, you are incredibly clueless about humans."

"I love it that you do not fear me." He took the pillow from her. "Ready when you are."

She gifted him with a heart-stoppingly gorgeous smile. "I'm glad that you can be reasoned with."

65

JIN

*J*in had the weirdest dream. Her mom was feeding her chicken soup and calling her honey, and her dad was sitting in a chair next to her bed and frowning.

That wasn't like him. Her father was more the brow lifting type, and she'd rarely seen him frown. And when she or Mey got sick, their mom would keep him away from them because he caught every bug and was the worst patient possible. She had also never fed them in bed. Jin couldn't remember ever being too sick to get up to eat.

A cool hand touched her forehead. "I think her fever has gone down a little. She doesn't feel as hot to the touch." That didn't sound like her mother's voice.

"That's a highly unscientific way to measure temperature." The male voice didn't belong to her father either, but it carried the same pompous self-importance that her mom always berated her dad for.

Her mom would tell him, "You're a history professor. That doesn't make you an expert on anything else."

And he would answer, "History encompasses everything. Even science and medicine."

"Outdated science and medicine."

Her father used to say that it was nothing more than his teacher tone, and that he was a humble man. But that was false modesty, and they all knew it but loved him anyway.

"You don't have a freaking thermometer. And until Julian gets here, my hand is all we have. Unless you think that your hand is better at measuring temperature?"

The voice sounded familiar, but it wasn't her mother's for sure. First of all, she would never say freaking, and secondly, she didn't have a southern accent. Hers was New Yorker.

Jin cracked her eyes open. "Jacki?" Her throat felt like it was on fire, and it hurt to talk.

"Oh, thank God. You're awake. Kalugal's guy found some Motrin. Apparently, immortals aren't immune to headaches. They get them when they are hungover. Anyway, you were delirious, and I had to shove it into your mouth and massage your throat for you to swallow it."

Jacki was talking a mile a second, which she'd never done before. She must think that Jin was dying.

As she hovered over Jin, her long hair was hanging like a curtain and blocking the view of a guy sitting on a chair next to the bed. Moving it aside, Jin looked at Kalugal. "Where am I?"

"In my bedroom. You fainted."

And she'd also puked, which explained the horrible smell. It had been that disgusting tea, or rather hearing about how it was made. Just thinking about it made her stomach heave.

"It was that horrible tea. I'm going to puke again." Jin slapped a hand over her mouth.

Jacki shoved an ice bucket under her chin. "In here."

It was full of cold water, with half-melted ice cubes floating around. Reaching inside, Jin pulled out an ice cube, stuffed it into her mouth, and crunched it into small bits.

The chewing helped with the nausea attack, and the icy water felt wonderful on her burning throat. Jin reached for another one.

Jacki grimaced and pulled the bucket away. "That water is not clean. I used it to dunk washcloths in." She turned to Kalugal. "Can you get Jin another glass of water with ice cubes inside?"

"Coming right up." He pushed to his feet and walked out of the room.

Leave it up to Jacki to boss around one of the most powerful immortals on the planet.

"Did I hear you saying that Julian is on his way, or was it part of the dream?"

"He should be here in less than half an hour. Kian sent him with a bunch of equipment, but I don't know what for. All you need are antibiotics."

"The doctor at the sanctuary checked me and said that I had a common cold, but I think she was wrong. This feels like strep throat."

"What sanctuary?"

Damn. Her brain was fuzzy, and she wasn't thinking straight. She needed to think before she opened her big mouth.

"Um, the clan runs a sanctuary for girls and boys that they rescue from traffickers. That's where I was hiding. They have a doctor there, and she examined me."

"I didn't know they were doing that. It's commendable."

"Yeah, I think so too." Jin looked at Kalugal who came in with a tall glass of water.

"Where is that sanctuary you've been telling Jacki about?" He handed her the glass.

She knew there was no point in trying to lie to him. He would just compel her to tell him the truth like he had done before she'd passed out.

"It's in Alaska."

"Alaska? Why so far away?"

Jin took a sip of water, sighing in relief as it cooled her throat. "I don't know. Maybe it's so the traffickers don't find them? Or maybe because houses in Alaska are relatively cheap."

None of what she'd said was an untruth, just not the whole of it.

Thankfully, Kalugal accepted her explanation. "Makes sense. I'm just thinking that those poor kids deserve better than freezing Alaska." He sat on the chair and crossed his legs. "I might consider contributing to the cause in exchange for some privileges."

Jacki glared at him. "You are so freaking rich. You can contribute without asking for anything in return."

He smiled. "That's true, but what I need from my esteemed cousin doesn't carry monetary value, only sentimental."

That piqued Jacki's interest. "What is it?"

"Talking with my mother. I'm holding you hostage until he lets me talk to her, but once is not enough, and I'll probably need to bribe him to let me keep in touch with her."

Jacki frowned. "Is he holding your mother prisoner? Why can't you just call her up?"

"That's a long story, and I'm not sure I want to share it with you. I can't make you forget anything, and you already know too much."

Jacki swallowed nervously. "What are you going to do about it?"

"Nothing. You are safe with me, but I don't know what Kian plans to do with you."

Jin bristled. "Kian is not going to harm Jacki. She's part of the clan."

Jacki lifted a brow. "I am?"

"Sure, you are. Do you think the clan is going to turn its back on you after you risked your life to save Arwel?"

Leaning forward, Kalugal steepled his fingers. "The question is in what capacity. Kian can't let you walk away. You will be a prisoner of the clan for the rest of your life."

66

KALUGAL

"What about Jin?" Jacki asked. "She is human, right? And so is her sister. How do they fit in with a clan of immortals?"

Kalugal glanced at Jin, who seemed uncomfortable, and not because of the illness.

Apparently, Jacki had been left in the dark about all things that had to do with immortality, which was a good decision on Kian's part. The less she knew, the better.

"Rufsur asked Arwel the same question. Apparently, Kian is not as careful in that regard as I am. He's allowed several chosen humans in on the secret."

Jin let out a breath. "Yeah. Being Arwel's girlfriend, I was granted that privilege. Same for my sister. She knows because she and Yamanu are a couple."

"That's not so smart." Jacki looked at her with sad eyes. "How long do you think it's going to last? You will grow older while he doesn't."

"I don't want to talk about it." Jin closed her eyes. "When is Julian getting here? I feel like I'm dying."

"Let me check." Kalugal pulled his phone out and called Kian. "When should we expect the doctor?"

"Has Jin's condition worsened?"

"No, she actually woke up and talked with Jacki and me for a little bit. But that was thanks to the Motrin Jacki forced down her throat, and the effect seems to be temporary. She says that she is dying, which I'm sure is an exaggeration, but she is obviously very sick."

"There was a slight delay. Julian should be there in forty-five minutes to an hour tops. He's coming with a lot of medical equipment, so make sure to prepare a room for him to set it up in."

"Tell him to leave it outside and come examine Jin first. I need to have that equipment checked."

"Relax. Now that I have my man back, I have no reason to blow your place up."

"Nevertheless, I'm still going to conduct a very thorough check."

"As you wish."

"She is sleeping," Jacki said as he ended the call. "There must be something seriously wrong with her. Jin is a healthy and strong woman, she shouldn't be that incapacitated by a freaking cold. Maybe it's one of those deadly flu strains. And if it is, I'm in trouble because they are usually highly contagious. And if it's a strep throat, that's not so bad because it's not life-threatening, but it's contagious as hell too."

Kalugal pushed to his feet. "May I offer you some tea?"

She scrunched her nose. "Not the one that made Jin puke."

"I don't think it was the tea that caused her to vomit. The Poo-Poo Pu-Erh tea is actually supposed to soothe upset stomach, and it also provides many other health benefits. I suggest that you drink it as a preemptive measure."

Crossing her arms over her chest, Jacki shook her head. "I'm not putting anything in my mouth that has Poo Poo as part of its name."

"Your loss. I'll have a simpler tea prepared for you."

"I'd appreciate it." She yawned.

As he walked out of the room, Kalugal thought back to the moments leading up to Jin's fainting spell. She'd looked bad, and he'd noticed her rubbing her middle when she'd thought he wasn't looking. Perhaps she had food poisoning?

It could have been caused by a virus, or by something she'd eaten before coming there, or it could have been an actual poisoning.

Why would Kian poison his own spy, though? That didn't make any sense. Unless it was all a ploy to get the so-called doctor and his equipment in.

A Trojan horse Kalugal couldn't refuse.

If that was indeed the plan, then he had severely underestimated his cousin's deviousness.

Most of his men were still in the bunker, and he was going to leave them there until the doctor and his equipment were gone. The question was whether Kalugal was going to join them there or remain in the house.

The smart thing to do would be to leave one of the men in charge, but that was not how Kalugal ran his house. He wasn't going to hide in the bunker and leave the skeleton crew he had in the house exposed.

Except, he had to admit that logic and strategy had little to do with his reluctance to go down to the bunker.

The truth was that he didn't want to leave Jacki and her crusty and yet surprisingly pleasant company. She was so refreshing, so different from the women he was usually attracted to.

Looks-wise, she was his type. He liked tall blondes with curvy bodies and peachy skin. But her character didn't match the profile of his companion of choice. He had a feeling that despite her intelligence, she had no higher education.

Jacki didn't sound like a hillbilly, but she was rough around the edges and not nearly as sophisticated as the women he usually picked.

Maybe that was precisely why he found her so fascinating.

67

ARWEL

When Arwel's phone rang, he nearly dropped it in his haste to pull it out of his back pocket. He'd been expecting a call from Bridget, but instead it was Kian.

"I have good news for you. Jin is awake, and Kalugal brought Jacki to take care of her. The bad news is that she is still very sick, and Julian is running a little late. He needed to pick up antibiotics and some other stuff that we don't keep on hand in the village. He should be landing shortly, though, and several Guardians are waiting for him on the strip to help him with the equipment."

"Is there a way I can talk to her or Jacki?"

"It's not advisable. In case Kalugal tries to compel me while I talk to him, I have Turner to take over and Onegus to stop me from doing something I'm not supposed to. You have no such protection. He could compel you to tell him what he wants to know, and no one there can stop him."

"What if you make a three-way call? If Kalugal tries his tricks, Turner can disconnect it. It's the same as if I were there with you. I'll have Kri chain me to a pillar, so if Kalugal commands me to come to him, I won't be able to do that, and if he asks me a question I shouldn't answer, Turner can disconnect the call before I reveal anything."

"Hold on a moment. I'll ask Turner what he thinks."

A long moment passed until Kian came back on the line. "Turner says it can work. Call me back when you're chained to that pillar."

"Thank you. This means a lot to me."

"No need to thank me. I get it." Kian ended the call.

Kri lifted a brow. "What do you want me to use for chains?"

"There must be something in the garage we can use."

"I have reinforced handcuffs." Gregor leaned over the second-floor railing.

Arwel looked up. "What can we attach them to that I can't rip off?"

Gregor scratched his stubble. "The railing is wrought-iron. Even if you tear it off the wall, you can't drag it with you through the door. And if you try, I'll knock you out."

"Sounds good to me. Get them."

"It could work. You can sit on the stairs and have one hand cuffed to the railing. That way, you'll still have the other one to hold the phone." Kri walked over to the railing and shook it. "It's sturdy."

When it was done, Arwel placed the call. "I'm ready."

"I hope Kalugal won't object," Kian said.

"If he does, let me talk to him."

Kalugal's parting words implied that he didn't want any hard feelings, and allowing Arwel to talk to Jin wouldn't cost him any advantage.

A short moment later, Kalugal came on the line. "Has the doctor arrived?"

"Not yet," Kian said. "Arwel is on the line, and he asks to speak with Jin if it's possible."

"She is asleep."

"Can I talk to Jacki?"

"Sure. I'm putting you on speakerphone. Go ahead."

That was easier than Arwel had expected. "Hi, Jacki. How is Jin doing?"

"I think she has strep throat."

"What's that?"

"Come on, you too? I thought that only Kalugal was so ignorant because he lives isolated from the world. It's a bacterial infection in the throat, and it can get pretty nasty. It's not life-threatening, though. You can Google it."

"How do you know it's that and not something else? You're not a doctor."

"Jin's throat hurts, she has a high fever that doesn't respond well to fever reducers, and when she talks, she sounds raspy. I've seen so many cases of strep throat that I can diagnose it like a doctor. Foster homes usually stick three to four kids in the same bedroom, and when one gets it, all the others get infected too."

"Can you do me a favor and call Kian when Jin wakes up? I want to talk to her."

"It's not up to me."

"I'll place the call for you," Kalugal said.

"Thanks. I appreciate that."

"No hard feelings, right?"

Arwel shook his head. "That still remains to be seen, but I'm grateful to you for allowing me to talk to Jin."

Kalugal sighed. "I'm a reasonable man, Arwel, and I'm not cruel when I don't have to be. As long as it doesn't endanger my men or me, I have no problem accommodating your or Jin's requests. You and Kian seem to forget that this whole mess was created by you, not me. I'm only defending myself and my men the best I can."

68

KALUGAL

"The doctor is here," Phinas announced from the other side of the door.

"I'll be right out." Kalugal pushed to his feet and looked down at Jacki. "I assume that you want to be here while he examines your friend."

"Naturally. He will want me here as well. When a male doctor examines a woman, a female nurse is usually present. I'm not a nurse, but I meet the first requirement."

He smirked. "You certainly do."

"Are you flirting with me, Kalugal?" Her eyes narrowed, but her lips were curved in a little smile.

"I'm just stating a fact. You are unmistakably female." He left before she had the chance to answer.

Spending time with Jacki was an interesting experience. He enjoyed the constant banter and the fact that she didn't give him an inch. He would probably grow tired of it shortly, like he did with most people, but that was okay. She was leaving soon, and until then, he was going to enjoy her company without analyzing the reasons for it.

Phinas was waiting for him out in the corridor. "A van full of medical equipment is parked outside, but the doctor says he can perform the initial examination just with what he has in his bag. The equipment will be needed only if the lady requires monitoring, whatever that means."

"It's what they do in hospitals. The equipment monitors the patient's vitals, like heartbeat, respiration, pulse, etc."

"How do you know that?"

"Movies. And I've also checked on doctor Google. These days you can find any information you want on the internet. No need to go to the library or attend lectures, it's all there at your fingertips."

Phinas assumed a smile. "At the ready for you to exploit."

"I'm just taking advantage of what's freely available to anyone who cares to investigate. The problem is that much of it is not reliable, and it takes a discriminating mind to know what's factual, what's speculation, and what's straight-up lies and manipulation. Where did you put the esteemed doctor?"

"In the library. Shamash is frisking him and checking his bag."

"Good. I don't want any more surprises tonight. We've had enough excitement to last us a year."

This time Phinas smiled for real. "I can't say that I don't enjoy it. Our lives are pretty boring, and sometimes I miss the old days of going out to fight."

How soon people forgot and romanticized the past.

"You've never believed in the cause, my friend. And you hated killing people for no good reason."

"That is true. What I liked about it was the adrenaline rush and also the camaraderie."

"You still have the second one. And if you need a rush, you can take up skydiving or something similarly dangerous."

Kalugal opened the door to the library and walked in.

"Doctor Julian, I presume?" He offered his hand to the immortal. "I'm Kalugal."

"I know." The guy shook it. "Your portrait hangs in our headquarters. Can you take me to Jin?"

Kalugal turned to Shamash. "Is the doctor clean?"

"Yes, sir."

"Follow me." Kalugal waited for the doctor to pick up his bag. "What is my portrait doing in your headquarters, and how did you get it?"

"That's a long story that I'm sure you'll find fascinating, but it will have to wait for another time. I have a patient to see."

"Of course."

Kalugal opened the suite's door and motioned for Julian to go ahead of him. "Jacki says that you need her present for the examination."

"I don't need her to be there, but I don't mind it either."

As they entered the bedroom, Jacki jumped up, ran up to the doctor, and hugged him. "You have no idea how glad I am to see you."

The rage gripping Kalugal was totally unexpected, and he struggled to stifle the growl rising up in his throat. Why had seeing Jacki embracing the handsome doctor evoked such an intense reaction in him?

What the hell was going on?

He'd never felt jealousy before or any overly intense emotions for that matter. He was a logical man, and not one who was ruled by basal urges. And what's more, he had no right. Jacki didn't belong to him, and if she wanted to wrap her arms around the neck of some guy that was too good-looking to be a doctor, it was her prerogative.

"Same here." Julian pulled her arms off. "Now, let me examine Jin."

"It's strep throat. I'm willing to bet on it."

"She shouldn't have passed out from a simple infection like that."

"She was tired and stressed out, and then Kalugal gave her Poo Poo tea, and it was the last straw."

The doctor shook his head. "I'm not even going to ask." He looked at Kalugal. "Can you please wait in the other room? You can leave the door open."

"Of course."

Kalugal would have liked to stay, but Jacki would probably threaten to scratch his eyes out if he insisted on it.

The doctor sat on the bed next to Jin and put his hand on her shoulder. "Jin, it's Julian."

Kalugal walked out into the sitting room and headed to the wet bar. Pouring himself a drink, he listened to the conversation in the other room.

"Can you open your eyes for me?" the doctor asked.

69

JIN

"Julian? When did you get here?" Jin whispered because talking hurt too much.

"A few minutes ago. I need to look at your throat."

"It hurts."

"I bet. Can you open your mouth?"

"Am I transitioning?"

"You are ill, Jin. But I'm here to take care of you."

Right. She wasn't supposed to mention transition next to Jacki. Although at this point, it was stupid. Jacki already knew about immortals, so what was the harm in telling her about Dormants?

Except, Jin lacked the energy to argue with Julian.

"She is delirious," Jacki said. "Before I gave her the Motrin, she thought that I was her mother."

Ignoring Jacki's comment, Julian lifted the tongue depressor. "Open and say ah."

As Jin followed the doctor's instructions, producing the ah sound hurt like hell, and it turned into a whimper.

"I'm sorry. I'll be quick." Julian shone his slim flashlight into her throat. "Just as we thought. Your throat is covered with pus. It looks like streptococcus, but it's always best to check. He pulled out a long cotton swab. "Open wide."

That was going to be a bitch, especially since she was starting to think that Julian was putting on a show for Jacki. Maybe she didn't have a throat infection and was transitioning?

Nevertheless, she opened her mouth as wide as she could and almost gagged when Julian swabbed the back of her throat.

"Where is the bathroom?" he asked.

"I'll show you." Jacki got up.

As the two left, Jin reached with a shaky hand for the glass of water on the nightstand. The thing almost fell out of her hand, but she gritted her teeth, tightened her hand around it, and brought it to her mouth.

Mey had said something about transition involving swollen glands, but that was supposed to happen only to the males. But then Mey had grown a pair of tiny fangs, which was an anomaly. None of the other Dormant females had lost or regrown teeth during their transition.

In Mey's case, the fangs had come without venom glands, but maybe Jin was going to get both?

That could be so cool. Talk about being a badass.

On the other hand, it felt like strep throat. The last time she'd suffered from it, Jin was eight, and all she remembered was that her throat had felt on fire and she couldn't even swallow her own saliva. Why would it come back so many years later, though? Strep usually affected kids, and Jin hadn't had contact with any for far too long to get infected.

It didn't make sense.

"It's strep," Julian announced as he came back with Jacki. "The culture tested positive in a matter of minutes."

Was he still putting on a show?

He sat next to her on the bed. "Are you allergic to penicillin?"

"No."

"That's good. I'll give you a Bicillin shot, which is an injectable form of penicillin, and you'll be all better in two to eight hours. It's a one-dose treatment. You won't even have to take pills for ten days."

"Really?"

"The streptococcus bacteria responds very well to antibiotics. The downside is that the shot is painful."

As the daughter of a pediatric nurse, Jin knew all about the shot. Her question wasn't about the speed of recovery or whether it would hurt.

"I know. I had it when I was a kid. But are you sure that I need it?"

"Do you prefer pills? I have those too. But it will take them longer to work."

More and more, it seemed like Julian was serious about it really being a bacterial infection and not the start of her transition. And in that case, Jin would rather heal faster than slower.

She still had a job to do.

"I'll take the shot."

Jacki grimaced. "Is it okay if I wait in the other room? I really hate needles."

Hallelujah.

Finally, she would have a moment alone with Julian.

"Go. I trust Julian."

"Thank you." Jacki scurried out of the room.

Jin put her hand on Julian's forearm. "Do I really have a strep throat, or am I transitioning and this is all for Jacki's sake?"

He chuckled. "If this was a charade, I would have given you sugar pills instead of subjecting you to a penicillin shot. You are not transitioning. In fact, you can't until you heal. We've learned from experience that unless the Dormant's body is healthy and in good physical condition, it's not going to enter transition. The process is incredibly taxing on the body, which is why it can be potentially fatal for older Dormants even if they are healthy."

"So, it's a defensive mechanism. The genes don't activate unless they have the right environment."

"That seems to be the case."

Jin sighed and turned on her side. "Do it quickly."

"Try not to scream. We don't want Kalugal and his men running in here to save you from me."

"I won't."

Just to make sure though, Jin grabbed a pillow and held it in front of her face. "I'm ready."

70

KALUGAL

"I won't be needing the equipment after all." The doctor walked into the sitting room. "It's a simple bacterial infection that responds very well to antibiotics. Jin is going to be fine in a matter of hours."

Kalugal rose to his feet. "Best news I've had today. Thank you." He offered the doctor his hand.

"I'm going to check on Jin." Jacki walked up to Julian. "Thank you for coming, and say hi to everyone else in the gang for me." She leaned and kissed his cheek. "Bye, Julian."

Even though there was nothing going on between the two, Kalugal didn't like her touching the male.

Forcing a smile, he turned to the doctor. "Would you like to stay the night, or are you going back to your people?"

"I doubt Jin will need my services, but I don't mind staying around if it's okay with you."

An unexpected relief washed over Kalugal. "I would very much like for you to stay. I find myself out of my element with an ill human, and I must admit that I didn't enjoy the feeling of not knowing how to help her."

The doctor nodded. "I know how you feel. Sometimes doctors can't help either, and that's incredibly frustrating, even depressing. It was difficult for me to work in a human hospital and be exposed to suffering I couldn't alleviate."

"Are you an empath?"

"Not a strong one. But it would have been hard for any immortal with a sensitive nose. I hate the scent of despair."

Kalugal nodded. "I hear you. There are many emotional scents that I find repugnant. My favorite by far is the smell of female arousal," he added to lighten the mood.

Julian cracked a smile. "Isn't it every male's?"

"You guys are gross." Jacki walked back into the sitting room, the color of her cheeks a deeper peach color than before.

Was she embarrassed?

"My apologies." Kalugal dipped his head while stifling a smile.

When they were waiting for Julian to administer the shot, he'd caught a very slight whiff of that best scent, and now that Jacki had heard his and Julian's exchange, she must've realized that her secret was out.

She waved a dismissive hand. "No need to apologize. All it proves is that all men are the same. Immortal or human, sophisticated or not, educated or not, it doesn't matter. Leave you alone for a few minutes, and you turn into adolescents, spewing locker-room humor."

Julian shrugged. "There's no harm in that. It just proves that we are female aficionados. Imagine a world in which males were indifferent to female charms."

"I could do without your appreciation for certain female-specific scents. But speaking of smells, I helped Jin to get into the shower. Can I borrow some clean clothes for her?"

"Certainly." Kalugal opened the door and motioned for Shamash to come in. "Can you show the doctor to a guest room?"

They'd never had guests before or had planned on having any, so there was no spare room in the house that was dedicated for that purpose. But since most of the men were still in the bunker, Shamash could put the doctor in one of their rooms.

"I don't intend to sleep," Julian said. "Point me to an armchair, and I'll spend what's left of the night reading."

"Then you will enjoy my library."

The doctor's eyes sparkled. "I definitely would. I'm also going to call Kian and give him an update if you don't mind."

"Not at all. It will save me the trouble."

Julian waved a hand at Shamash. "Lead the way."

"Bye, Julian." Jacki waved before turning to Kalugal. "You didn't tell your guy to get clothes for Jin."

"She can have some of mine. Follow me."

"Where?"

"To the closet, of course."

Jacki snorted. "That's the worst pick-up line I've ever heard."

"You have a one-track mind, Jacqueline."

As Kalugal walked back into the bedroom, he expected to be greeted by the smell of vomit. But Jacki had opened the windows, and most of it was gone.

"What do you mean?" She followed him into the closet.

"You keep insinuating that I'm flirting with you, but I am not." He was, but so far, he had been so subtle that it could have easily been interpreted as friendliness.

She rolled her eyes. "My mistake." Her tone dripped with sarcasm.

Naturally, a beauty like Jacki was used to a lot of male attention, and the best way to deal with someone like her was to appear unaffected by it.

He pulled out a set of silk pajamas and handed them to her. "If the pants are too loose, she can use only the top."

"Jin is tall. It might not be long enough to cover the essentials." Looking around his cavernous walk-in closet, Jacki pointed to a bank of drawers. "Do you have a pair of new boxer shorts by any chance?"

"I sure do." He opened the drawer and handed her a pair that still had the tag attached to it.

She ran the fabric between her fingers. "It's so soft. Is everything you wear next to your skin made from silk?'

Was she thinking about him in the nude, wearing only his boxer shorts or pajama bottoms?

The thought was very arousing.

"I like how it feels." His voice dropped half an octave.

The peach color of Jacki's cheeks deepened. "I bet. Only the best will do for you."

71

JIN

After showering, Jin already felt significantly better. First of all, the disgusting smell of puke was finally out of her hair, and secondly, much as she hated to admit it, Kalugal's silk pajamas were incredibly soft and luxurious.

Arwel would not have approved of her wearing another man's sleepwear, especially a sexy devil's like Kalugal, but he wasn't there, and she didn't have a choice.

Not much of the vomit had gotten on Alena's sweater and skirt, but they had still smelled horrible. Jacki had washed both in the bathroom sink, and then one of Kalugal's men had taken them to put in the washing machine and then the dryer. By morning, she could change back, and Arwel wouldn't know she had ever worn Kalugal's pajamas.

"I had tea made for you." Kalugal walked into the bedroom with a tray. "The regular kind." He put it on the nightstand.

Talk about ego-boosting. One of the two most powerful immortals on the planet was serving her tea in bed.

Sweet.

She smiled. "Thank you. Where is Jacki?"

"She fell asleep on the couch in the sitting room."

Lifting the chair that Jacki had moved aside, he brought it closer to the bed and sat down. "How are you feeling?" He poured the tea into a porcelain cup.

"A thousand times better. I can't believe how fast that shot worked." She took a sip from the tea. "Earl Grey?"

"Yes. I told Shamash to use the plainest tea we had."

Kalugal was such a snob, but for once she was going to keep her big mouth shut and not voice her opinion. "It's the one I like most."

"I'm glad that I was able to oblige your preference." He eyed her with that signature smirk lifting one corner of his perfect lips. "You must be disappointed."

"About what?"

"You thought that you were transitioning."

She nodded. "I'm glad it didn't happen now. I still need to show you that the tether is off. As much as I appreciate your hospitality, I want to be out of here by morning."

The smirk became more pronounced. "Given the way you were staring at my lips, I thought that you might want to stay a little longer."

Damn. The man was not only a snob but also full of himself. Still, she was going to tread lightly, and treat him as politely as a former Israeli soldier could. Some flattery wouldn't hurt either.

"You have the most beautiful lips I've ever seen on a man, and it's hard not to stare, but my heart belongs to another. Besides, your eyes can't compete with Arwel's."

He chuckled. "Indeed. He has the most uniquely colored eyes. But I'm sure that's not the only reason you gave him your heart."

"It was the first thing I noticed, but I fell in love with the whole package. There isn't a single thing I would change about Arwel." She scrunched her nose. "Except for his wardrobe, but that's a work in progress."

"A wardrobe is easy to fix." He sighed. "I want to wish the two of you the best of luck, but I have to be honest with you. If you can't prove to me that the tether is off, I won't be able to release you."

"I'll prove it." She scooted aside, clearing space on the bed, and patted the mattress. "Come sit next to me, and let's do it."

Gracefully unfolding his limbs from the chair, he shifted over to the bed and offered her his hand.

She took it and held it between her two. "I'm going to reattach the tether now. Close your eyes and turn your sight inward. You should experience a slight mental heaviness."

He nodded and did as she asked. "I'm ready."

Concentrating, she imagined inserting a hook into Kalugal's mind, and then attaching a thick strand of her consciousness to it instead of the wispy one she usually employed. Hopefully, he was going to feel it.

"It's attached. Can you feel it?"

Kalugal opened his eyes. "I think so, but it could be a placebo effect."

"Close your eyes again and focus on that feeling of heaviness. When I remove the tether, you should feel the difference."

"Okay."

"Did you feel it?"

He nodded. "I think so. Do it again."

She ended up tethering and releasing him five more times before he was convinced.

Partially.

"I felt the difference, but you might have been doing something differently to make me feel it. I can never be sure that the tether is really off."

"You can even remove it yourself once you know what to look for. One of the people I tethered was able to do it."

"I can attempt to do so, but that is not going to be conclusive either. I might imagine myself doing that, but I have no way of verifying that the tether is gone. I'll still need to take your word for it."

"Ask me. Compel me to tell you the truth."

"Is the tether off?"

"Yes, it is."

"Did you ever fail to remove the tether from someone you attached it to?"

"No."

"Have you ever encountered someone who you couldn't tether?"

"No. I could even do it to Jacki, who is immune to every other mind trick."

"How do you explain that?"

Jin sighed and looked down. "It's only speculation, but my sister and I think that we are the descendants of a different god. Someone who was not like the others. No one in the clan has ever heard of abilities like ours."

"What is your sister's talent?"

"She can retrieve echoes imbued in the walls. Not of everyday stuff, only conversations and events that were emotionally charged."

"Fascinating. I could use both your talents."

Jin smiled. "If you play nice with Kian, he might let you borrow us on occasion. But just so you know, I don't plan on a career in espionage. My sister and I are going to launch a fashion line."

His eyes widened. "That would be a terrible waste of two incredible talents. You could make millions by offering your special services."

"Or we could get conscripted into government service. That was what happened to me. If not for the clan, I would still be stuck in there. They saved me."

"Tell me all about it. And start at the beginning, please."

By the time she was done, it was light outside, Kalugal had ordered four more pots of tea to be delivered, and he must have asked her a thousand questions.

God only knew what he was going to do with all that information, but it wasn't as if she'd had a choice.

"One last question."

Jin rolled her eyes. "Go for it."

"Do you really love Arwel?"

"With all my heart and everything that I am. I can't imagine my life without him. We are fated mates." She smiled. "I didn't fully believe that until you captured him, but now I do."

He tilted his head. "You seem like an intelligent woman. I'm surprised that you believe in such romantic nonsense."

"It's real. Arwel says that the Fates reward those who have sacrificed greatly for others by giving them their one and only, a mate to form an unbreakable bond with. I haven't sacrificed much, but Arwel has, enough for both of us. Every day out in the field is torturous for him."

"How so?"

"That's more than one question, but it's not like I can refuse to answer. Arwel is a powerful empath, and he is constantly bombarded by human emotions. He would have been much happier in a job that didn't require interaction with humans, but despite the anguish it brings him, he chooses to be a Guardian and uses his special talent to protect the clan."

72

KALUGAL

Kalugal smiled. "That's admirable, and he deserves his reward." He rose to his feet. "I'll let you catch a little sleep."

"Are you going to let me go?"

Even though he wasn't sure about it yet, he nodded. "That's what I promised." He walked out into the sitting room.

Jacki was still asleep, covered in the throw blanket he'd wrapped around her. Hopefully, she hadn't been infected. The bacteria had wreaked havoc on Jin, and he would hate to see Jacki suffer like that.

Except, this time he knew what to do. He would bring a doctor and have him give her a penicillin shot. The thing worked like a miracle.

Sitting on an armchair across from Jacki, he was fascinated by the many shades of blond interwoven in her long wavy hair. He could have sat there for hours and just looked at her sleeping, but he had some thinking to do, and she was too distracting.

As Kalugal got up and walked out of the room, it occurred to him that it would be better if Jacki left as soon as possible. She was an unhealthy obsession that he had no business having, and she was too much of a distraction. A pleasant one, but still.

Except, he worried about the girl.

What was Kian going to do with her?

Perhaps he should continue his questioning to get a better insight into his cousin's motives and modes of operation. Jin didn't know much, and he doubted he could get anything more out of her. The doctor, on the other hand, would know much more.

Kalugal hadn't promised Kian not to interrogate him, but the fact that Kian hadn't insisted on it meant that the doctor didn't know any strategic secrets. Which was fine. He could still answer many of the questions that had been bugging Kalugal for decades.

When he opened the library doors, Kalugal found Julian flipping through one of his tomes on Sumerian mythology. "I see that you've chosen some light reading to pass the time."

Julian weighed the thick book on his palm. "Not as heavy as what's inside. Fascinating stuff."

Kalugal walked over to the library's bar and poured himself a small glass of whiskey. "Would you care to join me?" He lifted the bottle of twenty-five-year-old Macallan.

"Sure. I'm not a great whiskey connoisseur, but even I know that's a good one."

"What do you usually drink?" Kalugal handed him the glass.

"Beer."

Kalugal sat in the other armchair and crossed his legs. "Beer doesn't do it for me."

"Did you ever try Snake Venom?"

"Is it any good?"

"It's potent, and it's the only beer that can give an immortal a buzz."

"I drink for the taste, not to get drunk. Tell me, Julian, are immortal females blessed with the same advantages as the males?"

The doctor shook his head. "Are you using compulsion on me?"

"I'm not going to ask that you reveal clan secrets. Since I've never encountered an immortal female other than my mother, who I now know is a goddess, I'm curious about them and how different they are from the males. My father didn't share that information with his sons, real or adopted."

Julian struggled for a long moment, but Kalugal knew he wouldn't be able to resist for long and waited patiently.

"They are stronger than human females and have the same enhanced hearing and eyesight as the males. But they are not as strong, and they don't have functional fangs. Their sense of smell is not as developed either."

"What about thralling and shrouding abilities?"

"They have them, but since females don't need to use them, very few are good thrallers or shrouders."

"Is it because they are not soldiers?"

Julian chuckled. "It's because they don't bite their sex partners and don't need to erase the memory of it later."

"I see. Is there any way to distinguish them from human females?"

"Not unless they exhibit their strength."

The doctor was trying to resist by giving partial answers, but it was not going to work.

"Please list all the ways in which immortal females are different from human females and how to identify them."

That should close any loopholes Julian might cling to in an effort to resist giving Kalugal a complete answer.

"The scent of their arousal is different than that of human females. The caveat is that you need to know what to sniff for, and the female needs to be aroused at that moment for you to catch it. They also have the same rapid healing ability as the males. But it's not like you can go around scratching a woman's skin and watching how fast it heals."

"What about Dormants? How do you find them?"

"Usually, they find us."

Kalugal arched a brow. "Please explain."

"We've tried all kinds of methods to identify Dormants, but so far, the only indicator we've found was paranormal ability. It's not a sure sign because some humans with no godly genes have supernatural talents as well, and some Dormants have none. Most were seemingly random encounters or the work of the Fates, as some of us believe."

"Do you?"

Julian nodded. "You may say that I was compelled to. Meeting my mate must have been arranged by the Fates. There is no logical explanation for the bizarre set of circumstances that led to our coming together."

"How did you know she was your mate?"

Julian smiled. "One look at her picture was enough. I couldn't stop thinking about her. Every time I closed my eyes, I saw her looking at me, urging me to find her."

"Interesting. So, it can't be explained by pheromones or some other physical reaction."

"Precisely. When I saw her picture, I didn't know that she was a Dormant. All I knew was that the beautiful girl in the photo was much too young for me. The Fates had a different opinion."

"One more question. Can immunity to mind manipulation be considered a paranormal talent?"

Julian nodded.

"Is Jacki a Dormant?"

"She might be. There is no way to know until she is induced. She either transitions or doesn't."

"Has it been attempted with her?"

"No. She is new, and she doesn't know anything about transition or about being a possible candidate for one. We don't tell the suspected Dormants anything until they find a clan member to bond with, or in human terms to fall in love with. The bond guarantees their loyalty, and without it we can't risk the exposure."

That was excellent news. Jacki was a potential Dormant, and that explained why Kian accepted her into the clan and why he wasn't going to harm her when she came back to him.

Except, she might not.

Kalugal smirked.

Perhaps the Fates the clan believed in had arranged all of this to deliver Jacki to him. If she was indeed a Dormant, he could induce her transition and turn her immortal.

Suddenly his horizon appeared so much brighter.

Jacki could give him immortal children.

There was no guarantee that she possessed godly genes, but on the remote chance that she did, he couldn't let her go until he had seduced her and attempted to induce her transition.

73

JIN

After Kalugal left, Jin didn't go to sleep. She didn't even try.

Was he going to let her go?

He'd said he would, but he hadn't looked convinced. She could imagine him pacing the hallways of his sprawling mansion and plotting how to keep her without it causing a war with the clan.

Damn.

Now that she was feeling so much better, all kinds of crazy ideas were swirling in her head. The door to the suite was probably unlocked, and the Guardians were just outside the gate. Could she make a run for it?

Kalugal's men were not going to shoot her, so if she was fast enough and could scale that fence, she could get free.

How tall was that fence anyway?

Jin had watched it so many times from the balcony of the rented house, she should have known that, but for some reason, the details were hazy. Was it built from blocks or from bricks?

The master suite Kalugal had put her in faced the back yard, so she couldn't just look out the window and check.

If the fence was six feet tall, she could climb it with ease, she could even manage eight if there were small crevices that she could stick her fingertips into.

Except, she wouldn't make it to the wall before one of Kalugal's men tackled her to the ground.

Maybe Jacki could create a diversion?

Nah, those were all stupid thoughts. Kalugal would have no choice but to trade her back. The small suspicion still lingering in his mind was not enough for him to abandon Rufsur.

The sun was all the way up in the sky when Kalugal walked in with her clothes neatly folded in his arms. "You are awake."

"I couldn't sleep."

"How are you feeling?"

"As good as new."

"Excellent. That means that you can walk out of here on your own two feet, and Julian doesn't need to carry you out." He put the clothes on the chair next to the bed. "Get dressed. I'm letting you go."

Jin flung the blanket off and jumped up. "You don't have to ask me twice." She padded toward the bathroom. "I'll be out in a minute."

"No rush. I called Kian and told him to bring Rufsur back. We agreed to make the exchange at ten-thirty, which is two hours from now."

"Oh, okay."

"After you get dressed, come down and join Julian and me for breakfast."

"What about Jacki?"

"She stays. But you need to remove the tether from her as well."

"Why?"

"Because I don't want a spy in my house."

"Ouch."

"If you don't untether her, I will have to keep her locked up. If you do, she can be an honored guest instead of a prisoner."

Jin shook her head. "What's the difference? Jacki can tell us what she saw later, when you release her. I don't feel safe leaving her here with you without knowing what's going on with her."

"Do you want to go home, Jin? Because I can trade Jacki for Rufsur and keep you. You are a much better prize than your friend."

Damn him for leaving the choice up to her.

Maybe if he hadn't told her already that he was letting her go, she could have done the right thing and chosen to stay so Jacki could go. But with the taste of freedom already in her mouth, Jin couldn't bring herself to do that.

"It's only for a few hours, right?"

"Maybe a little longer. I don't know when Kian can arrange for me to speak with my mother."

That didn't sound too bad. Even if Jacki had to stay another night. After all, Kalugal would want more than one phone call with his mother, and if he did anything to Jacki, Kian would cut him off.

"Shouldn't Jacki join us for breakfast?"

"If you want to wake her up, you are welcome to do so. She is still passed out on the couch in the sitting room."

"I can't go without saying goodbye to her first."

He shrugged. "Then wake her up."

Why did she have the feeling that Kalugal had no intention of letting Jacki go anytime soon?

After Kian let him talk with Areana, it made no sense for him to keep her. Jacki didn't know anything useful, and even if she did, he couldn't compel her to tell him anything unless he planned to torture it out of her, but Jin doubted he would resort to that. Kalugal was a stuck-up snob who thought he was all that, but he wasn't evil.

Besides, Jacki seemed to like him. Maybe something had started between the two while she had been out of it?

That could be an interesting development.

DARK SPY'S RESOLUTION

After getting dressed, Jin combed her hair with her fingers because she didn't want to use Kalugal's brush, but she did use some of the hand lotion he had on the vanity to moisten her face. She looked like a damn ghost and there was nothing else she could do to improve her appearance. As they had suspected, it seemed that Kalugal never brought females home because there was nothing in his bathroom to suggest otherwise.

There was no leftover foundation, or eyeliner, or an extra robe. Even though the place was immaculately clean and luxurious, it screamed bachelor.

When she was done, Jin pulled on her shoes and walked into the sitting room.

Asleep on the couch, Jacki had a soft pillow tucked under her cheek, and a thick blanket tucked around her.

Had Kalugal done that? That was nice of him.

The two made a most unlikely pair, but maybe that was part of the attraction. Jacki had never met a guy like Kalugal, and he had probably never met a girl like Jacki, and not only because one was an immortal and the other still a human.

He was a prince, and she was a foster kid without a penny to her name.

Talk about Cinderella. Except, this one came with a sharp tongue and equally sharp claws. Jacki was no damsel in distress in need of a rescuer.

Or maybe she was?

Perhaps that was what Jacki had been looking for in a guy? Someone who would take care of her so she wouldn't have to worry ever again about where her next meal would come from or where she was going to sleep?

Except, if that was true, Jacki would have stayed in the program. She'd had a guaranteed income, including all-expenses-paid accommodations, and she'd given it all up for freedom.

Crouching next to her friend, Jin shook her shoulder. "Jacki, wake up."

"What? Why? Is it morning?"

"It is. Do you want to come down for breakfast?"

Yawning, Jacki stretched and sat up. "You look so much better. How are you feeling?"

"This is better?" Jin pulled on the skin under her eye. "I look like the walking dead."

"Trust me, this is better. Last night you looked like the non-walking dead. This is a big improvement."

Jin snorted. "Thanks for the compliment."

"You can always count on me to tell you the truth." Jacki put her feet down and got up. "I need to use the bathroom."

"I'll wait for you."

When Jacki was done, they took the stairs to the lower floor and followed the appetizing smells toward the dining room.

"I'm surprised that there were no guards posted outside the bedroom." Jacki stopped next to a painting. "Is this an original Picasso?"

"How should I know? It's possible. Kalugal likes expensive stuff."

"Who doesn't?" Jacki moved over to the next painting. "But I don't think those are originals. He wouldn't have hung them in the hallway."

"Probably. By the way, Kalugal is letting me go."

Jacki stopped and turned to look at her. "You managed to convince him?"

"Yes. After you fell asleep, he came back to the bedroom, and I attached and then removed the tether several times until he started noticing the difference."

"Thank God." Jacki pulled her into a crushing embrace. "It's over."

"Not yet. He is keeping you for a little while longer, and he wants me to remove the tether from you."

"I don't mind." Jacki waved her arm in an arc. "It's not every day that I get to stay in a place like this. More like never. This is a palace."

"You are not scared?"

"Of what?"

"You know, improper advances and stuff like that. There are no other women on Kalugal's estate, and without the tether, no one will know what's going on in here." She leaned closer. "Arwel says that all immortals are notoriously horny."

Jacki chuckled. "I hope that you know that from personal experience and not just hearsay."

Jin felt her ears warm up. "I certainly do."

Given the mischievous gleam in Jacki's eyes, she wasn't done teasing her. "Be careful not to set the house on fire." She leaned to whisper in her ear. "I'll be watching out for the smoke."

"Don't be silly." Jin slapped her arm and then leaned to whisper back. "With everyone fussing around us, we won't get the chance, and hopefully, by tonight, you will join us."

Jacki arched a brow. "I don't swing that way."

Jin laughed. "You know what I mean. Anyway, I'm done with my wandering days, and I hope to rekindle our passion in Arwel's home, not in the rented place or a hotel. I want days of doing nothing but making love, taking romantic walks, and having romantic dinners with my guy."

74

ARWEL

"Kalugal is releasing Jin." Magnus walked into the kitchen holding his phone.

Arwel's legs nearly gave out, and he leaned against the counter to steady himself. "When?"

"In two hours. We need to get Rufsur back here. Once he is at the gate, Jin is going to walk out with Julian. The antibiotics shot he gave her was an overnight cure."

"I'm ready to kiss him."

Kri snorted. "Who, Kalugal?"

"Julian. He cured my girl."

"What about Jacki?"

"I'll kiss her too."

"I meant, is he releasing her as well, or does he still want to keep her until he talks with his mother?"

Magnus shrugged. "As far as I know, that's still the plan. Kian told me to put you, Jin, and Kri on the plane and send you home. He wants all three of you out of here. "

Kri frowned. "Why do I need to go?"

"You know why. You are a head Guardian, and you know where the village is."

"I get it. But I could drive back with Michael." She cast Arwel a lopsided grin. "You and Jin probably want to celebrate on the plane. But if Kian insists, I can stay with Charlie in the cockpit and use these amazing earplugs Magnus has gotten us." She pulled them out of her pocket.

Arwel shook his head. "I just want to hold Jin in my arms and never let go."

"Still, I'd rather drive home with Michael."

"There is enough space for all four of you on the jet," Magnus said. "If you want to drive home, you will have to clear it with Kian first."

"Of course." She pulled out her phone and started typing a text.

"This is how I suggest we do it." Magnus leaned on the counter next to Arwel. "I'm going to bring Rufsur to the gate, collect Julian and Jin, and load them into my car. You and Kri will head to the airstrip and wait for us there."

Arwel wanted to argue that he could wait in the car, but he knew it wasn't prudent. Even staying in the rented house had been a risk.

Except so far, Kalugal hadn't tried anything underhanded or unexpected. He was holding up his end of the deal and doing exactly what he had promised to do.

In fact, Arwel had to admit that the clan had acted less honorably than Kalugal by sending Jin after him, and that he'd been very reserved in his response.

Was he reading the situation all wrong?

In the brief moments he'd had with Kalugal, Arwel had tried to read his emotional grid, but it hadn't been easy. Not because Kalugal was so complicated, but because he just wasn't the emotional type.

If they weren't on opposite sides of the fence, Arwel could have enjoyed the guy's company. Calm, collected, and logical were precisely the type of people Arwel liked to hang out with. That was why accountants were his favorites.

But what if Kalugal was just a cold and calculating bastard, and he was lulling them into a false sense of security?

Arwel needed more information about the guy, and he knew where to get it. "I'll come to collect Rufsur with you. I haven't had a chance to chat with him yet. I can continue from there straight to the airstrip."

"You're welcome to come, but don't expect to get any information out of him. The guy only appears easygoing and friendly. He has a sharp mind, and he keeps his guard up. I talked with him for hours last night and got basically nothing."

"I have a slight advantage over you. I can sense his emotional response, and that gives me additional insight. Besides, I promised him a chat, and I didn't make good on it."

"Sorry to disappoint you," Kri said after reading the return text from Kian. "He doesn't want me and Michael to waste time driving. We are coming with you and Jin on the plane. Julian is going to stay another day in case Jacki caught the bug from Jin and needs him, but the medical equipment that he brought with him goes back with us."

"That's okay. I wasn't planning on joining the mile-high club just yet."

He and Jin had eternity together, and there would be plenty of time to try new things. Making love in the sky could wait.

75

JIN

*E*xcitement swirling in her belly, Jin hugged Jacki. "See you soon."

"I hope so. Give Arwel a kiss for me." Jacki winked. "On the cheek. The other kisses are all yours."

"I can't wait."

"Then go." Her friend pushed her away. "I'll be fine."

Taking a deep breath, Jin nodded and walked over to Julian and Kalugal, who had been waiting patiently for her to say goodbye.

Jin pinned Kalugal with a hard stare. "Be good to her."

"Don't worry. I'll treat her like a visiting dignitary."

He sounded sincere, but Jin still felt like she was abandoning Jacki in a lions' den, and she wasn't sure whether Kalugal was more like Mufasa than Scar, or the other way around.

As the gate opened, Jin expected Arwel would be waiting for her, and her heart squeezed in disappointment when she saw Magnus standing on the other side of the street with Rufsur and not her mate.

With a nod from Kalugal, she and Julian started walking, and so did Rufsur. The guy smiled and winked when he passed them, but he didn't stop and kept walking.

She turned around, wanting to issue another warning about Jacki, but Julian's hand on her elbow propelled her forward.

"Welcome back." Magnus opened the passenger door for her.

Hoping to find Arwel inside the car, she ducked her head, but he wasn't there. "Where is Arwel?"

Magnus shook his head and got behind the wheel.

"He can't hear you. He has earplugs in," Julian explained as he got in the car.

"Oh."

That was smart. If Magnus couldn't hear Kalugal, he couldn't be compelled.

Glancing at the rearview mirror, Magnus drove for about fifteen minutes before pulling his earplugs out. "Arwel is waiting for you at the airstrip, but first, I'm going to drop Julian off at the motel."

Jin's heart sped up. They were finally going home. "Can I borrow your phone to call him?"

"Use mine." Julian handed her the device. "He's listed under Arabella."

Magnus chuckled. "That's clever, but not very imaginative. You should have listed him under Beatrice or some other name that bears no resemblance to his."

Julian shrugged. "That's the first thing that came to my mind."

Ignoring their banter, Jin placed the call.

"Julian," Arwel answered. "Is Jin all right?"

"It's me. I'm calling from Julian's phone."

She heard him release a breath. "Are you okay?"

"I'm great. The antibiotics shot cured me overnight. I can't wait to see you."

"I wanted to be there when you came out, but Kian didn't want Kri and me anywhere near Kalugal. We know too much."

"I get it. Are we going to the village? Or are we going back to the keep?"

He hesitated for a moment. "We are going to the village. I have some upsetting news for you. Wendy is a mole. She contacted the director."

Jin shook her head. "There must be some mistake. Why would she do that?"

"I don't have the details."

"Damn." Jin slumped back in the seat. "I should have tethered her like Kian asked me to do. I could have caught her before she had a chance to call. What did she tell him?"

"Just the location of the cabin they moved into after I was compromised, and the story we told your friends about who we are."

"Are you sure that this is all?"

"One of the Guardians thralled her and confirmed the information. What I'm afraid of, though, is that she might have an ability to shield parts of her consciousness. Otherwise, she wouldn't have been able to fool Edna."

"Do you think the Guardian saw a false memory?"

"It's unlikely with a fresh memory, but not impossible. The clan's psychologist should have a talk with her."

"Perhaps I should talk with Wendy. Where is she?"

"Kian had her locked up in the keep."

"Can we go there instead of the village?"

Magnus shook his head and mouthed *no* while looking at her in the rearview mirror.

Jin frowned. What was that about?

"You need to rest and regain your strength," Arwel said. "Let someone else take care of this for now."

"You don't have to twist my arm too hard. I really want to finally see the village, but I feel responsible for Wendy. How about I go see her tomorrow?"

"First, let's get home and then make plans for the future. Que sera, sera."

"Whatever will be, will be." She smiled and switched the phone to her other ear. "The future is not ours to see. But there is one thing I know for sure."

"What is it?"

"My future is with you."

Dear reader,

Thank you for reading the ***Children of the Gods***.

As an independent author, I rely on your support to spread the word. So if you enjoyed the story, please share your experience with others, and if it isn't too much trouble, I would greatly appreciate a brief **review** on Amazon.

Love & happy reading,
Isabell

COMING UP NEXT
Dark Overlord Trilogy

Read the enclosed excerpt

INCLUDES
38: Dark Overlord New Horizon
39: Dark Overlord's Wife
40: Dark Overlord's Clan

Don't miss out on:
The Children of the Gods Origins
Goddess's Choice
Goddess's Hope

The Perfect Match Series
Perfect Match 1: Vampire's Consort
Perfect Match 2: King's Chosen
Perfect Match 3: Captain's Conquest

FOR EXCLUSIVE PEEKS AT UPCOMING RELEASES
Join my *VIP Club* and gain access to the *VIP* portal at itlucas.com
CLICK HERE TO JOIN
(If you're already a subscriber and forgot the password to the VIP portal, you can find it at the bottom of each of my emails. Or click **HERE** to retrieve it. You can also email me at isabell@itlucas.com)

DARK OVERLORD EXCERPT

JACKI

As Jacki escorted Jin to Kalugal's front door, she had a sinking feeling that she was never going to see her bestie or her other new friends again. In the short time that she'd spent with the bunch, they'd become like a family to her, and finding out that most of them were immortal hadn't changed the way she felt about them. They were her teammates, and she was going to miss them.

Thankfully, a feeling wasn't a vision, so it might not come true. Jacki's gut had been wrong about things before. Besides, being left alone with Kalugal was reason enough for the churning in her stomach. The rest was just panic induced, and Jacki refused to let it bring her down.

She'd survived worse, and she was going to survive this as well.

"I hope that Arwel isn't still mad at me." Jin took a deep breath before walking out the door.

"He loves you too much to stay mad."

"I know that he loves me. But that doesn't mean that he's not angry."

During their imprisonment in Kalugal's bunker, Arwel and Jacki had become good friends, and at the beginning, they had even pretended to be a couple. The thing was, Jin must have witnessed some of their pretend flirting through the mental link she'd had to Jacki, and she must have also heard Arwel ranting about her decision to surrender herself to Kalugal.

Perhaps that had created doubts in Jin's mind?

Jacki wrapped her arm around her friend's shoulders. "I won't lie to you. When Rufsur told us that you were going to be traded for Arwel, your guy was majorly pissed, but that was because he was terrified of what Kalugal might do to you. Since nothing bad happened, and you are going back to him unharmed, all is good in Arwel's world."

Jin nodded. "I was scared too. Thank God that Kalugal turned out to be a decent guy. But while that might be true for me, I'm not sure about his intentions for you." She eyed Jacki with concern. "I hate leaving you behind. Without the tether, I can't check up on you." Glancing at Kalugal and Julian, who were standing further down the driveway, Jin leaned to whisper in Jacki's ear. "I don't like it that he demanded that I remove the tether from you. It should have been enough that I removed it from him, and it was also what he and Kian had agreed on."

"I think that it makes perfect sense for Kalugal to ask that," Jacki whispered back. "If you'd kept the tether to me, you could've spied on him through my eyes. If I were in his shoes, I would have done the same." She gave Jin a slight push. "Get out of here and go to your boyfriend. Everything is going to be okay."

Jin pulled her into a tight embrace. "See you soon."

"I hope so. Give Arwel a kiss for me. On the cheek, of course." Jacki winked. "The other kind of kisses are all yours."

"I can't wait."

"Then go." She pushed Jin away. "I'll be fine."

Thankfully, empathy wasn't one of Jin's paranormal talents, so she bought the lie and the fake smile that Jacki had plastered on her face.

Watching her friend walk down Kalugal's driveway, Jacki didn't feel fine. She was scared.

When Jin reached Kalugal, she pointed a finger at him. "Be good to her."

"Don't worry. I'll treat her like a visiting dignitary."

Taking a last glance at her friend, Jacki turned around and walked back in. With a sigh, she sat at the dining room table and reached for a piece of toast. Perhaps chewing on it would relieve the churning in her stomach.

So much for thinking of herself as tough, resourceful, and fearless. Except, there was a limit to how much she could take in such a short time.

Jacki felt as if she was staring down a tunnel, and it seemed that with each step she was tumbling deeper into an alternate reality.

The thing was, she knew precisely what had gotten her to where she was now. She'd been having visions her entire life, but the first tumble down the rabbit hole had started with one particular vision, which in hindsight, she regretted not keeping to herself.

As soon as she'd seen the old clunker that her friend Allison had gotten, the vision had hit Jacki hard. The car was going to break down, and Allison was going to end up in a ditch with multiple fractures and spend the next six months in rehabilitation.

Naturally, Allison had dismissed Jacki's vision as nonsense and had taken the clunker on a road trip to California. Jacki's prediction had come true, and a week after Allison's accident, she'd been contacted by Marisol, who had offered her a job in the paranormal talents' division.

Apparently, during her phone calls to Allison, Jacki had mentioned the words visions and predictions, and the bots had picked up on the trigger words, flagging her as a potential paranormal talent. When her prediction about Allison's accident had come true, her talent had been confirmed.

Still, all of that had been small potatoes compared to what happened next.

Meeting Jin in the program and foreseeing her rescue was the reason Jacki was sitting in the dining room of the fanciest house she'd ever seen, and until a few minutes ago, staring at the face of the most gorgeous, arrogant, sexy man ever born.

Correction.

Not a man, an immortal.

And not just any immortal, one of the two most powerful immortals on the planet.

Damn.

Up until three days ago, she hadn't known that immortals even existed, or that the people who'd helped her escape from the program weren't human.

Her biggest fear was that the knowledge could mean the end of her.

Humans were not supposed to know that immortals had been living among them since the beginning of civilization. If not for her immunity to mind manipulation, they could've erased the memory from her head like they did with all the other humans who had the misfortune of finding out about them. But there was no way to erase Jacki's memories, and she was stuck with what she'd learned.

Even if Kalugal released her in exchange for what Kian had promised him, she would never be free again. The way Jacki saw it, there were three possible outcomes.

One was being Kalugal's prisoner for the rest of her natural life, the other was the same fate at Kian's hands, and the third one was her death.

Was she being overly dramatic? Fatalistic?

Probably.

Jacki doubted that Kian and her new friends would kill her, but she was quite certain that she would never be allowed to go back to her old life.

There was also a fourth possibility.

Kalugal could fall in love with her, and they could live happily ever after.

Right. Talk about fairytales and fantasies.

A man like him might want her in his bed for a night or two, but no more than that.

Except, Jacki was not going to be his or anyone else's plaything, not even to save her life.

For her, it always had been and always would be all or nothing.

KALUGAL

"Welcome back, my friend." Kalugal pulled Rufsur into a one-armed embrace and clapped him on the back. "How was your stay with my cousin's people?"

"For the most part, uneventful." Rufsur dug a key out of his pocket and leaned down to open the lock on his leg restraints.

"They gave you the key?" As Kalugal looked down at the chain connecting Rufsur's ankle cuffs, he wondered whether they were the same ones that Phinas had put on Arwel.

"The only reason they did that was so I couldn't run. If I had stopped to open the lock, that would have achieved the same result. They wanted Jin to reach their side before I reached ours." Rufsur tossed the chain aside and straightened up.

"Come, Jacki is waiting for us in the dining room." Kalugal turned and started walking.

Rufsur followed. "She is still here?"

Kalugal arched a brow. "Where else would she be?"

"I thought that you'd already talked to your mother and released Jacki."

He stopped and turned to his lieutenant. "Didn't they tell you about what happened with Jin?"

"Only that the exchange was delayed because she didn't feel well." Rufsur cast Kalugal a regretful look. "You must have been disappointed to find out that she was not an immortal and therefore not a clanswoman. That ruined your plans to forge an alliance with the clan by marrying the spy."

It had been a contingency Kalugal had come up with in case Jin couldn't remove the damn tether she'd attached to him. If that had been the case, he would have needed to keep her by his side, and the only way he could have done so without starting a war with the clan was a political marriage. The alliance with Kian had been a secondary consideration. Luckily for them both, Jin was able to demonstrate that the tether was gone.

The problem was that he wasn't a hundred percent sure that it was.

"Those plans were irrelevant anyway. Jin is in love with Arwel."

"So I heard. Is she all better now? She looked fine to me when I passed by her and that guy. Who was he?"

"That was one of the clan's doctors. Jin got sick all over the gazebo floor before she could demonstrate the tether's removal, and then she passed out. I couldn't let her go, so they sent the doctor. After he gave her an antibiotic shot, she recovered almost immediately."

"And then she proved to you that the tether was gone?"

Kalugal shrugged and resumed walking. "I'm still not convinced that it is."

"So why did you let her go?" Rufsur followed.

"I didn't have a choice. It was either that or start a war with the clan."

"But you felt something, right?"

Kalugal nodded. "I did. But it might have been a placebo effect. I might have felt it because I expected to feel it. I compelled Jin to tell me the truth, but that's not foolproof either. She might have believed that the tether was gone while some of it still remained, or she might be able to re-establish the connection remotely. I've just realized that I didn't ask her about that."

"Do you mean that you forgot to compel her to answer that truthfully?"

"It didn't occur to me to ask about it at all. I've made a mistake, and it might cost me dearly."

"What are you going to do?"

"I don't know. I guess I'll have to trust her that it's gone."

Rufsur arched a brow. "That's not like you."

His friend knew him well. Kalugal had an idea of how to prove the tether's removal, but he couldn't tell Rufsur about it because it would defeat the purpose.

His plan was to pretend that he believed the tether wasn't there, do something that would provoke Kian, and then wait for his cousin to react.

As they entered the dining room, Jacki smiled at Rufsur. "We meet again after all."

He grinned and walked up to her. "You are a sight for sore eyes, Miss Jacqueline the Fair." He took her hand and kissed the back of it.

"I like it. You make me sound like a fairytale princess."

Kalugal didn't like it at all, barely stifling the impulse to grab his lieutenant by the throat and toss him across the room.

Fortunately, Jacki pulled her hand out of Rufsur's. "Are you hungry? There is plenty left over, but it's cold. I can take it to the kitchen and warm it up for you." She started to rise.

Kalugal put a hand on her shoulder. "Sit down, Jacki. Shamash can do it. You are my guest." He put a slight emphasis on the *my*.

But Rufsur hadn't been paying attention and pulled out a chair next to Jacki. "I don't mind that it's cold. I'm not a finicky eater like my boss."

Taking his seat at the head of the table, Kalugal glared at Rufsur. "Tell me your impressions from the time you spent with Kian's men."

Rufsur lifted the coffee carafe and poured the cold brew into a cup. "There was a female there as well."

"A female warrior?" Kalugal asked.

"I don't think so. Vivian is the commander's wife, and she's a very pleasant woman. She made sure that the warriors treated me well and that I was made as comfortable as possible given the circumstances. They had me chained to a chair."

Kalugal looked at Jacki. "Do you know her?"

"Vivian is Magnus's wife, and she is not a soldier."

"Is she an immortal?"

Jacki shrugged. "Did you forget that I didn't know anything about immortals until you captured Arwel and me and informed me about Arwel being one? They told me that they were a group of paranormally talented people."

"Point taken." Kalugal turned to Rufsur. "Is Vivian an immortal?"

"I didn't think it was polite to ask, but I assume that she is. Otherwise, what's the point of marrying her? It's just asking for heartache when she gets old and dies."

Kalugal turned back to Jacki. "Does the clan have female warriors?"

She shrugged again. "How the hell would I know? They didn't tell me anything."

Rufsur loaded his plate with eggs. "Before taking me to where I met Vivian, they took me someplace else to search me thoroughly. There was a female there, who I'm sure was a warrior." He lifted his hands and spread them wide. "She had shoulders nearly as broad as mine, but she was still fine to look at, and so was Vivian. If all the clan females are that pretty, then we should start negotiating with your cousin for visitation rights." He glanced at Jacki. "Not for me, but for the others." He winked at her.

She shook her head. "The reasons why I can't date you haven't changed since yesterday. And as you have mentioned earlier, getting involved with a human is asking for heartache." She leaned toward him. "After all, I'm going to get old and die."

Rufsur reached for her hand, but she snatched it away. Undeterred, he smiled suggestively. "I'll take whatever time you're willing to give me."

She let out a breath. "When you stop goofing around and give it some serious thought, I'm sure you'll arrive at the same conclusion I did."

Kalugal really needed to have a talk with the guy and make it clear that Jacki was his. Otherwise, the moment Rufsur discovered that Jacki was a possible Dormant, he would redouble his crude flirting efforts and get twice as bold.

The thing was, Jacki seemed to respond to his lieutenant's unsophisticated approach.

Kalugal had a feeling that Jacki simply didn't know any better because she hadn't met any high-caliber men like him before. All she was familiar with were the clumsy flirtation attempts of uneducated young men, who shared her lowly socioeconomic background.

He hadn't missed her comment about growing up in foster homes. She was a poor girl, with no family and no higher education, and the only things she had going for her were her beauty and her immunity to mind manipulation.

Except, that same ability was an indicator of a strong mind. Perhaps Jacki's lack of education was the result of lack of opportunity, and not the lack of intelligence or the drive to acquire knowledge. If that was the case, he could teach her all she needed to know.

It reminded Kalugal of an old musical he had once seen. *My Fair lady* was a story about a stuck-up professor trying to teach a poor girl to talk and act like a lady.

Had the musical prompted Rufsur to address Jacki as Miss Jacqueline the Fair?

Or was it the other way around, and Rufsur's remark had planted the idea in Kalugal's mind?

Since his lieutenant had probably never watched a musical in his entire immortal life, the second assumption was more likely.

Rufsur had just wanted to impress Jacki with his good manners and fancy talk.

Nevertheless, the idea was sound. Jacki wasn't the perfect companion Kalugal would have wished for, but he might turn her into one yet.

The question was whether she would let him.

Once he executed his plan to verify that the tether was gone, Jacki might never forgive him or allow him anywhere near her, and regrettably, he would not be able to erase the nasty memory from her head either.

DIRECTOR SIMMONS

Director Simmons opened the door to his office and motioned for his top recruiter to come in. "Good morning, Marisol."

"Good morning, sir." She walked over to his desk, took a seat in one of the leather chairs facing it, and put her hands on her knees.

"You look lovely."

"Thank you, sir."

"Please call me Edgar. You make me feel like an old man when you address me as sir."

"How about Doctor Simmons? Or Director Simmons?"

"We are friends, Marisol, and we are alone here. Save the titles for when we are in front of the recruits."

"Yes, sir. I mean, Edgar."

"That's better." He smiled and patted her bony back.

He wasn't flirting with the woman, but one of the things he had learned early on in his career was that personal touch always made his subordinates work harder for him.

Maybe if she were better looking and was a little more charming, he would have considered it, but Marisol had the sex appeal of a dull knife, and her personality bordered on sociopathic. Still, the new blonde hair softened her harsh features and made her look a little more feminine, which might help her with luring male talents into joining the program.

Sitting on the chair across from his recruiter, Edgar leaned toward her and steepled his fingers. "Wendy left a very interesting message on my voicemail."

Marisol's eyes widened. "She contacted you? Where is she? Are the others with her?"

He lifted a hand. "Slow down. When she left the message, they were in Big Bear, California, but Wendy must have gotten caught making the call because less than an hour later, there was no one at the address she provided. There was a for rent sign outside the cabin, and the guy that I'd sent to investigate found a cleaning crew preparing it for the next renters. They didn't know who stayed in it before."

"That should be easy to find out."

"Not really. Someone infected the rental records with a computer bug and turned everything into a jumbled mess. Not only that, the recording that Wendy left on my voice mail got erased. I tried to listen to it again, but it was no longer there. We are dealing with professionals, Eleanor."

He rarely called the recruiter by her real name, using it only when they were conspiring to do things that were not approved by the higher-ups.

"Did Wendy say anything else?"

"Yes, and it's more important than the location she provided. Apparently, an organization of paranormally talented people is collecting new members. Somehow, they knew about Jin and came for her. Jacki and Richard jumped on the opportunity to escape, and Wendy joined them so she could report to me and tell me where they were taken. She had to steal someone's phone to do so. Evidently, the organization that took them is not allowing them any more freedoms than we had."

Marisol snorted. "Fools. What did they expect? Some shady paranormal organization that is competing with us is not going to give them better terms or treat them better than we do. We need to stop the weekly leave until we figure out who we are dealing with, or at least beef up security."

Despite her abrasive and mistrustful nature, Eleanor was naive. But she wasn't entirely wrong.

Even though not everything was aboveboard, and not everything that the recruits had been told or promised was the truth, no one could compete with the US government's resources. He had no doubt that the program was leagues better than anything they could expect on the outside.

"We can't stop the outings. Not only are they good for morale, but they are also important for keeping up appearances. Trainees in other programs using this facility get to have days off. We can't treat ours differently. I can, however, increase security. We are already driving them to a different town every week, so the outings are not as predictable as they used to be before the escape."

Marisol's fingers drummed a nervous beat on her knees. "I don't remember much of what happened to me during the time I was gone, but I know that they got the information from me. That whole hotel room with drug paraphernalia was a setup. I've never used drugs, and I would have never gone to a hotel room with some guy I'd just met."

"I know, Marisol. We've been over that, and I don't blame you. It could have happened to anyone."

She looked down at her hands. "I don't know how they found out about me."

"You must have said something to Jin, and she told it to someone. She must have been resistant to compulsion."

Marisol shook her head. "She was so convincing. I can't believe that the girl managed to fool me."

Getting played bugged the hell out of Marisol, but what bugged her even more was that she'd had to change her name and her appearance once again. Her new name was Gina Voldachevsky, and she wasn't happy with it.

"I should start calling you Gina."

"It's confusing to the recruits who know me as Marisol." She touched her blonde curls. "This hair was adjustment enough."

"It looks good on you."

She smiled. "You are a bad liar, Edgar."

He laughed.

She couldn't have been more wrong. There were so many things he was keeping from her while pretending that she was his friend and confidant.

Eleanor, aka Marisol, aka Gina, had no idea that Wendy was his niece.

In fact, Wendy was his grandniece, but the distinction was not important. His sister's daughter was gone, most likely dead from a drug overdose, and his sister had passed away decades ago. He and Wendy were the only family members left.

The other thing Eleanor, aka Marisol, didn't know was that no matter where the missing trainees were hiding, he could find them quite easily. The only reason he hadn't done so already was that finding out who had taken them was more important than finding the trainees themselves.

Unlike Marisol, he was a patient man, and he was waiting for the dust to settle and for everyone to get comfortable and complacent. Not having a large force at his disposal, Edgar needed the recruits as well as those helping them to stop looking over their shoulders before he made his move.

DARK OVERLORD TRILOGY

THE CHILDREN OF THE GODS SERIES

THE CHILDREN OF THE GODS ORIGINS

1: Goddess's Choice

When gods and immortals still ruled the ancient world, one young goddess risked everything for love.

2: Goddess's Hope

Hungry for power and infatuated with the beautiful Areana, Navuh plots his father's demise. After all, by getting rid of the insane god he would be doing the world a favor. Except, when gods and immortals conspire against each other, humanity pays the price.

But things are not what they seem, and prophecies should not to be trusted...

THE CHILDREN OF THE GODS

1: Dark Stranger The Dream

Syssi's paranormal foresight lands her a job at Dr. Amanda Dokani's neuroscience lab, but it fails to predict the thrilling yet terrifying turn her life will take. Syssi has no clue that her boss is an immortal who'll drag her into a secret, millennia-old battle over humanity's future. Nor does she realize that the professor's imposing brother is the mysterious stranger who's been starring in her dreams.

Since the dawn of human civilization, two warring factions of immortals—the descendants of the gods of old—have been secretly shaping its destiny. Leading the clandestine battle from his luxurious Los Angeles high-rise, Kian is surrounded by his clan, yet alone. Descending from a single goddess, clan members are forbidden to each other. And as the only other immortals are their hated enemies, Kian and his kin have been long resigned to a lonely existence of fleeting trysts with human partners. That is, until his sister makes a game-changing discovery—a mortal seeress who she believes is a dormant carrier of their genes. Ever the realist, Kian is skeptical and refuses Amanda's plea to attempt Syssi's activation. But when his enemies learn of the Dormant's existence, he's forced to rush her to the safety of his keep. Inexorably drawn to Syssi, Kian wrestles with his conscience as he is tempted to explore her budding interest in the darker shades of sensuality.

2: Dark Stranger Revealed

While sheltered in the clan's stronghold, Syssi is unaware that Kian and Amanda are not human, and neither are the supposedly religious fanatics that are after her. She feels a powerful connection to Kian, and as he introduces her to a world of pleasure she never dared imagine, his dominant sexuality is a revelation. Considering that she's completely out of her element, Syssi feels comfortable and safe letting go with him. That is, until she begins to suspect that all is not as it seems. Piecing the puzzle together, she draws a scary, yet wrong conclusion...

3: Dark Stranger Immortal

When Kian confesses his true nature, Syssi is not as much shocked by the revelation as she is wounded by what she perceives as his callous plans for her.

If she doesn't turn, he'll be forced to erase her memories and let her go. His family's safety demands secrecy – no one in the mortal world is allowed to know that immortals exist.

Resigned to the cruel reality that even if she stays on to never again leave the keep, she'll get old while Kian won't, Syssi is determined to enjoy what little time she has with him, one day at a time.

Can Kian let go of the mortal woman he loves? Will Syssi turn? And if she does, will she survive the dangerous transition?

4: Dark Enemy Taken

Dalhu can't believe his luck when he stumbles upon the beautiful immortal professor. Presented with a once in a lifetime opportunity to grab an immortal female for himself, he kidnaps her and runs. If he ever gets caught, either by her people or his, his life is forfeit.

But for a chance of a loving mate and a family of his own, Dalhu is prepared to do everything in his power to win Amanda's heart, and that includes leaving the Doom brotherhood and his old life behind.

Amanda soon discovers that there is more to the handsome Doomer than his dark past and a hulking, sexy body. But succumbing to her enemy's seduction, or worse, developing feelings for a ruthless killer is out of the question. No man is worth life on the run, not even the one and only immortal male she could claim as her own...

Her clan and her research must come first...

5: Dark Enemy Captive

When the rescue team returns with Amanda and the chained Dalhu to the keep, Amanda is not as thrilled to be back as she thought she'd be. Between Kian's contempt for her and Dalhu's imprisonment, Amanda's budding relationship with Dalhu seems doomed. Things start to look up when Annani offers her help, and together with Syssi they resolve to find a way for Amanda to be with Dalhu. But will she still want him when she realizes that he is responsible for her nephew's murder? Could she? Will she take the easy way out and choose Andrew instead?

6: Dark Enemy Redeemed

Amanda suspects that something fishy is going on onboard the Anna. But when her investigation of the peculiar all-female Russian crew fails to uncover anything other than more speculation, she decides it's time to stop playing detective and face her real problem —a man she shouldn't want but can't live without.

6.5: My Dark Amazon

When Michael and Kri fight off a gang of humans, Michael gets stabbed. The injury to his immortal body recovers fast, but the one to his ego takes longer, putting a strain on his relationship with Kri.

7: Dark Warrior Mine

When Andrew is forced to retire from active duty, he believes that all he has to look forward to is a boring desk job. His glory days in special ops are over. But as it turns out, his thrill ride has just begun. Andrew discovers not only that immortals exist and have been manipulating global affairs since antiquity, but that he and his sister are rare possessors of the immortal genes.

Problem is, Andrew might be too old to attempt the activation process. His sister, who is fourteen years his junior, barely made it through the transition, so the odds of him coming out of it alive, let alone immortal, are slim.

But fate may force his hand.

Helping a friend find his long-lost daughter, Andrew finds a woman who's worth taking the risk for. Nathalie might be a Dormant, but the only way to find out for sure requires fangs and venom.

8: Dark Warrior's Promise

Andrew and Nathalie's love flourishes, but the secrets they keep from each other taint their relationship with doubts and suspicions. In the meantime, Sebastian and his men are getting bolder, and the storm that's brewing will shift the balance of power in the millennia-old conflict between Annani's clan and its enemies.

9: Dark Warrior's Destiny

The new ghost in Nathalie's head remembers who he was in life, providing Andrew and her with indisputable proof that he is real and not a figment of her imagination.

Convinced that she is a Dormant, Andrew decides to go forward with his transition immediately after the rescue mission at the Doomers' HQ.

Fearing for his life, Nathalie pleads with him to reconsider. She'd rather spend the rest of her mortal days with Andrew than risk what they have for the fickle promise of immortality.

While the clan gets ready for battle, Carol gets help from an unlikely ally. Sebastian's second-in-command can no longer ignore the torment she suffers at the hands of his commander and offers to help her, but only if she agrees to his terms.

10: Dark Warrior's Legacy

Andrew's acclimation to his post-transition body isn't easy. His senses are sharper, he's bigger, stronger, and hungrier. Nathalie fears that the changes in the man she loves are more than physical. Measuring up to this new version of him is going to be a challenge.

Carol and Robert are disillusioned with each other. They are not destined mates, and love is not on the horizon. When Robert's three months are up, he might be left with nothing to show for his sacrifice.

Lana contacts Anandur with disturbing news; the yacht and its human cargo are in Mexico. Kian must find a way to apprehend Alex and rescue the women on board without causing an international incident.

11: Dark Guardian Found

What would you do if you stopped aging?

Eva runs. The ex-DEA agent doesn't know what caused her strange mutation, only that if discovered, she'll be dissected like a lab rat. What Eva doesn't know, though, is that she's a descendant of the gods, and that she is not alone. The man who rocked her world in one life-changing encounter over thirty years ago is an immortal as well.

To keep his people's existence secret, Bhathian was forced to turn his back on the only woman who ever captured his heart, but he's never forgotten and never stopped looking for her.

12: Dark Guardian Craved

Cautious after a lifetime of disappointments, Eva is mistrustful of Bhathian's professed feelings of love. She accepts him as a lover and a confidant but not as a life partner.

Jackson suspects that Tessa is his true love mate, but unless she overcomes her fears, he might never find out.

Carol gets an offer she can't refuse—a chance to prove that there is more to her than meets the eye. Robert believes she's about to commit a deadly mistake, but when he tries to dissuade her, she tells him to leave.

13: Dark Guardian's Mate

Prepare for the heart-warming culmination of Eva and Bhathian's story!

14: Dark Angel's Obsession

The cold and stoic warrior is an enigma even to those closest to him. His secrets are about to unravel...

15: Dark Angel's Seduction

Brundar is fighting a losing battle. Calypso is slowly chipping away his icy armor from the outside, while his need for her is melting it from the inside.

He can't allow it to happen. Calypso is a human with none of the Dormant indicators. There is no way he can keep her for more than a few weeks.

16: Dark Angel's Surrender

Get ready for the heart pounding conclusion to Brundar and Calypso's story.

Callie still couldn't wrap her head around it, nor could she summon even a smidgen of sorrow or regret. After all, she had some memories with him that weren't horrible. She should've felt something. But there was nothing, not even shock. Not even horror at what had transpired over the last couple of hours.

Maybe it was a typical response for survivors--feeling euphoric for the simple reason that they were alive. Especially when that survival was nothing short of miraculous.

Brundar's cold hand closed around hers, reminding her that they weren't out of the woods yet. Her injuries were superficial, and the most she had to worry about was some scarring. But, despite his and Anandur's reassurances, Brundar might never walk again.

If he ended up crippled because of her, she would never forgive herself for getting him involved in her crap.

"Are you okay, sweetling? Are you in pain?" Brundar asked.

Her injuries were nothing compared to his, and yet he was concerned about her. God, she loved this man. The thing was, if she told him that, he would run off, or crawl away as was the case.

Hey, maybe this was the perfect opportunity to spring it on him.

17: Dark Operative: A Shadow of Death

As a brilliant strategist and the only human entrusted with the secret of immortals' existence, Turner is both an asset and a liability to the clan. His request to attempt transition into immortality as an alternative to cancer treatments cannot be denied without risking the clan's exposure. On the other hand, approving it means risking his premature death. In both scenarios, the clan will lose a valuable ally.

When the decision is left to the clan's physician, Turner makes plans to manipulate her by taking advantage of her interest in him.

Will Bridget fall for the cold, calculated operative? Or will Turner fall into his own trap?

18: Dark Operative: A Glimmer of Hope

As Turner and Bridget's relationship deepens, living together seems like the right move, but to make it work both need to make concessions.

Bridget is realistic and keeps her expectations low. Turner could never be the truelove mate she yearns for, but he is as good as she's going to get. Other than his emotional limitations, he's perfect in every way.

Turner's hard shell is starting to show cracks. He wants immortality, he wants to be part of the clan, and he wants Bridget, but he doesn't want to cause her pain.

His options are either abandon his quest for immortality and give Bridget his few remaining decades, or abandon Bridget by going for the transition and most likely dying. His rational mind dictates that he chooses the former, but his gut pulls him toward the latter. Which one is he going to trust?

19: Dark Operative: The Dawn of Love

Get ready for the exciting finale of Bridget and Turner's story!

20: Dark Survivor Awakened

This was a strange new world she had awakened to.

Her memory loss must have been catastrophic because almost nothing was familiar. The language was foreign to her, with only a few words bearing some similarity to the language she thought in. Still, a full moon cycle had passed since her awakening, and little by little she was gaining basic understanding of it--only a few words and phrases, but she was learning more each day.

A week or so ago, a little girl on the street had tugged on her mother's sleeve and pointed at her. "Look, Mama, Wonder Woman!"

The mother smiled apologetically, saying something in the language these people spoke, then scurried away with the child looking behind her shoulder and grinning.

When it happened again with another child on the same day, it was settled.

Wonder Woman must have been the name of someone important in this strange world she had awoken to, and since both times it had been said with a smile it must have been a good one.

Wonder had a nice ring to it.

She just wished she knew what it meant.

21: Dark Survivor Echoes of Love

Wonder's journey continues in *Dark Survivor Echoes of Love*.

22: Dark Survivor Reunited

The exciting finale of Wonder and Anandur's story.

23: Dark Widow's Secret

Vivian and her daughter share a powerful telepathic connection, so when Ella can't be reached by conventional or psychic means, her mother fears the worst.

Help arrives from an unexpected source when Vivian gets a call from the young doctor she met at a psychic convention. Turns out Julian belongs to a private organization specializing in retrieving missing girls.

As Julian's clan mobilizes its considerable resources to rescue the daughter, Magnus is charged with keeping the gorgeous young mother safe.

Worry for Ella and the secrets Vivian and Magnus keep from each other should be enough to prevent the sparks of attraction from kindling a blaze of desire. Except, these pesky sparks have a mind of their own.

24: Dark Widow's Curse

A simple rescue operation turns into mission impossible when the Russian mafia gets involved. Bad things are supposed to come in threes, but in Vivian's case, it seems like there is no limit to bad luck. Her family and everyone who gets close to her is affected by her curse.

Will Magnus and his people prove her wrong?

25: Dark Widow's Blessing

The thrilling finale of the Dark Widow trilogy!

26: Dark Dream's Temptation

Julian has known Ella is the one for him from the moment he saw her picture, but when he finally frees her from captivity, she seems indifferent to him. Could he have been mistaken?

Ella's rescue should've ended that chapter in her life, but it seems like the road back to normalcy has just begun and it's full of obstacles. Between the pitying looks she gets and her mother's attempts to get her into therapy, Ella feels like she's typecast as a victim, when nothing could be further from the truth. She's a tough survivor, and she's going to prove it.

Strangely, the only one who seems to understand is Logan, who keeps popping up in her dreams. But then, he's a figment of her imagination—or is he?

27: Dark Dream's Unraveling

While trying to figure out a way around Logan's silencing compulsion, Ella concocts an ambitious plan. What if instead of trying to keep him out of her dreams, she could pretend to like him and lure him into a trap?

Catching Navuh's son would be a major boon for the clan, as well as for Ella. She will have her revenge, turning the tables on another scumbag out to get her.

28: Dark Dream's Trap

The trap is set, but who is the hunter and who is the prey? Find out in this heart-pounding conclusion to the *Dark Dream* trilogy.

29: Dark Prince's Enigma

As the son of the most dangerous male on the planet, Lokan lives by three rules:

Don't trust a soul.

Don't show emotions.

And don't get attached.

Will one extraordinary woman make him break all three?

30: Dark Prince's Dilemma

Will Kian decide that the benefits of trusting Lokan outweigh the risks?

Will Lokan betray his father and brothers for the greater good of his people?

Are Carol and Lokan true-love mates, or is one of them playing the other?

So many questions, the path ahead is anything but clear.

31: Dark Prince's Agenda

While Turner and Kian work out the details of Areana's rescue plan, Carol and Lokan's tumultuous relationship hits another snag. Is it a sign of things to come?

32: Dark Queen's Quest

A former beauty queen, a retired undercover agent, and a successful model, Mey is not the typical damsel in distress. But when her sister drops off the radar and then someone starts following her around, she panics.

Following a vague clue that Kalugal might be in New York, Kian sends a team headed by Yamanu to search for him.

As Mey and Yamanu's paths cross, he offers her his help and protection, but will that be all?

33: Dark Queen's Knight

As the only member of his clan with a godlike power over human minds, Yamanu has been shielding his people for centuries, but that power comes at a steep price. When Mey enters his life, he's faced with the most difficult choice.

The safety of his clan or a future with his fated mate.

34: Dark Queen's Army

As Mey anxiously waits for her transition to begin and for Yamanu to test whether his godlike powers are gone, the clan sets out to solve two mysteries:

Where is Jin, and is she there voluntarily?

Where is Kalugal, and what is he up to?

35: Dark Spy Conscripted

Jin possesses a unique paranormal ability. Just by touching someone, she can insert a mental hook into their psyche and tie a string of her consciousness to it, creating a tether. That doesn't make her a spy, though, not unless her talent is discovered by those seeking to exploit it.

36: Dark Spy's Mission

Jin's first spying mission is supposed to be easy. Walk into the club, touch Kalugal to tether her consciousness to him, and walk out.

Except, they should have known better.

37: Dark Spy's Resolution

The best-laid plans often go awry...

38: Dark Overlord New Horizon

Jacki has two talents that set her apart from the rest of the human race.

She has unpredictable glimpses of other people's futures, and she is immune to mind manipulation.

Unfortunately, both talents are pretty useless for finding a job other than the one she had in the government's paranormal division.

It seemed like a sweet deal, until she found out that the director planned on producing super babies by compelling the recruits into pairing up. When an opportunity to escape the program presented itself, she took it, only to find out that humans are not at the top of the food chain.

Immortals are real, and at the very top of the hierarchy is Kalugal, the most powerful, arrogant, and sexiest male she has ever met.

With one look, he sets her blood on fire, but Jacki is not a fool. A man like him will never think of her as anything more than a tasty snack, while she will never settle for anything less than his heart.

39: Dark Overlord's Wife

Jacki is still clinging to her all-or-nothing policy, but Kalugal is chipping away at her resistance. Perhaps it's time to ease up on her convictions. A little less than all is still much better than nothing, and a couple of decades with a demigod is probably worth more than a lifetime with a mere mortal.

40: Dark Overlord's Clan

As Jacki and Kalugal prepare to celebrate their union, Kian takes every precaution to safeguard his people. Except, Kalugal and his men are not his only potential adversaries, and compulsion is not the only power he should fear.

41: Dark Choices The Quandary

When Rufsur and Edna meet, the attraction is as unexpected as it is undeniable. Except, she's the clan's judge and councilwoman, and he's Kalugal's second-in-command. Will loyalty and duty to their people keep them apart?

42: Dark Choices Paradigm Shift

Edna and Rufsur are miserable without each other, and their two-week separation seems like an eternity. Long-distance relationships are difficult, but for immortal couples they are impossible. Unless one of them is willing to leave everything behind for the other, things are just going to get worse. Except, the cost of compromise is far greater than giving up their comfortable lives and hard-earned positions. The future of their people is on the line.

43: Dark Choices The Accord

The winds of change blowing over the village demand hard choices. For better or worse, Kian's decisions will alter the trajectory of the clan's future, and he is not ready to take the plunge. But as Edna and Rufsur's plight gains widespread support, his resistance slowly begins to erode.

44: Dark Secrets Resurgence

On a sabbatical from his Stanford teaching position, Professor David Levinson finally has time to write the sci-fi novel he's been thinking about for years.

The phenomena of past life memories and near-death experiences are too controversial to include in his formal psychiatric research, while fiction is the perfect outlet for his esoteric ideas.

Hoping that a change of pace will provide the inspiration he needs, David accepts a friend's invitation to an old Scottish castle.

45: Dark Secrets Unveiled

When Professor David Levinson accepts a friend's invitation to an old Scottish castle, what he finds there is more fantastical than his most outlandish theories. The castle is home to a clan of immortals, their leader is a stunning demigoddess, and even more shockingly, it might be precisely where he belongs.

Except, the clan founder is hiding a secret that might cast a dark shadow on David's relationship with her daughter.

Nevertheless, when offered a chance at immortality, he agrees to undergo the dangerous induction process.

Will David survive his transition into immortality? And if he does, will his relationship with Sari survive the unveiling of her mother's secret?

46: Dark Secrets Absolved

Absolution.

David had given and received it.

The few short hours since he'd emerged from the coma had felt incredible. He'd finally been free of the guilt and pain, and for the first time since Jonah's death, he had felt truly happy and optimistic about the future.

He'd survived the transition into immortality, had been accepted into the clan, and was about to marry the best woman on the face of the planet, his true love mate, his salvation, his everything.

What could have possibly gone wrong?

Just about everything.

47: Dark Haven Illusion

Welcome to Safe Haven, where not everything is what it seems.

On a quest to process personal pain, Anastasia joins the Safe Haven Spiritual Retreat.

Through meditation, self-reflection, and hard work, she hopes to make peace with the voices in her head.

This is where she belongs.

Except, membership comes with a hefty price, doubts are sacrilege, and leaving is not as easy as walking out the front gate.

Is living in utopia worth the sacrifice?

Anastasia believes so until the arrival of a new acolyte changes everything.

Apparently, the gods of old were not a myth, their immortal descendants share the planet with humans, and she might be a carrier of their genes.

48: Dark Haven Unmasked

As Anastasia leaves Safe Haven for a week-long romantic vacation with Leon, she hopes to explore her newly discovered passionate side, their budding relationship, and perhaps also solve the mystery of the voices in her head. What she discovers exceeds her wildest expectations.

In the meantime, Eleanor and Peter hope to solve another mystery. Who is Emmett Haderech, and what is he up to?

For a **FREE** Audiobook, Preview chapters, And other goodies offered only to my **VIPs**,

JOIN THE VIP CLUB AT ITLUCAS.COM

TRY THE SERIES ON

AUDIBLE

2 FREE audiobooks with your new Audible subscription!

THE PERFECT MATCH SERIES

PERFECT MATCH 1: VAMPIRE'S CONSORT

When Gabriel's company is ready to start beta testing, he invites his old crush to inspect its medical safety protocol.

Curious about the revolutionary technology of the *Perfect Match Virtual Fantasy-Fulfillment studios*, Brenna agrees.

Neither expects to end up partnering for its first fully immersive test run.

PERFECT MATCH 2: KING'S CHOSEN

When Lisa's nutty friends get her a gift certificate to *Perfect Match Virtual Fantasy Studios*, she has no intentions of using it. But since the only way to get a refund is if no partner can be found for her, she makes sure to request a fantasy so girly and over the top that no sane guy will pick it up.

Except, someone does.

Warning: This fantasy contains a hot, domineering crown prince, sweet insta-love, steamy love scenes painted with light shades of gray, a wedding, and a HEA in both the virtual and real worlds.

Intended for mature audience.

PERFECT MATCH 3: CAPTAIN'S CONQUEST

Working as a Starbucks barista, Alicia fends off flirting all day long, but none of the guys are as charming and sexy as Gregg. His frequent visits are the highlight of her day, but since he's never asked her out, she assumes he's taken. Besides, between a day job and a budding music career, she has no time to start a new relationship.

THE PERFECT MATCH SERIES

That is until Gregg makes her an offer she can't refuse—a gift certificate to the virtual fantasy fulfillment service everyone is talking about. As a huge Star Trek fan, Alicia has a perfect match in mind—the captain of the Starship Enterprise.

Also by I. T. Lucas

THE CHILDREN OF THE GODS ORIGINS
1: Goddess's Choice
2: Goddess's Hope

THE CHILDREN OF THE GODS

Dark Stranger
1: Dark Stranger The Dream
2: Dark Stranger Revealed
3: Dark Stranger Immortal

Dark Enemy
4: Dark Enemy Taken
5: Dark Enemy Captive
6: Dark Enemy Redeemed

Kri & Michael's Story
6.5: My Dark Amazon

Dark Warrior
7: Dark Warrior Mine
8: Dark Warrior's Promise
9: Dark Warrior's Destiny
10: Dark Warrior's Legacy

Dark Guardian
11: Dark Guardian Found
12: Dark Guardian Craved
13: Dark Guardian's Mate

Dark Angel
14: Dark Angel's Obsession
15: Dark Angel's Seduction
16: Dark Angel's Surrender

Dark Operative
17: Dark Operative: A Shadow of Death
18: Dark Operative: A Glimmer of Hope
19: Dark Operative: The Dawn of Love

Dark Survivor
20: Dark Survivor Awakened
21: Dark Survivor Echoes of Love
22: Dark Survivor Reunited

Dark Widow
23: Dark Widow's Secret
24: Dark Widow's Curse
25: Dark Widow's Blessing

Dark Dream
26: Dark Dream's Temptation
27: Dark Dream's Unraveling
28: Dark Dream's Trap

Dark Prince
29: Dark Prince's Enigma

ALSO BY I. T. LUCAS

30: DARK PRINCE'S DILEMMA
31: DARK PRINCE'S AGENDA

DARK QUEEN
32: DARK QUEEN'S QUEST
33: DARK QUEEN'S KNIGHT
34: DARK QUEEN'S ARMY

DARK SPY
35: DARK SPY CONSCRIPTED
36: DARK SPY'S MISSION
37: DARK SPY'S RESOLUTION

DARK OVERLORD
38: DARK OVERLORD NEW HORIZON
39: DARK OVERLORD'S WIFE
40: DARK OVERLORD'S CLAN

DARK CHOICES
41: DARK CHOICES THE QUANDARY
42: DARK CHOICES PARADIGM SHIFT
43: DARK CHOICES THE ACCORD

DARK SECRETS
44: DARK SECRETS RESURGENCE
45: DARK SECRETS UNVEILED
46: DARK SECRETS ABSOLVED

DARK HAVEN
47: DARK HAVEN ILLUSION
48: DARK HAVEN UNMASKED

PERFECT MATCH
PERFECT MATCH 1: VAMPIRE'S CONSORT
PERFECT MATCH 2: KING'S CHOSEN
PERFECT MATCH 3: CAPTAIN'S CONQUEST

THE CHILDREN OF THE GODS SERIES SETS

BOOKS 1-3: DARK STRANGER TRILOGY—INCLUDES A BONUS SHORT STORY: THE FATES TAKE A VACATION
BOOKS 4-6: DARK ENEMY TRILOGY —INCLUDES A BONUS SHORT STORY —THE FATES' POST-WEDDING CELEBRATION
BOOKS 7-10: DARK WARRIOR TETRALOGY
BOOKS 11-13: DARK GUARDIAN TRILOGY
BOOKS 14-16: DARK ANGEL TRILOGY
BOOKS 17-19: DARK OPERATIVE TRILOGY
BOOKS 20-22: DARK SURVIVOR TRILOGY
BOOKS 23-25: DARK WIDOW TRILOGY
BOOKS 26-28: DARK DREAM TRILOGY

ALSO BY I. T. LUCAS

BOOKS 29-31: DARK PRINCE TRILOGY
BOOKS 32-34: DARK QUEEN TRILOGY
BOOKS 35-37: DARK SPY TRILOGY
BOOKS 38-40: DARK OVERLORD TRILOGY
BOOKS 41-43: DARK CHOICES TRILOGY
BOOKS 44-46: DARK SECRETS TRILOGY

MEGA SETS

THE CHILDREN OF THE GODS: BOOKS 1-6—INCLUDES CHARACTER LISTS

THE CHILDREN OF THE GODS: BOOKS 6.5-10—INCLUDES CHARACTER LISTS

TRY THE CHILDREN OF THE GODS SERIES ON AUDIBLE

2 FREE audiobooks with your new Audible subscription!

FOR EXCLUSIVE PEEKS AT UPCOMING RELEASES & A FREE COMPANION BOOK

Join my *VIP Club* and gain access to the VIP portal at itlucas.com
CLICK HERE TO JOIN
(http://eepurl.com/blMTpD)

INCLUDED IN YOUR FREE MEMBERSHIP:

- **FREE** Children of the Gods companion book **1**
- **FREE** narration of Goddess's Choice—Book 1 in The Children of the Gods Origins series.
- Preview chapters of upcoming releases.
- And other exclusive content offered only to my **VIPs**.

If you're already a subscriber, you can find **your VIP password** at the bottom of each of my new release emails. If you are not getting them, your email provider is sending them to your junk folder, and you are missing out on **important updates, side characters' portraits, additional content, and other goodies.** To fix that, add isabell@itlucas.com to your email contacts or to your email VIP list.

Made in the USA
Monee, IL
29 June 2025